"Alekos, what does it mean to be a man?"

"It means to have courage, to have dignity. It means to love without allowing love to become an anchor. It means to struggle and to win. . . . And for you, what is a man?"

"I'd say a man is what you are, Alekos."

A MAN

"A passionate document . . . utterly compelling."

—New York *Daily News*

"Like all good stories, this one is rich in ideas . . . it also traces a tortured, ecstatic, ridiculous and sublime love affair between two violently emotional people."

—*Philadelphia Inquirer*

"COMPELLING . . . CHILLING . . . A TRULY REMARKABLE BOOK."

—*Detroit Free Press*

ORIANA FALLACI

A MAN

Translated from the Italian
by William Weaver

PUBLISHED BY POCKET BOOKS NEW YORK

Distributed in Canada by PaperJacks Ltd., a Licensee of the trademarks of Simon & Schuster, a division of Gulf+Western Corporation.

POCKET BOOKS, a Simon & Schuster division of
GULF & WESTERN CORPORATION
1230 Avenue of the Americas, New York, N.Y. 10020
In Canada distributed by PaperJacks Ltd.,
330 Steelcase Road, Markham, Ontario.

Published by arrangement with Simon and Schuster
Library of Congress Catalog Card Number: 80-17838

ISBN: 0-671-43487-X

First Pocket Books printing November, 1981

10 9 8 7 6 5 4 3 2

Printed in Canada

Γιά σένα

FOR YOU

The hour of departure has arrived, and we go our ways—I to die, and you to live. Which is better only the god knows.

Plato, *Apology*

Prologue

A ROAR OF GRIEF AND RAGE ROSE OVER THE CITY AND boomed, relentless, obsessive, sweeping away any other sound, beating out the great lie. Zi, zi, zi! He lives, he lives, he lives! A roar that had nothing human about it. In fact, it did not rise from human beings, creatures with two arms and two legs and a mind of their own; it rose from a monstrous, mindless beast, the crowd, the octopus that at noon, barnacled with clenched fists, distorted faces, contracted mouths, had invaded the square of the orthodox cathedral, then stretched its tentacles into the nearby streets, jamming them, submerging them, implacable as the lava that overwhelms and devours every obstacle, deafening them with its zi, zi, zi. Escaping it was hopeless. Some tried. They shut themselves up in houses, shops, offices, wherever it seemed possible to find some refuge, at least not to hear the roar. But filtering through the doors, the windows, the walls, it still reached their ears and after a while they also succumbed to its spell. With the pretext of having a look they would come out, approach a tentacle and be swamped: to become a clenched fist, a distorted face, a contracted mouth. Zi, zi, zi! And the octopus grew, expanded in sudden leaps, at each leap another thousand, another ten thousand, another hundred thousand. By two in the afternoon there were five hundred thousand, by three a million, by four a million and a half, and by five no one was counting. They did not come only from the city, from Athens. They also came from far away, by trains, by boats, on buses, from the countryside of Attica and Epirus, from the Aegean Islands, from the villages of the Peloponnesus, from Macedonia, Thessaly: creatures with two arms and two legs and a mind of their own before the octopus swallowed them, peasants and fishermen in their Sunday suits, workers in their overalls, women leading their children, students. The people. That people which until yesterday had avoided you, left you alone like an irksome dog, ignoring you when you said, "Don't let yourselves be regimented by dogma, by uniforms, by doctrines, don't let yourselves be fooled by those who command you, by those who promise, who frighten, by those who want to replace one master with another, don't be a flock of sheep, for heaven's sake, don't hide under the umbrella of other people's guilt, think with your own brains, remember that each of you is somebody, a valuable individual, responsible, his own maker, defend your being, the kernel of all freedom, freedom is a duty, a duty even more than a right." Now they were listening to you, now that you were dead. Heading for the octopus, they carried your picture, posters with threats and defiance, garlands of bay, wreaths in the form of the letters A, P, and Z. A for Alekos, P for Panagoulis, Z for zi, zi, zi. Tons of gardenias, carnations, roses. And it was tremendously hot that Wednesday May 5, 1976, the stink of scorched petals fouled the air, robbed me of my breath, doubled my certitude that all this would last only one day, then the roar would die out, the grief would dissolve into indifference, the anger into obedience, and the waters would be calm again, soft, lazy, forgetful over the eddy of your sunken ship. Power would have won again. The eternal Power that never dies, falls always only to rise from its ashes; maybe you think you have defeated it with a revolution or a massacre they call revolution, instead there it is again, intact, its color changed and nothing else, black here, red there, or yellow or green or purple, while the people accept or submit or adjust. Was this why you were smiling that imperceptible smile, bitter and mocking?

I stood stony beside the coffin with the glass lid that displayed the marble statue, your body, and my eyes fixed on the bitter and mocking smile that curled your lips, I waited for the moment when the octopus would burst into the cathedral to pour over you its belated love, and a terror drained me along with suffering. The great doors had been barred, with extra iron bars propped against them, but angry blows shook them furiously and through invisible fissures the tentacles were already stealing inside. They were clinging to the columns of the arcades, they were hanging down from the railings of the women's gallery, they clenched the grilles of the iconostasis; around the catafalque a crater of space had been formed, but it was becoming more narrow by the minute. To escape the pressure at my sides, my back, I had to lean on the glass lid. This was a torment because I was afraid of breaking it, of falling on top of you and feeling again the cold that had stung my hands in the morgue when we exchanged rings again, when I placed on your finger the one you had put on my finger and on my finger the one I had put on yours, rings that we had exchanged without laws or contracts, on a day of joy, three years ago now, but there was nothing else to hold onto in there: even the rope which had marked off the catafalque had now been sucked away by the waves of sensation seekers, the curious, the vultures eager to find a place in the front row, to have a role in the play. Especially the servants of Power, the representatives of cultural and parliamentary respectability, who had reached the crater easily because the octopus always makes room when they descend from their limousines: "This way, Excellency, please step right up." Look at them now as they stand primly in their gray double-breasted suits, with their immaculate shirts, their long, manicured nails, their revolting propriety. Then the liars come pushing, the liars who tell how to oppose Power, the demagogues, the hacks of filthy politics, the leaders of the political parties with their privileges, they got here pushing and shoving not because the octopus refused to make way for them but because it wanted to embrace them. Look at them as they put on their mourning faces, with sidelong glances to make sure the photographers are ready to snap their pictures, they bend over to give the bier their Judas lick, clouding the glass with their snail slime. Then the ones you used to call pseudo-revolutionaries, future disciples of the fanatics, the murderers who fire revolvers in the name of the proletariat and the working class, adding new abuses to old, new infamy to old, also themselves Power. Look at them as they raise their fists, the hypocrites, with their little fake-subversive beards, their bourgeois mien proper for future bureaucrats, future masters. And finally the priests, synthesis of every power—present, past, and future—of every arrogance, of every dictatorship. Look at them as they strut about in their dark cassocks, with their inane symbols, their thuribles of incense, which clouds the eyes and the mind. In the midst of them the high priest, the patriarch of the orthodox church, who, swathed in purple silk, dripping gold and necklaces, precious crosses, sapphires, rubies, emeralds, chanted "Eonia imi tou esou. May your memory be eternal." But no one could hear him because the angry pounding at the doors was now mixed with the crash of shattered panes, the creak of locks unable to withstand the impact, the brawling of the protesters, the grim racket of the square where the roar had become explosive and, glued to the walls of the cathedral, the octopus was demanding impatiently that you be carried outside.

Suddenly a frightening thud, the central door gave way and the octopus spilled inside, foaming, rolling jets of lava. Screams of fear burst out, cries for help, and the crater compressed itself into a vortex that hurled me onto the coffin to bury me under an absurd weight and obliterate me in a darkness where the outline of your pale face could just be discerned, your arms folded on your chest, the glint of the ring. Beneath me the catafalque swayed, the glass lid creaked: a bit more pressure and it would shatter as I had feared. "Get back, you animals! Do you want to eat him?" somebody shouted. And then: "To the hearse, quickly, to the hearse!" The weight became lighter, through a crevice came a ray of light, six volunteers dived into the vortex and raised the coffin to safety, taking it out by a side door to the hearse trapped at the front steps. But the beast was now out of control and on catching sight of the exposed corpse, clearly visible beyond the fragile, transparent screen, it went mad. As if roaring were no longer enough, as if it did want to eat you, it arched its whole length, fell on the pallbearers who, caught in its vise and unable to go forward or backward, kept swaying and slipping as they pleaded: "Make way, please, make way!" The coffin rose up onto their shoulders, it dipped, pitched like a raft shaken by a stormy sea, slamming you back and forth, nearly overturning you. I tried to make room, kicking and hitting; distraught at the idea that the six might lose their balance, might abandon you to the ravenous madness, I shouted in despair: "Watch out, Alekos, watch out!" In vain though, because another current had formed and it was dragging us away from the hearse: instead of coming closer to us, it was moving farther and farther off. It seemed like an eternity passed before the coffin landed there, flung in askew so as not to waste time, an eternity before the door could be shut, a barrier against the claws that wanted to open it again, feet trampling, nails scratching. An eternity before I could slide along the side of the hearse, inch by inch, and sit beside the panic-stricken driver, paralyzed by the awareness that this was only the beginning. Because now we had to get to the cemetery.

That endless trip, with the coffin flung in askew and your body crudely on display like merchandise in a shop window, like an invitation, enticing and sluttish—Look but don't touch. That unending nightmare in the hearse, imprisoned by the lava, unable to go forward; if it gained a yard, it promptly lost it again. We were to spend three hours covering a distance that normally would have taken ten minutes: Mitropoleos Street, Othonos, Amalia, Diakou, Anarafseos. The police who were assigned to escort the procession had been lost at once in the sea of flesh, many wounded or beaten up; the dozens of young men who were supposed to keep order had been swept away at once, only five or six remained, covered with bruises and intent on shielding the shattered windows of the hearse. You can see this in the aerial photographs, where the hearse is a vague patch, sinking in the whirlpool of a compact mass, the eye of the cyclone, the head of the octopus. There was no eluding the octopus: it stuck to us so tight that we could no longer tell what street we were on, how far we were from the cemetery. And there was the downpour of flowers, sliding over the windshield, lowering a curtain of shadows, a darkness like the darkness that had buried me in the cathedral when I was flung against the catafalque. At times the curtain parted, giving a bit of light so I could see things that bewildered me with questions I couldn't answer. Could they have wakened suddenly, spontaneously, and were they no longer behaving like a flock that goes where those who command want them to go, those who promise, who frighten? And what if they had been sent again, regimented again, in the interest of some jackal who wanted to exploit your death? But I could also see things that dispelled suspicion and warmed my heart. Clusters of people hanging from lampposts and trees, leaning out of the windows, lining the rooftops, at the edge of the guttering, perched like birds. A woman was crying, and as she cried, she begged me: "Don't cry!"

Another, in despair, desperately screamed at me: "Courage!" A boy in a torn shirt forced his way through the teeming crowd and handed me a notebook of yours, from school days, certainly a precious relic for him, and he said: "I give this to you!" An old woman waved her handkerchief and, waving it, she sobbed: "Good-bye, my boy, good-bye!" Two white-bearded peasants with black hats, kneeling on the asphalt in front of the hearse, held up a silver icon as they cried: "Pray for us, pray for us!" The hearse was about to run over them, the people insulted them—"Get out of the way, idiots! Out of the way!"—and they remained there in the street holding up the icon.

It went on until a voice whispered, "We're here," and around us a channel of space opened, the driver stopped, someone pulled out the coffin, which was hoisted onto the shoulders of the pallbearers, and we proceeded very slowly along an unexpected passage, in an icy silence. Suddenly the octopus was no longer roaring or jerking or pressing. And yet it was there. With a pincer movement some of its tentacles had preceded the hearse, tens of thousands swarmed through the cemetery and around it—but quietly. Inside they covered every stone, every marker, they filled every flower bed, every path, they encircled every cypress, every monument—but quietly. And in that icy silence, along that passage that opened silently to allow us to go by, silently closed again behind us, I walked, heading for the grave which couldn't be seen. Suddenly I saw it: narrow, deep, a well that gaped beneath my shoes. I staggered. Someone caught me, held me, made me sit on the little wall of the next grave. And the burial began: final impossible task. But at the edges of the well the octopus had raised a bulwark of bodies, and to lower you as you should have been lowered, your head where the cross was to go and your feet at the path, the coffin would have to be turned around; but the bulwark was firm, hard as cement; the gravediggers asked, "Move back, please, back," in vain, and they had to bury you as you were: head toward the path and feet where the cross would be placed. The only dead person, as far as I know, with a cross over his feet. When you were at the bottom of the well, from heaven knows what crevice, the high priest popped forth with his cloak of purple silk and his gold, his necklaces of sapphires, emeralds, rubies. Pompous and hieratic, raising his pastoral crook to impart divine benediction, he promptly tumbled headlong into the well, shattering the glass lid of the coffin, plummeting onto your chest. He remained there a few seconds, flushed with embarrassment, grotesque, collecting his ornaments, groping for a foothold to climb up; then they fished him out and he vanished, offended, forgetting to impart the divine benediction. The first handfuls of earth fell on you. They fell with dull thuds, muffled, yet the entire octopus heard them all the same. And it shuddered, like an electric charge: the silence ended, rent in an apocalyptic tumult. Some shouted—"He's not dead, Alekos isn't dead!"—and some shouted words that I couldn't understand but later I understood them: they had shouted my name, and an order—"Write! Tell it! Write!" And while the clods fell by the shovelfuls, hammer blows on my soul, gradually covering the marble statue, the bitter mocking smile, while the banners swayed in flashes of futile red, the roar began again: relentless, deafening, obsessive, sweeping away any other sound, beating out the great lie. Zi, zi, zi! He lives, he lives, he lives!

I bore it until the well was filled and became a pyramid of withered wreaths, of doubly stifling petals, then I fled. Enough of the lies, the kermises—organized or spontaneous—the temporary and belated loves, the griefs and angers howled for just one day, enough. But the farther I ran and the more I rejected it, the more that cursed roar pursued me with the echo of memory, doubt, and therefore hope, consoling me and persecuting me like the tick-tock of a clock without hands. He lives, he lives. He lives, he lives. He lives, he lives. Even after the octopus had forgotten you, becoming once again a flock that goes in the direction desired by those who command and who promise and who frighten, even after your defeat had been crystallized into the perpetual triumph of those who command, who promise, who frighten, the roar went on: a ghost clinging to the walls of my brain, nesting in the crannies of my conscience, irresistible even if I fought it with logic or common sense or cynicism. I began to tell myself, at a certain point, that maybe it was true. But if it was not true, something had to be done to make it seem true or become true.

And so it was that, following paths sometimes clear and sometimes obscured with fog, sometimes open and sometimes blocked by thorns and lianas, the two sides of life without which life would not exist, retracing routes known to me because we had covered them together or almost unknown because I knew them only through the episodes that you had told me, I set off in search of your tale. The familiar legend of the hero who fights alone, kicked, despised, misunderstood. The familiar story of the man who refuses to bow before churches, fear, fashions, ideological formulas, absolute principles from whatever direction they come, in whatever color they are dressed; a man who preaches freedom. The familiar tragedy of the individual who will not fall in line, who will not resign himself, who thinks with his own head, and therefore dies, slain by all. Here it is, and you, my only possible interlocutor—there underground—while the clock without hands marks the journey of memory.

PART ONE

1

THE NIGHT BEFORE YOU HAD HAD THAT DREAM. A SEAgull was soaring in the dawn and it was a beautiful seagull, with silver feathers. It was flying alone and resolute over the sleeping city, and the sky seemed his, like the idea of life itself. Suddenly he swerved in descent, to plunge into the sea; he pierced the sea, raising a fountain of light, and the city wakened, full of joy because for a long time it had not seen a light. At the same moment the hills flared up in fires, windows were flung open, and from them people shouted the good news, thousands poured into the squares to celebrate their regained freedom: "The seagull! The seagull has won!" But you knew they were wrong, all of them, and the seagull had lost. After his dive, myriad fish attacked him, biting his eyes, tearing his wings, a terrible fight had broken out, with no possible escape. In vain he defended himself with skill and courage, pecking wildly, whirling in leaps that sprayed immense fans of foam and drove waves to the rocky cliffs: the fish were too numerous, and he was too alone. His wings torn, his body slashed, his head battered, he lost more and more blood, he struggled more and more weakly, and in the end, with a cry of pain, he sank, together with the light. On the hills the fires died, in the darkness the city went back to sleep as if nothing had happened.

You were sweating at the very thought of it: dreaming of fish had always been a bad sign for you, a premonition; the night of the coup you had also dreamed of fish. Sharks. You sweated and understood that the seagull's defeat was a warning, perhaps you should postpone it for a week, for a day, check once more the mines under the culvert, be sure you had made no mistakes. But the countdown had begun the night before, at eight in the morning the bombs in the park and the stadium would explode too, on the hills the woods would catch fire as in the dream, and the comrades assigned the mission were by now out of reach. Even if it were otherwise, what could you have told them? That you had dreamed of a seagull devoured by fish and that fish for you was a bad omen? They would have laughed and thought you were in a panic. You had no choice but to dress and go. You slipped on your bathing trunks, your shirt, slacks. It was August and the moment you got there you would take off the shirt and the slacks and remain in bathing trunks: anyone seeing you would assume you were an eccentric who liked to go swimming at dawn. Who would possibly set out to kill a tyrant wearing only swimming trunks? You put on the rope-soled shoes. Because the rocks were sharp, you would keep the shoes on. Or perhaps not? No, you wouldn't need the shoes in the stretch of rocky cliff between the road and the shore, because, once it was over, you would dive into the water and swim to the motorboat. You took your wallet with the money and the fake documents, stuck it into the waistband of the trunks, then changed your mind and took it out again. No documents, real or fake. If the fish seized the seagull, they wouldn't be able to pin an identity on him. And what if they killed him?

If they killed him, the newspapers would simply mention a corpse recovered along the Sounion shore. Age, about thirty. Height, one meter seventy-four. Weight, a scant seventy kilograms. Build, sturdy. Hair, black. Skin, very white. Distinguishing marks, none except a moustache. But many men in Greece have moustaches.

You looked at your watch: almost six. Soon Nikos would summon you with a hoot of the horn, and as you awaited that sound, the memory of the past few months seized you, tormenting you like an itch. The day you deserted, rather than serve under the tyrant, you went hunting from house to house in search of somebody who would take you in, but nobody would take you in, nobody would help you; hour by hour the net of the police tightened until you could feel them breathing down your neck, and as your willpower weakened, you asked yourself: suffer, fight, for whom, why? The day you understood that other people's fear, other people's submission, other people's obedience would destroy you and therefore you had to leave the country, escape, in search of other houses where you could be taken in, with a fake passport you took a plane at Athens airport and reached Cyprus, only to be pursued by the police there and to feel them also breathing down your neck and to become weakened and ask yourself again: suffer, fight, for whom, why? The day you understood that you would achieve nothing there, either, and the minister of the interior, Georgazis, was after you to hand you over to the junta, you had to run away again and you were hungry, you were cold, at night you slept in an abandoned hut, during the day you stole fruit in the fields to feed yourself, and you repeated: suffer, fight, for whom, why? The day that fate led you to the one man who could save you, President Makarios, and he had offered you a safe-conduct to reach Italy, telling you to go to Minister Georgazis, who would sign it for you, and you had gone with your heart pounding, had entered his office suspecting a trap had been set, ready to shout at him, "All right, arrest me. What's the use anyway of suffering, fighting, human beings don't know what to do with freedom?" And raising his moody face, framed by a coal black beard, like a hood that concealed everything but the piercing eyes, he smiled and said: "Hm, you. The very man I've been trying to catch for months. You realize the risks I would run, helping you?" "Don't help me then, hand me over to the police. What's the use anyway—" "Of suffering, fighting? It helps us to live, my boy. A man who gives in doesn't live, he survives." And then: "What do you have on your mind, boy?" "Just one thing: a bit of freedom." "Do you know how to shoot, how to aim?" "No." "Do you know how to make a bomb?" "No." "Are you ready to die?" "Yes." "Hm, dying is easier than living, but I'll help you." He really did help you. He taught you everything you knew. Without him you could never have made the two mines that were now under the culvert, beyond the curve. Five kilos of TNT, a kilo and a half of plastic, two kilos of sugar. "Sugar?" "Yes, it speeds up combustion." You had fun following his instructions, as if it were a game: "Will it be sweet enough? Let's add another heaping teaspoon." But now you were shuddering, thinking that it wasn't a game, it was the killing of a man. You never believed you could kill a man; you weren't even capable of killing an animal. This ant, for example. An ant was crawling up your arm. You picked if off with delicate fingers and set it on the table. A car's horn blew.

You checked the time, 6:00 A.M., and with determination you descended the stairs to meet Nikos, who was waiting at the wheel of the taxi. You sat on the back seat so you would look like an ordinary passenger. Nikos was your cousin and a taxi driver. You had chosen him because he was a cousin and you could trust him, and also because he was a taxi driver. A taxi is less conspicuous; what policeman would imagine that two men would carry out an assassination in a taxi? Besides you didn't have enough money to buy or rent a car; to have that kind of money, one must belong to a party, bow to its ideologies, its laws, its opportunism. If you don't belong to a party, if you don't offer the guarantee of a badge, who will pay any attention to you, who will finance you? In Rome, where you took refuge after leaving Cyprus, the professional politicians gave you nothing but talk. Nothing but alms. Comrade here, comrade there, long live the International and freedom, maybe a room where you could sleep and a cheap café where you could eat now and then, but that was all. At a certain point you were received by a Socialist functionary, one of those men who has the art of getting ahead written on his face, the ability of screwing his neighbor, and one of those who inevitably become a party leader. Staring at you from behind his thick eyeglasses, nearsighted, fat as a pig, he promised you heaven and earth, comrade here, comrade there, long live the International and freedom: however, you left Rome with empty pockets, and not one drachma ever reached you afterward. As for your fellow countrymen who should have helped you, like the one who considered himself the top chief of the exiled left, you knew them all too well. Compromise themselves with a madman who with a handful of other madmen wants to kill the tyrant? Never! If the assassination succeeded, naturally they would fall all over you like locusts on a field of wheat, they would take on the roles of accomplices and supporters, but now they offered you nothing but a glass of cognac: drink up, boy, and good luck. "Did you eat last night?" Nikos asked. "Yes, last night, yes." "Where?" "In a restaurant." "You showed yourself in a restaurant?" You shrugged, then you calculated whether or not there was time to drive past Glyphada, to see the house with the grove of orange and lemon trees. There you had spent your adolescence and your young manhood, there your parents lived: returning to Athens you had made a supreme effort to keep away from them. "Never give in to such romantic feelings," Georgazis had said. Romantic? Perhaps, but a man is a man also because he gives in to romantic feelings. "Drive past Glyphada," you ordered Nikos. "Glyphada? But it's late!" "Do as I say." Nikos drove past at great speed, you barely had time to glimpse the window of the room where your father was sleeping, and the garden where an old woman in black was watering the roses. The fact that your mother hadn't abandoned her habit of waking at dawn to water the roses moved you, the thought that your father was asleep gripped your heart, brusquely you turned to look again, but Nikos was already taking the next left and soon the taxi was on the road by the sea. The road that the tyrant traveled every morning, in his armored Lincoln, to go from his residence at Lagonissi to Athens. These past weeks you had covered it dozens of times, looking for the best spot to set the mines, and the first choice had been a natural arch: you would have liked to bombard him from above, like a thunderbolt from Zeus, a divine punishment. But it wouldn't have worked: dynamite acts from below, and you had to be content with the culvert beyond a bend in the road. It wasn't so much a culvert as a little cement cave, square, deep, over which the asphalt of the road passed with a thickness of only fifty centimeters. The distance from the bottom of the cave to the asphalt of the road was only eighty centimeters; they couldn't have invented anything more suited. Placed there, the mines would open gaps three or four meters wide, and the explosive force would be immense. The only problem was how to escape in the daylight. "It was no accident," Georgazis had said, "that assassinations take place in the dark. Nothing favors escape better than darkness." But what if they saw you getting away? To hell with it. For that matter you didn't like darkness. Bats move in darkness, and moles, spies, not men who are fighting for freedom.

You reached the culvert at a quarter to seven. Nikos quickly opened the trunk to give you the wire to attach to the mines, and you promptly let out a curse. The roll was a mess, a tangle of knots. "What have you done, you idiot, what have you done?" "Me? Nothing. I . . ." But there was no time to argue or to remedy things, so you undressed, handed Nikos the shirt, slacks, shoes, and barefoot, only in your bathing trunks, you ran toward the cave, clasping that knotted tangle of wire to your chest.

The culvert no longer exists. They filled it with earth when they widened the road and eliminated the curve: if you went back there you wouldn't even recognize the spot where you stood then. But I remember it very well because I saw it when you took me there, and I remember just as well what you told me about that morning: the beginning of your legend, of your tragedy, the beginning of everything. The sea was rough that morning, violent waves were breaking along the shore, and it was freezing. Or were you cold because of the tangled wire? You couldn't get over it, you couldn't understand how it had happened. Perhaps Nikos had flung the wire into the trunk too violently, perhaps he had forgotten to tie it, and the jolting of the taxi had caused the disaster. However it happened, the two hundred meters of smooth wire were now reduced to a tangle: no sooner did you undo one knot but another was formed; when you unwound that one, there was yet another. Exasperated, you gave a yank. You picked up the intact part, then measured it, and you let out a second curse. Only forty meters, a fifth of the length necessary! The rock chosen for detonating the mine was two hundred meters away: how could you change plans now? You had picked that rock after endless tests because it offered a perfect view all around. There was one moment, as the black Lincoln traveled along the stretch between the curve and the culvert, when the hood remained half-hidden by a billboard—according to your calculations, that was the exact moment when you should detonate the mine. Besides, the rock was near the water and you could quickly dive in. To set it off at a distance of forty meters meant having then to run a hundred and sixty meters before reaching the water. It also meant new calculations: at forty meters what would you be able to see? You attached an end of the wire to the mines and then, holding the other end in your hand, you went to see how far it would reach. Dammit, it reached a spot from which the road was invisible because of the embankment and, even worse, at that spot you would be completely exposed. You retraced your steps: with such a short wire there was nothing to do except take your place right under the road, ten meters or so from the culvert, with the risk of blowing yourself up. That would be suicide! But there was no other solution, and in any case this was an advantage: you could catch sight of the black Lincoln in good time. Advantage? What advantage? To see it well, you would have to peer over the edge of the asphalt and, dammit, again your calculations were not any good. You would have to make a new count, with new distances, pick a different moment for detonation, and you must hit it to the second: a fraction of a second off and you would miss the target. To work then! And quickly, very quickly. The black Lincoln usually passed over the culvert at eight o'clock, and it was almost seven forty-five.

Your brain started working with the speed of a computer: the car always travels at a hundred kilometers an hour, a hundred kilometers means a hundred thousand meters, one hour is three thousand six hundred seconds, one hundred thousand divided by three thousand six hundred makes about twenty-seven, so the Lincoln travels twenty-seven meters a second. Each tenth of a second, two meters seventy. But how could that tenth of a second be calculated? "Aloud," Georgazis used to say. "Kilia ena, kilia dio, kilia tria. One thousand and one, one thousand and two, one thousand and three." Good, that's what you would do. You rehearsed a couple of times, to establish the pauses between a thousand and one and a thousand and two, between a thousand and two and a thousand and three, you took a last glance at the mines, you connected the wire, and you were ready. Seven fifty-five. Five minutes to relax, to ask yourself . . . His name was George Papadopoulos, the man you would kill in five minutes and with whom, perhaps, you would be blown up.

What sort of man might he be, seen up close, in flesh and blood? You had never seen him in flesh and blood, only in photographs. In the photographs he looked like a little spider, he was comical: that insolent little moustache, those tiny bright eyes. But dictators are always comical, they always have tiny bright eyes. They open them wide as if they wanted to frighten children—Obey or I'll punish you! Once, examining his photograph, you had said to yourself: I'd like to look him in the face. But that was before preparing the assassination: afterward you never said that to yourself again. These past two weeks, for example, when you took up your position on that road to check the timing and the route, to make sure of the exact time he left his villa at Lagonissi and the speed of his automobile, the number of cars in the convoy, you could have satisfied that wish to look him in the face. But instead, as soon as the black Lincoln approached, you turned your back. Partly so they wouldn't recognize you, but even more because you did not want to look him in the face. If you look an enemy in the face and realize that in spite of everything he's a man like you, you forget what he stands for: killing him becomes difficult. Better to deceive yourself and imagine you are killing an automobile. Even when you were making the mines, when you were studying the times and the distances, when you were dividing one hundred thousand by three thousand six hundred, you were thinking of an automobile, not of a man inside an automobile. Or rather of two men since there was also the driver. The driver, for Christ sake! What sort of a man was he? A bastard or an innocent human being, a poor man who has to make a living? Surely he was a bastard: good people don't become a tyrant's driver. Or do they? You shouldn't think of that, in war you don't ask yourself certain questions. In war you shoot, and he who has to get it, gets it. In war the enemy is not a man, he's a target to be framed in the sights, and nothing else. If there's a poor man or a child beside him, that's too bad. Too bad? Too bad, be damned! Is it right to fight injustice with injustice, bloodshed with bloodshed? No, it isn't. And when you think about it, it isn't right either to take war as a comparison: nothing is more stupid, more reactionary, than the idea of war. When did war ever appeal to you anyway? You didn't even want to do your military service; with one postponement after another, you had finally put on a uniform at the age of twenty-eight. Even holding a gun nauseated you. Still, when you thought of the driver, you felt somehow ill, ashamed; you had to make an effort and repeat to yourself the things you repeated to your companions: violence provokes violence, the rage of the oppressed against the oppressor is legitimate, if someone slaps you don't turn the other cheek but slap him back, this man has assassinated freedom, in ancient Greece tyrannicide was honored with monuments and a laurel crown. And the phrase you had learned by heart: I am not capable of killing a man, but a tyrant is not a man, he is a tyrant. Suddenly it rang false to you, almost a lie. Was this why you were so cold? Nonsense: you were cold because you were naked and the weather was cold.

You crouched among the stones, clasping your legs with your arms to try to keep warm. The motorboat was arriving, punctually, heading toward the prearranged inlet. How far away it was, though. Would you manage to reach it? This morning the water must be icy: it would be difficult to dive into the icy water, to swim in the icy water. True, if you blew up with the automobile, or if you weren't in time to reach the shore, the problem of diving wouldn't exist. Life. How absurd life was. You turn a lever, you establish a contact between the negative pole and the positive pole and . . . The sound of the approaching convoy reached your ears. You sprang to your feet and murmured sadly: "Hang on, this is it."

It was a real convoy. The motorcycle squad led it, three cops on the right and three on the left, then the motor escort followed, two jeeps in a row, then the first aid ambulance, then the radio car, then four more motorcyclists, and finally it—the black Lincoln. Behind it another jeep, another squad of motorcycles. It had started along the last stretch of straight road and was advancing at the usual speed. Soon it would disappear behind the curve, would pass it, and then would appear again. The noise increased, and you craned your neck for a better look. The first two motorcyclists were emerging and coming toward you, so distinct that you could make out their features. At the billboard, however, they became a confused shadow and you realized then that you wouldn't be able to distinguish anything more and you would have to act solely on intuition, on your calculation of the times, remembering that from the billboard to the first mine was a distance of eighty meters, and to travel eighty meters at a hundred kilometers an hour takes approximately three seconds. Approximately! Your brain was working at wild speed and your body became rigid with tension: the trouble lay in that word "approximately." If twenty-seven meters can be covered in one second, three seconds means eighty-one meters, not eighty: so the first mine would explode too late. And the second would too, since it was a meter farther on, at eighty-one meters rather than eighty. Conclusion: the detonation had to be delayed. How long? Simple: if a tenth of a second corresponded to two meters seventy, it should be postponed approximately a third of a tenth of a second. Approximately. That "approximately" again! And all of this assuming that the black Lincoln maintained a steady pace! O Christ. How long does a third of a tenth of a second last? A blink of the eyes? No, less. A third of a tenth of a second is fate. You had to entrust yourself to fate and not waste time. Don't look at the stopwatch. Count more slowly. "Kilia ena, kilia dio, kilia tria. One thousand and one, one thousand and two, one thousand and three." More slowly? But what does "more slowly" mean? The two jeeps have gone by. The ambulance has gone by. The radio car has gone by. The motorcyclists have gone by. Now it is coming.

here it is—black. It approaches. It approaches nearer and nearer, black. It becomes bigger and bigger, blacker and blacker. In a moment it will reach the billboard and will become a vague shadow. Let's hope the Lincoln doesn't accelerate, doesn't slow down. It doesn't accelerate, doesn't slow down. It is about to arrive. It arrives. It has arrived. One thousand and one, one thousand and two, one thousand and three, contact!

For an eternal instant nothing happened. Then your eardrums were rent by a sharp, nasty crack, and a tumult of stones exploded, a cloud of gray dust rose. A single cloud, a single explosion. Only one mine had gone off. Was that possible? And not even a stone had struck you. Was that possible? You touched your body, incredulous. But there was little time to congratulate yourself on remaining unharmed because in a flash you realized you were unharmed because you had failed. An armored automobile exploding makes a much louder noise, raises a much thicker cloud, and not only stones fly through the air. What had failed, then? The charge? The timing? The system of counting kilia ena, kilio dio, kilia tria? Fate? The third of a tenth of a second, fate. But why hadn't the second mine exploded? Had you armed it badly? Had you failed to connect the detonator properly? Or had it been the sugar, the joke about the sugar—Is it sweet enough, shall we add another heaping teaspoon? You asked yourself these questions as you ran. Almost unconsciously, after touching yourself in disbelief, you had flung yourself down the embankment and now you were running, running, driven by a single impulse: to reach the sea, dive, vanish into the water, live. Live! Suddenly the sea was at your feet, was around your body that sank into the icy water as your mind repeated —It really is icy—and at a certain point it was so icy that you had to come up again for air. This allowed you to take a look at the road where the police were running with their revolvers in hand, and you were alarmed by what you saw. Immediately you filled your lungs with air and dived underwater again, swimming underwater again. You swam with confidence and strength, you had always been a champion, but the sea was angrier than you thought, a very strong current was driving you back toward land rather than toward the boat; you surfaced a second time, to breathe. You looked at the police a second time, to check if they were coming after you. No, they were all rushing toward the little cave under the culvert, they hadn't seen you, you could continue calmly. Too bad about this current! If it hadn't been for the current. And the lack of breath. You were out of breath. Every now and then you had to stop and catch your breath, losing valuable time. What waves! Feel those waves. A violent wave slammed you against the rocks and you clung to an outcrop, dazed. How much time went by as you were clinging there, dazed, unaware of the consequences? The consequences of that unforeseen pause were clear to you only at the moment your restless eyes sought the motorboat. You had told them to wait exactly five minutes, not one second more. You had told them this downright brutally, so they would understand: "That's an order!" When the five minutes had passed, they would surely go off. Something had to be done, immediately to save the situation. Emerge from the water and walk toward the inlet where the boat was waiting? They would certainly catch sight of you and wait. You pulled yourself from the water, painfully. You began to run, bent double, as before, over the rocks that were like knives here, every step a wound, a sharp pain, but at the same time you were nearing the inlet rapidly. Another fifty meters, thirty, and you would be able to call them: "Here I am! I'm coming, wait for me, I'm coming!" Then a plunge, a few strokes; they would come to meet you. Thirty meters. Twenty. Ten. "Here I am! I'm coming, wait for me, I'm coming!" The motorboat moved. It headed out to sea and went off.

It went off, and for the rest of your life you would suffer the haunting memory of that boat moving out to sea not waiting for you—I'm coming, wait, I'm coming

—the sense of emptiness that drained you at that moment. The desire to weep, to shout—Cowards, bastards, cowards! The despair. The question—Now what to do, what can I do? You raised your eyes to the road where the escort had set up a makeshift checkpoint and men in uniform were shouting, excited: "Watch the shore! Look out for anything that moves!" What to do? Hide, obviously. Hide, at once. But where? Your eyes roamed around, bewildered, in search of a hole, a grotto where you could take refuge. There! That tiny cave, that sort of niche that opened among the rocks of the shore. A bit too narrow, yes, but there was nothing else. You reached it, on all fours. You huddled up inside like a mollusk in its shell, a fetus in the womb: your forehead against your knees and your arms around your legs. Staying there until dark, you might make it, perhaps. At a certain point they would suspend the search and, with a bit of luck, you could move out and get to the road. Naturally there would still be plenty of problems, first of all the problem of roaming around naked and barefoot at night, but at various points along the coast you had placed your comrades with instructions to pick you up and . . . What would you say when you met them? How would you answer their questions, their mute reproaches? That things had gone wrong because of the short wire, the tangled wire, because of the calculations redone in desperate haste, because of a third of a tenth of a second, because of fate? You had waited too long, you realized now. You had counted too slowly kilia ena, kilia dio, kilia tria: the first mine had exploded when the Lincoln was almost three meters past the culvert. And the second mine? How would you justify the fact that the second mine hadn't exploded at all? Oh, Theos! Theos! Theos mou! God, my God! All that work, all that grief, all those sacrifices, those months for nothing. Nothing! You shouldn't think of it. You would go mad thinking about it. Better to turn your mind to a different thought: the token bombs, the fire on the hills. While you were to carry out the assassination, a bomb was supposed to go off in the stadium and one in the park, then the trees on the hills were to catch fire. A garland of fire that was to waken the whole city. The seagull, the seagull! Your instructions had been precise. But had the others carried them out or not? Fourteen apostles are few for a Christ who wants to overthrow a tyranny all by himself. And if you failed, they also were entitled to fail. Perhaps nothing had exploded at the stadium, either, nothing at the park, and on the hills nothing was afire. Nothing before, nothing after. What would Georgazis have said? And the professional politicians who had not lived up to their talk, their promises? Surely they would praise their own foresight—"That solitary fool, that presumptuous rebel who thinks he can take the place of parties, the discipline of parties, the logic of ideologies; we knew it, we sensed there was no point in taking him seriously." No more of that now. Now there was only one thing to be done: get away. But what torment it was to stay there, huddled like that, resisting the temptation to stretch an arm or a leg. Enduring these pins and needles in the joints. And what was this drowsiness? Fight it, stay awake. What an effort, though, what an effort. Especially with this helicopter. It was flying low, passing back and forth above you, and the pounding noise of its blades soothed you like a lullaby. A leaden curtain fell over your eyes.

How long had you slept? The watch couldn't say: waterlogged, it had stopped. At least one or two hours anyway: the sun was high, you could glimpse it through a fissure in the shell over your head, admitting a stripe of sky, and it was no longer cold, you were sweating, in fact. Perhaps it was the voices that had wakened you, voices very close, so close that you could hear distinctly what they were saying. "Search the area rock by rock!" The helicopter had come back, with a suddenly sinister racket, like the volleys of a heavy machine gun. It was as if the whole Greek army were there on maneuvers. "Send a squad down here!" "Sergeant, you're wanted!" "Not in a line! Spread out!" Finally an arrogant, angry yell, which hammered at your temples: "Search every inch, I told you!" "Yes Captain." And the stripe of sky over your head, the fissure in the roof of the cave, disappeared beneath a pair of shoes. You held your breath. You pressed yourself desperately into the shell and for a few minutes it was as if you had become a child again, the times when your mother used to look for you to punish you, and to avoid her blows, you hid under the bed, huddling under the side closest to the wall, and you remained there staring at her feet, listening to her grumbling, "Where's he got to, where's he hiding?" and your clenched lips prayed—O Christ, don't let her see me, make her go away. Sometimes she really did go away, not finding you, but you didn't trust your luck and you would stay under the bed, fighting off hunger, thirst, the need to pee. Sometimes, however, she would bend down and see you, and would reach out a threatening, triumphant hand, to pull you out: "I've caught you, you rascal, I've caught you!" But why, now, should they bend down and see you? You were a man now, and lucky: you had saved yourself dozens of times in those sixteen months. Why be frightened by a pair of shoes, by that officer standing over your head, implacable? A voice cried: "We've searched thoroughly, Captain. There's nothing here, there's nobody." "Take a look up above, then we'll go to the other side." A great breath swelled your lungs and you clenched your fists, thinking—Thank heavens, I've made it. But at the very moment you were thinking this the captain moved, stumbled. And he fell off the rock. He fell right in front of you. And he saw you.

"Don't shoot! Don't shoot!" Aiming his revolver with a trembling hand, he shouted these words, and you weren't able to answer him—Shoot with what? Then he shouted: "Come out, come out!" But in vain. Amazement, more than fear and anger, had paralyzed you: you couldn't untangle yourself, tear yourself from that shell. They did it. With the ferocity of the fish attacking the seagull in your dream, they fell on you, jostling one another, trampling one another. They pulled you out by the feet, they forced you to stand, not noticing that you couldn't stay erect because your legs were stiff, and any attempt to defend yourself like the seagull would have been madness. There were too many of them. It seemed as if a sea of uniforms was spreading, spreading, and wanted only to hit you, to search you. One struck you twice at the temples and on the eyes. One forced your mouth wide with both hands, to stick his fingers inside and poke for heaven knows what, shouting: "Spit it out, spit it out!" One ripped away your bathing trunks to see if you were concealing weapons. Then they put your arms on your head and pushed you up the slope. But you couldn't walk because under your bare feet, already torn in running over the rocks, every stone became a knife, and if you stopped to ease the pain a moment, they struck you impatiently with the butts of their pistols or the barrels of their rifles. Reaching the road brought a relief that changed abruptly into bitterness: where there ought to have been an abyss, a hole of barely two meters now opened, proving that you hadn't only mistaken the calculations of tenths of seconds, you had also mistaken the charge. They pushed you into a spacious automobile with jump seats. Sitting on the jump seats, they started interrogating you. "Who are you? Who paid you? Who are the others? Who was in the motorboat?" Then slaps, blows, kicks in the shins. The most ferocious was a heavy character in civilian clothes with the features of a monkey, his skin disfigured by a hive of craters, caverns, scars left by smallpox or some other infection. He struck with very heavy hands, a boxer's hands, and the more you opposed him with silence the more ferocious he became: "Talk, murderer, talk! Talk or I'll tear you to pieces!" "Answer me, you criminal, answer me, or I'll beat the skin off you." "Don't act surprised, murderer, you won't get away with it, if you don't answer me I'll kill you. You know who I am? Do you know who I am?" You didn't know and you didn't care. The only thing you cared about was being able to keep silent, not to give him the slightest hint, the slightest clue to identify you with: if he discovered your name, your companions wouldn't have time to save themselves. Suddenly a cop came over, an old, mild-mannered cop. He started tugging at the man's jacket. "Major, listen to me, Major, I know who he is. I know him, because I'm stationed at Glyphada; he comes from Glyphada. His name is Panagoulis and—" But the pockmarked man wouldn't let him finish and, opening his mouth and spitting a rain of saliva on you, he shouted: "Ah! It's you, you worm! So you hadn't disappeared, you hadn't escaped abroad, Lieutenant George Panagoulis? You were here, you dirty bastard, deserter, traitor, you were in Athens, you coward, and you thought you could get away with it?" Then an unbearable burning, a kind of stab, in the neck. He had put out his cigarette on your neck. You slumped down with a moan and your mind blacked out.

In the last years of your life, when you told me the story of your arrest, you didn't remember clearly what had happened after the cigarette was put out on your neck. Your memory could give you only scattered images, confused tatters: the old cop trying to attract the pockmarked man's attention to explain to him you're not George but his brother Alexander; the pockmarked man pushing him away, now certain of your identity, refusing to listen, driving him off—Get out, idiot, don't disturb me, can't you see I'm working! Again the old cop goes away with a shrug of resignation. Nothing else. Of the two hours you spent in that automobile and the beatings of those two hours you could say nothing. However, there was one thing you remembered sharply: the arrival of Ladas, the minister of the interior and Papadopoulos's righthand man. The wall of uniforms opens to allow him to pass. His big face, round, glistening, bends over you as the pudgy little hands slap you almost affectionately on the shoulder. His slimy voice oozes over you: "Listen to me, Lieutenant. I know your brother Alexander, I've known him since the days when he studied at the Polytechnic with my son. A difficult youth, to be sure, a kind of anarchist. He used to criticize Karamanlis, he hated the royal family, he had it in for Evangelos Averoff, communism didn't suit him, facism didn't suit him, nothing suited him. But he was intelligent, and if you handled him the right way, he would use his mind. And you know why I'm saying this to you, Lieutenant? Because if Alexander were here, he would say to you: 'Tell Ladas everything, trust Ladas. Confess to Ladas who's behind this plot. You'll save yourself a lot of trouble.'" You remembered this precisely because, as Ladas was speaking, you were filled with a great longing to cry. You shouldn't have wanted to cry: the fact that they thought you were George gave you a great advantage, you could gain a few days or at least a few hours, give your companions time to escape. But the more you told yourself the misunderstanding was an advantage, the more the desire to cry rasped your throat and moistened your eyes. "You must desert too, George." "But I'm a career officer, Alekos, I can't!" "Yes, you can. You must, therefore you can." "I can't manage it, Alekos, I can't!" "You'll manage it." You had convinced him. He deserted. Fording the river Evros he went to Turkey, from there to Lebanon, from there into Israel—without finding a country that would admit him, that would help him. A long suffering. Then in the port of Haifa, a moment before he was to board ship for Italy, the Israelis caught him. They handed him over to the captain of a Greek ship: it was to take him back to Athens, deliver him to the junta. The captain locked him in a cabin and . . . The pockmarked man had said "disappeared" because, when the ship reached Piraeus, the police found the cabin empty and the porthole open. But you knew George hadn't disappeared, he was dead. You knew this from a dream. The very night the ship was traveling between Haifa and Piraeus, you had that dream. You were walking with George along a mountain path, a path over a precipice that dropped to the sea. Suddenly the mountain shuddered, an avalanche engulfed George. "George!" you cried, clasping him. "George!" But you hadn't been able to hold on to him. And George had fallen into the sea, among the fish.

They took you away at noon. On your right the pockmarked man, on your left a colonel, who was quarreling with the pockmarked man, on the jump seats two guards with submachine guns, and two more beside the driver: eight in one car. The pressure of the bodies made it hard for you to breathe and irritated the bruises left by the beatings, a revolver pressed to your ribs redoubled the torment. The revolver belonged to the pockmarked man, who kept repeating: "You'll see, Lieutenant, you'll see!" Or else: "You'll stop playing deaf and dumb, Lieutenant, you'll stop that!" And after every threat he kicked your legs. You remained silent and stared at the road in the absurd hope that something unpredictable would happen. An accident, perhaps, that would allow you to escape. But nothing happened. The automobile traveled confidently, preceded and followed by the motorcyclists, nobody paid any attention to it. When it passed other automobiles and you tried to catch the eye of the people in them, empty glances answered you; when a passerby turned around, it was to display the indifference of someone who wonders: "Who've they arrested? A thief?" Or else: "They've caught a thief, good for them!" At one point a girl walking along the sidewalk with a young man seemed to sense the truth; anguish in her face, she grasped the boy's wrist and pointed toward you. This gave you a marvelous consolation, as if the girl represented the whole city and the whole city were preparing to fling open its windows and shout: "They've arrested him, they've arrested him! We must hurry and free him!" The young man, however, shrugged his shoulders, as if to say—Ignore it, don't get involved. The consolation turned into disappointment, you were overcome by a great weariness: you bowed your head and the flotsam of defeat rose to the surface. You felt ridiculous because you were naked among clothed people, you felt humiliated because you had failed, you felt alone because you were alone and because you were afraid of what they would do to you. A doubt pierced your conscience: would you be able to resist? The pockmarked man realized it. He shifted the revolver from your side, set it against your jaw: "We'll soon be there, Lieutenant. And I promise you, you'll talk. Oh, yes, Lieutenant, you'll talk. Because I'll cook you to a turn. You know what they say about me. That I even make statues talk. Haven't you realized who I am? I'm Major Theophiloiannakos."

You knew that name, and what he said was true: in fact, there was a lugubrious joke about him going around. An archeologist finds a statue and doesn't understand what period it's from. "Tell me!" he cries to the statue. And the archeologist's assistant says: "Professor, take it to Theophiloiannakos. He'll make it talk." But it helped, to discover who he was. It was as if a wind swept away fear and doubt and defeat and even the feeling of ridiculousness at your nakedness; in place of your fears and doubts there rose the pride of being alone, humiliated, the certitude that you were incapable of being defeated. You turned your eyes to the hive of craters, caverns, scars left by smallpox or some other infection, you burst out laughing. "Laugh, laugh," Theophiloiannakos scoffed. The automobile was going past the Olympic Stadium, and now past the Hilton Hotel, and now past the American embassy. After the embassy it turned right and your heart contracted. Beyond the acacias on the sidewalk you had immediately recognized the Special Investigation Section of the military police, of the ESA. The torture center.

This building also no longer exists. It was torn down to make room for a skyscraper that was never built because too many people said there was a curse on the place and living there would bring misfortune. Beyond the acacias on the sidewalk you see nothing but truncated concrete pillars, some dangling steel webs, and a vacant lot defiled by garbage. When the southwest wind blows from the sea and the garbage forms little eddies of rage and the webs slam hollowly against the concrete, it seems that voices of lament rise from the ruins. And yet it's a lovely residential neighborhood with airy green avenues, little white fin de siècle villas where the rich have a cook and a butler and a laundress and a chauffeur, elegant little art nouveau buildings where diplomatic missions maintain well-tended gardens and well-polished brass. It's hard to believe that here, right here, there was the hell from whose windows came the screams and the moans of the victims. Didn't the rich with cook and butler and laundress and chauffeur hear them? Didn't the officials of the consulates and embassies with well-tended gardens and well-polished brass hear them, especially those of the American embassy, since it was on the sidewalk directly opposite? Or did they hear them and remark with a grimace of ennui? "Good Lord, they're at it again. Let's hope they won't spoil the party this evening." It's also hard to imagine what type of building it was, this ESA headquarters. Perhaps a beautiful palace like the Lubyanka in Moscow, like the secret police building in Madrid, or else a barracks like so many other barracks in Mediterranean countries: old walls, squalid waiting rooms, armchairs of peeling fake leather, filthy ashtrays, bare offices with a picture of the tyrant on the wall and a sweating functionary behind the desk. Black fingernails, pompous moustaches, dull and greasy faces, cups of coffee brought in by soldiers sealed in fear—Yes, sir, Yes, Major—and then the cellars for those arrested, the special rooms for those being interrogated. One was on the top floor, near the flat roof, where a motor was turned on, to drown out moans and screams. This is mentioned in the pages you wrote a month before dying, which you tore up the day you reached the terrible page twenty-three, forbidding me to collect the pieces, but I did collect them and discovered, to my disappointment, that they were only a detailed catalog of the first twenty-four hours in there. Today it is that very catalog that awes me, the exacerbated abundance of tiny things, the fact that many years later you had forgotten nothing, not a name or a sentence or a gesture, as if every detail had been engraved on your memory like a brand.

The courtyard, you tell in those pages, was in a state of alarm when the automobile drove in, and Theophiloiannakos said to you: "Welcome, Lieutenant." Sentries aimed submachine guns, soldiers shifted their positions with nervous, snappy movements, sharp commands mingled with whispers, questions—Who was this half-naked, barefoot man, what crime had he committed? They pushed you up the stairs, brought you into an office, took a photograph of you for the newspapers. The one where you look like a tired handsome swimmer and your arms are limp at your sides, your head bent toward your left shoulder, and your gaze steeped in a heartbreaking sadness. Then they called a doctor to check if your silence was caused by shock. The doctor came and he was an odd character. He had a likable, shrewd face, his little eyes glistened with complicity and irony, he seemed to have turned up there by chance. With false surprise he examined the cigarette burns: "Who did this? Did they take you for an ashtray?" With almost excessive delicacy he studied the bruises and scratches: "Does it hurt here? And here? Here?" Then he asked you if your reddened temple hurt and pretended to be irritated because you weren't answering his questions. It was clear that he liked you, that he wanted to help you somehow. You liked him too even though he was wearing their uniform, but you could do nothing to show it, you could only hope he would stay a long time. He did stay. In fact, quite soon, Theophiloiannakos lost patience: "Well, Doctor, is he in shock or isn't he?" "Yes, I do believe he is traumatized by some fear, but I would have to examine him carefully, in my office, to make sure; I'd have to give him some tests." "Tests my ass, Doctor, this is a police office, not a first aid station!" "And I am a psychiatrist, not a veterinarian!"

"If you're a psychiatrist, can't you see he's playing dumb, that he's making fun of you, too?" "No, and I would like to treat him!" "We'll treat him, Doctor. You can go now." They pointed to the door, and seeing him go toward the door was like seeing the boat going out to sea without waiting for you—Wait for me, I'm coming, wait for me! You would have liked to run after him, cling to his sleeve, hold him back—Take me away, find an excuse and take me away! He seemed to hear it. He stopped, turned, gave you a look which said—I know you're faking, but they aren't sure, keep trying. The fact is that faking was less and less use, the moment was approaching when you would have to face them in a different way, showing that you were neither deaf nor dumb: now the moment had come, they were taking you into another room, a room that contained a table and two chairs to be sure, but also an iron cot without mattress. Beside the cot there were three sergeants, their arms folded, each with a billy hanging from his belt, the billies were so big that they looked like primitive clubs. The men were big too—and sturdy. You looked at them, you looked at the cot, and for a few seconds you did not understand what a bed without a mattress could be used for but then it was suddenly clear because the two grabbed you, serious, impassive, and stretched you out on it, impassive, paying no attention to the groan that escaped you at contact with the broken springs that jabbed like barbed wire. You bit your lip to fight your suffering: would they start at once, or not? No, not at once: a shy-looking captain was at the door, coughing a bit and blushing: "Excuse me, good afternoon, may I come in?" Looking as if he were unaware of the absurd spectacle of a half-naked man, covered with blood, stretched out on a cot without mattress, he settled himself at the desk. He put a folder on it, lined up some pencils, began to ask questions, which clearly were meant for George—What is your name, in what year were you born, what regiment did you belong to?—and, since you remained silent, he answered for you: "Oh, yes, it's written here, sorry. Born 1937. I know quite a few men of that year, all good chaps, I had a friend of that year, we were together in Camp 534." You stared at him, wondering what his role was. Was he there to fill a vacuum or was he part of the ritual? Had he been sent by some psychology department—You go there, act as if nothing strange were happening, treat him politely, win his confidence, and maybe you'll get some results? One thing was certain: he counted for nothing and they had scared him to death: when the door opened, he sprang to his feet as if they had stung him, or as if a general were entering. But it wasn't a general, it was two characters in civilian clothes. They pushed him aside, with a slow movement of the head they signaled him to leave, then they planted themselves beside the cot, waved a sheaf of papers, and said, enunciating clearly: "I am Assistant Inspector Malios of the anti-Communist section of the central police bureau." "I am Assistant Inspector Babalis of the same office."

Once, as a boy, you had seen a terrifying film. It was a science fiction picture and its protagonists were robots, created through a very special process by which they weren't born as babies but as adults, fully dressed with hats on their heads and shoes on their feet, and they all had the same face, the same stature, the same way of moving or of standing still. These two reminded you of that film. At a glance they seemed ordinary, innocuous types—unremarkable features, gray suits, shirts, and ties—but on closer examination, they inspired fear. And the reason was simple: though one was tall and one short, one thin and one heavyset, one with moustache and one without, they seemed monstrously the same, like the repeated shadow of the same person. Their way of standing, legs apart, belly thrust out: it was identical. Their looking at you as if you were in your own room or in a hospital: it was identical. Identical too was the tone of voice they used, alternating their remarks, perfectly synchronized. As soon as one finished a sentence, the other began the following sentence, completing the idea, but it did not express a separate notion, it expressed the logical or syntactical continuation of the previous sentence, so looking at them and listening to them was like following a tennis match between two players who never miss a stroke. Plok, plok! Plok, plok! Plok, plok! "Lieutenant, we have some information concerning you." "We also have the file on your brother Alexander." Plok, plok! "We know everything about you and we believe you know everything about us." "In fact, the foreign broadcasts devote considerable attention to us." Plok, plok! "To slandering us, that is. They say we torture people." "Lies. Our system doesn't need torture." Plok, plok! "We overwhelm the person under interrogation with facts, with evidence collected thanks to our patience." "So in the end he is always disarmed by our kindness." Plok, plok! "Some say to us: I'll spill everything but I want to protect a certain person." "And we understand, we let him have his way." Plok, plok! "One said to us: I was hidden in such-and-such a person's house, but don't do anything to him, he has a family." "And we didn't do anything to him; we just paid him a visit and gave him some advice." Plok, plok! "Friendship is a fine thing, we said to him, but friendship could make you spend the rest of your life in prison." "He flung himself on his knees and swore he'd never do it again." Plok, plok! "That's why the Communists hate us." "Because of our professionalism, our ideological preparation." "But we don't want to tire you with this talk, Lieutenant." "We just want to ask you a few questions." "For example, the address of the house where you have been hiding." "Afterward you can have your clothes back, you can get dressed. You certainly can't go on being naked." "Where were you living, Lieutenant?" Plok, plok! Plok, plok! Plok, plok!

You followed them, shifting your eyes from one to the other, with the alternating movement of a pendulum, exactly like people at a tennis match, and since you didn't remember which of the two was Malios and which Babalis, they became more and more the split image of the same person, with the same voice, repeated by an echo. "Where were you living, Lieutenant?" "Yes, where were you living, Lieutenant?" You had to stop them, unwind them, separate them. You had to answer them, or you would go crazy. "I don't remember." "You don't remember?" "No, I don't remember." "Lieutenant, do you know the meaning of the word interrogation? Under interrogation, everyone gets his memory back, we can assure you." "I said I don't remember, and there's no hope I will remember." "Perhaps you're too tense, Lieutenant. You need a cognac, a coffee." "I don't need anything." "Perhaps your position is uncomfortable. Would you like to sit on this chair?" "I'm fine us I am." "Come now, Lieutenant, you're acting like a child." No, it was no use. They wouldn't unwind, they never missed the ball, not even in answering. You had to try something else. Insults, perhaps. You tried: "Shut your trap, Malios! Shut your trap, Babalis!" It worked. They separated. They flung the papers into the air, started shouting with different, distinct voices. "You tell us to shut our trap, you murderer? Why don't you say—Yes, it was me and I'm proud of it, I assume full responsibility—why don't you act like a man?" "Man, Man? Can't you see he's not a man? He's a coward, he's shaking, he's afraid!" "Fuck you, Malios. Fuck you, Babalis. You're the one who's afraid, you eunuch. Everybody knows you're castrated, a eunuch, Babalis." "Criminal!" Babalis flung himself on you, Malios was just in time to hold his arm. "No, Babalis. It's no use losing our temper. The lieutenant is going to be reasonable." "Reasonable? We speak to him politely and he, an unsuccessful murderer, insults us?!" "Calm down, I said. He'll soon stop insulting us. He won't have the breath." "All right." But the door opened and Theophiloiannakos burst in, bawling: "You tried the polite approach, eh? Leave him to me. Poor fools, don't you realize that for him a special system is what's needed?"

You used to say that in every repressive regime, in every dictatorship, whether of right or left, west or east, yesterday, today, tomorrow, a good interrogation is like a theatrical script, with characters who enter and exit according to precise instructions and a director who moves them from offstage: the inquisitor who has been put in charge of the investigation. You used to say that each of those characters has a different role but they all have a single purpose: to make the victim talk. In the interest of their success the inquisitor gives them carte blanche and waits. He has a terrific weapon at his disposal, the weapon of time; he knows that if he is patient, sooner or later the victim gives way. To keep from losing, the victim has to make that weapon impotent: he has to react with a counteroffensive that will prevent the normal performance of the script. Hunger strike, thirst strike, aggression, violence opposed to violence, anything to drive them to hit harder and make him faint. When the victim faints, overcome by beatings and other tortures, or goes into a coma after fasting, the interrogation obviously is suspended. This allows him to rest and to face the resumption of the tortures in fresh condition and with the advantage of knowing the lines, the scenes, the style of the production. You hadn't known these things but sensed them the moment Malios and Babalis began that double monologue. It was precisely through listening to them and observing them that you began to suspect they were reciting the speeches of a script controlled behind the scenes by a very skilled director, interpreting the characters of a play whose aim was to wear down your mind already upset by the shy and awkward captain. More through instinct than through reason, you understood that you had to defend yourself, making them beat you at once, because if you fainted from their blows, not only your body but also your mind would get some rest and after that you wouldn't make mistakes. The essential thing was to seize the right moment. And this was offered you by Theophiloiannakos the instant he burst in yelling, "You tried the polite approach, leave him to me, poor fools, don't you realize that for him a special system is what's needed?"

And then, turning to you: "We know who you are anyway, criminal! We discovered that without any trouble! You're the deserter who ran off to Israel, the traitor who escaped that ship! Lousy faggot!"

With a leopard's spring you jumped from the cot, with a leopard's claws you seized his hand, forced his head back with your other claw, and roared: "Theophiloiannakos! Faggots wear majors' uniforms!" And immediately it happened, what you wanted to happen, what had to happen: as if hurled by a spring that had blocked them till that moment, Malios and Babalis lost their control, the three sergeants with clubs lost their immobility, they jumped on you, freeing Theophiloiannakos, and your attack became a duel against six men stronger and fresher than you. Two in front, two behind, two at your sides, under a hail of blows, clubbing, fists, as you slipped, fell, rose again, slipped again, rose again, dealing out kicks, blows with your elbows, your head, fierce as a leopard caught in a net but determined to rip the net. The table was overturned, a chair went flying, grazing the body of Babalis, who ran to the door in terror and called for reinforcements, in spite of Theophiloiannakos's protests, who didn't want more witnesses to his humiliation—"Reinforcements my ass"—but an officer with a submachine gun was already barging in, and this was more than you had hoped for. You broke the net: you hurled yourself on the gun to gain possession of it, you grabbed it, and though the officer clutched it with iron fingers, you yanked at it with such rage that you didn't even feel the clubs on your head, your shoulders, your arms. You only heard their shouts, and along with the shouts the dull sound of the blows given at random, so much at random that now the club came down on Malios's forehead, and Malios turned, infuriated, to kick the man responsible, but Babalis caught it instead, Babalis in a rage gave Malios a slap across the mouth, and this started the brawl between them. Then the brawl spread and involved the others, mindless, grotesque, more and more grotesque as they hit one another and kept urging one another not to do it: "Stop, what do you think you're doing? Stop! Cut it out! Can't you see this is just what he wants? Tend to him, instead!" Alone with the officer, you kept pulling, and yanking, you felt his fingers loosen, give way little by little, and there, you were about to snatch the gun from him: you gave a tug, it was in your hands! You aimed it. And immediately the heavens crashed over your head. Blackness. A thousand talons gripped you. A thousand bonds.

Unfortunately you hadn't fainted. The blow of the club had only dazed you. You raised your eyelids, you looked around to try to figure out where you were and what had paralyzed you. You were on the cot again. They had bound you this time, by the ankles, the wrists, and one sergeant was sitting on your chest, another on your legs. Bending over, Theophiloiannakos was gasping: "We'll make mincemeat of you, bastard! Mincemeat!" You stared into his eyes. If only you could spit in his face. Find a little saliva and spit in his face. And your tongue collected the few drops of moisture remaining, brought them to your lips. He understood, flew into a rage: "The club!" Babalis came forward with the club. "Now you'll see, you traitor!" The club struck the soles of your feet. Once, twice, dozens of times. The falange. The torture known as the falange. What suffering. What unbearable suffering. Not just suffering, an electric charge that rises from the feet to the brain, from the brain it descends to the ears, then to the stomach, the guts, the knees, where the spasm concentrates. As a voice repeats methodically: "Take this. And this. And this. And this. And this." As your mind pleads—Let me faint, O Jesus, let me faint, not scream, faint. But how can you help screaming? You began to scream. And then something worse happened: Theophiloiannakos covered your mouth so you wouldn't scream. He covered your mouth and nose, thumb and index finger pinching your nose, palm of the hand over your mouth. No, don't suffocate me, no. I can't stand it. Give me all the blows in the world, but don't take my air away. A little air, just a little air, for Christ sake. Jesus, if I could only bite him. If I could bare my teeth and bite his finger. For a moment he would take his hand away, for a moment I could breathe. You summoned all the energy you had left, you concentrated it in your jaws. Slowly, very slowly, you opened your jaws and you bit the little finger of his right hand, with force, until it cracked. A savage yell. And it was Theophiloiannakos yelling, holding up his hand full of blood, his little finger broken in two. Then they went wild. "Traitor, whore, whore! Spy! Bastard! Traitor!" They all yelled in chorus, a chorus of uniforms, and one slapped you, another slammed your head against the cot, another hit you in every part of your body until there wasn't a single part of your body that would respond to your impulses anymore, the springs dug into your flesh, the suffering alternated with a paralyzing numbness Faint, O Jesus, make me faint, let me rest, let me die for a bit, just a bit. And finally darkness. A long darkness into which you plunge as if into a liberating abyss. And silence. A silence that buzzes in your ears like the buzz of wasps, while your mouth fills with blood, and your temples burst, and your consciousness vanishes in the longed-for relief of losing your senses, of dying for a little while.

When you reopened your eyes, you were bound not only at the wrists and the ankles. A strap held you tight across the stomach, and you had no feeling in your legs or arms or torso. You could feel your face, and nothing else, as if they had decapitated you and your severed head went on living. You ran your tongue over your lips. They seemed immense to you and you thought they must be frighteningly swollen. You tried to raise your eyelids. They were glued shut and you thought they must be frighteningly swollen also. Beyond the curtain of your sticky lashes, vague forms were gasping for breath. One laughed: "What a job!" A shadow, breathing normally, came forward and Theophiloiannakos said to it: "Here he is. Is this him?" The shadow came close to you, bent over you, covering you like a cloud, a hesitant voice asking you: "Do you recognize me?" You sighed a very faint no. Theophiloiannakos intruded: "Liar! You did officer training together and you claim not to recognize him?" The shadow bent again. Maybe it had realized you weren't George but was unwilling to say so for sure. "Well?" Theophiloiannakos insisted. The shadow was silent, raining drops of sweat on you. "Go on, is it him or isn't it?" Theophiloiannakos repeated. "I can't say. It must be him, but he seems changed to me. Maybe because of what you have done to him." "All right, then come back tomorrow." The next day he came back. And the day after that, but every day he gave the same answer because every day you became more unrecognizable, they battered you even more. Officers, sergeants, soldiers: sons of the people, that people for whom we weep, suffer, struggle, always absolving it, justifying it for any crime because "it's not their fault." Five years later, when I took you for X rays to check on some respiratory troubles you were having, the radiologist held up the negative in dismay and cried: "But what did they do to this man? He doesn't have one rib intact!"

You didn't. The sons of the people had broken them all with blows of a crowbar. They had mangled your left foot with a club, and this is why you used to walk as if one leg were shorter than the other. They had dislocated your wrists, roping them and letting you hang from the ceiling for hours until your shoulders and arms would atrophy, the carpus and metacarpus come loose. This is why the right wrist was deformed by a kind of callused edema that became horribly irritated at any contact with your watch—"I can't even wear a wristwatch!" You had lots of little holes on your chest because you had been burned there many times with cigarettes; years later your back and hips still bore the marks of the steel lash. There were other scars on your legs, your thighs, around your genitals. But the most terrible one was the consequence of a cut made by Theophiloiannakos with his jagged letter opener, while

Constantine Papadopoulos, the brother of Papadopoulos, aimed his revolver at your temple: "I'll stick it into your heart, I'll stick it into your heart!" The flesh had grown back badly, in excrescences that looked like a bas-relief of white tears, very hard to the touch, as hard as grains of rice. On the day of the X rays, the doctor, incredulous, ran his finger over them and stammered: "Good Lord! Incredible!" Not to mention the tortures that leave no mark: such as waking you the moment you fell asleep, exhausted, or the suffocation torture. They had realized this was the one you could bear the least, so they used it always. However, after Theophiloiannakos's finger was bitten, they used a blanket.

Finally the sexual tortures. You would never tell me what tortures, specifically; if I asked you precise questions, you would turn pale and lock yourself up in silence. Yet, you made no mystery about one of them: the needle in the urethra. They would strip you, tie you to the cot, grope your penis until it was erect, and when it was hard, they would stick an iron needle into it, about the size of a knitting needle. Then they would heat it with a cigarette lighter, and the effect was exactly like electroshock. To make sure you didn't die, there was a doctor in attendance with a stethoscope.

This went on for two weeks, while they hammered you with questions many of which you couldn't have answered even if you wanted to because they were meant for George. "Answer, Lieutenant! Who helped you? What barracks did you take the explosive from? Who was going to benefit from the plot? What are the names of your accomplices, where are they? Where is your brother Alexander? When did you see him last? In whose house did you hide after you escaped from the ship. Who opened the porthole for you?" And you kept quiet. You opened your mouth only to moan or to scream. Then, on the fifteenth day, a man arrived in a blue suit with a white shirt and blue tie. His hands were carefully manicured, his nails shone as if they were covered by a fine polish; this was the first thing you noticed about him because those hands were holding a dossier with George's name written on it and the stamp TOP SECRET. You looked at his face afterward—you couldn't take your eyes off that dossier—and it was a face that reflected the hands: neatly shaved, well massaged. The features were sharp and stern: high forehead, long nose, thin mouth. The eyes were steady and penetrating behind the thick glasses. He examined you a moment, with extreme detachment as if you were an object and not a person. He started leafing through the papers in silence. Finally his lips moved and with an icy voice he said: "I am Major Hazizikis, the commanding officer of the ESA. Let's have a little talk, Alexander. Do you feel better, Alexander? Or should I call you Alekos?"

"The true inquisitor never hits you. He talks, intimidates, surprises. The true inquisitor knows that a good interrogation doesn't consist of physical tortures but of the psychological torments that follow the physical tortures. He knows that when the victim's body is nothing but a mass of sores he will be happy to take refuge with someone who torments him only through words. The true inquisitor knows that after so many sufferings nothing will sap the victim's physical and moral resistance as much as the calm announcement of further sufferings. The true inquisitor never appears with the characters in the drama of interrogation: he waits and reveals himself only when the curtain has come down on the first act. Only then, like a director who coordinates the work of his cast, does he step forth: patiently gauging the questions, studying the answers intelligently, accepting silences with civility. Extraordinary or immediate revelations aren't what matter to him. He is more interested in scraps of news with which he can compose the mosaic that will allow him to discover his victim's vulnerable points, provoking a sense of uncertainty and fear and at last total surrender. Therefore, when the inquisitor appears, it isn't enough to refuse him answers. You must also refuse him any form of dialogue, and keep your brain alert. Naturally this is difficult: the physical tortures diminish the functioning of the brain. But you must make the effort if you want to understand how far the investigation has gone, what they have discovered and what they haven't. Eyes and ears open. And memory, imagination, because the inquisitor has no imagination: he's the sort who sees power as an external phenomenon, an accumulation of means for maintaining the status quo without bothering himself about theoretical problems. Not that he's a fool or vain and thirsting for glory: often he is not even driven by personal ambition and is content to be an unknown with a certain authority, to remain in the vestibule of Power. Not that he is necessarily wicked or corrupt: often he is inspired by a sincere hatred for disorder and a sincere love of order. But totalitarian and oppressive Power is his god; his model of order, the symmetry of crosses in a cemetery. Into such symmetry he fits himself, without argument: he cannot imagine anything new or different, the new and the different frighten him. Devout as a priest to already tested systems, he considers regulations divine and obeys them just as he obeys the banal canons of elegance: blue suit, white shirt, blue tie. The real inquisitor is a gloomy creature. Philosophically he is the true fascist—the colorless fascist who serves all fascisms, all totalitarianisms, all regimes provided they serve to keep men in line like the crosses in a cemetery. You find him wherever there is an ideology, an absolute principle, a doctrine that forbids the individual to be himself. He has offices in every locality of the earth, chapters in every volume of history; yesterday he served the tribunals of the Inquisition and of the Third Reich, today he serves the witch-hunts of the tyrannies of East and West, right and left. He is eternal, omnipresent, immortal. And never human. Perhaps he falls in love, when necessary he weeps and suffers like us, perhaps he has a soul. But if he does, it lies in a grave too deep to be dug up. If this is not understood, you can't stand up to him and resisting him becomes simply an act of personal pride. Mind you, personal pride is legitimate, indeed a duty. Closed off to itself, however, it is a political error: to stand up to interrogation does not mean only displaying a heroism like Saint Sebastian or the martyrs of the Colosseum, it means also humiliating the inquisitor on the professional and intellectual level, leading him to doubt himself and the system he represents, avenging all those who were crushed by his graceful ferocity."

You wrote this brief essay for the book you were planning to do many years later, the book that never went past page twenty-three. It is the rationalization of your hatred for Hazizikis: the only torturer you would never forgive. A grim, painful, stubborn hatred. A hatred that burst out at the very moment when he pronounced your name, showing he knew who you were. "Do you feel better, Alexander: Or should I call you Alekos?" And you stared at him, unable to answer yes or no. You would have given a great deal to answer yes or no. But the words wouldn't come out of your mouth, as if they had cut off your tongue. It wasn't so much the fact of being recognized that made you mute or even the awareness of what this meant: the arrest of Nikos and the others, the implication of Georgazis, the scandal that would develop because if they were capable of discovering your identity, it wouldn't take long to find out who had given you the explosive and how it got to Athens. It was his offensive self-confidence, his contemptuous condescension, the detachment with which he treated you. Theophiloiannakos and his assistants were human in their bestiality: so human that they were afraid of you and became angry. He, on the contrary, was not angry and was not afraid of you: he sat there behind the desk, with his beautiful hands and his impeccable clothes, he calmly removed his eyeglasses, wiped them, looking at the lenses and not at you, he replaced them, hesitating with a slight cough; he behaved as if he ran no risk at all. In fact he had not wanted anyone there to guard you, he had ordered your handcuffs removed, had offered you a chair, and now he spoke in the tone of a man conversing in a bar, not interrogating at ESA headquarters. "You won't speak? Good. Silence is assent. It means you feel well. I'm glad, because somebody in the family has to feel well. Your father had a heart attack when he heard the news and your mother nearly went mad. The things she said to us when we went to search the house! She didn't want us to rip the upholstery of some armchairs, she became indignant when we confiscated photographs from her album and when we wanted to know where a certain roll of money came from. Screams, yells, insults. We were forced to arrest her. Your father as well, you understand. I don't mind telling you, it's always unpleasant to arrest a couple of old people, but I had no choice. We're holding them at headquarters. We'll have to keep them for a little while. A few months, let's say. Ah, yes: you're causing too much trouble for too many people. If such things as borders and diplomatic immunity didn't exist, we'd fill all our cells. But none of this interests you, does it?" A hoarse sound: "No." "Well, that's your privilege. If I'm not mistaken, the good revolutionary has no feelings, or doesn't allow himself any. He is ready to sacrifice his father, his mother, his friends, anybody. It's no effort because they don't matter to him. He has no heart. Do you have a heart?" "No." "As I feared. However, your lips are parched. I see you have trouble forming words. Would you like a glass of water?" "Yes." "Very well." He rang, Babalis came in, very deferential and without his other half: "Yes, Major." "Our friend would like a glass of water. His lips are parched." Then he addressed you again: "Now, where were we? Ah, yes: the heart. You're not married, are you? You don't even have a steady girl. A brief affair every now and then when the occasion arises, when there's time, but no ties. No loves. Your only love is politics, I'd bet you've never been in love. But I understand this too: the good revolutionary must not allow himself to be distracted by such foolishness. Or is my information wrong, am I mistaken, do you have a woman?" Another hoarse sound: "And you, Hazizikis?" "No, me neither. I am unmarried like you, and, like you, I am not in love. We have something in common, the two of us, sooner or later we'll understand each other. But here is the water." Babalis had come back with the glass of water and it all happened before either one had time to realize you weren't raising it to your lips. They heard the crash, felt the wetness, and you were already leaping on Hazizikis's desk, to cut his throat. He ducked to one side just in time. Babalis was slower. Between you and Babalis there were no obstacles and it was easy to strike, at least a grazing wound, a second choice since your objective remained Hazizikis: for him you had accepted the water and you turned toward him with the broken glass, shaking with anger because of the imperturbable calm with which he had eluded you. But he didn't blink. He didn't even change expression. He merely rang his bell for reinforcements and enjoyed the scene that immediately followed. Among the reinforcements were the three sergeants who had been beside your cot the first day. They swiftly pounced on you to block the arm brandishing the glass and you fought them as Babalis was shouting: "Grab him! Hold him tight!" It was a battle because, even held tight, you wouldn't let go of the glass, you clenched it the way rugby players clasp the ball to their chests, you were heedless of the glass that was tearing your fingers; when they managed to unfold your hand, your right little finger was almost cut off, the tendon was severed. "Well, I see that today we can't converse," Hazizikis said in his usual voice. Then he left you to Babalis, who tied your arms behind your back and, forbidding the doctor to anesthetize you, had your finger sewn up. But a week later Hazizikis appeared again with his blue suit, blue tie, white shirt, manicured nails, and asked: "How's the finger? They told me you are brave, that you refused an anesthetic. Congratulations. By the way, aren't you the man who bit the little finger of Major Theophiloiannakos in two? Now both of you are wearing bandages and, if I'm not mistaken, it's the same finger for both. As the Muslims say, an eye for an eye and a little finger for a little finger. Now then, let's have a talk."

That's what he always said: "Now then, let's have a talk." He said it for two and a half months. For two and a half months without interruption they continued tormenting your body and soul. The body belonged to Theophiloiannakos, the soul to Hazizikis. But you never talked. You opened your mouth only to insult them or to say: "Yes, I did it. I failed, and I'm sorry. If I don't die, I'll do it again." The others talked. One by one all of them had been arrested, not a day went by that they didn't bring this one or that one to you, hoping to make you give way, to make you understand that your resistance was useless. With their swollen faces and their gazes that had lost all willpower, the others would say to you: "Stop, Alekos, it's no use anymore. We couldn't hold out. We told them everything." And you, tied to the cot or hanging from the ceiling, would answer: "Who is this man? What does he want? I don't know him." At the end of September, exploiting what the others had said, Hazizikis and Theophiloiannakos prepared a confession and asked you to sign it. A signature and nobody would torment you anymore. You refused. They gave you the falange and during the torture they asked you again to sign. You refused again. They whipped you with the metal lash, and afterward they tried once more. And you refused once more. You kept refusing. You would have died under their tortures if he hadn't appeared one night: Brigadier General Ioannidis, supreme chief of the ESA.

It was a cold night, October was cold that year in Athens, and you were lying naked on the cot bound by the ankles and wrists. A thread of blood trickled from your mouth because their fists had knocked out another tooth, your face was a white mask because you hadn't slept for weeks and for days you hadn't eaten. You were breathing with effort, a rattle deep in your throat, and Theophiloiannakos stood there and shouted: "It's all the same whether you talk or not, we'll say you talked anyhow! Whether you sign or not, we'll say you signed!" The door was flung open and Ioannidis entered with his military stride. Chest out, arms folded behind him, he stopped at the cot. You recognized him at once, you knew who he was: not only supreme chief of the ESA, but the strongest man in Greece, so powerful that he was feared by Papadopoulos himself. Taciturn, ill-tempered, gruff with anyone who approached him, he inspired fear in everyone, and though he did nothing to attract attention and indeed liked to remain in the shadow, everyone knew his hardness, his incorruptibility, his obstinacy. It was said that if he considered it necessary, he would shoot his mother—or even destroy his rose garden, the only thing he allowed himself to love. It was also said that he was openly contemptuous of the tyrant and it was only out of principle, reluctantly, that he had assisted in the coup, which without his participation would have been impossible. Eight years later, when the irony of history put him in your place, namely behind bars, I was amazed to realize that you respected him as one respects an adversary rather than an enemy and that for this reason you were unable to hate him. Was your inability to hate him born that night from the words that he said in front of Theophiloiannakos? His face rigid, his icy eyes staring into yours, Ioannidis remained silent for a few seconds. Then brusquely he thrust Theophiloiannakos aside and said to him: "That's enough. Don't touch him anymore. It's no use insisting: he won't talk. It happens once in a hundred thousand times that someone won't talk. That's the case with him." Then he stretched his hand toward you, the rest of his impressive figure remaining frozen, and not moving a muscle of his evil face, he seized an end of your moustache and slowly tweaked it: "I'll shoot you, Panagoulis." Nineteen days later, when November had come with the winds from the north, the trial began.

2

THE COURTROOM WAS SMALL AND STANK BECAUSE OF THE clogged toilets along the next corridor. On the central wall there was an icon of the Virgin with child in the act of blessing the victims of that smell. Under the icon was the long table with the judges of the court-martial; choked in their bottle green uniforms with gold buttons and red insignia, they were all officers devoted to the regime. To the left of the judges was a bald magistrate, Liappis, with a pudgy, greasy face; he was the representative of the public prosecution and his presence could have invalidated the trial since he wasn't an officer. To the right was the cage of the defendants: fourteen besides you. Perpendicular to the cage and facing the court was the desk of the defense attorneys, named at the last minute and not supplied with the conclusions of the investigation. Swollen with cold and fear, huddled in their black robes, they looked like tiny birds perched on an electric wire. One peeped: "There ought to be a postponement! There ought to be a postponement!" Behind them was the desk for the journalists, admitted sparingly and under a hundred prohibitions: no tape recorders for those from the radio, no film cameras for those representing television, no other cameras, unless the presiding judge gave special authorization. Finally there was the enclosure for the public; admission was determined by a kind of examination: relatives and friends of the accused could not witness the trial. You entered in a stony silence. You walked with your head high, handcuffed, pressed between two policemen clutching your elbows. With them you reached the front row, just next to the railing of the cage, and it was only then, still clutching your elbows, however, that they took off the handcuffs. You were wearing a soldier's uniform, too big for you, deliberately chosen to make you clumsy. Two hours before, they had brutally slapped you because you didn't want to put it on and demanded civilian clothes like the other fourteen. They pulled the uniform on you, snickering and declaring it was a fine fit, especially at the neck and the shoulders. Your neck swam in it, your shoulders were actually swamped. You had grown very thin in three months, you were twenty-five pounds below your normal weight, and this was obvious from your haggard face, your sunken cheeks. The only relative who had managed to steal inside, an aunt of yours, did not recognize you: "I can't see him, he's not there, when is he coming?" she murmured, looking at you in the cage. But your eyes were two wells of life and you smiled with such pride, such happy insolence, that it was hard for people in the courtroom to feel any pity for you. These people, besides, did not know your case, the rumors of your torture had never gone beyond the confines of the ESA. What they knew about you was limited to the portrait of a fearful, obscure mercenary, a common criminal who performed his deed for pay. The information had been supplied by the press of the regime, by the cowardly inkslingers who under a democratic regime portray themselves as masters of courage and freedom but the minute a dictatorship comes along they bed with it like whores, and to serve it they slander the very people they praised before, and praise those they condemned before; they obligingly describe the oceanic rallies of a Mussolini in Piazza Venezia, or the athletic prowess of Mao Tze-tung who at the age of seventy-four swims in the Yangtze River, and when the fear is past, democracy restored, they start all over again, shameless, nothing happens to them because they are needed, as needed as cobblers and gravediggers and whores. What would the new masters do without an obedient pusillanimous press? How would they manage without it, the witch doctors of those who command, who promise, who frighten? Eight years later, after your death, they would praise you. And they would describe you in their newspapers—athanatos, immortal. Now they insulted you freely, well knowing that they didn't risk anything in the future: there was no political party to protect you, no organized ideology, no recognized religion.

They read the charges: attempted subversion of the state, desertion, attempted assassination of the chief of state, possession of explosives and arms. You listened without batting an eye, maintaining your smile. It was all true and you had no thought of denying it. But then they claimed that you had admitted your guilt in a signed document in which you denounced your accomplices, and then even the blind saw who you were. They saw you break free of the grip of the cops, spring to your feet, point your forefinger at the judge and cry: "Liars! My signature is not on any papers, and you know it! Any document with my signature on it is a fake by Hazizikis and Theophiloiannakos, and you know it, servants of the tyrant!" "The accused will be silent!" "Accused by whom? By you? You dare accuse me? You! I'm the one who accuses, I accuse you, I denounce you, I condemn you, for your lies, your torture!" You tried to unbutton your shirt to show the scars on your chest, Theophiloiannakos's stab wounds in your side. "The accused must not undress in the courtroom!" "I'll undress, if it's necessary to supply proof!" "Proof of what?" "Proof of the tortures I underwent during interrogation! Stabbing, clubbing, whippings with a steel lash!" "Silence!" "Cigarette burns on the genitals! Falange on the soles of the feet!" "Silence!" "Needles up the urethra, sexual tortures!" "Silence! The accused will keep silent!" "Suffocation, kicks, blows! I was beaten just before I was brought into this courtroom! And for ninety days—ninety days!—they haven't removed these handcuffs! Not even to let me sleep, not even to let me urinate! I ask, I demand that a doctor examine my body here in this courtroom and ascertain the truth of what I say! I ask for the opening of an investigation of Major Hazizikis and Major Theophiloiannakos on a charge of fraud. I ask that those two as well as Assistant Inspector Babalis, Assistant Inspector Malios, the brother of your president, Costas Papadopoulos, and the ESA officers be tried for torture. I ask—" "Accused! These things are not connected with the trial!" "If they are not connected with the trial, gentlemen of the court, then I am doubly right to call you servants of the regime." They sentenced you then and there to two years imprisonment for contempt of court, for insulting the authorities.

The trial lasted five days and from a legal point of view it was a farce. The witnesses were the same men who had conducted the investigation or had tortured you; one after another, in haste, they confirmed their statements, and the lawyers didn't dare raise any objections. In your defense they called only two or three people, who were threatened before they could testify, so on the stand they said whatever the prosecutor Liappis wanted. Afraid of displeasing the tyrant, Liappis played his role to the hilt and every time he spoke he aimed at discrediting you, insisting you were a hired killer in the service of foreigners, especially of Polycarpos Georgazis, and you were an outlaw, a bandit, a troublemaker universally detested. To prove it he used the confession whose authenticity you had denied, and when your defense lawyer asked that your denial be considered, he was refused. Your lawyer couldn't communicate with you, they allowed him to approach you only for a few minutes during the sessions, while the two policemen at your side could listen, make remarks, interrupt. Soon the two were joined by a third, who stood behind you and wouldn't let you speak. Yet you never abandoned the attitude you had decided on, there was always a moment when you managed to stand up to protest, unmask, give the lie, producing an almost admiring awe in the judges; had anyone ever seen a man under threat of death who transformed himself from accused into accuser with such steadfastness, such lucidity? But was this man crazy or suicidal? Didn't he realize he was demanding his own death sentence? Yet you realized that. It was obvious. You knew that with this behavior you were gambling away your life, throwing it on the judges' desk like a chip on the roulette table: rouge ou noir et rien ne va plus. But you weren't gambling blindly, you were playing scientifically, calculating with shrewd detachment the consequences of every action, every phrase, gauging every gesture of bravado with reasoning and courage, impulse and astuteness: like a great gambler who doesn't approach the roulette table to win petty sums. You were to explain this to me years later. True, you said, you had only a remote chance of surviving. Let's say one in a hundred. It was ninety-nine to one they would shoot you. But for this very reason you had to play for high stakes, following a system that would amaze and upset them, that would sow a seed of doubt in your accusers—He's so sure of himself, could he be right? So every day you became more decisive, more aggressive, you stood prouder above the other defendants, who instead humbled themselves, denying, apologizing, even accusing one another, or casting all the blame on you. And the hope of winning that one percent grew and grew.

But then the day came for your plea and the final speech by Liappis, and something happened that you hadn't foreseen: you fell in love with the idea of dying. Why continue the game? To see them inflict what you might have demanded proudly? To play the role of victim? The role of victim must always be rejected, nothing is ever achieved by the role of victim, and here was the great opportunity you had dreamed of: a chance to show the world who you were and what you believed in. The regime's press would pay no attention, but the foreign reporters would. They risked nothing in disobeying, so they would tell the truth about this man who lived and died as a man, without bending, without being frightened, without resigning himself, preaching the only possible good, the only thing that matters, freedom. And maybe someone in your own country would tell about it too. Some judge, some lawyer, some repentant policeman. And many would find out. Once you were dead they would love you, maybe imitate you. And you wouldn't be alone anymore. "The accused will rise!" The chief judge called you. According to the regulation, the accused was to speak before the public prosecutor. The three policemen relaxed their grip. You stood up. You looked the judges in the face, one by one. And your voice rose, steady, ringing. Beautiful.

"Gentlemen of the court-martial, I will be brief. I won't bore you. I won't even dwell on the unspeakable interrogation that I underwent: what I have already said about that is enough for me. Before examining the charges that have been made against me, I prefer to go into another aspect of the shameful case that concerns me: your attempt to sustain the accusation with faked evidence, false statements, prearranged testimony forced on the witnesses of both sides. This plea of mine is not intended as self-defense; it will not be that. It is intended, on the contrary, as an accusation, and that it will be, beginning with the fake document attributed to me, which has been the recurrent motive of the whole trial. An important document, in my opinion, because it is typical of all the trials that take place in countries where the law is slain along with freedom. In fact you are not alone in this shame. Certainly, as I speak to you, patriots in other countries without law and without freedom are being tried by a court-martial serving a tyrannical regime and are being sentenced on the basis of fake evidence, false statements, prearranged testimony or testimony forced on the witnesses, confessions similar to the confession that I never made and never signed. This is clear from the fact that it does not bear my signature but instead the signatures of those two torturers Hazizikis and Theophiloiannakos. Torturers without any respect for grammar, moreover. Last night I was able, at last, to read those pages, and it would be hard for me to say whether I winced more at the lies or at the crude grammatical errors they contain. If I had seen them before, I assure you, even in a state of coma I would have suggested corrections. Alas, what illiterates this regime employs! One would say that ignorance and cruelty go hand in hand. Well, gentlemen of the court-martial, you know very well that using a fake document is unacceptable both from a moral and from a legal standpoint. And since this trial was based on such a document, I would have had the right to declare it invalid. I didn't because I didn't want you to think I was afraid of facing the accusation. Obviously I accept the accusation. I have never rejected it. Not during the interrogation, and not before you. And now I repeat with pride: yes, I planted the explosives, I set off the two mines. I did this for the purpose of killing the man you call president. And I am only sorry I didn't succeed in killing him. For three months that has been my greatest suffering, for three months I have been asking myself with grief where I went wrong, and I would give my soul to go back, to succeed. So it is not the charge in itself that arouses my indignation: it's the fact that through those pages you try to besmirch my name, declaring that I was the one who involved the other defendants, giving the names that have been spoken in this room. For example the name of the Cypriot minister Polycarpos Georgazis. The infamy lies here, and this is also typical. To support it my accusers even said that I have a police record, that I was a hoodlum as a boy, a criminal as an adult, a thief and a mercenary. My police record is in front of you, gentlemen of the court-martial, and from it you can see that I was never a hoodlum or a criminal or a thief or a mercenary. I was always, and I am, a fighter in the struggle for a better Greece, a better tomorrow, a society, in other words, that believes in man. And believing in man means believing in his freedom. Freedom of thought, of speech, of criticism, of opposition: everything that the fascist coup of Papadopoulos eliminated a year ago. And now we come to the first charge that is made against me.

"The first charge, also in order of importance, is attempted subversion of the state: article 509 of the penal code. Isn't it paradoxical that those who make this charge against me are the very men who on April 21, 1967, violated article 509? Who then should be in this cage? I or they? Any citizen with some brains and balls would answer—'They.' And he would add what I add now: in becoming an outlaw, refusing to recognize the authority of the tyrant, I respected article 509 and did not offend it. But I do not deceive myself that you will understand me on this point because, if the coup had failed, you also would be in this cage, gentlemen of the court, not only the chiefs of the junta. Therefore I will say nothing further about this charge. I will go on to the second charge: desertion. It is true: I did desert. A few days after the coup I abandoned my unit and went abroad with a fake passport. I should have done it the very day of the coup, not afterward. But on that count I should be absolved: the day of the coup the situation with Turkey was extremely tense, and if war had broken out, my duty as a Greek would have been to fight and not to desert. Precisely because the war did not break out, I hastened to perform my other duty: to desert. Gentlemen of the court, to serve the army of a dictatorship would truly have been treason. I chose to be a deserter then, I am proud of my choice, and having said that, I come to the charge that is most important to you: attempted murder of the chief of state. I will begin by saying that, contrary to the nonsense offered by my torturers, I do not love violence. I hate it. I do not like political assassination either. When it happens in a country where there is a free Parliament and the citizens are granted the freedom to express themselves, to oppose, to think in a different way, I condemn assassination with disgust and anger. But when a government is imposed with violence and with violence prevents citizens from expressing themselves, from opposing, even thinking, then the use of violence is necessary. In fact, imperative. Jesus Christ and Gandhi would explain it to you better than I. There is no other way, and the fact that I failed doesn't matter. Others will follow. And they will succeed. Be prepared, and tremble. No, Mr. President, don't interrupt me, please. I am coming to the fourth charge and soon you will be able to shout to the four winds that your uniform does not tremble. Fourth charge: possession of explosives. What can I say to you beyond what I have already said? I have explained that only two of my fellow defendants knew I was preparing an attack, but they didn't know what kind. I have assumed responsibility also for the two bombs that exploded that same day in the park and in the stadium. I have explained that they were only a demonstration, a warning; they were exploded in such a way as to cause no victims. If my codefendants claimed something different in the documents they signed, this doesn't matter. Those documents were extorted under torture; if I were to torture Hazizikis and Theophiloiannakos I could make them say even that their mothers are prostitutes and their fathers are faggots. And I suppose that similar systems are responsible for the slander regarding Polycarpos Georgazis. I know that Papadopoulos would give a lot to make that slander the truth. Ioannidis also. That way they would have an excuse to invade Cyprus, destroy its independence just as they have destroyed democracy here. But they must both resign themselves; no foreign political figure is involved in the struggle I represent. It is taking place here in our country, gentlemen, not abroad; rightly my group is called the Greek Resistance. And if Polycarpos Georgazis were working for the Resistance, for me, it would be the first time that a private soldier has recruited a minister of defense. But in that case, you ask, where did this explosive come from? Gentlemen of the court-martial, I will not tell you. If I refused to confess that under the most horrible tortures, do you expect me to confess it in a speech to the court? That secret will die with me. And now I have finished. I must only add one personal thing. If you like, a small matter of personal pride. Your witnesses have said I am an egoist. Well, if I were, I would have remained calmly abroad. Instead I came back to fight and to risk my life. I knew the dangers awaiting me. Just as now I know the sentence you will inflict on me. I know, in fact, that you will sentence me to death. But I will not draw back, gentlemen of the court-martial. Indeed I already accept this sentence. Because the swan song of the true fighter is the death rattle he emits when shot by the firing squad of a tyranny."

There was a stony silence in the room. The judges, not reacting, stared at you, and it took a minute or so for the chief judge to find his voice again, to invite Liappis to make his concluding speech. Liappis spoke for a long time and with no reference to what you had said, demanding the death sentence for you and for another defendant, Eleftherious Verivakis, life imprisonment for Nikos, heavy sentences for almost all the others. Then the trial was suspended for a week, with the excuse that one judge had a fever. They no longer knew what to do. There were rumors that after your speech the members of the court-martial were in disagreement among themselves, that even Papadopoulos hesitated to have you shot because he realized how unpopular that would be, rumors that there were anxious meetings to persuade Ioannidis, unyielding in his determination not to spare your life. And then Sunday November 17, 1968, arrived, the day of the final hearing. You were very calm; during those seven days and seven nights you had had no second thoughts; if anything, you criticized yourself for not saying more, and you wrote a poem in praise of death: "The white doves have gone / the sky is filled with ravens / black birds / Wild rustlings of terror / have hidden the blue / the last moments / Throw earth in the grave / so the white doves will return / Earth, quickly, earth / But graves do not want only earth / they want ashes and blood / they want the dead / throw in the dead / Knead the earth with blood / For the white doves to return / it takes much blood." You entered the courtroom with your usual smile, your usual confidence, and your voice didn't break even when the chief judge a little later asked you if you had anything further to say and you stood up to utter the words that would eliminate any probability of salvation. "Gentlemen of the court-martial, in his concluding address the public prosecutor Liappis mentioncd Themis, the goddess of justice. But when we bring up mythology, we must do so without the errors he makes as soon as he opens his mouth. Your public prosecutor is ignorant, gentlemen, he doesn't even know that two Themises exist: the one who holds scales in her right hand and a sword in her left, looking at the scales with serene eyes; and then there is the Themis who holds scales in her left hand and a sword in her right, looking at the sword with a blindfold over her eyes. This is a political trial: all the crimes that have been attributcd to me, from subversion to desertion, from possession of explosives to attempted assassination, are part of the same accusation, which is political. Furthermore, gentlemen of the court-martial, you cannot allow yourselves any tenderness. Each of you staked his head on April 21, 1967: failing to condemn me would mean condemning yourselves, admitting your guilt. I understand this so clearly that I will not argue any attenuating circumstance that might lead you to a lighter verdict. On the contrary, I will repeat: I am the one who demands the death sentence the public prosecutor has called for. Send me in front of the firing squad: it will also serve to clarify my struggle morally, the struggle of everyone who opposes the foul regime crushing Greece today."

And the verdict: death for attempted subversion of the state, death for desertion, fifteen years' imprisonment for attempted murder of the chief of state, three years' imprisonment for possession of explosives and arms, besides the two already inflicted for insulting the court and the authorities. Total: death twice over and twenty years of prison. Verivakis was given life imprisonment. The others had sentences ranging from four to twenty-four years in prison. General Phaedo Gizikis, commander of the presidium of Athens, immediately signed the papers required for carrying out the sentence.

Not a muscle of your face had moved. You hadn't even blanched. Afterward, your lips twisting in an ironic grimace, you asked your lawyer: "How can anybody be shot twice?" Not waiting for an answer, you held out your arms to the policemen so they could slip the handcuffs on again. You felt strangely relieved, you told me years later, almost happy, and not because you were tired of living but because you were tired of suffering. Usually people are kind to those about to die, they are given a decent mattress, offered good food, perhaps even a swig of cognac; the priest comes for a little chat, and the condemned man is allowed to write to his family and friends. And, above all, he isn't beaten anymore. No more torture, no more torments. But you realized it wasn't going to be like that the moment they took you back to ESA headquarters and flung you into that cell without windows and bed, there were three officers waiting inside with lashes, and Theophiloiannakos promptly arrived with Malios and Babalis. "We have no respect for grammar, eh? We make mistakes in writing, eh? We're illiterate idiots, eh? Now you'll see how illiterate we are, what idiots we are, because we're going to interrogate you as we've never interrogated you before! And nobody will know whether you died here or in front of the firing squad." Then the lash came down on your back, your sides, your legs: they wanted to know if a certain Angelis had taken part in the plot to kill Papadopoulos. You fainted almost at once, and when you recovered consciousness, you thought you were dreaming: Hazizikis, with his blue suit, his carefully knotted blue tie, his clean-shaven face was standing in front of you. "Good day, Socrates. Or should I call you Demosthenes? No, the comparison to Socrates seems more correct. He too was a learned man, he also made an impressive last speech. Congratulations, your art as an orator almost moved me. Who would have said you were capable of such a thing? Well, after all, it's useful for great men like you to be brought to trial and sentenced to drink hemlock: otherwise history would never know they existed. Will I go down to posterity, too, the Meletus of our time?" You felt like crying. "Get out, Hazizikis." "And first, O men of Athens, I have to reply to the charges that have been falsely brought against me, the slander by which Meletus has brought me into this court . . . You see? I may be weak in grammar, but I have a good memory. I could also quote the dialogue about the immortality of the soul." "Get out, Hazizikis." "If death were the end of everything, O Simmias, the wicked would have a good bargain in dying, happily quit of their body, since with it they would be free also of the soul that committed their wickedness." "Get out, Hazizikis." "Not until I've asked you a few little questions, O Socrates. You should know me by now: you can't think I'm here to amuse myself, that I took the trouble to come here to discuss philosophy with you. Now what are you doing? Crying? Who would ever have said it! You're capable of crying. If you cry, you can't answer me. And you have to answer me, my dear man, because I want to know—" Then you turned and showed him a face streaked with tears. "Hazizikis! I won't die, Hazizikis! And one day I'll make you cry, Hazizikis! Because one day you'll end up in prison, Hazizikis! And while you're in prison I'll fuck your wife, Hazizikis! I'll fuck her and fuck her again until she pisses blood, until her guts fall out, Hazizikis! And you won't be able to do anything about it but cry, I swear it." "Impossible, my dear chap. I'm not married, as you know. But tell me if—" "Hazizikis, I'll kill you, Hazizikis!" "All right, I'll go. I'll pass my questions on to others who don't mince matters. You have to die anyway." And he left you in the hands of three officers who this time whipped you till you bled in order to find out if a certain Kostantopoulos were involved in the plot.

During the following twenty-four hours nothing happened. The next morning was November 20 and they put you into a motor launch. They took you to the island of Aegina where you waited three days and three nights to be shot.

They had taken many precautions on the island. They had chosen an uninhabited guardhouse in the old wing of the prison; they took you in through a side entrance in the most absolute silence and without anyone's knowing, and in the tiny courtyard they had posted twenty guards with submachine guns, in the vestibule of the guardhouse another five, in the corridor another nine, and three more in your cell. Thirty-seven armed men for one man, alone and handcuffed. You smiled and called a sergeant, to take off the handcuffs at least for a little while. The sergeant answered that it was impossible: the strictest order specifically concerned the handcuffs. "The minute his wrists are free, he attacks like a wild animal. He's a very, very dangerous criminal." The only concession was the door of the cell: it could remain open. But actually this was not a concession, it was a security measure: if you attacked one of the three guards, the open door would allow those in the corridor and the vestibule to come to his rescue. But how could you attack them, with what? The cell was emptier than a husk; they hadn't even given you a cot or a mattress, to rest you had to huddle on the floor. An officer came in with a paper in his hand. There was no time to lose, he said: by martial law, unless the president of the Republic intervened, the sentence would be carried out within seventy-two hours of the time it was pronounced. Forty-eight hours had already gone by, so here was the petition for pardon: you had only to sign it. You took the paper, read it, handed it back to him calmly. "No." The officer's eyes widened: "You won't . . . sign the petition for a pardon? Did I understand you?" "You understood perfectly, papadopoulaki, little Papadopoulos. I won't sign it." The officer insisted: "Listen to me, Panagoulis. Maybe you think there's no use, but you're wrong. I'm authorized to tell you that the president is prepared to commute the death sentence to life imprisonment." "I believe it. He'd like to be able to tell the world how I asked him to make me a present of my life. It would suit him not to kill me." "It would suit you even better, Panagoulis. Sign." "No." "If you don't sign, there's no hope." "I know." The officer put the paper back into his pocket. He seemed sincerely sorry. He also seemed uncertain whether to leave, as if he were hunting for words to convince you and couldn't find them. "Do you . . . do you want to think it over for a minute?" "No." "Then it's set for tomorrow morning at five thirty," he said, irritated. And he went off, shaking his head. In a corner one of the three guards was moaning: "Oh, no! Oh, no!"

He was a boy, almost beardless, his uniform still fresh from the quarter-master. He had followed the scene, gaping, and now he was looking at you as if he were going to cry. You went over to him: "What's wrong, papadopoulaki?" "I—" "You also wanted me to sign?" "Yes, I did! Yes!" "Didn't you hear what I said to the officer?" "Yes, but—" "No buts, papadopoulaki. When it's necessary to die, a man dies." "Yes, but I'm sorry all the same." "Me too," the second guard said. "Me, too," the third said. And that upset you deeply: it had seemed like centuries since a human being had not been bad to you. In all that time there had been only the old woman at the military hospital where they took you when tortures and your fasting had sent you into a coma; the old woman cleaned the toilets and one day, seeing you tied by the hands and feet, had come over with her pail and gently stroked your forehead: "Poor Alekos! Poor little creature! Look what they've done to you! And you're always alone, you never talk with anybody. Tonight I'll come here and sit beside you, and you can talk to me, eh?"

But a policeman grabbed her, carried her off with her pail, and you never saw her again. You cleared your throat now, to check your emotion. "Come here, all of you, papadopoulaki. Let's talk this over a bit." When they were around you, you began to explain to them why they weren't to be sad, or passive, why they should fight and see to it that your death served some purpose. You even recited some poems to them about freedom, and they listened respectfully, politely: if they liked a poem, they would write the verses down on a cigarette package. "That way we won't forget it." All three were very young, recruits who came from distant villages, all they knew about you was that you had tried to kill the tyrant, and their ignorance was so moving that it was hard for you to express yourself, to find the right words to make them understand you. "Really it doesn't matter that somebody tried, and afterward somebody else will try—and succeed, because when you walk along the street and you're not bothering anybody and a character comes along and hits you, what do you do?" "I hit him back!" "Bravo. And if he beats you up, again for no reason, what do you do?" "I beat him up." "Bravo. And if he prevents you from saying what you think and puts you in prison because you think differently from him and the law doesn't defend you because there isn't any law, what do you do?" "I, well, I—" "You kill him. You don't have any choice. To kill somebody is a terrible thing, I know, but in tyrannies it becomes a right, or rather, a duty. Freedom is a duty more than a right." In the end an officer in the corridor became annoyed and ordered you to be silent. "Shut up, Panagoulis! Are you looking for disciples when you're practically dead?" But another one took your side—"Shut up yourself, lousy pig, or I'll bust your face"—and he came to offer you a cigarette. Again you were moved. Was it possible that suddenly they were all so kind to you? Human beings are really odd: as long as you expect something of them they give you nothing, when you no longer expect anything they give you everything.

Around five in the afternoon the three young soldiers went off duty, and when they left, you felt a great emptiness: there was no telling what bastards would be sent now. Instead the three newcomers were the same: same age, same innocence, same sadness. And your uneasiness now became an emotion that found its release in bravado: "Come on, papadopoulaki, earn your bread! Who knows how to sing around here?" They pointed to a big fat boy, clumsy, with a peasant's hands. "Him, him! He sings in the choir in his village church, he does!" "Really? Then sing me the requiem from the funeral mass." "No! Not that!" "Sing it, I said!" He obeyed you and you wished he hadn't, because listening to him gave you a cramp in the stomach. "May he rest in peace, O Lord! May his burial be meet, O Lord! Earth that returns to earth! Receive thy servant, O Lord!" You interrupted him: "I don't like your requiem, papadopoulaki. I don't like the words 'servant of the Lord.' You have to make me a promise: when you sing it for me, you won't call me 'servant of the Lord.' Nobody is anybody's servant. Not even the Lord's. Understand?" The boy nodded, embarrassed. But the cramp wouldn't pass. "Come on, papadopoulaki, let's sing something better! Who knows 'The Smiling Boy'?" "Me!" "Me!" "Me!" "Good. Now then, all together! 'What can ever heal / my broooken heart / I've lost my smiling boy / I'll see him never-mooore / cursed be the hour, cursed be the moment / when our enemies killed / my boy with the sweeeeet smile . . ." You sang with them. But still the cramp wouldn't go away. That whole evening you sang, joked, preached, trying not to think of that requiem, not to think of that cramp, but the cramp wouldn't go away. There were moments, in fact, when it got worse. And these were the moments when you asked yourself the most absurd questions or took refuge in the craziest hopes: where it would be, what it would be like. You thought somebody had said it would be on the other side of the island, at the navy's firing range, but you didn't know whether this firing range was walled or in the open and you hoped it was in the open, that it wouldn't rain because once you had seen a movie where they shot a partisan in the rain, and it had distressed you because the partisan fell in the mud. You hoped too that they wouldn't shoot you in the face, you also wondered how to tell the soldiers to aim at your heart and not your face, and finally you wondered if it would hurt. This was stupid, you knew that; there is no comparison between the hurt you feel when you're tortured and the hurt you would feel being shot, it takes at least fifty seconds to become aware of the burning of a bullet in the flesh and before those seconds have passed you're dead. You had read this somewhere, or perhaps somebody who had been in the war had told you. Anyway the curiosity remained and you had to make an effort to overcome it, to meditate on more serious things, for instance on what you would say before the execution squad opened fire. It wasn't enough to say, "Long live freedom," you had to add something or else say a sentence that contained everything freedom included. Something, yes, like the cry of the Italian officer the Germans had shot at Cefalonia in 1944: "I am a man!" The cramp in your stomach passed at the idea of shouting at them: "I am a man!" But it returned a moment later because the cramp came not from the phrase you would shout or not shout, the pain you would feel or not feel, the rain that would soak you or wouldn't soak you: it came from the fact of having to die at a given hour on a given day. It's one thing to die under torture or in war or when a mine explodes—to die with an element of the unexpected—but it's another thing to die knowing that you have to die at a given hour on a given day with the same kind of precision of a departing train. One more night and you would cease to exist. In spite of your strength and your faith and your pride, you couldn't resign yourself to the idea of ceasing to exist. You were unable even to imagine what it meant, to ask such a question was worse than trying to establish whether the universe was finite or infinite, if time was time and space was space, if God existed or not, and if God and space and time had had a beginning or not, if before the beginning there had been something else or nothing, and what nothing is. What is nothing? Perhaps it is what we are or are not when we have ceased to exist, shot at a given hour of a given day, after a day and a night spent playing the role of the brave man even with a cramp in his stomach.

As it became dark you began to grow tired. The effort of dividing yourself in two, on one hand the pain of those secret reflections and on the other the show of proud indifference, had worn you out. Your legs were heavy, the handcuffs, your eyelids. You were terribly sleepy. And the sleepier you became, the less you wanted to sleep. The guards said: "Get some rest, Alekos. Why don't you rest?" But every time they said it you answered rudely. Wasn't it unbelievable that they should say, "Get some rest, why don't you rest," to a man who was on the point of resting forever? Wasn't it madness to fall asleep when you had so little time to live? To keep from giving way to sleep, you walked up and down, up and down, you even refused to sit. Then, toward three in the morning, weariness overcame you, the need to close your eyes. You stretched out on the floor, telling the guards to be sure to wake you in ten minutes, no more than ten minutes, and you fell promptly to sleep. Then you had a dream. You were like a seed, and gradually the seed's size was doubled, trebled, decupled, becoming so swollen and so big that its hull could no longer contain it; with a shattering explosion it burst, flooding the earth with a thousand seeds, and each of these seeds was quickly transformed into a flower, then a fruit, then again into a seed which in turn doubled, trebled, decupled, to burst again, flooding the earth with a myriad of seeds. At that point a very strange thing happened: from one flower a woman bloomed, and from another flower another woman, and from yet another flower yet another woman, and you wanted to possess them all, but you thought—O Christ, how can I manage, I don't have the time, soon the firing squad is coming and they will take me away, I have to hurry—so you seized the nearest one; without looking at her face, without asking yourself if she attracted you, without asking her if she accepted you, and you entered her, ravenously, with a haste, brutally, then you flung her away and took a second woman in the same way, you entered her and flung her aside in the same way to grasp a third, and a fourth, and a fifth, and a sixth, until you lost count, every thrust of your loins, a woman, and then the anguish of having to break off because somebody was waking you, was tugging at your shoulder and waking you. Who? You peered through your lashes. It was the clumsy young soldier who sang in the church choir: "It's five o'clock, Alekos. You slept two hours."

You sprang to your feet. You stared at the guards one by one, with dull fury. Two hours! You had begged them to wake you after ten minutes and they had let you sleep two hours! One part of you would have liked to hit them, sob and hit them, shouting—Wretches, idiots, thieves!—but another part realized they had disobeyed you out of affection and kindness—Let him sleep, poor man, but he said ten minutes, let him sleep anyway—and with an effort you controlled yourself, with an effort you whispered: "Shits. You stole two hours of my life." Then you said you wanted to bathe your face, use the toilet, and they led you into the corridor where there was a faucet and a primitive water closet. In front of everyone, awkward because of the handcuffs, you sat on the can, you washed, and it was five twenty. When you went back to the cell, you asked for coffee, drank it, and it was five twenty-five. Another five minutes to live then. And what does a man who is going to be shot think about during the last five minutes? Many years later, when I asked you this question, you answered that it was very difficult to express it, in fact you had had a lot of trouble representing those sensations in a poem, but there were three writers who had conveyed the idea: Dostoyevsky in *The Idiot,* Camus in *The Stranger,* Kazantzakis in *The Life of Christ*. These were three books in which you had recognized yourself. You made me a summary of the last two, but not of the first because we were sidetracked in an argument. I insisted that there's nothing of the sort in *The Idiot,* but you answered that I was wrong, that as a young man Dostoyevsky had been sentenced to death for a political crime and reprieved twenty minutes before being tied to the stake; in the book it was Prince Myshkin who told the story, but you couldn't remember the chapter with the episode. To prove it to me, you started hunting for it, leafing through the two volumes of *The Idiot* for hours in vain, and in the end you said: "Maybe I'm wrong." You weren't wrong: I was to discover this after your death. It was after your death that I found the passage you had looked for that day in vain. Who knows when, you had slipped a little piece of paper between the pages, and the book opened at those pages as soon as I picked it up; you had underlined the words, the words in which you later recognized your own feelings of your last five minutes: "He then had five minutes left to live, no more. He said that those five minutes were like an eternity to him, riches beyond the dreams of avarice. It seemed to him that in those five minutes he could live many lives, but for the moment he should not think of that last instant, so he came to various resolutions. He calculated the time necessary to bid his comrades farewell and he decided that it would take two minutes, he allowed another two minutes to think of himself again, the rest to look around for a last time." Then these words: "He said that for him the most unbearable thing was the constant thought: what if I had not had to die! What if I could turn life around? Everything would be mine. I would turn each minute into a whole century, I would lose nothing, I would count every minute, I would never waste one. He said that this thought finally filled him with such anger that he wanted only to be shot as quickly as possible." You had underlined the question of Alexandra Yepanchin: "What did he do with that wealth afterward? Did he count every minute?" And Prince Myshkin's answer:

"Oh, no. He told me himself—I asked him about it—he didn't live like that at all and wasted many, many minutes." But alongside the words of Prince Myshkin you had placed a big question mark.

Your last five minutes lasted three hours and then thirty hours. At half past five you were ready, but the squad didn't come. You asked a sergeant why not, and the sergeant answered that obviously they would come at six. You gave yourself a present of the half hour and at six you were ready again. But the squad didn't come at six either. Again you asked the sergeant why not, and the sergeant answered: "They'll come at six thirty." You granted yourself another half hour, at six thirty you were ready again. But again the squad didn't come. And the same at seven, at seven thirty, at eight. From one half hour to the next you prepared to die, and you didn't die. Once, twice, three times, four times, six times, each time a relief and a torment, a hope and a disappointment, while your anxiety grew and became raving impatience, a suicidal haste. At eight thirty you shouted: "What are we waiting for?" And when an unfamiliar shuffling echoed in the courtyard and the captain appeared on the threshold, you heaved a satisfied sigh: "Here I am." It took a while for you to understand what he was stammering, half-surprised, half-irritated: today was the Feast of Mary Virgin and Mother, the execution had been postponed until the next day, November 22, hadn't they told you? "No." Christ, what a hateful mix-up, what a cruel error, had some evil person perhaps been making fun of you? You turned your back on him, in silence, you remained in silence the whole morning and could never explain to me what a man feels when he discovers he has another twenty-four hours of life before him. Not a half hour but twenty-four hours, one thousand four hundred and forty minutes, a day and a night to think, breathe, exist. When I asked you, you remained puzzled, pursuing a memory that perhaps eluded you and perhaps didn't exist, as if the second agony had swept it away in outrage, and you always ended by repeating the sentence you had spoken the evening we met: "At dawn the waiting began again and it was all like the day before, like the night before." The heart-rending torture began all over again: five, five thirty, six, six thirty, seven, seven thirty, eight, eight thirty, nine. At nine the officer who had brought you the paper with the petition for a pardon came back and announced the execution was for the following morning. With identical movements he waved the identical paper, with an identical voice he urged you: "Sign it, go on, sign it." You tore the paper from his hand, crumpled it into a ball, threw it in his face, threw yourself on him, gripping him by the lapels of his uniform. "Coward, coward, coward, lousy coward, you knew they weren't going to shoot me yesterday! I'll strangle you, coward!" They tore him away from you, he ran off screaming that you were ungrateful, he had done it so you would sign. "You don't deserve anything, ungrateful bastard, you won't see me again." Immediately afterward a sharp command resounded, a guard blanched, and you thought—This is it, this time this is really it. But nothing happened, and again you began waiting. At eleven you were extremely restless, the wish for no further delay had become a need, a fever. You cursed with clenched teeth, you asked for a watch, you looked for explanations. Was Liappis missing? Liappis had to witness the execution in the name of the law. Was the sea rough? With a rough sea, the boats won't travel and maybe not even the navy's motor launches. You called a guard: "What's the sea like?" The guard looked into the corridor and repeated the question to the sergeant: "What's the sea like?" "Calm. This morning it was calm. Why?" "Just asking." Was Liappis coming in a helicopter and could the wind prevent it from landing? You called the guard back: "What's the wind like?" The guard looked again into the corridor to ask the sergeant: "What's the wind like?" "What wind? There isn't any wind. Why?" "Just asking." You bit your lip: "I don't understand. I don't understand at all." The thought that Papadopoulos might have decided to let you live never crossed your mind. You never imagined that, while you were being worn out by the inhuman waiting, all over the world people were fighting for you: processions in the streets, rallies, demonstrations in front of embassies, clashes with the police, frantic telephone calls among chiefs of state, thousands of cablegrams, diplomats shuttling between Rome and Athens, Paris and Athens, London and Athens, Bonn and Athens, Stockholm and Athens, Belgrade and Athens, Washington and Athens, and even messages from the pope, from Lyndon Johnson, U Thant, with a plea to spare you. But how could you have imagined it? They hadn't even allowed you to say good-bye to your father, your mother, exchange a word with your lawyer. After the sentence the only people who had come near you had been Theophiloiannakos, Hazizikis, Malios, Babalis, and those little soldiers who knew less than you did: for you the world began and ended in that cell where you thought you were ignored like the least strand of seaweed.

In the afternoon the squad came. "Get moving, Panagoulis." You embraced the guards one by one, you apologized for having been nervous, you thanked them for keeping you company. The guards were crying. There was also the beardless boy and the fat soldier who sang in the church choir, they were both sobbing without restraint and you slapped the first on the nose and held the other by the chin: "Courage, papadopoulaki." He blew his nose: "Can I ask you one thing, Alekos?" "Of course, papadopoulaki." "Why did you always call us papadopoulaki, what does it mean?" A smile: "Sometimes it means little papadopoulos and sometimes servant of Papadopoulos. It depends on how I say it." "But I'm not a little papadopoulos, and I'm not a servant of Papadopoulos!" "Good! Then shout with me: down with Papadopoulos! Down with fascism! Long live freedom!" "Yes, but—" "All together! Shout all together: Long live freedom!" "Long live freedom!" "Good! Now who wants to do me a favor?" "Me—"

"Me—" "Me—" "Fine. At ESA headquarters there's a certain Major Hazizikis. Telephone him and tell him not to forget to offer a cock for me to Asclepius." "What?" "He'll understand." And you followed the squad. Outside there were two automobiles, a truck, a jeep. You got into the jeep after taking a long look at the sky: it was a fine day, the blue sky as clear as polished glass. The convoy set off. But you realized at once that it wasn't heading for the firing range because you knew Aegina, you knew that the road to the firing range was in the opposite direction, up the mountain, and the convoy turned into the little lane that goes down to the harbor. "Where are you taking me?" "To Athens. We'll shoot you in Athens." They took you on to the same motor launch you had come in. They locked you in a cabin, running the chains of the handcuffs through a metal ring. At Piraeus they thrust you quickly into an automobile. "Where are you taking me?" "To Goudi. We'll shoot you at the army camp at Goudi." But they didn't take you to Goudi, they took you to the ESA. Here there was a commandant you didn't know. He wore black eyeglasses and had bad breath. Blowing the bad breath into your face, he said: "The papers say that you have already been shot, Panagoulis. Now we can really enjoy ourselves as much as we like." So you spent the whole night waiting to see them come and tie you to the torture cot. But they didn't come, and at dawn, when they pushed you toward the same car as the day before, you were so exhausted you couldn't stand on your feet. You walked with your eyes half-closed and nothing interested you anymore, you only hoped they would hurry and they would shoot you somewhere nearby, not at Goudi. A great contentment filled you when you saw that the tree-lined avenue was not the road to Goudi: thank heavens, at least they had chosen a barracks in the city. But which one? "Where are you taking me?" you asked again. "We're taking you to be shot, idiot. Where do you think we're taking you? The jokes are over." Instead they took you to Boiati.

3

THE LEGEND OF THE HERO DOES NOT CONCLUDE WITH THE great exploit that reveals him to the world. Both in myths and in real life the great exploit represents only the beginning of the adventure, the start of his mission. This is followed by the period of the great tests, then the return to the village or to normality, then the final challenge, which conceals the snare of death, which has always been eluded before. The period of the great tests is the longest, perhaps the most difficult. And this is because the hero is then completely by himself, irresistibly exposed to the temptation to surrender, and everything conspires against him: the oblivion of others, the exacerbated solitude, the monotonous repetition of his sufferings. But woe to him if he fails to overcome that second ordeal, woe to him if he doesn't resist, if he gives way: the great exploit that revealed him becomes futile and his mission fails. Well, your period of great tests is named Boiati. There, in that inferno where you wasted the best years of your existence, your heroism was confirmed, your legend took on consistency. And you knew it. That's why, like a sick man who always tells about his sickness or a war veteran who always tells about his war, bringing up one or the other no matter what he is supposed to be talking about, you never tired of returning in your memory to Boiati. Even at the end, when the memory of the bomb and of the trial and of Aegina had faded and your legend had been enriched with far bolder feats, and surely more important, the Boiati chapter remained for you the ache of an incurable disease, the pride of an impossible victory, as if the time there had cost you more than the tortures and the hours spent waiting to be shot. You talked about Boiati obsessively with everyone, and you didn't worry about repeating the same things to people who had already heard them or who couldn't appreciate them: you offered to anyone the story of your journey into hell. How you enjoyed amazing, horrifying, amusing where your sense of humor found a comic element in the tragedy. The only thing you never mentioned was the resignation that had exhausted you before you arrived there, the hope that they would shoot you quickly: you cannot twice ask the guards to telephone Hazizikis to offer a cock to Asclepius.

Boiati is about thirty kilometers from Athens and the road that leads there is easily recognized because it is marked with many signs. But you didn't see the signs, you stared dully at the asphalt, and suddenly the avenue opened out in a landscape of gray hills: on the opposite hill loomed a building like the prison on Aegina, with an outer wall and sentry towers and machine guns on the towers, and over the gate the sign MILITARY PRISON, BOIATI. The automobile entered, reached an open space where six little doors, painted green, stood in a row. The guards made you get out, they pushed you toward the last door on the left, muttering something to which you attached no importance, then they flung you inside with such violence that you slipped on the floor, striking the back of your head. The blow dazed you, a few minutes passed before you could look around and collect your wits. Where were you? In a cell obviously. As usual, an empty one: no cot, no mattress, and not even a blanket. The only object, in this emptiness, the slop bucket. The space was not too small, however. Say nine paces by seven. And the guards? There weren't any. Strange, according to regulations a man under death sentence must never be left alone. But what had he said, as you fell down, that character with the black eyeglasses and the bad breath? "Here you are, home," he had said. And after that? "If all goes well for you, you'll stay here till you croak." What did he mean? That they weren't going to execute you this time either? Impossible, unless the sentence had been suspended. Suspended for a day, a week, a month. The idea gave you no joy: it's terribly hard to get used again to the thought of living when you were already resigned to the idea of dying. You dragged yourself to the wall, to rest your back against it. You huddled there, your back to the wall, your legs stretched out on the floor, and you started looking around. Near the door there was a cockroach and he was moving slowly toward you. He kept approaching until he was a foot or so from your shoes, then he stopped: fat and black, disgusting. You kicked your feet: "Go away, go!" Then you repented and called him back: "Come on, come!" The cockroach seemed to hear. He made a turn and approached once more, then stopped near your right heel. "Come on, come ahead!" you urged him on. The cockroach moved an inch or two, avoided your heel, and continued his advance along the side of your pants until he was at your knee, when he stopped again, puzzled. You bent over to observe him. He had long hairy legs and erect antennae like two bristles, but the amazing thing about him was his wings. The shiny and hard carapace concealed beautiful wings. So even a cockroach could fly! You held out your arms to him: "Fly!" No, he refused to fly. "Jump, at least! Jump!" After great hesitation, he climbed onto the chain of your handcuffs, then onto the handcuffs themselves, then onto the back of your right hand, reached the base of your fingers, where he seemed again to hesitate, in doubt: which path to take, which finger? Finally he decided on the thumb, where unexpectedly he lost his balance and dropped headlong to the ground. A laugh escaped you. Hearing it gave you a kind of happiness: who would have thought you were still capable of laughing? And simply because a cockroach had fallen off a thumb! You stroked his back, delicately. You wondered how long a cockroach lives, how long his company would last, if they didn't shoot you at once. You also wondered if a cockroach can be made a pet. As a child you had tried to tame a beetle and you had almost succeeded. Your happiness grew. What luck to have someone you could play with, talk to, without being judged or reproached, what providence! To a cockroach you can say anything that comes into your mind, even that courage is made of fear, that in these past months you had often felt fear, that you had felt it especially when the firing squad came. They hadn't realized it, but forcing yourself to seem always calm and bold had been a terrible effort: on the motor launch you could hardly bear it any longer. An hour ago you still couldn't bear it. And a half hour, a minute ago. As if living no longer attracted you. Suddenly, instead, thanks to a tiny creature which at other times would only have disgusted you, you realized you wanted to live, and after all you can live also in a cell of nine paces by seven. You only need a cot, a table, a chair, a flush toilet, and a cockroach. And maybe a few books, some paper, a couple of pencils. If they weren't going to shoot you! You could study, read, write poems: you weren't the only person in the world forced to be in prison, and in some cases being in prison is a form of battle. Tyrannies are measured by the number of political prisoners, don't you agree, Dalí? You would call him Salvador Dalí because of those antennae that looked like a moustache, and calling him by this name you spoke with him until the key turned in the lock and six guards entered with your food. Dalí stayed there nice and quiet, his antennae lowered. Perhaps he had become bored with your talk and was sleeping. "Watch out for Dalí, papadopoulaki!" "Watch out for who?" the soldier carrying the tray asked. "My friend Dalí." "What friend?" "Him." And you pointed to the cockroach. "Ah!" the soldier said, his mouth twisting in a grimace of revulsion. And bringing his boot down sharply, he crushed it. On the floor there remained a whitish blob.

You used to say that it wasn't so much the whitish blob that distressed you; it was the crack of the carapace under the boot. And together with that crack, the shrill sound you thought you heard: as if, dying, the cockroach had let out a cry of pain. You said you almost felt they had crushed a creature with two arms and two legs, not a cockroach, and that the idea of losing him made the blood rush to your head because suddenly it brought back to you the awareness of your solitude, the image of the empty cell, furnished with a slop bucket and nothing else. You said that all these things aroused a bestial fury in you and restored your energy. "Murderer!" With that absurd shout you flung yourself on the soldier, slamming your handcuffs into his face. The tray with the food flew against the wall, and the soldier fell backward. Then you hurled yourself against the other five, giving one a kick in the belly, another an elbow in the stomach, a punch in the nose to one, and it was worse than throwing a lighted match into a wood in summer: in a few seconds they were all on top of you, you were reduced to a red mask of blood. The commandant of the prison also came, and in his rage he couldn't utter a word. Now who had they sent to him, who was this? Lunatic, he kept repeating, tirelessly, lunatic, in his long career he had seen all kinds but never a monster who tried to beat up a poor guard sent to bring him food, and what had the guard done, he had killed a cockroach, he had done you a favor, so the ESA men were right in saying you're a wild animal, you were to be treated with extreme severity, the system that tamers use in handling ferocious animals at the zoo, personally he was opposed to such methods but he realized he had no choice, he would inflict every kind of punishment on you, for a start he wouldn't give you the cot he had planned to give you, in spite of orders, no newspapers or books or paper or pen, just as they had told him, absolute severity, not even a daily walk in the open air, no family visits. And handcuffs twenty-four hours a day, because if you managed to wound people with your hands bound, what would you be capable of with your hands free? You listened to him, pretending to be indifferent, but actually weighing every sentence with extreme attention: O Christ, if he was announcing disciplinary measures, it meant they weren't going to shoot you. And this was the only thing that counted for today, tomorrow some saint in heaven would help you. But tomorrow is another day.

Tomorrow is not another day when existence has nothing human about it. You had been there a month, and there were moments when you couldn't see any difference between being alive and being dead, you knew you were alive only because you were breathing. First of all, the cell. It was damp, cold, because they wouldn't give you even a stove, and fouled by an unbearable stink because the bucket was emptied only every other day. When they entered, the guards held their breath, or they pressed a handkerchief over their nose and mouth, turning purple, and with an about face they ran outside to vomit. You were used to that stink, but the moment the door opened, letting in a gust of pure air, you realized the contrast, and at times you were overcome with nausea, you couldn't swallow a morsel. The absence of a cot increased the torment. Though at ESA headquarters and on Aegina it had been the same, you couldn't resign yourself to the idea of sleeping on the ground like a mangy dog; besides the floor was icy, the tiles covered with mold, this certainly didn't help cure your eternal cold, your cough. And you had no pillow. Give me at least a pillow, you shouted. But Patsourakos, that was the commandant's name, played deaf, fearing that his superiors would accuse him of being soft. For a pillow you used your rolled-up jacket, and without the jacket you froze. To keep from freezing, you interrupted your sleep, rose, and started walking up and down, but after a while your legs grew stiff, you had to stretch out again on the floor or sit with your back to the wall, your teeth chattering as you waited for the sun. Not that you could see the sun: they had put a piece of cardboard over the window. Still you could feel its warmth, and you were more impatient waiting for that warmth than waiting for food. You didn't care much about the food because the sight of the tray on the floor revolted you and because you couldn't manage to eat with the handcuffs on. The handcuffs! The big torment was the handcuffs: you still wore handcuffs. The first day you thought they would take them off. For sure they won't keep me in prison with handcuffs on, they don't force any prisoner to stay with handcuffs on, it must be an oversight, yes, they've forgotten to remove my handcuffs, and when the guard came back to empty the slop bucket, you held out your arms. "The handcuffs, papadopoulaki. You forgot the handcuffs." But the guard didn't answer, and when a week had passed, Patsourakos explained to you that the most specific order concerned the handcuffs. "I've had handcuffs on since August 13!" "I have nothing to say about it, Panagoulis. They told me to do this, and I have to do it." They took them off only twenty minutes every twenty-four hours so that you could use the bucket, and those twenty minutes never coincided with the moment you wanted to go. The act of taking down your pants afterward was a delicate and complex gymnastic exercise, the chain that joined the two steel circles measured thirty centimeters. As for the circles, they were so tight that they scraped your wrists and blood and pus from the sores oozed constantly.

And yet these weren't the things that exasperated you. It was the solitude, the isolation. You hadn't the slightest notion of what happened outside beyond the wall or in the prison proper, you didn't even know how many prisoners it contained and who were the men in the next cells. The only people you laid eyes on were the guards who came to bring your food or empty the bucket, and whether you greeted them cordially or else insulted them, they never opened their mouths. They had been forbidden to speak, and to hear the sound of a voice different from your own, you had to wait for the echo of some quarrel or a song. That obstinate silence nearly broke your nerves and at times made you nostalgic for the interrogation and for Aegina. Death can be faced, you used to say, tortures can be undergone, but not silence. At first it doesn't seem harmful, on the contrary it seems to help you think more and better, but soon you realize that in silence you actually think less and worse because the brain, working on memory and nothing else, becomes impoverished. A man who talks to nobody and to whom nobody talks is like a well that has no spring feeding it: little by little the water stagnates and becomes putrid, evaporates. Every now and then you would speak to a stain on the wall. A stain on the wall can be great company because it moves, its outlines are never the same; shifting constantly, they give you an object, then a profile, then a face, then a body, perhaps the face of a friend, the body of a desired woman. And you talk with it as with a cockroach. But there is quite a difference, if you think about it, between a stain on the wall and a cockroach: when you made the comparison, you suffered. You missed Dalí the cockroach so much. You missed him so much that you began to worry about your sanity: a man can legitimately weep at the death of a dog, a cat, but not at the death of a cockroach. And how you deceived yourself, thinking another would appear! For days you actually looked for him, saying to yourself that where there's one cockroach there's another, no animal lives alone, but you never found anything except some tiny ovoid balls that appeared to be mouse excrement. And this excited you very much, you would have been overjoyed to have a mouse: you would have preferred it to a cockroach. Mice are intelligent, cute, easy to tame. But this hope also quickly faded: it wasn't mouse excrement, it was the excrement of a spider. Without the spider. No, there was absolutely nothing alive in that cell. Only silence. Naturally, if they had given you a book or a newspaper, the act of reading would have helped to exercise your brain, a dialogue with written words at least, but this veto continued and it fed the silence, the monotony, the boredom. The boredom! When you are shut up within four walls with a stinking bucket and nothing else, even idleness is a torment, a minute seems like years, you lose all sense of time.

You no longer knew how to calculate time. You had no watch, they hadn't given yours back after your arrest, and there were moments when you couldn't tell if it was morning or afternoon. You kept asking yourself: what time can it be? At ESA headquarters you never asked yourself that, you couldn't have cared less about hearing them say it was nine in the morning or five in the afternoon, you never asked the time at the trial either. But at Boiati the curiosity to know the time devoured you convulsively, and the bastards refused to tell you. "What time is it?" Silence. "Tell me! What time is it?!" Silence. As if their tongues had been cut off. But even worse was another thing: you had also lost count of the days, the weeks, the months. During the first week, when darkness fell, you would make a scratch on the door, but after the eighth scratch you fell ill and made no more marks. "What day is it? What month is it?" Silence. In vain, you became angry, you shouted. "Answer me, for Christ sake! What difference does it make to you?!" Silence. When you decided that at least three months had gone by, by pure chance you discovered that only one had passed. It was the day when they made you come outside for the first time. "Come out, Panagoulis! Outside!" "What is it? What's going on?" "A visitor." "Who?" "You'll see." Half-blinded by the sunlight and staggering in your weakness, you reached the visitors' room. What if it were your mother? You hadn't seen her for almost two years, since the day you deserted. It actually was your mother. There she stood in her Sunday coat, her little turban, looking like a peasant woman dressed for a holiday. But why didn't she greet you? Why did she look away? You approached the grille to call her, but your emotion choked you and your lips wouldn't move. You coughed. She turned, observed you for a moment casually, then looked away again. After a few seconds she addressed the guards, infuriated: "Well, is he coming or isn't he?" "He's here. Can't you see him?" Her eyes grazed you again and went past you, in search of someone who was supposed to be there and wasn't: that white skeleton with the livid hollows under his eyes and the handcuffs on his thin wrists didn't resemble you even in his features. "No, where is he?" You summoned a faint voice: "I'm here." And immediately a cry shook the room: "Murderers! What have you done to him, murderers?!" You would never have believed your mother capable of crying: you had never glimpsed a tear on her lashes. But now she was crying and it took a while before she could calm down and speak, a while before you were reminded how beautiful it is to listen to another voice. Yes, of course, she had so many things to tell you: she had been arrested too and so had your father, did you know that? They had been released on November 24 and he wasn't well, those one hundred and three days of suffering seemed to have stunned him, but you weren't to worry, now he was better. For that matter he didn't know you were in prison. He didn't even know you had stood trial, she was keeping it from him. As for the death sentence, it had been suspended. Yes, it remained in effect for three years but everyone was sure Papadopoulos wouldn't shoot you, in spite of Ioannidis: in Europe there was too much talk about you, you had become a symbol, your name was on everyone's lips. This was why they had finally allowed her to come and visit you, and this morning Patsourakos had also allowed her to bring you some food, especially since the day after tomorrow— You interrupted her: "What day is today?" "You don't know the date? December 23! The day after tomorrow is Christmas!" "Christmas?! You mean I've only been here a month?" "Yes, of course, yes."

It was after that discovery, that trauma, that you rebelled: no, it couldn't go on like this. A man cannot live without having even a notion of time. Cockroaches or spider shit was not the solution: you had to escape.

But meanwhile you had to have humane treatment. You wanted a cot, for Christ sake, and a watch, and a decent toilet, and the newspapers every morning. And you wanted them to speak to you as well. What sentence decreed that you had to be always alone, without a watch to keep track of time, without a calendar to know what day it was, without anyone to answer your questions or say a word to you? What gave Ioannidis the right to avenge himself on you because you weren't dead and buried? You would go on a hunger strike, you would continue it until you went into a coma, and if Patsourakos didn't give in, the question would end up in Papadopoulos's lap, and rather than outrage public opinion, he would grant your requests. To be sure, starting a hunger strike with all that food in front of you was almost madness. You marveled at what your mother had brought you. Ah, that rabbit must be really delicious, was there any dish you liked better than rabbit? Maybe pork livers. Christ! There were pork livers, too, cooked with bay leaves! What else? Stew! If you had to choose between rabbit, pork livers, and stew, you would have had a harder time than Paris when he was to give the apple to the most beautiful goddess: how many eons had it been since you had eaten food like this? And there was enough for days, would three days be enough to consume a part of it? Today the livers because they spoil quickest, tomorrow the stew, otherwise it might turn sour, and for Christmas the rabbit! Yes, Paris's apple went to the rabbit: browned just right, smelling of sage. Afterward, the fast! For two days you stuffed yourself so full that on Christmas you couldn't even swallow a coffee. It was hard not to enjoy Christmas by eating the rabbit but the next day it would be yours, and you said to it: "Just wait, handsome, just be patient! We'll postpone the hunger strike twenty-four hours, today I just can't handle you, forgive me!" Then, contented, you shuffled a few dance steps between the door and the wall opposite, the wall opposite and the door. At the fourth turn, however, you stopped, frowning. Strange, there was something different about the door: the light didn't pass through the peephole as it usually did. Why not? You approached, you put your forehead to it, and immediately you sprang back: there, on the other side of the hole, an eye was watching you. Damn it! They had seen you converse with the roast rabbit, dance, behave like a fool! The embarrassment of it, the shame. Who was it? What did it matter who it was, whoever it was, he had to be punished. You raised your chained arms, you thrust your right forefinger in the hole, and a cry of pain answered you, then a chorus of excited voices: "Hurry, to the infirmary! He hurt him. He almost blinded him! What do you mean, almost? He did blind him! That animal, that beast! Let's teach that animal a lesson!" And another voice said: "No, no, I can see. He didn't blind me. I can see, I swear I can! It was an accident! He didn't do it on purpose. I tell you, leave him alone: it's Christmas!" But it was useless. The door of the cell was flung open and, furious, determined to avenge the offense, seven of them burst in. "You animal, filthy animal, beast, we'll give you Christmas!" It seemed they had suddenly found their vocal cords again, the silence of a month had suddenly been broken, to deafen you. And soon they weren't just shouting: they were hitting. All together, all seven. Made clumsy by the handcuffs, you couldn't even try to defend yourself, and soon you were a little heap of scratches and bruises on the floor, between the trampled rabbit and the excrement from the overturned bucket. Merry Christmas, Merry Christmas.

And yet, paradoxically, that Christmas beating made things easier. It made your first hunger strike in Boiati almost bearable. With a hunger strike it's actually the beginning that proves difficult. The first three days. When they've passed, a great weakness takes over and all desire for food disappears. So, if you begin your fast after a fine beating has dazed you, you don't even notice your stomach is empty, the last thing you want is food, and this is what you did from the moment the seven left you alone: for seventy-two hours you refused even water. After that you accepted a little cup of coffee, then you started all over again until you sank into a lassitude so profound that you lost consciousness, and it was in this condition that the ESA doctor found you: the same man who had tried to help you on the day of your arrest. You were half-dead this day because you hadn't touched food for two weeks. Suddenly you felt a needle prick your arm and a rush of warmth stirred your blood, along with a sense of well-being. You raised your eyelids and there he was standing over you, with his shrewd face, his little eyes sparkling with complicity and irony. "Hello, Alekos." "Who are you?" "You know me. A doctor. My name's Danaroukas." "What do you want?" "To help you." "Like that other doctor who watches tortures?" "I don't watch tortures." "Liar." He answered by thrusting a sliver of chocolate into your mouth. "Tell me why you won't eat." "Because I want a calendar. A watch and a calendar. And I want them to speak to me!" "Not enough. What else?" "I want them to take off my handcuffs." "Still not enough. Then what?" "I want them to give me a cot." "Still not much, so?" "A decent toilet." "And then?" "Newspapers. Books. And pen. And paper." "That's better. If you ask for only one thing they'll never give it to you. If you ask for a lot of things, they'll give you one of them. Or two. I'll report. Meanwhile hide this chocolate. It'll come in handy next time." He went off with the list of requests and the next day the cot arrived. Two days later a soldier appeared, with a meek, likable face: "Good morning, Alekos."

Christmas Day they had assigned him to guard your cell, without telling him who you were. They had only explained that you were a very, very dangerous criminal, so he wasn't to say even one word to you, and this had aroused an immense curiosity in him: he had started watching you through the hole in the door to see what a very dangerous criminal looked like, and he had promptly got a finger in his eye. You examined him, with hostility: "Who are you?" "I'm the one whose eye you stuck your finger in." "That'll teach you to be a spy." "I'm not a spy." "All spies say, 'I'm not a spy.' " The little soldier smiled and without answering went toward the bucket to take it away. What if he was sincere? You had to provoke him, to make sure. You deliberately set to provoking him: "I see you like collecting shit, papadopoulaki." "No, but I'm glad to collect yours, Alekos. Because I admire you." O my Christ! he seemed sincere. You waited until he came back with the cleaned bucket and you began tormenting him again. "Unfasten my pants, papadopoulaki. I want to piss." He smiled again, meekly. He set down the clean bucket and then, gravely, unfastened your pants. "Now help me piss." "No, Alekos, not that. It isn't right. I'll take off your handcuffs and you can do it by yourself." "Ah! they've given you permission to take off my handcuffs, papadopoulaki?" "No, they haven't, but I've been wanting to do it for a long time." "I don't believe it." "Don't believe it then." You softened a bit. "Why didn't you talk to me before?" "Because I didn't know you." "Or because you didn't have the courage, because they had told you that talking to me is forbidden?" "I knew it was forbidden, but still, these past few days, when you were delirious, I talked to you all the time. Well, do you want me to take off these handcuffs or not?" "If you take them off, I'll run away." "If you run away, they'll catch you and instead of me they'll send somebody who isn't a friend." You held out your wrists to him. He took off the handcuffs. "What if I stole your keys now and your revolver?" "No, you won't do that." "Why not?" "Because it would be foolish. You want to pee, or not?" Disoriented, you urinated and at the same time you studied him out of the corner of your eye: no, he wasn't lying. You could feel with all your instinct that he wasn't lying, and after a slight hesitation you held out your wrists again so he could put the handcuffs back on. At your right wrist, the more infected, the sore had eaten into the flesh, to the bone. "What's this? You must be treated, Alekos, bandaged!" "Slip on the handcuffs, papadopoulaki, and stop the playacting." "You're being unfair. And I won't put the handcuffs on a wound like that. I'm going to get some medicine right away and I'll bandage you." "No." "I'm going anyway." He went off and came back an hour later, with salve and a bandage. "You took your time, papadopoulaki. Did you go and report on your progress?" "No, I strolled around to give you more time with your hands free." Then he medicated you, bandaged you, put the handcuffs back on, with an expression that convinced you more than any word. "Thanks, papadopoulaki." "My name isn't papadopoulaki. My name is Morakis. Corporal Morakis."

It took almost a month for you to be convinced he wasn't lying, and during that month you were often cruel, as you so effectively knew how to be whenever you wanted to make sure something was true. The more you liked a person, in fact, the greater was your fear of being deceived, of letting yourself go, so you made that person suffer. In the end, however, his goodness convinced you. He was extremely devoted to you. There were moments when you asked yourself how you would have managed without him: it was he who, besides emptying the bucket even three times a day, brought you the newspapers, the pencils, the writing paper that Patsourakos hesitated to give you. Not that Patsourakos was despotic, for some time he had even allowed you to see your mother in the chapel rather than in the visitors' room with the grille. Nevertheless one day the guards caught you passing her a note, and, rather than get into trouble with Ioannidis, Morakis took away your newspapers, pencils, paper, everything you had gained by the hunger strike that Danaroukas had interrupted. He left you the cot, and that was all. Still he took off your handcuffs, risking being caught each time, and this was what convinced you you could really trust him, confess to him your desire to escape. He didn't seem surprised: "I know, but it's very hard." "No, all I need is a uniform. Do you have one?" "I have my extra one for the times I go out on a pass." You measured yourself, you measured him: he was shorter than you and his shoulders were less broad but by and large you had the same build. "All right, you'll give me your extra uniform and you'll wear the one you have on." "Me?!" "You'll come with me, naturally." "But I—" "Don't make that face. You'll have plenty of time to get used to the idea. To begin with, I have to regain my strength. I'm still so weak I couldn't reach the gate." "And when are you thinking of—" "I don't know. There's no hurry. Now bring me a healthy supper." He brought it to you and you ate heartily. You ate like that every day: you became so docile that Patsourakos even allowed you a table, a chair, and some time out in the yard. The only thing he didn't do was have the handcuffs taken off: the ESA had denied him authorization: "Are we playing good samaritan, Commandant?" Handcuffs or not, you improved rapidly: by spring the sores on your wrists had almost healed, you had recovered some of your weight, and you could even be heard singing in a festive voice the gloomy poem you had written during the week the trial had been suspended: "The white doves have gooone! The sky is filled with raaaavens! Blaaaack birds!" You liked singing it because, as you were tone-deaf, you knew it was doubly irritating to the guards. "Shut your trap, Panagoulis!" Then May came, with its warmth, and the terrible thing happened.

One morning they removed your handcuffs, brought you a bucket of warm water, gave you a bath, cut your hair, shaved you, offered you a clean shirt and a freshly ironed pair of slacks, and they said you could go into the yard and stretch your legs as much as you liked. The offer surprised you but didn't arouse your suspicions: obviously they had decided to give in and why should you reject a bit of comfort? You left the cell. There was nobody in the yard. You leaned against the wall, turned your face to the sun, and a football landed at your feet. You narrowed your eyes to see who had thrown it, but the sun blinded you and again you saw no one. Was it

Morakis? You kicked the ball away lazily. The ball came back. Yes, it must have been Morakis, hiding somewhere or other, wanting to joke. With greater enthusiasm you gave another kick. The ball slammed against the wall opposite, bounced, and for the third time you found it at your feet. Ah, Morakis! He wanted to challenge you, eh. All right, you'd go along with him. It was ages since you'd played football, but you'd prove to him that even with your breath gone you could show him a thing or two. "There! There! There!" You kicked it once, twice, three times, until you were out of breath and you stopped, gasping: "I'm tired, Morakis!" But nobody answered you. Could it have been someone else? Not Morakis? And, as you asked yourself this, you had the unpleasant sensation of being watched. Still the yard was deserted. Deserted? No, now that you were growing used to the sun, you could make out a sergeant, there at the end. And he was waving: "Go on, Alekos, go on!" You didn't know him. Who was he? "Go on, Alekos, play! Kick!" Blushing, you turned away from him and walked back to your cell. Then you waited for Morakis, and when he arrived, the next day, you had only to see the way he handed you the newspapers and you understood everything. They all featured your photograph taken while you were playing football, and all deplored the outrageous slander of the foreign radio that said you had been kept handcuffed for nine months and slept on the floor like a dog and never saw the sun, as if you were buried alive: Greek reporters as well as correspondents from every country had been able to see for themselves that, on the contrary, you were in good health, clean, well dressed, without handcuffs, that you left your cell whenever you liked and you had so much sunlight that you even went back inside before being told to. Morakis was the image of dismay: "It was my morning off . . . If I had been here it wouldn't have happened . . . I'd have warned you . . . I heard about it only last night and . . ." "Tell me: where were they?" "In the visitors' room. They hid them in there. They watched you from the windows." You remained silent for a few minutes, then you burst into tears and told Morakis to be ready: in a week you wanted to escape.

It was the night of Friday June 5, 1969, and the prison was asleep. Morakis came with the uniform in a bag, and you put it on at once. Then you stuffed your clothes in the bag, arranged the blankets to imitate a human form, to deceive anyone who looked in through the peephole, and you gave the order: "We're off!" It was as if you were about to go on a picnic. Morakis, on the contrary, seemed nervous: the realization that he was transforming himself into a deserter and becoming responsible for the escape most feared by the regime made his hands shake. "You lock it, I can't," he said, pointing to the door of your cell and handing you the ring of keys. You locked it with steady hands, headed off in the darkness, not knowing how the two of you would solve the first problem: getting past the prison gate. What if the sentry recognized you? What if he asked for your papers? The sentry was half-asleep. "You do the talking," Morakis said. You stepped forward. "Wake up, slacker!" Then you flung him the bunch of keys: "Open the gate, slacker!" "But, Corporal, sir—" "Come to attention when you speak to a superior!" "Yes, Corporal." "What's your jacket doing unbuttoned like that? Is this a new way of wearing a uniform?" "No, sir, Corporal. I'm sorry, Corporal." "Let me make sure everything's in order here." "Yes, Corporal. Check, sir." Behind you, Morakis was groaning faintly. "Oh no! What's the need? Oh no!" But you didn't even listen to him, and carried away by the farce, you went on shamelessly playing your role. "Look at this! Is this any way to keep the keys! Shame on you! With carelessness like this, anybody could escape, dammit! Anybody! All right, I'll let you off this time. But tomorrow I want you to report yourself, you understand?" "Yes, Corporal." "Open the gate." "Right away, Corporal." "And if we come back don't shout any 'Who goes there?' or any nonsense like that, you understand?" "Yes, Corporal." He opened the gate, you were in the army camp itself, of which the prison was part, and now you had to face the second difficulty: getting out of the camp. How? Presenting yourselves to the sentry and repeating the same farce was inconceivable, to climb the outside wall and jump down was very risky: spotlights from the towers illuminated it every fifty seconds. And yet there was no other choice. You crouched down at the point farthest from the barracks, waiting for the right moment, and when it came: "Go!" Morakis quickly climbed on your shoulders, grabbed the wall, reached the top, held down his arms to you, pulled you up: "Watch out for the barbed wire!" The barbed wire or the band of light that was inexorably approaching and in an instant would illuminate you. "Jump!" A double tear was heard: both of you had ripped your trousers, and your jacket too. But the jump had gone well, no twisted ankles, no bruises, you could run down the hill and reach the road: the only obstacle was a shepherd with his flock and his dog exactly halfway down. "Will the dog see us?" "Let's hope not." "Go ahead!" Morakis went first. Bent double, he ran like a hare; but you had to stop every now and then to catch your breath, and the dog saw you. It barked and barked. It kept barking until, covered with dirt, gasping, you touched the road. Now there was the question of getting to Athens.

As a rule an escaping prisoner can rely on the complicity of somebody on the outside, a man waiting for him with a car, who helps him continue his flight. But in your distrust and your taste for the impossible gamble, you had rejected this solution and forbidden Morakis to look for aid. No one was to know that you and he were going to escape, everything had to be entrusted to chance and to your initiative, so on the road there wasn't a living soul. "Now what?" Morakis asked. "Now we take the bus." "The bus?" "Yes, the bus, just as two corporals on a pass should do." The bus was arriving, you boarded it with Morakis, and you quickly realized this had been a mistake: with your uniforms torn and soiled, you looked like anything but two corporals on a pass. The conductor stared at you, bewildered: "Been in a fight?" "Yes, yes. A lousy bum allowed himself to insult the army." "Are you going into the city?" "No, we'll be getting off at the next stop." You got off. Morakis seemed more and more uneasy. "Now what?" "Now we take a taxi." The taxi also came along. It carried you only a few kilometers because it was confined to the Boiati area. Afterward you were on foot again, protected only by the darkness. "Now what?" "Now I take off the uniform." You hid behind a tree, took out the clothes you had put in Morakis's bag, changed with a sigh of relief: now they would lose the trail of the two corporals in uniform. "Now what?" "Now we look for a second taxi, and then a third, to Athens." The third taxi took you into the city at midnight, and it was then that the disturbing fragility of a plan relying on luck became evident: where to hide? During the preparations Morakis had asked you several times: "Afterward where will you go? I can hide out at a girl's, a relative's, but you? The police are watching your family. Your friends are all in prison. How will you manage?" And you had always answered him: "Don't worry, a thousand people are ready to welcome me." Who were those people? The ones who always come forward when the risk is past, when freedom has been regained, the big talkers, the cowards who as soon as they are put to the test melt like candles in a fire? Some wouldn't even open their door. "Who is it?" "It's me, Alekos, I've escaped, let me in." "Go away, you must be joking, get out!" Others opened a crack, with the chain on, and were panic-stricken at the very sight of you: "I can't, it's too dangerous, I can't!" Even a girl who said she loved you drove you away like a beggar, a leper: "Get out, fast! You don't want me to end up at the ESA on your account?" At three in the morning you were still wandering from one neighborhood to another, and Morakis was in despair: "What are we going to do? Where can I leave you?" You were exhausted, all this walking had worn you out, and you dragged yourself along, murmuring: "I'm not used to it anymore, I have to rest, I have to rest." Finally you noticed a building being demolished: "What if we rested here?" "All right," Morakis answered. You fell asleep at once, stretched out side by side like children, and at dawn you were wakened by a yell: "Faggots! You don't come and do your filthy things on a worksite, understand? Police, police!" There was just time to get up and run away, pursued by a group of threatening workmen. After turning the corner, you stopped: "We have to separate. Fast!" "I can't leave you alone, Alekos, I can't!" "Yes, you can! Clear out, I tell you. Go!" "But where will you go? Where?" "I don't know, don't think about it, run!" The workmen were approaching: "Police, arrest them, police!" Morakis vanished. There wasn't even time for you to say thanks, see you again.

And there you were alone in the city that was beginning to wake. There you were exposed to the light of the sun, with that face that six months before had been photographed for every newspaper, that moustache that made you recognizable even in a country of men with moustaches: if you had at least thought to shave it off! "He is wearing a pair of dark trousers, a blue T-shirt, and has a moustache," the police descriptions would say. No doubt by this time, seven in the morning, they had already discovered the escape and the police alerts had already been circulated: so taking a taxi was out of the question. Taking a bus, worse. To continue walking the streets, crowded or deserted, the same. The question had to be resolved immediately, here in this neighborhood. What neighborhood was it? Ah, yes: Kipseli. Who lived in Kipseli? Patitsas! Demetrios Patitsas! Why hadn't you thought of him last night? Demetrios was a distant relative, a second cousin, and he had been involved with the Resistance: Theophiloiannakos had asked you to confirm that, during the interrogation, hitting you with the falange. "Who is this Demetrios who supplied the fake passports? Who is he?" Once again not a word had escaped you: out of gratitude, if for no other reason, Demetrios would put you up for a night. But what was his address? Ah, yes: Patmos Street number fifty-one. But what was the way to Patmos Street? Let's see: from here, you turn right, then left, then another right . . . Patmos Street! How long it is, though, endless: this is number one hundred forty-nine, one hundred forty-seven, one hundred forty-five . . . ninety-nine, ninety-seven, ninety-five . . . Keeping your head down, afraid someone might turn and say: "Why, isn't that Panagoulis?" Fifty-seven, fifty-five, fifty-three . . . fifty-one! Finally you reached fifty-one, you rang the bell. The next to the top, on the left. A sleepy voice came through the intercom: "Who is it?" "Me." "Me, who?" "Open up, Demetrios! Don't waste any time, for Christ sake!" A sharp sound and the front door opened. There was no concierge. A brief hesitation—elevator or stairs?—and then up the stairs, panting. Oh no! All these stairs, for a man who hasn't climbed any for eleven months and whose legs are gone! Eight flights to reach the fifth floor where a terrified little face stares at you, unable to send you away. But you didn't waste time pleading now. With one leap you were in the apartment and you shut the door behind you: "I've escaped, Demetrios. You have to keep me here at least one night." "Escaped?! Tell me—" "Later. First give me a razor. I have to shave off my moustache."

Without the moustache you were almost unrecognizable. You looked smugly at yourself in the mirror and then you began inspecting the house. One glance was enough for you to realize you had happened on an excellent hiding place: Patmos Street was in a kind of casbah, and Patitsas's apartment was in a building identical to the others. It also had a double terrace from which you could jump to the next roof and get away if necessary. But the necessity would not arise: who could possibly discover you were hidden there? Nobody had seen you enter, nobody had seen you on the stairs, and from the windows opposite there was no way to observe what went on in here because the windows were much lower. You counted the rooms: living room, bath, kitchen, and a room with the door shut. "What's in there?" "A friend." "Don't you live alone?!" "No, but don't worry. He's a real friend, a comrade." "What's his name, what does he do?" "His name is Perdicaris, he's a student." "I want to talk with him." Patitsas opened the door. Under pictures of the Kennedy brothers and a poster showing Red Square with the onion spires and the Kremlin a young man was sleeping. You restrained a smile and went in. You waked him and confronted him firmly: "I'm Panagoulis. I've escaped from Boiati. No false moves, understand?" After a moment of amazement, he jumped from the bed and answered you with kisses, hugs, oaths of loyalty. "Alekos, you've no idea how much I admire you, Alekos, I'd lay down my life for you!" And Patitsas, pointing to the photographs of the Kennedy brothers, Red Square with the onion spires and the Kremlin: "What did I tell you? Don't worry! You're among comrades, for heaven's sake, you couldn't have struck a better place, why didn't you come here right off? Now rest, eat, tell us how you managed, you devil!" He went on like that, with assurances and flattery, until the moment when the radio announced the news. The escape had been discovered at eight in the morning, the radio said, when the guards had had to force the door of the cell because they couldn't find the keys entrusted to Corporal Morakis. Along with Panagoulis, Corporal Morakis had also disappeared and was now being sought as accomplice and deserter. An argument broke out at once: you had to leave the country, obviously, but how? Would it be better to go by land or by sea? Patitsas said by sea, with a foreign freighter or a yacht; Perdicaris said by land, across the Albanian or Yugoslavian border; you said a plane was better, without moustache and with eyeglasses nobody would recognize you, provided you had a passport. But Demetrios would take care of that. "Right, Demetrios?" "Of course. Tomorrow." But the next day the matter was postponed. It's Sunday, you know, on Sunday everybody goes to the beach, you can't get anything done on Sunday. Besides they had a date with a couple of girls and if they didn't show up, they would arouse suspicion. So long, see you at suppertime.

At suppertime they hadn't come back. Not at midnight either, or late in the night, or even Monday morning, or Monday afternoon. Why not? Soaking in anxiety, you counted the minutes, and each minute was a grim hypothesis. What if they'd been arrested? No, no, in this case the police would have come looking for you. What if they'd had an automobile accident? No, no, in that case somebody would have got in touch. What if they were going to . . . Oh, no, you didn't even want to think about that. It was obvious: they'd stayed at the girls', slept with them, and . . . Obvious, hell! Didn't they know you were alone, worried, nervous, and with the problem of not wasting time, of getting out of the country? You were also without food. They had left two eggs in the refrigerator and a tomato and the rest of the cheese from Saturday night. The eggs and the cheese you had eaten at once, the tomato you had eaten later, so nothing was left but a crust of bread. And didn't they even consider that? Unless . . . No, Demetrios was someone you could trust, Perdicaris was a good boy, no doubt they were hunting for a passport for you and this was why they hadn't got in touch. You told yourself this. Still the doubt lingered, poisoned you, and in the grip of it you became restless, you flung yourself on the bed, got up again, turned on the radio, turned it off, stiffling with anger, helplessness, uncertainty. Leave, or stay? To leave would be almost insane, and yet staying was a mistake too. Let's suppose that in spite of their welcome they had been overcome by fear. The most infamous things are done out of fear, and you could almost see them with their pimply little faces, their greasy hair, their vulgar blue jeans, you could almost hear them: "It had to happen to us, eh? I'm not going to jail for him!" "Me neither!" "Suppose we go to the police?" "Simpler not to go home, starve him out: sooner or later he'll cut and run." Yes, it had been a mistake to seek refuge in Patmos Street, you realized that now. A mistake and a waste of precious time. When darkness fell, you would leave. You waited for the darkness and just as you were about to leave, the door burst open: "Here we are! Ah, women! What whores they are! Whatever happens, it's always women's fault. They kidnapped us. We kept saying 'If we could only telephone him!' Still, we were thinking of you the whole time. We went to the port too. And we found the ship. It's a freighter, leaving Piraeus Wednesday, bound for Italy."

In the years we lived together, the years that revealed you to me, I noticed there was one subject of which you spoke little and reluctantly: the days spent in the house of Patitsas and Perdicaris. Whenever I tried to learn more, you would turn pale and say: "Skip that." Once, however, you abandoned your reticence and, telling me what I have told so far, you said that on hearing the voices of the pair—Here we are, what whores women are!—you felt your stomach contract. Looking into their faces, you were overwhelmed by a strange uneasiness. Something about them didn't convince you: they were too jolly, too cordial, they talked too much and they contradicted themselves. Had they really been with the girls or had they been busy on your account? The two things didn't fit. And the freighter, what sort of freighter was it? How had they found it, who had dealt with them, what story had they used? You became hard: "Less talk and more details." "Of course, Alekos, of course, but what are you getting nervous about, be patient, be calm, we have all night ahead of us, and we also have to eat, don't we? Aren't you hungry? Look at all the good things we've brought: eggplant, kid, veal birds." First the news, then the food. "Ah, you don't trust us? We left you alone too long, eh? It's made you nervous, Lord only knows what's got into your head. Sure we should have come home last night. But those two whores . . . This morning I wanted to drop by here a minute, but it was so late, I wouldn't have made it to the office on time." You addressed Perdicaris: "Would you have been late for work, too? Do you also go to an office?" "No, I had a class at the university." "At noon you had a class at the university too? In the afternoon too?" "Come on, Alekos, you're being unfair. I went to the port in the afternoon. And I looked for the captain—" "What's the name of this captain?" "Honestly, I don't remember, Alekos. A foreign name, a hard name. Was he Japanese or Swedish, Demetrios?" "Swedish, I think." "And the ship?" "Swedish, right?" You grabbed him by the neck: "Don't try anything funny, kid." If Patitsas hadn't butted in, you would have strangled him. "Calm down, your nerves are shot, I understand you. But why take it out on him, poor boy? Why don't you take it out on me? I sent him to the port. Don't you trust me? I'm your relative, your friend. We played together as children, have you forgotten that?" You pushed him aside: "I'm leaving." "Are you crazy? You want to get yourself killed?" And the other one said: "No, Alekos, no. You've got us all wrong!" Meanwhile they sought your hands, they stroked you, whining. In the end you gave in: "All right, let's eat these birds, this eggplant." You ate and drank. There was plenty of wine, white, the kind you liked, retsina, and you hadn't touched wine for almost a year. Your anger soon became gaiety, and the gaiety became stupor. "Now, boys, let's talk about this ship that's leaving Wednesday." "Later, Alekos, later. We've had too much to drink. Let's get some sleep." "Yes, yes, another glass, and then some sleep, Alekos!" Yawning, you ended up taking Perdicaris's room and, under the pictures of the Kennedy brothers, the poster of Red Square with the onion spires and the Kremlin, yes, they were comrades, friends, and you fell into a tormented sleep. With the fish. You were with Morakis, on the seacoast road of the assassination attempt, but he was halfway down the embankment and you were on a rock near the water. Morakis was shouting: "Four eyes see better than two, why have we separated?" Then a wave flung two fish on the rock. You wanted to catch them but they were alive and so slippery that when you barely touched them they flopped away, rapidly, and if you caught one, the other eluded you, so you flung yourself on the other and lost the first one, suffering because you realized that catching only one was no use: you had to capture both. Morakis, you called, Morakis, come help me! But Morakis didn't hear you, and you fell down from the rock, and at the moment of drowning you realized Morakis had fallen before you. Patitsas was shaking you: "What's wrong? Are you sick?" "Why?" "You were tossing, groaning." "I was having a bad dream. Something's going to happen." "Nothing's going to happen, Alekos. Sleep in peace."

The next morning was Tuesday and Patitsas went out very early, when you were still dozing. "Ah, we didn't talk about the ship last night! All that wine! We'll talk at noon. I'll be home around twelve. So long, I have to run, sorry." There wasn't even time to answer him—No, dammit, we'll talk now. That brought back the uneasiness the wine had dispelled, but you forced yourself to master it and a couple of hours later, when you got up, you felt almost confident. Whistling, you made coffee, drank it, turned on the radio, and immediately the uneasiness returned. The announcer was saying that no trace of you or Morakis had been found and the government was offering half a million drachmas to anyone who furnished information leading to your capture. Damn, half a million drachmas was a handsome sum, more than enough to whet somebody's appetite. You had to be careful, avoid making noise when Patitsas and Perdicaris weren't home, keep the lights off, the radio low, or the neighbors might get suspicious. Half a million drachmas. Did they know, the two of them, that you were worth half a million drachmas? You woke up Perdicaris sleeping off the wine in the next room: "Hey, did you know I'm worth half a million drachmas?" "They've been talking about it at least since yesterday," Perdicaris mumbled, then he rolled over again and resumed snoring. Since yesterday? What did he mean? And why hadn't they told you? And who had told them? Certainly not the radio. You hadn't missed a single news broadcast and this was the first time they had mentioned a reward. The newspapers maybe? No, the newspapers don't come out on Monday. If it really had been in the papers, the announcement would have been made Sunday and . . . You went back to Perdicaris: "Hey, you! Who told you about the reward?" "Oh, I don't know, I don't remember, I drank too much, let me sleep, what difference does it make?" He seemed sincere, you believed him. Enough of this mistrust! Enough suspicion: had you lost your optimism? Didn't you know the meaning of patience anymore? You would stretch out on the bed and wait for Demetrios. "I'll be back at noon," he had said. At twelve sharp the key turned in the lock. You raised yourself up on one elbow: "Demetrios?" A scuffle replied, then the sound of a chair overturned, and the house was invaded by about twenty plainclothes cops pointing their revolvers: "Hands up, or we'll shoot!"

I'm looking at the photographs snapped as they displayed you to the reporters that afternoon, before taking you to the army camp at Goudi. Your eyes are staring at the ground, your mouth is sealed in a heartrending bitterness, your hands hang limp from the irons clamped over your wrists: you seem the very symbol of defeat and humiliation. A humiliation that came not so much from having been recaptured as from the minister of public order's statement to the press: "He was betrayed by members of his own organization, to collect the reward. There are two of them, and their names are Patitsas and Perdicaris." To you, however, the police inspector had said much more. "You thought you had obedient, devoted slaves, eh? Since Sunday we knew you were at 51 Patmos Street! We didn't come in sooner because we were hoping you would come out: we had promised your little cousin that we wouldn't grab you in the house. He came here to us and said: 'He's so nervous, he'll come out. I didn't even leave him anything to eat!' Two days we waited, watching every move you made. Then we got tired and we yelled at your cousin and his friend: 'What kind of game is this? He's capable of staying there for months, he's so used to prison!' And he said: 'I'll make him come out, I'll take him to the port.' We got fed up. We made him give us the keys to the apartment. But half a million drachmas weren't enough for him, he demanded a job with Olympic Airways as well. We got that for him. We're gentlemen, we are, we keep our word; we're not liars like your friends." Later he told you Morakis had been captured too. They were already interrogating him very, very firmly. And he was confessing, confessing.

4

HOW A MAN SENTENCED TO DEATH AND CAPTURED AFTER A miraculous escape could overcome his despair and immediately plan another escape is something only somebody who knew you would be able to understand. But this is what happened a month and a half later when they took you from Goudi back to Boiati. Patsourakos was no longer in command at that time, the disgrace had cost him his job; waiting for you at the door of your cell was a big man of about fifty with a huge bald head and a great beak of a nose. "Good morning, Alekos, welcome back." Welcome back! You observed him through your lashes. Porcine eyes, at once dull and malignant. Fat mouth, nasty. Heavy, shaky hands, hands that could plead or strike with the same ease. "Who are you?" "I am Nicholas Zakarakis, Alekos, the new commandant." "What do you want?"

"I want to talk to you, Alekos, to explain how I see things." "And how do you see things, Zakarakis? Tell me." "As I see it, well, I think you're a hero, Alekos, and you've got balls. And since I think you're a hero and have balls, I quickly came to an agreement with Brigadier General Ioannidis. I said to him, General, what's past is past, let's forget about it, say nothing more to the subject. Let's forget the mistakes that boy made, show him we're human, give him no excuse to behave badly, and in the end he'll be sorry, he'll come to his senses. And the general said: what do you suggest, Mr. Zakarakis? I suggest showing him consideration, I replied, talking to him, taking off his handcuffs. Yes, we should take off those handcuffs, he's been wearing them for almost a year; let's allow ourselves a gesture of good will! Naturally the general was not enthusiastic, but he gave in. Mr. Zakarakis, he said, you're in charge, you're the man who matters. You have a free hand, use whatever methods you like." O Christ! An idiot but also sly, threatening but also conciliatory: you knew the type. The type who bows before any power, any authority, any bullying. Long live Papadopoulos, long live Stalin, long live Hitler, long live Mao Tse-tung, long live Nixon, long live the pope, long live whoever happens along: provided there's no trouble. The type, moreover, who takes it out on those more unfortunate than himself because this is the only way he can make up for his insignificance and take revenge for the abuses he has undergone. Dictatorships are born from him, totalitarianism is strengthened by him. It is no accident that, as a rule, he makes an exemplary jailer. You had to force a showdown at once, remind him who you were, reject him and provoke him in order to renew the fight. You interrupted him: "Have you finished, Zakarakis?" "No, Alekos, I was going to add that—" "Save your breath, Zakarakis. I know what you're here for. You're here to tell me I'm handsome and you like me and you want me to fuck you. It's an old story, everyone knows that all the servants of the junta are faggots. But I don't want to fuck you, Zakarakis. Not today. Never. I can't do you this favor, you're too ugly, too fat. You're disgusting. I couldn't even pull down your pants and take a look at your big fat ass." "Criminal! Communist traitor! Hired killer!" And he went off, gesticulating.

A few hours later he reappeared, stubborn. "Eh, I'm sorry about the scene. It's my fault, Alekos, I hadn't realized you were joking. And yet they told me you like to joke, you're a comical sort. I should have remembered. Eh, to make you excuse me, I've brought you this. Here." Your eyes brightened: he was handing you a koboloi. For at least a year you had been dreaming of a koboloi: toying with that sort of rosary was a mania of yours and in your idle solitude it became a necessity. But you didn't dare accept it. It would have been tantamount to absolving him, to saying—I understand you, Zakarakis, you have a family too, you too are a son of the people, let's make peace. And you would have surrendered to his game for good. You had to hold out, show him that you couldn't be swayed by the carrot or the stick, that you and he were enemies and such you had to remain. So you stifled the impulse to reach out toward that precious gift and, pretending indifference, you said: "I don't want it." "Oh, come, take it. I'm happy to give it to you." "I said, I don't want it. I want only one thing from you, Zakarakis: a flush toilet." "A flush toilet?! Why?" "Because I won't live with a bucket. It stinks. It's unhealthy." "But all the cells here have buckets. None has a flush toilet!" "Mine will." "Come, be reasonable. And accept my present." "I don't accept presents from fascists. From fascists I accept only a flush toilet. Because it's my right." Zakarakis fumed. He had known you would utter the word fascism sooner or later and he had prepared an answer on the word fascism. "Eh, you're young, Alekos, my friend. You don't understand certain things. At your age, I talked about fascism too!" "Don't tell me you talked against it, Zakarakis." "But I did. I had no brain. And besides Mussolini had attacked us, I had no regard for him. I remember one evening in Rimini. In 1940 I was a prisoner of war, you know, in Rimini, sometimes I used to argue with the Italians, and that evening I said Mussolini was a criminal, the ruin of mankind—" "Good for you, Zakarakis, bravo!" "And they answered me that Mussolini had created a nation, restored order and calm to the whole country—" "And you believed that, didn't you?" "No, I didn't. I told you, I was as single-minded then as you are today. I didn't believe it at all, and I protested. I yelled: can't you see all the misfortunes you're undergoing because of him? But they said no: our misfortunes are caused by the English, the Jews, the Communists. But I . . . Listen to what I answered. Because I know how to handle a situation, you can't imagine what a diplomat I am. I answered: I don't like the Jews myself, but what made you come into Greece? Looking for Jews?" "Cut it short, Zakarakis, get to the point." "No, listen! You know what they answered me? They answered: We came because of Albania, otherwise you Greeks would steal it and call it North Epirus." "That was true, Zakarakis." "Ah, you simply don't want to listen. Because that was when I said to them: Yes, Albania is ours, but fascism is a crime. And you know their conclusion? Their conclusion was that the worst crime, for anyone, was fighting fascism, because if you fought fascism, you were lending a hand to communism! They were right, my boy. Absolutely right, I know that now. And I'll add: In good faith you're committing the same crime." "Do you really believe that, Zakarakis?" "Do I believe it? I'm certain of it, mathematically certain, my boy. Anyone who's an antifascist is working for communism and the Soviet Union." "Uhm." You pretended to be puzzled and you flashed him one of those smiles nobody could resist: "Interesting. Yes, by heavens, that's interesting. Can I ask you a question, Zakarakis?" "That's what I'm here for, my boy, at your disposal." "Do you speak Italian, Zakarakis?" "No, not I. I only know Greek. I never even wanted to learn English, or French, or German. I'm a nationalist, that's what I am." "I see. And in

Rimini do the Italians speak Greek?" "Not a word." "Then how did you manage to chatter so much, idiot, when you don't even know Greek and express yourself worse than an illiterate?" He forgot the promises he had made to himself and to Ioannidis. He beat you with a stick until you fainted. But you didn't hold it against him: that was what you wanted. Because then you had a legitimate excuse to inflict one of your hunger strikes on him and to obtain the flush toilet, an instrument indispensable to your next escape.

Never having experienced a hunger strike, Zakarakis didn't know the importance of the first three days, the only time one feels a desperate need for food, and after they have passed, a gentle torpor takes over, killing any stimulus of hunger. So he made the mistake of not coming to you until you had been fasting for three whole weeks: to stay alive you accepted only a bit of water. You no longer had cheeks, your legs had wasted to the thickness of your wrists, and such an unbearable smell came from your mouth that it was difficult to stay near you. At the mere sight of you, he took fright and decided to inform the Ministry of Justice: "He's dying, he's dying!" "If he dies, you'll end up in jail, we can't allow ourselves an international scandal," they answered at the ministry. In jail? O Jesus, he really had to persuade you to eat something! Zakarakis went into the kitchen, examined the supper they had prepared for him, discovered to his dismay that it was his favorite dish, lentils, and brought it to you. "Kalimera, good day, here we are!" A wisp of a voice: "What do you want, Zakarakis? What is it?" "My supper, cooked for me! And I'm giving it to you. Lentils?" Lentils? "Get out, Zakarakis." "Come on, taste them. At least taste them. They're good, you know, they're good for you too!" "Get out, I said!" "Don't you like them? Would you rather have a steak? Soup? Broth?" Broth, yes, you would have liked that, what wouldn't you have given for a cup of broth! "No, Zakarakis, no broth. No soup, no steak. I want a flush toilet and that's all." "But I explained to you, nobody has a flush toilet!" "You have one." "I'm the commandant!" "And I'm me. I want a flush toilet." "I can't give it to you!" "Yes, you can. You only have to buy it and have it installed." "No! No, no!" "Then I'll die. And you'll end up in this cell yourself, for second-degree murder. Or first-degree. Wait and see. Reporters will come from all over the world, they'll accuse you of having killed me, depriving me of food and beating me, and all countries will declare sanctions against Greece, because of you our country will be kept out of the Common Market." "What are you saying?" "This is what I'm saying. And Papadopoulos will never forgive you, and neither will Ioannidis. Now leave me alone. I want to die in peace. In heaven I'll find a flush toilet." Zakarakis went off almost in tears. He didn't sleep that night and during the next few days he kept coming to feel your pulse or touch your brow, heaving sighs of anguish. You were worsening visibly and you did everything to make it obvious. As soon as he approached, you would move your lips: "I'm dying . . . dying." Finally he gave up: "Alekos, can you hear me?" "Yes . . ." "If by chance I were to give you the flush toilet, would you accept some broth?" "I don't understand . . . say it again . . ." "If I give you the flush toilet, will you drink some broth for me?" "No. First the flush toilet and then the broth." "Oh, all right, all right! You'll have the flush toilet!" "Now." "Now!" Half an hour later, the cell was invaded by workers with trowels and axes. And you accepted the broth, you started eating again.

The idea of the flush toilet or rather the idea of an escape based on the flush toilet had been in the back of your mind for many months, but it became clear at Goudi when you realized that sooner or later you would return to the familiar cell at Boiati. For escape purposes that cell had many good points. It was on the ground floor and flanked a seldom-used path, and, besides, its walls were so rotten from dampness that they almost seemed to demand being broken through. You only had to get hold of a tool to dig with, find some object to hide the hole as it widened, and discover a way of getting rid of the rubble as you went along. Well, this last could only be a flush toilet, and now that they were preparing to install it, you felt you were already halfway to your goal. You could even joke with Zakarakis: "Hey, papadopoulaki, where's that plate of lentils?" "I don't have any today. I can offer you a piece of chicken." "Chicken it is then!" Meanwhile you were pondering solutions to the other two problems. First of all, what digging tool could you find? You didn't even have a fork, at meals they gave you only a spoon and . . . Yes, the spoon! What more did you want: a pick, a drill? You hid the spoon under the cot, and when the guard looked for it, you shrugged. "What do I know about your fucking spoon? Somebody must have taken it away." Then you scratched the wall for a test. It worked! The soft plaster came away at once, and the bricks crumbled more easily than you had imagined. You restored everything with some soft bread and you faced the problem of covering the hole. A curtain was needed. But how could you justify the request for a curtain, what stratagem could you invent to get it? Surely not another hunger strike, the strike was a weapon not be wasted in excessive use. Maybe some kind of blackmail. Yes, you would wait until Zakarakis came to reap gratitude and you would blackmail him. He came. "Are you happy? Do you like your flush toilet?" "Yes, only the curtain is missing." "What curtain?" "The modesty curtain. Now that I have a flush toilet, you certainly don't expect me to keep on relieving myself while someone's looking at me through the peephole." "Who looks at you through the peephole when you're relieving yourself?" "Everybody. You included." "Me?!" "Yes, Zakarakis. Don't try to act smart. I saw you." "You pig, you bastard!" "If you insult me, I'll tell everything." "Tell what, blackmailer?" "I'm not a blackmailer, I'm just modest. Is it my fault if I'm modest, if I blush easily? And besides a curtain would cheer the place up, I don't even have a table, a chair—" "I see, you want to decorate your room a bit. And I want to prove to you how big-hearted

I am: I'll give you a table and a chair." "And a curtain." "Curtain, hell! Where can I find a curtain?!"

Blackmail didn't work. Begging didn't work either. "Zakarakis, please, a curtain." "I don't have any curtains." "Any old rag will do, and a couple of nails to hold it up." "No." "Why not?" "Because I'm the one who decides, you understand? I'm in charge here, you understand? If I paid attention to you all the time, you'd soon be running this prison! I've had enough of your demands! I gave you a table, I gave you a chair, and I won't give you a curtain!" "If you give it to me, I'll return the table, I'll return the chair." "No, it's a matter of principle. And besides, you're crazy." Crazy. That was the solution. You would make him believe you were crazy, and he would end up humoring you. That evening you waited until he went to bed, then you set the table under the window, put the chair on top of it, climbed up to the bars, and shouted: "Zakarakis! Are you asleep, Zakarakis? You shouldn't be sleeping, Zakarakis! You should be sewing my curtain! I want a blue one! With a ruffle!" Or, "Zakarakis, have you sewn my curtaaaaaain? Did you put a ruffle on it?" This continued for three, four, five nights, while the other prisoners complained: "Commandant, give him the curtain! We can't get any sleep around here!" On the sixth night Zakarakis burst in with his guards and beat you. But, after beating you with a club, he granted you the curtain. Blue, with a ruffle. And you could start digging. You worked day and night, tireless, using your hands when the spoon bent double: your fingers were all scratched and bleeding. You didn't even feel the pain, to see that hole widening until it reached a diameter of forty-five centimeters was an anesthetizing joy. And you sang, whistled, laughed. Especially when you threw the rubble into the toilet and flushed it: heedless of arousing suspicion. You weren't alarmed even when Zakarakis came to you, frowning: "What is this? Are you sick? Do you have dysentery?" "Me? No. Why?" "You keep flushing the toilet." "I flush it because I enjoy flushing it. Is that forbidden?" "No, it's not forbidden." But in his little porcine eyes there was a glint of understanding.

And the day came when the thickness of the remaining part of the wall was only two or three centimeters: a few sharp blows and you would knock through it. You had only to wait until night, and so with a great sigh you stretched out on the cot to daydream: once on the path, would it be better to turn left or right? To the left were Zakarakis's quarters, to the right the kitchens. Better to the right. Yes, but how would you deal with the sentries? Well, the sentry problem could be solved, you had seen that in your escape with Morakis. And the same was true of the outside wall, which you'd have to scale alone this time. Luck never abandoned you, after all Zakarakis himself had been a stroke of luck. Poor Zakarakis. He had offered you the koboloi, the lentils, he had given you the flush toilet, the curtain with a ruffle, and you had driven him out of his mind, you had exploited his stupidity. But were you really right to say it was characters like him who caused and sustained tyrannies? When you think about it, they are the first victims: he was really a prisoner too. Always shut up in that prison, cursed and insulted, always at the mercy of the Ioannidises and the ministers of justice, always in the grip of fear, the fear of those who command now, the fear of those who will command next. You would have liked to tell him you weren't really against him, you really considered him a prisoner too. You would have liked also to save him, to explain to him that in flogging you and people like you he was flogging himself, the man he could have been: free, disobedient, not a servant. Too bad there wasn't time. You were thinking of these things when Zakarakis came into the cell. He seemed very tired and he spoke politely. "Alekos, I have to ask you a favor." "What is it, Zakarakis?" "I don't feel well this evening, I need my rest. Don't sing tonight, don't amuse yourself flushing the toilet." "All right, Zakarakis." "Really. You promise?" "I promise, Zakarakis." "I know you've got it in for me. Of course, I'm your jailer—" "I don't have it in for you, Zakarakis. I'm against the people you serve. You're a prisoner too, Zakarakis, just as Patsourakos was, as all wardens of all prisons are, in a dictatorship or not. When this country is free again, you'll understand what I mean and why I behave like this now. You're all victims of ignorance and cowardice, you're not guilty. The guilty are those in command, the cruel are those who command. You're not cruel, Zakarakis. You're only stupid." Zakarakis smiled strangely as he had the morning when he asked you if you were suffering from dysentery. This time you noticed it, and with a painful stab you were alarmed. But it was too late for precautions or second thoughts, the night was advancing; dismissing your uneasiness, you waited for taps and for silence to fall.

Eleven. Two sharp blows, a jab with your elbow, and the shell of the wall caved in. You stuck your head out of the hole: the path seemed deserted. You pricked up your ears for any sound: you heard nothing. The coast was clear! Holding your breath, you stuck your head into the hole, then one arm, one shoulder. You thrust yourself forward. Just as the other shoulder was to pass, you remained stuck. Had you misjudged the width? No, it was your clothes: the leather jacket, the wool shirt, the sweater. Naked, you could slip through easily. You undressed completely, wrapped your things into a bundle, and flung it out on the other side. It landed with a light thud, there would be a drop of barely half a meter. Perfect! You stuck your head through again with one arm and shoulder, drew the other arm and shoulder to the outside, and slid forward to the waist. Now you had to draw in your abdomen: so. Plant your feet: so. Slide some more: so. And . . . just then a snicker wounded your eardrums, followed by a mocking voice: "It's cold, Alekos. What are you doing here without your clothes? Have you lost your modesty?" It was Zakarakis, with about twenty soldiers lined up along the path. Zakarakis was laughing, laughing. The soldiers laughed too. They laughed so hard that the barrels of their rifles were swaying like the branches of a tree stirred by the wind.

"And you thought I was stupid, eh? 'You're only stupid, Zakarakis.' Stupid, blind, and deaf, eh? You thought I hadn't understood what all that scratching was, that flushing the toilet, that hiding behind the curtain, eh? You're so vain! Fool! You know why I let you do it? Because you stopped bothering me, you criminal! Because I wanted to catch you in the act, amuse myself! Yes, amuse myself!" And then came the blows: on your face, chest, genitals. "So I don't count for anything, eh? I'm a poor fool, I'm a prisoner the same as you! Idiot, I'm in command here! I'm the chief! The chief! And an intelligent chief: I had even calculated how long it would take you, bastard! I knew very well you would try it tonight! We all knew it, all of us! They had all seen the crack in the wall! You never guessed there was a crack on the outside, eh?" And more blows: on your face, chest, genitals. But it wasn't the blows that hurt, it was the humiliation, the sound of those words, the memory of the snicker that had hurt your eardrums when with half of your body outside and half inside you had raised your eyes and seen the soldiers lined up along the path and him as he repeated mockingly, "It's cold, Alekos, what are you doing here without your clothes?" You had felt your cheeks flush purple with shame, you would have liked to die. O Theos, Theos mou! Oh, God, my God! To be beaten, yes, to be tortured, torn to pieces: not made ridiculous. It isn't right, it isn't human. "You really thought I had gone to bed, eh? That I was all cosy and warm in my bed, meditating on your gab, eh? You know how many hours I've been waiting for you, with my guards? Three hours! Three!" Your swollen eyelids were raised to his contemptuous gaze, your swollen lips could move only with effort: "You'll pay for this, Zakarakis. I don't know how, but I'll make you pay, Zakarakis. I'll give you a nervous breakdown, I'll send you to the insane asylum." Zakarakis replied with a final kick and then, sweating, tired of beating you, he turned you over to the ESA men, who wrapped you in a blanket and took you to the army camp at Goudi. And here they resumed the usual interrogations, the usual tortures. Even the pilgrimage of the familiar characters was resumed: Malios, Babalis, Theophiloiannakos, Ioannidis.

The most infuriated this time was Theophiloiannakos. "Tell me what you dug with? What was it?" "With a spoon, Theophiloiannakos." "It's not true, it's not possible, I don't believe it. Tell me who helped you! Who are your accomplices, eh?" "Nobody, Theophiloiannakos." "Liar, hypocrite, that's not true! You'll confess soon enough!" "With one of your fake documents, Theophiloiannakos? Don't you know me yet, Theophiloiannakos? Wipe your ass with your confessions, illiterate. Wipe it, it needs wiping!" "I'll kill you!" The least surprised was Ioannidis. He stared at you without saying anything, his icy face almost relaxed in a grimace of indulgence, and only after a long time he said, shaking his head: "Panagoulis, Panagoulis! I kept saying you had to be shot, Panagoulis! It's all the fault of Papadopoulos, who didn't have the balls to knock you off!" And then Phaedo Gizikis, commanding officer of the Athens zone, who had signed the decree for your execution. He was stern, sad. On the left arm of his jacket there was a mourning band: his wife had died a few days before. He bent over you as you were lying handcuffed on the floor, beside a tray of untouched food, and: "Mr. Panagoulis! Please, Mr. Panagoulis, eat something." The first person, in fourteen months, who addressed you formally. You returned the compliment: "Without cutlery, sir? Forgive me, General, but I am not a dog, sir." "I know, Mr. Panagoulis, I know. But you must understand their hard feelings. The minute they give you a spoon, you use it to dig a hole in the wall!" A flash. Here, this was just the right person, the opportunity to avenge yourself on Zakarakis and on those who had humiliated you, mocked you. If you could manage to convince this polite and authoritative man, the trap would shut tight without difficulty. You looked into his ingenuous eyes, you contracted every muscle of your face into an exaggerated amazement: "General! You surely don't believe that spoon story? A wall isn't made of custard!" "What are you saying, Mr. Panagoulis? What are you saying?!" "I'm saying it was the guards who helped me, General: the same ones that arrested me afterward. I'm saying it was Zakarakis, General. The whole idea came from Zakarakis! He was the one who suggested it to me. He was hoping to get a transfer after my escape attempt, to get away like Patsourakos! How was I to imagine he was playing a double game, General? I believed him, forgive me for saying so, but you would have done the same! When the commandant of a prison comes into a prisoner's cell and says to him, 'Let's make a deal, you want to escape, I want to be transferred, we can help each other,' and so on, when he puts his guards at the prisoner's disposal, lets him glimpse the mirage of freedom . . . General, I actually wonder if the double game was always part of his plan: he seemed so sincere with me! Maybe he changed his mind, afraid that one of the guards would talk. He was so anxious to be removed from Boiati, like Patsourakos!" "Mr. Panagoulis, I can't believe my ears. It's unheard of! Absolutely unheard of!" "I agree, General. And I'm glad to confess this business to you because you're a gentleman, a civil, proper person, a real soldier. You've never mistreated me, never. And you know full well I'd never open my mouth to the others: under torture I don't talk." "I know, Mr. Panagoulis, I know. And I have to admit it: you're a man of honor. But what you've confided in me is so scandalous, incredible!" "I know it is, sir, but it's the truth. Unfortunately it's the simple truth. Imagine: when the hole ran into a snag, Zakarakis would come to me and say: try again, keep trying! I'll give you a hatchet! And one day, when I was tired, I absolutely couldn't make it, he became angry. He said: 'You certainly don't expect me to make this hole in the wall myself?!' Afterward, all the same, he sent some guards to help me. 'So I'll get out of here like Patsourakos.' Uhm! And what he said about officers and in particular about you, General! I don't mean the military, which I also feel contempt for, the servants of the junta: I mean army men like yourself, General!" "Thank you, Mr. Panagoulis. You are a very fair enemy, Mr. Panagoulis. But surely you realize that I can't keep this information to myself, I will have to report it." "I realize that, sir. I'll be the one to pay, but it doesn't matter. Report it, General, report it." "Then, good-bye, Mr. Panagoulis." "Good-bye, General." "I'll have you brought a spoon, Mr. Panagoulis." "Thank you, General." "And eat something, eh? Please." "Yes, General."

He saluted you, raising his hand to his cap, as if you were his superior, and he went off in the grip of searing indignation. A few minutes later he reported everything to Ioannidis, who with identical indignation summoned Theophiloiannakos. "So the hole was dug with a spoon!" "Yes, sir, General. That rascal confessed as much." "A normal soup spoon." "Yes, General, we're certain of that now." "And nobody helped him, nobody gave him a hatchet, for example." "No, General. He's an animal, that one, we all know it." "And you're an idiot! A fool, an incapable fool!" "General, sir!" "A half-wit! A cheap inquisitor, an amoeba!" "General!" "Get out of my sight or I'll kick you in the ass!" The guards who had laughed at you in the path, meanwhile, had been brought to Goudi and from the rooms where they were being beaten you could hear their cries, sweeter than harp music. "No! Help! No! I didn't have anything to do with it! I'm innocent, I swear I am! Innocent! No, I didn't help him, I didn't! Stop! Please, stop!" They brought you in for a confrontation with some of them, and they were in such bad shape that for a moment you were tempted to let them off. But the memory of the shame that had burned your cheeks was too fresh, so you confirmed the things you had said to Gizikis, and you twisted the knife: "Yes, they're the ones. Zakarakis had given them the hatchet, and they helped me with the job. Then they carried away the rubble so the toilet wouldn't be stopped up." "It's not true, it's not true!" "It's true, unfortunately. And because they were lazy and not even Zakarakis could make them carry away the rubble quickly, at a certain point I threw everything into the toilet and it did stop up. And they were so angry with me they didn't want to fix it." You didn't see Zakarakis, however. Ioannidis wanted him all to himself. To tell the truth, Ioannidis had some doubts. He understood you better than anyone else and he knew you were capable of anything: even of sacrificing credit for that escape, lying to get Zakarakis into trouble. But the doubts also followed a certain line of reasoning, and from whatever angle he examined the thing, that reasoning seemed perfect. Send Zakarakis away? Why? If you had lied, from now on no jailer would be more reliable and inflexible than Zakarakis. If, on the contrary, you had told the truth, Zakarakis should be punished, but not in the way he had hoped. So inquiries or reproaches were futile: a bit of contempt would suffice. He summoned him and said: "So, Zakarakis, you wanted to retire on your pension." "I don't understand, General." "You understand, Zakarakis, you understand. The man who doesn't talk has talked this time. I know everything, you can stop acting." "General, I must insist that I don't understand. I'm tired, yes, you can't imagine what these past five months have been with that wretch. I'd like to be transferred, yes, I'd like not to see him again, not to hear him again, to forget that he exists. But retire?! No, no!" "Transferred, Zakarakis? Did I hear you correctly? You said transferred?" "Yes, General. If it were possible, yes. I can't go on, sir. That man is a demon, I assure you, a demon!" Ioannidis's voice became more icy than ever. "I know him better than you do, Zakarakis. He's a demon, yes, but he's honest. Exactly the opposite of you, who are a fool and dishonest. I should have you arrested, Zakarakis, drag you in front of a court-martial for treason. But it would be too little for you, it would be a gift, and—" "Court-martial,

General? Treason?! General, I was the one who caught that criminal, I was the one who—" "Don't interrupt me, Zakarakis. I told you I don't like acting. And I repeat that the court-martial would be too little for you, a present. I know the punishment you deserve. And you know what it is? You will stay at your post, Zakarakis. You will stay at Boiati! With him! You'll have him on your back as long as he lives, I swear!" "No, General, no! Not that!" "Yes. And from this moment on, I'm giving you another assignment, Zakarakis: to build a special cell for him, a cell from which he can't escape, not even if you open the door for him. Now, get out of here. And be careful, Zakarakis! If you fail, I promise you something worse than a court-martial. I'll lock you behind bars with him!"

For two weeks Zakarakis lay still, like a ghost. The clash with Ioannidis had so distressed him that, as he was to confess to you in a moment of weakness, he couldn't even perform his conjugal duties and his wife taunted him in vain with mocking words: "It seems they've commissioned him to make the Parthenon!" The desperate listlessness that enervated him, the helpless awareness of his inability left him only when he dreamed of having you back, in a cell from which you wouldn't escape. But what sort of cell?! This was the question that robbed him of sleep, appetite, sexual capacity. Ioannidis had given him even the responsibility of the choice: "This is your business, Zakarakis. I give you three months. After Christmas, it has to be ready." After Christmas! Only three months! In the hope of solving the problem, Zakarakis leafed through catalogs, books on architecture, he learned difficult expressions, potential energy, stress resistance, the Maxwell equation, Betti's theorem, Clayperon's. But in vain. To be sure, it had to be a cell in reinforced concrete and with foundations so solid, walls so thick, that it couldn't be pierced even with a pneumatic drill. It had to have double doors of steel, almost invisible windows, roof reinforced by an electric current that would knock you out if you so much as looked at it. But not even this would be enough, he could feel it: something better was needed, something more. Something, yes, this was it, that would imprison not only your body but also your imagination: something that would prevent the brain from thinking. In his crude mind he had somehow realized that this was the point, to prevent your brain from thinking, because the next time you wouldn't try a hole in the wall but some completely new devilishness. And if you were to succeed, O Christ! Ioannidis would have no mercy. "Be careful, Zakarakis! If you fail, I promise you something worse than a court-martial. I'll lock you behind bars with him!" Then one day at the end of November, as he was wandering around in a cemetery, he saw a tomb in the form of a chapel, and the idea came: a tomb! That's the thing for that demon: a tomb! A cell that had the form and the dimensions of a tomb. He would build you a tomb. Maybe even with a little cypress beside it. Wasn't there a cypress already in the big central yard? Like an artist afraid of losing the creative impulse if he doesn't immediately obey the call of inspiration, Zakarakis went straight back to Boiati, designed a parallelepiped, determined its measurements. Two months later the cell was ready. The terrible cell where you were to remain for three and a half years, beginning on a February morning.

That horrible February morning. You were at Goudi that horrible February morning, and you certainly didn't imagine that Zakarakis had built his Parthenon. You had the illusion that you had been removed from his authority. You weren't too badly off at Goudi, the commandant never had you handcuffed, the guards often lingered to chat with you, and, above all, there you had come to know another Morakis: a soldier willing to help you escape. "Look at me, Alekos, don't you remember me?" "No." "But you know me, Alekos, you've seen me before." "Where? When?" "At ESA headquarters, right after you were arrested, during a beating." "A beating?" "Yes, they ordered me to beat you and I beat you with a stick. But afterward I felt terribly ashamed." "I don't believe it." "It's the truth, Alekos, the truth. I felt so ashamed that I swore I would help you at the first opportunity and—" "I don't believe it." "I swore I would help you and I said to myself—If they don't kill him, one day I'll do something for him." "Look, Morakis got sixteen years." "I know." "And the next time they won't bother to arrest me, they'll shoot me and anyone with me." "I know." "What do you know, clown?" Using your old system, you mocked him, threatened, humiliated him, but in the end you were convinced he wasn't lying and together you prepared a plan. No foolishness this time, no bravado. In addition to a uniform he would supply you with military documents, to get out of Goudi, a fake passport, a pair of eyeglasses to alter your features, and a car waiting for you at the exit, a yacht to pick you up in the bay of Vouliagmeni: ready to cast off for extraterritorial waters. The only difficulty was the two padlocks on the door of your cell: a captain kept the keys. "I can't steal them from him, Alekos." "There's no need. Go to a locksmith and buy all the keys that you think might possibly work." He went, came back with about fifty keys, and one of them opened the first lock. Not the second. "What'll we do, Alekos?" "That's easy: buy more. Buy all the keys on the market. If we keep trying, we'll find the right one." He went again, came back again, with about a hundred keys. From eight in the morning till eleven, the length of his daily shift, and then from ten in the evening to midnight, his evening shift, he worked at the second lock, sweating, trembling at the idea of being caught. "Try this one." "It doesn't work." "This one." "Doesn't work." "This one." "Doesn't work." Then the thirty-eighth key: "It works!" It opened. "Good. Can you manage everything for tomorrow?" "Yes, it's all ready." "Even the car and the yacht?" "Yes, they've been waiting for days." "At midnight then. See you tomorrow." Midnight was a perfect time. At midnight the camp slept.

You sang that morning, as in the days of the flush

toilet. But you didn't sing long because around nine a squad entered the cell: "Out, Panagoulis. You're leaving." "Leaving?! For where—?" "For Boiati, Panagoulis. You're going back to Boiati." A truck, a journey that was endless, a longing to cry that stopped your breathing, and there was the gray mass of Boiati with its outer wall and its towers. Zakarakis was waiting for you at the entrance, his hands on his hips, and his big, sallow face could barely conceal a look of triumph. "Look who's here, look who's back again! Come in, dear boy, come in. You can't imagine what I've prepared while you were on vacation at Goudi." He took you by the arm, thrust you along the little road that led to the courtyard with the cell from which you had escaped, passed it without stopping. He turned to the right, then to the left, then again to the right, and your heart was pounding furiously: you sensed something evil was about to happen when Zakarakis said, "Here we are, dear boy, we're there." Something terrible, something that would torment you more than all the torments undergone till now. "Here we are, dear boy, we're there! Do you like it? It's for you, all for you, only for you!" And in the midst of the open space there appeared to you, like a blow on the eye, the tomb with the cypress. "The cypress is short, but it will grow."

You used to say it was impossible to imagine that cell without having seen it. And that's why after the fall of the junta you asked the minister of defense, Evangelos Tossitsas Averoff, for permission to photograph it. But he refused. You asked him again when you were a member of Parliament, explaining that it wasn't a whim of yours, it was necessary, to show the world how prisoners are treated under tyrannies. But again he denied you permission. You asked him for three years, obstinately, each time underlining your suspicion that he wanted to hide the outrage from the world, that he actually meant to erase the memory of it by leveling it, but he kept on denying permission. He wouldn't even let you past the gate at Boiati so you could take a look, to say to yourself—There, I was walled up in there, and I survived, I won. You never saw it again, you never photographed it. But after your death, in the days when I went like a pilgrim to seek the traces of a submerged past, streets or buildings that often no longer existed, truncated concrete pillars, steel webs slammed by the wind, I saw it again for you, I photographed it for you. Evangelos Tossitsas Averoff's bulldozers were demolishing it by that time. Having knocked down the towers, a good part of the outer wall, the central barracks, everything was crumbling into nothingness, so I had trouble recognizing the courtyard where they made you play football that humiliating day, Zakarakis's office, the cell from which you escaped with Morakis and to which you had returned to wage the battle of the flush toilet. I recognized this, the cell, because of the hole in the wall: from the path outside you could still distinguish the patch. But then I reached the big yard where Zakarakis had chosen to erect his Parthenon, and I recognized it in a flash because a mere glimpse of it made my heart stop. It really was a tomb, you hadn't been exaggerating. It had a tomb's color, proportions, appearance: only one little window, thirty centimeters by thirty, broke the flat uniformity of the cement, and the tiny door that led to the antechamber of the cell proper. Inside it was worse. Because, inside, you realized that everything was much smaller than it seemed on the outside: two thirds of the space was taken up by the antechamber. The actual cell was in the back, beyond a barrier, a steel slab up to the chin, then bars. Its whole area didn't come to two meters by three: the size, you might say, of a double bed or a bit more. This comparison, all the same, is wrong because it suggests the area to move in was that of a double bed. It wasn't. You could move only along a strip one meter eighty long and ninety centimeters wide, the rest of the cell was occupied by a cot and a closet with a rudimentary wash basin and toilet. The cot, fixed at fifty centimeters from the ground, was set between one of the corners and the wall of the closet. Lying stretched out there was like lying in a coffin, because of the extremely low ceiling and the darkness. The darkness was almost total. In addition to the weak blue bulb only a bit of light came from the antechamber, where the ceiling was replaced by horizontal bars. It wasn't exactly daylight, however, because beyond the bars there was a grille, then an iron lattice, and the sun filtered through that iron lattice as if through a colander: shedding a dim glow, faint strands of yellow. But rain passed through easily, as did the cold in winter and heat in summer: it was, in short, a tomb exposed to all the elements. I shut myself inside. I tried walking along the strip ninety centimeters by a meter eighty, remembering the poem that went, "Three steps forward / and three back again / a thousand times the same journey / today's walk has tired me . . ." Three steps?! You could take two at most. I tried stretching out on the cot. The oppressive ceiling and the walls that held it prevented me from breathing. I clung to the bars, to catch my breath again; with great effort I made myself resist the temptation to fling the little door wide open. When it seemed I had spent hours and hours in there, I looked at my watch: barely ten minutes had gone by. Then I tried again, with all my willpower, but time trickled away so slowly that I lost any sense of progress, the mind became crystallized in a silence of death, and in that silence a single idea took over: get out, out, out!

And yet not for a moment did you show Zakarakis that you despaired; with a big smile you answered him: "Bravo, Zakarakis! You did this yourself?" "Yes, all by myself." "I don't believe it, Zakarakis. You're not intelligent enough." "But I did! I did it myself, I swear! I designed it!" "Congratulations." Then you pointed to the antechamber. "Is this for me, too?" "No, this is for the guards when they come to bring you your food. But if you're good, I'll give it to you, to take a walk in, for thirty minutes a day." "Fine, Zakarakis, fine." "Is that all you have to say to me?" "Yes, Zakarakis. I'll escape, Zakarakis." "No, you won't escape from here." "I'll escape. Shall we bet?" "All right. What do we bet?" "A colonel's uniform." "All right." He unbarred the gate, the entrance door, and left you alone, to think. You had to make your brain work, think, without letting anger swamp you, without pitying yourself for your bad luck, the fact that you hadn't found the key to the second lock twenty-four hours sooner. There had to be some solution to getting out of there, a few days would be enough to discover it, and with these thoughts the first day passed, and the second, and the third, the fourth, the fifth. Meanwhile you were collecting information, impressions, and you were developing them: there were sixteen guards around the tomb, three on each side and one at each corner; four of them brought you your meals. New, blank faces. Perhaps the solution lay in those new, blank faces, perhaps it wouldn't be hard for you to trick the guards, find the way of getting out of the cell. The obstacle wasn't the cell, it was the outside wall with the barbed wire: was it normal barbed wire as it had been at the time of your escape with Morakis or was the wire now electrified? You couldn't come out and ask, you would have aroused suspicion. You could only gamble, this time blindly, rouge ou noir et rien ne va plus: if you were electrocuted, then the wire had been electrified; if you remained unharmed, then the wire was normal. It was worth the risk also because the ruse you invented to get out of the cell was such a beauty. The most beautiful, the most amusing trick your imagination had ever concocted. And on the sixth day you made up your mind. Evening was falling, the four guards came in with your food, two stopped in the antechamber, one opened the inner gate, one crossed the threshold with the tray and immediately the tray fell to the floor. Jesus Christ, the cell was empty! And on the cot there was a note: "Dear Zakarakis, I'll come back to collect the colonel's uniform. If you see Theophiloiannakos and Hazizikis, tell them I'll make them piss blood. If you see Ioannidis, tell him to retire you. Yours most affectionately, Alekos."

The two guards from the outer room also ran in.

"Where is he?!" "He's not here!" "It's impossible." "Impossible? Look!" "Who brought him lunch this morning?" "You did, you brought it to him!" "Liar!" "Who're you calling a liar?" "You." "Calm down, you guys. Let's think this out. Did you lock everything carefully when you left?" "Of course!" "And the keys? Who did you give them to afterward?" "I gave them to you!" "To me? Liar!" "Boys, let's not fight among ourselves! Let's look for him instead!" And their eyes ransacked the ceiling, the walls, as if you were a fly. Huddled under the cot meanwhile, you were holding your breath, restraining your desire to laugh. Exactly what you had foreseen was happening: they weren't looking in the one place where you could hide. Would they be stupid enough to commit also the second error and go out without locking the inner gate and the door? There, they were sitting on the cot, groaning, "But how did he do it, for Christ sake, how did he do it?" They said, "We've got to give the alarm," and rushed out, not closing the gate and the door. "Alarm! Alarm!" Now the camp was a single cry: "Alarm! Alarm!" You waited a few seconds and then off, shouting with the others, "Alarm, alarm!" You reached a tree, from there the kitchen hut. A shadow grazed you, a soldier. He asked you: "Did you see him?" "Yes, down there!" you answered, pointing to somebody running in the opposite direction. He thanked you and ran on, yelling, "Down there, down there." Nobody paid any attention to you, nobody thought of turning on the spotlights, you could think of trying to reach the outside wall. You reached it, you began to climb it, you got to the top, rouge ou noir et rien ne va plus, you touched the barbed wire. No, there was no electric current in it, but it tore your flesh worse than the evening you escaped with Morakis. How long would it take, this time, to disentangle yourself? The darkness was a help but the alarm had to stop. You made a megaphone with your hands: "Cease alarm! Cease alarm!" A voice repeated: "Cease alarm! The alarm's off!" Then a sergeant's angry shout: "Who gave the cease alarm?" "Him!"

"Him, who?" "That guy in civilian clothes." "What guy in civilian clothes? Idiots! Look for him!" You tore the wire from one leg, and an arm was caught. Your sleeve filled with blood. Had you slashed a vein? The suffering paralyzed you a second too long. "I saw him!" "Where?" "On the wall! Catch him!" A spotlight came on, it flooded you with light. And you were about to jump when you felt someone grab you. "Sergeant, I've got him!"

A fairly brief fast followed. Abroad they were still concerned about you, and Zakarakis was more and more afraid you would die. "Eat!" "No." "Eat, please!" "No." "Your mother brought this food." "Let her eat it." "Come on, tell me what you want." "I told you: I want a colonel's uniform. I have a right to it. I escaped, didn't I?" "No, because I caught you." "That doesn't count. I escaped from the cell and I proved you're an idiot." "Idiot yourself!" "No, I'm intelligent. And I want the colonel's uniform." "What will you do with a colonel's uniform?!" "I'll wear it. It's carnival. At carnival people wear costumes, and the funniest costume that exists is a colonel's uniform, because your master, Papadopoulos, wears one." "Bastard!" "Clown!" The next day the same dialogue. And finally a desperate cry from Zakarakis: "Bring him a colonel's uniform!" "We don't have one, sir, there aren't any colonels here." "Find one!" They found one, you put it on, and you ate. Zakarakis returned. "Now give it back to me." "Not on your life." "I only gave it to you so you would eat. You've eaten, now give it back." "No." "Take that uniform off him!" Five of them were on top of you. Hindered by the scant space, bumping into one another, banging their elbows against the walls, they took it off you. They also took away your shoes, for days, and it was cold. You resumed your fast. "Eat." "No." "What do you want?" "My shoes." "Here are your shoes. Will you eat now?" "No." "What else do you want?" "I want to have a bath. Because I stink and I have lice. Like you, Zakarakis." "I do not stink! I do not have lice!" "Yes, you have. You have one that weighs ninety kilos. It's you yourself." "I'll kill you!" "And you'll end up in front of a court-martial, for murder. Ioannidis told you that." "Oh, all right. Give him a bath!" "Hot. I want a hot bath. Otherwise I'll get pneumonia and you'll end up in front of the court-martial all the same, for manslaughter." "Give him a hot bath then!" "I want the barber, too." "Call the barber!" The tub came with hot water, the barber came. They washed you, they shaved you, they cut your hair. But they cut your hair to half a centimeter, by order of Zakarakis, and the battle broke out once more. "You lousy pig, you had them scalp me." "I didn't have them scalp you, I had your hair cut short. Didn't you tell me you had lice?" "Lice don't nest only on the head, they're wherever there's hair. So you have to shave all of me, under the armpits too, and around the balls." "You're crazy! They've given me a madman to look after!" "I'm not crazy, Zakarakis. You know very well I behave like this to drive you crazy. And I'm going to succeed, as sure as I'm in this tomb." "Cut all his hair off!" "Not them, you. Because I know you like touching me, because besides being a pig and a bastard you're also a faggot." He had you tied to the cot. He beat you personally. He beat you so hard that he then had to call the doctor, who was horrified on seeing you: your body was one bruise from head to toe. "Who did it?" "Zakarakis did it. He wanted to shave me." "Shave you?!" "Yes, in order to rape me. He says that that's how they do it in the brothels in Istanbul. I defended myself, and he beat me." "Rape you?!" "Of course. He tried it with everybody, everybody knows it. He's a faggot." This time Zakarakis had a liver attack that kept him in bed for a week.

By now each of the two was at once victim and torturer of the other: the relationship was based on a constant exchange of roles or in a simultaneous interpretation of them, and it would have been hard to decide which of the two was more cruel toward the other. You perhaps, because you understood Zakarakis well; whereas Zakarakis didn't understand you. How could he? What you expressed and represented was farther from his world than Alpha Centauri is from Earth. He would have burst out laughing if they had explained to him that the true hero never surrenders, that he is distinguished from the others not by the great initial exploit or the pride with which he faces tortures and death but by the constancy with which he repeats himself, the patience with which he suffers and reacts, the pride with which he hides his sufferings and flings them back in the face of the one who has ordered them. Not resigning himself in his secret, not considering himself a victim, not showing others his sadness or despair. And, when necessary, exploiting the weapons of irony and mockery, obvious allies of a man in chains. And so, when your new offensive erupted, he was again taken by surprise.

While you were recovering from the aches of the last beating, the new offensive erupted with the din of a cannonade. One evening you gripped the bars of the inner gate, and aiming your voice at the grille ceiling of the antechamber, you called all the guards and prisoners together: "Your attention, please! Attention! This is the Boiati news broadcast! Special bulletin! Nicholas Zakarakis, commandant of this shit farm, is suffering from liver trouble. Rumor has it that this disease is a consequence of the violent fury that seized him when he was unable to rape a prisoner who doesn't like faggots, but this rumor is mistaken. We are in a position to reveal that Zakarakis's liver attacks are due to his disappointment in not having his posterior desires satisfied by that same prisoner. Anyone wishing to volunteer for this gruesome operation is asked to report to the proper office, leaving his name, rank, and serial number. Zakarakis pays in lentils." And the next evening: "Your attention, please! Attention! Boiati news broadcast. Special bulletin. Zakarakis is a liar. He doesn't have liver trouble, he has hemorrhoids. This prisoner knows the truth because that pig showed them to him. He also explained that he got them from the

Turks when he was working as a whore in a brothel in Constantinople. Zakarakis's disease has had a relapse as a result of his recent conversation with the minister of justice, who kicked him in the ass." Every evening it was like that, with paralyzing punctuality, and in the barracks beyond the wall the amusement was so great that requests for an evening pass sharply declined. "What are you doing tonight? Going to the movies?" "No, I want to listen to Panagoulis's special bulletin." Or: "Did you go into the city last night?" "No, I stayed here to listen to Panagoulis's special bulletin." Often, and with fake indifference, some officers also joined the audience, eager to hear what you had invented for the latest broadcast. A bit at a time, in fact, the broadcast had become a serial about the erotic experiences of Zakarakis in the legendary brothel of Constantinople, and your skill lay in always breaking off at a dramatic twist. "Tomorrow, dear listeners, you will learn the rest." I don't remember the plot well, but if I'm not mistaken, at a certain point Zakarakis gave up being a whore and was castrated in order to become the eunuch of the grand vizier. This led to a series of incredible obscenities that involved other characters, including the grand vizier himself who was named Papadopoulos, a caliph who was called Ioannidis, an executioner named Theophiloiannakos, a wily councillor named Hazizikis. The grand vizier and the caliph hated each other mortally, the executioner and the wily councillor played many spiteful tricks on each other, but all formed an iron alliance when they could humiliate the eunuch, who to defend himself underwent trials of abject submission.

In the end Zakarakis came to you. He came, he leaned wearily against the gate, he looked at you with spent eyes. "Alekos, I have to speak with you." "Make yourself at home, Zakarakis, there's plenty of room here. It's an immense salon, do you prefer the sofa or one of these easy chairs? But don't caress me, eh? Don't touch me. Today I feel particularly chaste." "Listen to me, Alekos. I know you're joking. I know that you know I'm a clean, normal man. I have a wife and two children." "Zakarakis, your wife is a front. Lots of faggots have wives, and Lord only knows whose children those are." "You bastard!" "Don't insult me and don't touch me, Zakarakis, otherwise I'll tell the radio you're a cuckold too. In fact, I hadn't thought of that, you know; tonight I'll relieve you of your position as eunuch and have you marry the favorite of the grand vizier, that way you become a cuckold right away while your wife is screwed by the caliph." "Listen to me, Alekos, I understand you. I read a book on psychology and I understand certain things. You're young, you have your sexual needs. They're what make you so restless. Me too, when I was at Rimini, a prisoner of the Italians, I was always restless, because I needed a woman. So, if you like, I'll have a woman come for you. Once a month. No, once a week. You'd like that, wouldn't you? Wouldn't you?" "I understand, Zakarakis. It's the same old story: you want me to screw you. Poor Zakarakis, you've really fallen in love with me. You've got it bad, all right. You've lost your head so badly you make me feel sorry for you, and if I could, I'd make you happy. Yes, you'd deserve a fuck. But I've told you a thousand times: I can't manage it, you don't appeal to me!" "Criminal!" "Don't be hysterical, Zakarakis. Don't be unjust. Is it my fault if I can't get it up for you? You're even bald! Listen, Zakarakis, why don't you bring me your wife? It's all in the family then." "Hanged! I'll have you hanged!" "Oh, all right. I'll make this sacrifice. I'll screw you." In a flash you shut the gate, with your left hand you held his arms fast, with your right you tore down his pants, with your knees you pressed him against the wall: the guards were just in time to rescue him from you, as his screams of terror summoned them.

A few days later, on April 9, your pallet caught fire. Zakarakis was always to insist, swearing by his wife and children, that you were the one who had set fire to it. Knowing your histrionic gifts, I would be inclined to accept his hypothesis. As a stratagem, in fact, it would be anything but foolish: the guards run in, leaving the door wide open, in the smoke and confusion you slip out and jump over the wall. But it is a fact that, just two days before, they had taken the pallet away and then had brought it back with curious precautions. It's a fact that a friendly guard had whispered to you: "Alekos, had you hidden anything in the straw? I saw Corporal Karakaxas searching inside." It's a fact that after your attack on him Zakarakis punished you by depriving you also of matches and cigarettes. It's a fact that when you recovered, a certain Major Koutras of the ESA came to you and said: "If you don't tell anybody what happened, you have my word of honor that we'll leave you free to escape abroad." It's a fact that, to the end, you continued repeating to me with impassioned sincerity: "I swear to you, I wasn't the one who set fire to it. They did it. I've lied about other things out of expediency or necessity but not about that. I didn't even have a match. Even if I had wanted to, I couldn't have done it. Why won't you believe me? Around seven in the evening I heard a whistle, then a little explosion, and the pallet caught fire. I'm certain they had put something inside it, plastic or sulfur." However it had happened, Zakarakis did everything to let you die. Clinging to the bars, you begged them to open up—"I'm burning, I can't breathe, I'm dying." And nobody moved. With your cries, the smoke came billowing out, more and more dense, from the grille of the antechamber, and yet none of the sixteen guards around the cell made a move to help you: as if Zakarakis had forbidden it. The guard who had told you about Karakaxas was near him, and he called out: "We have to do something, Commandant! He'll be roasted alive!" And Zakarakis said: "Calm down, don't worry, calm down. It's one of his usual tricks." It took quite a while for him to make up his mind, and by then the cell was an oven, flames were rising from the pallet, you were lying on the ground unconscious. When the doctor arrived, alarmed, and said you had to be taken to a hospital or you would die, Zakarakis wouldn't even allow them to pull you out into the open air: "He must be kept in the antechamber." They kept you there two days, stretched out on a blanket. The second day it rained, the water soaked into you as if you were a tree, the doctor succeeded only in making them give him an umbrella to cover your face. It was necessary to telephone the Ministry of Defense, then to ask Papadopoulos to intervene, before Zakarakis would capitulate. By now you were in pathetic condition, moustache and lashes and eyebrows burned, the skin of your face and hands covered with blisters: you couldn't see and you didn't speak. At the Goudi infirmary, where they took you, it was ascertained that there was ninety-two percent carbon dioxide in your blood. You remained in a coma for seventy-two hours. And returning to Boiati, Zakarakis received you with these words: "Hey, good news for you. Your friend's croaked." Then he handed you a newspaper with the headline KILLED YESTERDAY ON CYPRUS EX-MINISTER OF INTERIOR AND DEFENSE POLYCARPOS GEORGAZIS.

He had been found in his automobile, murdered by submachine gun fire, the paper explained. The assassins had escaped and there was no hope of discovering their identities. Clues led nowhere. The evening before, Georgazis had agreed to meet some mysterious individuals in a remote village; on leaving he embraced his wife with particular affection and said to her: "If I'm late, have them search for me." You burst into loud sobs, and not only from grief. Yes, during the interrogation and the trial you had stoutly denied any help from him. But nevertheless Hazizikis had discovered the role Georgazis had played in the assassination attempt, the evidence he had provided was so overwhelming that relations between the Greek and the Cypriot governments had deteriorated once and for all, Ioannidis had redoubled the number of his officers on the island, and in the space of a few weeks Georgazis had lost power, the friendship of Makarios, the respect of the other politicians who now considered him a freebooter capable of any rashness, and finally he won the hatred of Papadopoulos, who even in public swore he would make him pay. Who organized the trap, the meeting in the remote village? Papadopoulos's personal executioners or their CIA opposite numbers? Both, perhaps, in a coordinated operation, and anyhow your great friend was gone: the man who had believed in you, helped you, taught you, the man you admired enthusiastically like a child with a crush on his teacher. He too was dead, like George. Because of you, like George. At a certain point the sobs became so convulsed that you began to vomit, and you fell ill. You were ill for a month. You had barely recovered when Zakarakis brought you new sorrow: "Come on, get dressed. Hurry. The president is allowing you out for a few hours." "Why?" "Because your father is dying and the president is allowing you to go and say good-bye to him. A magnanimous gesture, eh? If it were up to me, I wouldn't let you see him, not even a photograph of him."

You loved your father dearly. Years later you would confess to me that you had never felt the same tenderness for your mother, so tough and self-sufficient, but you had always felt a melting tenderness for your father. Perhaps because your father was much older than she: he had married as an old man and had had his sons as an old man, had brought them up with an old man's indulgence. When you were a child and you hid under the bed to escape your mother's blows, you would stay there for whole days resisting hunger and the need to pee, and she would cry: "Come out, I haven't finished with you yet." He, on the contrary, would murmur: "Come on out, nothing will happen to you, I'm here." When you were a schoolboy and couldn't stand spending afternoons in the house studying, she would double-lock you in your room, and he would wink at you, saying: "Run along! I'll handle it." And yet your father had never been a rebel. A career man in the army, he had grown up in the school of obedience and he had always squandered his courage in wars with cannons and rifles. The army was his world, the nation's flag his god, and you knew the sadness he had felt when you chose to study mathematics instead of wearing an officer's uniform like George! What grief when you deserted, what bewilderment when you ended up in prison, what torment when they arrested him too and held him for a hundred and three days. You learned later what happened to him in those hundred and three days. Blows and insults and maltreatment of every sort despite his seventy-six years, his medals, his rank of colonel. "If you're not guilty of anything else, you're responsible for bringing a criminal into the world!" Or: "Why do you want to go home? Your wife's left you, she's decided to have some fun, she's tired of an old wreck like you." A specially hard blow had made him almost blind in one eye, still deeper humiliation had come from a physical and mental paralysis: for eight months he had been hovering in a limbo without sadness and joy, and he remembered nothing of what had happened. He didn't even imagine that you were serving a life sentence with a suspended death sentence; from his chair or his bed he always asked the same things: "Where's Alekos?" "Abroad." "What's he doing there?" "Studying." "Why doesn't he come to see me?" "He'll come." "I want to see him, I want to embrace him before I die." You, too, wanted to embrace him. There were moments when you wanted it so poignantly that you felt like a child again and . . . Zakarakis became agitated, impatient: "Well are you going to get ready to go see your father before he dies or aren't you?" "No." "No?! Did you say no?!" "I said no, Zakarakis. Your friend Papadopoulos isn't going to exploit me in his farce of being magnanimous. He's not going to call in the press and television to document the journey of the prodigal son to the bedside of his dying father. Get out, Zakarakis." "You heartless animal!" "Get out, Zakarakis." "You'll change your mind! You will!" "Get out or I'll strangle you, Zakarakis." Zakarakis went out and the following evening he came back: "He's dead, you bastard! Dead without embracing you!"

At first you didn't react, as if you were deaf or dumb or didn't care. But then Zakarakis spat on the ground, perhaps outraged by what seemed to him indifference, and your body snapped, from your mouth came a roar that had nothing human about it: "Zakarakiiiiiiis!" You grabbed him by the throat. You squeezed until his face turned purple from lack of oxygen, his tongue protruded horribly. By the time the guards managed to loosen your fingers you had almost choked him.

5

LIKE WATER DRIPPING MONOTONOUSLY FROM A FAUCET, always the same, an obsessive tolling in the silence of the empty night until, as you keep hearing it, you feel you're going crazy and you pray for a different sound, an explosion perhaps, a shot that kills, anything but that ghastly uniformity, that darkness, as the years went by after the evening that Zakarakis told you your father was dead. During those years, in fact, you never left your sepulcher illuminated only by the blue bulb, you never passed the threshold beyond which lay day and night, sun and stars, rain and wind. Not even to stretch your legs, to get a breath of air. Not even to be confined in the infirmary when you went into a coma, not even to see your mother when they allowed her to visit you. Previously the meetings with her had taken place in the visitors' room like the other prisoners' visits, you went out and walked one hundred and twenty-six steps to go there and one hundred and twenty-six steps to come back, and as you walked you saw the sky. After that evening, however, you always saw her in your cell, with the barrier between you. And yet many things happened in those years. First of all you began to know me through the books I had written and articles of mine that sometimes were printed in the Athens papers. And as a result you learned my language, studying it at the rate of twenty words and two irregular verbs a day: so we would be able to talk once we met. You needed this effort of memory in particular to combat the mental inertia that comes with isolation, the terrible fog that kills the ability to concentrate or even to pursue a memory, to abandon yourself to a fantasy. And then, as we shall see, you wrote your most beautiful poems in those years. But the most important thing was that you never became resigned, that you never abdicated your role of the hero who refuses to give in. Seventeen times you were caught sawing at the bars of the gate with the tiny files that are used to open ampuls of medicine, fifty-two times you were punished for your rebellion by the confiscation of your pen, your writing paper, the Italian grammar, the Rapaccini dictionary, your newspapers and books; twenty-nine times by the confiscation of your shoes and cigarettes. Eighteen times they beat you until you fainted, and the same number of times they put you in a straitjacket, shouting that you were crazy. As for the hunger strikes, they were so numerous that you soon lost count of them. Speaking of this with me and reciting that scrupulous list, you remembered only the longest ones: seven fasts that lasted for fifteen days, four for twenty-five days, two for thirty, one for thirty-seven, one for forty, one for forty-four, one for forty-seven. Your only nourishment was water and sugared coffee, a sliver of chocolate concealed in the mattress, and you became so skeletal that the doctor was forced to feed you through a tube up your nose. The worst torment. You couldn't bear that tube, which went through the nasal passage, down your throat, and then down into the esophagus; it stifled you like the hand of Theophiloiannakos at the time of the interrogation and it also made you want to vomit though you weren't able to vomit. As soon as they stuck it in your nose, you thought, enough of this fasting, enough! Then you began again, and naturally you began again only to keep yourself in practice: there were times when everything seemed to you the monotonous repetition of a ritual and you would have liked Zakarakis to invent some new outrage to rouse you a bit, to keep you from yawning. The first time he confiscated your shoes you had almost enjoyed yourself although it was winter, and also when he had put the straitjacket on you for the first time. In a way it was a curiosity. But with time you became accustomed to it and now your only diversion came from the little files with which you insisted on sawing at the bars of the gate. It was a joy to discover them in the food your mother brought you, to put a piece of rabbit into your mouth and feel between your teeth that little strip of metal, because when Zakarakis heard the sound of iron being rasped, he would rush in. "Criminal, what are you doing?" "Me? Nothing." "Where have you hidden it?!" "Hidden what?" "The file, murderer, the file!" "What file?" "I heard you! You were filing at the bars!" Then he would call the guards, who would search you everywhere, the cuffs of your trousers, the collar of your shirt, the hems of your underwear, the soles of your shoes, but they never found anything because the little file was where nobody would ever think of looking for it: in your hair, between your teeth, in the pages of a book. "But you were filing, damn you!" "I wasn't filing, Zakarakis, I was making music." And laughing you would take a glass, wet the rim with some saliva, and run your forefinger around it to produce the sound of rasped iron. "Listen, idiot."

You were entertained also by your jokes, they helped you fight boredom: and you never gave up making fun of the others with your ruses worthy of Cagliostro. The business of the revolver made of bread and soap, for example. Patiently with the soft part of bread and some soap scraps, you fashioned a facsimile revolver, then with burnt heads of matches you stained the butt black, you wrapped the barrel in some aluminum paper, and one evening you were ready to aim it at the guards bringing you your supper. "Hands up! Give me the keys!" This time there were only two guards and they were unarmed, and the one holding the tray immediately dropped it, the other, trembling, handed you the keys. You gave them back to him with a chuckle, you couldn't have used them anyway, the sixteen sentries were still outside. "Fools!" Or the business of the wire with which you wanted to have the gate opened for you. There was a poor dimwit guarding you in the antechamber of the cell, a recruit fresh from the country. Zakarakis had put him there to keep you from filing the bars, he had told the boy you were a very important prisoner, and the words "very important" had so impressed him that while he never let you out of his sight, he obeyed you with the eagerness of a servant. He actually called you Excellency. "Slacker, light my cigarette." "Yes, Excellency." "Slacker, fan me." "Yes, Excellency." That day, on the floor of the outer room there was some wire. "Slacker, come here." "Yes, Excellency." "Open the padlock, I have to go piss." "Yes, Excellency, I'll just run and get the keys." "What do you need keys for, you fool? You don't open the padlock with a key! Can't you see that length of wire? Why do you think they keep it there? To open the lock, right?" "Yes, Excellency, excuse me, Excellency; in my village they open padlocks with keys!" "What makes you think I care about your stupid village? Open, hurry up! I can't hold it much longer!" "Yes, Excellency. Right away, Excellency. But in the meanwhile couldn't you urinate in your toilet, Excellency?" "Imbecile, can't you see it's stopped up? Didn't you hear the commandant when he asked me not to piss in it until it's been fixed? Hurry, pick up that wire, open the lock! That's right!" All excited, the poor boy worked and worked on the lock, but with no success. "Forgive me, Excellency, I can't manage it, I'll call the sergeant." "If you call the sergeant, I'll report you! Go on, keep trying!" Nothing happened because, attracted by your raised voice, three other guards intervened and stopped him: "Imbecile! What do you think you're doing?!" But like the bread-and-soap revolver the incident helped you to conquer the melancholy a bit, the sense of an emptiness that studying or reading couldn't fill or, if anything, worsened. In fact it's through studying and reading, you used to say, that you measure the weakening of the intellect in prison. At first you believe you have learned a verb, then half an hour later you realize you've already forgotten it. Then you repeat it, you keep reciting—I go, you go, he goes, we go, you go, they go—but your eyelids grow heavy, you lie down on your cot for a little nap and you sleep the whole afternoon, and when you wake, your mind is so sluggish that instead of a man you're like a vegetable.

Not that you had given up the idea of escape. Until habit intervened, inevitable, inexorable, and made you accept the tomb and redirect your resistance into your poetic vein and nothing else, you never stopped cultivating that mirage. But with less and less conviction, more and more indifference, with a humor that was an end in itself, as was shown by the escape attempt that concluded with a renunciation obviously deeply rooted in your subconscious. This was the attempt involving the guard who had replaced the dimwit of the padlock joke: a young man who dreamed of being an actor. A few sentences allowed you to deduce that his intelligence was also scant and you could exploit him as you liked, so you immediately began working your wiles on him: "Uhm! So you want to be an actor. You're right, with a face like yours. Let's see your profile. Ah, yes, a splendid profile. You have a great career ahead of you." "The trouble is I don't know anybody, Mr. Panagoulis, nobody at all." "You mustn't let that worry you. Now tell me: are you really sure you want to be an actor? It's a fine career, I agree: all the women you want, villa with swimming pool, billions. At the beginning it demands a lot of sacrifices, however. Some men have even risked their lives in order to become an actor: just think of Laurence Olivier and what he did for Churchill." "What did he do?" "It's a long story.

I'll tell you one of these days. Meanwhile let me ask you something. Have you studied acting?" "Yes, as a boy." "So much the better. Acting is like languages. If you learn when you're a child, you never forget them afterward. Are you photogenic?" "Oh, yes. But why do you ask me that?" "Because I can help you." "Here? While you're in here?" "Not exactly. We'll talk about it tomorrow. The important thing is for you not to say a word about this to Zakarakis. He hates actors, theater, the movies. He's envious." "Don't worry, Mr. Panagoulis." "You can call me by my first name." "Don't worry, Alekos." "Good. Tomorrow bring me your photographs." And the next day: "First rate. No doubt about it: you're photogenic. Uhm! Have you ever been to Rome?" "Never." "Marvelous city. My dearest friends are all in Rome. Sophia always used to say to me—" "Sophia? Sophia who?" "Don't interrupt me. Sophia Loren, of course. In Rome I used to live in a wing of her castle. Ah, yes. That's where I prepared the assassination, but don't tell anybody. Her husband, just imagine, actually helped me make the mines. In exchange he asked me only to write a script for him." "A script? You wrote a script for Sophia?" "Not for Sophia, for Carlo! Carlo, her husband, the producer!" "Oh!" "Under an assumed name obviously." "Oh!" "What's strange about that? Could I have refused to do a favor for a friend who was risking jail for me?" "No, no!" "So then, as I was saying, Rome is the ideal city for breaking into the movies. The only city. Even Marlon Brando these days, if he wants to make a picture, he has to go to Rome. And if you really want to become a star, Hollywood's out! You have to go to Rome. Uhm. Let me see those photographs again." "Here they are." "Excellent. The nose is excellent. So is the right profile. The left profile isn't quite as good. How odd, just like Laurence Olivier. Remind me to tell you the story of Churchill and Laurence Olivier. Well, yes: I believe I can recommend you to Sophia. Or rather to Carlo. Sophia, in these matters, doesn't count. At most, when Carlo has got you under contract, she might ask for you as her co-star. Because of your strong, manly features." "What are you saying, Alekos? Really?!" "Calm down, boy. You don't honestly think I have a magic wand, do you? Besides, Carlo's cautious. He'll let a year go by before he gives you a part with Sophia. He'll test you, he'll throw you some television jobs." "For me television is all right too." "Yes, but I don't want to get your hopes up. Television doesn't offer the same kind of money as the movies. You'd be lucky if they give you as much as fifty thousand drachmas a month." "Fifty thousand?!" "That seems a fortune to you, eh? Well, it's peanuts. But later you can make even five hundred thousand."

And so day after day he grew more and more excited, and you kept waiting for the right moment to give him the finishing stroke. The moment came when he asked you to write a letter to Carlo and Sophia. "Are you crazy? You want me to ruin my friends, the man who helped me prepare the bomb? Don't you know he works with the Americans? Don't you know that if the letter went astray, he could end up in prison too? Besides, does it seem to you the kind of favor you can ask in a letter? I'd have to speak to him in person, of course. I'll have to go to Rome with you! That seems obvious to me! If you don't lend me a hand and help me escape, how can I help you become an actor?" "Escape! But that's difficult, Alekos, that's dangerous!" "Difficult? Dangerous? My foot! Even Laurence Olivier succeeded, with Winston Churchill. Idiot! Fool! Why don't you study history? You don't even know that Winston Churchill escaped from that Nazi prison because Laurence Olivier helped him! And Laurence Olivier wasn't even a guard; he was a cook's helper! For him it really was difficult, dangerous. But Churchill never forgot that favor. And when he became prime minister he made them all hire Olivier. I know, he said, one profile isn't so good, but Larry is my friend, profile or not I want him to become Laurence Olivier! The fact is that Laurence Olivier had balls, and you don't! I've wasted all this time worrying about you, and look what comes of it. Get out! Out! I never want to see you again!" "No, Alekos, listen—" "Out! Get out!" For two weeks you acted hurt, and he begged you in vain to forgive him, he explained that his hesitation had been a moment of weakness, it would never happen again. "I refuse to listen to you!" You only spoke to him again when he flung himself on his knees and begged you to allow him to help you escape: you were his only hope, nobody else would give him a hand to become an actor, to follow his vocation; if he were to go to Rome without you, Carlo and Sophia wouldn't so much as look at him. You accepted his offer as if you were giving him an immense present. But he was to get one thing straight, however: you were giving in only because of a damn weakness of yours, known as generosity. In fact you didn't see why you should turn to him rather than to Laurence Olivier who was so brave and had telephoned your mother offering his services. "Laurence Olivier?! Honestly?!" Of course. Not that Larry did anything for nothing, you knew very well he was offering you his services in order to bring you to London and get hold of your screenplay of *Oedipus Rex*, but you didn't like London, too much fog and too much monarchy, so—"I'll do what you want. Let's get organized." The usual uniform, the usual hour of night, and then you would find some way to get out of the country. As for the sixteen guards around the tomb, they weren't worth worrying about: up to that point Operation Sophia had been carefully worked out. In that period the evening meal was still brought by only two guards, and frequently the aspiring actor was one of them. The other was a boy whose brain was worth still less: you only had to stun him, undress him, tie him to the cot, slap a bandage over his mouth, and put on his uniform. "Just get me a rope and a bandage, boy."

The next day the aspiring actor brought the rope and the bandage: "Tonight he and I are on duty." "Good." You hid the rope behind the toilet, the bandage under an armpit, and you waited. But you felt no enthusiasm, you were to tell me, and at nightfall a terrible sleepiness overcame you: you fell asleep dreaming you were possessing a woman. It happened rarely that you dreamed of possessing a woman; after the night on Aegina it had happened to you maybe four times and every time it had been very brief because of the fear of not making it, of being led in front of the firing squad before the final orgasm, had remained with you like a complex. But this time, on the contrary, it was a very long dream. It was as if you had eternity before you and you entered the woman calmly with the quiet, smooth movements of a serene sea that grazes the beach in caresses of foam, then withdraws slowly, lingers patiently before returning, to graze again with new slowness, and it was sweet to postpone the explosion, the moment when the sea would swell and crash in a release of roaring water, it was exquisite to expand the waiting for a conclusion that could not be denied, that now was approaching, closer, always closer, a little more and the final wave would break, scattering its glorious spray. There it was swelling, closer, it was about to sweep you away, and—"Wake up, Alekos, wake up! I'm here, we're here!" The aspiring actor was shaking you with both hands and his gaze hinted, implored, indicated the companion you were supposed to attack. You looked at him furiously: "Bastard, you didn't let me finish!" Then, still shouting—"You didn't let me finish, you didn't let me finish"—you drove him out, throwing your supper tray after him. He went off sobbing. Crazy, he kept saying, you were crazy, they were right to put you in a straitjacket. Then he asked Zakarakis to remove him from duty at your cell and you never saw him again. Nor did you mind. Your cot wasn't all that uncomfortable, your cell wasn't all that small: by now you had become accustomed to the sepulcher.

Habit is the most shameful disease because it makes us accept any misfortune, any pain, any death. Through habit we live with odious people, we learn to bear chains, to submit to injustices, to suffer, we resign ourselves to sorrow, to solitude, to everything. Habit is the most merciless poison because it enters us slowly, silently, grows little by little, nourished on our unawareness, and when we discover we have it in us, our every fiber has adjusted to it, our every action is conditioned by it, there is no medicine in existence then that can cure us. What had happened the evening you renounced another escape attempt was something you would never have believed possible: you no longer missed open spaces and green grass and blue skies and people. In the summer, when the sun filtered through the ceiling of the antechamber and formed a compact stain of light on the pavement, the glare so annoyed you that you took refuge, blinking, in the darkest corner of your cell and there you stayed until sunset like a mole that never comes out of its lair. If Zakarakis had built you a window to allow you to see the sky in the day and the stars at night, you would have covered it with a newspaper. And yet something existed that habituation to darkness, lack of space, and monotony had not extinguished: your capacity to dream, to imagine, and to translate sorrow, anger, thoughts, into verses. The more your body adjusted, atrophied in laziness, the more your mind resisted and your imagination, unrestrained, gave birth to poems. You had always written poems, ever since you were a boy, but it was in this period that your creative vein burst forth, irrepressible. Dozens and dozens of poems. Almost every day a poem. "Don't weep for me / Know that I die / You can't help me / But look at that flower / the one that is withering I tell you / Water it." Or: "I loved the light so much / that I could light a candle / But I wasted that opaque faint light / before enjoying it / I sensed in desperation / a heavy darkness projected elsewhere / because the very light that I held / made the shadow of my body / fill with darkness my streets." Or: "I don't understand you, God / Tell me once more / Are you asking me to thank you / or to excuse you?" You wrote them even if Zakarakis confiscated your paper and pen, because then you took a razor blade that you saved for this purpose, you cut your left wrist, soaked a match or a toothpick in the cut, and wrote with blood on whatever you found: the wrapping of a bandage, a scrap of cloth, an empty cigarette box. You waited till Zakarakis gave you back paper and pen, then you copied in very small handwriting, careful not to waste a millimeter of space, you folded the paper into tiny strips, and you sent it out into the world to tell the story of a man who doesn't give in even to habit. There were various stratagems: throwing the little ribbons of paper into the garbage so that a friendly guard could retrieve them, slipping them into the hem of the trousers you sent home to be washed, or passing them to your mother when she came to see you. But first you learned the verses by heart to prevent their being lost or destroyed. And what arguments you had with Zakarakis when he demanded to read them, to censor them or approve them. "Where have you put them? Give them to me! Don't you know the commandant must censor anything that's written in prison?" "I know, but I can't give them to you, Zakarakis. I've locked them in my storeroom." "What storeroom?! I want to see the storeroom!" "Here it is, Zakarakis!" And you pointed to your head. "I don't believe you, you damn liar, I don't believe you!" But he should have, because years later we would find in that storeroom all the lost or destroyed poems: to publish them in a book many critics thought was the beginning of a literary career.

And it's obvious that the squabbles weren't caused only by the poems. On the pages that Zakarakis insisted he had to censor, at times, there were strange numbers alongside the words, mysterious calculations: clinging like a shipwrecked man to the raft of your mind, you had resumed studying mathematics. "Tell me what this is!" "It's a theorem, Zakarakis." "What theorem?" "Even if I told you, you wouldn't understand." "Because I'm a fool, eh." "Yes, you are. So shut your trap and leave me alone." As a rule, defeated by his ignorance, he would beat a retreat. At other times he would be stubborn, and grotesque brawls developed, tensions that harked back to the days of your brutal war. Mathematics, in fact, gave rise to the conflict that was to poison your last months at Boiati. It was the spring of 1973, the day Zakarakis had come back to search for the storeroom where you hid your poems. "Where is it? Tell me where it is?" "I told you, Zakarakis, in my head." "That's not true, it's not possible, you can't remember all of them!" Suddenly his gaze fell on a piece of paper where you had written the equation $X^n + Y^n = Z^n$. He seized it with one bound. "And what's this? I don't see any numbers here. Ah, this is a code, you bastard!" "No, it's not a code, Zakarakis." "It isn't? You want me to call the brigadier general? You want him to force you to tell who X and Y and Z are? And the n's? Who are the n's?" You pointed to the cot, you invited him to sit down. "Come here, Zakarakis." "No, otherwise you'll take off my pants and try to rape me like that other time." "I won't rape you, Zakarakis. I promise." "And you'll tell me who X and Y and Z are? And who the n's are?" "I'll tell you, Zakarakis. Then n's are numbers. X and Y and Z are unknown quantities." "Bastard, liar! You think you can make fun of me, eh? I'll discover who these unknown quantities are!" "You'd be a real genius, Zakarakis, because nobody has ever succeeded in doing that, for three hundred years." "Three hundred years? You see? You're making fun of me! You see? Guards, tie him up!" They tied you to the cot, and you were strangely submissive. Zakarakis, on the contrary, was more and more furious. "Now you'll talk, eh? You'll talk." "I'll talk, Zakarakis. And if you don't understand, as soon as you let me loose, I'll pull your pants down." "Talk!" "All right. Try to follow me. If n is a given integer superior to two, the theorem cannot be satisfied with integers, none of which is zero. Therefore—" "Liar! Criminal! That's what you are, a liar, a criminal!" "And you're an idiot, Zakarakis. Is it my fault if that's what the theorem says?" "What theorem, you bastard?" "The one you have in your hand: X to the nth power plus Y to the nth power equals Z to the nth power. It's a theorem, Zakarakis, a mathematical theorem. You know I studied mathematics at the Polytechnic. And if you start with the assumption that differential calculus—" "Stop this! Stop!" He went out almost in tears. He was holding the paper in his hand and was going to uncover the plot. Because it could only be that, by Christ, a plot to escape once more. And he had to nip it in the bud.

For nights Zakarakis studied it, determined to win Ioannidis's praise. Naturally he could have turned to the espionage service, to the KYP, but this would have meant handing others on a platter a triumph he wanted all for himself. And without consulting anyone, he arrived at the following conclusions. The three n's were three soldiers who were part of the plot to help you escape: Mr. X, Mr. Y, Mr. Z were three civilians working on the outside. X for Xristos or Xristopoulos or Xarakalopoulos. Unless, instead of standing for people, X and Y and Z indicated names of countries or cities. In that case X could refer to Khania (Xania), capital of Crete, and Y to Yemen, Z to Zurich. Or did X stand for Xristougenna, that is, for Christmas? Of course, Christmas, that's what it meant: with the help of three soldiers you were going to escape on Christmas Day to Zurich by way of Yemen. He came back to you. "You thought I was stupid, eh? I've discovered the whole thing, I've worked it all out." "All?! No, Zakarakis! No, it's not possible. I swear it's not possible." "Yes, it is. I know who X is, who Y is, and who Z is. You wanted to escape to Zurich, eh, you bastard?" "What did you say, Zakarakis?" "I know that Z stands for Zurich." "And what if it stood for Zakarakis?" A tragic silence followed, Zakarakis looked at you in a stupor. O Jesus, he hadn't thought of that! If Z stood for his name, that meant only one thing: that with the complicity of the three soldiers and a Mr. Y you wanted to kill him at Christmas. "You want to have me killed, eh? I should have imagined it!" "No, Zakarakis. You're such a fool, it would be a mistake to kill you. I'd be bored to death without you. I swear it isn't you. It's

Fermat." "Who's he? I don't know him!" "You couldn't, Zakarakis. He lived three hundred years ago. He was a mathematician who was also interested in politics and literature, and especially an expert in differential calculus and in the calculation of probabilities. This theorem—" Again he ran out and didn't give you time to explain to him that the theorem existed, it was Fermat's famous last theorem, he had proved it but his text had been lost, so for three centuries they had been trying to show how X raised to n plus Y raised to n is equal to Z raised to n, nobody had succeeded, and the British Academy of Sciences had set a prize, and now you wanted to try to win the prize, not so much for the money as for the pleasure of shaming those who were keeping you in that sepulcher. But something worse happened: Zakarakis gave orders to confiscate paper and pen, and they were to search carefully, you weren't to be left even with a stub of pencil, a card, a bandage. They searched well, they even found the rusty blade. Without paper and pen, without even the blade to cut your wrists and squeeze out blood to use for ink, solving the problem became an impossible enterprise. You tried. It was like catching an eel in your bare hands. As soon as you fixed in your memory a passage of the theorem, it slipped away, it's one thing to imprint some verses in your mind but quite another to imprint mathematical calculations. Yet one afternoon it seemed to you that you had found the solution. All excited, you gripped the bars and shouted: "Paper! Pen! Quickly! Please, I beg you!" But nobody answered, and when Zakarakis gave you back paper and pen, it was too late. You had forgotten everything.

Years later you still spoke of it with bitterness. Or rather, you would begin telling the story laughing, and toward the end your voice and your face would turn grim, bitter. You used to say that episode had wounded you more than many beatings, that after it you had developed a strange feeling toward Zakarakis, a kind of indulgence that undermined your insistence on the responsibility of the individual, the single person. Because the conclusion of the story was heartbreaking for both. Unable to establish whether X and Y and Z stood for Xristos or Xristopoulos or Xania or Xristougenna, and Y for Yemen, Z for Zurich or for himself, Zakarakis had in fact turned to the KYP. And the KYP with contemptuous hilarity had answered him that you were right, it wasn't a plot but the famous last theorem of Fermat, a French mathematician of the seventeenth century: the commandant would please avoid ridiculous alarms. You saw him arrive full of dismay, holding in his hand a notebook and two ballpoint pens, one red and one blue, and: "I . . . er . . . I came to say that I'm sorry because I've found that your Fermi really is dead." "Not Fermi, Zakarakis, it's Fermat." "Fermi or Fermat, it's the same to me. Here are two ballpoints and a notebook." "I don't need them anymore, Zakarakis. I can't remember anymore what I had found." "Maybe it'll come back to you." "I don't think so. Get out, Zakarakis, go!" But at the door you stopped him. "Hey, Zakarakis!" "Yes—" "Listen, Zakarakis. I told you the moment we met and I'll repeat it now: you're an unbelievable shit but it isn't your fault. And when you're in the defendant's cage and I come to testify against you, I'll say precisely that: he was an unbelievable shit but it wasn't his fault. And I'll ask that you be sentenced only to spend one week in here." "I'm the head here! I'm the commandant!" "You're nothing, poor Zakarakis. Nothing but a symbol of the flock that submits and always obeys whoever is in command. You don't count for anything, you'll never count for anything, and you'll always be screwed by everybody else, poor Zakarakis, whether you want it or not. This is the point: whether you want it or not." Then you stretched out on the cot to laze and ponder the sadness of an unsuspected truth: hating him, by now, cost you effort.

It was Sunday, August 19, 1973. The previous night was so sultry you couldn't sleep, the cell was roasting like an oven: you got up, looking for a breath of air, and immediately you flung yourself down on the cot again, exhausted. A procession of ants was marching with extraordinary lineality across the floor. They came from the antechamber, passed beneath the gate, crossed the cell on the diagonal, and then ended under the water closet in a compact ribbon. You had noticed them a week before and at first you wanted to kill them but you remembered the cockroach that died under the guard's boot and you restrained yourself. You determined to be careful not to trample on them, and every time you went to the toilet or walked up and down, you stepped over them. They deserved such consideration: they were very polite ants, they never climbed on the cot, and it was pleasant to observe them. You counted them: there were one hundred and thirty-six and the hundred and thirty-sixth was dragging a wisp of cypress. The cypress! How it must have grown in these years. You hadn't seen it since the day you came back from the infirmary at Goudi, after the fire, and isn't it absurd to live beside a tree that can't be seen? A tree is better than a procession of ants, better even than a cockroach. When had the cockroach died? On November 23, 1968. Almost five years ago, incredible! You wondered how much you had aged in those five years. You couldn't know because Zakarakis would not let you have a mirror, he was afraid you would use it as a weapon, he said he had already gone too far, giving you the glass on which you played your little music, and to see your own face you would have to wait till the barber came to cut your hair or shave you. But the barber seldom brought a mirror. At Easter he had brought one, and you had taken a glance in it and were aghast. You didn't recognize yourself in that ragged little face, those cheeks furrowed by wrinkles, then buried in the moustache, that greenish skin: you looked fifty. And you were barely thirty-four. "Do I always look like this?" you asked. And the barber said: "No, no."

You yawned. You picked up the Italian grammar to devote a few moments to the subjunctive: "If I were loved, if you were loved, if he were loved, if we were loved, if you were loved, if they were loved . . ." "If I were understood, if you were understood, if he were understood, if we were understood, if you were understood, if they were understood . . ." After the Fermat business you no longer felt any desire to wear yourself out with mathematics. As for the poems, you were beginning to feel sated with them also. The fertile year had been 1971, then you wrote the one you were most proud of, "Journey," and the one for George, the one for Morakis, the one for Georgazis, and the finest sestinas. In 1972 you wrote "Quatrains of Autumn" and other things, good but brief: a poor year. And this year you hadn't produced more than about thirty verses. Too little. The fact is that there were weeks of complete listlessness, days in which the body did not respond to the activity of the brain, and even a pen seemed heavy in your hand. You threw the Italian grammar aside, you picked up an old newspaper. You knew it by heart but still you never tired of rereading it. It told of the unsuccessful revolt of the navy and the brief arrest of the ex-minister Evangelos Averoff. You didn't like that Averoff. Before the coup, you hadn't liked him because he was a monarchist and a reactionary, now you didn't like him because he had been released from jail a bit too quickly. Really! A man admits having participated in a plot to overthrow the regime and then he comes home without their touching a hair on his head? "Please, Mr. Averoff, step this way, that's the exit, best regards, keep well." Unless—Hadn't he been the one to conceive of the so-called bridge policy? "To build a bridge between the junta and the opposition." Opposition! What opposition? His own?! Yes, his release covered up a trap: even inside that sepulcher you could smell the whiff of a trap. You wouldn't have been surprised if, with the direct or indirect help of Averoff, Papadopoulos were to do something tricky, creating a fake democracy for example, to legalize the junta, constitutionalize it. In fact, you'd bet anything the proofs of all this existed. Ah, if you could get hold of the proofs, the documents! To be able one day to reveal the truth, show that the really guilty ones are those who hide behind a screen of respectability, the dignified gentlemen who exploit anyone and always come out on top, whatever regime rises and whatever regime falls. The Averoffs. Power that never dies, that dresses in all colors, all falsehoods. You were gripped by a great anger. Your energy returned. You sat erect on the cot, and with Zakarakis's red ballpoint you wrote on the wall: "Tha martirizo. I will document." At the same moment the Sunday silence was rent by joyful shouts: "Zito, zito! Hurrah, hurrah!" You jumped down from the cot, gripped the bars, to hear better. Who was shouting like that, the prisoners or the soldiers? "Zito, zito! Hurrah, hurrah!" It was the prisoners shouting. And in a flash you understood. There is only one thing that makes them shout hurrah in a prison: amnesty. So what you feared had already happened: the bridge policy had borne its fruits, Power had realized that the ropes had to be slackened, and had convinced Papadopoulos to grant an amnesty in order to jabber more easily about normalization, democratization. Unless the dictatorship had fallen and the shouts referred to the miracle. You waited for the guards to arrive with your meal. "What is it? Why are they cheering?" "They're happy, tomorrow they're going home." You bowed your head, crushed by the confirmation. And what if they were to release you as well? Christ, that would really be a problem! Afterward who would be able to talk about real tyranny? Come, come, they would say, that Papadopoulos isn't so bad: he didn't shoot his would-be assassin although the man refused to ask a pardon, and now he's actually turning him loose! And your five years of battle, your sacrifice, your sorrow would go for naught. No, you didn't want them to release you. You didn't want to become his instrument, his accomplice! It's one thing to win freedom by escaping but quite another to receive it as a gift from your enemy. Saying this to yourself, you paced up and down, you trampled on the ants, forgetting their existence.

You thought about the amnesty all night, sometimes

believing it, sometimes not, and when you didn't believe it, you felt serene, when you did believe it, your conscience was split in two. A man is a man, and a man is made of generosity and egoism, of courage and weakness, of coherence and incoherence: if one half of you hoped that it wouldn't happen, the other half desired it madly. You were young, by Christ, you were alive, you couldn't bear staying any longer in that tomb! Never seeing the sun, never seeing the sky, unable to touch a woman, to caress her, to say to her, I love you, always alone, alone, alone, moving only in a tunnel a meter eighty by ninety, buried without being dead! And outside was life. Space, life. Light, life. People, life. Love, life. Tomorrow, life. How difficult it is to be a hero. How cruel it is and inhuman and basically stupid, futile. Would anyone ever thank you for having proved yourself a hero? Would they raise monuments to you, name streets and squares after you? And if they did, what did that matter to you? Would a monument, a street, a square give you back your lost youth, the life not lived? No, stop, this was blasphemy. You don't do your duty simply because someone will say thanks, you do it out of principle, for yourself, for your own dignity. Who knows how many human beings at that moment, left and right, East and West, were in prison, in solitary confinement, buried alive because of their own dignity and without expecting any thanks? People whose names weren't even known, would never be known. Anonymous, unsung heroes, also thirsting for sun and sky and love, company, also oppressed, deprived of space and light, also tortured by a Zakarakis, who punished them by taking away their shoes, cigarettes, books, newspapers, pen, paper, confiscating their poems, thrusting them into a straitjacket: "He's crazy! He's crazy!" The world is full of these madmen. The best, the crazy, almost always end up in prison. The ones who adjust, who compromise, who are silent, who obey, submit, betray, agree to be slaves, are those who never end in prison. Come on, were you perhaps giving in? Was a desire to run through a meadow or along a beach, to have a woman, to lie beside her in a bed, enough to make you forget who you were, who you wanted to be? You had remained steadfast through tortures, the trial, the waiting for the firing squad, the ghastly solitude of a darkness where for five years you had encountered only a cockroach and one hundred thirty-six ants: you would remain steadfast in the face of the amnesty, at all costs. And if that door were to open, if Zakarakis were to come in and say—You're free, Alekos—you would answer him—O Christ, what would you answer him? You closed your eyes, exhausted. You dozed off. It was late morning when the voice of Zakarakis wakened you. "Get up, Alekos. You've been granted a pardon."

The silence is long that is frozen by the sound of a sentence much feared or much desired, for better or worse, as the brain is silent and the body paralyzed, the feet do not move, the arms do not move, the head does not move or even the tongue: only the heart beats. Then from the abysses of a rediscovered will an impulse starts and you will never know what it is: and a foot moves. An arm moves, a leg moves, and the head, and the tongue: the brain resumes thinking. You stood up. "What pardon? I haven't asked anyone for any pardon, Zakarakis." "You haven't asked for it, but the president has granted it to you." "President, my ass!" "Bastard, I'm telling you that tomorrow you're leaving, bastard, can't you understand?! You're leaving! You're getting off my back!" "What if I don't want to, Zakarakis?" "We'll carry you out bodily! Bodily!" You leaned against the wall of the toilet, slipped your hands into the pockets of your trousers, crossed your legs, provokingly. "Then you'll have to carry me out bodily because I'm not moving from here, Zakarakis." "You'll move, Alekos, you'll move. You're talking to hear yourself talk, you don't know what you're saying. Once you're outside you'll change your mind. You'll realize that life is sweet out there and—" "And you, all of you, will realize that putting me in here is easier than taking me out." This time Zakarakis didn't answer and with a shrug he went off: leaving the inside gate open. By accident or on purpose? You called him: "The gate, Zakarakis. You forgot to close the gate." Again Zakarakis didn't answer and went on toward the door. Here, however, he had a spark of genius because after a moment's hesitation he went out leaving that open too. You called him again: "The door, Zakarakis. You forgot to close the door." You didn't move. You didn't even start toward the antechamber, the doorway, to look into the yard. You were dying to, you would confess to me one day. You wanted to do that more than anything in the world. Yet you remained motionless. And an hour later, when Zakarakis returned, you were still there: back against the wall, hands in your pockets, legs crossed. So his spark of genius died. He began to scream—Ingrate, madman, villain—he shut all the padlocks, and you spent your last night in Boiati the usual way.

The procedure that accompanies release from prison because of pardon or amnesty involves a regular ceremony with the public prosecutor, who reads the decree, the prison authorities, who are present at attention, a soldier holding the flag, and a squad that presents arms. You knew this, so nothing of what happened on Tuesday, August 21, was accidental. Except for the chair business, every action of yours, every word was a part of the script you had worked out to the smallest detail. To begin with, you were waiting there in your underwear when Zakarakis came to get you. "What? You aren't even dressed?!" "No, why?" "Because there's the ceremony!" "What ceremony?" "The release ceremony!" "I haven't released you, Zakarakis. You're still my prisoner." "Not *my* release! Yours! Will you dress or won't you?" "No, I prefer to come in my underwear." "Listen to me, Alekos. You've had your revenge. Now be good, don't make me ridiculous in front of the public prosecutor. You can't come in your underwear." "Yes, I can." "I beg you on my knees,

Alekos." "On your knees? Really?" "Yes, if you'll put your clothes on, I'll get on my knees." "Don't talk shit, Zakarakis. I don't like seeing people on their knees, not even when their name is Zakarakis." And very slowly you put on your trousers, shoes, a blue T-shirt. Then: "Oh! My beard! What about my beard, Zakarakis?" "Shave him! On the double!" "Why on the double? I'm in no hurry." "I am! The public prosecutor is waiting! And the commandant too! The authorities are all here!" "What do I care about the authorities? I like to take my time with the barber." The barber came. He shaved you. This wasn't enough: you wanted him to cut your hair too. This still wasn't enough: you wanted him to trim your moustache as well. Zakarakis was beside himself: "Are you ready now?" "No, there's no cologne." "What's cologne got to do with it?" "It's vital. I'm not a stinker like you. I use cologne." "Panagoulis, don't provoke me!" "And if I provoke you, what will you do, Zakarakis? Will you put me in a straitjacket? Will you beat me? Will you drag me to your ceremony in a straitjacket or on a stretcher, covered with blood?" "Bring him the cologne!" They brought it. You didn't like it. "This isn't French. I use only French colognes." "Find some French cologne!" Nobody had any, but an officer of the camp had an English lotion, and after you had made a long speech on the difference between French cologne and English lotion, you sprayed yourself with English lotion. Finally, toward noon, you were ready and you came out. But it was three years and five months since you had crossed that threshold and at the second step your head swam, you felt so ill that they had to carry you back into the cell so that you could lie on your cot for a few minutes. Afterward it took you twenty minutes to cover the distance to the commandant's quarters. And you were supported by a corporal because you had to keep your eyes half-closed. The sunlight seared your pupils.

In the commandant's quarters a little crowd of uniforms was waiting impatiently. At your entrance they came to attention, pompously, and it was then that you glimpsed the chair. You sat on it, deaf to the protests of Zakarakis. "That's the public prosecutor's chair!" "Why, did he buy it?" "Give it back!" "No." The public prosecutor spoke: "Panagoulis, stand up!" "Why? I'm not going to give you the chair anyway." "Because I have to read the presidential decree." "It may be a presidential decree for you, busboy of the junta. For me it's only a clown's paper. With the papers of your Papadopoulos I wipe my ass." "Panagoulis, you're going too far!" "Then arrest me. Send me back to my cell." "That can't be done. You've been pardoned!" "That's what you say. I don't accept any pardon." "Come on, stand up." "No, not even if you kill me." A bewildered silence followed: what to do? Risk a brawl forcing you to stand or pretend indifference allowing you to remain seated? Better to leave you seated, it was the wiser course. "Let's begin," the camp commander said. The squad presented arms, the soldier with the flag raised the flag, the public prosecutor read the first lines of the decree. Sprawled on the chair, meanwhile, you yawned, whistled, never stopped scratching yourself. Especially your ankles. The public prosecutor broke off his reading: "What are you doing?" "Scratching myself." "What are you scratching?" "I'm scratching my balls. They're so limp with boredom they come down to my ankles." The public prosecutor blushed, Zakarakis gritted his teeth, the camp commander made an irritated gesture, the reading was resumed. When it was finished, to the immense relief of everyone but you, they invited you again to stand up. "Panagoulis, come on!" "Where? I'm fine here. I like it. And besides I'm tired." "You have to go back to your cell until the lieutenant colonel comes." "Carry me!" "How?" "The way they carry the pope around on his chair so he can bless people." Now the camp commander was laughing, Zakarakis was crying. "You see, sir? You see? Almost four years of this! A criminal, I tell you, a criminal!" And you said: "Cry, Zakarakis, go ahead and cry. I'm not budging from here." And you held the chair with both hands, you twisted your legs around it. They had to carry you out chair and all, they were more and more embarrassed, you were suddenly grave and prim, just like a pope on the sedia gestatoria. But at the moment of leaving the cell you started all over again. With a lieutenant colonel, this time. "Collect your things, Panagoulis, you're free." "I'm not collecting anything. You collect them." "Don't you want to leave?" "No, I've already told all of you a thousand times that I'm fine here, I prefer to stay here." "Outside you'll change your mind and—" "And I'll discover that life is sweet: Zakarakis says the same thing. Carry my stuff then." Half-amused, half-resigned, the lieutenant colonel took your baggage: a flight bag full of dictionaries and files. The files were hidden in the handle, you had put them there as a joke, and anyway by now they were souvenirs. "Let's go, Panagoulis." "All right, let's go." You took a last look at the cell, a very strange look of both sadness and regret, you stared with painful intensity at the words, "I will document," then you went out and you were in the courtyard on the little path that curves to the left and then to the right, on the path where that terrible night of the second escape Zakarakis had mocked you. You walked with your head down, your eyes half-closed as when you had gone to the ceremony, stubbornly avoiding looking at the sky, it was an effort for the guards to support you, you leaned so heavily on them. You felt very tired, all that farce of provocation and insolence had exhausted you, at every step you asked yourself what you would do once you were at the gate, where the guards would leave you, and there was no sign of joy on your face. Finally you were at the gate, you moved away from the guards, you passed the threshold. And you stammered, bewildered: "Oh, Theos mou! Theos mou! Oh, God! My God!"

Before you there was a chasm so broad, so deep, so empty that merely perceiving it made you nauseated, made you want to vomit. And this chasm was space, open space. Inside the sepulcher you had forgotten what space was, open space. It was a terrible thing, because it was like a thing that wasn't there. There was no wall to limit it, no ceiling to cover it, no door to close it out, no lock, no bars! It gaped before you and around you like a mysterious, insidious ocean, and the only reference point was the earth that stretched down through the valley and up over the hills, barely interrupted by clumps of grass or by trees: ghastly, nightmarish. But the worst thing was the sky. Inside the sepulcher you had also forgotten what the sky is. It was a void above the void, a dizziness above the dizziness: so blue, no, yellow, no, white. So evil. It burned your pupils worse than an acid, more than fire. You closed your eyes so as not to be blinded, you stretched out your arms so as not to fall. And at once the thought of your cell gripped you, along with an irresistible homesickness, an irrepressible desire to go back there, to take refuge in its darkness, in its narrow and safe womb—My cell, give me back my cell. The officer who was carrying the bag with the dictionaries and the files understood, overtook you, touched your shoulder: "Courage." You reopened your eyes, blinking, you took a step, then another, then another, then yet another. You stopped again. It wasn't a question of courage, it was a question of balance. To walk in all that space, that light, and alone, was not like walking along the paths of the prison, pressed between two guards who support you by the elbows: it was like groping on the edge of a precipice. Even walking straight was very difficult because without walls, obstacles, you couldn't tell what was straight and what crooked, front and back, you could only tell that there was an above and a below, sky and earth, the dazzling sun. But little by little, as the nausea developed and the uncertainty and the fear, as everything expanded and rotated and turned over to make you repeat—My cell, give me back my cell—you found yourself again. And you discerned something. What? There were shadows over there, moving spots. They were coming toward you, swaying, waving, strange appurtenances that seemed at first like wings, or were they arms? Birds or people? They must be people because they were making strange sounds that sounded like voices: "Aleeeekos! Aleekoos!" What a terrible effort to head in that direction. "Aleekoos! Aleekos!" Suddenly one spot stood out among the others: a black stumpy form. And it became a woman with a black dress and black stockings and black shoes and a black hat and black glasses. She ran toward you with her arms outstretched, her fingers outstretched. Your mother. You fell on her. And then all were on top of you, friends and relatives and reporters, to touch you, hug you, call you so you would no longer regret your cell, in fact, abruptly, you no longer regretted it, you felt inexplicably happy: though you had a great need to weep. You didn't want to weep, you wanted to say something important, historic. But the more you asked yourself what this something could be, the more the need to weep grew, swelled, became a tingling in the throat, a film of water over the eyes. The bewilderment you had felt on seeing that chasm was now being translated into a precise intuition, into the awareness that freedom for you would mean another suffering, another grief.

And this was the man I would meet the next day, at last, crashing into him like one train colliding with another, traveling in the opposite direction on the same track.

PART TWO

1

The bitter discovery that God does not exist has destroyed the concept of fate. But to deny fate is arrogance, to declare that we are the sole shapers of our existence is madness; if you deny fate, life becomes a series of missed opportunities, a regret for what never was and could have been, a remorse for what was not done and could have been done, and the present is wasted, twisted into another missed opportunity. With regret you asked me: "Why didn't we meet before? Where were you when I was detonating the mines, when they were torturing me, when they tried me, sentenced me to death, shut me up in that tomb?" With remorse I answered Saigon, Hanoi, Phnom Penh, Mexico City, São Paulo, Rio de Janeiro, Hong Kong, La Paz, Cochabamba, Amman, Dacca, Calcutta, Colombo, New York, then São Paulo again, Saigon again, Phnom Penh again, La Paz again; and as I listed those distant cities, it seemed to me I was lining up the stages of a betrayal. I never answered you that I was where fate had demanded because that very fate had determined that we would meet on this day at this hour and not before. Until that day, at that hour, our paths were so separate, so far apart that even the most iron will could not have made them cross. Only once we grazed each other in a flash: the day you fled to Italy from Cyprus. In fact, examining dates, we discovered that as you arrived I was leaving. But fate has a logic, nothing happens at random: if we had met on that occasion or before, we wouldn't have recognized each other. We recognized each other afterward because we had already seen each other a hundred times in Saigon, in Hanoi, in Phnom Penh, in Mexico City, in São Paulo, in Rio de Janeiro, in Hong Kong, in La Paz, in Cochabamba, in Amman, in Dacca, in Calcutta, in Colombo, and then in São Paulo again, Saigon again—all rotations of the wheel to bring me to you, all stages in a great faithful love.

You were to have many faces, many names, in those years. In Vietnam your name was Huyn Thi An and you were a Vietcong girl with cheeks and chin and forehead defaced by scars. In your house a stick of dynamite, which you had wanted to use to kill a tyrant called Van Thieu, exploded, and they caught you. They tortured you with boiling water, smothered you with towels, and the officers in bottle green uniforms were about to sentence you to death when we met in a room of the special police headquarters and you looked at me with hatred because I was wearing an army uniform. I said to you: "I'm not a soldier, Huyn Thi An. I'm a journalist, I come from a country that is not at war with yours, and I want to write well about you. Talk to me, Huyn Thi An." And you answered me: "I don't want you to write about me. I don't need that. The only thing I need is to get out of here and start fighting again. Can you get me out of here?" "No, Huyn Thi An, I can't." "Then you don't interest me. Go away. Good-bye." Your name was also Nguyen Van Sam, a little barefoot man, dressed in black, with frail shoulders, skinny little hands. You had done a tremendous thing, you had set off two claymores at the My Canh restaurant—the one on the river—and you had slaughtered dozens of people: for nothing. On the eve of another attempt they set a trap for you and you ended up at the premier arrondissement, the ESA headquarters of Saigon, where Malios and Babalis and Theophiloiannakos hadn't succeeded in making you talk. Hazizikis, that time, did. His name was Captain Pham Quant Tan, your Saigon Hazizikis, and he blackmailed you: "If you talk, I'll shoot you with honor. If you don't talk, I'll crush you under a truck and you'll die without glory." You weren't a hero, that time, you couldn't resign yourself to the idea of being run over by a truck instead of being shot, and painfully moving your lips, swollen by blows, you asked Pham Quant Tan: "Will you really give me a trial and shoot me?" "Yes." "Then I'll tell everything." We met in the same room where I had met Huyn Thi An and you were very polite, you liked being with me because they would free your hands and let you smoke. I interviewed you for two nights, and it was beautiful to listen to you because you had become a poet there too, in the Saigon prison. You told me about a god with a yellow beard whom they call Jesus Christ and he has wings and flies over the clouds and dies like a Vietcong partisan, shot; you told me about your village where at sunset the sun turns red and drowns in the rice paddies as a light breeze bends the tops of the rice plants; you told me how useless it is to kill, how idiotic, you said to me that men are innocent because they are men and do useless things, idiotic things like killing their enemy, therefore we must look at them with great pity. We were both sorry to part—you because you would no longer have the opportunity to smoke so many cigarettes and sit with your hands free, I because I had begun to love you. Saying good-bye, I wished you a good death. That was what you were dreaming of: a good death.

In Bolivia your name was Chato Peredo and you were the last of the Peredo brothers, the first had died with Che Guevara and the second in a conflict with the police. To organize armed resistance you had run off into the Illimani forests and I was about to come to you when General Miranda's army surrounded and captured you. It was your comrades in La Paz who told me so that I would do something, and I rushed to President Torres, who was a good man, such a good man that Miranda later murdered him. I said to him, "Mr. President, they have caught Chato and they want to shoot him, please save him." Torres saved you and you never knew that he had been the one to save you and that I had pleaded with him. In fact we never met when you were called Chato, but we met when you were called Julio and were being held in the central prison of La Paz. With a trick, a faked document, I got inside the prison and reached your cell: to discover its location and to report to the others, who were preparing to liberate you. You had a great black beard at that time, and you didn't write poems, you wrote books: in your tiny, neat, elegant handwriting. We were together only a few minutes and you trusted me, you told me what I had to know, and it helped: the day I learned they had succeeded in freeing you I wept for joy. And I came to find you in Brazil. In Brazil your name was Carlos Marighela and you were an old Communist, an ex-deputy whom Fleury was after, like a hare in a shooting gallery. The infamous Fleury, head of the police of São Paulo, accomplice and protector of the uniformed murderers who formed the so-called Squadron of Death. You lived in hiding at that time, constantly changing address and wig, but you wanted to meet me to tell me the truth about those who were fighting the dictatorship in Brazil and three times you made an appointment. Twice I was unable to reach you because Fleury had put his agents on my heels; wherever I went, I found them after me with their tan raincoats, and the one time I shook them off you didn't show up at the meeting because they were tailing you. Then Fleury killed you. At the corner of Lorena and Casabranca, he set a trap for you with two monks of the Resistance he had already arrested and with many plainclothes police, men and women. It was two women who riddled you with bullets and for their exploit they were promoted and their pay was raised. That was November 5, 1969, and I believe the awareness of my love for you erupted after Fleury had you killed at the corner of Lorena and Casabranca by the hand of two women to whom he would give in gratitude a promotion and a raise.

And then your name was Padre Tito de Alencar Lima, a Dominican monk whose face and age I didn't even know. You became Padre Tito de Alencar Lima on February 17, 1970, when Captain Mauricio came with his squad to collect you and took you to ESA headquarters, which in São Paulo went under the name of Bainderantes Operations, and he said to you: "Now you will know the local office of hell." Then he stripped you completely naked and tied you to an iron pole that swayed from the ceiling. The pau de arara. In Portuguese that means parrot pole; in fact it looked like a parrot's perch, but at the Bainderantes Operations they used it for men and women, not for parrots: they wrapped a body around it in such a way that the pole supported the elbows and the knees, they tied ankles to wrists, and they left the victim in that grotesque, terribly painful position until the blood stopped circulating and the body swelled and breathing ceased. They hung you there and kept you there all one afternoon and evening, untying you only to give you the telephone, a torture that consists of hitting the victim's ears with both hands, and afterward they threw you in a cell like the cell in Boiati, without a cot or mattress, without a blanket: "Tomorrow you'll talk, monk, you'll talk." But the next day again you didn't talk, and then came Captain Omero, a specialist in the falange and in beatings on the genitals. You didn't talk even for Captain Omero and so there came Captain Albernaz who had the most determined team of all. "Monk, when I come to Bainderantes Operations I leave my heart at home; to find out what I want to find out, I spit on the Virgin Mary. Every time you say no or remain silent, I'll increase the charge," he warned you. And he immediately tied you to the dragon chair, which was a kind of electric chair, and he attached the wires to your temples, your hands, your feet, your genitals, and he released into you a charge of two hundred volts. "Will you talk or not?" "No." At each no, two hundred volts. By ten that night he was tired and he concluded that for you a special little job was required, you had mocked him long enough, tomorrow he would arrange it. The special little job consisted of sticking the electric wire in your anus, and so the next day he stuck the electric wire in your anus and gave a charge so intense, so long, that you thought you would explode into a thousand pieces: the sphincter gave way spattering a rain of feces on the floor. Albernaz stepped over the feces and said: "For the last time, monk, will you talk, yes or no?" "No." "Then get ready to die." And he said, "Open your mouth and I'll give you the Host." You opened your mouth, happy to die, and Albernaz put the electric wire on your tongue, released a charge of two hundred and fifty volts. Forty-eight hours later you tried to commit suicide, which for you, a Catholic, a Dominican priest, was a mortal sin twice over. They had come to shave you and had shaved only a part, in contempt. You called a soldier, you asked him for something with which you could shave off the rest, he gave you a blade, and as soon as it was in your hand, you dug it into your left arm near the inside of the elbow. The blade severed the artery, blood spattered the walls. You regained consciousness in an infirmary room. Six men were guarding you and Captain Mauricio was insisting, like Zakarakis: "Doctor, he mustn't die, otherwise we're lost." You didn't die and some time later I learned of your calvary. I learned about it from a letter you had written to your archbishop; I had come looking for that letter in São Paulo, to publish it, to explain to the world who you were, to do something for you.

And this is the point. In the years when the wheel of fate was turning with stubborn coherence to lead me to you, not once did I call you by your name, not once did I give you your own face. For the man who bore your name, who had your face, I hadn't signed one document of protest, I hadn't attended one rally, I hadn't written one line. I hadn't even read the thirty poems that had escaped from Boiati and had been translated and published in Italy. I hadn't made any attempt to learn more about a story I knew only slightly, superficially. I had learned about the attempted assassination very late, from an agency report while I was in Vietnam: a few lines about some Greek officer who had wanted to kill the tyrant. I read them saying—Good, something's stirring back there—then I forgot them; in Vietnam a whole nation was dying, to be rid of one oppression and to succumb to another, the stink of corpses polluted the air along with the futile odor of heroism: in all that tragedy there was no room for you. Of your trial and your death sentence, however, I learned when I was in the hospital after the Mexico City massacre. I was wounded in the massacre, a bullet in my left leg and one in my back; the wound in the back became a growth and they operated on me. "The would-be assassin of Papadopoulos will be shot," the paper said. And it added that you yourself had asked to be shot. I was distressed by this story, but this distress soon faded at the thought of the hundreds of people massacred before my eyes in the great square of Mexico City, those bodies that rolled down the steps or jerked forward in a somersault, that little boy whose brain was ripped open by a burst of automatic fire, the other who flung himself on the first one, in tears, and the second volley hit him as well, cut him in two, that pregnant woman whose womb they tore open with bayonets, that girl who lost half her face and the doctor repeated, "I'm letting her die, yes, I'm letting her die." And the dead, among whom they flung me and left me for hours, the dead who died in prisons and were burned or buried secretly so nobody would ever speak of them, nobody would ever exclaim with admiration—He himself asked to be shot. I learned late that your sentence hadn't been carried out, and felt a brief, abstract joy about it; I learned casually that in prison you were undergoing inhuman sufferings, and I felt an anger equally brief and abstract. If fate did not exist, if I hadn't had to become an instrument of your fate, we would have to ask ourselves why I telegraphed you on that August day and then rushed to Athens with the urgency of someone obeying a long-awaited summons and why the moment I arrived in your city I had the presentiment that something was about to crash down on me, crash down on us, something irreparable.

It was very hot in Athens. The heavy early afternoon heat that inflames southern countries in summer. The soft asphalt gave way beneath one's shoes, clothes stuck to sweating skin, there wasn't a breath of air. I came out of the airport, got into a taxi, gave the driver your address, and at once I was caught by a strange uneasiness, the same feeling I had in Vietnam when I was following a patrol along trails that were probably mined, alert to every rustle as I tried to set my feet where the others had already stepped, knowing it was useless, that my shoes could have pressed the firing pin the others had missed by a hair, and sorry I had even said—I'll come too—I would have liked to turn back, to run away shouting—I don't give a damn about your war. That's how I felt. And soon the uneasiness became anguish, the same feeling I had that morning when I had gone hunting for Padre Tito de Alencar Lima's letter on the outskirts of São Paulo and Fleury's agents followed me with their tan raincoats; the same I had felt that afternoon when I was going toward the massacre in the Zocalo Tlatelolco, knowing it was going to happen. The same expectation of some unknown disaster, some unknown sorrow, but a disaster that will certainly destroy you, a sorrow that will make you suffer too much; the same contradictory impatience as the taxi speeds through that stifling heat and the driver doesn't know the neighborhood so he takes all the wrong streets and keeps finding himself back at the same place, a garage with a Texaco sign. Under the garage a narrow ramp, a black pit that rivets my gaze each time around and unnerves me like a threat. The pit into which they will hurl you, three years later. Texaco,

Texaco, Texaco. The driver is in despair, he apologizes in a mysterious, remote language, sounds that remind me of words learned in school, the *Iliad* and the *Odyssey*. "Den xero, den katalaveno. I don't know. I don't understand." But suddenly he waves the paper with the address and brakes at a pavement flanked with olive trees. Beyond the olives, a narrow garden of orange and lemon trees, rosebushes and succulents, in the midst of the garden a path leading to a little yellow house with green shutters and a veranda running all around it, crammed with excited people, to the left of the path a big palm tree with bunches of garlic hanging from a gash in the trunk, heaven knows why. "Edo, edo! Here, here!" He makes the sign of the cross. Is it to thank the Lord for having finally arrived or to exorcize this thin little foreign woman, dressed like a man, who smooths her long sweaty hair and doesn't get out, as if she were afraid, then she does get out abruptly, determined, and goes to her appointment with fate?

I hadn't the slightest idea of what you looked like, I had never seen a photograph of you. I had never even wondered if you were young or old, handsome or ugly, tall or short, blond or dark. What sort of person you were was a question I asked myself all of a sudden as I pushed through the crowd, went up the path, stepped onto the veranda, and found myself in a little hallway full of more excited people, then in the buzz of a shabby little living room, where the men were sitting on one side and the women on the other, Arab-fashion. The men seemed all alike, any one of them could have been you. I looked for you, convinced I wouldn't recognize you. But I did recognize you, immediately, because immediately our eyes met and clicked and because this thin, almost ugly man, with the burning little black eyes and the big moustache that stood out, black, against the sick pallor of the face could only be Huyn Thi An and Nguyen Van Sam and Chato and Julio and Marighela and Padre Tito de Alencar Lima. And it was Huyn Thi An who sprang up with extended arms, it was Nguyen

Van Sam who came toward me, it was Chato and Julio and Marighela who grabbed and hugged me in a vise before I had time to introduce myself, say my name, it was Padre Tito de Alencar Lima who stroked my cheek with soft fingers. But it was your voice that said: "Hello, you've come." And it was such a voice that just hearing it meant losing a sense of peace forever.

"I was waiting for you. Come in." You took me by the hand and led me away from the crowd, you drew me along the corridor to a bedroom, where the wardrobe had been transformed into an altar. Icons of Christ, of the Virgin, saints, one above the other in a glitter of superstitious silver, and burning candles, incense, missals. In the opposite corner a bed covered with books in Greek. On top of the books a great bunch of red roses. You grabbed it happily and handed it to me. "For you." "For me?!" "Yes, for you." Then, with authority: "Andreas!" The young man you had called Andreas came in, tall and elegant, blue suit and white shirt; he stood as if at attention and in that absurd pose he listened to what you said in your language, then he translated into English. You knew Italian, he translated, you had studied it in prison, but during those years you had conversed only with the grammar book, so you preferred him to act as interpreter. You wanted first of all to apologize for receiving me in a bedroom, it was your mother's room and the only place where we could talk undisturbed; you wanted moreover to explain that those were my books translated into Greek, that to procure one of them you had gone on a hunger strike, that in the solitude of your cell they had often kept you company and this is what the roses meant. You had sent two friends to me at the airport with them, but the friends hadn't found me there because my telegram didn't say which flight I would be on, so here they were. I listened, amazed, unable to answer with any kind of words: what man was this who, barely out of prison, took the trouble to receive me with such a tribute, and why, instead of flattering me, did all this redouble my uneasiness, my anguish, the inexplicable menace I had sensed in hearing his voice? I had to be free of him as quickly as possible, that was vital, the meeting had to be shifted to another plane, I had to make it clear I was on an assignment, here for an interview. And without asking myself if I was wounding you, in fact avoiding the strange expression of your reaction, at once mortified and ironical, I thanked you in a curt tone: "Molto gentile, very nice." Then I laid the roses on a bench, set the tape recorder on a low table, sat down, asked you to sit facing me, please, right, now let's get started, and I began questioning you: professional, cold. But at the same time I was desperately, frantically studying you, trying to resolve the enigma, decipher the fascination or rather the magic you emanated. There was something in you, I said to myself, that attracted and repelled at the same time, something heartrending and terrifying. Like looking down from the top floor of a skyscraper: you feel you're flying, but at the same time you seem to be plunging into the void.

What was it? The face perhaps. No, no, the face was far from exceptional. The only beautiful thing about it was the forehead: high, broad, sublime in its purity. The only interesting feature was the eyes, because they weren't identical, either in shape or size, one was wide and one was narrow, one was open and one was half-closed. The wide and open one glared with almost evil harshness, the narrow, half-closed eye had a childish tenderness, but together they blazed like a forest on fire in the night. The rest was not very impressive. The eyelids were two shapeless spoons of flesh, the nose was boneless and slightly crooked, the nostrils just a bit imperious, the chin was short and petulant, the cheeks too round. Haggard by hardship and yet round. Only the moustache, limp and thick, and the heavy eyebrows, like two brushstrokes of ink, restored importance to that face. As for the body, it was well built: solid shoulders and hips and legs; when the thinness was past, it might even become seductive, but it would always remain the body of a working-class man of middle height, a bit crude. No, in the physique I saw absolutely nothing that could enchant me or make me nervous. So? Perhaps the voice. That voice that merely grumbling—"Ciao, you've come"—had entered me like a stab: guttural, deep, rich in an undefinable sensuality. Or was it the authority with which you moved and handled people? "Andreas!" The calm of a man who is very sure of himself and brooks no reply to what he says because he has no doubts. You took out your pipe, filled it casually, lighted it casually, and started smoking it with long puffs, like an old man, and this underlined your detachment as you answered my questions. There was no detachment, however, in what you said, nor had there been in your leap as you came to meet me, embrace me. Best not to think about that. Better to seek again for Huyn Thi An and Nguyen Van Sam and Chato and Julio and Marighela and Padre Tito de Alencar Lima, to give you his face again, look at the wrists deformed by the ropes with which you hung from the ceiling, the foot broken by the falange, the gash in the rib, the scar that at the left cheekbone bloomed like a violet excrescence. "You remind me of a Brazilian monk, Alekos." "Padre Tito de Alencar Lima." "How did you know that?!" "I know. I know his letter, the one you published. I was hoping you would do the same thing for me." "I've never done anything for you." "It doesn't matter. Now you're here." You put down the pipe, you clasped both my hands, you pressed them hard, piercing my eyes with yours. "You're here, we've found each other."

It was awful. Because suddenly everything was clear, and understanding it was the same as making rational the presentiment that had gripped me on my arrival in Athens, admitting that in this room before the absurd little altar of Christs and Virgins I not only had to add up my ideals and my moral commitments, deciding what you represented or what I wanted you to represent, but I also had to face a duel, the meeting between a man and a woman that led to a love for each other, the most dangerous love that exists: the love that mixes ideals and moral commitments with attraction and with emotions. I withdrew my hands, I hid them under the table. With the cowardice of a snail who, merely being grazed, hides in his shell, I began a dogged resistance, avoiding your gaze, or shielding myself behind a bulwark of questions, or clinging to the presence of Andreas, addressing him instead of you. However, the things you recounted, the tortures, the trial, the death sentence, the hell in which you had lived for years without losing your faith, without renouncing your individuality, brought me back to you like a wind that sweeps away even the will. And behind that wind there was that voice, there were those eyes, those fingers that stubbornly continued to seek me. In the end I gave way. I stopped avoiding your gaze, I allowed my eyes to sink in it, I put my hands back on the table so that you could find them each time you wanted to press them, and the interview went on like that: as Andreas's presence became somehow inopportune, indiscreet, and we ignored the hours that passed. The sun was high when we began, the silver icons gleamed in its light. Then the sun became twilight, the twilight darkness, an old woman dressed in black came in and lighted the lamps, but not even this distracted us. The fear that had dissolved came back suddenly when I asked you what politics meant for you, not the politics that is made in secret, underground, but the politics that goes on in freedom, and first you answered me that you had never engaged in politics, but had flirted with politics, in the style of Garibaldi not Cavour, then you shut yourself up in an unexpected silence, and in that silence, you slowly moved your fingers closer to mine. Very slowly you clasped them. And very slowly you said in my language: "I like flirting, but I prefer love. Love with love."

As if stung by a wasp I stood up. I said I had to leave you and go find a hotel. You answered categorically:

"You're not going anywhere. You stay here." Then limping on the foot Theophiloiannakos's clubbings had broken, you headed toward the old woman dressed in black, who was shuffling about the kitchen. It was night by now and the visitors, disappointed by your abandonment, had left the house.

Four policemen were positioned on the sidewalk, but on the veranda it was cool, the air was scented with jasmine, and a light breeze stirred the strange clusters of garlic hanging from the gash in the palm tree. I pointed it out to Andreas: "What's that for?" He smiled. "To ward off the evil eye, the police, and complications. Are you really staying?" "No, you explain it to him." "You'll have to do that yourself, and it won't be easy. When he decides something, it's practically impossible to disobey him." "I'm not here to obey him." "Oh! They all say that and then they all obey him. Fourteen people ended up in jail for obeying him. However, you could leave at once, there must be even a night flight to Rome. If you like, I'll take you to the airport." "Why? Are you worried about me? Are you afraid those policemen will arrest me?" He smiled again. "No, it's not the policemen." "I don't understand." "I'm saying that what went on here wasn't an interview, it was a mating of souls. And he has to remain calm, at least for a while, he needs rest. Love isn't a rest, and when it's born from a mating of souls, it can become a tragedy." "Don't exaggerate," I said sharply. His presumption irritated me, besides the fact that he had seen more than I feared. But while I wanted to tell him to be silent, at the same time I couldn't help listening to him and in a way encouraging him to speak. "Don't exaggerate." "I'm not exaggerating. Or am I? We Greeks are obsessed by tragedy. Since we invented it, we see it everywhere." "But what kind of tragedy are you talking about?" "There is only one kind of tragedy, and it is based on three elements that never change: love, pain, death." And just as he was saying this, you burst out, with your slight limp: "All arranged! You sleep in the living room. It isn't as comfortable as a suite at the Grande Bretagne, but it's better than a cot in Boiati. And in a little while we eat." "Listen to me, Alekos—" "Do you like melitsanosalata?" "Alekos—" "And spanakopitta?" "Alekos—" "Ah, you don't even know what spanakopitta is. It's spinach pie! And melitsanosalata is an eggplant salad. Very good, you'll see. Better than Zakarakis's lentils: did I tell you the story of Zadarakis and the lentils?" You talked and talked, interrupted every sentence of mine, preventing me from replying—I'm not staying, thank you, I must leave, thank you—and any subject served your purpose: Zakarakis and the lentils, eggplant salad, spinach pie. Finally you put your arm around my shoulders possessively, leaned on the railing of the veranda, sniffed the air greedily. "This is the first time in five years and ten days that I've smelled the perfume of jasmine. It wasn't there, last night." "Yes, it was there," Andreas said. "It wasn't there, I tell you." "It wasn't there," Andreas repeated.

The supper was harmless. Even Andreas, who had been invited, seemed to think so. You appeared in high spirits, you described Boiati as a superdeluxe holiday hotel, heated swimming pool, golf course, private movie theaters, and restaurants with caviar fresh from Iran, first-class service, and you never gave me a look that was too intense, made a gesture too intimate, never did anything that could rekindle the prophetic fears discussed on the veranda. So at a certain point I concluded that the play of hands, the looks, had been a simple display of friendship, the pronouncement about love had been a political statement of great acumen. If I wanted, I could easily accept your hospitality and leave the next afternoon: little by little the house had filled again with acquaintances, people who wanted to say hello to you, embrace you, and the sight of you receiving them with the nonchalance of a leader returned from a long journey aroused my curiosity. I was interested also in observing the way you conversed with them, instructed them, put them on their guard. Yes, meeting again was beautiful but it mustn't go to the head, the amnesty was a trick, an alibi to strengthen the dictatorship with the consensus of the right wing, of the Evangelos Averoffs. Yes, to sleep in one's own bed was a comfort, but a man doesn't come out of prison to sleep in his own bed, he comes out to take up the fight again. You said the name Averoff with an almost obsessive frequency, and from what Andreas translated, it was clear you hated him almost as much as the tyrant. "What's he saying?" "He's saying that one day he'll document it." "What's he saying?" "He's saying that the Papadopouloses pass and the Averoffs remain." Just as frequently, however, and with opinions just as severe you said the name of Andreas Papandreou, the official representative of the left wing in exile. "What's he saying?" "He's saying he's leading an operetta opposition." "What's he saying?" "He's saying that characters like Papandreou replace dictatorships with other dictatorships and at best they smooth the way for some form of authoritarianism." This confirmed your libertarian personality, the ideological independence which I had recognized as my own during the dramatic hours of the interview, and confirming it could explain the mysterious transport that had upset me, could reduce it simply to an ideal brotherhood. Yes, I could stay, I thought, reassured. And I got up to help the old woman dressed in black, your mother, who was muttering obscure complaints, shuffling and patting her gray bun back into place, clearing away the remains of the supper. "I see you're calm," Andreas remarked. "I am," I answered. "So you are really staying?" "Yes, I honestly think I am." "Ah! Good night." "Good night." I said good night to him, to you, and overcome with fatigue, I shut the living room door. The door was opaque glass, and the light in the hall shone through it. But once I had stretched out on the daybed, I fell asleep immediately.

I was wakened two hours later by an echo of footsteps and a vague impression of a looming danger. I propped myself on one elbow, to listen better, but I heard nothing. The house was shrouded in silence, not even the rustling of leaves came from the garden. Yet I hadn't been mistaken, the echo of footsteps had resounded with such precision through the curtain of sleep that I recalled even its cadence: inexorable, slow, the tread of someone who bears down on his heel to spare the broken sole of the foot. One, two. One, two. I looked more carefully toward the glass door: in the hall there was one bulb, and in its weak glow I could make out no one. Odd. Perhaps the concern that you might come to me was so acute that it had pierced the barrier of my unconscious. I stretched out on the daybed once more, hoping to fall asleep again quickly. I shut my eyes and almost at the same moment the footsteps that had wakened me reechoed a second time, and beyond the glass door the outline of your body appeared. Black, motionless. I sprang to my feet, holding my breath, I stood there staring at the form for a time that seemed endless. The form hesitated, stepped back, moved away, then the footsteps resumed: inexorable, slow, in the direction from which they had come. One, two. One, two. One, two. Finally they stopped, only to come back again, with the same cadence, and the form reappeared, closer, more distinct. An arm rose, rested on the knob, withdrew quickly, as if the knob were red hot. The obsessive march started over again. One, two. One, two. One, two. And at every sound of the heel there was the anguished expectation that the door would open and we would be face to face in the darkness, to say and hear the word, the sentence, that I didn't want to hear, didn't want to listen to. There, the footsteps stopped, again. The arm rose, again. The fingers touched the knob, again. They remained there, now. And the knob turned, slowly, very slowly, creaking. But suddenly and so rapidly that everything was clear only when it was over, you let go, turned, and went off, entered your bedroom again, slamming the door. Bang! The house shook at the blow. My lungs expanded in mad relief.

I knew that relief. I had felt it in war every time a bullet passed near me, whistling, missing me.

The cruel thing in war is that usually you are hit at the very moment when you tell yourself you've made it. As long as you are alert or when you risk your life, advancing with bare head under fire, nothing happens; the minute you relax or feel safe, the projectile arrives. Maybe a small fragment, perhaps heaven-sent, the fragment that offers you the welcomed wound, the trifling wound that will allow you to go home or be transferred to the rear lines, but instead it proves mortal because it has severed an artery or has lodged in the heart. This is what happened the next day. The first bullet I was expecting: it was the moment we would meet again in the morning, and I dodged it easily when, on meeting in the corridor, we both stiffened like a pair of cats getting ready to fight: "Kalimera." "Buon giorno." As for the fusillades that broke out afterward, a pressure of your shoulder against mine, a touch of your arm, fleeting yet alarming contacts. I always emerged from them unharmed. The mortal risk wasn't there. It was in the word, the sentence you wanted to say to me which I didn't want to hear. To prevent you I sought safety among the others, the people who gradually turned up, a journalist or a photographer, and if we happened, all the same, to be left alone for a few minutes, I crawled down into the trenches, distracting you with point-blank questions: "Have you read Proudhon, have you read Bakunin, have you ever been a Marxist?" And it's no use asking why I didn't just leave. My flight was at seven that evening, I couldn't even conceive the idea of leaving you a moment earlier than necessary, and the expectation of that hour filled me with sadness: whenever a plane roared overhead, my heart twisted and I had to make an effort not to move close to you. Andreas came around one in the afternoon, then a couple of friends you had invited to lunch, you became involved with them in a discussion that I was excluded from because it took place in your language, and this relaxed the tension a bit. I began to say to myself that a man who's been in prison for years obviously feels attracted by a woman who admires him and understands him, obviously he would try to enter her room to satisfy a hunger suffered too long and too deeply: what does this have to do with love, pain, the threat of a dangerous and profound bond? I had interpreted too sensitively some episodes that were basically banal, tomorrow these twenty-four hours would obviously appear in a different light, and the good Andreas after all wasn't Cassandra. Then I got up and went down to the garden to congratulate myself on my recovered well-being. Three thirty in the afternoon. The cicadas were singing in the olive trees by the sidewalk, but a wisp of air made it easier to breathe. I leaned against the palm tree and lighted a cigarette, giving the cluster of garlic heads an amused glance. Then I raised my eyes and I saw you.

You were advancing in the sun and you were so pale that the scar on your cheekbone glowed redder than a ripe cherry. You came forward, staring hard at me, and your step had the same cadence of your march to and fro in the night. One, two. One, two. One, two. When you were in front of me, you stopped, without saying anything you grabbed me by the wrist, without saying anything you led me back to the house, without saying anything you thrust me into your little room and I barely had time to glimpse Andreas's frightened gaze before the door was closed. You pointed to a chair. "We'll talk. Sit down." You sat on the bed and folded your arms. "You're not leaving." "Not leaving?!" "No. You're not leaving." "Why shouldn't I, Alekos?" "Because I don't want it. And if I don't want it, I don't." "Listen to me, Alekos. I've finished what I came to do. There's no reason for me to stay." "Finished what?" "The interview, the assignment. I was here for an interview, an assignment, remember? And I've completed it." "You weren't here for an interview, you were here for me. You're here for me." "For you, the way I was for others I wrote about, in Bolivia, in Vietnam, in Brazil." "Liar." "Listen to me, Alekos—" I had to make an appeal to common sense, wield the weapon of reason, address myself to the man who twenty-four hours earlier had spoken to me with detachment of his sufferings, smoking his pipe casually with an old man's long puffs. "Listen to me, Alekos. I don't go around looking for affairs and—" "Neither do I." "Being on the same side of the barricade, having the same ideas and feelings isn't enough to be more than friends, comrades, and—" "I know." "I don't even speak your language and—" "That doesn't matter." "I live in another country and—" "Doesn't matter." "I couldn't, I can't change my life for—" "Doesn't matter!" "But it does matter. All these things matter, and I believe I would have said them to you last night if you had come in." You started imperceptibly, as if I had pricked you with a pin. "I saw you last night, Alekos. And I hoped you wouldn't come in because—" "Because you have no courage!" I sprang to my feet, offended. Perhaps I had no courage, I answered, but I also had no need of you because I didn't need the suffering that was in you. I wasn't superstitious, I was a modern woman, but instinctively I knew that going into this encounter with you would bring me only suffering. All right, I was afraid of you. Of you, not of coming to bed with you. And here I played my trump card: "Do you want to go to bed with me? If this is what you want, let's do it right now. Because this evening I'm going away." Slowly the grimace of incredulity became an expression of irrepressible anger. Your chest swelled. "But I love you!"

That hoarse, angry cry of a wounded, humiliated animal. That savage flaring, those arms extended to grab me and shake me and finally lock me in an iron grip. That warm breath, that greedy mouth. And those eyes, those incredible eyes in which I had seen the blaze of a burning forest. For a brief instant I was on the point of apologizing, admitting that I too loved you, even though I didn't want to. But then I met those eyes and a terror restrained me: because there was death in those eyes. However irrational and exaggerated it might seem, I tell you there was death in those eyes, the announcement of everything that was to happen in the years to come and couldn't have happened without me, if I were not the instrument and the vehicle of your fate, already written. There was the defeat born with you, the curse that was to pursue you until one night in early May and hurl you into a black hole on the Vouliagmeni Road, the ramp of a garage with a Texaco sign. And there were the agonies, the servitude you would inflict on me, reducing me to a Sancho Panza on his nag, robbing me of my identity, my life. It would be disastrous to accept your love and to love you: I knew that with certainty, in an instant. And I freed myself immediately from your embrace, from your mouth, from you, I rushed into the next room, I threw my things into my case, I called Andreas, I asked him if he could take me to the airport: there should be a flight around five, with a bit of luck I could manage to catch it, was ten minutes enough? "It's enough," Andreas answered, springing into action. Erect against the wall, hands in your pockets, an enigmatic smile beneath your moustache, you observed the scene in silence and did nothing to stop me or to calm me. But then after I had said good-bye to your mother, you exclaimed: "I'm coming too." And you led me to the automobile, where you sat beside me, composed: "Let's go." You said nothing else the whole way, nor did I open my mouth for that matter. It seemed there was nothing more to say. On reaching the airport I got out, said good-bye to Andreas, shook your hand; you shook my hand and said: "Iassou, good-bye." But when I had taken a few steps your voice rose, sharp as a command: "Agapi!" I turned. Your right hand was thrust out of the car window with the index and middle fingers raised in a V sign, and on your face there was an affectionate, trepid irony. "You'll come back! I'll win! You'll come back!"

I came back very soon. The first telegram arrived the next day and said: "I'm waiting for you." The second, two days later, said: "What are you waiting for?" The third, after four days, said: "I'm very sad because you still have no courage." Then the following week when I was in Bonn, I was given a letter in which you announced you were entering the Polyclinic in Sacratous Street. With this news there was a short poem: "Forgotten thoughts of love / revive / and restore me to life." There was also a note: "For you." From Bonn I was supposed to go to New York. I canceled my departure and looked for a direct flight to Athens. There was only the one, from Frankfurt in the afternoon, but by hiring a car to drive me to Frankfurt I could make it in time. And a few hours later I was landing in your country, drawn by the inevitable lot I would no longer be able to elude. Because it overpowered even the instinct of survival and the ambiguous snare of happiness.

Happiness is laughter that explodes at nine in the evening when my taxi stops in front of the hospital and a shadow darts from the darkness, opens the door, falls on me, and says to the driver: "Grigora! Hurry!" When I had first arrived, I found you in a little room in the Pathology Ward, surrounded by doctors and medicines, and you seemed the sickest sick man in the world: in a wisp of a voice you asked me to come back at nine. "I'm ill, very ill . . ." And now here you were, all energy, resurrected, hugging me in a taxi. "Grigora! Hurry!" "Why, what are you doing? What's got into you?" "I escaped!" "What do you mean, escaped?" "I mean that I got up, dressed, gave the orderly a bang on the head and came out here to wait for you." "A bang on the orderly's head?!" "Yes, he didn't want to let me go. He said it couldn't be done. I put him there and I said to him: just watch and see if it can be done." "Put him where?" "In my bed. He'll be there until tomorrow morning at five. At five I have to go back and untie him." "Untie him?!" "Yes, I had to tie him up. And also put adhesive over his mouth. Otherwise he would have yelled." "I don't believe you." "You're right, it's not true. It wasn't an act of force, but of intelligence. Listen, I said to him, when does your free shift begin? At nine, he said. And when does it end? At five, he said. Do you live far away? Very far away, he said. Would you like to sleep comfortably, without having to go home? Sure, he said. Well, this is my bed and these are my pajamas. I'll take your shoes. I pushed him into a chair, took his shoes off, and I was on my way. He's a fool, he won't move from the room until I get back." So I laugh and laugh, free of all hesitation, all fear, amused to discover in you an aspect I didn't know or even suspect, your loutish histrionics, your gaiety. And you laugh with me. You confess that you fooled me, you weren't sick today, you were faking, they put you into the Polyclinic for some tests, that's all, tomorrow you'll be discharged. The driver laughs too, without knowing why, he watches us in the little rearview mirror and laughs as the taxi crosses the bright city, turns into the Vouliagmeni Road, passes in front of the garage with the Texaco sign, takes us to the restaurant where three years later you will eat for the last time, shortly before going out to die. But if the gods were to announce it to us, to put us on our guard, if they were to tell us that this is your fate, our fate, already written, we wouldn't believe it and I would answer, mocking, that fate doesn't exist. "Where are we going?" "To Tsaropoulos's." "What's there?" "It's an outdoor place, by the sea, you eat fish there. Do you like fish?" "Yes." "I don't. The night before the attempt I had supper there and ate fish." "Why are we going there then?" "Because tonight I can defy even fish."

Happiness is a pride that vibrates when we enter the restaurant pierced by the inquiring and hostile gazes of those for whom you aren't a hero but an unsuccessful assassin, a subverter of order, at best a visionary who should have stayed where he was: in a well-guarded prison. From their tables come offensive coughs, frightened murmurs: "Isn't that?!" A proper young man from an embassy cries in English: "Look who's there!" You understand him and for a moment you are overcome by a kind of bewilderment, you lean on me like a cane, uncertain whether to go forward or turn back, then you stand boldly erect and lead me to a table exposed to their curiosity. The murmurs increase and each one wounds you like a stab, I can see it, and at moments you bow your head as if to repress the hurt, to bear it better: what a disappointment freedom is, what an effort! But my fingers seek yours, press them hard to repeat to you that you are not alone, and your face glows. "I know." It is beautiful to live the challenge together. It is beautiful also to notice that some smile at you, even if secretly, with the caution of people afraid of getting into trouble. Then a brave waiter advances with a bottle of wine and says to you in a loud voice: "This is on me. It's an honor, Alekos, to have you here." The sky is a deep blue enamel and thick with stars, next to us there is a tree with broad, orange blossoms, gradually we are isolated in a spell that grants us a kind of oblivion. Or heedlessness? A flower seller comes in with a basket of roses, you grab a bunch and throw them in my lap. A hunchback comes in holding a stick with lottery tickets pinned to it, you buy a long string of them and put them on my plate. Every act of yours is a naive transport of love, a clumsy prayer to be loved, and your earlier boldness has gone. You drop your fork, you drop your spoon, and suddenly you blush like a child, you hand me the present saved for my return: a folded wrinkled paper, covered with tiny writing. "Alekos! What is it?" "My favorite poem, 'Voyage,' I've dedicated it to you, look: now it has your name as its title." You translate it for me with that voice that scours the soul: "I voyage through unknown waters on a ship / like millions of other ships / that roam oceans and seas in long voyages with perfect schedules / And many more / many too / are at anchor in harbors / For years I have stocked this ship / with everything they gave me / and I took with unconfined joy / And then / I remember it as if it were today / I painted it with bright colors / and I was careful / that not a drop would spill / I wanted it beautiful for my voyage / And after waiting long really long / finally the hour came to set sail / and I set sail—" Here you broke off, you explained to me that the voyage is life, that you are the ship, a ship that has never dropped anchor, that never will, not the anchor of affection, or the anchor of desires, or the anchor of a well-earned rest. Because you will never resign yourself, will never tire of pursuing the dream. And if I were to ask you what dream, you wouldn't be able to answer me: today it's a dream you call freedom, tomorrow it could be a dream you call truth; it doesn't matter whether or not the goals are real, what matters is chasing their mirage, the light. "Time went by and I / began to chart the route / but not the way they had told me in the port / though even then my ship seemed different to me / And so my voyage / also seemed different now to me / Anxious no more about harbors and trade / the cargo now seemed useless to me / But I went on voyaging / knowing the value of the ship / knowing the wealth I was bearing . . ." And I never tired of listening to you.

Happiness is surrender that at midnight leads us to the house with the garden of orange and lemon trees where we enter on tiptoe ignoring the police who observe your every movement: two at the corners of the street and two on the sidewalk. It is a jasmine tree blooming under the window where we look out and you can pick a clump and offer it to me together with your shyness. It is a room whose squalor I no longer see, the greasy, peeling chairs, the ugly bric-a-brac, the absurd framed diplomas: because you are there. It is an unexpectedly chaste kiss on my brow, as the wind rustles among the olive boughs and brings us the chant of the sea. It is a tear that unexpectedly glides down your cheek as you murmur: "I have been so alone. I don't want to be alone anymore. Swear you will never leave me." It is your grave face approaching my grave face, your rapt eyes drowning in my rapt eyes, your uncertain arms that seek my uncertain arms, as if we were two kids at their first love encounter, or as if we knew we were preparing to carry out a rite on which all our future years would depend. It is a long, awesome silence as our lips touch without hesitation, join with decision, and our bodies entwine without fear, to lie down groping in the darkness, swept away by a river of sweetness that dazzles, as we seek forgotten, longed-for gestures and find them to enter each other with harmony, again and anew, and again and again, as if it were to last an eternity. Time belongs to you now, no firing squad is advancing at harsh commands to take you to the range and shoot you. Afterward we look at each other, exhausted, heads resting on the same pillow, and you cry: "S'agapo tora ke tha s'agapo pantote." "What does that mean?" "It means: I love you now and I will love you always. Say it." I say it in a whisper. "And what if it isn't like that?" "It will be like that." I attempt a last, futile defense: "Nothing lasts forever, Alekos. When you are old and—" "I will never be old." "Yes, you will. A famous old man with a white moustache." "I will never have a white moustache. Or even a gray one." "Will you blacken it?" "No, I'll die long before. And then you will really have to love me forever." Are you speaking in earnest or are you joking? I force myself to believe you're joking, a mocking light glints in your black irises and a happiness made up of many tomorrows spurs your body which immediately, insatiable, covers me. Nor must I think anymore of a dialogue on the veranda: "We Greeks are obsessed by tragedy. Since we invented it, we see it everywhere." "But what kind of tragedy are you talking about?" "There is only one kind of tragedy, and it is based on three elements that never change: love, pain, death."

Happiness is opening my eyes beneath your voice that cries almost with amazement: "You're beautiful!" It is realizing that it's almost five and you have to hurry to give back the shoes to the confined orderly. It is going out into the cool air that heralds the morning, still ignoring the policemen who follow us to the taxi rank, it is embracing for the whole ride, saying good-bye but knowing we will soon see each other again. It is going back to the house with the orange and lemon trees without regretting the responsibility that from now on will weigh upon me like a heavy stone. It is waking to come to the hospital and hear you tell me triumphantly that nobody noticed your escape in the night. And the doctor says you can be discharged without serious complications, nothing irreparable has emerged from the tests and the X rays. Naturally torture and imprisonment have affected your health but your heart is strong and your lungs are in excellent condition, little by little you'll regain your strength, it's all a matter of becoming accustomed to life again.

Finally, happiness is knowing that last night, just as we were loving each other, in the house next door a child was born and they've given him the name Cristos: can anyone imagine a more beautiful omen than the birth of a child next door as we were making love? We must celebrate the arrival of Cristos, and the day is full of sunlight, of blue sky. Let's go to the sea! For five years you haven't seen the sea, you've dreamed of seeing the sea again. Since the day you left Boiati, when you rediscovered space, you have left the house only to go to the hospital and to take me to Tsaropoulos's: let's go to the sea! And we are on the beach of Glyphada. You advance hesitantly, your head down as if you didn't dare raise your eyes, and when you bring yourself to raise them, you start, you blink, stunned, an expression I don't understand appears on your face. Joy or fear? Suddenly you spring forward and run toward the water. You run with the broad stride of an agile, carefree colt, the very image of youth, and as you run you shout: "I zoi! I zoi! I zoi! Life! Life! Life!" At the sea's edge you leap and turn, exuberantly you call me, hold out your arms to me, I run too and we roll laughing on the hot sand. "I zoi! I zoi! I zoi! Life! Life! Life!" Today no one is chasing you over the rocks, today the sea is not evil as it was one August morning you don't want to remember. Wait for me, I'm coming, wait for me! Soft and smooth, the water curls slightly on the beach in little rolls of white foam. Who is afraid of the fish? "Nobody!" Do they announce defeats perhaps, disasters? "Nonsense!" Let's dive in then. We undress quickly, impatiently. We dive together, we swim side by side in the warm, still water, we stop every now and then to exchange a kiss fresh with salt. S'agapo tora ke tha s'agapo pantote. Afterward it is exquisite to stretch out in the sun, hand in hand, exhausted, to shudder with pleasure and cold, to sense a desire that shakes your white body jealous of my tan, to think that at home we will fulfill it. Does there really exist a tyrant named Papadopoulos! Who knows any Ioannidis? And Theophiloiannakos, Hazizikis, and Zakarakis? Never saw them. For a week we will not even say those names. Happiness is an oblivion that lasts a week.

That unreal week to which my memory will always return with incredulous amazement: isolated from everyone, sufficient to ourselves, we vegetated in an unknowing bliss. There were so many little things to be done to reaccustom you to life. For example, to teach you how to cross a street again without the terror of being run over by the cars, to walk on sidewalks avoiding people and not let yourself be frightened by shoves, by the chaos of the city. In the Boiati tomb you had forgotten this too, and after the outing to the sea a kind of reaction had taken place inside you: in the daytime you no longer wanted to leave the house. Or else you left it only to shut yourself up in an automobile, where you felt protected, and when you got out of the automobile, everything frightened you. To make you cross a street, I had to encourage you with a thousand reassurances: "Come now, come, there is the green light!" And to make you walk along a sidewalk, often you had to be encouraged. In fact you wouldn't walk straight, you went in a diagonal until you bumped into a wall. And so in the mornings I took you downtown in the most crowded streets, and, clinging to my arm like a blind man clinging to the leash of his seeing-eye dog, you gradually found again your lost habits. "You see? He was coming straight at me, but I didn't bump into him." "You see? You didn't notice there was a red light, but I did." The afternoons we spent in the house, where the sultriness and the silence barely broken by the shrilling of the cicadas enervated us in the silence of endless embraces. We spoke very little, we had no need for words. As evening fell, however, you would wake up with the instinct of a bat who sniffs the darkness and you would become talkative, and off we would go to supper somewhere. At times we went all the way to Piraeus, at times we stayed in Glyphada where there were the taverns of your adolescence and where an old guitar player with watery blue eyes would sing to us in a stentorian voice "A Bed for Two." You adored that song because it told about a pair of lovers who sleep in a narrow little bed. Our bed was narrow and little, it was the one you had had as a boy, and if we didn't sleep in each other's arms, we would fall on the floor. Everything ended abruptly, without any warning sign, the day we went to Aegina.

2

YOU HADN'T SAID WE WOULD BE GOING TO AEGINA, YOU had simply said an island. Nor had I asked you what island: I let myself be guided by happiness like a leaf blown by the wind. The ship had barely left the harbor, we were on the deck, spellbound, I was watching the prow cleave the water in fans of spray when a dolphin surfaced. I gripped you, crying: "Dolphins! You see them? Dolphins!" A toneless voice answered me: "I couldn't see anything, they put me down on the floorboards." "On the floorboards? I don't understand,

Alekos. What are you talking about?" "I'm talking about the day they took me to Aegina, to shoot me." That said, you shut yourself up in a silence that admitted no approach, no need of company; you opened your mouth again only on landing when you pushed me into a taxi and gave the driver an address I couldn't understand. The taxi drove off, in silence we left the town, in silence we reached a deserted road that climbed up, bordered by cactus, then by olives, then pistachio trees, then again cactus. Here and there a little villa, a house coated with whitewash, a white shrine with a black icon. "Where are we going, Alekos?" "Over there." "There, where?" "There." It was impossible to penetrate the mysterious barrier behind which you had isolated yourself. Face tense, brow furrowed, pupils alert, you stared at the landscape as if every meter, every curve, every stone concealed a trap or as if there were a secret behind those cacti, those olives, those pistachio trees that either were lost in fields of green or plunged down in grim gorges or were mingled with the scrub of the undergrowth. Were you searching for someone, were you going to a dangerous rendezvous? No, instinctively I decided not. Did you want to show me the prison where you had waited the three days and the three nights? Yes, this was possible. But the prison was fairly close to the port, and the taxi was going in the opposite direction. "Alekos—" "Shut up!" "Listen to me—" "Shut up!" "Why don't—?" "Shut up!" We had been traveling like that for half an hour when the driver turned into a track, smothered by weeds and so narrow that we could just get through. It climbed for another couple of kilometers, jolting over the rocks and holes, then emerged into a steppelike heath, and finally stopped at a rail which along with rolls of barbed wire barred the path. Beyond the barbed wire, a sign read MILITARY ZONE. NO ENTRANCE. We got out and with rediscovered sweetness you took me by the hand. "We're there. Come."

Puzzled, looking around blankly, I followed you. We were on a peak of the island, toward the side facing the southwest coast of Attica, and below us the mountain dropped sharply into the bay; to the right it broadened into a barren promontory: not a house, not a hut, or a tree. Wherever the eyes lighted they saw only rocky cliffs or sea, and an awesome solitude like something out of Genesis stagnated with a sense of desolation, an almost anguished stillness. And yet it was one of the most beautiful places I had ever seen. Especially the promontory that sloped down and spread out in the water, a harmonious tongue of land, and little inlets veined with phosphorescence, tiny beaches, snowy and uncontaminated, brought on a kind of yearning. Almost a need to sink down and thank the Lord for being alive. Was this why you had brought me up here? Was this why you had shut yourself up in that strange silence? To surprise me, to enjoy my wonder? I turned to tell you but you were paying no attention to me. Pale, your arm outstretched toward the tongue of land extending into the water, you were pointing something out to me, something I couldn't identify: "Down there, there." "Where down there, Alekos? And what is it?" "The enclosure." "What enclosure?" "That gray rectangular space. Can't you see it?" No, I really couldn't see it. "Down there, farther down. The place begins a few steps from the shore and ends at a low wall." Ah, yes, now I could see it: a rectangle of cement, bounded by a wall. But what was it, a bowls court? A heliport? An army heliport, perhaps. That explained the signs forbidding access. "I see it," I said. "It's a helicopter pad." And you said: "No, it's the target range, the place used for killing those sentenced to death. That's where they were to shoot me. With my back to that wall." Pause. "For five years I've been wondering what it was like, where it was. I knew only that from up here you could see it." Pause. "Is it sad, I always wondered, is it ugly? Sad! Ugly! Hell. It's perfect, a really perfect place to die: with the Saronic Gulf stretching out in front, the blue above and below, Athens—Look, there to the far right is Cape Sounion, the ruins of the temple. Just before it is Lagonissi, Papadopoulos's villa. Farther on there is the culvert where I set the mines, and then Vouliagmeni, then Glyphada. My house at Glyphada. There's Piraeus at the end on the left, and above Piraeus you can see the Acropolis. Think! If they had shot me, I would have died looking at the Acropolis and my house and the place where I tried to kill the tyrant. It would have been a beautiful death, a really beautiful death. I missed out on a really beautiful death."

It was as if death with a view of the Acropolis and of your house and the place of the assassination attempt were a splendid woman you had always desired, who had maliciously eluded you the moment before you could possess her. Your pallor was gone, your cheeks were flushed, and so were your lips and ears: your eyes glistened with desire. Or regret? Then I couldn't get you away from there. Let's go away, I kept repeating, please let's go, and you remained motionless, staring at the rectangle of the beautiful death you had lost. It was almost dark when the taxi set off again along the melancholy succession of cactus, olive, pistachio trees; dark when we reached the prison of the three days and the three nights, the second stop of your pilgrimage. But you no longer recognized the building, you couldn't even find the door where you had entered; in vain you moved around the outer walls, insisted, racked your memory. "Maybe they brought me in at the back. Yes, there must be a half-hidden path in the back that leads to an iron gate, a kind of shutter, and beyond it an enclosure that on the left becomes a very narrow passage. So narrow that only one person can go through at a time. Beyond the passage there is a little yard with the blockhouse for those condemned to death. Very old, very dirty, one story. The vestibule is only a few steps wide because immediately after it you enter the corridor with the cells at left and right. Mine was the last one on the right. It was four meters long and three meters wide, the walls were painted a pale blue, faded, the floor was of tiles, no lights because the light came from the lamps in the yard." Then with your cheeks flushed again, your eyes glistening with desire, again you said: "How I would like to see it once more! To go inside once more, at least for a few minutes. I would really like that! Can you believe it?" "Let's go away, Alekos, please let's go." "Just a little longer." "Let's go home, please. Let's go home." "Just a little longer." "I'm tired, it's late, it's cold." "Just a little longer." You had sat down on the ground, your back against a hedge, and you wouldn't get up. You didn't even say what was holding you there. But when we were finally aboard the last ship you told me that it was nostalgia that had held you there. The nostalgia for death. "Because a man who has been sentenced to death, who has lived three days and three nights waiting for death, will never be the same again. He will always carry death with him, like a second skin, like a frustrated desire. He will continue always to pursue it, dream of it, perhaps using the excuse of noble causes, duties. And he will never find peace until he has caught up with it."

You gave me a demonstration of this even before we got home. A taxi was taking us to Glyphada when in Thessaloniki Street the traffic was halted to allow a procession to pass, coming from the opposite direction. Four motorcyclists arrived, roaring, and a little police truck, then two more motorcyclists and another truck, and finally a black automobile appeared. Papadopoulos's limousine. I barely had time to glimpse a round, grayish face, a little dark moustache, then your mouth twisted in a fierce cry and your hands reached for the door: "Clown! Son of a bitch!" "No, Alekos, no!" "Let go of me, I want to get out, let me go!" There was a terrible strength in your arms, I couldn't hold you back, prevent you from grasping the handle. The limousine was coming closer and closer, the round and grayish face became more and more distinct, now I could also see the shrewd little eyes, the enigmatic smile that curled the spiteful little mouth. Another moment and you would have hurled yourself out, to throw yourself against him and get yourself killed. "Help me!" I shouted to the driver. He understood, turned around, and blocked you, throwing you backward. "Are you crazy, my friend?" I felt a great weight on me and I knew that you had fainted, that the happiness was over. Because the loss of happiness often helps to clarify thoughts, to wake from a sleep that has befuddled the intelligence and prevented judgment, I now understood that loving you would be an agonizing job.

"Did anyone notice?" Andreas asked. I shrugged. "I don't think so. It happened so fast, all eyes were on the convoy." "What about the driver?" "The driver was fine. I gave him the address and he brought us home. He shook his head, that was all." He also shook his. "And this is only the beginning, you realize?" I nodded. "I realize." Then I asked him why he had come: to predict misfortunes? He shook his head again. "No. Because he called me. There's a singer, in Athens. He's fairly famous and disliked by the junta. He has a club in Plaka and he's invited the two of you various times these past few days. This morning Alekos called me and told me to go and say that you'll both be there this evening. But on one condition: that they play songs forbidden by the junta, the songs of Theodorakis." "And what will happen?" "The police will intervene, I suppose. And he will do everything possible to get himself arrested, to prove nothing has changed, the dictatorship continues. Yes, I'm afraid this is exactly his plan. Unless—" "Unless what?" "I don't know, maybe he's planning something more complicated. It would have to be—" But just as he was saying this, you burst in on us: "Plots, plots! What are you two plotting? Come on, hurry up and get ready. Let's go have some fun, listen to music. I want you to be elegant, this evening, in a red dress!"

We went. And now, huddled in your arms, I listened to your heavy breathing in sleep, as I tried to find a meaning in what had happened. But it was like untying one knot only to create another knot and make the tangle worse than ever. When you entered, the singer began an anthem by Theodorakis, and from that moment the orchestra played banned music; we were on an open terrace so surely the racket could be heard in the whole neighborhood. But the police didn't intervene. At a certain point you even insisted that everybody sing with you the march based on your poem "Forward the Dead," and dozens of voices were raised, bold, loud, to shake the violet night: "Forward the dead / flag bearers without end in the struggle / and after us / eager to raise the standards / a whole people / living and dead together . . ." But even then the police didn't react. Only toward one in the morning two gendarmes looked in to ask for less noise, some people in the building were complaining, so sorry and thanks. No arrests, no mention of the law. Why? When your challenge failed, you went down into the street to yell fierce insults against Papadopoulos, against Ioannidis, even against the passersby who tried to calm you, and not content with this, you accompanied every insult with the arrogant cry: "Ime Panagoulis! I am Panagoulis!" Again nothing happened, as if every policeman had received orders to accept whatever you said or did with complete indifference. Why? As soon as you were back in the house, you grabbed the telephone and called the ESA switchboard: "Ime Panagoulis! I am Panagoulis! Thelo Ioannidis! I want Ioannidis!" And then more hair-raising insults, but the agent on duty maintained his composure: he said Brigadier General Ioannidis was not in his office at night, would you care to leave a message? Yes, you growled, here's the message, now write the message down carefully, don't miss a word: "Ioannidis, faggot, cocksucker, it's true that Papadopoulos didn't have the balls to shoot me but you don't even have the balls to arrest me. And you're making a mistake, Ioannidis, a mistake, because I'll make you piss blood, Ioannidis." Then you hung up the receiver, saying calmly: "Let's see if they come to arrest me." And, wonder of wonders, nobody came. Soon it would be ten in the morning and still nobody came.

Why not? I couldn't understand. For that matter I couldn't understand why, instead of using your newly found freedom in a serious effective way, you squandered it in these histrionic actions, superficial and rhetorical challenges, like a dinosaur who advances in the primeval forests trampling on trees like blades of grass. What sense did it have, what was the use of it? Was it really to seek the death that had been denied you on Aegina? I freed myself from your arms: "Alekos—" You woke with a great smile. "They didn't come to arrest me, eh?" "No, they haven't come." "I knew it!" "You knew it?" "Of course, I knew it. Ioannidis is no fool. Who takes seriously a lunatic who makes scenes or telephones the head of the ESA to insult him?" "Don't tell me you did it on purpose?" "Yes, I do tell you. And just wait and see, today we'll have a calm day, you'll see, we'll be able to go comfortably to Cape Sounion." "What is there on Cape Sounion?" "A very beautiful temple. The temple of Poseidon."

It was a glorious afternoon and the ruins of the temple rose white in the cornflower sky, the sea glistened like mother-of-pearl, the foreign tourists let out little ecstatic cries: "How marvelous! Wunderbar! Superbe!" I thought the same as I walked beside you; every now and then I bent over to pick up a pebble I would have liked to keep as a souvenir, but, shocked, you took it from my hand. "You can't do that! It's stealing! Shame on you!" "What do you mean, stealing? What do you mean, shame on me? It's only a stone!" "If everybody took a stone, what would be left?" "The columns, the slabs of marble—" "And then you would steal the columns, and the slabs of marble! You would even steal the cliff. What a beautiful cliff! There is where Aegeus threw himself into the sea. The legend goes that Aegeus waited here for the return of his son Theseus, who had gone off to slay the Minotaur. Aegeus had told Theseus to hoist a white sail on entering the harbor if he returned victorious, but Theseus was drunk: excited by his triumph, he drank too much, forgot to hoist the white sail and—" Something was slipped into my shoulder bag, making it very heavy. "Alekos, what did you put in there?" "Stop, don't look, don't touch it. Two fragments of the stairs." "Two fragments of the stairs?! You didn't want me to steal a pebble and you took two fragments of the stairs?!" Smug laugh: "Ah, what wouldn't I do for you? A thief! You've made me a thief!" "When did you take them?" You hadn't moved from my side, you hadn't bent over to pick up anything: when could you have taken them? "Don't be such a bore. I took them. What do you care when? And don't touch that bag, I told you. You want to send me back to Boiati for two little pieces of marble? Let's move, come on. Look innocent. Like this. We're lovers admiring the landscape. Like this." Your left arm slipped through my right arm, the bag was between us, and you pushed me toward the edge of the promontory, away from the crowd, and you were trembling, excited by the theft. Then, at the point where the cliff descends in a kind of terrace open over the bay, you stopped. "Let's sit here, with our backs to the temple. No, you sit sideways, and make sure nobody has seen us." I checked. Disciplined, serried, the tourists were intent on the beauties of the Doric propylaea and nobody was bothering about us. There was only a young man in a checked shirt off to one side, he appeared to be reading the pillar on which Byron carved his name, but actually he was glancing at us. "Maybe one boy, over there. He must have noticed, he's studying us. Now he's moving away, though. He's leaving. You think he's going to report us?" "Absolutely not." "Good. Let's see what you stole." I pulled on the zipper of the bag, with joyous eagerness, and immediately my smile died. There were no marble fragments inside, but instead two tin cans, an apple green color. "Alekos, what's this stuff?!" "Tobacco. It's written on the tins: Golden Virginia hand-rolled tobacco." "Tobacco? Who gave it to you?" "A friend." "A friend in a checked shirt?" "Yes." "But when?!"

"When I was telling you the story of Aegeus and Theseus. Fast work, eh?" "And did we have to come to Sounion for this?" "Obviously we did. A good conspirator always loves archeology." "Alekos, what's in those tins?" "I told you: tobacco. Golden Virginia hand-rolled tobacco." I weighed them in my hand. Against the apple green, three other words stood out: "Fifty grams net." Fifty grams! Each weighed at least two hundred grams, maybe three hundred. "Alekos—" I lifted a lid, opened the aluminum foil, and immediately all doubts vanished. I knew well that rough yellow stone. I could illustrate for you all its characteristics and properties. What you had put in my bag as a toy or as a gift was TNT. Two nice cakes of TNT.

Now the sun was burning in pink and purple flames as it was beginning to set, and the shrill little cries of the tourists were redoubled. Some gulls were also darting among the pink and purple flames and one was diving headlong into the waters of the bay, like the gull in the dream. I looked away. "What are you going to do with it, Alekos?" You answered me with a question: "Tell me, what is love?" "Maybe it's carrying two sticks of TNT in your bag." "Good. Carrying them or entrusting them. I entrusted them to you deliberately, to show you that love is friendship, complicity. Love is a companion with whom you share a bed because you share a dream, a commitment. I don't want a woman to be happy with. The world is full of women you can be happy with, if happiness is what you're looking for. In fact I've had so many women that if you look at it one way, those five years of prison were a rest. But I've never had a companion. And I want a companion. A companion who will be my comrade, friend, accomplice, brother. I'm a man in battle. I always will be. I would be anywhere, no matter what. Even in paradise. I can't conceive of a different way to live and to die. How many people are there on this planet? Three and a half billion? Well, if three billion and four hundred ninety-nine million nine hundred ninety-nine thousand

and nine hundred ninety-nine people chose not to fight, which would be all of mankind minus one, I would fight just the same. The TNT has nothing to do with it. The TNT is a moment in the existence of a man in battle. For that matter I don't like TNT. I don't like violence, any form of violence: I would never be capable of blowing up a bus full of children the way some do in the name of their country or for some other screwed-up ideology. I don't believe in war. I don't believe in bloody revolutions. I'm convinced that they serve only the change of masters. I don't like shooting, explosions: I told you that I prefer the Cavours to the Garibaldis. But when freedom is involved, and the only thing that counts is freedom, when—" "What do you mean to do with it, Alekos?" "What? Listen to me: five hundred grams of TNT is nothing. But you can do lots of things with five hundred grams of TNT. All you need is a detonator, a fuse, a bit of imagination. And a companion who helps. I need you. I can use you." "To go on an excursion and collect tins of Golden Virginia without attracting attention?" "No, for much more than that. To not be alone. If you help me, if you don't leave me alone, I'll tell you what I want to do with it." That voice. Those eyes. There was a demon in that voice, in those eyes: a cold, lucid passion, beyond restraint, the passion of an obsessed man who in the name of his faith can commit any absurdity, can ruin his own life and the lives of others, sacrifice his own feelings and the feelings of others, his own intelligence and the intelligence of others. But your words contained the most extraordinary declaration of love. They were worth a thousand embraces in a bed, a thousand enchanted nights, a thousand jasmine plants, a thousand "s'agapo tora ke tha s'agapo pantote." And the dinosaur I had seen yelling the night before, advancing through the primeval forest trampling on trees like blades of grass was no longer a dinosaur: he was a man. A man alone, moreover. So alone that denying oneself to him would have been base. "A companion who will be comrade, friend, accomplice, brother. Will you help me?" "Of course," I answered. "Good. Now picture the Acropolis—"

The Acropolis plan was a glorious folly. It consisted of occupying the archeological zone at the time when it is closed to the public, then raising the red flag on the Parthenon, not because you liked the cliché of the red flag but because the red irritated the junta and stood out well against the white of the marble, and then finally holding the Parthenon hostage under the threat of blowing it up. "Alekos, two cakes of TNT won't be enough to blow up even a column!" "Of course. But they don't know we have only two. And as soon as I've set one off, as a demonstration—" "They won't believe you." "They'll believe me. Because they think I'm capable of anything, even of destroying the Parthenon." "Would you really destroy it?" "Not on your life." At first you thought of also capturing a certain number of tourists, Americans if possible, but then you decided that they would be too much bother: they would try to escape, they would need food, water, maybe medicines. They would have been a pain in the ass. The Parthenon, on the contrary, doesn't drink, doesn't eat, doesn't escape, and doesn't need medicines. And what hostage could be more precious than the Parthenon? Anyone who loved beauty and culture, you said, was still cursing that Koenigsmarck who had cannonaded it in 1687 to root out the Turks, when the Turks had installed a powder magazine there. To lose what was left of the Parthenon would have been like losing the very symbol of civilization: the whole world would rise up in defense of its forty-six columns, all the embassies would intercede with the junta, begging them to accept your demands. "What demands?" "In a dictatorship there's never a shortage of demands and I have one that's worth the Erechtheum and the Caryatids." That the enterprise might fail was an eventuality you dismissed a priori. The Acropolis, you repeated, cannot be captured: it stands on a promontory with sheer cliffs around and there is only one entrance, by the Propylaea. A dozen well-armed guerrillas would have been more than enough to keep the army and the police at bay. The only problem was to find them. "Twelve guerrillas, Alekos? A couple of helicopters and a few sharpshooters could eliminate them in five minutes. To say nothing of tear gas—" "No, not if at the first shot or the first cylinder of gas I blow up a little piece of the Parthenon. It's a question of psychology." "You said that you wouldn't harm the Parthenon for your life." "And who says it would really be a little piece of the Parthenon? How do they know whether the stones flying around are from the Parthenon or not?" "All right, let's assume that works. How long do you think you could hold out? A day? A night?" "With a few provisions, even three days and three nights. Can you imagine, the red flag flying three days and three nights from the Parthenon? In all that white it'll stand out like a poppy, and they'll see it from every part of the city. Television cameramen, reporters, photographers will come from every country. The junta will be made a laughingstock, and he will be forced to capitulate." "He, who?" "Why, Ioannidis. It's Ioannidis I want. Papadopoulos counts less all the time, and sooner or later Ioannidis will eliminate him." "You want him where, for what?" "To come to terms, right? On the Acropolis, right? He'll have to climb up there and—" "Is this the idea that would be worth the Caryatids?" "Yes." "Listen to me, Alekos: Ioannidis would never come." "You listen to me: I know Ioannidis, and I tell you he'll come. Because he has courage. And because he hates me."

You evinced no doubt on this point either. Your certainty that the plan would succeed was so unshakable that any attempt to be rational about the thing fell on deaf ears. Yes, Ioannidis would climb up to the Acropolis and you would receive him inside the Parthenon. With a charge of TNT on you. You would say to him: "Congratulations, Ioannidis. You've never disappointed me, Ioannidis. Five years ago you were the one who declared that once in a hundred thousand times you come across someone who won't talk. Today I'm the one to say that only once in a hundred thousand times do you come across a general who will accept such an invitation. However, that day I was wearing handcuffs, Ioannidis. And today you should wear them. Or rather, we'll wear them together." Immediately afterward you would handcuff his right wrist to your left wrist, and say: "You see this explosive I have on me, Ioannidis? It's attached to a fast-burning fuse. If you make a move, we blow up together." "I don't believe it, Alekos. You wouldn't do it." "I'd do it, I'd do it. If needs be, I'll do it. Wait and see." "And then?" "Then I make the demands and we go to Algeria." "Algeria?!" "Yes." "Straight from the Acropolis?!" "Yes." "With Ioannidis!?" "Obviously. We'll take him along as hostage, still handcuffed to my left wrist. We'll insist on a plane all for ourselves and—" "And what if Ioannidis were ready to die, to prevent you?" "He would be, but his supporters wouldn't. He's the strong man of the regime and he has a large part of the army with him, Attica is his. Anyone who wants to eliminate Papadopoulos would never allow him to die and so would grant what I ask. For that matter, I'll still have the explosive ready to set off. If necessary, I'll die with him like that German general who wanted to be blown up with Hitler." "You're crazy." "Perhaps. But it's the crazies who make history, it isn't logic that makes history. If we were always to reflect on what's sensible and what isn't, what's possible and what isn't, the earth would stop going round. And life would lose its purpose."

The role you were assigning to me in the course of this folly wasn't very clear. At times I seemed simply moral support, at times I was to play a part of great strategic importance. "If I put three men on the north side, three on the south side, two on the east side, four between the gate and the Propylaea, I'm left exposed at the Parthenon and I don't have anyone to keep an eye on my rear. Can you use a submachine gun?" The thought that I might have objections about anything, for instance, about the use of the machine gun, never really crossed your mind. You weren't even interested in finding out if I agreed on the whole business: that afternoon at Cape Sounion had sealed a pact that precluded any desertion on my part. The only point that worried you, you said while illustrating the plan, was finding those twelve guerrillas. With no party behind you, no packaged ideology, it wouldn't be easy for you to get them together. You would have to hunt for them, groping in the dark, and aware of this, you shut yourself up in the house to make lists of names, study them, reject them: "No, not him, I don't know him well enough. No, not him, he'd tell. No, not him, he'd be afraid." And heaven help anyone who tried to talk to you about something else, to distract you. "It doesn't concern me, it doesn't interest me!" Only when the news came that there had been a coup d'etat in Chile and they had killed Allende did you come out of your shell: the Acropolis seemed to disappear from your thoughts. But it soon reappeared, with the malignant strength of a cork that the more one pushes it underwater, the more it bobs to the surface, and even the death of Allende became nourishment for your glorious folly. "Beside the red flag we'll fly the flag of Chile. Freedom has no fatherland." You had composed a list of candidates and decided to see them personally and scrutinize them one by one, not revealing the aim of the meeting. You received them with an innocent expression, and flinging out your arms, slapping them affectionately on the back, you would lead them into the living room where a cassette player was playing Resistance songs very loud. It was your method of understanding at once the sort of man you were dealing with. If the person became nervous or said that playing certain songs was dangerous, you rejected him immediately; if on the other hand he became impassioned or remained calm, you took him into consideration. Character, aptitude for risk, degree of intelligence, will to fight: with the coldness of an entomologist observing an ant or a tailor examining a fabric, you studied him, you tested him, you analyzed him. But almost always without success. And in the end, when you picked the five who you thought would form the nucleus of the team, three immediately confessed that they lacked the courage. What happened with the other two was worse.

The first asked for a few hours to think it over, then he came back with a page full of calculations and explained to you why the bluff wouldn't work: to make them believe the temple was mined was an enterprise not so much absurd as impossible. The Parthenon, he said, is less fragile than it seems: any engineer or architect knows that its blocks of marble cannot easily be knocked down. To blow it up, therefore, there are two possible methods. And both are based on the collapse of the columns, column by column. One of the two methods consists of setting a charge of dynamite at the base of each column, inside holes about fifteen centimeters deep and about the same width. Fifteen centimeters is the maximum possible and the minimum necessary because, mined from within, each column requires ten kilograms of dynamite, that is to say, twenty sticks: a stick weighs half a kilo. However, one hole will not hold more than ten sticks, so you need two holes spaced well apart. Since the Parthenon has forty-six columns, a total of ninety-two holes is required. To make a hole in marble with an electric drill takes an hour. Ninety-two hours of work divided among twelve guerrillas who put down their guns and turn into workmen, drilling three or four columns each, amounts to almost eight hours of uninterrupted activity. Let's say from ten in the evening until dawn. For such a job you would need at least twelve electric drills and a very powerful generator, but, worse than that, the noise would be something incredible: a nonstop racket that would waken the city from Piraeus to Kifissia. Naturally the work could be reduced to an hour, but then you would need ninety-two men and—

You interrupted him, angrily: "I didn't ask you for an

essay on demolition and I've never had any intention of turning the Parthenon into a colander or a piece of Swiss cheese. So all this talk is pointless." But he answered: "No, it's reasonable. The same reasoning an expert would give Ioannidis if Ioannidis were to ask what chance there was that you really had mined the Parthenon. The answer would be: no chance at all unless he has half a ton of dynamite. Ten kilos of dynamite inside each column, multiplied by the forty-six columns, makes in fact almost half a ton of dynamite. Does that seem too much to you? The other method doesn't require electric drills or powerful generators, because it is based on charges set outside the columns: it needs ten tons of dynamite. That's two hundred kilos of dynamite per column. And two hundred kilos comes to four hundred sticks. To simplify the operation, the sticks can be put in a sack: then you attach the sack to the column with strong adhesive tape, like sealing a bundle. One sack per column makes forty-six sacks, so finally, if you manage to convince the junta and the world that you've carried ten tons of dynamite or at least half a ton up to the Acropolis, you're all set." You interrupted him again, but this time with unexpected calm: obviously the business of the sacks had struck your fancy. "There's no need for that dynamite, but you've given me an idea. We only have to carry up forty-six empty sacks, two or three hundred meters of very strong adhesive tape, and a bundle of wire. The Acropolis is full of stones and nobody will know what we've put in the sacks." The young man looked at you, dismayed. Then he got up and left.

The second didn't argue the practicality of the empty sacks scheme. Yes, he said, in a conciliatory voice, he knew your imagination: it vied with your courage and you had demonstrated it clearly during the five years in Boiati. So he wasn't at all in agreement with anyone who underestimated the chances of your bluff's success. Knowing you, neither the police nor Ioannidis would ask themselves whether or not the sacks really contained explosive. The only thing he questioned was whether you would emerge alive from such an exploit, and in any case, whether you survived or were killed, what was the final purpose? "I told you: to focus the world's attention on Greece, mobilize the national and foreign press, make the junta look ridiculous." He nodded, cleared his throat, and as if seeking my approval, now translating the most important sentences into English, so I would understand, he launched into a kind of sermon. Nobody, he said, had forgotten that during World War II a hero named Glazos had climbed the Acropolis and had torn the German flag from the flagpole near the entrance. A spectacular gesture, a feat of bravado that was now part of legend and children studied in their schoolbooks. But what had that gesture achieved besides amazing the world and mocking the invader? Had it perhaps inspired the people to rise up, had it affected the course of events? Spectacular gestures, private heroisms, never affect reality: they are displays of individual and superficial pride, romantic deeds but without results precisely because they remain exceptional. Unfortunately the Greeks were masters at this, there was an essay by Bertrand Russell on the subject. Well then: Russell maintained that the citizens of the Greek polis had been animated by a primitive patriotism, imprudent, not wise. The power of their passions did lead to personal successes but such successes did not help the whole polis, and in the final analysis they were signs of political incapacity. For that matter you didn't need Russell's help to understand that the great example is no good in mobilizing the masses, instead it discourages them because, feeling themselves excluded and intimidated by the valor of one man or a few men, they become blocked by an inferiority complex. Conclusion: the hero's sacrifice is an act of egoism. "Egoism?" Your question exploded, as sharp as a slap. "Yes, an act of egoism. Or should I say narcissism? An error, to be sure." "Narcissism? Error?" And this time the question sounded like a whiplash. "Yes, Alekos, error. You are suggesting again the same error of five years ago:

I've already explained that you don't wipe out dictatorships by playing the lonely hero or by individually eliminating a tyrant. They are wiped out by educating the masses to collective revolt, to organized struggle. Otherwise, when one tyrant is dead, another comes along, and everything goes on as it had before." I saw your teeth bite hard on the pipe. "So I was no use for anything, I'm no use for anything." "I'm not saying that, Alekos, I'm discussing the ideological basis, I'm examining things from an ideological point of view, rationally. It's necessary to admit that there is quite a lot of vanity in the hero!" "Vanity!?" There was a leap, yours, then a kind of death rattle, his: you had grabbed him by the necktie and were twisting it around his neck. "Listen to me, preacher! Anyone without balls takes refuge under the umbrella of ideological reasons! Anyone without faith hides always behind the screen of being rational! Where were you, preacher, what were you doing when I was on the torture cot and was waiting for the firing squad? Writing books, to educate the people? Organizing the masses of the year two thousand three hundred and thirty-three? Get out of here. Ooooout!" Then you slumped down, in desolate tears. Sticks of dynamite, electric drills, division, multiplication, forty-six times two equals ninety-two, ninety-two divided by twelve equals seven and eight left over, Bertrand Russell, egoism, narcissism, the masses: was there then nobody in this city, nobody, prepared to lend you a hand and believe in you?

I hoped this would be a beneficial crisis. But instead it did nothing but feed the bewilderment I had begun to feel that evening when you tried to throw yourself under Papadopoulos's automobile: what trap had I fallen into, what labyrinth had I entered?

Like a wayfarer lost in a foreign and hostile country whose roads are unfamiliar, where he has to stop at every crossing, puzzled, hoping in vain to glimpse someone or something to tell him how to go forward or turn back, that's how you appeared to me after the refusal of the five candidates. The last two, in fact, had given me proof that also in your world, among those who spoke your language, you were considered a creature impossible to comprehend, indeed an eccentric plant born to create disorder in the woods, a beautiful mushroom nobody picks for fear of being poisoned. And this substantiated my puzzlement, it confirmed the fears that had tormented me since the trip to Aegina: what did you have to do with Huyn Thi An, Nguyen Van Sam, Chato, Julio, Marighela, and Padre Tito de Alencar Lima? Were you really what I had believed you were, had I really been right to come back, to agree to be your companion, or had that Cassandra, Andreas, been right and was there only suffering ahead of me, tragedy? Everything about you represented a challenge to reason, a revolt against common sense, a slap in the face of logic: the blind, deaf, exaggerated ardor with which you hurled yourself into an adventure; the exaggeration and rhetoric with which that ardor was expressed; the caprice with which you bestowed it or imposed it on your fellowman ignoring his arguments or making fun of them; the lust to wear yourself out in constant danger, incessant strain, continual struggle. Not the struggle to gain a specific goal, but struggle for its own sake, as if the goal didn't matter or were only an excuse, a mirage that is called freedom, a mirage of windmills, and therefore is pursued in vain, merely to live. Because to live means moving, and stopping is tantamount to dying. Loving you, or rather accepting you, really meant putting on the costume of Sancho Panza, who follows Don Quixote and sings his poetic, mad falsehoods, living the impossible dream, fighting the invincible enemy, bearing the intolerable pain, correcting the incorrigible error, reaching the unattainable stars. And all the time wondering whether deep in his heart he doesn't know that they are only poetic, mad falsehoods, and so at every crossroads feeling anew the impulse to flee, which would always mar yet also seal my relationship with you. Because the same things that drove me away from you, as I was already realizing, also drew me to you. As if the difference or rather the incompatibility of our natures were the cement the gods used to keep us together.

Blocked by the dilemma, the choice of going forward or turning back, and at the same time confusedly aware that I couldn't escape the will of the gods, the already written fate, I tried then to adapt myself and to understand you through the kaleidoscope of your thousand contradictions. The brusque shifts of mood that transformed you one moment into a boy and another into an old man, both of them alien to the man I had known, the man the world thought it knew, yet fused in him like two rivers in a sea. The old man walked with bowed head, sagging shoulders, never let go of the pipe he smoked slowly, with eyes half-closed, and he was tender, benevolent, he bore adversities with infinite patience, spoke with that same splendid voice that one August afternoon had seduced me. His words were solemn. Then if you asked him about the boy, he would answer: "He is me. He is true wisdom. The appearance of wisdom is not dark and grim, is not thoughtful, it is jolly, filled with joy. The end and the fulfillment of wisdom lie in happy gaiety." He called me kid, alitaki. The boy on the other hand leaped and darted, like the moment he believed he had found the guerrillas to occupy the Acropolis; the boy moved in starts, nervously, was festive or quarrelsome according to his whim and when he was festive he attacked you with the small blows of a puppy's paw, happy to have found a bone; he swept you in a merry, childish spin: "Want to play?" If you asked him about the old man he would answer with singsong nonsense: "I am I. I with him am I with him, I with you am I with you, so I remain always I." He also made rather silly plays on words, happy to be a master of my language: "Non voglio te, voglio il tè! I don't want thee, I want tea!" Moreover he collected little glass balls, bottles, boxes, any object that could become a toy. He adored toys and appropriated for himself the present I bought for Cristos, the child born in the house next door when we loved each other for the first time in a bed: a silver bell with a music box that played a sweet lullaby. And I need hardly add that the mixture was irresistible: proceeding along parallel and opposing paths, in contrasting yet harmonious rhythms, the boy and the old man cohabited in a single body that even without the glamour of a glorious past would have been seductive. It was no accident that women fell madly in love with you. And sometimes men as well, though you didn't notice. Or pretended not to notice. With women you would always have an extraordinary success, I rarely saw such crushes, such passions, as you aroused to the last day of your life, particularly in the period just after Boiati, when girls and old women, rich and poor, stupid and intelligent, offered themselves to you in a plebiscite of sexual greed that was almost sinister: telephone calls, letters, presents, messages entrusted to go-betweens, little notes thrust into your hand or your pocket before my eyes, since not even the fact that we were living together could discourage them. Indeed it stimulated them. Now that you had regained your confidence in crossing streets, walking along crowded sidewalks, and you limped less and less on your broken foot, even those who had ignored you before wanted you now. Fascinated, I observed the phenomenon, seeking also in it a key that would open the doors of your character: if men and women fell so desperately in love with you, why did you remain so alone, why could you find no one who would lend a hand in fighting the dictatorship in the way you wanted? And why didn't you adjust a little to reality, why didn't you act from within an organized movement, a recognized political group, why did you stubbornly insist on changing things by yourself, perhaps with feats or exploits that had the taste of a game, the Acropolis plan in other words? It would take me a long time to understand that it was here that your great intuition lay, as rebel and artist, your great coherence.

It refused to leave your head, that plan. Nothing, not

the impossibility of collecting a command prepared to carry it out, not the reasoning of the man you called preacher, not time, which went by with its distractions, its temptations, had been enough to rid you of it. And one morning you said: "We're going to Crete." "What for?" "To hunt for guerrillas. We'll find them in Crete."

Waiting for the trip to Crete was the acid test of your stubbornness, of the monomania that afflicted you every time your faith spawned an idea and the idea became a psychosis. The business of tying the sacks to the columns had so appealed to you that it had inspired a supplementary devilry: besides filling them with stones and ballast in place of explosive, you would use them to spell out a slogan running all the way around the Parthenon. "We can't write anything on the marble: for one thing the fluting would prevent it, and besmirching the Parthenon with paint would be a real crime. But on the sacks we can write whatever we please. One sack on each column, and one letter on each sack: the slogan will be legible from miles away. Isn't that a great idea?" It was. The problem was to select words whose letters corresponded to the number of columns at the front and rear of the temple and along its sides. The facade and the rear had eight columns, so the words there could not have more than eight letters; the sides had seventeen columns, on them therefore the words could not have more than seventeen letters. But the four corner columns could not contain letters at all, that would cause confusion, so there could be only six letters in the words on the facade and the rear or else only fifteen letters in the words on the sides.. Not to mention the blank spaces, which drove you crazy because, thanks to them, all words seemed too long or too short. "Oppression! Katapiesis!" "Too long." "People! Laos!" "Too short." In the end we found a sentence that almost worked because it was made up of eight words coming to a total of forty-three letters: "Agonas dia tin elefteria Agonas kata tis tirannias" (Fight for freedom Fight against tyranny). The problem lay in that "almost." The two "agonas," in fact, fitted perfectly on the facade and the rear: they even left the two corner columns blank. The words "dia tin elefteria" (for freedom) fit just as perfectly along one side. But "kata tis tirannias (against tyranny), on the contrary, had one letter too many. This annoyed you, but it didn't discourage you. The sentence had a meaning, you said, it moved around the Parthenon in a harmonious way, and to hell with aesthetics: you would compress the article "tis" onto two columns, using there a single, extra-large sack. We actually went up to the Acropolis to check all this, the first of many excursions on which you insisted I should behave like an archeology maniac: admiring, photographing, studying friezes and capitals, so as not to attract attention. You, in the meanwhile, looked for possible hiding places, measured in paces the distance from the Propylaea to the Erechtheum, from the Erechtheum to the Parthenon, from the Parthenon to the Propylaea, you examined carefully the rock that at the northeast edge of the cliff climbs up the wall, the one Glazos had climbed to tear the German flag from the pole, you counted the number of tourists, watched the behavior of the guards, picked out the places suited to setting off the charge of TNT for demonstration purposes. "I want to take a complete plan with me to Crete, perfect, down to the minutest details." And you didn't listen to me when I ventured some doubts about the usefulness of the trip. "Everything will go well. You'll see."

You were sure of this because you knew you hadn't made any mistakes: no appointments, no flight reservations, and the hotel reserved under a phony name. You had told only a very few, trusted companions that we were coming. Obviously there was still the risk that the police would trail us when we left the house for the airport, but during the drive, we didn't notice anybody following us and even as we were boarding the plane nobody seemed interested in us. "You see? They barely glanced at us among the other passengers." The illusion vanished when we were onboard. They hadn't lost sight of us for a second, everything had been organized in such a way that they could check every breath we took. The seats assigned us, for example. They were the last two on the left, different from the others because between them and the wall behind us there was a space of about half a meter, and in this space two plain-clothesmen promptly took their positions. Their hands clutching the backs of our seats, they loomed over us, their breath stinking of garlic; they made no secret of the fact that they were there because of us. They actually taunted you, touched your hair, provoked you with little laughs and remarks: "Katalaves italiki? Do you understand Italian?" "Ne. Yes." "How do you say buon viaggio in Greek?" "Kalon taxidi." "Heh, heh!" I questioned you with a look: if they did this and also were traveling standing up, against regulations, it meant they were on an official mission with very specific instructions. You nodded slightly and then remained in a taciturn immobility that lasted until we disembarked and were met by Marion and Phebo. She was a dear friend from your days at the Polytechnic and he was a Resistance fighter freed from prison by the amnesty. When you had hugged them, explained what was happening, the stink of garlic had disappeared, the pair had vanished. To be replaced by whom? Again nobody seemed to be bothering about us. In the streets of Khania not one automobile followed the Renault in which Marion and Phebo drove us to the hotel. "Maybe they were simply afraid you would hijack the plane." Marion smiled. And almost at that same moment a cry escaped her. "Oh, no!" We had reached the hotel and right there at the sidewalk a white police car was parked. We went up to the room, a lovely room with a window over the sea, you looked onto the balcony and stepped back inside at once with a hoarse command: "Turn off the light, quickly." "Why?" "Turn it off, I said!" I turned it off, came over to you: "What is it? What's happening?" "Look!" I looked and for a few seconds I saw nothing but a splendid night illuminated by the moon, the calm water of the little port where the waves splashed in light, silvery slaps. But then, with my stomach contracting, I saw what you were pointing out to me: a boat anchored twenty meters from the shore. And in the boat three men watching us with a big spyglass.

It was to stay there each night, anchored at the same spot. At a certain hour of the morning it went off and at sunset it came back: with the three men onboard and the spyglass trained on our balcony. It was a persecution at once subtle and absurd. Subtle because it aimed at exasperating you with an apparently innocent system, absurd because it forced the three men to perform a far from easy job: in turn, but without pause, they had to stare into the darkness. To make matters worse, you refused to change rooms or the hotel or even to close the shutters: you said it would be an act of weakness, of surrender, that we had to behave as if we hadn't noticed anything or as if we didn't care. When we came in at night you always accepted the challenge of turning on the lights, flinging the window wide open. And we moved in that orgy of light; knowing we were watched made both of us painfully uneasy. But you more than me. Already strained by the effort not to react to the two in the plane, touching your hair, provoking you, mocking you, then wounded by the dismay of finding the police car at the sidewalk, you were succumbing every hour to the battle of nerves. You became convinced that our room concealed microphones, and you were constantly shifting the furniture, examining the drawers, poking the mattresses, you communicated with me by writing little notes that you then burned in the ashtray. In bed, when the darkness was not enough to make us forget the unpleasant sensation of being spied on, and we hesitated even to exchange tenderness, as if the walls were of glass, you would become agitated, repeating obsessively: "How hard it is to go on!" With this refrain the wait for dawn was endless, and the sunrise brought new persecutions. No, I hadn't been wrong to express doubts about the usefulness of this trip: to attempt even preliminary meetings with potential guerrillas represented an almost insoluble problem. As soon as we left the hotel, the white police car would start its engine and follow us. Dead slow if we were on foot, a few meters behind if we took a taxi or Phebo's Renault, and we were never able to determine whether we were also shadowed by plainclothesmen. The first morning you thought that Marion's architectural office, on the sixth floor of a building full of offices, was a perfect place to meet anyone you were interested in: however, as you went up in the elevator, you sniffed the stink of garlic you had smelled in the plane and you canceled the appointment. To conduct your search, therefore, you resorted to suppers in restaurants, a trick that consisted of having a large party at the table, including the candidate that interested you; but this made the examination superficial, with useless talk, and afterward your dejection increased. "Time wasted, time wasted!" Occasionally you were so depressed that I didn't dare ask if you were making any progress. That things were going badly I could sense from the words I caught despite the language barrier: "Den ine practicos. It's not practical." "Den ine pragmaticos. It's not realistic."

And the day came, the fifth I think, when the tension and the disappointment exploded with the force of a gas too long compressed. We went to see the grave of Venizelos and, as on Aegina, the call of death bewitched you. You started saying that no man can say as much when alive as he can say when he is dead, and the proof was here in this grave: if Venizelos had been alive and had conversed with you, taking you by the arm, you wouldn't have heard what you heard now, knowing he was under ground. Then you started talking about Jan Palach, about his sacrifice in flames at Prague in front of the statue of Saint Wenceslaus. "You know what I say? The Parthenon is better then the statue of Saint Wenceslaus. Only the Czechs knew who Saint Wenceslaus was, but everybody knows the Parthenon." I repressed a feeling of horror, and pretending not to understand, I answered you lightly: "What's the Parthenon got to do with it?" "A lot. Think what a defeat for the junta if somebody killed himself on the Acropolis, in front of the Parthenon. The whole world would say that—" "It would say he was crazy." "Why? Was Jan Palach crazy? Were the Vietnamese monks crazy when they set fire to themselves in Saigon? There are lots of ways to carry forward a struggle, a resistance. One is suicide. I never considered suicide, not even when they were torturing me and I couldn't stand it anymore. But then I felt less alone, I knew that people outside were concerned for me, helped me by believing in me. But when nobody helps you, and nobody listens to you, and you can't attempt anything because you're alone, killing yourself has a meaning. It's useful." "A can of gasoline is enough, eh?" "No, five hundred grams of TNT are enough, plus a fuse and a match." "Alekos!" "Don't take it to heart. Characters like me die alone even if they love and are loved. Oh, tonight I'm going to get drunk, sick drunk." And you kept your promise. Glass after glass, bottle after bottle, mixing wine with anger, anger with sorrow, sorrow with mortification, mortification with helplessness, or rather with solitude, a solitude so deep that any thought of alleviating it would have been like the illusion that one could drain the sea with a spoon. You drank more than I would ever have believed a man could drink. We had chosen an outdoor tavern, almost opposite the hotel, and we were sitting at a table just at the edge of the street. A blue car passed back and forth, slowly, with two men in it who stared at you insistently. But you didn't see them, your drunkenness also made you blind. If I said to you—"Let's go, there's a car that makes me suspicious"—you would open your glazed pupils wide. "I don't see any cars. It only takes five hundred grams of TNT, a fuse, and a match." When you finally made up your mind to come away, you couldn't stand on your feet. You fell on me with the weight of a tree falling on a weak shrub, and I had to make a cruel effort to get you across the street, up the steps, into the hotel, to the elevator, then open it, close it, open it again, close it again, reach the room, fling you on the bed.

Later, in the months and in the years to come, I was to repeat that cruel effort other times. But later I was to learn the movements, the little ruses to make you shift a foot, a leg, to give you a bit of balance, and above all I was to learn that drinking for you was not a physical indulgence but rather a desperation whose every technique, every secret you knew. I was actually to learn how to distinguish what you called the first stage, the second stage, the third stage: the first stage is the one that stimulates the mind, loosens the tongue, transforms the act of drinking into an intellectual and social rite following the rules of the Socratic symposium; the second stage, the one that breaks the bonds of inhibition, shatters the barriers of self-control, and freeing you from thought, leads to the limbo of forgetting; the third stage, the one that shatters and leads to the boundless plains of oblivion and the unknown. A mysterious drowning in the self, an indefinable plunge into the abysses of nothingness, an absolute rest, a temporary death. Through your stories I would finally learn that each stage was willed in advance with cold calculation, and each corresponded to a given degree of sorrow. Knowing this, I would force myself to the indulgence that allows us to love someone in his faults, in his weaknesses, and I would become inured. But now I wasn't, and I felt only dismay, incredulity, pitying disgust: can a hero be so fragile? "Five hundred grams of TNT, a fuse, a match." "Hush, Alekos, hush!" "How hard it is to go on." "Hush, Alekos, hush!" Then, suddenly, you were stretched out on the bed, your body now marble, and your head on fire; the fever raged, became delirium. If I bent over you, you shrank back, covered your face with your elbow, all huddled up, staring at me with eyes brimming with terror. "Oiki! No! No! No!" Or else: "Ftani! Enough! Enough!" And trying to calm you was useless because it wasn't me you saw, it was the ghost of a past unforgotten and unforgettable, the faces of Theophiloiannakos, and of Malios and of Babalis and of Hazizikis, which, I was to discover, materialized always when an anger was added to a sorrow, and a sorrow to a humiliation, and a humiliation to a helplessness, or rather to your solitude, and that knot became awareness of a defeat. Then from the delirium you plunged into a prostration soaked with sweat which dripped down like an oil, drenched your clothes, the sheets, the pillow. Finally you fell into a stony sleep, almost cataleptic.

I sat watching over that sleep until the first lights of dawn when you woke up, completely cured. "Good morning! Sleep well? What beautiful sunshine! You know where I'm taking you today? To Herakleion! Pack your bag!" "And what's at Herakleion?" "You know very well: the temple of Knossos!" "And besides the temple of Knossos?" "Somebody I want to see." You called Phebo, you asked him to drive you in his Renault, and we prepared to leave. Wasn't it a great idea, you said, to travel in the early morning with this beautiful sunshine? And wasn't it wonderful luck to have a friend like Phebo? If it hadn't been for Marion, you would have already asked him to take part in the action: he wouldn't have made any fuss. But you couldn't ask him, you couldn't take him from the children and from her. That was the trouble with having a wife, a family, also back in 1968 you had not wanted men with a wife and family. You chattered on and on, heedless of the microphones that according to you were hidden in the walls, in the furniture, who knows where, forgetting what you had said in front of Venizelos's grave about the dead who speak, about Jan Palach, about the idea of blowing yourself up with your cakes of TNT. And about what had happened last night, about the terrible drunk, the fever, the delirium, not a word.

"It's not there!" "Who? What?" "The white police car." "Are you sure?" "Absolutely. Look!" I looked. It was true. "It's probably only gone off for a moment.

Don't get your hopes up." "No, the concierge says it's been gone since yesterday evening." I searched my memory, but in vain: during the trip from the restaurant to the hotel I had been so absorbed in the job of keeping you on your feet that I had paid no attention to anything else. A strange business, though. Phebo shrugged: "Maybe they've decided to leave you in peace." "Maybe." "Maybe they'll catch up with us on the road." "Maybe." We got into the Renault. He at the wheel, you beside him, me on the back seat. We crossed the city, undisturbed, soon we were on the highway to Herakleion. And still nobody bothering about us. Every now and then some vehicle would pass us, a little truck or two, and that was all. "I don't understand." "Neither do I." To see whether we were being followed at a distance, we stopped at a village tavern, left the Renault clearly visible, and sat at a little table. We stayed there about thirty minutes. But in the end we had to convince ourselves that the persecution had actually stopped: for some reason that eluded us, they were ignoring your trip to Herakleion. And yet, speaking with Phebo on the phone, you had clearly said Herakleion: had they resigned themselves to accepting this stay in Crete as a harmless vacation? It was not a hypothesis to be rejected, and relieved, we went back to the Renault: "In less than an hour and a half we'll be there!"

The drive from Khania to Herakleion is very beautiful. For long stretches the road lies above the bluest sea of the archipelago, or it passes among harsh, rocky mountains, a warm reddish brown, and the sky has the color of the sea: in September there isn't a cloud to mar it. There aren't even houses to deface the landscape, only goats live there; if you know you aren't being followed, you feel a kind of happiness. You can laugh, chat about pleasant things, even recall episodes that weren't amusing in the past but are today. "What a nice woman, the proprietress of the hotel! Imagine: she didn't want us to pay the bill!" "And she asked us to sign the ledger of honored guests, and she was moved when I wrote 'Freedom' in it." "She gave me a bag full of fruit." "Fruit! On Cyprus there was a time when I was starving, so I stole fruit in the fields. Have you ever tried stealing a watermelon when you don't have a knife? You become Tantalus." "Alekos, tell Phebo about when you stole the cigarettes in Athens. Tell him how it's done." "You do it like this. You know those hole-in-the-wall shops where they sell newspapers and cigarettes? You have the man give you the cigarettes, and when it's time to pay for them, you pretend to drop the money. Or rather you throw it on the ground. You bend over to pick it up, and in that position you crawl around the corner of the stand, and you run off." "Shame on you!" "I didn't have a drachma, I was a deserter!" "Tell him how you steal cakes in a pastry shop." "This is what you do. You stop a child and say to him: 'Would you like to eat your fill of pastries?' The child nods. Then you say to him: 'Come with me, I don't like eating pastries by myself.' You go into the shop and the two of you stuff yourselves with pastries. Then you say to him: 'Wait here for me, I'll be right back. If the waiter asks for me, say that your Dad has gone to the bathroom.' And instead you go out and don't come back. They won't arrest the kid!" "You crook!" "You say that because you've never been hungry. Tell me: what did you eat on Easter Sunday in 1968?" "Let me think. Easter of 1968 I was in Vietnam, on the Danang front. I must have eaten the American soldiers' rations, canned stuff. And you?" "A can of caviar." "And you're complaining?" "Listen to me. You were in Vietnam but I was in Rome, setting up the assassination. And as usual I didn't have a cent, I was dying of hunger, in the house there was just this little can of caviar. Not even a slice of bread. Have you ever made a meal off a can of caviar and nothing else, not even a slice of bread? Ever since that day I've loathed caviar, I can't understand why so many people like caviar. Phebo, do you like caviar?" But Phebo wasn't listening. Incredibly pale, he was glancing nervously into the rearview mirror. "Bastards! The bastards!"

"Phebo, what is it?" "We were kidding ourselves. They're behind us."

I turned, but it wasn't the white police car, it was the blue car that had driven back and forth the night before past the tavern where you were getting drunk. It was traveling about three hundred meters behind us and it was highly visible because it was the only thing moving on the straight, deserted road: I could hardly believe the two of us hadn't noticed it before. Phebo had seen it shortly after the stop in the village. He had said nothing to us, assuming at first it wanted to pass, he explained; then he suspected nothing because it had lagged almost half a kilometer behind us. It seemed harmless, until a little while ago when it had started tailing us like a shadow. If he accelerated, it accelerated; if he slowed down, it slowed down. And not so much as a dog in sight, coming or going, even from the opposite direction. "Skata. Shit!" "Not shit, fate," your icy voice remarked. You also turned around and your face expressed neither surprise nor rage but rather a calm heavy with irony, as if the matter were completely normal and confirmed what you were expecting. But the left eye was a pool of hatred. "Try again, Phebo." Phebo pressed on the accelerator and gained about fifty meters. At once the blue car imitated him, regaining its position. "Uhm. I see. How much longer is it to Herakleion?" "That depends." "Have we already passed Rethymnon?" "Yes." "And Perama?" "Yes." You smiled at me bitterly: "General police strike." "Strike?" "Of course. Did you think that was a police car? It isn't a police car, they aren't plainclothesmen." "Then who are they?" "Fascists." "How do you know?" "I know. Ask Phebo." I asked him. I got no answer. Bent over the wheel, Phebo was trying to double the distance from the blue car and he was speeding along at a minimum of a hundred and thirty kilometers an hour. When he took the curves badly, the wheels screamed, and since that stretch of road ran between two walls of rock, it seemed we would slam into them. "Watch out, Phebo, watch out!" "Let him drive, don't be afraid. We'll have plenty to be afraid of when they attack us." "Attack us?" "Obviously. And the idea is not stupid. Afterward who could prove it was a crime and not an accident?" "If they wanted to do that, they wouldn't have waited so long, Alekos." And as I was saying this, the rock walls ended: I understood the reason why they had waited so long. From there until the distant curve where an embankment rose again, the road had no rail or parapet, and the mountain dropped away sharply, in chasms. To cover that stretch of road with the prospect of being hit was like crossing a bridge flung over the void with a blindfold on your eyes. We began moving along it. And immediately the blue car spurted forward.

It darted with a kind of leap, aiming inexorably at us, and in a flash it caught up with us: only to slow down at the very last moment, avoiding the crash by a hair, then settling with its muzzle against the tail of the Renault. The space between one car and the other was so slight that you could see with absolute precision the faces of the two men in it, their greasy black moustaches, their olive skin, the driver's evil smile. I heard myself cry: "You were right! They want to force us over!" I heard you murmur: "In the middle, Phebo, keep in the middle." Phebo nodded, shifted to the middle lane, moving from the cliff, but the blue car followed the maneuver and fell in behind us to the left. The right end of its front bumper was almost attached to the rear bumper of the Renault. "Faster, Phebo, faster." Phebo obeyed with a grunt: he couldn't go much faster, all we could hope was that they meant only to scare us. And at that same moment the blue car's muzzle grazed the left side of the Renault. A very light bump, like a kitten's playful slap, but enough to make us veer to the right: toward the precipice. I saw Phebo grip the wheel hard, yank on it, recover control before the wheels came too close to the edge of the road, move back to the center, and continue straight for a moment. Then the second blow came. Harder, this time. This time the Renault skidded as if on a carpet of grease, and for a brief moment, no longer than the idea of death, it slid along the rim of the void. A few centimeters more and the void would have sucked us in, shattering us down in the valley. But Phebo made it once more. Back in the middle, he even managed to gain about ten meters on the blue car and the distance quickly became twenty, forty, eighty, a hundred, as you lighted a little cigar and said: "Bravo, Phebo." For me it was incomprehensible that you could think of lighting a cigar in such a circumstance and then actually light it. And yet you did, and you were smoking it, and as you smoked it, your face continued to express a calm heavy with irony, your voice continued to be icy, nothing now recalled the vulnerable creature racked by the delirium of the previous night. On the contrary one would have said that risking your life and making two people who loved you risk theirs was a negligible trifle for you and perhaps a secret cruel pleasure. "They'll be back. They're coming back. Give me a pen, quickly. I want to take the number of the license."

They really were coming back. With a determined roar the blue car darted forward again and was devouring the hundred meters it had lost. I barely had time to glimpse its evil muzzle, its white eye sockets, its almost human form, and at once it was at our side: it passed us in a whoosh, only to move in front of us and suddenly slow down. "Oh, Christ!" Phebo moaned, swerving to the left, narrowly avoiding a crash. This irritated them, and with the same pass, the same whoosh, the blue car again positioned itself in front of us, forcing Phebo to repeat the dangerous maneuver. And this was more than we had foreseen, this attempt to wear Phebo down until he should lose control of the car and plunge over the cliff, this game of cat and mouse. In fact their car was more powerful, more solid. It never skidded, it passed us whenever it wanted and however it wanted, it cut us off, not caring about being hit. There, it passes us for the third time, slows down for the third time, and the fourth, and the fifth, and the sixth, but at the third we skid, and at the fourth, the fifth, the sixth, to the right and the left, then again to the right and again to the left, in a zigzag that leads inevitably to the rim of the void. It seems to go on interminably, not just a few minutes, for hundreds of miles, not a few dozen meters, and Phebo seems more and more tense, more and more exhausted, his face no longer pale but green; he is the very opposite of you, imperturbably smoking your little cigar, as you direct him, advise him, congratulate him: "Excellent, Phebo, Kala. Watch out, Phebo, that's right. Grigora, Phebo, faster." "If only somebody would come along!" Phebo answers, gasping. But nobody comes, not even from the opposite direction; on the ribbon of asphalt there is only us and the blue car with her evil muzzle, her white sockets, her somehow human quality. I say her because she is the one you're addressing, not the two men inside, and because death, from today on, will have for me (and also for you?) the form of an automobile, it doesn't matter what automobile, what make, what color, today it's blue and tomorrow it'll be black, it will be dull green, it will be red, tan, and finally apple green. You watch it once more as it stops the zigzagging, presses us against the edge and prepares for the definitive attack, knowing that the bridge flung over the void will not last long, that soon, beyond the curve, the embankment will rise and the rock walls will begin again and if we can reach there we're safe. But will we reach there? Every turn of our wheels brings her closer, her side is almost glued to ours; unable to restrain my fear I dig my fingers into your shoulders, I bend over Phebo and beg him: Hurry, Phebo, hurry, make a last effort and when you're near the embankment slow down, so if she hits us there the impact is less violent, there are only two hundred meters. Two hundred, a hundred, fifty, forty, thirty, twenty, there's the embankment, there it is, ten, five, three, two, one—

She struck us at the beginning of the embankment, sideswiped us, halfway along our left side, and we swerved to the right but not too much because Phebo had slowed down and was holding the wheel firmly. He held it also when the Renault whirled around in a spin that seemed to swallow us for eons, with the certainty that it would never stop. But it did stop, and we looked at one another, dumbfounded, incredulous, and discovered we were unharmed, on a completely deserted road. The blue car had disappeared, and waving the paper on which you had written the number of the license plate, you said: "Now we can really have a good time in Herakleion."

We realized we wouldn't have a good time in Herakleion the moment the white police car appeared, a few kilometers before we entered the city. It was coming from the opposite direction, at the slow, cautious pace of someone looking for something or somebody, and merely seeing it we were outraged: was it coming to look for three live people or for three corpses down the ravine? There could be no doubt that it was looking for us: after passing us it veered brusquely and tailed us into town. Here it was joined by a red car full of plainclothesmen; the surveillance was taking on alarming proportions. When we stopped at a tavern to eat, one agent stood guard at the door, another in back of the building, another at the corner of the street. It was a big job persuading you to stay calm, to leave the tavern without paying attention to them, assuming the attitude of a tourist on a sentimental holiday: all your aplomb gone, purple with rage, you wanted to face them and perhaps hit them. Then, while Phebo telephoned to call off the meetings you were scheduled to have in the afternoon, you and I went to the palace of Knossos. But, on the ramp that surrounds the archeological zone, again there was that stink of garlic and the taunting voice: "Katalaves italiki? Do you understand Italian?" You flared up once more in grim wrath, spoiling for a fight, you hurled yourself against the more malicious, shouting at him—Servant, cocksucker, bastard—and only the intervention of the armed policemen prevented your arrest. It was wiser to return to Khania at once. But how could it be done without being exposed a second time to the risk we had run on the trip out? If they had decided to eliminate you on the highway, surely they would try again at sunset, with the darkness. An argument broke out. I said it would be a good idea to call on the uniformed police: in the palace of Knossos they had actually helped you, and if we told them about what had happened this morning, they would protect us; you wouldn't even discuss it and you shouted: "Me? Have myself protected by the police? Me?! Ime Panagoulis! I am Panagoulis!" In the end Phebo suggested a stratagem: we should behave in such a way that the police would be reluctant to let us out of their sight for a second. And he followed this tactic. Taking half-hidden alleys, going down one-way streets the wrong way, doubling back, pretending to give them the slip, he made them so suspicious that the white police car accompanied us from Herakleion to Khania. There we remained just long enough to discover that the blue car's license plate was a fake.

Walking up and down now in the garden of orange and lemon trees I was pondering that fake license plate, and my meditation provoked questions without answers. Who had hired the two in the blue car? Who had ordered a murder to be passed off, if it succeeded, as an automobile accident? Papadopoulos? Perhaps. But it was useful for him to keep you alive if he wanted his farce of political tolerance to gain credibility. Ioannidis? Perhaps. But he wanted to have you shot, not killed in a Renault by accident. Theophilioannakos, Hazizikis, the band who had shuddered with fear of vendetta on hearing the bad news of your release from prison? Perhaps. But it seemed strange to me that they would risk a tricky card like a faked automobile accident. The secret services, then, or some marginal figure of the regime? Perhaps. Obviously they were all suspect. But one thing was certain: the order to eliminate you came from high up, from people in positions of power. Otherwise there was no explaining how the white police car had been sent to Herakleion before we left Khania, or why the boat from which they trained the spyglass on us had remained undisturbed for three nights in the little port. And why had they attacked you on Crete instead of in Athens? Was the reason geographical, or rather strategic, or had the Acropolis plan been discovered? And assuming that it had been discovered, was it conceivable that such a mad joke, destined to flower only in the gardens of your imagination, would frighten them to the point of wanting your death? Wouldn't it have been simpler to forestall it by keeping an eye on you and guarding the citadel? Then, gradually, came the answer I was looking for. No, the Acropolis plan had nothing to do with it, or very little. What Power feared was not five hundred grams of TNT and the more or less spectacular use you could make of it: it was your personality, the disorder it caused everywhere and in every way. You hadn't been still one second since the day you left Boiati. Statements to the national and foreign press, interviews, protests, legal quibbles. You had even questioned the amnesty, demonstrating the decree was illegal since it applied also to torturers: can you grant an amnesty to those who have not stood trial or received sentence? And isn't granting them an amnesty perhaps the equivalent of admitting that the tortures the regime denies had in fact taken place? To say nothing of the scenes you made in public, the rowdy telephone calls to ESA headquarters, and the popularity you enjoyed. You could never walk in the street unnoticed. There was always someone bold enough to stop you and embrace you. And as if that weren't enough, the newspapers devoted a lot of space to us. Our unpredicted and unpredictable relationship aroused a kind of morbid interest, we were a couple that made news, which made you even more of a nuisance. But above everything else there was your intransigence, your intractability, your imagination. They could never guess what you would do a minute from now or tomorrow, and anyone who asked himself that question became a Zakarakis, waking in the heart of the night and shouting: "Where is he? What's he doing?" In other areas this can be amusing, pleasing; in politics and, worse still, in a dictatorship it is an unwritten death sentence. You had to leave Greece at once.

"What are you brooding about?" You suddenly appeared at my back and looked at me as if you had heard every word. "I wasn't brooding, I was thinking that—" "I understand: you were thinking that sooner or later somebody's going to knock me off. 'Which one of them, however, that's the problem.' Forget it, it's a problem that doesn't matter. I will always be a nuisance to anyone at any moment, in any country, under any regime. And the one who knocks me off won't be one of those you're thinking about." "Alekos, I was thinking that—" "That I have to get the Acropolis plan out of my head? No, it's an excellent idea, I won't give it up. At worst, if I can't find anyone to help me, I can reduce it: limit it to a token action. No TNT, no weapons, no hostages, only the slogan 'Agonas dia tin elefteria Agonas kata tis tirannias.' Uhm! It would take only forth-three pieces of cloth and . . . at night nobody would see us." "They would see us, Alekos. At night the Parthenon is illuminated by floodlights." "Uhm, that's right. We could do it at dawn." "They would clear everything away before the city was awake." "Then instead of cloth we'll use paint: to hell with the sacred marble. We only have to take a spray can with us." "Listen to me, Alekos. You have to get this idea out of your head. You have to leave Greece." "Ah! So this is what you were plotting! Sooner than do that I really would blow myself up—in front of the Parthenon." "Because no man when alive speaks like a dead man speaks?" "Right." "No, you're wrong, Alekos. The dead are always silent. When they seem to be speaking it's because they are forgotten. At first it seems impossible to forget them, it seems they will last for eternity: after a while, however, nobody even remembers they were born." "That's not true!" "It's true, Alekos. It's true, unfortunately. The dead depend on the living in everything." "You're wrong!" "No, Alekos, no. It's the dead who are always wrong.

Because they're dead. You have to live, Alekos. Live! And to live you have to get out of Greece." "To hell with you!" You went back into the house and shut yourself up in the little bedroom. When you came out again you seemed relaxed. "You know what? This Acropolis business is a bore. I don't want to hear the words Acropolis or Parthenon again. I'll invent something else." "With the TNT?" "Oh, that? I got rid of the TNT last night, as soon as we got back from Crete. I gave it back to the person who got it for me. I said to him—Here, enjoy yourself with these fireworks, I have more important things to do."

Overcome with relief and convinced that my rational discussion was responsible for it, at first I didn't wonder what had really inspired it. Nor did I wonder afterward, as long as you were alive. But years later, when your ghost became a nightmare of memory and memory an instrument of research, as I pieced together the mosaic of the man you had been and I tried to understand you through death, the recollection of your sudden abandonment of the Acropolis plan revealed you to me. No, my rational discussion had not determined that abrupt switch; the cause instead was a curse that hung over you. And that curse stemmed from your inability to conclude the things you set in motion, to materialize the things that you dreamed. The more obstinate and unshakable you seemed when a thought became an obsession, a monomania, the more you proved inconstant and impatient in the task of carrying it out. For a certain period you would fling yourself body and soul into the project, tormenting your existence, ruining the existence of others, ignoring obstacles like a tank overriding every object or creature it finds in its path, and then abruptly the pirouette: you gave it up and you never spoke of it again. Only in two instances did your obstinacy win: in the attempted assassination of Papadopoulos, which was to determine your life, and in the capture of the documents, which was to determine your death. That is, at the beginning and at the end of your hero's tale. It happens often to poets, to artists. It happens especially to the lonely rebels who know they will soon die: as a rule their existence is a blaze of a thousand unfinished adventures, a storm of seeds cast on the wind or sown at random, without knowing whether the plant will bloom, without waiting to see the shoots. Rebels don't have the time, or the desire, because they have always to pursue something new, always to begin again and again, with an incoherence which, if you think about it, is an extraordinary coherence. Everything serves the purpose, even the ideas of others. In some cases, in fact, the idea that replaced the discarded idea was not yours: you heard it from others. After having heard it, you would reject it, bury it in the abysses of your unconscious. "I don't want advice, I don't want opinions." But down there at the bottom of the abysses, if it struck a response in your fantasy, it would immediately surface again, so you could develop it and make it yours. This is exactly what happened with my suggestion that you leave Greece. One night, when I was sleeping quietly beside you, you shook me awake and said: "Open your eyes! Open your eyes!" "What is it? What's going on?" "I've found it!" "Found what?" "I must go away." "Where to?" "To Italy, Europe. Away from Greece." "Ah!" "You don't agree, eh? If you don't agree, you're wrong. I can't achieve anything here now, my hands are tied. They keep too close a watch on me, and people are afraid: they all draw back. Abroad it'll be different: I can organize myself, form action groups. Among the exiles, you understand. Europe is full of them. Then I'll come back secretly or rather I'll come and go and—Tomorrow I'll apply for a passport. Papadopoulos won't have the nerve to refuse it to me." "What about Ioannidis?" "Ioannidis would." "And what if Ioannidis has his way." "In some things Papadopoulos still counts."

3

TYRANNIES, WE KNOW, WHETHER OF THE RIGHT OR THE left, of East or West, of yesterday or today or tomorrow, all resemble one another. The systems of repression are identical, the arrests, the interrogations, the solitary confinement, the stupid and wicked jailers who confiscate even pen and writing paper, and the persecutions are identical when the reprobate, who dared disobey, is released from prison, the controls, the threats, the attempts to eliminate him if he is incorrigible. And one thing in particular makes all tyrannies of our day kin, a thing that at first sight seems bizarre: their refusal to allow the reprobate leave when he asks to go to another country. In fact you would think that by going to another country he is doing the oppressor regime a great service—I'm leaving, I'm getting out from under foot, I won't trouble you further. But no. It irks them, if he goes away, it offends them. Because if he's leaving, if he's removing the source of irritation, how will they manage to avenge themselves on his disobedience? How will they control him, torment him, put him back into prison or the gulag or the mental hospital? Above all how will they prevent him from thinking or from expressing himself? For tyrannies the reprobate in exile represents a bigger problem than the reprobate at home because in exile he thinks, he expresses himself, he acts, and to be rid of him they have to go to the trouble of sending an assassin who will kill him—with a pistol or even a hatchet. The pistol in Paris for the Rosselli brothers; the hatchet in Mexico

City for Trotsky. A pain in the ass, better to have him at home and kill him easily, little by little with prison, mental hospital, gulag, with his helplessness, as the people remains silent. Passport? What passport? Oh, yes, of course: you simply have to present your birth certificate, a good conduct certificate, and . . .

To apply for a passport you have first of all to present your birth certificate. But at the town hall of Glyphada, where it was kept, the clerks said that they couldn't give it to you: the page with your name was missing from the ledger. Lost because of a banal mishap or torn out by order of Ioannidis? The ledger seemed intact, the pages with the names of the other members of your family were there all right, but not the one with your name. And the clerks stammered in confusion: what could they say except that legally speaking you didn't exist? This answer was brought back by your mother who, in her most ladylike outfit, with little black hat, black suit, black purse, black stockings, black glasses, had gone to get the birth certificate: "You weren't born." "What are you talking about?" "They say you weren't born, you're not in the ledger." This was something you weren't expecting. Among all the insults, all the provocations they could inflict on you, this was the worst, and your roar made the windowpanes tremble. "I'm not born? I'm not born?!" If they had told you that you were dead, you wouldn't have been upset: but to say that you weren't born, that you didn't exist! Few people in the world had shown more clearly than you that they were born; you yelled, choking on tears: you were so born that they wanted to shoot you, and how can they shoot somebody who isn't born, somebody who doesn't exist? Now you would go to the town hall and you would beat them up one by one, from the mayor to the lowest traffic cop, and you wouldn't stop until they were singing in chorus: "You're born, Alekos, you're born!" It was a job persuading you that this was exactly what they were counting on, a furious reaction from you: better to pretend to believe it was an error and keep insisting. And with little black hat, black suit, black purse, black stockings, black glasses, your mother went there again to seek the missing page. She went there every day, and each time to cry that you were born for goodness' sake; she certainly knew it, for she had kept you nine months in her belly and then given birth to you: and they knew it too, the dogs, thieves, servants of the dictatorship: out with that certificate. Many clerks, instead of taking offense, were on your side, and they asked her to return the next day. But the next day the same thing happened. "You're not born, you're simply not born," she would say, coming back into the house, then she would withdraw to the room with the little altar in the wardrobe and grumble to the icons of the saints. She accused them of egoism, of indifference, cowardice, she threatened to blow out their candles, to shut the door of the wardrobe, to let them mold in the dark unless they worked a miracle and found the page again; but the saints were silent, deaf to blackmail and threats, and the page still couldn't be found. The passport application couldn't be presented. So one evening you spread out a big map on the dining table. "Come here and have a look." I went over, suspiciously. "What is it?" "Something I've been studying since they started insisting I was never born. Illegal exit from the country." "Oh, no!" "Oh, yes! Now listen."

There were two solutions, you said, one by land and one by sea. It was hopeless even to think of planes. In theory the land solution offered the possibility of escaping into one of the four countries that shared borders with Greece to the northeast and northwest: Albania, Yugoslavia, Bulgaria, and Turkey. But Turkey had to be rejected out of hand because the tension between Ankara and Athens made the border almost impossible to cross, Bulgaria had to be avoided for the same reason, and Albania refused to accept outsiders: at least three Greeks who had fled to Albania after the coup were in the Tirana prison, serving heavy sentences for illegal entry. "Overland, I would favor Yugoslavia. I say 'would' because it would be fairly easy for me to cross the border at Ezvonoi, and it would be fairly easy to obtain political asylum too. But the problem isn't crossing the border, it's getting to Ezvonoi. From Athens it's at least six hours by car or by train. They would have plenty of time to follow me and catch me or send a bullet into my head. So I prefer the sea solution: the bay of Vouliagmeni. Vouliagmeni has two advantages: it's only a half hour from Glyphada and it's a small harbor, you can reach the open sea quickly. But this time of year there are not many yachts at anchor there and your yacht might arouse curiosity." "My yacht? What yacht?!" "The one you're going to get. A foreign yacht with four or five rich-looking, carefree people, prepared to make an Aegean cruise." "And where am I going to find a yacht with four or five rich-looking, carefree people, prepared to make an Aegean cruise?" "In Italy I suppose. How should I know? Don't interrupt me. Hypothesis number two: Piraeus. It's heavily guarded, every vessel is thoroughly checked by the police and by cus.oms. On the other hand it has the advantages of a crowded port, you attract less attention. Yes, if I could choose, I'd choose Piraeus. Anyway, whether we sail from Piraeus or Vouliagmeni, the problem starts the moment we set sail because we have to tell the port authorities where we're headed. We'll say we're going to Crete and we'll turn south, along the Peloponnesian coast. When we're off Kithira, instead of heading for Crete, we'll swing right." "Alekos—" "We'll pass Kithira, the island at the extreme south of the Peloponnesus, and we'll enter the extraterritorial waters of the Ionian immediately. If we're lucky, the Coast Guard won't have time to stop us. Then we'll land at Brindisi or at Taranto. Naturally the shortest way would be via Corinth and Patras, but that would be too risky: that's the route of the commercial liners." "Alekos—" "From Piraeus to Kithira, or from Vouliagmeni to Kithira, would take a day and a night. Too much time. Obviously we have to cut the length of the voyage to the minimum. So you'll have to pick a very fast yacht." "Alekos—" "I want to sail in a week." "A week?!" "Make it ten days. It's almost October, and in early October a cruise is still credible." "Alekos! Be reasonable, Alekos, a yacht isn't a taxi you can call with a whistle, and finding four or five people willing to stage a phony cruise to get you out isn't simple." "It's very simple. You'll find them. Because if you don't then I'm forced to try the Yugoslav border and I'll get that bullet in my head before Ezvonoi."

The thought that you were asking something impossible of me never even crossed your mind. Or else it did and you paid no attention to it. So it was useless to insist that an escape like this required at least a month of preparation: to organize it in ten days I would have needed Aladdin's lamp. As always when you fell in love with a dream, your unshakable optimism made you blind to the obstacles and deaf to the appeals of reason; any argument I opposed to the plan was dismissed by your heartbroken cry: "You don't love me!" You wanted me to leave the minute the details were agreed on, so you thought only of them: with the same fervor as when you were measuring the distance from the Propylaea to the Erechtheum, from the Erechtheum to the Parthenon, from the Parthenon to the Propylaea, or counting the number of letters necessary to compose the slogan, now you were working on routes, winds, autumn storms, habits of the Coast Guard, harbor regulations, techniques of searching boats, measurements of territorial and extraterritorial waters. The same persistence you showed before, when you took me to the Acropolis, you showed now on the way to Piraeus. "Yes, I've decided on Piraeus." There wasn't an evening when we didn't have supper in one of the taverns near the roads where the yachts are berthed and here, pretending to admire the reflections of the moon in the water, you observed, annotated, invented new expedients, announced new devilries to me. "Let's suppose that yacht is the one. Who can see me if I board it in the dark? Look at that group coming back in a taxi; the taxi can go right up to the dock, from the taxi to the gangway is three meters: one leap and, mingling with the others, I climb onboard, I take the place of a sailor. Yes, I'll shave my moustache and dress like a sailor. At dawn we cast off and we're on our way." Or else: "Two days in Athens will be enough, but you must come ashore as little as possible. You could be recognized. You'll be wearing a black wig and you'll have a fake passport. Borrow the passport of some friend who looks a bit like you. But not the others, it's best for them to come with their documents in order. Make sure they act nonchalant, like real tourists. And no phone calls, no contact with me. All I need to know is the name of the yacht and the date of arrival. I'll handle the rest. To let me know, you will send a postcard signed Giuseppe. Write the information under the stamp." "Under the stamp?!" "Of course, it's a very simple system, I discovered it myself. You write in the little square that's the size of the stamp, then you glue the stamp on and you mail the card. The person who receives it only has to wet it, remove the stamp, and read what's written in the space." I listened, resigned, desperately hoping for my sake that in the meanwhile the page from the ledger would be resurrected to show you were born and it would get this whole business out of your head. In this hope I caught myself actually glancing toward the little altar in the wardrobe, joining my pleas to those of your mother, who, grumbling, shuffling, threatening, kept demanding a miracle. Demanding with a new strategy. Ever since she had learned of the plans for the secret flight, she no longer addressed all the saints. Saint George was fired, as patron of the army he was suspected of ties with the junta; Saint Elias was also discharged, patron of mountaineers, hence suspect of favoring escape to Yugoslavia; Saint Nicholas eliminated, patron of sailors and suspect of favoring the yacht plan; and so her prayers and her candles were concentrated entirely on Saint Phanourious. Saint Phanourious, the patron of lost persons and therefore of lost things. And it was on the very Friday that the ultimatum was to end that Saint Phanourious performed the miracle.

I was packing my bags to go to Rome when a joyous cry shook the house: "Ghenitica! Ghenitica!" I rushed out and it was you, waving a piece of paper with your name on it: "I'm born! I'm born!" Immediately my bags were unpacked, my departure canceled: now the passport application could follow its course and the hope of getting one had some meaning. Of course the page hadn't been found by chance; rather Papadopoulos had permitted the document's being issued. But now we had to see how much time he would take to impose his wishes on Ioannidis. Ioannidis, you said, would do everything to prevent your leaving the country. And you were right: we noted at once that after the document was issued, the surveillance around the house was increased. Two more policemen at the street corners, an extra three in the side street, and behind the windows of a nearby apartment there was always someone spying on you. We learned also that an ESA officer had warned many people against being seen with you. And obviously there would have been no need of this: on your return from Crete, a kind of void was created around you. Those who came to see you could be counted now on one hand, and also those who invited you to supper or to their homes. Even your most assiduous vamps kept clear now, and the fans, the self-styled friends who had invented a thousand excuses to see you—"I'd like to but I can't, I've a family, you understand."

"Someone has to go and see if it's ready. Have you called to ask if it's ready? Ask again if it's ready." Like a peasant praying for rain on his fields parched by the sun and examining the sky at every breath of wind, seeking a cloud that signals the end of the drought, you waited for the moment when the passport office would say to you: "Here it is, have a nice trip." With the same feelings, intensified, however, by my eagerness to reenter my world, return to my life, my work, I longed for the moment when the plane would rise from the Athens runway and tear me away from that barrage of troubles, violent emotions, constant alarms, dramas alternating only with an inanimate idleness. The idleness of soldiers who between battles don't know how to spend their time and, unable to fill those intervals of peace, lie there yawning, homesick for cannon fire. Everything was hateful to me by now: the Levantine atmosphere of that city that reminded me of Tel Aviv or Beirut, no longer West but not yet East, its squalid, stupidly modern buildings, its hills without green, rocks and stumps of trees carbonized by neglect and ignorance, its Turkish habits, coffee served in dolls' cups with a gulp of muck at the end, the afternoon nap that until six in the evening paralyzes everyone in a cataleptic laziness, and finally the stupidity, the resignation with which the majority submitted to the tyranny. The age-old stupidity, the age-old resignation, to be sure, the same that, when required, is in each of us—I want to but I can't, I've a family, you understand—and which, still, when you come up against it, when you see it in others, drives you crazy. And the squalor of that house whose only pleasant feature was the garden of orange and lemon trees, but you wouldn't go into the garden because of that character spying on us from the window, so we were always shut up in the ugly rooms where the glass doors erased the very idea of privacy, every room had at least two doors, some had three: through that glass you felt always a pair of eyes staring, barbarous and irritated, maternal. And the little nuisances which, as the enchantment of a love at its beginnings had lifted and adjustment was exhausted, you realize you can't bear: the stink of the chicken coop behind the kitchen, the hens that deafened us during the day with their clucking, the cock that at sunrise shattered our eardrums with his crowing. I hated that cock whose ancestor, embalmed, dominated the dining room with his glass eyes and wax crest. To look at him make me repeat, like you: "Someone must go and see if it's ready. Have you called to ask if it's ready? Ask again if it's ready."

In the hope of hurrying things up, knowing your

telephone was tapped, I devoted myself to tricks, such as calling New York and pretending that a group of American universities had invited you to give a series of lectures. A friend in cahoots with me played the role of literary agent assigned to expediting your departure, and when I didn't telephone him, he would telephone me, protesting because the date was approaching and they had to print the posters, send out the invitations, inform the newspapers, reassure the faculties as well as the mayors of the various cities that would be giving dinners in your honor. When it wasn't a question of a lecture series, it was an honorary degree that in your infinite modesty you hesitated to accept and then accepted, but how to solve the problem of the passport? The passport didn't exist, they hadn't given it to you yet, I would answer with a sigh, and then angry voices would call also from Chicago, Boston, Philadelphia, passing themselves off as university presidents, city officials, leaders of the Democratic or Republican parties, other friends roaring their indignation. In short, it was already serious that the Greek authorities should create problems for American culture by having your lecture postponed, but for these same authorities to insult American culture by causing your absence from the honorary degree ceremony was an outrage, only in Russia did such shameful things occur; if the passport weren't given you and in plenty of time, the senators would raise an international scandal. Which senators, which universities, which degree we never specified for fear that the secret services would check: but the thing became more and more credible, and two years later we were to learn that it had affected Papadopoulos's decisions. "The matter of the American senators worried his advisers quite a lot," a secret service official was to confide to you. And obviously my stratagem didn't amuse you at all, it depressed you, in fact, caused you fits of dejection and the more I telephoned the angrier you became; you cursed yourself, saying that giving up the yacht plan had been idiocy, that you weren't going to wait for any passport, that if they gave it to you, you would reject it and would escape to Yugoslavia: if you caught a bullet in your head, all the better. The worst crisis came on the night you announced that before noon you would take a train for Ezvonoi, and it was then that your mother made an armistice with the saints that had been rejected in favor of Saint Phanourious. Lighting candles to all of them, promising perpetual devotion to all of them, she swore that if you were given a passport she wouldn't reproach them anymore. And one was moved, and granted her wish. At the break of dawn we were wakened by shuffling in the corridor: it was she, packing your bag. We asked her why and her answer was categorical: Saint Christopher, patron of travelers, had appeared to her in a dream. On his head he wore a crown of stars, his hand clenched a sword of fire, and his tunic shone so brightly that just thinking about it made her eyes smart. Raising his sword of fire, Saint Christopher smiled at her and then revealed that the passport was ready: you could collect it when the offices opened and leave the country before sunset. We shrugged. If Saint Phanourious had been right about the birth certificate, why should Saint Christopher be any less efficient? "Let's go." We went, the passport was really there. And as you snatched it with greedy fingers, your only remark was: "What time is it?" "Nine thirty." "When is there a plane for Rome?" "At two in the afternoon." "Will you go and buy the ticket?" "Yes. One-way?" "No. Round-trip."

I felt light as a bird gliding through open space, and every ugliness seemed to me forgotten. Every nausea, every anxiety. Tomorrow had the colors of the rainbow. I smiled, running under that rainbow, and people turned in amazement to look at me; but as soon as I had the ticket in my hand all this vanished. It was a simple ticket, a rectangular cardboard with the name of the line, and yet touching it filled me with a mysterious uneasiness: the indefinable anguish of the day I landed in Athens to meet you. Why? Was it the color perhaps? The color was apple green, the same apple green of the tins of Golden Virginia tobacco. I tried not to think about it, I jumped into a taxi, telling myself that if you live with superstitious people you acquire superstitions, the taxi headed swiftly for the Vouliagmeni Road and for a few minutes I was happy again. Then I reached the Vouliagmeni Road, I was outside the garage with the Texaco sign, the black pit that went down into darkness, and the mysterious uneasiness reappeared. The indefinable anguish. Why was I so hot? Could it possibly be so hot in October? Maybe I was getting a fever, I was tired. The crisis during the night with the threat of your going to Ezvonoi, the early waking caused by Saint Christopher, the unexpected delivery of the passport, the sudden departure: as usual, too many emotions at once. And with this diagnosis I stifled my questions, entered the house, handed you the ticket: "Here it is."

"They don't want to let us leave." Your voice was a hiss heavy with outrage. "What makes you say that?" "I smell the stink of garlic. There must be at least twenty police around us." I looked around but saw nothing that justified this statement. The airport waiting room looked the same as always, dozing travelers sprawled in the chairs, children running back and forth disturbing everyone, tourist groups buying souvenirs, and nobody resembling a plainclothes cop. Garlic or not, plainclothesmen have something that never eludes a practiced eye. Something concentrated in the face at once blank and shrewd, and the eyes, empty but alert. You feel those eyes on you even if you turn your back on them, as if they were hands pressing on your nape. And if you turn, seek them, they slip away, falsely distracted, then they return cautiously, passing over you with indifference, as if you were a negligible object, simply an obstacle in the path of their gaze, but there is always a moment when they give up the farce and stare at you with the foolish and malign arrogance of the man holding the stick, the man who believes himself powerful because he serves Power. "I don't see them, Alekos." "Haven't you learned how to recognize them yet? That man's a plainclothes cop. And that one. And that one. And that." "How can you tell?!" "By their shoes. They all wear shoes with laces. Including the kid in blue jeans." I examined the ones you had pointed out. They had the innocent, absent look of people minding their own business, and they were all wearing shoes with laces. "You're right, but I don't understand how they could prevent us from leaving. We've already gone through passport control and we have our boarding passes: if they had wanted to stop us, they would have done it earlier." "Earlier there were the reporters." This was also true. The news of your departure had reached the papers immediately, and up to passport control, we had been protected by reporters taking our picture, asking us questions, recording every detail: if the police had stopped us earlier in front of such witnesses, there would have been a lot of publicity. "Yes, but I still don't understand how they could prevent us, Alekos." "You'll understand very soon." And as you were saying this, the loudspeaker announced the Rome flight was ready for boarding, departing passengers would please leave through gate number two. We headed that way. We got in line. We were at gate number two. We held out our boarding passes. A frightened hostess pushed us back. "No, you, no." "Us no? Why not?" "Stand back." "Back? Why back?" And again I held out our boarding passes to her. In a flash the characters with the laced shoes stepped forward, and hands in their pockets, lips clenched, they surrounded us in a ring: deaf to my protests. "We've already completed the formalities! Our documents are in order!" Silence. "We have a right to board the plane!" Silence. "We have a right to know why we're being kept off it!" Silence. "I'm a foreign citizen: if we miss the plane I'll inform my embassy and my government!" Silence. Then your voice, that hiss charged with outrage. "Don't argue. Never argue with shit. Den sizitas. Den sizitas me skata." A policeman took his hand from his pocket and was about to fling himself on you. "Watch out, Alekos!" But there was no need to warn you: an extraordinary control made you stiffen, an iciness like the calm that had saved us on the road to Herakleion when we were struck by the blue automobile. "What are we to do, Alekos?" "There is nothing to do except see who wins: Ioannidis or Papadopoulos." The frightened hostess, meanwhile, continued collecting the boarding passes of the other passengers, who filed in front of us, uninterested or neutral. In the space of five minutes we were the only ones left, locked in the mute circle of laced shoes.

Five minutes, ten, fifteen, twenty. And each minute a stiletto stab in the heart, the torment of Tantalus dying of thirst and holding his mouth to the spring where the water vanishes at the very moment he is about to take a sip of it. The plane was there, a few meters away, it was almost in front of gate number two, visible beyond the glass, the plane's door was still open and the gangway still attached: we had only to cross that threshold, walk those few meters, climb on board and we would be safe. But no, not you. An airline official came by. I stopped him, asked him if the captain was keeping the gangway attached and the door open to wait for us. He whispered yes, but nobody knew how long he could hold out. I asked him if the veto on our boarding was final. Again he answered in a whisper, no, telephone calls were flying back and forth, they were quarreling among themselves, then surprised by his own boldness, he went off. Twenty minutes, twenty-five, thirty. The official reappeared. "Be ready. They're talking with the president of the Republic. If they give us authorization, we'll have you board at once and forestall any countermands." "Countermands?" "There've been three already. One moment!" His walkie-talkie was flashing. I saw him raise it to his ear, nod, head for the police, argue with them with an I'm-only-following-orders tone, then he came back to us, his face flushed, he seized our boarding passes, and murmured: "Hurry up! Go!" And almost without our realizing it we found ourselves on the plane: watching the steward seal the door. "We've made it, Alekos!" "Maybe." "Why maybe?" "Because he still hasn't turned on the engines." He really hadn't turned them on, and he didn't. Why not? As we waited, as we wondered, time started passing, dripping slowly. Five minutes, ten. Ten minutes, fifteen. Fifteen minutes, twenty. Twenty minutes, twenty-five. The air conditioning wasn't working, people began grumbling: "Enough of this! It's an outrage!" Twenty-five minutes, thirty. Thirty minutes, thirty-five. Thirty-five minutes, forty. Had the countermand come? It surely had. From the window we could make out two policemen busy arguing with the official who had made us board in such haste, and he was holding out his arms, as if to say, terribly sorry. I pressed your hand. It was so sweaty that it slipped through mine. Your whole body was pouring sweat. Huge drops trickled down from your brow, your temples, your chin, and soaking through your shirt, they spread damp stains on your jacket. Was it the heat or the tension that your apparent self-control was hiding? You couldn't even manage to speak. "It'll leave now, Alekos, you'll see." "Uhm!" "They won't dare take you off." "Uhm!" "It would really be a scandal." "Uhm!" Suddenly, with a glorious explosion, the engines roared, the plane moved, glided lightly away, reached the runway, where it stopped, with a shudder that grew. And grew, and grew, to become thunder. And thundering, the plane was launched on its race, it rose to plunge into the great blue sky. Immediately Athens was a geography of minuscule houses, trees as tiny as heads of pins, a gray stain, the memory of an August night with the scent of jasmine. You heaved a great sigh and said grimly: "Once I buggered a general." "What?!" I stammered. "And I don't regret it. I'm only sorry I never told Ioannidis." Then you slumped back, closing your eyes.

When you opened them again, we were flying over the gulf of Corinth. You raised the glass of champagne the hostess had brought and recited: "I have earned a life / a ticket for death / and I voyage still / At certain moments / I have thought I had arrived / at the end of the voyage / I was wrong / They were only unexpected events / along the way." "It sounds like a poem," I said. "It is. An old poem written in Boiati two years ago, when the deadline for shooting me had expired. They had three years to do it in." "But the poem's sad!" "Every postponement is sad when you know it's a postponement." Two fighter planes arrived, black and disturbing as two insects. For about a minute they remained at the side of our plane, maintaining the same altitude and the same speed, as if they were there to escort us, then they veered to the left, leaving two ribbons of white smoke, like two gigantic question marks, and they turned back. But by now the tension had vanished, and drunk on the champagne, forgetting the sad poem, you had found yourself again. Armed resistance on the mountains, attacks on the barracks, radio stations to stir the people to revolt: the thousand plans that you could carry out in Europe. I couldn't hush you. At a certain point, however, it was only the sound of your beautiful voice, and the word "postponement" took the place of what you were saying: clarifying the mysterious uneasiness, the indefinable anguish that had gripped me at the sight of the apple green ticket. Postponement, postponement. Nothing was going to change in Italy, in Europe. You wouldn't suffer less, you wouldn't risk less. You had said it clearly that afternoon after the trip to Crete: "I will always make everyone uncomfortable, in whatever country, at whatever moment, under whatever regime." Wherever you went you would remain that plant that defies cataloging, that is born to bring disorder into the forest and therefore must be uprooted, extirpated. Here or there, they would eliminate you, in the end. And not for what you wanted to do, armed resistance on the mountains, attacks on the barracks, radio stations to stir the people to revolt, but for what you were, for your singularity, the rebel poet, free of any restraint, any pattern, any taboo, even from the concept of licit and illicit, because of your uniqueness as solitary hero, clinging to the chimeras of the dream, the imagination. The rebel poet, the solitary hero, is an individual without followers: he doesn't sweep the masses into the streets, he doesn't provoke revolutions. But he paves the way for them. Even if he doesn't achieve anything immediate and practical, even if he expresses himself through acts of bravado or madness, even if he is despised and rejected, he stirs the waters of the silent, stagnant pond, he weakens the dams of repressive conformity, he saps the crushing power. Whatever he says or undertakes, even an interrupted sentence, a failed enterprise, becomes a seed destined to blossom, a perfume that hangs in the air, an example for the other plants in the forest, for us who haven't his courage and his clairvoyance and his genius. And the pond knows it, the Power knows that he is its real enemy, the real danger to be liquidated. It even knows that he cannot be replaced or copied: the history of the world has given us clear proof that when one leader dies another is invented, when one man of action dies another is found. But when a poet is dead, a hero is eliminated, there is a void that cannot be filled and you have to wait until the gods resurrect him. The gods know where, the gods know when.

So taking you away from Greece was useless and that escape was truly a postponement. A desperate attempt to keep you alive for as long as possible.

PART THREE

1

The tragedy of a man condemned to be a poet, a hero, and thus to be crucified, can be measured also by the incomprehension of anyone who, out of love, would like to rescue him from his fate and his role: to try to rescue him by distracting him with the wiles of tenderness, the lures of luxury, the mirage of a victory attainable through a well-earned rest. One who loves him, in fact, is not willing to hand him over to death; and to save his life, to prolong it a little, the one who loves him will exploit any weapon, any stratagem. In this sense no one would ever understand you less than I, no one more than I would attempt to rescue you from your fate and your role. And especially on our arrival in Italy, when I wasn't yet resigned to the fact that perpetual defiance was your food, constant danger your drink. You understood it the moment we were in the suite of the hotel I had chosen in Rome, and you did nothing to hide from me the fact you had understood. You entered, you examined carefully the three rooms, the balcony overlooking Via Veneto, the elegant furniture, the expensive carpets, the crystal chandeliers, then you stopped at the lovely basket of flowers that stood on the table next to a bowl of fruit and an ice bucket with wine, and you asked: "Are the flowers for you or for me?" "For you." "Is the fruit for you or for me?" "For you." "Is the wine for you or for me?" "For you. It's all for you, Alekos." "Uhm. I see." A great silence followed. Heavy, immobile. And in that silence you sat down, loaded your pipe, lighted it, and spoke finally in a voice brimming with sadness. "You know, one night in Boiati I had a dream. I dreamed I was in a hotel exactly like this. The same furniture, carpets, chandeliers, balcony. Yes, there was also a balcony. And the basket of flowers, the bowl of fruit, the bottle of wine. And the woman who had brought me there was saying: 'For you. It's all for you, Alekos.' But I felt unhappy. It wasn't very clear at the beginning why I felt unhappy: the hotel was beautiful and I liked it very much. But soon it did become clear: I felt unhappy because I had handcuffs on. Strange. When I had lain down to sleep, Zakarakis had taken them off me. In the dream, however, they were still there, and they were tight. They were so tight that I wasn't able to open the bottle. At a certain point it fell on the floor and broke. Then I ran out of the hotel, shouting: 'Skata, shit, skata!' And I came back into my cell, where I didn't have handcuffs." I smiled and handed you the bottle from the bucket: "Open it. It won't fall today." You took it, you raised it level with your head and dropped it on the parquet floor where it shattered, with a crash. "Skata! Shit! Skata!"

The tragedy of a man condemned to be a creature who cannot be cataloged, and hence is alien to the phenomenology of the time in which he lives, is measured moreover by the involuntary cruelty of anyone who confers on him a personality that is not his and consequently bestows on him advice, criticism, warnings, thoughtful questions that make him suffer. One who looks at him, in fact, hasn't the slightest idea of his true nature and sees him only through the tried-and-true formulas: the clichés that out of expedience or bad faith or laziness were used to create his portrait. In turn the portrait of the dynamiter, the martyr, the revolutionary, the leader. In that sense no one would ever be as cruel as those who in the first hours of your arrival in Rome fell on you with kisses, embraces, welcomes. Curious, they were often people to whom you didn't matter at all, who sought you out only because you were an acquaintance to boast of, or else demagogues who considered themselves your creditors because at the time of the trial they had organized a public meeting or had participated in a protest rally. Rarely people who were truly fond of you, friends from the time spent in Italy, companions. However, even these saw you through those formulas, those clichés. Advice to the martyr: "Enough sacrifices now, enough hardship. You must take a long rest, a real vacation, and not think of anything: you've done your part. Eat, drink, sleep, amuse yourself. To hell with politics, you surely didn't come here to be bored with politics? Tomorrow we'll organize a big party." Warnings to the dynamiter: "Be careful whom you see, be careful whom you speak to, don't get involved with the wrong group, and the next time don't use mines, mines are tricky. And besides they're heavy, awkward, better the plastic the Palestinians use. You should go to Lebanon and train for a while with the Palestinians." Criticism of the revolutionary: "What a handsome tie, what a beautiful shirt. You do yourself proud, eh? By the way, why are you staying in this hotel? It isn't the right place for you, it's where movie stars stay, and Kissinger and the shah of Iran. What will the working classes think, what will the people think? You must leave it at once. Come to my house, we'll make up a cot in the corridor." Questions to the leader: "What do you plan to do, what is your program, how do you propose to reach the masses? You must clarify your ideological position, you must realize that fighting a dictatorship isn't enough, insisting on the problem of freedom isn't enough. Why don't you hold a press conference? Why don't you write an essay?" And not one bothered to ask you what you had come to do, what you were looking for. Suddenly you lost control. You were listening to one of those with the picture of the revolutionary who has to sleep on the cot in the corridor—This is a palace, you can't stay in a palace like this, you're forgetting who you are, what you represent—and the patience with which you had suffered him, in silence or mumbling meager monosyllables, turned into a scene. Why didn't they all lay off, why didn't they stop cutting off your balls, you would stay in your palace as long as you liked, and you would buy yourself twenty-four silk shirts, twenty-four English raincoats, twenty-four pairs of shoes with buckles: now get out! But then, immediately afterward, you burst into tears so desperate that I even forgot the bottle deliberately broken and the cry, Skata, shit, skata. "I'm leaving," you sobbed, "I'm leaving, I'm going back to Athens, let's go back to Athens."

The tragedy of a man condemned to be alone because he makes everybody uncomfortable and serves nobody is measured finally by the desert he has to face when he emerges from his natural environment, politics seen as dream, and enters an environment that is unnatural for him, which is politics understood as profession or religious sect. This you were to understand completely eleven months later on going back to your country; however, your apprenticeship took place on your arrival in Italy. Fatuous types led only by the search for their own triumph, careerists concerned only with the personal advantages of a seat in Parliament, tradesmen concerned only with filling their pockets with tips, decrepit leftovers sealed in the sarcophagi of their extinct virtues, the best of them grouchy witch doctors, perched on the grim tower of dogma; on the other side the adventurers of easy disobedience, the worshipers of bloody fanaticism, the frauds for whom the word revolution is a chewing gum to be kept in the mouth, a pretext for fighting ennui, a substitute for the Foreign Legion. This is the political landscape that greeted you when, overcoming the shock of feeling yourself handcuffed by me and exploited by the others, you went looking for help to continue resistance against the junta. Like discussing the immortality of the soul with a bunch of deaf-mutes. Yet you tried. You got on the telephone and began calling the leaders of the parties that had inspired some hope in you: Socialists, Communists, Republicans, left-wing Catholics. "Hello, this is Panagoulis." "Who?" "Panagoulis. Alexander Panagoulis. Alekos. I'd like to speak with Comrade So-and-So." "What about?" "Well . . . I . . . I'd like . . . to say hello to him." "He's not here; he's in a meeting. Try tomorrow. No, tomorrow is a holiday, there's a long weekend. In a few days." "Hello, this is Panagoulis." "Taragoulis?" "No, Panagoulis, Alexander Panagoulis, Alekos. I'd like to speak with Deputy So-and-So." "You mean with His Excellency the Minister!" "Ah, I didn't know. Yes, His Excellency the Minister." "His Excellency the Minister can't be disturbed." "Then I'll leave him a message, to please call me as soon as he can." "See here, His Excellency the Minister has important things to do, very grave problems. If he had to call back all the people who call him!" "Hello, this is Panagoulis." "Speak up, can't hear a thing. Who are you?" "Panagoulis, Alexander Panagoulis." "Are you a comrade?" "Yes—" "Are you Russian? I can hear an accent." "No, I'm Greek." "And what do you want?" "I'd like to speak with the party secretary-general." "Ah, but if you're Greek, you have to go by the foreign affairs office." Either they had someone say they weren't in, or they told you they were very busy solving the problems of the human race, or they passed you on to assistants of their assistants. Which produced nothing except some very affectionate slaps on the back—Dear Alekos, dear Alexander, what joy to see you again, what an honor to meet you. But in the depths of their eyes a kind of question mark flickered—What'll I do with this character, how can I use him? As long as you were a man under threat of being shot, sentenced to life imprisonment, a man in chains, you suited them beautifully: you offered them an excuse to do their international commitment act, stir up a bit of fuss. Now that you were free, well-fed, well-housed, what could they do with you? And besides, what did you want? Why did you ask to meet the chiefs? Better spare them this nuisance, steer clear of you, tire you with waiting to be received. The only ones who would listen to you in those days were three old men.

The first was Ferruccio Parri, the man who had led the Resistance in northern Italy. Speaking to him did you good, it lifted you in a high tide that swamped your disappointments, drowned the refrain "Tomorrow I go back to Athens, I want to go back to Athens, let's go back to Athens." In fact a deep understanding was to develop between the two of you, which was strange considering the age difference: later you would never tire of telling about the day you met him. He frightened you at first because you couldn't see his face. Parri was eighty-three years old at that time, age and a disease of the spinal column bent him double like a pine twisted by the wind, and even if he stood up, all you could see of him was a pair of black trousers, a black jacket, a tangle of wavy ivory-colored hair. No face. With the humor of the old who enjoy making fun of themselves, he exacerbated this infirmity, crumpling himself more than necessary, delaying more than necessary the moment he would finally raise his head, finally show his face. White, thin, accented by absurdly brown moustache and eyebrows, and illuminated by eyes that were flares of sarcasm, the stings of a spiteful elf. That day he had behaved as usual. But immediately the sarcasm melted into sweetness, and as the fleshless hands were lifted to stroke your cheeks, your chin, your mouth, he exclaimed: "My boy, my boy. You were right to leave Greece, you were absolutely right. Now you can really organize the struggle, start again at the beginning. Sit down, my boy, sit down here beside me: I have so many things to ask you. The first is: What can I do for you? You need help, I know, you're so alone." Speaking with the second old man also did you good, Sandro Pertini, then president of the Parliament. With him too you were to establish an understanding that would last until your death, and you would often tell of the comfort you felt when he sprang to his feet to come to meet you: small and wiry, nervous, strangely like you in his bursts of joyousness and his sudden ill-humor, identical also in his way of holding and smoking a pipe. "Bravo, Alekos, bravo. You made a wise decision in settling in Italy, we'll find a way to lend you a hand in making armed resistance. I too, after having been so many years in prison, did the same. Armed resistance, yes, there's no other way." He talked and talked. He encouraged you and encouraged you. And the high tide swelled and swelled. Then there was the meeting with the third old man, Pietro Nenni. We went to see him at his house in Formia, and the tide suddenly sank, waking you, leaving on the beach of your consciousness dead fish, dry seaweed, tar. Flotsam, reality.

I can still see him as he examines you from behind his thick, near-sighted glasses, not a muscle moving to stir the cobweb of wrinkles that spreads from the leathery face to the great bald head, motionless and inaccessible as the mummy of a pharaoh, disenchanted as an ancient sage who is no longer surprised by anything because he has seen everything, now knows everything, and perhaps no longer believes in anything. He received you with a long embrace and a hoarse sound: "Alessandro." He kissed you twice, moved, but immediately he sat on the high-backed chair, a kind of throne, and began studying you with the coldness of a scientist examining a specimen under the microscope. He doesn't mention the past, what you have suffered, he doesn't say it's a good or bad thing for you to have left Greece, he asks you practical and specific questions. How long will Papadopoulos last? How much time will it take Ioannidis to defenestrate him? Will a change of guard be for the better or for the worse? What is the percentage of officers supporting the junta? You are facing him, sunk in a too-soft divan, which embarrasses you, and you answer him, weighing each word, but without enthusiasm. You have no desire to convey news, you want to shift the conversation in the direction that is urgent for you, and in the end you succeed: "Armed resistance is the only way to defeat the junta." "Armed resistance?" Nenni repeats. He knows armed resistance is impossible, but he also knows it would be useless to tell you that, so he is silent and listens to you, continuing to study you. He seems to be pursuing a thought, an idea that eludes him, then suddenly he brightens and exclaims, to me: "He reminds me of a boy from Turin I loved very much, a socialist who died in the Spanish Civil War. His name was Fernando De Rosa. Actually he was more an anarchist than a socialist. Just like him. Like him, he made an unsuccessful assassination attempt, on Prince Umberto di Savoia, when Umberto went to Brussels to be engaged to Maria José. He shot at him and missed. Then he came to Spain, joined the brigades, and went to the front: straight to the front. He died almost immediately: a bullet in his head. It was 1936. Yes, he resembles De Rosa, though De Rosa was blond and had blue eyes. The same dreamy, touchy manner, the same impatience. And the same courage, the same purity." A murmur, as the scar on your left cheekbone becomes inflamed and a purplish flush burns your ears: "What's he saying?!" "He's saying that you look like Fernando De Rosa, a socialist or rather an anarchist who died in the Spanish war. He loved him very much." "Anarchist?" I sense that you want to say something in rebuttal, but the grand old man goes on talking: of utopia, of realism, of doubt. The doubt that assails us, for example, when we wonder if the men like you and like De Rosa are right or whether it's those like him, who act in the name of common sense and sweet reason; that doubt that torments us when intelligence poisons the optimism of the will, and we realize that men do not correspond to the idea of man, that people do not correspond to the idea of the people, that socialism does not correspond to the idea of socialism, and we discover that being rational means being pessimists. Here he stops and says: "But you will have time to ponder these things too, now that you are in exile. By the way, I too was in exile during the period of fascism, you know. Thirteen years! In exile in Paris and in the south of France, in the Auvergne."

It was the first time that someone had used the word exile in speaking to you. Nobody had uttered it in those days. Exile. Nobody had summed up with such clarity, such candor, the reality of your presence in Italy. Exile. And there was no concept or noun that you loathed more. Exile. Secretly I sought your eyes. They were clouded with grief, humiliation, anger: isolated in yourself, wounded, you weren't even listening to the names and addresses Nenni was giving you. People who would help you: at least so he hoped. And almost at once you muttered that it was late, we had to leave. We left. For the entire return trip to Rome you slept. Or did you pretend to sleep? Because when we arrived at the hotel you suddenly raised your eyelids, quickly got out of the car and ran to the elevator, and five minutes later a howl shook the three rooms: "My ticket!" I ran into the bedroom: all our clothes were flung on the floor, on the chairs, on the bed; every jacket, every pair of trousers had its pockets inside out. My bags had also been opened, and my papers scattered everywhere: it was as if a cyclone had gone by. I looked at you, dumbfounded. "Ticket? What ticket?" My ticket back! It was round-trip, wasn't it?" "Yes, it was round-trip. Why?" "Because I've lost my ticket back! Where is it?!" "Calm down, you can't have lost it. You had it in your wallet, and it was such a tight fit that it couldn't have slipped out. Look more carefully. We'll look together." "I've looked, everywhere! It's not there!" "Don't worry, you'll find it. Anyway for the moment you don't need it, you don't have to rush to Athens." "What did you say?" "I said for the moment you don't need it, that you don't have to rush to Athens." "I understand! You took it! You stole it from me! You stole my return ticket! To keep me from leaving! To keep me here in exile! You want me to stay in exile! In exile!" "I didn't steal anything. If you've lost your ticket you simply inform the airline and have them give you a copy. I'm not keeping you in exile, you're free to leave, right away if you like." Then, outraged, I locked myself in the other room and it wasn't until morning that I realized you hadn't gone to bed. You had slept on the floor in your clothes. "Because that's how a man sleeps when he's in exile and not on vacation. Or rather a man who is tired of himself, who needs to find himself again." You seemed penitent, crushed. I forgave you. But that ticket was never found again and I was never to know whether you had really lost it or whether you had staged a histrionic scene, perhaps after having destroyed it, to stifle the impulse to run to the airport and return immediately to Athens. Something that, as usual, you partly wanted and partly didn't.

Tuscany is beautiful in autumn. You can walk along paths that smell of mushrooms and broom, listen to the voices of the wind calling from the hillocks edged with cypresses and firs, fish for eels in the gullies where the stream rolls over stones slippery with moss, hunt hare and pheasant in the underbrush of red heather, and it is the time of the vintage, the grapes swell and turn violet among the thick leaves, the figs hang sweet from the branches that quiver with chaffinches and larks, in the woods the leaves turn yellow and orange burning the green monotony of the summer. If you feel tired of yourself and need to find yourself again, wash away your doubts, there is no better place than Tuscany in autumn: let's go to Tuscany, I said to you. Come, and the old house on the hill had never been so enchanting as it was that autumn. The ivy bound it in flames of red that climbed to the windows of the third floor and the battlements of the tower, the rosebushes blossomed unexpectedly in a springlike jubilation, and the wisteria from the railing of the terrace burst in cascades of tender blue. The arbutus also bloomed outside the chapel, deep red berries that the greedy blackbirds fell upon, and in the pond the water lilies floated, white, proud. But you cast an indifferent look and then shut yourself up in a confinement that barred any interest or curiosity. For days and days you hardly went out. You never ventured among the rows of vines to pick a grape, you never went to the woods to breathe the air scented with broom and to admire the landscape from the brow of the hill. Only once you stirred thirty meters beyond the gate to discover, surprised, that chestnuts ripen in a hull all bristling with spikes and walnuts in a husk, called *mallo* in Italian, and another time you went down into the garden to see, with horror, that in the lily pond there were fish and to ask if there were dead in the chapel. But the detail that most dismayed me was something else: though the house was very big, full of stairs, doors to open, rooms to discover, objects to examine, books to read, you stayed always in the same room, dozing with the shutters closed and the electric light on. When you weren't dozing, you would walk up and down, up and down, the usual three steps forward and three steps back, or else you would toy with your koboloi, or listen to music, vacillating in a lethargy. "Do you feel ill, Alekos?" "Me? No." "Then why don't you go out, why do you always keep the shutters closed and the electric light on? Turn out the lamps, let the sun in!" "No, not the sun. It disturbs me, it distracts me." "But you need distraction! Come on, let's take a walk." "No, no walk, it tires me. Let's stay here, come here, beside me." "But, Alekos, living like this is the same as living in prison!" "That's why I like it. Haven't I ever told you how free a man is in prison? Idleness allows him to meditate as much as he likes, isolation allows him to cry or belch or scratch himself as much as he wants; in the outside world he can meditate only in the intervals that the others allow him. And crying is weakness, belching is rude, scratching yourself vulgar." "So this is what you do in here: cry, belch, and scratch yourself?" "No. Here I work." "You work? What work?" "I think." "You don't think. You sleep." "You're wrong."

I couldn't even make you angry. Like clouds swept away by a sudden wind, your irritability had vanished, and the crises of anguish, the attacks of rage. In their place hung a kind of indifference, or a calm laziness that seemed to me indifference, and you emerged from it only at specific intervals at specific stimuli. You emerged at the dinner or supper hour when you sat at the table and ate with appetite, drank with gusto, and even joked. "Let's sing together: 'Ah, if the sea were wine and the mountains were cheese!' " Or else when you peered through the cracks in the windows looking for Lillo, a black rebellious mongrel, and you discovered he was on a chain, and you rushed to free him. "Not even a dog should be humiliated with chains! Go on, Lillo, run away." Or else after supper when you tried to remember the poems you had preserved in Boiati by storing them in your memory, and tense with the effort, your eyes half-closed, your brow furrowed, you pursued them like fireflies throbbing in the darkness. In fact, as soon as a verse came back to your mind, you yelled with the joy of a child who has caught a firefly in the darkness: "I've got it, I've got it!" Afterward we would translate them, quarreling because you insisted on using Italian words that don't exist—This word doesn't exist, if it doesn't exist I'll invent it—and the quarrel would degenerate into little brawls that were appeased in the night when you sought me under the quilt. But these too were sparks stolen from the ash of inertia, and in the morning the apathetic lazing in bed began again, the indolent shuffling around the room with the shutters closed and the electric light burning. "Open the windows at least, let the sun in!" "No." "Go outside, move about a little!" "No." "Do you want a book, do you want to read?" "No." "But what are you doing here in the darkness?" "I'm working." "What work?" "I'm thinking." "You're not thinking. You're sleeping!" "You're wrong." Until, in the end, my bewilderment faded into indifference, I went off telling myself I couldn't dedicate every minute of my existence to the analysis of your metamorphoses and your eccentricities, and besides I really was working in furious haste. I was finishing a book I had interrupted to go to Athens, and it was hard for me to accept the notion that idleness nourishes talent. At times, however, I was worried because I noticed some alarming things: the poems that you fished up from the well of memory were almost all poems about death. As if that weren't enough, there was also a song that haunted you, a song full of vivacity and yet sad, with a refrain that seemed a sob, and you never tired of listening to it: your lips curled in a grimace that could have been ironic or pained. When I asked you why you like it so much, you answered: "Because it says something I mustn't forget." "What?" "I zoi ine micri. Poli, poli, poli micri. Life is short. Very very very short." Even your solidarity with Lillo was a death pact. I was convinced of that the day he was almost run over because you had set him free, and there was that quarrel between us: "Why did you turn him loose?! I don't keep him on a chain to be cruel! Can't you see he hates cars and when he's loose he chases them and tries to bite them? You want him to be run over, killed by a car?!" You answered: "If he wants to be run over by a car and be killed, that's his right. You can't deny him that right. Love isn't putting chains on someone who wants to struggle and is ready to die for it, love is letting him die in the way he's chosen. That's another truth you can't manage to understand." Then you turned on your heels and with slow, heavy steps you went up to the tower and stayed there until late listening to the silence sung by the crickets. Like a mystic transported in contemplation of the self.

Yet Athens was burning in those days. And you knew it. The very week we went to the country, thousands of demonstrators had marched in the streets and squares of the city shouting, "Down with the tyrants! Down with Papadopoulos!" Near the temple of Zeus the clashes with the police had been very violent: stones, Molotov cocktails. The police had fired and dozens of protesters had been wounded, dozens and dozens arrested; more trials were in the offing, more sentences. You also knew that the demonstrators had shouted your name, finally using it without fear. So why were you staying there like a sphinx, motionless, listening to the silence sung by the crickets like a mystic transported in contemplation of the self? Why did you retire in that gloomy isolation from which you stirred only to love me under the quilt or to remind me that life is short, very very very short? Were you preparing to tear off the leash with which I had bound you to prevent you from being run over, or was your spirit so tired that you could accept the chains and not react even to the summons of those fighting and calling your name? An answer had to be found, or rather someone to whom you could confide it. And just then, with the inexplicable logic that often unties the knots of life, someone came to the house on the top of the hill, a man of fifty with a gentle and alert face, a polite and articulate manner, with something reassuring in his eyes, steeped in patience and perhaps kindness. His name was Nicholas, and in your Polytechnic days, when you had been seized by your political passion, he was the one who had first experienced the seduction of your personality, giving you assignments in the Young Socialists Front of which he was president. He was the one who had come to see you in Italy after you had left Cyprus with the fake passport given you by Georgazis, and it was he who, in the period when you were preparing the assassination attempt, had believed most in you, becoming your adviser, your protector, sharing hunger with you, embitterment, the waiting for the day when you would set the mines on the Sounion Road. You had spoken to me about him many times, each time with a respect approaching deference, even if you enjoyed underlining his aversion to risk and his fussy meticulousness, the white handkerchief folded to make three points, which peeped from the pocket of his blue jacket, and you always regretted being unable to see him because he was living in Zurich. "Nicholas is the only one I trust, because he's the only one who knows me." He came, then, and his arrival flung open the doors of your confinement, broke the dams of your indifference. Suddenly you went out walking in the fields, in the woods, you discovered a desire for the sun, and you were revived in a loquacity so torrential that the concern which had made me suffer disappeared. But when I asked him what you two were talking about, my knees went weak in fear.

"Madness. Pure, simple, genuine madness. Clandestine returns, attacks on barracks, armed resistance: alone. He says that here too nobody listens to him, nobody helps him, that only three old men would see him, and so he will do it all alone and if they kill him, what the hell. But with precise plans, worked out to the minutest detail!" "But when did he make them, Nicholas? Where?" "Where? In this house, in these days, when you thought he was dozing or toying with the koboloi. Instead he was really working, planning his madness with the meticulousness of a mathematician. That's his system, always has been." "I thought he was thinking about death: he always talked about death." "Of course. Each of those plans, carried out without a party, without an organization backing him, is suicide. And he knows it. The simple fact of returning to Greece would be suicide. They consider him the instigator of the uprisings and . . . they'd kill him like a dog." "Return to Greece? Now?" "Yes, he's got it into his head to go back on November 17, the anniversary of his death sentence." "Without telling me!" "Obviously." "In Athens he had no secrets from me." "In Athens he hadn't realized that you aim only at keeping him alive, keeping him safe. Now he's realized it, and the day he goes, he will catch you by surprise. He'll leave the house saying he's going to buy a pack of cigarettes and instead he'll go to Greece. Or else he'll start a quarrel so he can pretend to be offended, provide an excuse for going away, and . . . a few hours later he'll land in Greece with a fake passport." "He doesn't have one." "He'll find one, he'll find one." "Have you tried to dissuade him?" "Obviously. I reminded him that one lamb ready to sacrifice himself isn't enough, I've shown him the reasons why the present uprisings won't achieve anything and will be put down with bloodshed, I told him that history doesn't repeat itself and today his role is changed: it's to exploit his popularity and do things abroad. But if you advise him to do something, that's the very thing he won't do, and if you advise him not to do it, that's what he'll do, and dissuasion only makes him more stubborn. There's only one way to distract him from an idea: feed him another which he considers his own and which challenges him. How did you manage to get him to Italy?" "More or less like that." "Try again, get him set on something else, take him far away."

Distract you from an idea, get you set on something else, take you far away, as far as possible. Where? To the other side of the globe, to America! I'd do it, I told him. But when I said it, I didn't bear in mind one reality. There is one thing that the terrible Leviathan, the great monster, the self-elected champion of democracy, America, has in common with the tyrannies of right and of left. And this thing is the state, strong, arrogant, merciless, supported by its Manichaean laws, its crippling regulations, its pitiless interests, its fear or rather its hatred for the creatures who do not represent a mass, the individuals who don't match a specific card in its computer, a code of conformity, a religion. The solitary reprobates. The solitary reprobate cannot leave and cannot enter, he is not given a passport to leave the frontiers of tyranny, nor a visa to enter the frontiers of the great monster, self-elected champion of democracy. Precisely because he is solitary, because he does not have a party behind him, an ideology, and hence a power that guarantees him. Paradoxically, the dissidents who leave the Soviet Union are not solitary reprobates: behind them there are statistics, there is the doctrine of the opposing barricade; the payoff for Leviathan for whom they are barter goods, money to spend in the name of international equilibrium. I give you a Corvalan and you give me a Bukovsky. I'll return spy X or Y and you let me have a Solzhenitsyn. Not because I care about saving him personally, but because I can use his brain to show you are bad, his case is emblematic. But who backs a Don Quixote, who is of no use to any power, isn't convenient to any barricade, a nuisance to all, who doesn't belong to any conformism or organization, who goes out to set off a bomb in a taxi driven by a cousin, who acts only according to his own morality, his own imagination, his own mad dreams? What state guarantees for him, intervenes for him, what political group? Does he fit into the statistics, can he be used as barter goods, as money to spend in the name of international equilibrium? Since there can be no barter, you understand, the Leviathan would have to deal with him. And the Leviathan doesn't deal with individuals, in particular with individuals who have no file card. It deals with other states, other doctrines, other religions, on occasion with the parties that are states within the state. And so much the better if they are parties of the opposing barricade. If you're not at least a Communist, America doesn't want you. Communist or fascist or socialist or Buddhist, in other words an *ist* who obeys an established authority, a mass-man who can be cataloged, filed, predicted, traded, not an eccentric particle that represents only itself, that doesn't correspond to a precise form in the computer, so its gears jam in questioning him. Theodorakis fitted into America: he was a Communist, therefore cataloged and filed and guaranteed, and moreover a musician known to the crowds, therefore a weight to throw into the scales, so he was given permission to enter America. Without remembering all these things, without taking into consideration this reality, distracted moreover by the eternal illusion that the Leviathan is a basically kindly monster and never forgets that it was born from the rejected, from the solitary reprobates, I didn't even think they might refuse you a visa: the only problem I foresaw was making you apply for it.

"Alekos, I have to go to America. I'll be gone two or three weeks." "To America?! Two or three weeks?!" "Yes, I have to. Too bad you can't come with me. Not on a vacation, I mean: but to make contacts, look for support." "Support in America? With a president named Nixon and a secretary of state named Kissinger and a CIA that hands Chile over to Pinochet, that has Allende killed? Are you perhaps forgetting who helped Papadopoulos, who protects him, who has the greatest interest in keeping him where he is?" "No, Alekos, no, but America isn't all Nixon or Kissinger or the CIA: I know more civil disobedience protesters in America than in Europe. And you have to admit: a lot of new ideas are born there." "And die there sooner than anywhere else. Their disobedience doesn't count for anything, doesn't achieve anything, doesn't exercise the slightest influence on the decisions of the Nixons and the Kissingers and the CIA. It doesn't prevent unjust wars, sordid alliances, purges, witch-hunts." "I know, still some members of Congress behaved well when you were sentenced. And they persuaded Johnson to protest to Papadopoulos against your being shot." "Uhm!" "There are also lots of Greeks in America. Just think: seven hundred thousand in New York, seven hundred thousand in Chicago, three hundred thousand in San Francisco, at least two hundred thousand in Washington. Not to mention the other cities. There are more Greeks in America than in Italy, Germany, and Switzerland put together." "What of it? The Greeks in Italy, Germany, and Switzerland are still Greeks, they speak Greek, they care about Greece. The Greeks in America are Americans by now, they don't speak Greek and they don't care anything about Greece anymore." "You're wrong. They will speak Greek, even the young ones. The man who sells me flowers in New York is Greek and speaks Greek. The waiters in the restaurant next to the florist's are Greek and speak Greek. And if you were to come to America I'd introduce you to a lot of Greek students who speak Greek, who are enemies of the junta. And then I'd take you to the senators and the congressmen who went out on a limb for you. And to U Thant and to other friends at the UN. And you would talk in the universities. And on television—" "Sure, on American television they let someone like me talk!" "Why not? America is a country that receives anyone, including those who criticize it." "America is an elephant that can allow itself any luxury, even the luxury of tolerance. If you criticize it, it doesn't even feel a tickle, or if it does, it laughs as if you'd given it a pinch under the armpit. And there's also the fact that for America I don't represent a criticism, but an obstacle. I tried to kill one of their protégés, remember? When it comes to an obstacle, the elephant doesn't fool around: it tramples, it crushes." Well, I had brought you this far, now I only had to cast the real bait. I threw it out: "But would you go to America?" "Why?" "Because so many people can't conceive even the idea of going there, of knowing its culture, its people. To them it would seem a betrayal if they went there, and Manichaeism . . ." I felt a string vibrate. You frowned: "What does Manichaeism mean." "It means splitting the world in two, life in two: good on one side and evil on the other, beautiful on one side and ugly on the other. Black and white, in other words." "Uhm. Fanatics." "Yes." "Dogmatism." "Yes." "You're surely not implying I'm one of them?" "No, but—" "But what?! Do you dare think there are any iron curtains in me? Who said I wouldn't go to America? I'll go to America, Russia, China, the North Pole, wherever there's anything to learn! Wherever there's somebody who'll listen to me. And who said I can't go there?!" It was working. Yes, by heavens, it was working! "Nobody said that, Alekos. But you don't have a visa, and—" "A visa can be applied for, can be gotten. Where do you apply? Where do you get one?" "Why, I don't know . . . As a rule at the consulate in Milan, it doesn't take more than ten minutes." "Good. Pack the bags." "The bags?" "Yes, we're going to Milan." "To Milan?" "Yes, and then to America. I want to see the elephant. I want to meet those senators, those congressmen, those waiters, those young men who speak Greek. And U Thant. And that florist. And anybody who's willing to help me a little. It'll be a very useful trip, why didn't I think of it before?"

In Milan you wouldn't even enter the hotel, you were so furiously impatient. It was almost five in the afternoon, the hour when the offices closed, so we left the baggage at the desk and ran at once to the consulate where the official on duty received us in front of the flag of the Leviathan which was born from outcasts and solitary reprobates. The official on duty was a little blond man with a freckled face and a delicate nose, with a sign saying vice-consul on his desk. His name was Carl MacCullum and he had the irritated look of a man caught just at the moment when he ought to be hurrying home to rest after a day spent doing nothing. To avoid wasting time he had you quickly fill out the form which asks if you're a Communist and if you believe in God, then he stamped on the passport the visa stamp and wrote in it your personal particulars, date of issue, date of expiration. He was about to sign it too when his secretary gave you a maternal and affectionate look, then exclaimed: "Poor thing, how much suffering you've had to bear these past few years!" Immediately he lifted his pen, examined you suspiciously and asked: "Why? Where have you been these past years?" Rather surprised, I translated his question from English into Italian: "He wants to know where you have been these past years, Alekos." "Tell him!" I told him. He didn't understand. "Boiati? What's Boiati? Is it a clinic, a hospital?" Again I translated, with the vague presentiment that my faith in the Leviathan was about to be trampled on once again, this time at your expense. You smiled, unaware, as if the suspicion that things were taking a nasty turn wouldn't even cross your mind; evidently I had been very convincing in expounding to you the virtues of the great Leviathan that "receives anyone even those who criticize it." "Hospital? No, sir. I wouldn't say a hospital.

Not exactly a hospital." The vice-consul understood. "Not exactly? What do you mean by not exactly?" Again I translated, as the presentiment grew. "It means that Boiati is a prison, a military prison. An ugly military prison," you answered with another unaware smile. The vice-consul's pen fell with a tiny thump. "A prison?! A military prison?! And why were you in prison, in a military prison?" "He wants to know why you were in prison, a military prison," I translated. Your smile died, your voice became hoarse. "Tell him." I told him: "This is Alexander Panagoulis, the hero of the Greek Resistance, sir." "Greek resistance?! What resistance? Resistance for what? Against whom?" "He wants to know what resistance, for what, against whom," I translated. Your voice became more hoarse: "Tell him to give me back my passport." "Without visa?" "Without visa." I turned to the vice-consul again: "Sir, will you please—" But before I could finish the sentence, the passport had vanished inside a drawer. "Sorry, I can't sign it. Nor can I give it back."

I looked at you. Suddenly pale, you were staring at him with eyes so stony in their amazement that the pupils seemed blind. "What did he say?" "He said he can't sign it, Alekos, and he can't give it back." "Tell him he has no right, as an American, to confiscate a Greek passport in Italy. Tell him that if he doesn't give it back to me, I'll take it back." I translated, adding something of my own, namely that he was committing a misappropriation punishable with prison, thus I would call my lawyers, his embassy in Rome, the police, and he would end up in jail, diplomatic immunity or not. But my words had the sole effect of overwhelming him with indescribable panic. No, he stammered, no, he shouldn't, he couldn't because there was the stamp on the passport now, what an awful mistake, what an unpardonable error, merciful and mighty Lord, it was all his fault and how could it be remedied, O my Lord, my Lord. All this time, he was trembling. You know the convulsive shudder that seizes rabbits when you approach their hutch and, boneless with panic, their heart bursting beneath their fur, they don't know what to do, where to go, how to defend themselves, so crazed they jump from one part of the hutch to the other, their paws rigid, they cling to the bars whimpering. There: now he was locking the drawer, hiding the key in the inside pocket of his coat, so we wouldn't try to snatch it from him, now he grabbed the telephone and put it on his lap so I wouldn't really call the lawyers, the embassy, the police, now from his lap he shifted it to a little table, from the table to another drawer, trying to shove it inside, but it wouldn't go, so he took it out again and handed it to the secretary, who was trying in vain to calm him, sir, Mr. MacCullum, sir, don't take it like this, the stamp isn't valid without the signature. But it was useless, and the grotesque agitation continued, enriched with pleas to his merciful and mighty Lord. Suddenly he stood up, to go to the consul, confess his crime, ask him for advice; and when he came back, he was almost serene. "Are you a Communist?" "No, sir, I'm not a Communist," you answered. "Do you belong to any party?" "No, sir, I belong to no party," you answered. No barter goods. No exchange to be spent in the name of international equilibrium, no card to slip into the computer. No established authority or ideology or power that would guarantee for you. Really? Really. In that case, before returning your passport he would have to ask the authorization of the Greek government. "Of who?!" "The Greek government." You looked at him again: the contempt that now numbed your face was transformed into a grim rage, terrifying. You stood up. You extended your right arm, stuck out your forefinger until it grazed his nose: "American, give me back my passport, American. At once!" "But then . . . I must cancel . . . the stamp . . ." "He says that he must cancel the stamp," I translated. "Answer him that he can also cancel his balls, if he has any." I nodded. "Mr. Panagoulis says you may cancel your balls too, if you have any." Immediately the key hidden in the inside pocket of the jacket reappeared, the drawer was opened, the passport was in the paws of the rabbit, a choked voice announced that he had to confer for a moment with the consul, but please don't be upset. And when you got your passport back, the page with the stamp was stained with a big black spot. The eight letters that in English form the word "canceled." A man alone equals canceled.

Canceled and slandered. The next day I wrote to the Leviathan's ambassador, a Mr. Volpe, whom the Italians called Mr. Golpe. And instead of apologizing, he had the consul in Rome, Margaret Hussman, reply. She wrote two short letters, one to you, one to me, in these she said that after careful consideration, Ambassador Volpe wished to inform us that the vice-consul, Carl MacCullum, had behaved in a perfectly correct manner and that in view of regulations 212(a)9, 212(a)10, 212(a)28 F(ii) of the Immigration Nationality Act you were denied a visa. As to what those regulations covered, those cabala figures, the rude paper said nothing, but I soon found out that they referred to your "moral turpitude": tyrannicide committed or attempted, actions performed to subvert a legitimate regime, being a crime that the Immigration Nationality Act indicated with the expression "moral turpitude." I also found out that the verdict had been approved and confirmed in Washington by the secretary of state, a certain Kissinger, who was in command at that time. Hence there was no hope that the visa would be granted through someone else's intervention. Yet the paths of fate are impenetrable. Stubbornly insisting on going to an America that didn't want you, you rushed with your ink-stained passport to Nicholas in Zurich. Thus on November 17, the anniversary of your death sentence, you were not in Athens, where Ioannidis was looking for you, determined to fulfill his old promise—I'll shoot you, Panagoulis.

"Now how will I go back? How? How?" In Athens, in the space of two days, the unrest had assumed incredible proportions. The newspapers told of barricades in almost every part of the city, emblems of the junta torn down and shattered, demonstrators driving confiscated buses, signs reading JUNTA MUST GO! DOWN WITH FASCISM! DOWN WITH THE AMERICANS AND THEIR LACKEYS! and in one photograph there was your mother, in her little black hat, black purse, black eyeglasses, black stockings, black dress, and a basket of provisions over her arm, being carried in triumph by the boys of the Polytechnic. In another there was the crowd spilling from the grounds of the university along the length of Stadiou Street in a whirl of red flags: no less than ten thousand people, and not one policeman. However, these were photographs of what had happened twenty-four hours earlier and, while publishing them, the morning newspapers also reported news of quite different import. Shortly after midnight tanks had invaded the capital, about fifty tanks with heavy guns, and most of them had headed for the Polytechnic, where the barricaded students were the focus of the revolt. Knocking down the gates, shooting, the tanks killed them by the dozens: among the dead was the boy with the checked shirt who at the temple at Sounion had given you the two cakes of TNT. He had died singing verses of yours. "Now how can I go back? How?" And with the fury of a trapped tiger struggling in a net, you strode, limping, up and down the living room of Nicholas's house. If I replied—Calm down, even the most iron will comes up against unforeseen twists of fate—you spewed on me a bitterness bordering on hate. "It's your fault, yours, yours, yours! You're the one who made me waste time with the idea of the trip to America! You're the one who distracted me with that shitty consulate, with those hypocrite fascists who haven't even the courage to be what they really are! You're the one who took me to that stammering rabbit! I'd be in Athens today if it weren't for you! I could have gone back there with my passport, and now I'll never be able to go there even with my passport! Never! Never!" And your eyes were filled with tears of helplessness, despair.

Nicholas came in with the evening papers. The Polytechnic had been cleared at the first light of dawn, he said, the government admitted a dozen dead and hundreds of wounded: the word massacre was already being used. Repression had spread to Salonika, to Patras, and among the peasants of Megara, but the epicenter remained Athens, where the tanks were stationed even in front of Parliament and a curfew was set for four in the afternoon. The most important thing, in any case, was the message broadcast by Papadopoulos. A message in which he announced the return of martial law, which had been abolished in August, and committed himself to restoring the "order disturbed by anarchist minorities in the hire of international communism and unscrupulous politicians." "He said that?" "Yes." "Over the radio and not on television?" "Yes." Immediately the fury of the trapped tiger seemed to abate and you looked at me with eyes from which all reproach had vanished. "Then Papadopoulos is talking with a revolver held to his temple. Ioannidis's revolver. Papadopoulos is a puppet now in the hands of Ioannidis, his pseudo-democratization has failed, his regime is finished, along with the attempt to legalize it with a farce of an election. The army has turned against him. Those tanks aren't his, they belong to Ioannidis: it's Ioannidis who made the uprisings worse, first allowing them to grow, then brutally cutting them down; it's Ioannidis who wanted the massacre at the Polytechnic to show that Papadopoulos is a weakling and incapable; it's Ioannidis who commands today, however you look at it, supported by the hard-line faction." "If you go back now, I give you five minutes to live from the moment you land in Athens," Nicholas murmured. You mustered a melancholy smile: "There's no need for me to go back now. It wouldn't achieve anything except ending up in the cell next to Papadopoulos's." "What are you saying?!" "I'm saying we were all of us mistaken: it wasn't a people's uprising but a coup d'etat within the coup d'etat. This time Ioannidis is the one who has made the coup: to oust

Papadopoulos and stabilize the dictatorship, or rather to make it a military dictatorship again. In a week all this will be obvious and official."

And the prophecy was to come true. A week later Ioannidis was to put Papadopoulos under house arrest. In his place, as president of the Republic, Ioannidis installed a general named Phaedo Gizikis. The same Gizikis who in 1968 had signed the decree for your execution and who the following year had come to see you in your cell at Goudi to urge you to eat. "Please, Mr. Panagoulis, eat something." "Without cutlery, general? I'm not a dog." "I agree, Mr. Panagoulis, but you must understand their hard feelings. The moment they give you a spoon, you use it to dig a hole in the wall!" In your tale the characters are almost always the same: as if the gods took delight in using and reusing them as bait for you.

We had come back to the comfortable hotel in Rome, and to my amazement you asked for the suite that on your arrival in Italy had aroused guilt complexes in you and shocked the partisans of conspicuous sacrifice. We had arrived in the morning and since then you had done nothing but silently inspect the curtains, the chandelier, the table lamps, the inside of the fireplace, the upholstery of the chairs: as if a bomb were hidden somewhere. "What are you looking for?" "Nothing." "What are you ransacking now?" "Ssh!" In the end, after having examined every object for the thousandth time, you sat on the sofa in the living room and exclaimed in a loud voice: "Uhm! Nenni says I'm in exile, but Ioannidis doesn't think so. It seems that these past few days he was convinced I was in Athens, and he searched for me even among the stones of the Parthenon. Ioannidis never gives up. He has the stuff of a little Robespierre. Besides he knows how power works in a military dictatorship, he knows that in a military dictatorship the one who commands isn't the head of the government or of the cabinet, it's the one who controls the army. Poor Averoff. He'll have to start all over again, with his bridge policy. And this time he'll have to deal with Ioannidis." "Averoff?" When you least expect it, that name emerges again. "Yes, Averoff. The one who organizes revolts of the navy and then spills the beans, the one who always comes out on top. The Lord only knows what he promised Papadopoulos, knows how he's planning to deceive Ioannidis. Making use of Gizikis perhaps." "But what does Averoff have to do with all this?" "Plenty—Ugh, it's hot in here!" Flinging open the French window, you stepped onto the balcony, where you anxiously signaled me to follow. I followed reluctantly: winter was approaching and it was cold outside. "But why—?" "Sssh! Not so loud!" "Loud? But you were shouting in there!" "Because I wanted to be sure they'd hear everything." "Who?" "The ones who are listening. I'm sure they've planted microphones somewhere." "Don't be ridiculous! Who would plant microphones?" "Anybody. The Greek embassy, the American secret services, the Italian secret services to do a favor for the American secret services and the Greek embassy—" "Is that what you were looking for all over the place? Microphones?" "Right." "Then why did you come back here and ask for the same suite?" "Because no place is safer than a place that's under surveillance. When you know it, you take your precautions and you can even trick them with false information. Let's make a test." "What test?" "Wait and see. Now we'll go back inside and I'll say I'm about to go to Athens. You just play along with me. No laughing, eh?" Well, it was better than shivering with cold in this late November wind. Besides, if you had got it into your head that there were those microphones, there was no contradicting you. "All right, Alekos." We went back into the living room, and you started speaking again in a loud voice, enunciating each sentence clearly. "I'm leaving tomorrow then. I'm taking the plane that gets to Athens at seven in the evening." "Did you reserve a seat, Alekos?" "Never make reservations. Never let them know in advance. You turn up at the last moment and ask for a seat. I'm not that stupid, to put my name on the passenger list two days ahead of time!" "You surely aren't going to travel under your own name, Alekos, with your own passport?" "Yes, perhaps." "Will you really?" "It'll be all right, I promise." "Alekos, why are you going to Athens?" "Don't be naive! Why should I go? To make an attempt on someone's life, of course." "Who?" "Ioannidis, who else?"

You organized the trick with diabolical care. To begin with, you alerted a friend in Athens, telling him to go to the airport and see if anything unusual happened. Police activity, for example, around seven in the evening. Then you arranged to be at the Rome airport forty-five minutes before the scheduled flight, and this was the most malicious detail because it involved an innocent Nicholas. That week Nicholas was to accompany you to Stuttgart to make contact with some Greek émigrés, and instead of meeting him in Zurich, as would have been normal, you persuaded him to join you in Rome. That way you would be seen with him before your supposed departure for Athens and any doubt about the authenticity of the dialogue picked up by the hidden microphones would vanish. "Alekos, they'll catch on that you're bluffing, all the same." "They won't catch on, let me handle this. For me it's enough for them to see us together when he comes through customs, then I know how to slip away, and they'll believe I boarded the plane." So there you are, ordering a taxi with impatience—Hurry, please, I have to get to the airport—and there you are leaving with a briefcase, which could be an overnight bag, and there you are saying good-bye as if you were leaving, while instead you murmur final instructions to me. I must not go back into the hotel before you, no matter what, not risk being asked if you have left or not; I was not to see people who might ask me where you were. We would meet again, with Nicholas, at suppertime, rendezvous in a restaurant, and at midnight we would go to the central post office to telephone the friend in Athens, to ask what had or had not happened. I nodded, to please you, convinced that it was futile and childish, that the hidden microphones notion had no basis in reality. But I was wrong. At midnight, in fact, the friend reported that an uproar had started at the airport in the early hours of the afternoon. Soldiers on the runway, radio cars, ambulances: only tanks were missing. At the seven o'clock arrival the situation had become downright dramatic because all the passengers had been searched like criminals and a Spaniard had been arrested. A dark Spaniard, about thirty, with moustache: your type. "Are you convinced? Are there hidden microphones, or not?" A smile of triumph made you radiant. Nicholas, on the contrary, seemed so nervous that even his submissiveness had vanished along with the symmetry of his white handkerchief folded with three points. It had been a useless joke, he repeated, and sooner or later they would make you pay for it. You had to give up these private challenges, these personal duels. You had to change methods, or you would never achieve anything. Did you want to carry on the armed struggle? Well, the armed struggle is not achieved by wasting yourself in private challenges, personal duels; it requires the participation of many people. You had to seek out these people: without being discouraged, without losing patience if you didn't find them in a week or a month. "Come on, let's go to Stuttgart. We'll begin with Stuttgart, with Germany."

Germany, France, Switzerland, Austria, southern and northern Italy: I can imagine nothing more disappointing than those journeys in search of guerrillas among the Greek exiles and emigrants. A resigned Nicholas accompanied you, I never went along and therefore did not witness your defeats, but to understand them I had only to see your wan face when you returned, the way you would drop your suitcase, abruptly, as if it contained the baggage of your embitterments, hear your voice when you murmured: "Words, words, words!" Then the story of what had happened, always the same. Triumphant welcomes at your arrival, applause at the speeches you made in some theater, endless suppers in taverns deafened by bouzouki, bodyguards who protected your sleep with a Colt superautomatic in their belt, kisses, hugs, offers of women, and at the end of all this not one soul who said yes, let's go fight Ioannidis with guns. "Why? Tell me why?!" Superfluous question, since as usual you refused to consider the reality that Greece had prevented you from assembling a handful of volunteers willing to occupy the Acropolis and that Italy had raised a barrier of uneasiness and distrust. Here too nobody was ready to sacrifice himself in suicidal ventures, particularly ventures not commanded by a party, by an ideology. Here too there was the problem of your political position, of the solitude that eliminates the advantage of being possible barter goods, money to spend in the name of international equilibrium—Who's he? what's he want? who guarantees for him? When the poison of doctrines pollutes consciences and causes people to act as a herd, it isn't only the brain of the foreign leader or the computer of the great Leviathan that jams, the brain of your brothers reacts in the same way, raises the same questions—Is it possible that he doesn't have a card, a party membership, that he doesn't belong to a church? And it's no use to answer—But he is Panagoulis, the one who tried to free you from the tyrant, the one who was sentenced to death for it and who remained buried for years in a chicken coop without windows! It's his past that guarantees for him, his present, his purity! Their eyes look up, spent, their ears listen, deaf. Yes, but the card, the membership: where is it? Is he a socialist, a Communist, a Buddhist? And even worse if he can't explain in scientific terms the reasons why he doesn't even conceive of identifying himself with a doctrine, a formula. He isn't a philosopher, after all, he isn't a thinker: he has never reflected deeply on this puzzle, he has never rationalized his awareness of certain things. He can say only that he wants to be a man, that to be a man means to be free, to have courage, to struggle, to assume one's responsibilities, so let's go into action, let's fight this dictatorship.

In this guise, with your name as your only guarantee, your past as your only introduction, you presented yourself to the Greek emigrants in Germany, in France, in Switzerland, in Italy, and again you banged your head against the wall. Either your call to armed resistance was rejected with the fatal sentence—I'd like to but I can't, I've got a family—or else it was invalidated by the fact that the majority didn't understand for *whom* you wanted to enlist them, to *whom* you belonged, *who* was behind you. To say nothing of the fact that many had already been signed up by the Communists or by the Papandreists. Any dialogue with the former group was practically impossible because your libertarianism clashed with their dogmatism, while for the second group you harbored an unshakable contempt: the contempt due the followers of a demiurge who sustains a party of his own last name, or rather on the name of his famous, deceased father. Above all you despised the demiurge: I had realized that clearly the night we met, when I heard the scorn with which you judged him. Someone had only to say Andreas Papandreou and you would let the insults fly: "That word spinner! That irresponsible clown! Deceiver of the people!" And with such anger, such bitterness, that at first I thought it was some personal hostility, inspired by the way he had disappointed you before the assassination attempt. Useless trips to ask for his support, promises not kept, lies. I had also some resentment of his easy, comfortable exile in Toronto, in accord with the habits of certain leaders who as long as danger is hot keep themselves in a safe place, and as soon as the danger is past, return to the homeland to exploit the sacrifice of others. But during the Polytechnic massacre, when he came to Rome to say that he had conceived and directed the revolt, that the rebels had telephoned him every day for instructions, that the dead were not forty but four hundred, five hundred, six hundred, a thousand, my misunderstanding was cleared up. I understood that for you Papandreou embodied a disease typical of our time, contagious as dogmatic ideology: the bogus populism of those who bark but don't bite, the Mussolinian revolutionism of those who deceive themselves or want to deceive us into believing that they aim at the good of the people, the abstract maximalism of those who put on the adjective socialist like a fashionable dress, a lie that pays off. Far from being a private matter, your contempt for him included the professional leftists, the opportunists, whose yelling offers pretexts to the right wing and sparks its coups d'etat, its squalor masked as "law and order."

Most of those who turned their backs on you belonged to this left wing. I really can't imagine anything more disappointing than those journeys from which you returned with the wan face of a man who has lost once again. Or else with the swollen face of one who has got drunk once again. In fact it was in those weeks that drinking became for you a daily and perverse masochism, symbol of the desperation that was tearing you apart. It was in those weeks, moreover, that Sancho Panza, the squire, became nurse and tried in vain to trap you with the lures of serene love, with the house in the woods.

2

IN EVERY HERO'S LEGEND THERE'S A HOUSE IN THE WOODS, a secret refuge where the hero stops to rest or to prepare himself for the next test, and so also in your legend there's a house in the woods, the one in Florence to which we moved in secret, at the beginning of the new year. I say in secret because only a few trusted friends knew of its existence and very few knew the address, which for that matter was hard to find: the place was secluded, the number plate was so faded by the weather that it was almost illegible, and our rare visitors lost their way even if they had been there before. Remember? Halfway along that avenue, bordered with plane trees and lindens, that climbs up through the most elegant neighborhood of the city, there was a wall; in the wall, directly opposite the bus stop, there was a gate half-hidden by shrubbery, and after the gate was a little private road that, first straight and then curving, plunged into a park of pines, cypresses, horse chestnuts. At the end of the straight stretch, beyond a laurel hedge that sheltered it with exquisite hauteur, there was a four-story villa, art nouveau style, formerly the exclusive residence of a patrician family, now broken up into apartments and inhabited by three or four tenants. We didn't have a real apartment, of course. We had a room on the fourth floor, a kind of studio that we reached through a private entrance, then a climb of six flights of stairs where we never encountered anyone except a hysterical dachshund or a snarling fox terrier. But the room was vast, made habitable by the addition of a bath and kitchen, very bright thanks to the immense windows: one window opened onto a wrought-iron balcony over the spot where the road forked in two curves and the laurel hedge joined the clump of lilacs, and the other window looked out on the back of the park. And from those windows only trees could be seen: so splendid, so thick, some so gigantic that they had to be two hundred years old, I often thought, and others so close that you could touch them. The boughs of the horse chestnut grazed the railing and, without stretching your arm, you could pick its chestnuts or stroke the shiny, enameled hulls. But the most beautiful feature of the room was something else: on the wall opposite the south window there was an enormous wardrobe with mirrored doors, reflecting the horse chestnut and a cypress, so that instead of being in a room it was like being in a wood. When we opened the windows, the illusion deceived even the birds, who, unawares, darted toward the mirrors to light on a branch, and as soon as they realized that the branch didn't exist, they would pause, frightened, their wings fluttering against the invisible barrier of the deceit, then they would fly off, darting between ceiling and wall in search of a leaf or a bush that should be there and wasn't, and finally they would perch on the chandelier to complain or to twitch their heads, staring first at the reality then at the mirage: unable to understand which was reality and which was mirage. To get them back outside, we had to help them, waving a towel. "There! Outside! There!" One morning a robin came in. It entered with such enthusiasm that it banged straight into itself and fell to the floor, breaking a wing. It was very small, perhaps a fledgling, and you picked it up with trembling delicacy, you bound the wing fast with toothpicks and adhesive, you made him a nest inside a hat, where he stayed for two days and two nights chirping faintly until dawn of the third day, when he was still, so you sprang from the bed. "He's healed, he's healed!" But he wasn't healed, he was dead, and stroking the inert little clump of feathers, you murmured: "You are killed by the mirage, my little one. See what happens when you seek something that doesn't exist?" Then you put him in a tin box and buried him under the cypress. "Anyone who dies for a mirage deserves a good funeral."

The house in the woods also had serious defects. The avenue with the plane trees and the lindens offered no protection because not only was it almost unfrequented but also it passed only houses with gates sternly barred: not a shop or a public building or a gathering place, except for the bus stop where nobody ever got on or off. Our gate, on the contrary, remained always open, there wasn't even a streetlamp to illuminate the passage, so at night the little private road lay in total darkness and to reach the villa you had to cover about a hundred meters in that darkness: if anyone wanted to attack or kidnap or kill he had only to wait in the darkness, hidden behind a tree or the laurel hedge. In the evening, true, we did take the precaution of going and coming by taxi, but only rarely would the driver accompany us all the way to our door, and when he did, he abandoned us before we could fit the key in the lock: any aggressors then had time to slip from the darkness and attack us. I had foreseen these things and they were the reason why I questioned the feasibility of renting the house, but you answered that beauty has its risks, that it was worth running them for such an enchanting place, and so the contract had been signed, the house furnished. Pictures on the walls, books in the shelves, the desk placed in the correct corner, the rocking chair beside the balcony, even a precious Tiffany lamp on the table. And the promise: "I'll be calm here, you'll see!" You even kept it, at the beginning. There had been moments at the beginning when I thought we were reliving the week of happiness. At night we loved each other with joyous passion, then we fell asleep in a tight embrace that made the double bed too big. In the daytime we allowed ourselves little luxuries like working at the same table without disturbing each other, walking together in the park, making a date to meet at a café downtown, playing lovers who exchange rings gaily. One afternoon you came home with a little diamond wedding ring for me, I immediately ran to buy a white gold band for you but I got the wrong size and instead of the ring finger you had to put it on your left little finger, where it was to remain, to my amusement, because while complaining about it, you pronounced the word for ring, *anello,* as if it were the one for lamb, *agnello.* "This little lamb! Questo piccolo agnello!"

There were also spells of ill-humor. They came when you collected your mail at the central Post Office, used as an address to protect the secrecy of the house in the woods, and among the letters from Athens you would find one that renewed your guilt complexes, the sensation of being in exile. Still an unhoped-for equilibrium seemed to have replaced the hysteria of the weeks wasted in Germany, Switzerland, France, and the things you did now showed sense: the column entitled "Greek Resistance," which you wrote for a Roman daily paper, the collection of your poems in a book which contained the Greek text as well as the Italian translation so that it could also be distributed in Greece, the rubber stamps for making little on-the-spot handbills against the junta. These were an inspiration of genius because in Athens the problem of handbills lay in finding an underground printing shop and these shops were luxuries that only the Communists and the Papandreists could allow themselves: but with the rubber stamps it would suffice to procure a bit of paper and some ink pads and print the slogans on the rubber stamps. Among these there was the one that was to have been placed around the Parthenon: "Agonas dia tin elefteria Agonas kata tis tirannias. Struggle for freedom, Struggle against tyranny." You ordered a hundred and fifty of these, each the size of two packs of cigarettes and therefore easy to handle, then you packed them in bags with false bottoms, to be entrusted, one at a time, to people going to Athens. Three of these bags had already reached their destination; four were waiting inside the mirrored wardrobe. And you were drinking very little, until suppertime you quenched your thirst exclusively with orange juice: in the space of a month, only two or three suppers had ended in drunkenness. But it was the drunkenness of the first stage, the stage that flinging open the gates of eloquence also unleashed your humor. "All right, I wasn't sober tonight. But can you imagine Socrates conversing with Crito and Phaedo and Simmias while drinking orange juice?" I had only one reason for uneasiness, the mysterious trip you had made to Sweden. "I have to go to Stockholm." "To look for more emigrants?!" "No, no." "Then why do you have to go to Stockholm?" "Uff! Is this an interrogation?" You returned from Stockholm with a little package and an envelope which you locked up in a desk drawer, then you put the key in your pocket without telling me why.

"Alekos, what did you hide?" "Nothing." "It isn't TNT, is it?" "TNT? Christ, no!" I didn't like this business and every time I looked at the drawer I felt anxious. But you talked no more of armed struggle, or even of going back to Athens.

I was soon to realize that all this equilibrium, this good humor, was a performance, staged to deceive me.

"Art is born in need and dies in wealth." "That's only true in some cases, Alekos: you can't deny that the statues of Phidias are art, you can't deny that the Sistine Chapel is art, and yet neither of the two was born in need. They were born in wealth." "Shut up. I'm not talking to you, I'm talking to him." We were having supper with the publisher who was issuing your books of poems and who had come to Florence to bring us the proofs. So I reacted more strongly than I would have if we had been alone. "Don't talk to me like that!" "Shut up, I said. What do you know about Phidias? You don't even inhale when you smoke! Look, she doesn't even inhale. What's the sense of smoking if you don't inhale?" "Everybody smokes in his own way," said the publisher. "I don't like to inhale either, and anyway I can't see any connection between Phidias and smoking and inhaling." Then, with the obvious intention of diverting my rising anger, the publisher started smoking a cigarette, just puffing on it. But it served only to encourage that unjustified attack. "Are we forming alliances? Defending the weak? She's not weak, not her. Don't worry: she's stronger than me. She's made of iron. Her heart's made of iron, too! Have you ever seen her cry? Have you?" Strange, really strange. Nothing like this had ever happened. "And smoking isn't the only thing she doesn't know how to do properly: she can't use a lighter, either. She keeps it open at least thirty seconds before spinning the wheel, so she wastes gas. For that matter everything she does, she does badly. You know how she sticks stamps on. With the picture upside down, the head of Italy, for example, upside down. And if you tell her, she shrugs and says it makes no difference. She doesn't respect anyone, not her. She doesn't believe in anyone or in anything." If you had been drinking, I would have said the alcohol was taking effect. But you had only had one glass, wine didn't interest you this evening. Nor were there any disagreements between us. In fact, until you produced the theory on art being born in need and dying in wealth, you had been affectionate, sweet. Were you going mad? The publisher seemed to be asking himself this, as I was, though the first incredulity was turning into hostility: "Certainly anyone would have to be made of iron, Alekos, to put up with your manias. An iron heart, too. In her place I'd have had a massive coronary by now." "Alliances! The alliances continue!" "It isn't a question of alliances, Alekos. It's—" "It's the fact that you don't know who painted the Sistine Chapel. Come on: who painted the Sistine Chapel?" "Winston Churchill, Alekos." "Good. Fine. And what was Winston Churchill's real profession?" "Basketball champion." "Perfect. And when did Winston Churchill die?" "In 1965, at the age of ninety-one." "Wrong! Wrong! Winston Churchill died in 1967, at the age of eighty." Well, you had broadened your range to include him, too, but joking, thank heavens. I could interrupt my haughty silence, now, and join the game. "He's right, Alekos. Churchill died in 1965 at ninety-one." "I said 1967 at eighty." "No, Alekos, I'm sorry to contradict you, but it was really in 1965. January 24, 1965. I remember it well because I was in London that day and the next day my son was born." The publisher's voice sounded sharp, belligerent. Just what you needed to make you change your tone: "You're lying." "I'm not lying, and anyone will confirm the date. Call the morgue of a newspaper." "I'll call," I said. Then I got up, came back: "They also looked in the encyclopedia. Churchill was born on November 30, 1874, and died on January 24, 1965. That's history." "The morgue's wrong. The encyclopedias are wrong." "And you're a pain in the ass." "I am? Very well." And, throwing a handful of money on the table, you left the restaurant without finishing the meal. Without saying good-bye to us.

I was certain I would find you at home when I came in, at midnight. But the house was empty and the drawer which had always been locked was now wide open, there was only the little package in it. The envelope had disappeared. Oh no! suppose it contained—? I flung open the mirrored wardrobe: if the four bags with the rubber stamps were still there, my suspicion had less probability of being justified. But two bags were gone, and so you really had left for Athens. With a fake passport: the envelope contained a fake passport. And the little package? What was there in the little package? I opened it. A wig. Dark blond, a man's wig. Then perhaps you hadn't gone to Athens. Had you gone to Zurich? I called Nicholas: "Are you expecting him? Is he supposed to come to you?" "No." "Would he perhaps come without telling you?" "No. Why do you ask?" "Because—" "I'll leave right away." And the next morning, there he was, with his white handkerchief in his pocket and his eyes more patient than ever. "What was his mood when he came back from Sweden?" "Excellent." "What was this envelope like?" "Normal." "The size of a passport?" "More or less." "Then, yes, at this moment he is traveling with a Swedish passport made out in a name like Bersen or Eriksson." "But why didn't he tell me?" "For the same reasons that made him keep silent in the country about what he was planning: to keep you from trying to stop him. It's all in his style, isn't it? In fact, the way he provoked you, insulted you, is his style. His stratagems, rather. If he hadn't insulted you, you wouldn't have insulted him. And so he would have had no excuse to go off, certain that he wasn't being followed: only a quarrel makes a sudden departure plausible and eliminates the necessity of justifying it with explanations or lies." "I should have realized." "He would have managed to exasperate you all the same. He's a master in the art of provoking others, and who knows how long he had been planning that scene. In certain things he has an inhuman patience." "He wouldn't trust me." "No, he followed his reasoning: someone who doesn't know, doesn't speak. If we don't know where he is and what he's doing, it's no effort for us to remain silent. If we know, remaining silent becomes a choice and a risk of giving something away. And besides there's the other rule he always follows before plunging into an enterprise that could end badly: no ties with people he loves and who love him. As a rule he cuts them off with brutality, with insults, considering that someone who has been brutalized or insulted suffers less on learning he's been imprisoned or killed. And it's an effort for him, believe me; in fact, he must have been very distraught yesterday evening. The proof is the open drawer, and the wig left behind. Hm! Let's hope he isn't planning some special act of bravado, some new challenge that will compensate him for his disappointments. But there's no use fooling ourselves: now that the emigrants have rejected him, he wants more than ever to prove he can do everything on his own. He'll never change." "Now what, Nicholas?" "Nothing. All we can do is wait. And hope he comes back."

You came back on the fourth day. The phone rang and: "Sono me! Sono io! It's me! It's I! I'm here!" "Here? Where?" "At the Rome station! I'll catch the train and come right away!" Three hours later there you were, unshaven, dirty, rumpled, in worse shape than a beggar who has slept three nights in a gutter. But your smile was that of a child who has won a race or passed his exams. "I've been there! I've been there! I'll take a bath and tell you everything!" Then you filled the tub, you plunged into it with blissful cries, and the mad story flowed out: without a word of apology for the Churchill business or an explanation that justified your insults. You had been in Greece, naturally. With your moustache, your pipe, your koboloi, recognizable among a thousand, you landed at Athens airport on the first morning flight, and calmly producing the Swedish passport of a certain Bjorn Gustavsson, you presented yourself at the border police. You were counting on the fact that sometimes the police look at the passenger without really seeing him or they compare the photographs of the wanted list only with the picture in the passport, and the rare times that that doesn't happen, tough luck: when you have no other choice, you have to trust in luck, believe in fortune. Rouge ou noir, le jeu est fait, rien ne va plus. The policeman leafed absently through the passport, looked for the name Bjorn Gustavsson, then he thanked you, in English, with a yawn: "Thank you very much." In your left hand you carried the larger bag, the one with the false bottom so deep that twenty-seven rubber stamps fitted in it, and in your right hand you carried the smaller bag, with twelve stamps; heading toward customs, you felt anything but relieved: at customs they could check your passport again or might realize the bags were a bit too heavy. But if a man thinks about these things, he'll never accomplish anything, will he? Act as if they were light, then. Head for the exit, handle the guy in customs with the absent tone of someone with nothing to declare, no sir, no cigarettes, no alcohol, no presents, only a few dozen rubber stamps for making handbills against the junta but I won't tell you that and you're too stupid, too lazy to find them. And what if they weren't stupid, weren't lazy at all? Again rouge ou noir, le jeu est fait, rien ne va plus. It went smoothly there too, and then you were in the city with a great longing to run to the house with the garden of orange and lemon trees, embrace your mother, but you didn't do that, of course, and for twenty-four hours you remained hidden in a friend's house. There you left the rubber stamps and met four companions whom you called the People's Army of Armed Resistance. A name you liked because in Greek the initials formed the word laos, people: or laikos, people's; antochi, resistance; oplofri, armed; stratos, army. In fact, the stamps were all signed Laos. "But what will you do with an army of four soldiers?!" "You'll see. I've divided them into regiments: Laos 1, Laos 2, Laos 3, Laos 4. One man to a regiment." "You'll never stop bluffing, will you?" "No."

You spent the next day doing what at heart was most important for you: humiliating Ioannidis. The method you chose was simple: displaying yourself in various spots in the capital: sudden, fleeting appearances, scarlet pimpernel-style. You would go into a bar, stand on a sidewalk, get into a taxi, get out, linger in the lobby of a hotel, and as soon as you heard that little stifled cry—"Panagoulis! Is that Panagoulis?!"—you would vanish, only to reappear elsewhere, perhaps in a distant neighborhood, creating amazement and uncertainty. Panagoulis is back, he was seen in Constitution Square. No, outside the Polytechnic. No, in Kolonaki. No, in Kypseli. No, in Pagrati. No, in Plaka. No, in Piraeus. No, in Glyphada. It isn't possible, yes it's possible. I saw him clearly, it was him all right with his moustache and his pipe and his koboloi, I even said hello to him, I called him. Or else: I wanted to say hello to him, I wanted to call him, but when I crossed the street, when I looked around, he was gone. Soon the rumor became news and the news reached ESA headquarters, the trouble was that Ioannidis wouldn't believe it. "And how do you know?" "I know because I telephoned ESA twice. And I said to them: 'Look, Panagoulis is here, tell the brigadier general.' And the operator said: 'We've already been told: the information is not true.' After a while I telephoned again and I said to them: 'See here, it is true: I'm Panagoulis.' And you know what he answered me, the idiot? He answered: 'Then I'm Karamanlis.' So I got an idea, the idea of giving them undeniable proof, and I climbed up to the Acropolis with a friend, I had myself photographed in front of the Parthenon, holding an open newspaper in my hands. So they could read clearly the headlines and the date, you see? If they couldn't have read the headlines and the date, it would have seemed an old snapshot. Finally I had it printed in postcard format and I sent it to Ioannidis, with this inscription: 'From Alexander Panagoulis, who comes to Greece when he likes, and wants you to know it.'" "I don't believe it." "I swear!" And jumping out of the tub you ran to get the copies you had kept for yourself. It was as you had said. "And what about coming back?" "Uhm! That was difficult. No, it was a miracle. A friend of mine collected the boarding pass but then I had to go through passport control again, and I can't tell you how scared I was. I noticed about thirty tourists traveling in a group and I mingled with them. They were making such confusion that the poor cop lost his head. He didn't even know which one of us was Bjorn Gustavsson. He just stamped the passport, and that was all. Look."

I looked, and my knees went weak. Not because of the stamp, which was indeed the stamp of the Athens airport, fresh that day, but because of the passport you had used to go and to come back with. Bjorn Gustavsson was a boy who looked about as much like you as a white Pekingese looked like a black Great Dane. His face was delicate, beardless, features so fine that at first glance you would have thought him a girl or an ephebe, and hair so blond and eyes so pale he seemed an albino. As if this weren't enough, his birthdate corresponded perfectly to his appearance: eighteen years old. "You're crazy, Alekos." "Uhm . . . Maybe you're right. I have to change the picture. Or else shave off my moustache."

You would never shave off your moustache and would never change the photograph. But you were to find a passport of an Italian whose physical appearance bore some relation to yours, and the trips continued, always with the continuation of that absurd comedy. You rarely confided the truth to me. Faithful to the principles Nicholas had explained to me—If you don't know, you don't suffer and don't talk—and also seduced by the delight of conspiracy, every time you left for Greece you managed to trick me, to draw me into some quarrel which would justify your abrupt, "I'm leaving." And though I knew the trick by now, I fell for it every time. "You don't even know how to make a phone call. Why do you have to keep your finger in the hole after you've dialed the number? The disk goes back by itself, doesn't it?" "Cut it out, Alekos. I'll dial numbers any way I like." "I won't cut it out, remove your finger, you make me nervous." "Alekos, will you stop nagging me, or won't you?" "All right, I'll stop. I'm leaving." Or else: "Venice is a dead doll." "Perhaps, but I like it all the same." "Because you have no taste." "Well, you can say anything, but you can't say people who like Venice have no taste." "Well, I do say it anyhow. Smell this perfume: it's bad taste, it stinks. It stinks like a dead doll, that's why you like Venice." "Idiot, boor." "Idiot? Boor?" "Yes, and I'll say something else: you're right: I have bad taste: in fact, I live with you." "Not anymore, you don't. I'm leaving." You went off alone and the next day I realized I had fallen for it again like a dimwit. Then, after three or four days had passed, you would come back: "It's me! Guess where I've been!" Or else: "Ciao, alitaki. I brought you some perfume from Athens. This doesn't stink." I didn't take offense anymore. While the trip lasted, my irritation was replaced by the anguish of knowing you were in danger; afterward it was overcome by the relief of seeing you again. If anything, I wondered what sense there was in those scarlet pimpernel returns to Greece, what good they did beyond keeping you in trim, maintaining your skirmish with death. To make contact with Laos 1, Laos 2, Laos 3, Laos 4? To organize exploits that regularly failed to come off? To attempt to wrest some soldier away from the Communists or the Papandreists, to reduce a solitude that was beginning to weigh on you? Rather than humiliate you, I even avoided asking you questions: I pretended to believe these were highly useful expeditions, from which memorable things would result. Then one evening at the end of February we were at home reading the newspapers, and my gaze fell on a news story from Athens. Ten lines, no more. The night before, the article said, four bombs had exploded in a factory, but there were no victims. A fifth, however, had blown up while two men, a civilian and a soldier, were defusing it. The two men had been killed. On the scene the police had found the handbills of a group calling itself Laos 8. I sought your eyes: "How are your four regiments going?" "There aren't four now: there are eight," you answered with a happy smile. "I've recruited Laos 5, Laos 6, Laos 7, and Laos 8. You'll see what happens in a few days!" "It's already happened, Alekos. Last night." "What?" "Five bombs. One exploded while they were trying to defuse it. It killed a civilian and a soldier." "Where?" "In a factory." "I've nothing to do with it." "Yes, you have. There were the handbills of Laos 8." The smile vanished. You sprang to your feet, tore the paper from my hands. "I have to leave." "Leave? Why?" "Because they disobeyed me! Disobeyed me!" "How?" "In every way! It wasn't supposed to explode there, not there! It wasn't supposed to kill anybody! Idiots! Fools!" "Alekos, when you plant bombs the least they can do is blow up people trying to defuse them." "I know. I must leave." "Alekos, it isn't their fault if those two men died. Six years ago the same thing could have happened, one of your mines didn't explode, either." "I know. I have to leave." "Armed resistance is a war, Alekos, and in war you don't shoot candy bars: if your attempt with Papadopoulos had succeeded, who knows how many people would have died with him." "I know. I must leave." "You won't leave! This time I'll prevent you!"

You didn't leave. Nor did I attach importance to it: it was one of your characteristics to do exactly the opposite of what you announced you would do. Obviously, I said to myself, the trauma of the two deaths had caused a passing crisis in you and immediately afterward you realized it would be wise to stay far away from Greece for a while. You didn't even mention it again, and since that dialogue a month had gone by, with the dramas we will see later, when we went to Rome but, as soon as we reached Rome, you began saying you had to go to Milan. This made me suspicious, especially since you offered no plausible excuse for going to Milan. "Look me in the eyes, Alekos.

Milan, or Athens?" "Athens? What's Athens got to do with anything? And besides, if you want to be sure I'm going to Milan, all you have to do is come to Milan with me." "All right." "This evening?" "This evening." "Reserve a sleeping compartment." "Sleeping compartment? But you never take one! You always say it's dangerous, a trap, that anyone can steal the keys from the porter and enter the compartment, that the plane is better." "No, not the plane, not today." I reserved the sleeping compartment, and in the course of the day you publicized the trip by every possible means: telephoning from the suite with the hidden microphones, checking with the desk clerk several times to make sure he had the compartment, asking the exact train schedule in a loud voice. When we left the hotel there wasn't a soul who didn't know your plan, and after all this publicity, finally we are at the station, we are in the compartment, where the porter arranges the suitcases and where unexpectedly the curtain rises on the play. "You don't want to come to Milan with me!" "Don't want to come, Alekos?! But I'm here!" "You're here with a long face, and I can't bear people with long faces." "You're mistaken." "I'm not mistaken and I'm not going to Milan with you. I'm not staying in a compartment with somebody who's looking at me crossly." "Now listen to me, Alekos: the idea of going to Milan is yours, I don't have any reason to go to Milan. I don't have a long face, I'm not looking crossly at you, and you're trying to pick a fight. You're not about to insist that Churchill died this morning, are you? At the age of twenty?" And as I was saying this, I realized the whole business of going to Milan by sleeper was a farce to deceive me and whoever was watching your movements. You had worked it out in order to fly to Athens without my following you and once again you had lied to me, once again I had fallen for it in the most foolish way. I glanced at my watch: one minute till the train left. Soon the station master would blow his whistle, the train would move out, and there would be no time to unload the suitcases. Besides, that would have attracted attention and spoiled your plans. There was nothing to be done then, nothing. I sank down on the bunk, I heard my voice murmur: "You could have avoided it." Then your voice answered: "No, I couldn't." The station master blew his whistle. You rushed into the passage, reached the door, opened it, got out. The train moved off as you were slipping along the platform, head down, not looking back.

A day, two days, three days: I thought I would never be able to forgive you for this latest trick, and in fact I had gone back to the house in the woods only to collect my things, leaving you a letter explaining my refusal to continue such a relationship. I wasn't Penelope who weaves her veil waiting for Ulysses, the letter said, I was Ulysses myself, had always lived like Ulysses, and the fact that for you I had betrayed my own nature by becoming Sancho Panza didn't authorize your arrogance in certain instances; anyway Sancho Panza follows Don Quixote, enjoys his confidence, is not left behind on a train like a suitcase. But four days later, when I saw you in that condition, my revolt evaporated. You looked like a carnival mask: half of your face was a purplish red, the other half was white, bloodless. The line that divided the two colors started at the brow, went along the nose and down to your chin and neck, and although the eye on the white side was normal, on the red side it seemed monstrously swollen. "What have you done?!" Instead of answering, you took a flask of wine, opened it and began to drink. In silence, with cold determination, glass after glass. The only words that came at intervals from your lips were: "I can't get drunk, I can't get drunk." And you really couldn't, your gaze remained clear and your voice distinct, you could stand steady on your feet. Halfway through the flask you turned and went to the bar, where we kept hard liquor, which you didn't like, you took out every bottle it contained, lined them all up on the table, and started drinking again, first from one bottle then from another. You deliberately mixed, perhaps even pouring them into one glass, vodka, whiskey, cognac, then drained the mess with the determination of someone swallowing a disgusting medicine, and finally you were drunk to the degree you wanted. The third stage, temporary death. But this time it didn't lead you to the boundless plains of the dream, you didn't plunge into the sweet limbo of forgetfulness, into the soft abysses of the void. Soon you came to, and the waking was a heartrending weeping, tears and sobs that stifled you, broken words that filtered through the wet handkerchief in a monotonous refrain. "Go away, they said to me, go away! Away! away! away!" "Who said that to you? Who?" "They did. Go away, they said to me. Away! away! Away, away, away!" It took all night before I understood what had happened in Athens, that, after the five bombs and the death of the two men, nobody had the courage to approach you, nor were you allowed to get near them. Only two agreed to a meeting on the beach, not to listen to what you wanted to say but to tell you that this was good-bye: your kind of struggle didn't interest them, so they had decided to join a party, and they would join it. Good luck and so long. Then I asked you where you had slept, and pointing to the red side of your face, you answered: "Where beggars and stray dogs sleep." Then you confided that, after looking in vain for somewhere to rest, toward dawn you returned to the beach. You lay down on one side, half your face resting on a pillow of sand, half-exposed to the rising sun, and immediately you were taken ill, unconscious, you remained like that until afternoon, when you opened your eyes to find yourself surrounded by a troop of kids, amusing themselves by poking at you and spattering you with water. "He's dead! He's dead!" Without reacting, you didn't have the strength, you stood up and got to the airport. "One cheek and one eyelid were itching, in this season at Athens the sun burns almost as badly as in summer, and I was afraid they would see. But nothing could be seen. It turned red later, in the train." I treated you with a lotion for the burn, I tried to console you: "On the next trip, Alekos—" You interrupted me: "There won't be a next trip. From today on I am really in exile. So much the better, because I don't believe in bombs anymore, in explosions, in arms. Any imbecile can squeeze a trigger, set fire to a fuse, kill two men and even a tyrant. And then what? What changes? When one tyrant dies, they create another, and often the future tyrants are the very ones who fired the shot. No, it isn't by strewing corpses about that you make the world a little more bearable. It's with ideas! The real bombs are ideas! Oh, Theos! Theos mou! All the years I've wasted! It's time I started thinking. The trouble is I'm tired. Terribly tired."

It was the first time you said to me—The real bombs are ideas, any imbecile can squeeze a trigger or set fire to a fuse or kill two men and even a tyrant. I looked at you, amazed. When had you begun to understand this, what had sparked a conclusion so contrary to your personality? Had it been the death of the two men, had it been the trauma of seeing yourself rejected by your scant army, or had those episodes made a seed that had always lain dormant in the back of your conscience suddenly blossom? What a victory, if you would really start reflecting, give form to the intuitions that until today you had expressed only through brief statements or poems! What a gift if you had really succeeded in facing the truths that are never faced because it wouldn't be advantageous or because we lack the courage or because a blindfold, the blindfold imposed by intellectual dictatorships, prevents us from seeing them! For example, the reasons you were alone and remained alone no matter what you did. And the reasons this was a boon, far from being a disadvantage. A sorrow and a heavy burden, yes, but a boon: the only human way to fight, to believe in freedom, to make the world a bit better, a bit more intelligent, a bit more bearable. Because the world isn't an abstract notion: the world is me, it's you, him. And if I don't change, if you don't change, if he doesn't change, separately, individually, spontaneously, nothing changes and we remain slaves. The fact is that you had admitted you were tired. And I had already realized that this weariness existed. If I retraced the story of the last few weeks, I could see when this had become obvious to me. Now I'll tell it to you.

At the beginning of spring, long before the tragic journey to Athens killed every hope of giving your exile a meaning, the house in the woods was discovered. We realized this when we noticed a group of young men in blue jeans who lingered from morning to dusk outside the gate near the bus stop. They were strange young men: to look at them, they really seemed to be waiting for the bus but when the bus came they didn't board it; and also from a distance you could see them having lively arguments but when you came closer they went dumb. As if they didn't want us to hear what language they were speaking. Their number varied between three and five, but two were always part of the group and they were the two who wore a swastika on their belt buckle. Italians or Greeks? Naturally we also considered the possibility that they were simply loafers who liked to hang out at that spot, or that the two wearing the swastika lived in the villa, but we hadn't once encountered them on our side of the gate, and in the end we were forced to admit that the reason for their presence was you. Were they sent by someone who was interested in knowing your every move, checking on your trips abroad, or was it someone preparing to kidnap you, to kill you? The first week you wanted to confront them, then you had second thoughts, remarking that if they didn't bother us with words or actions we couldn't take any initiative; in fact it was wise to pretend not to have noticed them. The only warlike action you allowed yourself, both leaving the house and returning, was to brandish your pipe like a sword: holding it, in other words, by the bowl. "You know what weapon this is? If somebody attacks you, all you have to do is poke him in the eye." "And if you miss the eye?" "Doesn't matter. Wherever you hit him, you make a hole. Provided the stem is straight, of course, and not curved." And it was no good replying that we had better buy a revolver, that I would buy a revolver, that I would keep it in my purse. "No weapons! I forbid you!" Your faith in the warlike use of the pipe with a straight and not a curved stem was so boundless that you were deaf to any worry on my part, and for that matter I had never seen you with a revolver in your hand. You, who were considered a dynamiter, a devotee of explosives and of weapons, felt a kind of physical repugnance for arms. You didn't know how to use them, you weren't even capable of holding a hunting shotgun correctly: you held the butt low, didn't put your cheek to it, and you always missed the target. Even if it was a bird sleeping on a branch two meters away. Then you consoled yourself, saying: "If I see him again, that one, I'll hit him with my pipe and knock him out!"

But the presence of the young men in blue jeans: spring was slipping by, full of warmth, and it was getting on toward summer when the silent persecution of the group outside the gate ended and in its place another developed, more subtle and cruel. Every night, as soon as we turned off the lamps and went to bed, a round glare, like a stone of light, burst through the window with the wrought-iron balcony and struck us. How they managed to direct it into the room with such precision we never understood. Peering into the darkness of the park, we saw clearly that the electric spotlight was far away, beyond the pines that flanked the outside wall of the park: to strike our window that stone of light had to pass among dozens of trees and find an open path through the trunks and boughs. Still it succeeded perfectly, and despite the barrier of the shutters, the glare tormented us endlessly: now moving slowly over the walls or the ceiling or the bed, now darting nervously from below to above and from right to left, in the sign of the cross, now flashing maliciously in a zigzag striking us in the eyes, hot, impalpable. And this was the moment you lost your head. Since you really couldn't bear that penetrating light in your eyes, you would run to fling open the shutters, hurl yourself onto the balcony, and yell: "Cowards, come out of the darkness, cowards, if you don't come out, I'll come down and find you." And naturally you never went down: you knew very well that this was just what they wanted, to exasperate you and make you go down and they would have you at their mercy, afterward saying that you had been the one to attack them. But that time, no. At the very moment the glare struck our eyes, I saw you spring from the bed, pull on slacks, shoes, and before I could take it all in, you were already on the balcony roaring: "I'm coming!" Then you ran toward the door. I was just in time to rush in front of you, slip out the key, take possession of it, and with all the charge of your fury you try to force my hand open, loosen the grip of my fingers; you clutch at my fingers, but the more you tug the harder I grip, then you seize my wrist and twist it wickedly, you bend my arm, and you seem to want to wrench it from its socket, you fling me to the floor and fall with me and I defend myself badly because I can use only one arm against you, one hand, still I defend myself and I accept the combat. A deaf, dumb, mean combat, a struggle of serpents who twist around each other trying to strangle, both determined not to succumb, and meanwhile they inflict blows on each other, hurt each other without a word escaping their mouths, the only sound is a pained gasping, a kind of rattle, and suddenly a hammer blow rips my stomach. A sharp pain. The key is in your hands. My voice breaks the silence to say what you don't know: "The baby."

You went numb as if struck by a rifle shot in the forehead. You stared at me for a few seconds, eyes wide, lips parted. Then you exhaled the invocation: "Oh Theos! Theos mou! Oh, God! My God!" Then you stood up and, heedless of the glare that continued to turn and flash mercilessly on us, around us, heedless even of me lying on the floor, pierced by that pain in the womb, unbearable and now exasperated by a thousand knives, you burst out in an exultation so frenzied that you seemed to have lost your mind. You laughed, cried, leaped, danced, applauded. You weren't even aware of my suffering, in fact it wasn't to soothe it that at last you picked me up gently, lay me on the bed with tenderness, rested your head against my body, murmured—Good morning, baby, anchor of anchors, chain of chains, joy of joys, wine of all wines, you don't know who I am, I am you, you don't know who you are, you are me, you're life that doesn't die. Life, life, life. I zoi, i zoi, i zoi. Escape from the darkness, baby, escape soon and we'll go far, to a place where they can't find us, where we can play. Enough of this suffering, enough of this struggling. That mad monologue, sweet, wondrous, heart-rending, as the blows of the knife increased in number and intensity, and remorse for not having told you before silenced me, the remorse for not having realized before that a child would have been the only rival of your fate. If I had realized sooner, I wouldn't have had to hurl myself on the door and slip out the key and engage in that bestial combat, undergo that terrible kick that had mortally wounded it. The fact that the blow had wounded it mortally was beyond doubt, the symptoms already spoke out, unmistakable: no miracle, I was sure, could revive the inert creature buried inside me. And still I was silent, unable to sweep away your futile happiness: better to leave you some hours of illusion, I thought, and in the meanwhile remain motionless, recover the strength to drag myself to a doctor. In the morning, careful not to wake you, I gently detached myself from you, went to hear the confirmation of what I knew. But I had made my plans without reckoning that telling you afterward would be much worse because you would be overwhelmed in a much more violent way: renewing the guilt complex in which you drowned, always, thinking of those you had loved and lost. Your father, your brother George, Polycarpos Georgazis. "I'm death. I carry death with me and I sow it," you murmured when you saw me and saw that inert shapeless bundle. Then you vanished for four days and the evening I saw you again I had a hard time recognizing you. The livid hollows under your eyes, the unshaven face, the shirt stained with lipstick, breath stinking of alcohol, you staggered, the caricature of a wretch who has spent four days and four nights guzzling in unrestrained excesses. Lord knows where. Heaven only knows with whom. And offering no explanations, not even asking me how I was, you collapsed into the rocking chair, began a disjointed lament about the weariness that drained your body and soul—I'm old, I'm already old, look I have white hair, I've got lumbago too, and liver trouble and a cough.

The white hair was a silvery clump that you already had in Boiati, the lumbago was a slight, passing rheumatism, the liver trouble was the obvious result of the drinking, the cough the obvious result of the smoking. But at that moment you really believed you were old. Because you felt defeated by existence.

Yet you did start thinking. Painfully at times, naively at other times, perhaps dismissing with a certain superficiality concepts worth deeper investigation or presenting obvious truths as if they were new discoveries, often repeating principles declared a hundred and fifty years earlier by an individualistic anarchism that Nenni had immediately perceived from behind his thick glasses, but you started thinking: marvelously free of the formulas of the intellectual dictatorships that, especially in those years, blindfolded and gagged others. You read, you wrote. Coming back into the house or the hotel, I would almost always find you reading or writing. Little notes, pages, jottings that you then translated for me or read to me with the pride of a boy who has written a good composition in school—Listen to what I decided today, I'll read it to you. "This is the epoch of the *ism*. Communism, capitalism, marxism, historicism, progressivism, socialism, deviationism, corporativism, unionism, fascism: and nobody notices that every *ism* rhymes with fanaticism. This is the period of the *anti:* anticommunist, anticapitalist, anti-marxist, antihistoricist, antiprogressivist, antisocialist, antideviationist, anticorporativist, antiunionist: and nobody notices that every *ist* rhymes with fascist. Nobody says that real fascism consists of being *anti* on principle, out of caprice, denying a priori that in every trend of thought there is something right or something to be used in seeking what is right. It is through locking oneself up in a dogma, in the blind certitude of having gained absolute truth, whether it be the dogma of the virginity of Mary or the dogma of the dictatorship of the proletariat or the dogma of law and order, that the sense or rather the significance of freedom is lost, the only concept that is beyond appeal and beyond debate. The fact is that the word 'freedom' has no synonyms, it has only adjectives or extensions: individual freedom, collective, personal, moral, physical, natural, religious, political, civil, commercial, legal, social, artistic; freedom of expression, of opinion, of worship, of the press, of a strike, of speech, of faith, of conscience. In the final analysis it is the only fanaticism that is acceptable: because without it a man is not a man and thought is not thought." "Bravo!" "You like it? You really like it? Then listen to this other one, because this other is more important, it talks about the left and the right, the shithead intellectuals with their fake left who've really given me a pain in the ass." You were waving a paper covered with scrawls, crossings-out, and you began to declaim again.

"Many intellectuals believe that being an intellectual means enunciating ideologies, or developing them, treating them, and then linking them together to interpret life according to formulas and absolute truths. This attitude does not care about reality, man, the intellectuals themselves; in other words they refuse to admit that they themselves are not made only of brain: they also have a heart or something resembling a heart, and an intestine, and a sphincter, therefore feelings and needs alien to the intelligence, not controllable by the intelligence. These intellectuals are not intelligent, they are stupid, and in the final analysis they are not even intellectuals, they are the high priests of an ideology. With the stupidity of high priests they do not recognize that, once they are married to the ideology, or worse still if they married the ideology in a marriage that denies adultery and divorce, they are no longer free to think. Because everything is bent to fit that solution, everything is judged according to those formulas: on the one side hell and on the other heaven, on one side the licit and on the other the illicit. Therefore to be coherent they become incoherent or, rather, dishonest. Take the intellectual of the left, the intellectual fashionable today, or rather the intellectual who follows the fashion out of convenience or fear or lack of fantasy: he will always be ready to condemn the dictatorships of the right, nothing wrong with that, but he will never or almost never condemn the dictatorships of the left. The former he dissects, studies, combats with books and manifestos; the latter he remains silent about or excuses or at most criticizes with embarrassment and timidity. In certain cases even falling back on Machiavelli: the end justifies the means. What end? A society conceived on abstract principles, mathematical calculations, two plus two makes four, thesis and antithesis make synthesis, and so forgetting that in modern mathematics two plus two does not necessarily make four, maybe it makes thirty-six, or forgetting that in advanced philosophy thesis and antithesis are the same thing, matter and antimatter are two aspects of the identical reality? It is thanks to their calculations, to the lugubrious fanaticism of the ideologies, to the illusion or rather the presumption that the good and the beautiful are all on one side, that a genocide or a murder or an abuse is illegitimate if it takes place on the right and legitimate or at least excusable if it takes place on the left. Conclusion, the great disease of our time, is called ideology and the bearers of its infection are the stupid intellectuals, the lay high priests not prepared to admit that life (they call it history) furnishes on its own a way of reshuffling their mental masturbations, and thus proves the artificiality of the dogma. Its fragility, its unreality. If this were not so, why would the Communist regimes repeat the same outrages of the capitalist regimes? Why would they have the same Ioannidises, the same Hazizikises, the same Theophiloiannakoses, the same Zakarakises of the fascist regimes? And why would they fight among themselves, supported by feelings and needs like love of country and egoistic nationalism? It's time to denounce the disease, without timidity, without embarrassment, without fear. And to do so it is not enough to stop at Marx and the Marxists, we have to go back at least two thousand years, refer back to the Christian ideology. That is the ideology that conceived of the unnatural division, the licit on one side and the illicit on the other, paradise on one side and hell on the other. Today the masters of our brain, the theologians of the left, simply repeat the errors of those masters: take the cross from the flagpole, put the hammer and sickle there, and you will see that it remains the same thing: a rag that waves the usual privileges, the usual ambitions, the usual frauds." Then: "Do you like it? Really like it? They're just notes, of course. Too bad I didn't make them in Boiati. The fact is that in prison you can't think. You have all that time and yet you can't think, it's a lot if you can yell out some poem."

You studied. Proudhon, for example, whose libertarian socialism, opposed to violence, was suited to your search. Then Plato, though I couldn't understand what you were looking for in Plato, and then writers like Albert Camus whom you called Camis because in Greek the *u* is pronounced *i:* nor was there any way of making you pronounce it Camus. "Camus!" "Camis!" You adored Camus—Camis because in your late adolescence you had happened to read the text of his debate with Sartre. "An idealist who can oppose the messiah complex of absolute principles," you said of Camus—Camis. And sometimes inserting something of your own, a sentence or a comparison or a thought, or altering the form to suit yourself, you often recited the passages from it that summed up your position. "Listen to this: 'Organized religions do not answer the needs of modern man, religious pantomimes make no sense in our time, whether they come from the churches, or whether they present themselves with the new or pseudo-new dress of Marxism.' Now listen to this: 'An intelligent man cannot accept an ideology that delivers him over to the state, that considers him the state's passive subject. It is outrageous to speak of men in terms of historic missions, it is dangerous. Because after it has been said with books, it is said with the police: establishing at what time I must or must not go to bed, at what time I may or may not drink a bottle of wine, finally lining me up in Red Square to make me go and kneel before the Holy Sepulcher of Lenin. No, you cannot justify anything at all in the name of logic and of history. It is not logic that makes history!' " "That isn't what Camus says, Alekos. He says that history isn't everything. And besides he doesn't mention any bottle of wine or the Holy Sepulcher of Lenin." "Who cares? I'm completing him, improving him." At times, on the contrary, you would copy out the passage with the scruple of an amanuensis copying the New Testament on illuminated vellum, and you would recite the words to me faithfully: "We must, today, ask two questions. Do you or don't you accept, directly or indirectly, being killed or being made the object of violence? Are you or aren't you willing, directly or indirectly, to kill or to use violence? Those who answer both questions affirmatively will automatically be committed to a series of consequences from which a new way of posing the problem of the struggle will result." And also: "Since man has been delivered totally to history, he can no longer turn toward that part of himself that is as real as the part connected with history, and we live in terror. To emerge from this terror, it is necessary to reflect and to act according to our reflection. At stake is the fate of millions of Europeans who, sated with violence and with lies, disappointed in their greatest hopes, feel repugnance at the idea of killing their fellowmen, even to convince them, or at the idea of being convinced with the same system." These were pages in which you seemed to seek a confirmation of your own change of heart: to believe no longer in bombs, explosions, arms, the struggle conducted in bloodshed.

Yet this change was so total that I had actually stopped wondering if it had bloomed from a seed buried in the depths of your unconscious mind or if it derived from a need for peace whose detonator had been the lost baby. You never showed any sign of regret, of nostalgia for the bold enterprises, the impossible challenges. Everything you did now seemed the quintessence of reason and of reasonableness: participating in conferences and rallies, distributing among the emigrants the volume of poems that had meanwhile appeared, going to Brussels to meet the leaders of the Common Market. Even your new monomania was as peaceful a one as could be imagined: it consisted simply in obtaining from the Italian radio the time necessary to transmit a biweekly broadcast that could be picked up in Greece. Programs of the sort already existed in France, England, Germany, but they were barely audible because of the distance; the Italian radio, on the contrary, had a wavelength capable of covering the whole region between the Ionian and the Aegean. So you kept going to Rome to explain it to ministers, undersecretaries, party leaders: insistent, patient, stubborn, determined not to allow yourself to be discouraged by the indifference, the hypocrisy, the jesuitism of the "we'll see, we'll look into it, we'll consider." And even when it was clear that you weren't going to get anywhere, that the indifference and the hypocrisy and the jesuitism would triumph as always, you didn't alter your conduct. "Too bad," you said. "Here's another disappointment, another price to pay." It was your favorite remark by now. And every time I heard it I couldn't believe my ears because the temptations to resume the old way echoed around you like the sirens' song that called to Ulysses. "Odysseus, Odysseus! Come, O brave Odysseus! Hear us, son of Laertes! Land!" In Europe the Palestinians were still sowing massacres everywhere; in Germany urban guerrilla warfare had become a constant system; in Italy the philosophy of violence was mounting every moment. Kidnappings, blackmail, shoot-outs, murders were no longer the exclusive property of the right wing; they represented a grim fashion of the extreme left and it didn't take much to understand that far from dying out it would grow and become habit. What if these sirens loosened the ropes with which Ulysses had bound himself to the mainmast of his ship? And what if Ulysses succumbed to their call to forget his change, his new battle against the windmills. I was answered by a savage cry: "You don't understand me at all. Not at aaaalllll! How dare you insinuate I have something in common with those altar boys of fanaticism, those bureaucrats of terrorism, those irresponsible killers who shoot like John Wayne on the convenient territory of democracy, bad but still democracy, sick but still democracy, those dogmatists who aren't risking the tortures and the firing squads of a dictatorship? I'm no terrorist! I never have been! I believe in democracy! I fight against tyrants, have you forgotten that? I forbid you, forbid you to confuse me with those wretches who shed blood to apply the ideological formulas of their abstractions! Those fascists dressed in red, these pseudo-revolutionaries!" And the phrase pseudo-revolutionaries was to become from that day on one of your favorite slogans. To condemn the timidity and the weaknesses of the democracies that give in, you were to grow fond instead of the slogan "This isn't freedom, it's a fiesta of freedom." And one evening when Rome was teeming with disorder, windows smashed, shops attacked, automobiles burned, I also knew why next to Proudhon and Camus you also placed Plato. You opened to a page of Plato and began to declaim: "When a people consumed by thirst for freedom has clumsy cupbearers for leaders, who pour as much as is demanded, until the nation is drunk, it then happens that if the rulers resist the demands of the evermore demanding subjects, they are declared reprobates and accused of wanting to destroy freedom. And it also happens that he who shows himself disciplined toward his superiors is called a man without character, a servant, the frightened father ends by treating his sons as equals, the son no longer has any fear or veneration for his parents, the master no longer dares reproach the pupils and flatters them, so that they mock him and claim the same rights and the same consideration as their elders. And the elders rather than seem too severe agree with the young. The soul of the citizens then becomes sick unto death, and wherever there are cases of submission the majority becomes indignant and refuses to obey, and in the end all are heedless of the written laws and of those unwritten, and they have no more regard or respect for anything. In the midst of such license the weed of tyranny is born and flourishes there. In fact every excess habitually leads to the opposite excess, in seasons as in plants and in bodies, and all the more in government."

But how stupid established power is, the Power in power that exploits everything, everyone, and never dies. How blind it is, how deaf, how ignorant. On this very evening, that same Mr. Kissinger who had confirmed the refusal to grant you a visa for the United States came to Rome on an official visit, and escorted by a hundred and ten bodyguards, smeared with honors like a Persian satrap, he installed himself in our hotel. From that moment nobody in the city was more closely watched than you, who were preaching against violence and reciting Plato. The rooms next to ours were occupied by his bodyguards; unmistakable in their ghastly Hawaiian shirts, their hairy hands clutching cans of beer, their colleagues spied on us constantly from the half-closed windows of the opposite building. As if this weren't enough, the whole corridor of our floor teemed with plainclothes agents with revolvers stuck in their belts. They were assigned, among other things, to rummage in our drawers: twice, on returning to the room, we found objects shifted or altered. But perhaps I am wrong to call Power in power blind, deaf, stupid, ignorant. Power sees all, hears all, knows all. Power knew that indeed the real enemy of that pathetic figure was not the ambiguous barricaderos who in the years to follow would shoot harmless and unarmed people. It was you.

3

IT WAS MID-JULY AND ONE MORNING YOU WOKE UP TO announce: "The junta is about to fall." Then you told me the dream you had had during the night from which you derived the prophecy of the junta's fall. You were at the bottom of a well filled with fish and it was so dark that the sky, seen from those depths, was only a remote glow. You had been down there for an incalculable time, perhaps centuries, and you wanted only one thing: to escape, up, toward the sky. But the sides of the well were smooth, without a single hole, no kind of outcrop to offer a foothold, and you could only hope for a miracle. Suddenly the miracle occurred, holes and outcrops appeared, and you began to climb. A terrible effort because often you slipped, you fell among the fish and you had to start all over. A very long effort. Finally you reached the edge of the well and clung there to catch your breath and look at what was outside. There was a desert of gravel. In the center of the desert a mountain with a boulder balanced on its peak. And suddenly from that mountain rose a roar, a dull roar heralding a landslide, the boulder began to sway, tilted forward, broke from the peak and rolled down: to shatter into countless little pebbles like those that made up the desert. You were swept up in a surge of happiness. As brief as a blink, however, and followed by a blind rage because on the peak of the mountain a second boulder promptly appeared: identical with the first, but stable. It was the stability that made you angry, filled you with the irresistible need to demolish it, and then you started to climb over the side. But in vain. A mysterious power transformed your legs into blocks of lead, your arms into rivers of weakness. You tried again and again: the attempts did nothing but discourage you, leave you there on the edge of the well. You were suffering horribly, you realized that the new boulder had to be demolished; if you didn't demolish it, it would never tilt, never break from the peak to roll down and be shattered like the first, and how long that suffering lasted you couldn't remember. In the dream it had seemed very long to you. The seasons ripened, heat alternated with cold, cold with heat, sun followed rain, and rain followed sun, and you kept clinging there, half of your body outside the well and half inside, your eyes glued to the boulder. But you seemed to remember that at the beginning it was summer and afterward the snow had fallen twice, the swallows had passed twice. The swallows in fact were passing again when you decided to try something, not just to look. You reached out to grasp a stone, to fling it against the boulder, make it lose its equilibrium. A dangerous act, you realized, because for some time you had known that the holes and outcrops in the wall had disappeared: if you should fall, you would never climb up again. Still you had to try, you also knew this, and leaning out, you picked up a stone. You raised it to fling it. But at the very moment when you were preparing to hurl it, a terrible wind came from the direction of the boulder. And it struck you with merciless violence, tearing you from the edge of the well. And you plunged down to the bottom, among the fish, forever.

"What a horrible dream, Alekos." "Yes, horrible. I can't get it out of my mind." "And yet, a dream that announces the fall of the junta shouldn't be horrible." "No, but it didn't only announce the fall of the junta. What made me fall back into the well forever wasn't the junta: it was the heir of the junta." "Oh, stop it! You're not going to fall into any well. You dream these things because you think them up during the day: the dreams we have when we're asleep are only confused reflections of the thoughts we have when we're awake. Science shows that—" "Science doesn't exist. Science is an opinion. And it doesn't show a damn thing, least of all life and death." We had no argument, however, on the meaning you attributed to the rest: the mountain represented Power, the eternal Power that looms over us, offering no avenue of escape, and the boulder teetering on the mountain represented the regime which Power uses until it decides to get rid of it, replace it with another that in different circumstances is more useful. Dictatorship, democracy, revolution: boulders balanced on a mountaintop. The same boulder, the same curse that human beings have borne since the day when they gathered into a tribe. But if the boulder that falls and is shattered into gravel was the junta, who was the boulder that appeared in its place? And why did you want to destroy it, since it had replaced the junta? Because it kept you glued to the edge of the well, half your body outside and half inside, preventing you from climbing over it? This was what I wanted to know. "But what about the boulder that takes the place of the junta? Who is it?" "You mean does it have a name, a face? Of course, it does." "Then tell me." "No, it'll soon be revealed anyway." "Soon?" "Yes, it's a matter of days now, maybe of hours." And twenty-four hours later there was the coup d'etat on Cyprus, the attempt to assassinate Makarios, the Turkish invasion of the island; a week later the junta summoned the political leaders that Papadopoulos had ousted and gave them the responsibility of forming a government that would save the country from a war with Turkey. But you didn't rejoice. You merely murmured: "The boulder has broken from the mountain, the boulder remains on the mountain. When are you leaving for Athens?" "When am I leaving, or when are we leaving?" "You. I'm not going." "Why not? I don't understand."

"You'll understand when you hear a little voice greet you: dear friend, my dear young lady, what a pleasure to meet you, I read all your books, your articles, I'm an admirer of yours, a colleague, I write too, you know."

I left without you. And, though not understanding your words, I began to sense their meaning as soon as I landed at the Athens airport, where I was promptly held, shut up in a kind of closet. Everybody was going by, now, at that moment Theodorakis went by, coming from Paris, but my name was on the blacklist and, before they would cross it out, let me out of the closet, quite a while had to pass. One policeman seemed favorable, another not; trying to come to an agreement they quarreled among themselves and didn't know who was supposed to authorize my entry: the new Ministry of the Interior or the ESA? The night before, Karamanlis had returned from exile and had taken the oath as prime minister, now the government was made up of civilians, the majority of them formerly persecuted by the dictatorship. But Gizikis continued to be president of the Republic, Ioannidis still maintained control of the army and of the ESA, not one member of the regime had been arrested, and the political prisoners remained in prison: from whatever angle one looked at things, one's mind encountered the puzzles of an ambiguous comedy. Everybody, for that matter, was saying that nothing was clear, nothing was sure except the fact that the junta had not fallen: it had abdicated. And not of its own free will but by order of the Americans, obviously opposed to a war between Greece and Turkey, two NATO countries. But a regime that abdicates is not always a dead regime, and if it abdicates while retaining the key posts such as the presidency and retaining control of the army and the police, it can actually snatch power back in the space of a night. So the situation could change again suddenly. Everything depended on Ioannidis. It was an open secret that he had given in only when the U.S. ambassador had relayed the ultimatum of Washington; Ioannidis had still cried betrayal, accusing the CIA of having suggested to him the error of the Cyprus coup, hissing, "They screwed me, I was too naive." But now he considered himself anything but defeated, he constantly hinted at the troops with which he would defend his honor, the tanks with which he would react to any offense, and people were afraid. Once the first flush of enthusiasm was past, most of them stayed shut up in their houses to avoid being compromised, and nobody spoke of freedom: at most, they spoke only of an odor of freedom. Karamanlis himself, always touchy, in a bad humor, seemed to be expecting the worst. The one person who apparently harbored no fears or worries was the new minister of defense, Evangelos Tossitsas Averoff. The man who greeted me now with his little piping voice: "Dear friend, my dear young lady, what a pleasure to meet you, I read all your books, your articles, I am an admirer of yours, a colleague, I write too, you know."

He was in the doorway of my room, escorted by a naval officer, and his hands imprisoned mine like a seashell that no knife can open. Soft, nevertheless; without bones. I observed him with curiosity. Under his arched eyebrows, his black, round eyes penetrated mine like the eyes of a hypnotist, yet restless and so slippery that they resembled two olives swimming in oil. Below the gray-streaked moustache the mouth, very funny because it had the shape of a toothless mouth and yet it was full of teeth, smiled with the ecstasy of the lover who for too long has remained far from his fair one and finally is preparing to make love to her. A role not suited to his appearance or to his age: he was a little man of about sixty, with narrow, sloping shoulders, wide hips, and a fat belly; a great crooked nose, a bump at the end, dominated an equally unseductive face. But the forehead was high, intelligent, you sensed his intelligence long before you grasped it with your reason. If he wasn't intelligent, he was shrewd with that shrewdness that can't be distinguished from intelligence. Moreover he was tough. You could sense this too. Sensing it, you were amazed, you said that nothing in such an appearance and in such behavior could justify the idea of toughness, yet the toughness existed, hidden in the folds of an unctuous flaccidity. I freed my hands from the shell's valves, which had parted slightly for a moment: "Come in, sir, do make yourself at home." He came in, dismissed the officer with a sharp, haughty gesture, sat in the armchair, and the minuet of compliments resumed. "But, sir, I didn't expect you to take the trouble of coming here. I should have come to you." "My dear, my very dear friend! A gentleman would never allow a lady to be so disturbed, to come to him. And such a fascinating and charming and famous lady! If I hadn't come, I would have been rude almost to the point of the most unforgivable boorishness. Do you understand my Italian?" He spoke excellent Italian, without mistakes and without accent. "Your Italian is impeccable, sir, both in your choice of words and your pronunciation. Not even Panagoulis speaks it as well as you do." I said your name deliberately, to see how he would react, but he didn't react at all, as if he hadn't heard it. "My dear, my very dear young lady! I learned Italian in Italy, you know. When I was a prisoner of war, in Rimini." "Rimini? Zakarakis was also a prisoner of war in Rimini." "Zakarakis who?" "The commandant of Boiati, Panagoulis's prison." Again he didn't pick it up. "Rimini, Rome. Great times. We all learned Italian in those years." "Not Zakarakis. By the way, Excellency, what has happened to people like Zakarakis, Theophiloiannakos, Hazizikis? Or should I ask first of all about Ioannidis? That's what everyone is wondering about. If the junta is no longer in power, people ask themselves, why has Ioannidis remained head of the ESA?" He sighed. He shifted twice in the easy chair. He shut his eyes, opened them again, and finally launched into an impassioned preamble. Before answering my delicate question he had to give me some background, he said, background that nobody knew about: too many people believed that the reason for the change was Cyprus, the stupid coup on Cyprus. "Ah, no, dear friend! No, that was only the beginning. What made the military abandon the government of the country was the discovery that the catastrophe would arrive from Bulgaria." "From Bulgaria?!" "Yes, dear friend, yes. From the Communists. They always have their finger in everything. In fact, what did the Bulgarian Communists do the moment we started having trouble with Turkey and Cyprus? They massed tens of thousands of troops at the border. And five hundred Russian fighter planes, I said five hundred, landed in the Bulgarian military airports. And two thousand Russian technical advisers, I said two thousand, came into Bulgaria from Rumania. And the officers of the junta let themselves be overwhelmed by panic. A panic that lasted thirty-six hours. The most desperate thirty-six hours of their life because . . . well, because they are patriots, patriots with a capital P. Ioannidis included. Ioannidis, first and foremost. And Gizikis assembled his chiefs of staff and said to them: 'The nation is lost, gentlemen; to save it, the only course is to give control to the civilians.' Then he called us . . ."

He talked and talked, and a mysterious uneasiness irked me, along with my regret at having got in touch with him. Why had I? Who had suggested it to me? Not you. You had never mentioned his name, never hinted that his was the little voice of the "dear friend, dear young lady." Who then? Ah, yes. Kanellopoulos, the former prime minister who had been arrested on the night of the coup and who today should have occupied the place of Karamanlis. I knew Kanellopoulos, I had met him in the days when you were asking for a passport, and from that meeting a warm friendship had developed. I liked his ascetic, weary face, his manners, the manners of an elderly disillusioned gentleman, I admired his courage, his old-fashioned liberal culture, and the moment they had released me from the little room at the airport I had hurried to see him again. We talked at length, without reticence, but he glossed over the unexpected summons to Karamanlis to return, he glossed over it with a kind of embarrassment—I can't answer that, I don't want to discuss it. And suddenly he said: "Ask Averoff. Question Averoff." I telephoned Averoff and he volunteered to come to my hotel. A strange business. Could he possibly be the boulder at the top of the mountain? Despite his clever chatter about the Bulgarians and his even more clever praise of the members of the junta, his almost shameless concern with exculpating them, there was a link missing in the chain of evidence. A link that perhaps was there, within reach, and that still I couldn't identify. Like looking for your eyeglasses when they're on your nose. It had to be found. I had to pay closer attention to what he was saying. "And now, dear friend, let me explain how Gizikis and his chiefs of staff behaved toward us, like true gentlemen. For that matter, they have always behaved like true gentlemen toward me. You surely know that I was involved in the unsuccessful revolt of the navy, last summer, and they arrested me. Well, they didn't harm a hair on my head. Impeccable. Ah, I must underline that: impeccable. And yesterday . . . imagine, my dear, we arrived one at a time and Gizikis received us standing, polite, jovial, then he invited us to sit down and offered us orange juice or coffee. When we were all there he also sat down and with the greatest simplicity he declared that the country was about to undergo the final tragedy, and to save the country the whole junta had decided to renounce all command, except military command. Afterward he called his chiefs of staff and one by one they repeated the same thing. Then we began the discussion. We spoke of responsibilities. And here Gizikis was admirable. Honest, human, friendly. He offered himself as scapegoat. 'I realize the end of the regime demands a scapegoat,' he said, 'and therefore I offer myself as such. I didn't want to become president of the Republic, gentlemen, but I agreed to accept the position and it is right that I pay.' Well, I needn't add that there was no thought of entertaining such a proposal and indeed we had to commit ourselves to avoiding reprisals, uprisings, punishments. And we did commit ourselves in that sense. Finally we confronted the decisive question: the choice of the man to form the government. The majority wanted Kanellopoulos. But I wanted Karamanlis." "Why Karamanlis and not yourself, Excellency?" The smile reappeared: "Simple, my dear, very simple! Because I wouldn't give up the Ministry of Defense! Ah, on this point I have always been categorical! Cat-e-gor-i-cal!" "And you won." "Yes, dear young lady, yes. When I want something, I get it. And when I want two things, I get two."

The Ministry of Defense, the army! That was the link that was missing in the chain. What was it you said about the army? "In Greece whoever commands the army, commands Greece." I sought the round black eyes, the two olives swimming in oil: "Excellency, who commands in Greece today?" The two olives hardened and the piping voice became icy: "Who do you think, dear friend?" "An hour ago I thought Ioannidis, Excellency." "My dear friend! I am the man from whom Brigadier General Ioannidis takes orders. I am the man who commands the army." "And whoever commands the army in Greece, commands Greece. Isn't that true, Excellency?" "Who says that?" "Panagoulis." He leaped to his feet. "It has really been a pleasure meeting you, an exquisite pleasure. What a pity I must leave now." He started toward the door, held out his boneless hands to me, clasped my right hand again in the valves of the shell. "I hope soon also to meet our friend. Tell him that. By the way, when is he coming back?" And without awaiting a reply he went off, erasing in my mind any residual doubt. Only two days later it started pricking at my mind again. The political prisoners were beginning to leave the prisons, the people were looking festive again, the odor of freedom was gradually assuming the shape of freedom: what if I had been mistaken.

You smiled, mocking. "The boulders on top of the mountain are not necessarily malevolent, and if the prisons weren't emptied of political prisoners, what would be the sense of talking about freedom? He would never behave like a tyrant, not him: he's intelligent. You know how he managed to liquidate Kanellopoulos? At a certain point of the meeting with the orange juice and coffee he suggested a pause, for meditation, and he went out with the other politicians. On the pretext of going to the toilet, he remained in the president's palace. 'You go ahead, we'll meet later.' He went back to Gizikis's office and the two of them called Karamanlis in Paris. 'Leave at once, come and head the government.' When the others reappeared with the results of their meditations, Karamanlis had already accepted the assignment and was flying to Athens in the personal plane of Giscard d'Estaing. A masterpiece. And I'll bet my arm that the masterpiece had been prepared by Averoff before the junta abdicated." "Anyway he said he hopes to see you soon." "That son of a bitch." "And then he asked me when you're coming back. When are you going back?" This time, instead of answering, you went to the window of the hotel and pointed out a couple, sitting at the bar opposite the hotel: a young man in blue jeans and a woman. She was about thirty, elegant, attractive. Full bosom and ash blond hair. "Who are they, Alekos?" "I don't know. I've never seen him before. Her, yes. Again yesterday, in Geneva." The day after my departure for Athens you had gone to Geneva to follow the conference on Cyprus. "In Geneva?" "Yes, at least twice. And the first time I didn't recognize her. I just felt a kind of uneasiness. But the second—" "Recognized?" "Yes, from Stockholm. In Stockholm, wherever I went, she turned up. At the beginning I didn't pay any attention, I thought she was some Swedish fan. But then I was forced to convince myself that she was no fan and she wasn't Swedish either." "Why not?" "Because she didn't speak Swedish." I looked at her again, puzzled. "Are you sure?" "Quite sure. Besides she loves wigs. In Stockholm she was blond, like here, but in Geneva she had brown hair. That's why I didn't recognize her the first time." "Think carefully, Alekos. Maybe the Geneva woman isn't the same one sitting there on the sidewalk. Maybe they just look alike. It's hard to tell from a distance." "I'm not judging her from a distance. She was on my plane. I had time to look at her carefully." "Did she notice?" "I hope not. Come away from that window, I wouldn't want her to catch on now." I moved back. "And the boy?" "Never saw him before. Anyway I'm sure he doesn't count. She's the one who counts, she's the one who's following me. And very cleverly. She's a top-level professional, a really smart spy." "Spy for whom?" "I don't know. To find that out I have to catch her, and to catch her I have to let her go on for a little longer. She could work for anybody: for the KYP, for the SID. And if she's following me for the SID it's to do the KYP a favor. The Italian secret services and the Greek secret services are always trading favors: everybody knows that." "Alekos! But the KYP was working for the junta!" "And now it's working for the new government. Secret services are always at the disposal of Power, they don't change just because a regime changes or a policy. At times to save face they change their men, or rather their directors, but it's like slipping a new glove, exactly like the old one, on the same hand. And I don't think Averoff has even bothered to slip a new glove on the KYP." "Yes, but why would the KYP be shadowing you or ask the SID to shadow you now?! A man with your past, with—" "Certain people aren't interested in my past. They're interested in my present, or rather, my future." The future. Your future. That question tormented me since the fall of the junta. What would you do now with your future, with your life? I sought your eyes: "Well, Alekos, when are you going back?" But again you evaded the question, pointing to the woman and the boy in blue jeans. "Uhm! I bet those two would like to know that too. In fact I bet their bosses would be very happy if I went back to Greece in a coffin." And for the second time you didn't answer me.

Same thing the next day. And the day after and the day after that. One by one they were all going back: politicians, actresses, students, writers, and frequently liars, who had been abroad only to save their skin or to play the comfortable role of the political exile. "I'm a victim of the junta, down with the junta!" Welcomed as heroes and heroines by yelling, sweating masses, maybe by the same people who had slammed the door in your face, they landed at Athens airport and raising a clenched fist, shouting "Long live the people, long live freedom!" they rushed off to lay the foundations of a parliamentary career. Liberals, socialists, anti-fascists of opportunism. And you were silent, still. Hailed like an ancient warrior, an Agamemnon returning from the ramparts of Troy, Papandreou informed the press that he would go home by sea and land in Patras to march on the capital with a procession of cars and buses, a forest of red flags. "Andreas! long live Andreas!" And you, still, silent. As my puzzlement increased. Were you delaying because you didn't want to mingle with the return of the dogs who bark when the danger is past, the jackals who fatten on the sufferings of others? Was it that without dictatorship your country interested you less, that the idea of facing a normal existence filled you with ennui? It is the drama of many fighters, I thought: when the war is over they can't adjust to peace. And remarks to which I had never attached great significance reechoed in my ears, in support of that thesis: "How I understand Guevara! Rather than bore my ass off in Cuba, I'd have gone to die in Bolivia, too!" Or: "This morning I met a Greek who's really fighting, a Trotskyite. Too bad he has a party card and we can't work together. He said to me: 'My dear friend, if the junta falls, the two of us will be unemployed and we'll be bored stiff!'" In Italy you weren't yet bored stiff: there were the boys with the swastika on their belts, the blonde with wigs, the suspicion that someone would like to see you go home in a coffin. The mysterious persecution continued in fact, aggravated by a far from negligible episode. When I had turned in my piece on the July 23 events, we went to Zurich, and as we were having supper in a restaurant near Nicholas's house, you cried: "Oh, no! But I didn't see her on the plane." "Alekos, don't tell me she's here." "Yes, she is. Behind you. Don't turn around." "Alone, or with somebody?" "Alone." "What color hair, this time?" "Black. She has black hair." "What shall we do?" "A test. We'll go out and we'll move to another restaurant. If she follows us there too—" Interrupting the meal, and with ostentation, we left and went to a tavern with garden at the opposite end of the city. There, a few minutes later, she showed up, as if looking for someone, she glanced at us for an instant, absently, it seemed, then went off, as if saying: "Too bad, he's not here." "Let's run after her, Alekos. Confront her." "With what pretext? It's no crime to change wigs and to be in the same cities as me." "And in the same streets, the same restaurants. If you don't want to confront her, let's go to the police." "Good girl! And what would you say to the police? There's a blonde, no she has brown hair, no it's black, who happens to be wherever we are? Apart from the fact that the secret services actually make use of the police. Let's give her some rope. I really want the satisfaction of catching her red-handed." Yes, perhaps this was what kept you from returning to Greece, I decided finally. The obscure fascination of knowing that you were in greater danger abroad than at home, the fear of being bored with normalcy and with the applause that they would surely also give you.

But suddenly one evening: "I've made up my mind. I'm going back on August 13, I'll go back on the anniversary of my attempt on Papadopoulos." "So this is what you were waiting for?" "Not exactly, though the idea of refreshing a few memories rather amuses me. And when I say some memories I don't mean only Ioannidis or Averoff. I also mean my pals on the other shore, those who have never done anything." "Alekos, what does 'not exactly' mean." "It means . . . You remember when you asked me if I preferred Garibaldi or Cavour?" "Yes, and you answered that you preferred Cavour." "That is to say, politics. Well, after having thought some things over, the right and the left and human beings, I'm not so sure I love that kind of politics. And returning to Greece means returning to that kind of politics." Then, curtly changing the subject, as if discussing it irritated you, you said that anyway the immediate problem was something else. It was to survive until August 13.

To survive until August 13 some precautions had to be taken. And the first precaution was keeping far away from the places where the mysterious persecutors so interested in your moves knew they might find you: the house in the woods, the house in Tuscany, the very city of Rome. We then decided to spend a few days at the sea, thus giving ourselves some rest, some privacy, and we chose the island of Ischia, where a friend who had a hotel would lodge us even if we arrived unexpectedly. "The important thing is not to tell, not to reserve rooms, and travel almost without luggage. Nobody will notice, nobody will find us." Twenty-four hours later, on the contrary, she had already found us. Assuming she had ever lost sight of us. With her fake, absent air, her full bosom, her ash blond hair, again ash blond, she was at the Rome station and about ten meters away from us she was waiting for the same train: the Naples express. Not alone, however: with a boy in blue jeans similar to the one with her in the bar opposite the hotel in Milan. "I don't understand, Alekos. Why are they so anxious to know what you're doing and where you're going?" "Maybe that's not all they want. Maybe they want something more. I'm really beginning to believe they want something more." "Shall we go anyhow?" "Of course. It would be the same anywhere, now. And I'm interested to see what her next move will be." "Good." We got into a carriage far from hers, we settled in a compartment occupied by an old couple and, almost at once, there is the boy in blue jeans, holding a package inside a cellophane bag. He puts the package on the rack, sits down beside you, starts leafing through a pornographic comic book. On his belt buckle a swastika similar to the swastikas of those characters who used to loiter near the gate of the house in the woods. But the repulsive detail wasn't the swastika, it was his nervous agitation, as if he were tormented by some terrible problem or by fear. Throwing away the comic book he sighed, huffed, cast strange glances at the package. At a certain point he stood, picked it up, put it down again, picked it up again, frightening the old couple, and finally he went off, cursing: Christ this, Madonna that, asshole here, asshole there. "Let's go after him, Alekos." "No, that's what he wants: a brawl. If I react, I'll draw attention away from her and then I won't even be able to see if she takes the Hovercraft for Ischia. But she will take it, just wait and see. And that's fine: it's a confirmation and an excuse to grab her, to find out who she is and who sent her and what for. This time I'll grab her. I'll make her spill everything."

The Hovercraft was very crowded. With difficulty we managed to board it, and closed behind a barrier of bodies, we were pressed on the deck: trying in vain to make our way through, to find a comfortable corner. Even moving half a meter was impossible. "We've lost her," I murmured. "Maybe." "It would have been better if we confronted her the minute we left the train." "Maybe." As soon as we had left the train, in fact, she reappeared with the boy in blue jeans. They were at the end of the platform and the boy no longer had the package in the cellophane envelope, she was speaking furiously as if reproaching him. About what? For not having provoked you enough? Maintaining your composure and still pretending not to have noticed her, you pushed me out of the railway station: "Come on, don't turn around." The trip from the station to the dock was short, we made it on foot, the better to see if she were following us. But she didn't follow us. "Unless she took a taxi and got there before." "Perhaps." "In that case she's down below with the seated passengers." "Maybe." "Or else she isn't following us anymore, she's staying in Naples." "Maybe." The engines rolled, the Hovercraft slowly moved away from the dock. "So much the better." And just as you said so much the better, there she was on the opposite side of the deck, waving to two people remaining ashore: the boy in blue jeans and another boy with a round face covered with moles. She was waving her right hand, putting it to her ear as if holding a telephone and repeating: "At eight! I'll call you tonight at eight!" A fresh, bold voice, and speaking perfect Italian. The two nodded with the disciplined look of those obeying a leader. I saw you blanch and then with an abrupt movement dive into the barrier of bodies, heedless of the protests—What do you want, where do you think you're going, who're you shoving. Ten minutes later you were back. "She's gone." "Gone?" "I couldn't find her. I've covered the whole boat. She's not here." "I'll go." I went, raising more protests—What do you want, where do you think you're going, who're you shoving. I looked everywhere for her. Even in the rest rooms. But I didn't find her. "But she's on board!" "Of course, she's on board." "Let's try again together." "No, we'll surprise her on landing. We'll be the first off and we'll surprise her." We were the first off. We positioned ourselves at the foot of the gangway, watching every passenger, determined not to let her escape us. We were never distracted for a moment except when a tourist started yelling that they had stolen his wallet and there was a little brawl that shoved us aside. And perhaps that was when she slipped off unobserved because a moment later an automobile drove away and her blond head was quite visible through the rear window.

The first day nothing happened. The first day we were almost serene. Our friend who owned the hotel had given us a pleasant room on the sea, the hotel was excellent, with two restaurants and a private beach and a fine swimming pool and a bay protected by a No

Entrance sign, and we were so consoled by it that we decided it was useless to let ourselves be overcome by anger or anguish: we might as well enjoy our holiday. At most we would be careful: no going out on the roads, no swimming far out to sea, staying always near other people, near possible witnesses. But the next morning you cried: "Wake up, wake up!" "What is it?" "Look." Five or six hundred meters from the shore, on a direct line with our room, there was a big covered motorboat. "Alekos, we're at the seaside, and it's August. Don't you think it's normal to see a motorboat on the water and in August?" "In the daytime, yes; at night, no. It's been there since last night." "So what?" "I'll tell you; motorboats don't go cruising around at night, and they don't stay in one place like that." "Like what? Maybe they're fishing!" "They're fishing, all right. But I'd swear they're not fishing for fish. Ever since it arrived, it hasn't moved." "Maybe the engine broke down." "If the engine had broken down, they would already have gone out to fix it or to have the boat towed. The engine works very well. You want to bet?" I bet and I lost. In a few minutes the motorboat roared and went off, only to reappear very soon, stopping at the same point as before. It stayed there until noon when it roared again and went off again, only to reappear again and stop again: a hundred meters closer to the shore. At three in the afternoon, the same thing. And also at sunset. At intervals of about three hours it went off and came back, each time moving about a hundred meters closer. Onboard there were four people: was it possible that no one would come ashore? We asked the life guard and he grumbled that summer people are crazy, you can't count the crazies in summer, last year a couple had stayed off shore almost a week: they were called resistance contests. The answer so convinced us that at suppertime, with our friend the proprietor escorting us, we went to a restaurant in the port where you ate heartily and drank gaily. That night you slept peacefully. I didn't. I hadn't taken the life guard's remarks seriously for a moment, at the restaurant I had done nothing but look around, and now I got out of bed constantly, went constantly to the window to see if the boat was still there. It was still there: in the moonlight it rocked on the calm sea and to anyone else it would have looked like the most harmless vessel in the world. At dawn, the same, and it was rocking. During the morning, the same, and it was rocking. At noon the same, and it was rocking. Not even at three in the afternoon, when instead of going up to the room we went down to the bay protected by the No Entrance sign and, not worrying about its being deserted, we stretched out in the shade of a cliff, not even then did it move. It stayed there, rocking: splashing a good deal now because, as it had moved closer and closer, it had come to within two hundred meters of the shore. I pointed it out to you: "Doesn't it really worry you anymore?" You smiled nonchalantly: "Last night in the restaurant they could have got me easily. I was wrong. They aren't here for me. They're not dangerous." "Maybe not dangerous. But strange. Don't they suffer the heat, staying there, not moving, in the blazing sun?" "It's a covered motorboat." "And don't they ever feel like taking a dip?" "They must be lazy." "Why are they never visible?" "I don't know." "There's one thing that puzzles me: it rocks and rocks. I mean, it doesn't seem anchored. Why don't they drop the anchor?" Immediately your smile disappeared, as if I had given you an idea that had never occurred to you. You sprang to your feet, you said: "Don't move. I'm going to take a look." And before I could stop you, you had dived into the water and were swimming straight toward the boat.

What took place next happened in great haste. When I think of it now I see everything like a film projected too fast, at a tempo that chases itself, precipitously, frantically, which is strange because our movements weren't precipitous, weren't frantic: you moved with calm, I moved with calm. Calm was indispensable if we wanted to succeed, and also a display of absolute indifference: I understood that the minute I heard the motorboat engine turn over. You had swum very close, now you were about fifty meters from it, and suddenly you turned around and swam back, with broad, determined strokes, slow but determined, every stroke a vigorous thrust and a long wake of foam, while the boat moved, just as slowly but just as determinedly, as if it were amused by giving you a head start, delaying the pleasure of crashing into you, aware of its own superiority and sure of winning. The four young men were quite visible at last. The one at the helm was young and blond; the other three dark, about thirty, and they stared at you with hostility, frowning, more and more hostile, frowning more and more as the distance gradually diminished, and certainly you felt it diminishing, but you went on swimming with the same steady, precise rhythm, not turning, not looking at them, not betraying any nervousness, aiming for the entrance to the bay, the narrow point where there was the No Entrance sign, because the passage was narrow and the motorboat would have trouble entering. You gained at least two meters with each stroke, another bit of effort and you would reach the rocks of the little pier, provided you didn't tire, didn't lose heart, but you didn't tire, you didn't lose heart, and you were almost inside the bay, you clung to the rock, climbed onto the little pier, walked along it at a steady, calm stride, still not turning, not looking at them, as if you were indifferent to the fact that the motorboat had stopped and some young men were arguing, undecided whether to come ashore. And meanwhile I was moving toward you, trying to imitate your sangfroid, ignore your face contracted by the tension, green, your eyes wide and incredulous; my heart pounded riotously. I had left behind our towel, shoes, your slacks, your sandals, everything had to stay there, as if we were only going off for a little while, I knew that soon you would grasp my wrist and thrust me into the swimming pool's enclosure, then onto the terrace, then into the elevator. "Do you have the room keys?" We were in the room, you peered through the slats of the blinds: "Two of them have come ashore. They're waiting down there for us. You were smart to leave everything behind." "What if they come here?" "They won't come. They haven't any balls. They're waiting for us to go down and get our things, I tell you. Now we'll get dressed. Hurry." "And then?" "Then we go out, jump into a taxi, go to the port, and take the first boat we find. No luggage. That stays here. We'll telephone tomorrow for them to send it to us, and the bill. Until tomorrow morning nobody must know we've left. Nobody."

Your voice was cold, but your face was still contracted with tension, white, and your hands trembled as you dressed. They were trembling also as with assumed nonchalance you walked past the desk clerk and as we got into the taxi, went to the port, boarded the boat for Naples, as we ran to the central station to mix with the teeming crowd of second-class passengers boarding a slow local train. I had never seen you like this. Your hands didn't stop trembling until we were in the train, and then a bit of color returned to your cheeks and you broke the silence in which you had barricaded yourself: you told me why you suddenly turned in the water and came back. "You had noticed the right thing: they hadn't dropped anchor. You don't drop anchor if you have to stay ready to start the engine. I had a moment of hesitation and the blond one said: 'There he is!' The other three looked out. One of them seemed to have a gun. But I don't believe they wanted to kill me. If they had wanted to, they would have had plenty of time. I'm sure they wanted to kidnap me." "They can do it in the next few hours, Alekos. Your plane leaves day after tomorrow." "I know, but tonight they won't do anything, they didn't see us leave. Who saw us leave? The luggage is in our room, the bill is still unpaid, nobody suspects we've gone back to Rome!" You seemed so sure of this that you wouldn't let me express doubts or advice, and in Rome you wanted to go straight to the hotel and from there to Trastevere where you chose an outdoor restaurant. And here we were having supper when a deep breath emptied your lungs: "What is a man's limit, the point where he risks not being able to go on?" "Why do you ask that?" "Because they've found us. The green car, look, over there." I looked. It was a dark green Peugeot, parked on the other side of the square, and inside a character with dark glasses could be seen. "Maybe he's waiting for somebody, Alekos." "Right. He's waiting for me." "Maybe he'll go away in a little while." "He won't go, he won't go. He's been there for half an hour." "It could be coincidence." "It could be. But it isn't." You paid the check. You called a taxi. The taxi came, and the moment it moved, the Peugeot also moved, shadowing us so impudently that the driver stuck his head out of the window twice to yell back at him: "Dope, what do you want?" And soon he found out because on the broad street flanking the river the character with the dark glasses pulled alongside us, showing us, distinct in the glow from the headlights, his sardonic smile, his clean-shaven face, his gloved hands, his elegant checked jacket, his blue tie. After driving beside us, he passed us, slowed down, fell back again alongside us, only to pass us again, slow down again, and finally, repeating the Crete maneuver, strike us in front, strike us behind, then he hit us hard, flinging us onto the sidewalk. The driver was clever. He managed to avoid the tree that otherwise we would have crashed into, and afterward, with you urging him on, he launched into a pursuit that allowed us at least to copy down the number of the license plate. As usual, fake.

It was the fake license plate, always a fake license plate, that made my exasperation explode and, shouting that I wasn't going to send you back to your country in a coffin, I asked the police to intervene. And the police sent an escort of three plainclothesmen. You didn't want them naturally, you yelled at me, wretch, fool, making me ridiculous like this, putting the day laborers of Power on my heels, can't you understand that having yourself protected by the police is naive, besides it means giving up any hope of learning who those others are and who sent them? And you were right: after your death I was to discover that the Italian police were more interested in keeping an eye on you than on those who wanted to kidnap you or kill you; they even knew the blonde with the wigs, a Croat by the name of Jagoda, alias the Salamander because of her endurance and her venom, in the service of the SID and of the CIA, friend of an MSI neofascist general and the den mother of fascist groups. It was no accident that the three agents assigned to you seemed sent deliberately to alert the reckless—Watch out kids, keep your distance, otherwise we're obliged to arrest you. They exhibited themselves in a grotesque fashion, pressing you in a kind of protective embrace like hospital orderlies keeping a patient on his feet, sniffing and examining the passersby like hunters advancing in a jungle infested with wild beasts, unbuttoning their jackets so everyone could see the guns stuck in their belts. We quarreled about this, and so bitterly that I canceled my trip to Athens, changed it for a trip to New York, and we spent the last twenty-four hours like strangers who stay together to save appearances, for the sake of others. And so the question that for several days had been burning my lips, that I had tried in vain to repeat after the curtly interrupted hint—How would you go back to politics, *that* kind of politics, that is, how would you employ the things you had understood when you set yourself thinking, remained a question mark—suspended.

The plane for Athens and the plane for New York were to take off almost at the same moment and our quarrel was now past: a joking remark from Sancho Panza who is leaving Don Quixote to become governor of Barataria but will return, happy to be his squire, had broken the ice. You asked me to forgive you, I asked you to forgive me, and now we were sitting, calmed down, waiting for them to announce the departure of the two flights, to say to each other some of the things not said in those twenty-four hours. That we would keep the house in the woods, that in two weeks' time I would come to you or you would come to me, that in no circumstance would we stay far from each other for long, that living at different addresses in different countries would give us again the relief of reciprocal everyday freedom, without changing anything. But we both knew that a chapter of our existence had ended and the sadness pierced us with a thousand regrets, from the regret that we hadn't always understood each other or had competed in superfluous toughness to the incurable regret of having lost a child that now would never be born, and from time to time painful silences fell, your hand sought mine, your eyes, mine. We also interjected useless remarks, the ones that fill gaps when the train is about to leave but doesn't leave, so a minute becomes long, endless. "Are you going on to Washington or staying in New York?" "I'll telephone you as soon as I arrive." "Yes, and write." Suddenly you asked: "What happened to Padre Tito de Alencar Lima?" I looked at you, amazed. I had told you his story a year ago and in a year you had never spoken his name, you had never asked me what happened to him. "He's in Paris. You were still in Boiati when the Brazilian government released him, with another seventy political prisoners, in exchange for a kidnapped ambassador. He went to Santiago de Chile, stayed there until after Allende's death. Then, thanks to the intervention of the UN, Pinochet allowed him to leave. He chose to return to Paris and enter a convent of Dominican monks. Why are you suddenly interested in Padre Tito de Alencar Lima?" You smiled evasively. "Didn't you used to compare me to Padre Tito de Alencar Lima?" I smiled too. "Only before I knew you. I compared you to lots of people before knowing you. But why are you suddenly interested in Padre Tito de Alencar Lima?" "Because I dreamed of him last night." Another dream! Would you never be cured of this disease of having dreams? "Let's hear it. What was Padre Tito de Alencar Lima doing in the dream?" "He was walking on some leaves and raising his arms." "What does that mean?" "I don't know but I sense . . .

I sense he's very unhappy. Perhaps he doesn't feel like fighting anymore. And when you don't feel like fighting anymore, that's bad. You raise your arms and you die." The loudspeaker crackled, announced your flight. We got up to go to the gate. "Ciao then." "Ciao." "There'll be a lot of people waiting for you, eh?" "Just imagine the crowd." "Be careful then." "Don't worry. We still have a lot of time to spend together. At least two years. While I was clinging to the edge of the well, in the dream of the mountain, a summer went by, and an autumn, a winter, a spring, and another summer, another autumn, another winter. The swallows were flying when the wind sprang up: that makes almost two years." "Don't talk nonsense." "It's not nonsense. How many times do I have to tell you that dreams aren't nonsense?"

About two weeks later, I happened to pick up a newspaper with a headline that read: DOMINICAN PRIEST SUICIDE IN PARIS. The suicide was Padre Tito de Alencar Lima. The news story said that his body had been found in a wood, with the veins severed, and that it had been difficult to identify him because he had been lying there for at least two weeks. In all likelihood his death had taken place on August 13.

PART FOUR

1

IN THE LEGEND OF THE HERO IT IS THE RETURN TO THE native village that justifies the sorrows undergone and the exploits performed in the realm of the impossible: without this return his long absence would lose all meaning. But the return is also the most bitter experience that he has to face, a grief that rends him more than he was rent by the battles sustained in the period of the great tests, and not only because up to the very gates of the village he is opposed by the gods, who never tire of trying him or tormenting him, but also because returning among common mortals he must endure their ingratitude, their indifference, their blindness. In only one myth is the hero spared this bitter experience, this grief: that of the Hindu warrior Muchukunda who, to avoid being disappointed by human beings, asks the gods to compose him in a sleep that lasts millennia; waking from it he discovers that mankind did not deserve his sacrifice, so he shuts himself up in a cave to get free of himself, to fall into a sleep from which he will never wake. And these things were not unknown to you at the moment you boarded the plane that was to take you back to your country. The renunciation of your secret trips, after everyone had rejected you and you woke on that beach with half of your face burned by the noon sun, had been born also from the definitive confirmation of the ingratitude of people, their indifference and blindness; your lingering in an exile that with the fall of the junta no longer had any reason was also derived from the awareness of the new solitude that would engulf you on your return. Right and left, ideologies, parties, conformities, cards for the computer. What you didn't know, what you didn't even suspect, was the disappointment that would assail you on your landing in Athens. "Will there be a lot of people waiting for you?" "Imagine the crowd!" You hadn't the slightest doubt that at the airport you would be given a triumphant welcome. Neither did I. In periods of transition from one regime to another any occasion is an excuse to cheer, I repeated to myself as I was flying to New York; for heaven's sake, they had come by the thousands to receive that Karamanlis who for eleven years had lived comfortably in Paris, that Papandreou who for seven years had stayed easily in Canada; by the thousands they had shouted themselves hoarse for the petty victims of the dictatorship or for the timorous who abroad had done nothing but wait for better days; there was no telling what would happen on your arrival on August 13. For sure, I repeated to myself, the newspapers would underline the significance of that date, your decision to return on the anniversary of the day you had tried to restore dignity and freedom to the country. But when I called you from New York, your words hit me with the weight of a bludgeon: only a couple of newspapers had carried the news, in a few lines so hidden that few people had noticed them, and those who had noticed didn't get excited. The sparse group waiting for you beyond the gate of the customs area was made up of friends, acquaintances, girls eager to take you to bed, uncles, aunts, nephews, first and second and third cousins, people collected by a few frantic phone calls. Someone raised a pathetic poster—Long live freedom—someone raised an even more pathetic red flag, someone shouted excitedly, "Make way," as if there were any way to be made, an applause crackled, like the clapping one hears when the candles are blown out on a birthday cake; manhandled and pecked at by hasty mouths, squeezed by sweaty hands, you then disappeared into an automobile and nobody saw you again until the next morning. "Alekos, what did you do?" "I got drunk as a pig. And I also went with a whore. A fat one." "Why, Alekos, why?" "Because she won me, like a kewpie doll in a shooting gallery."

It wasn't so much the story of the fat whore that struck me as the gloomy tone of your voice. And much later, pondering the acts of cynicism, the incoherence with which you would often degrade your beautiful body, women taken and thrown away, friends insulted, senseless binges, I was to ask myself if all this had not begun on the afternoon of August 13, 1974, after that dismal return. Something broke inside you when you discovered that the date of August 13 meant nothing in the country for which you had fought, that thousands had rushed to welcome Karamanlis and the son of Papandreou and the petty victims of the dictatorship, but not the man who had dared the impossible and had been condemned to death. Something made you nasty, at a certain point almost bestial by a rage of masochistic degradation, and this despite a reality you knew very well: had you been on the side of Karamanlis or of Papandreou, had you fitted into the patterns of right or of left, in the dogmas that divide the world and herd people together like players of a football team no matter how inept or how lazy, then the newspapers would have printed the news of your arrival with great prominence and everyone would have remembered that August 13 was the anniversary of the attempt on Papadopoulos; thousands would have come to greet you as well. Because they would have been sent, lined up and sent, just as they had been lined up and sent for

Karamanlis and for Papandreou and the others. "But were some people there, or not?" You exploded like a bomb: "The people! The good people that is always absolved because it is exploited, manipulated, oppressed! As if armies were made up only of generals and colonels! As if only chiefs of state made war and kill the helpless and destroyed cities! As if the soldiers of the firing squad that had to shoot me weren't sons of the people! As if those who tortured me weren't sons of the people!" "Calm down, Alekos." "As if those who accept kings on thrones weren't the people, as if those who bow before tyrants weren't the people, as if those who elect Nixons weren't the people, as if those who vote for the masters weren't the people!" "Calm down, Alekos." "As if freedom could be murdered without the consent of the people, without the cowardice of the people! What does the word 'people' mean? Who is the people! I'm the people! It's the few who struggle and disobey! The others aren't people! They're herd, herd, herd!" And you hung up.

Then I wrote you a letter, one of the few we were to exchange from then on. I was saddened, I wrote, and not so much by the swinish binge, by the sordid little sexual party with which you had spoiled a return full of meaning, unfortunately there would be other binges in your life, more fat whores and thin ones and others neither fat nor thin, but rather I was saddened by what I had heard before you broke off the call. It showed your thinking had gone for nothing. Didn't you already know certain things? Wasn't your poem about the herd written in Boiati? "Always without thinking / without their own opinions / One time shouting, Hosanna / and the next, Kill him, kill him!" Hadn't we discussed at length this people who always goes where it is told to go, does what it is told to do, thinks what it is told to think, victim of every established authority, of every dogma, every church, every fashion, every *ism*, absolved of all guilt and cowardice by the demagogues who care nothing about it and in absolving it aim only at enslaving it further to exploit it more? Hadn't we concluded that for those demagogues the people is a numerical abstraction, a concept to separate the individual from his identity and his responsibility, whereas the only real fact is the individual, and every individual is responsible for himself and for the others? In a book of mine about the war, about Vietnam, you had read about the M16 bullet, a bullet that travels almost at the speed of sound, and as it travels it spins, and entering the flesh it goes on spinning and breaks and tears and shatters, so that even if you're wounded only in a muscle you die in a quarter of an hour. A horrible bullet, and even more horrible to think that someone had invented it, that a government had adopted it, that an industrialist had got rich from it. But it was just as horrible to think that the workers in a factory would make it, scrupulously, conscientiously, with the approval of their unions, their socialist and pacifist parties, rejecting it if a tiny flaw made it slower and prevented it from breaking and tearing and shattering; equally horrible that the soldiers of an army would fire it, aiming carefully so that it wouldn't be wasted, feeling themselves absolved by the foul slogan "But I'm obeying orders." Well, I'm fed up with the slogan "I'm obeying orders, I was obeying orders, I obeyed orders," I wrote you; I'm fed up with responsibility being attributed only to the generals, only to the rich, only to the powerful: what are we, then? Statistics, numbers to be manipulated at will in wars and elections, in the propagation of their damned ideologies and churches and *isms?* It's also our fault, mine, yours, his, the fault of anyone who obeys and submits, if that bullet is invented and manufactured and fired. To say that the people is always the victim, always innocent, is a hypocrisy, a lie and an insult to the dignity of every man, every woman, every person. A people is made of men, women, persons, each of these persons has the duty to choose and decide for himself; and you don't stop choosing, deciding, because you're not a general or rich or powerful. But the reason I was writing you, I concluded, wasn't to remind you of things you knew: it was to tell you something that concerned you. A story set at the beginning of the nineteenth century, in New York State, among the pioneer Dutch colonists in America, a story whose protagonist was named Rip Van Winkle. "When Rip returned to his village, like you, things were greatly changed: elections were about to be held. And since twenty years had passed and his beard was full-grown and white, nobody recognized him and also he didn't recognize anybody. With his fowling piece, followed by a swarm of women and children, Rip started wandering through the town and came to a tavern where a political meeting was being held. He went inside to listen, and since he was different from everyone else, he attracted the attention of the politicians, who eyed him from head to foot with great curiosity. When the meeting was over, the orator also bustled up. He drew Rip aside and asked him for which of the two parties he was going to vote. Rip stared in vacant stupidity. Then another man came up and, tugging at Rip's beard, asked him the same question: was he Federal or Democrat? Again Rip gaped, astonished, and a great silence fell. In that silence a self-important old gentleman with a cocked hat made his way through the crowd. With one arm akimbo and the other resting on his cane, he planted himself in front of Rip and demanded that he explain what brought him to the elections with a gun on his shoulder, a mob at his heels, and whether he meant to breed a riot in the village? Rip's astonishment changed to dismay and he answered that he was a poor quiet man, a native of the place: he had come back to make himself useful, to assume his personal responsibilities, he had a gun because men like him carry a gun at times, but he had never misused it, and anyway he wasn't voting for the Federals or for the Democrats. Then a general shout burst from the bystanders. 'A man who doesn't vote either for Federals or Democrats! A refugee! A spy! Away with him! Arrest him!' Then Rip was taken and beaten by both factions. There, Alekos, for the herd and for men wearing cocked hats, that is to say, for the politics of politicians you really are Rip Van Winkle!"

Actually that isn't quite the way the story goes, I had changed it a little here and there for my own purposes. To justify himself, for example, Rip answered: "Alas! gentlemen, I am a poor quiet man, a native of the place, and a loyal subject of the king, God bless him!" Moreover Rip wasn't a real hero or one who had suffered, he had simply fallen asleep and his feats with the gun had been performed in his sleep. But you didn't know that, and as soon as you received the letter, you called me: "I like that Rip Van Winkle story, but there's a difference between me and him. He is beaten up right away. Not me. Soon there will be elections, and would you believe it? They all want me: Karamanlis, Papandreou, even the Communists and the Union of the Center." "Impossible!" "Sure, it's possible, in the politics of politicians everything is possible. In the politics of politicians anybody is utilized, even if it means offering him a seat in Parliament." Your voice sounded almost festive: obviously the trauma of the first day had been forgotten. "And what do you plan to do, Alekos?" "I specially liked the detail of the self-important character with the cocked hat." "Alekos—" "Yes?" "I asked you a question." "What question?" "You heard it." "Yes, and I'll ask you another: do you know any way of making politics without entering the politics of politicians? I want to go into politics. Politics for me is a duty, it's a weapon in the struggle. What's the use of fighting for freedom if when there is a little freedom you don't use it to make politics? I tried to kill a man so we could make politics, I sowed sorrow so we could make politics, I was in prison and in exile so we could make politics: should I perhaps retire to private life now that we're about to have a Parliament? I have to enter that Parliament, I have to enter it like Ulysses entering the city of Troy in the wooden horse. So I need a wooden horse." "A party, in other words." "Yes, a party. So what?" "So it's the same as giving in to blackmail, Alekos." "Not if once inside the city of Troy, I go off on my own way. And besides I have no choice, I tell you. The only problem now is—Ciao, it costs too much to talk about these things between Athens and New York."

For a few days I didn't call you back. I knew what the dilemma was anyway. It was the usual dilemma of those of us without a party card, without a church, without a fatherland, the usual problem of anyone who wants to change this world a bit without being regimented in the codes of the computer: whom to campaign with, whose blackmail to accept. Not with the party of Karamanlis, obviously, nor with the party of Papandreou. However, having discarded those two poles of your contempt, only the Communists and the Union of the Center remained. The latter was a kind of liberal-socialist club, formed in the 1960s from a coalition of Socialists, Social Democrats, and vague left-wing groups. I couldn't believe that you would go with the Communists: imagine the uproar when they would hear you repeat your favorite remark that all dictatorships of the right fall sooner or later but the dictatorships of the left never fall. The idea of your handing yourself over to the Union of the Center seemed to me a kind of masochistic jest. Apart from its leader, George Mavros, whom you considered a good man, they were all opportunists without ideas and without a future. Still you had no choice: if you wanted to become a deputy and fight in Parliament, you had to join one or the other, even if you ran as an independent. So, stung by curiosity and at the same time alarmed by a silence that boded no good, I telephoned you. But this time your voice did not sound festive, it was more like a river of angry discontent. "Have you decided, Alekos?" "Yes." "Who with?" "What does that mean, who with?" "It means which left-wing party?" "Left-wing, what does left-wing mean? The left is a lie, it's an alibi with the word 'people,' a pair of underpants with the word 'people' on it, that's the flag of the left, cataramene Criste, cursed Christ! A pair of underpants to play chess with the right—I take the rook, you take the bishop, I take the king, you take the queen! The pawns are all the same, only the color changes, cataramene Criste! And if you don't want to sit and twiddle your thumbs, you have to wear those underpants, you have to wave that flag, you have to campaign with that label: yes, it's blackmail. Filthy blackmail. Yes, I gave in to the blackmail." "Who with, Alekos? Who with?" "Who do you think I could stand with? I picked the blackmail that seemed less like blackmail, the party that seemed least like a party: the Union of the Center." "Ah!" "It's not a great choice, I know, but it doesn't have any demagogues, no semi-gods, and not even any priests who light candles on the altar of the goddess History. I may even find myself fairly comfortable." "What do you mean? Aren't you standing as an independent?" "No, I joined." "Joined?" I was speechless. So you had capitulated totally. So the helplessness of us without a party card, without church, without fatherland, had won. But what was the alternative? To go preaching in houses and squares, like Socrates? To go back to throwing bombs like those you called the pseudo-revolutionaries? "Hello? Hello? Where are you?" "I'm here, Alekos." "I thought you had hung up." "Oh no. I was thinking." "What about?" "About nothing of importance, dear. Nothing." "Then you'll wish me luck?" "Yes, dear, I wish you luck." "And when are you coming? Eh? When are you coming?"

"When are you coming?" Now every telephone call ended with the question: "When are you coming?" And you called almost daily, direct call, reserved call, day rates, night rates, prepaid, collect. Not always because you missed me or because you had something to say to me but also because the telephone was your favorite toy, one of your overwhelming passions. It went back to your adolescence, that passion, and what originated it, I don't know: but I do know that it had never lost its power and not even the taps of the secret services and the police had managed to kill it. On the telephone you conspired, flirted, preached, seduced, organized, formed friendships, got over your spells of gloom or boredom: "Ah, if I had had a telephone in my cell in Boiati!" The first thing you asked me on arriving in Italy was: "How many phones do you have?" And you were disappointed to learn that there were three phones but only one number: in the house with the garden of orange and lemon trees you had two phones and two numbers, and in your office as a deputy you were to have six phones and three numbers. Even if they all rang at once and in different rooms you weren't upset; on the contrary you relished it: that racket became music to your ears, a concert of harps and violins and clarinets and flutes, and to see you leap from one to the other like a happy cricket was an unforgettable spectacle; to hear you answer, downright incredible. You never turned anyone away on the telephone, you never complained of being disturbed, you clung to the receiver like a starved man falling on a sandwich and cried: "It's me! It's I!" But you especially enjoyed making calls. In the period of your exile in Italy there were days, when you never lifted your finger from the holes of the dial, at the end of the month bills arrived so astronomical that merely glancing at them plunged us into a fit of dejection as deep as your guilt. Then, repentant, you exorted yourself, in the plural—"We must cut down, we must cut down"—and for a few hours you kept this vow. Immediately afterward, however, you forgot it and dialed a number, always in a distant city, a distant country. "It's me! It's I!" The long-distance calls enchanted you, international calls made you ecstatic, intercontinental calls raised you to paradise: you said that talking with somebody at the other end of the world was like a fairy tale, practically supernatural: especially direct dialing. You always sought people who lived in faraway places where you could call them directly, and you were terribly downcast to discover that it was possible to direct-dial Japan when in fact you didn't know anybody in Japan to call. For months you kept asking me: "You're not going to

Japan by any chance, are you?" And the evening I asked, suspicious, why in hell do you want to send me to Japan, what do you need from Japan, you confessed: "Nothing! But if you go there, I can telephone you!" The calls to New York took the place of those you had never made to Japan, they gave you an excuse to enjoy the fabulous, almost supernatural thing, and thus I didn't grasp the dramatic undertone of the when-are-you-coming refrain. So when I did come to Athens, everything caught me off guard.

It seemed as if a year of illnesses had passed over you. Your face looked wizened, worn, now that the fullness of the cheeks was gone, it was reduced to a very vast brow, two livid hollows under the eyes, a thin nose and a moustache. Your body seemed drained, bent, the sturdiness of the shoulders and of the solid chest gone, and now it drooped in the listlessness of a plant without water and support. But the most dismaying detail was not even that physical decline, it was the shabbiness that diminished you, a kind of deliberate degradation, as if you wanted to express with it some protest or discontent. Hair greasy and rumpled in bangs of vulgar curls, black fingernails, shapeless jacket covered with food stains, uncreased trousers baggy at the knees, shirt dirty and unbuttoned, necktie askew, and you stank. The harsh smell of someone who hasn't washed for a while, who sleeps in his clothes. I was so shocked that instead of letting you take me to your house I took you to the hotel, to throw you into the bathtub, send those clothes out to be cleaned, and make you go to the barber; but even cleaned up and shaved, you looked so wretched it was heartrending. And I couldn't imagine the reason. In the end, as we were going to the office you had opened in Solonos Street, I asked you: "Come on, Alekos, what's wrong?" What was wrong, you began, coming to the point in a roundabout way, was that you felt annoyed because a family is a great burden, yes, a great comfort but also a great burden, a blackmail that accompanies us for the whole cycle of our existence, first as infants, then as children, then as adolescents, then as adults, a kind of party of which you find yourself a member on coming into the world, a dictatorship you can't shake off even if you offer resistance, because in spite of everything you love it, by Christ: take a mother, for example. She is earth and sun and the planets and the galaxies and the cosmos of every cosmos, the law of every law, the love of every love: she's universal, in India she's portrayed with four arms and a garland of human heads on her head, the heads of the children she has eaten, in fact she is called Kali the Bloody; in the West she is portrayed with a halo of light and the sweetest of smiles, a face grieving and mild, they call her the Virgin Mary, it took that poor Christ thirty years before he could go off about his business because she blackmailed him with her love, she demanded that he work as a carpenter; in Greek mythology, instead, she is Thetis of the round shoulders, she is Gaea of the broad bosom, she is Juno of the wide hips, she is Pallas Athena of the owl eyes, shining and warlike, she is Jocasta, the most terrible of all because she marries her Oedipus, she bears him and later she marries him, and it costs him his sight. And whatever you call her she is always the same, the great genetrix who creates us and destroys us, protects us and punishes us, castrating us with her affection and her jealousies, cataramene Criste.

"No, Alekos, that's not it." A resigned sigh. "You're right. That's part of it, but that's not it." "What is it then?" You launched into another tirade, this time against the women who were after you, who wouldn't leave you alone, more pitiless, more carnivorous than any Jocasta, any Virgin Mary, any goddess Kali, and the whole trouble was that instead of coming to Athens I had gone to New York, leaving you available like a kewpie doll in a shooting gallery, and a man is made of flesh, and the flesh is weak, now don't look at me like that, they steal my balls and I'm trapped, there are some who would sell their souls to be plugged for a couple of minutes in the elevator, and if you do them the favor you can't get rid of them again, but the worst is the fat onc who's cheating on her husband, I can't get rid of her, she won't let go of me, that whore, don't look at me like that, I told you, it's your fault, I said, cataramene Criste! "No, Alekos. That isn't it either." Second sigh. "No, that isn't it, either. That's part of it, but that isn't it." "Come on then, what is it?" And there was the third philippic, this time against your city, "Just take a look at it, to understand it you only have to take a look at it, this square, for example, I used to live here as a child and I remember how there were houses full of charm then, with handsome iron balconies, red roofs, facades with the patina of time, now just big blocks, symbols of the ignorance that doesn't know how to change or how to preserve, knows only how to destroy and forget, we've forgotten everything, even Socrates, even Plato, all we have left is the sea and the sky, the sun to make tomatoes grow, the old pride is lost, for that matter they supported the dictatorship for seven years, it took the blood of Cyprus for them to rediscover a shred of freedom and with Evangelos Tossitsas Averoff, these people capable of living only on gossip, only on intrigue, on petty fraud, they call us Levantines and they're right, traitors, deceivers, I don't trust anybody, I can't trust anybody, cataramene Criste!" "No, Alekos, that isn't it." "No, that isn't it. That's part of it, but that isn't it." "Well then, Alekos, what is it?" You raised your face, charged with dismay. "It's . . . it's that I've done it all wrong." "Done it all wrong?!" "Yes. Because these elections are a farce, an alibi of those who wear the other underpants, with the word 'freedom.' Elections! While Ioannidis is still head of the ESA, while Theophiloiannakos, Hazizikis, Malios, Babalis, and the others like them are impudently strolling around, while Papadopoulos is living comfortably in his villa at Lagonissi! While the only person brought to trial is his wife Despina for the ten thousand miserable drachmas that the KYP slipped her every month! She didn't do anything to earn it, they say, she was defrauding the state. But anyone who did earn his pay is a worthy citizen. And if you shout, 'It's disgusting,' they answer you: 'What do you mean? We have democracy now, we have freedom. There are the elections, even Panagoulis is standing as a candidate!' I don't want to be an accomplice in this farce! I was wrong to say yes! I was wrong to come back! I did everything wrong, yes, everything! And I'm leaving! I'm leaving, I'm leaving!" "Leaving? And where are you going?" "Where I should have gone when the junta abdicated! Chile, the Basques, hell! Wherever fighting means fighting and not boxing with shadows, with alibis!"

This was what had wizened your cheeks, hollowed your eyes, drained you in a deliberate, physical decline. But then you hadn't changed, I had made a mistake believing that a few months spent thinking had developed a new personality—The real bombs are ideas. Ideas weren't enough for you, the challenges to be hurled by the intellect, and perhaps you had not forgotten even the fascination of death, the mysterious regret I had seen on Aegina. I looked at you as we might look at a door we are struggling to open without realizing it is open already. What to reply? With what words to help you? With the old saying that to die is easy, the hard thing is to live? With the simple argument that in war anybody can be a hero, in peace almost nobody manages to be one? It would have changed nothing, especially since what you said was the plain truth: those elections would be of use only to men like Karamanlis, Papandreou, Averoff, and it's as easy to defraud with the word "freedom" as with the word "people." "I don't know what to say to you, Alekos." "I can believe it. Come on." We had reached Solonos Street and you were thrusting me toward the door of the building where you had your office. We entered, we went up in the elevator, we reached a long landing, with a door that had your name on it, and immediately I let out a cry. Under your name there was a big cross and under the cross two dates: November 17, 1968—November 17, 1974. "Alekos! What does that mean,

Alekos?" "It means what you think," you murmured. "It means that somebody who was unhappy when I remained alive six years ago wants to see me dead on next November 17." Then with renewed liveliness: "You know what I've decided? I'm not leaving. No, I won't give up that candidacy. I'll stand in the elections. I will! Ah, I wish it were November 17!" As the authors of the laconic threat knew, the elections were to be held on November 17. The news was released a short time after that.

It was like watering a plant sick of drought, in the space of a week you blossomed, also physically. The worn air had vanished, and the livid hollows under the eyes, the bent shoulders, the shabbiness, the sadness. Don Quixote had found himself again and his imagination galloped again in the realm of mad whims, of amazing enthusiasms. "An idea! Those two dates under the cross have given me an idea! I'll print ten thousand handbills with the slogan: 'On November 17, 1968, the junta sentenced Alexander Panagoulis to death; on November 17, 1974, the people will elect him deputy in Parliament.' So I'll stick in the word 'people' too and the wearers of underpants will vote for me." "Yes, Alekos, but—" "No, half handbills and half stickers. That way you save on glue: one lick and they're ready to go. And you can stick them wherever you like: on taxi windows, buses, bars, on chairs, tables, on people. Somebody goes by and wham, you stick it on his back, on an arm. Or else on his behind. Can you imagine Averoff with my sticker on his behind?" "Yes, Alekos, but—" "Listen to this: instead of the usual handbills I want to distribute my book of poems. Let's say a thousand copies. Isn't that chic? And it also contributes to the spread of culture." "Yes, Alekos, but who's taking care of your campaign? The party?" "The party? What's the party got to do with anything?" "A campaign costs money." "Money? What money?" "For example, the money to print those handbills, those stickers, and to buy those thousand copies of the book." "We'll buy the book ourselves, with a discount, and we'll print the handbills and the stickers ourselves, somehow. I'm not accepting anything from the party!" "Alekos, surely you don't imagine you can conduct an electoral campaign with a book of poems and some stickers to paste onto people's behinds?" "No, there are the rallies." "But rallies cost money too! It takes a lot of people to organize them, and—" "I have my friends." "You'll need telephones and—" "Yes! Telephones, yes!" "And you'll need an office." "I already have an office." "The one in Solonos Street? But it's a hole hardly bigger than your cell in Boiati! Listen to me, Alekos—" "No, I won't listen to you. Because if I listen to you, you'll produce logic, and logic discourages me. If I get discouraged I won't win. We'll find the money. If we don't, tough luck. I'll do without offices, without automobiles, without telephones, I'll buy a few cans of paint, some brushes, I'll write with coal—'Vote for me.'" No obstacle frightened you, instead it kindled your pride and your imagination: if the way of conducting democracy was wrong, you said, why not begin to oppose it by rejecting the immorality of the electoral machine? "They spend billions to turn political meetings into kermises, fairs! They cut down forests to make the paper that will be wasted in posters! They burn rivers of gasoline to transport the candidates in automobiles! An honest candidate should make do with a bicycle and a megaphone. Apart from the fact that your so-called supporters don't give you anything for nothing: a contribution is always a bribe ante litteram, a debt that sooner or later will be presented to you, with requests for favors or frauds." The way you had blossomed also became evident the day you smuggled into Greece the five million with which you were to conduct your entire campaign.

Finally persuaded that with a bicycle and a megaphone you wouldn't get far, nor with writing "Vote for me" with coal on walls, you decided after all that some handbills were needed, as well as an office more spacious than the cubbyhole in Solonos Street. And determined not to accept a drachma from your fellow citizens, you named me your personal treasurer abroad and sent me to Italy to beg for help among those whose underpants had the word "people" printed on them. We made a naive mistake, since Papandreou was the great protégé of the Italian Socialists and their internationalist generosity was concentrated solely on him. But then one fine morning: "Victory! Victory! Prompted by Nenni, a marginal group had disobeyed the Central Committee and taken up a collection, which was now awaiting you in Venice. And since the Venice Biennale had invited you to the opening ceremony, air fare included, you could go at once to pick up the money without spending a cent." "What's the sum, Alekos?" "Huge!" "How huge?" "You'll see." Twenty-four hours later, there you are in Saint Mark's Square and nice men from Modena hand you a packet tied in string. You thank them with hugs and kisses, you run to the hotel, you break the string with trembling hands, and a hail of ten thousand lire notes scatters on the bed. "Alekos . . . is this supposed to be the huge sum?" "Yes, five million! Just think, five million! You know how many things I can do with five million?" And meanwhile you were counting it, in ecstasy, feeling the bills, stroking them, lining them up in a briefcase that from then on was to follow us everywhere, in motorboat, gondola, in restaurants, museums, even at the inauguration in the Doges' Palace, where you insisted I keep the case on my lap so I could guard it while you made your speech, and at the banquet, where you hid it under the table, clutched between your legs. "I won't leave it in the hotel, no. Otherwise they'll steal it from me, and that'll be the end of my campaign." Since the eventuality of a robbery was your only concern, I imagined that you hadn't considered the problem of transferring that money to Greece: not a negligible detail, given the severity of Italian laws about smuggling money. Yet you had indeed considered it: I realized this when I accompanied you to the airport and you locked yourself in the men's room, coming out half an hour later with a walk that aroused my suspicions. You moved so oddly. It was as if you had wooden legs, you didn't even bend your knees. Worse, you didn't raise your feet from the ground: you dragged them, as stiff as a robot: "Alekos! What have you done?" "Eh? Half a million in one shoe, half a million in the other, one million around the left leg, one million around the right leg, and the rest in my underpants. Ciao." And with a marvelous smile you presented yourself at the police control, where an agent frisked you from armpits to hips, looking for weapons, he opened the case, rummaged among the papers, examined your wallet. "No Italian currency?" "Not a lira." "Have a good journey, thank you." Not at all, thank you, and off you went, stiff as a robot, without raising your feet or bending your knees, with the treasure that no bank in Athens would want to change, it was all so crumpled, tattered, evil-smelling. "Is this money? Or dirty socks?" Still you were able to change it into drachmas, and with a part of it you would also rent what you called "my headquarters."

The headquarters consisted of two big, dirty, peeling rooms, with a plate-glass window half-covered by a photograph taken of you at the time of the trial and the sign that you had chosen as your symbol: a raised fist clutching an olive branch and a white dove. "What's the dove for? Why?" "It's not for anything. I like it." "And the olive branch?" "I like that too." "But what does it mean?" "Who knows!" The interior decoration was limited to a couple of rough tables, a borrowed desk, eight rickety chairs, contributed by eight different donors, a lame easy chair, a flower pot, a hot plate for making coffee, and many telephones, including a red pay phone. The people encountered there were without political experience, young men whose only merit was blind devotion, girls whose only strong point was their being in love with you, doting relatives, and an old woman with a little hat and myopic bifocals. Anyone who offered to work free, in fact, was received and exploited by you without limit and without mercy, including the poor woman whom you cynically called "that fat whore." Medical doctors were employed to stick up posters, graduates in architecture to write your name on walls, old aunts and paralytics to answer the phone or make coffee; but though each of them wore himself out with a will, the campaign was proceeding disastrously. First of all, propaganda material was scarce. Apart from the stickers with the dates November 17, 1968—November 17, 1974, and a few dozen posters with the olive branch and the dove, it was confined to perhaps a hundred handbills with your passport photograph on them. As for the thousand copies of your book of poems, they were lying in a customs warehouse, held up by a large duty you refused to pay. Moreover the press didn't mention you. Intent on publicizing their clienteles of right and left, the papers didn't even mention you were a candidate. Finally you did nothing to seduce the voters, to ask for their vote. You confined yourself to speaking at rallies and these were your Achilles heel. Only at the trial, with death staring you in the face, had you managed to express yourself effectively: under normal circumstances you didn't have a shred of oratorical talent. You couldn't put together a fluent speech, you lacked animation, you let shyness overcome you, and trying to seem confident, you would make ill-advised gestures like sticking your hands in your pockets or brandishing your pipe. In all this catastrophe even the fascination of your beautiful voice disappeared; it became weak, gray, impoverished by your constant slips of the tongue or else distorted by vulgar yelling. To make matters worse you hated rallies on principle. You insisted they are only exercises in bombast, lies, spectacles to deceive people, to manipulate them, get them drunk on promises that will never be kept, and rather than be guilty of those crimes you fell into the opposite excess, underlining brutal truths, expounding unpopular notions: the poison of ideologies, the blindness of dogmas, the dishonesty of alibis, the falsity of progress, the cowardice of the masses who obey. Perhaps summarizing everything in slogans and dismissive remarks. Listening to you was such anguish that I followed you every time with my heart in my mouth, asking myself—Good Lord, what will he be up to today?

Not that I came often, as a rule I preferred to spare myself the torment; and not that I understood well what you were saying in your language. However, if I did come, I had only to catch the nouns sossialismos, socialism; fassismos, fascism; epanastassis, revolution; laos, people; sovraca, underpants; o ghios tou Papandreou, the son of Papandreou; and I could reconstruct a speech that now I knew by heart and that went more or less like this: "Socialism? What socialism? Today anybody talks about socialism, the word 'socialism' has become the sauce of every dish, the badge of every lie, a fashion. Have we perhaps forgotten that Mussolini also chattered about socialism, indeed came from the ranks of socialism, and Hitler too? Isn't Nazism after all the abbreviation of National Socialism? Somebody says socialism and you all follow him, without asking yourselves what kind of socialism, without looking squarely at who is saying socialism. The son of Papandreou, for example, he has the word 'socialism' written on his underpants, and the 'revolution' the same, the word 'resistance.' What resistance? What revolution? Even Papadopoulos called his takeover a revolution, and even Pinochet: also on the right there isn't a dictator who doesn't use the word 'revolution.' They all want to achieve it, this revolution, but then nobody does, least of all those who call themselves revolutionaries, because their revolutions change nothing but the master, the regime. Revolution cannot be commanded. There exists only one possible revolution and it's the one that is made personally, the revolution that takes place within the individual, that develops in him slowly, with patience, with disobedience! The revolution is patience, it's disobedience; it isn't haste, it isn't chaos, it isn't what the demagogues with magic wands tell you. Pay no attention to those who promise you miracles, to those who say they will change everything in a flash, like a wizard. Wizards don't exist, miracles don't exist. The demiurges are making fun of you, ugly fools, who are accustomed to letting yourselves be led by anybody, to submitting; this facade of democracy can be knocked down with one breath if you follow the chatter of the fake revolutionaries, the pseudo-revolutionaries! We must hold on tight to this shred of freedom given us by the blood of Cyprus. Given, yes, and freedom that comes as a gift always produces fruit with a salty taste: if you are not careful, these elections will help only the heirs of the junta. Because the junta did not fall, it simply changed tactics, delegated its power to some louts dressed as liberals, and to lurid pigs like Evangelos Tossitsas Averoff, to the filthy right wing that has been holding sway for centuries, that until yesterday danced minuets with Papadopoulos, with Ioannidis, and that today will dance them with the barricaderos, with the worshipers of other totalitarianisms. And you don't notice it, because you don't think. There's always somebody who thinks for you, who decides for you—Master, tell me what I should do, comrade, tell me what I should think."

People would listen, sometimes disappointed, or offended, or bewildered: why, what was this man saying, why did he maltreat them and frustrate them in their hopes? What did he mean with the business of underpants, of patience, of freedom as a gift, of socialism that is a word, a sauce, a fashion, and in his conclusion what was he talking about with thinking and not thinking—Comrade, tell me what I should think? They had always believed that good was good and evil was evil, that the bad were on one side and the good on the other, they had never heard anyone say, on the contrary, that they were the same and that to improve things you had to make the revolution personally: how can you make a revolution by yourself? The majority of them were poor folk with callused hands, the faces of those who have been obeying since the beginning of the world, the doormats of every power, the tools of all ambition, real barter goods between the Brezhnevs and the Pinochets, the Averoffs and the sons of Papandreou: you had only to look at them to realize that they came to the rally to receive a bit of hope and not to be scolded. No, they really couldn't understand this young man who spoke humbly, stammering, monotonous, then suddenly reared up to shout madness. And so the meeting would end coldly, at best with faint, polite applause, more hesitant and light than a summer rain, and, grouchy, you would go off in a pickup truck that surely didn't help give you a semblance of authority. The truck had been lent by somebody or other and was covered with stickers and posters bearing the horrible passport photograph, a vehicle so old that if somebody didn't push it the motor wouldn't start: to see you shoving it, gasping, was a sight that few appreciated and that many considered disheartening. Add to this the fact that often your adversaries took their revenge mercilessly, especially the intellectuals, and behaving like those who have read or pretend to have read the forty volumes of Marx and Engels as well as the forty-five volumes of Lenin and the *Wissenschaft der Logik* of Hegel, they castigated your ignorance or your superficiality or the fragility of your thinking. Or else they simply sneered: "Let him talk, he doesn't know what he wants, he's crude, a romantic, an unsuccessful dynamiter. What are his merits, after all? He planted a couple of bombs. And one didn't even go off, the other made only a hole in the road." These were words that wounded you mortally, even though you wouldn't show it and went on, undaunted, with your pitiless truths, your rickety pickup trucks, your borrowed desks, your donated chairs, your wretched five million now reduced to a few drachmas, and the unshakable certainty of winning the great bet: "People understand me at heart. They'll vote for me." Until election day came.

Like waiting for the verdict of a jury that will decide our future or the result of a medical examination on which our health depends, and the longer it takes the more we are assailed by the fear it will announce an incurable disease, a sentence beyond appeal, so I waited for your telephone call from Athens, pacing up and down my room in a squalid hotel in Jordan. I hadn't attended your last rally, my courage had failed me. However, from a balcony of the Hotel Grande Bretagne in Sintagma Square I had seen the Karamanlis rally taking place at the same time on the same evening. I had seen the people, who you believed understood you and would elect you. I had seen them arrive: orderly, disciplined, regimented, a real flock that goes where those who command want it to go, those who promise, who frighten, it proceeds with closed eyes since there's no need to see the road, the road is a solid stream of fleece that will arrive at the square chosen by the power in charge, in this instance Sintagma Square in Athens and long live Karamanlis, in other instances Piazza Venezia in Rome and long live Mussolini, Piazza San Pietro in the Vatican and long live the pope, Alexanderplatz in Berlin and long live Hitler, Trafalgar Square in London and long live Her Majesty the queen, Place de la Concorde in Paris and long live De Gaulle, the Square of Celestial Peace in Peking and long live Mao Tse-tung, Red Square in Moscow and long live Stalin or rather long live Khrushchev or long live Brezhnev, long live whoever comes along, long live whoever is at the top of the mountain, never long live the poor bastards who die so that the sheep may become men and women. The poor bastards are applauded only at their funerals, when they no longer disturb. I had seen the people fill the square, seen it become a solid mass, an army of eight hundred thousand, and it had frightened me. Not so much by its number as by the geometric severity with which it had been lined up in squads and platoons, the method with which they waved their flags and shook their signs and held up their torches, the regularity with which they enunciated the "long lives," obeying coordinators with walkie-talkies. One, two, three: "Ka-ra-man-lis!" "Ka-ra-man-lis!" And each Ka-ra-man-lis was four cannon shots fired at a precise distance one from the other, an intensifying of the bombardment already so heavy and frightening that it swamped the entire speech of the old politician who, illuminated by spotlights and accompanied by Evangelos Tossitsas Averoff, yelled himself hoarse saying Lord knows what. The only words that could be distinguished were the name of his party, Nea Democratsia. Perhaps he was explaining what this new democracy was, how it was preparing to screw them, but they didn't want to know, they wanted to cheer him and nothing else, so that if he had shouted the result of a soccer game, "Real Madrid versus Manchester two to one," or if he had shouted a recipe, "Take the pork chop, dust with flour, then season and fry," it would have been exactly the same thing, they would have gone on firing the quadruple cannonade, waving flags, shaking signs, obeying the squad leaders, who in turn obeyed the platoon leaders, who in turn obeyed the coordinators with the walkie-talkies, who in turn obeyed the great producer of the apotheosis. Who was the producer? He had also thought of fireworks and pigeons though he hadn't foreseen the pigeon incident. At a certain point the night was inflamed with red, green, violet, golden lights, fountains of stars, and from cages hidden behind the roof of the presidential palace hundreds and hundreds of pigeons were turned loose toward the square. Instead of flying harmoniously, they started flapping their wings like drunken butterflies, and terrified by the racket, the fireworks, the flags, the human imbecility, they lost control of their intestines, dropping on the crowd a rain of hot liquid excrement. Then Karamanlis and Averoff left, both cleaning their jackets on which the pigeons had defecated in accord with the undiscriminating principles of equality that only animals respect; to the tune of the national anthem that rang from the loudspeakers the eight hundred thousand cleared the square: always orderly, disciplined, regimented. About face, forward march! In the square there remained the filth of handbills, torn papers, lost shoes, empty bottles, pistachio hulls that the automatic sweepers quickly collected, and something happened. Perhaps by accident, perhaps on purpose, one of the technicians working on the loudspeakers put on a record of Theodorakis: the song written by Theodorakis after your death sentence. Instead of the national anthem, that sad music spread out, those words: "Otan Ktipissis dio fores, k'istera tris ke pali dio, Alexandre mou . . . When you knock twice, and then three times, then twice again, my Alexander . . ." Upset and incredulous, I went down to see how people were reacting, but in the now-deserted square there were only two youths, two sons of the people, two lambs in the flock, and one was saying: "Ti ania! Pios ine aftos Alexandros? What a drag! Who's this Alexander?" The other shrugged and answered: "Den xero. I don't know."

I hadn't wanted to wait for the election returns either, again my courage failed me. But I spent the night of the election in your headquarters and that was enough for me to understand how things were going. Everyone wore the expression of those who can't get their hopes up, the phones rang only to report bad news, hour after hour the party of Karamanlis rose higher in the results and your party went down. As for the personal preference votes you garnered, they were so few that the press bureaus were already taking your defeat for granted. Five votes in this district, ten in another, fifteen at most, and in many cases none. In vain, surrounded by the boys and girls who had worked for you for a month and a half, you added and readded the sums with the hope of reaching the number of votes necessary to be elected. In vain the old woman with the little hat telephoned again and again to learn the final figures, repeated the sums, discovered that you had made a mistake of three votes, no five, no six: the substance of the bitter reality didn't change and your face became more and more haggard and white. At dawn, unable to witness that agony to the end, I left and I saw you again only the next morning. You were sleeping, destroyed. But as soon as I lightly touched your hair, you woke up and burst into irritated weeping. "The people vote for those who tell them lies! The people vote for those who make fun of them! The people vote for those who spend billions to get elected with fireworks and pigeons! The people want to be slaves, they like to be slaves, they like it!" Then you sank back into that destroyed sleep and I moved away from you in order to leave, to avoid being in Athens at the moment your defeat would become official. In three days I was supposed to go to Jordan to interview King Hussein, and I used this as an excuse: lying, I left a note on your pillow in which I said the meeting with Hussein had been moved forward and so I had to go immediately to Amman. Then I really did go to Amman. From there I called you a couple of times, receiving vague answers, convincing me that, at best, you would enter Parliament by the skin of your teeth, namely with the reservoir of the votes transferred into the national list, and at a certain point I actually stopped calling you: "Call me, as soon as you know something specific." And that's why I was waiting the way we wait for the verdict of a jury that will decide our future or for the result of a medical examination on which our health depends. What if the party failed to get you elected even by the skin of your teeth? What would then be the use of your sacrifice in entering, an unwelcome guest, into the politics of politicians? How else would you sow the seed that you urgently wanted to cast on the river of fleece, among the motionless stones of the gravel that sleeps at the foot of the mountain? To say nothing of the fact that a seat in Parliament would have protected you a little. Or was it the opposite? I looked at my watch. Eleven. The meeting with Hussein was at noon. I started for the door. The telephone rang. I went back. Your joyous voice poured into my ears: "It's me! It's I! I'm an honorable deputy, I'm a dishonorable one!"

What was it that so quickly extinguished my relief? The bitterness at knowing you had become a deputy through the leftover votes of others, the crumbs remaining on the table? The awareness of the new disappointments that you wouldn't be able to withstand? Or else the legend that Hussein told me? His Majesty seemed sadder than usual that morning and at a certain point, talking about his fatalism, he asked me: "Do you know the legend of Samarkand?" Then he told it to me. Once upon a time there was a man who didn't want to die. He was a man of Isfahan. And one evening the man saw Death waiting for him at the door of his house. "What do you want with me?" the man shouted. And Death said: "I came to—" The man wouldn't allow Death to finish the sentence, he leaped onto a fast horse and fled full tilt toward Samarkand. He galloped for two days and three nights, never stopping, and at dawn of the third day he reached Samarkand. Here, convinced he had put Death off his track, he dismounted and went to seek an inn. But when he entered his room he found Death waiting for him, sitting on the bed. Death stood up, came to him, and said: "I'm happy you have come, and so punctually. I was afraid we would miss each other, that you would go somewhere else or arrive late. In Isfahan you wouldn't allow me to speak. I had come to Isfahan to make an appointment with you, at dawn of this third day, in this room, in this inn, here in Samarkand."

"I'm going to have great fun in the politics of politicians. Wait and see! And now that I can start searching for the proof—" "Proof of what?" "The ESA documents, the proof about the scoundrels! It'll take me a while, but I'll do it. The important thing is for me not to mix with anyone. Like today." "Like today?!" "Yes, like today." "Does it seem right to you not to mix with anyone today?" "Absolutely right." In Athens they were holding a great rally to commemorate the Polytechnic massacre, by chance I had returned from Amman just in time to participate, and as we were heading for your office, quite near the street where the procession was to form, you were announcing that you didn't want to mingle with anyone. "Alekos, explain to me why not." "I told you: to make things clear right away, to show right off that I won't play the game of liars, opportunists, that I won't walk with their flags, their signs. All the parties will be there, each party has hired its extras, so they'll fling them into that procession for only one purpose: to make a show of power, to compete in vanity. 'Look how many I have, I have more than you, I also have more flags, more posters.' The parties don't give a damn about those deaths at the Polytechnic. The parties never give a damn about the dead. And when I think that also the servants who kept their mouths shut are going to parade in this game, the ones who were shitting their pants in fear, and wouldn't even listen to the word 'resistance,' you know what I say? I'd rather walk with Theophiloiannakos." "Those who really were in the Resistance will also be here, Alekos." "Of course. Requisitioned by the parties, utilized by the parties like carnations to wear on their lapels, overwhelmed by the servants who kept their mouths shut and shit their pants with fear. It's always like that. No, thanks, I repeat: I don't want any part of it." "You'll have to be with somebody, Alekos. You can't think of parading all by yourself or only with me." "I won't parade by myself or only with you. I'll parade with those who are alone like me. They exist. They are very few, but they exist. I'll find them." "Where?" "On the sidewalks. And some are already there. Look!" We had reached your office, and with a broad gesture of your hand you were pointing to the little group that had worked for you during the campaign. There was the old woman with the little hat and the bifocals; there was a dwarf, no more than a meter forty tall, carrying a purse bigger than herself; there were about ten boys, the same number of girls, and a cripple. "My friends! We'll form a little island, see?" "You don't even have a flag, Alekos, a sign." "You want a flag? You want a colored one?" And with a spin, you took a flame-red scarf from the neck of the old woman with the little hat, "Sorry, I'll buy you another," then with a ballpoint you wrote on it "Elefteria ke Alitia. Freedom and Truth."

"There. Now we have a flag, brightly colored too. We only need a pole. Look for a pole! Some nails! A hammer!" The hammer was there, but no nails, nor a pole. "Take the chairs apart, unscrew the door handles, break the table!" "Alekos, what are you doing?" "The banner. The signs. Didn't you say we need signs too?" But they were already taking the legs off the chairs, unscrewing handles, finding sticks and screws, making signs, industriously, swiftly, and a half hour later we were in the street, making our little island. In the lead the old woman with the little hat and the dwarf with the big purse: the old woman raising her scrawled-over scarf, now bolted to a chair leg, the dwarf holding up an illegible sign, made from heaven knows what. In the first row you and I and the cripple and two of the boys, with the others behind us. "And now what do we do?" "Now we parade. On our own. Singing. On our own." "What do we sing?" " 'Forward the Dead,' what else?" We set off singing: "Forward the dead!! Flag-bearers endlessly of the struggle! And after them we come! Eager to raise high the banners!" We looked like a band of beggars. Nor was there any hope of not attracting attention: to keep us detached from the rest of the procession that preceded and followed us, you would stop singing and shout: "Pente metra, five meters! Stay five meters' distance!" And a student with an armband, assigned to maintain order, approached, begging you in vain to shorten the distance, repeating that the rest of the procession was united and you had to follow suit: you answered him with such roars that the poor boy beat an immediate retreat. "Pente metra. Five meters!" From the sidewalks people watched, puzzled: who were those bums who walked by themselves, led by a dwarf and an old woman with a little hat? Why didn't they march with the others? Why didn't they sing what the others were singing? Why didn't they wave the same signs, the same banners, why were they carrying that wrinkled rag, those illegible signs? And that character who kept ordering pente metra and drove away anybody trying to make him join the rest of the procession: who was he? At times your name could be heard: "It's Panagoulis, I tell you, can't you recognize the moustache, the pipe?" And, pleased, you would respond with broad gestures of benediction, like a shepherd of souls: "Come, come!"

We were marching like that, making every strand into a rope, when I sensed a sharp shudder run through you and you nodded to point out two young men to me, one almost blond and one dark, standing at an intersection. Well dressed, both of them, and firm in a kind of severe hostility. "You see them?" "I see them: who are they?" "Two former ESA guards. Two of the ones that beat me with clubs." Then you broke from the chain, raised your arms: "Halt!" Pushing and shoving, the second row bumping into the first, the third into the second, the fourth into the third, our group stopped, blocking the whole procession; only the old woman with the little hat and the dwarf with the huge purse continued a few more steps but they soon realized they weren't being followed, so they too turned back, surprised, confused. Yet everyone seemed surprised and confused, nobody understood the reason why you had suddenly halted our advance, and from the last row came questions, protests: "Who said to halt? Come on, move! Forward, empros!" I touched your elbow. "Let's go on, Alekos." You didn't answer. "What do you want to do anyway?" Again silence. Isolated, as you were to confess to me later, in a dilemma of questions—How do I react, do I hit them or use them, treat them as enemies or friends?—a hesitation resolved as usual in an unforeseen way, with the irrationality of the gambler who ponders, then stops pondering and acts on impulse—rouge ou noir, le jeu est fait, rien ne va plus—you stared at the two exactly as someone stares at a roulette table before betting at random on red or black, odd or even, one number or another, it's all the same anyhow; what matters is to act, risk, defy luck, not to remain neutral. And the decision was made, the impulse snapped, you broke from the island with your slow, heavy step, your phlegmatic disdain, as if the street belonged to you and nobody had the right to protest against such ownership, you reached the two who, faces ashen, frightened, were staring at you, and raising your pipe to your mouth, you sketched a smile, taking the pipe from your mouth again and holding it toward the procession, you pointed to your group. "Come. I'm waiting for you." Then, turning your back, with the same slow step, the same disdain, you went back to wait for the little ball to stop spinning in the bowl, to remain fixed in a red slot or a black, odd or even. Rouge ou noir, le jeu est fait, rien ne va plus.

How long the wait lasted, I couldn't say. Months later, talking about it, you were to insist it was very brief, the whole scene took place in a couple of minutes, three at most. But to me and to those who had understood it, it seemed an unbearable time before the ball stopped, and the two young men stepped down from the sidewalk, came over to you, and you welcomed them with outstretched hands, and ignoring the complaints of the man with the armband, now furious and very impatient—Move on, really, are you moving or not. You took their arms. You made us step aside and you took their arms: one on your right and one on your left, you formed the chain again, resumed the parade, and what a glaring look when you noticed my hesitation. A look that would have been enough for anyone to realize that your gesture hadn't been one of forgiveness or compassion but of pride, indeed of contempt. Not contempt for the two ESA guards, contempt for the hypocritical laws of the community, for the politicians now shedding very profitable tears over the Polytechnic massacre, for the people who now took part in the procession but during the tyranny had been silent or had collaborated, for the banners of opportunism, the signs of expedience with which you refused to mingle; and if they didn't understand, if they didn't even guess, too bad for them. They didn't understand, they didn't guess, and immediately the rumor went around that Panagoulis had forgiven two of his most ferocious torturers, that he was walking arm in arm with them through the streets of the city, one on his right and one on his left, like the two thieves crucified to the right and left of Jesus Christ, and it wasn't a lie, anyone could see them, they were coming along Stadiou Street, leading the little group that was marching by itself. And the rumor stirred those who were watching with detachment that well-organized procession, too well organized to seem sincere, those who weren't participating because they didn't care about it or they felt excluded from it, both groups crowded now to see Jesus Christ advancing between the two thieves, and when he appeared, with his moustache and his pipe and his disdain, they applauded; convinced, moved, some shouted your name, some responded to your invitation, "Come come." But little by little what you had not foreseen happened. The game ceased being a game, and in the wake of an illusion, your pride was transformed into humility, your contempt into gratitude for those who applauded from those sidewalks without having understood anything. The independents, you said, who stay out of processions not because they don't care or aren't interested but out of protest, refusal to flock with the river of fleece. The rebels, you persuaded yourself, who oppose the liturgy of commemorative ceremonies not out of aridity or indifference but because they are looking for something else. Who knows what, but something. Perhaps themselves, their downtrodden individuality, their oneness offended by the concept of mass and mass man. And you plunged headlong into the role you thought they were attributing to you. You changed expression, look, walk, you began to say thank you to those who joined the group, often with glistening eyes, and they really did join. Men and women, lots of women with children by the hand or astride their shoulders; young men and old, many old people encouraged by the old woman with the little hat, I suppose. And cripples, drawn by the cripple in the front row, I suppose. And kids, attracted by the dwarf with the huge purse, I suppose. After about a hundred meters I counted five cripples, three with canes and two without, and the climax of this was a fat lame young man, a poliomyelitic who didn't dare enter our island, which was now a vast island, but proceeded alongside it, clinging to a pair of enormous aluminum crutches. How he managed to keep up with us, not dropping behind, is a mystery. But he succeeded, struggling, gasping, dragging his poor swaying legs, his poor contorted body, so that at a certain point you stopped the procession again, went to him and kissed him, then brought him inside, placing him in the center of the first row, which then set off again marching at his swaying pace. And after this there was no need for you to say "come come": so many people came that in Sintagma Square there were almost a thousand of us. From thirty we had become almost a thousand.

And thus you made your debut in the politics of politicians. Thus you began the series of your poetic, tragic errors in the politics of politicians. Because thanks to that makeshift and improvised army, incapable of struggle, joining you through a misunderstanding of other formulas, the formulas of forgiveness, compassion, Christian love, Jesus Christ, seeking something perhaps, but without knowing it, you fed the illusion that you were no longer alone. And riding on this illusion you hurled yourself against the windmills of your chosen dragon.

2

THE DRAGON, IN THE LEGENDS OF THE HERO, IS TERRIFYing to see, he is a winged serpent with many heads and forked tongues or a gigantic lizard with flaming eyes and steel talons. He feeds on virgins and youths, blows smoke from his nostrils, devours anyone who approaches the bridge that protects his realm; the landscape around him is strewn with skulls, gnawed bones, torn limbs. The remains of those who tried to kill him and failed. In real life his essence is the same but his appearance is different. At times you can't even define him because he symbolizes an abstract reality, a situation that exists but cannot be seen. At times you can't even recognize him, because he presents himself as a human being, a normal body, a torso with two arms and two legs, a head with a nose and a mouth and two eyes, perhaps a pair of round eyes, like a hypnotist's, but so slippery they seem like olives swimming in oil, and soft hands, boneless, and a smooth, caressing voice: "Dear friend, dear young lady! What a pleasure to meet you, what an honor!" In other words the features of Evangelos Tossitsas Averoff had nothing to make anyone identify him with a dragon, and despite the uneasiness I had felt on meeting him, even the discovery that he was the new boulder on the mountaintop, I would never have depicted him against a landscape of skulls and gnawed bones and torn limbs. His way of living also had all the marks of inoffensiveness. Devoted to Saint Reparata, patroness of his village, every Sunday he struck his breast in front of the icons to have his sins forgiven; friend of bishops and archbishops, he believed in heaven and hell; a loving father, a respectful husband, he was a dedicated family man and clothed himself in the dress of the most absolute morality; fairly cultivated and a compulsive writer, he published books that nobody gave any notice to but also did nobody any harm; very rich, proprietor of an estate near Ioannina in northern Epirus, he made every effort to contradict the gospel that states it is easier for a camel to pass through the eye of a needle than for a rich man to enter the kingdom of heaven. I mean, he didn't indulge in slothful laziness, he was full of initiative and industry. For example on the farm of his estate, the farm of Metsovo, he had imported the best cows from Canada and with their milk produced an excellent parmesan which he called metsovan, an excellent gorgonzola which he called metsovola, an excellent ricotta which he called metsotta. He also produced a decent wine. Averoff White and Averoff Red, and he was so proud of all this that it would have been hard not to believe him when he insisted that for him politics was a noble hobby, a way of serving the banner of liberalism. He very often used the words "freedom," "liberalism," and just as often he expressed an outraged condemnation of dictatorships. In fact he claimed to have been a true antifascist ever since the days of the Italian and German occupation.

Yet he was a dragon. Perhaps the best dragon that in those days and in that situation your country could offer a hero seeking the final challenge because, with all his apparent inoffensiveness, his metsovan and his metsovola and his metsotta, his liberal facade and his declared antifascism, in those days and in that situation he represented Power more than anyone else. The irredeemable, inextinguishable, indestructible Power that even in its most camouflaged forms, in its most sanctioned dress, now in the name of the fatherland and now of the community, now in the name of law and now of civilization, now in the name of order and now of justice, now in the name of democracy and now of revolution, commands us, manages us, defrauds us, blackmails us, stultifies us, screws us—Master, tell me what I must do, comrade, tell me what I should think—or even devours us like the winged serpent of legends and myths, the gigantic lizard that guards the bridge. Nor does it do any good to kill him with Don Quixote's lance, because he is always reborn from his own corpse, perhaps with a different face, a different language, by will of the people instead of by will of God. It has always been so, it will always be so. But if you don't fight him, all is lost, if you don't denounce him, if you don't give him the lie, his realm is extended, the landscape around him becomes even more filled with skulls, gnawed bones, torn limbs. He is greedy, never satisfied with what he has, he takes advantage of every armistice, every surrender. And those who along the way serve him or represent him, those who allow him to materialize—the boulders on the mountain peak—have the same characteristics of greed and resuscitation. Consider the case of the dragon you had chosen for yourself: having attained command by ancestral right, inheritance and family name, having become minister for the first time after World War II thanks to his monarchist faith, in the next thirty years politically dead yet revived a thousand times, never dead actually and quite alive even when he seemed buried. A detail demonstrated by the fact that not even the Papadopoulos coup had disqualified him, not even his arrest after the unsuccessful revolt of the navy had hamstrung him. The position he occupied in the government the electoral test had made legitimate, needless to say, he had remained minister of defense. Yes, from now on you had to concentrate all your energy on him. And you would do it, you said firmly. "What about the others, Alekos?" "What others?" "The sultans of demagoguery, the ideologues of despotism, the pseudo-revolutionaries." "I'll bother about the others afterward, if I'm still alive. And if I'm not alive, too bad; somebody else will deal with them in my place. A man can't fight two battles at the same time and on opposite fronts. Especially if he's alone. He has to fight the urgent enemy, the immediate enemy, according to the period and the country he's acting in. If I were in the Soviet Union or in Poland or in Czechoslovakia or in Hungary or in Albania or in China, my enemy would be the authority that in the name of a doctrine kills freedom and shuts people up in gulags or mental hospitals. I would fight their abuses and their lies. But I'm in Greece. And yesterday in Greece my enemy was named Papadopoulos, was named Ioannidis, tomorrow he'll be named Papandreou or who knows what, but today his name is Averoff. His name is the right wing. The arrogant and slimy right wing that wears underpants printed with the word 'freedom' and utilizes democracy to keep us in their grasp. If I weren't to concentrate my battle on it, on him, what would be the sense of having given in to the blackmail of the party card, of having accepted the label of a party I don't believe in? What would be the use of having entered Parliament? And besides there's no time to lose. Because the next coup will be backed by Averoff himself, whose dream is to become master of Greece and return his king to the country."

On December 8 there had been the Republic-or-monarchy referendum and the Republic had won sensationally and definitively, but this was a detail you apparently did not take into consideration. You seemed to bother still less about the fact that Ioannidis had finally been arrested and shut up in Koridallos prison along with Papadopoulos, Pattakos, Makarezos, Ladas, the members of the junta. The two things were of scant importance, you said, a referendum can be annulled, the doors of a prison can be flung open. You worried only about fighting the dragon while remaining true to yourself, not falling into the protesting poses of the Papandreists or into the ecclesiastical abstractions of the Communists, not allowing yourself to be infected by the conformity of official anticonformity. And while the other left-wing deputies spitted out their sacred words or bombastic banalities, you began tormenting Averoff with specific accusations: "Why doesn't his Excellency reappoint the democratic army officers that the junta discharged? Would it disturb the minister if there were also honest men in the army? Why does the minister allow the followers of Ioannidis to command regiments and divisions which could march at any moment on Athens and dissolve this Parliament once again? Does the minister like the idea of a coup which can be exploited by those who wave the flag of liberalism?" "Is the minister aware that in Koridallos prison Brigadier General Ioannidis continues to control his gheddafists, the officers capable of carrying out that coup?" You called them "questions or rather superquestions." You had even invented a new nickname for yourself: Questioner-or-Rather-Superquestioner, and now your telephone calls began: "It's I! It's me! The questioner-superquestioner! Guess what I did today!" "You asked Averoff a question." "No, a superquestion!" "And what did he do?" "He gave me a subanswer." You never granted him a moment's truce. You persecuted him like a wasp: the more we ignore it or drive it away, the more it buzzes around us, nagging, intrusive, determined to sting us. It was almost as if rather than a dragon he were your new Zakarakis. Your new monomania. In fact mindful of your remark—Wait and see what fun I have in the politics of politicians—at the beginning I thought you were playing to some extent. But when I visited Parliament and saw you at work, I became convinced you weren't playing at all, and if anything, he was the one who was having fun at your expense. You had only to address him and your face contracted, your voice went hoarse; his face, on the contrary, remained serene, his voice mild. His young and brave colleague had to be patient, understanding, the situation was delicate, difficult, the reason why the reserve officers hadn't been recalled to duty couldn't be revealed nor the reason why Ioannidis's followers hadn't been discharged; he could only say that little by little things would be adjusted to everyone's satisfaction. And he thanked his young and brave colleague, thanked him from the bottom of his heart for having made Parliament aware of such a serious problem. About the coup which you kept on announcing, not one word.

Finally the question about George. George's death had never ceased to be an obsession for you, you would have given a year of your life to know who had induced the Israelis to capture him and hand him over to the junta; you wanted to recover the file Theophiloiannakos had waved in your face during the interrogation. "Here's the file on your brother George. Here it is! You'd like to read what's written in here, wouldn't you?" You would have given as much to see his rank of lieutenant restored to him post mortem; after his desertion they had taken it from him. Thus you would establish the principle that deserting from the army of a country oppressed by a military dictatorship is not a crime but a duty. So on this subject you addressed Averoff with a voice hoarser than usual, a face more contracted than usual, and this time it wasn't a question but an order: the minister must trace and make public the file on Lieutenant George Panagoulis, whose life had served as barter goods between Papadopoulos and the Israeli government; the minister must restore to Lieutenant George Panagoulis the rank and the honors denied him by the junta; the minister must cleanse that officer's offended memory. Averoff asked time to search for the file, then answered that it couldn't be found or rather it didn't exist, but even if he had found it he couldn't make it public because secret documents must be protected. And you lost control. Raising your forefinger you shouted at him that your brother had become a deserter rather than serve the junta, that the same could not be said of those who today were in the government for the purpose of shielding criminals and hiding the crimes of their old friends, that in a truly democratic regime documents must not be secret, that one day you would find them and give the lie to him and his government. Or rather you would find more, something that concerned him very closely, and there would be a fine Watergate. It was so merciless, your reply, so threatening, that he was seriously alarmed and the next day, meeting you outside the chamber, he came toward you with outstretched arms: "Dear friend, my dear man, there is a misunderstanding between us that must be cleared up, why don't you have supper with me and we'll talk it over like civilized people? My wife would like very much to meet you too, dear friend, and my daughter is a great admirer of yours!" But pretending not to see the outstretched arms and keeping a hand in your pocket while the other held your pipe, you aimed the mouthpiece at him: "Listen to me carefully, Averoff. When there is a Parliament, the ills of the country are discussed in Parliament: not at supper between the roast and the dessert." A few days later, on February 24, the officers Averoff hadn't purged really did attempt the coup you had talked about.

A plan for a coup, not even an attempted coup, many were to insist. The army had supported it only in part, the navy and air force would have nothing to do with it, and in fact it hadn't been hard to smother it at birth, arresting thirty-seven officers. But a week later when I came to Athens you were still distraught and without a smile you gave me ten handwritten sheets of paper. "Read this." "What is it?" "Notes for an article I want to publish in Italy." "Why in Italy and not in Greece?" "Because in Greece nobody would publish it for me." And I read what it said: "*One.* It seems too diabolical to be true, and yet it is true because it is diabolical. The attempted coup of last February 24 was not at all an attempt; it was a coup that, far from failing, succeeded to the degree that Minister of Defense Averoff wanted, for the furtherance of his plan. And Averoff's plan was, or rather remains, to bring his king back to the country and to become master of Greece as the CIA would like. (Explain that Averoff has the CIA behind him, always has had, that under the junta he worked for the KYP and hence for the CIA.) *Two.* Averoff was in the know about what was to happen the night of February 24. They had carefully informed him that Ioannidis's officers, the so-called gheddafists, were about to take over the country and that in Athens sixty percent of the army was with them. (Explain that the secret services are now in Averoff's hands since as minister of defense he is in charge both of ESA and KYP.) *Three.* A few days before the coup Averoff had actually allowed one of the authors of the coup, an infantry general in the Greek Pentagon, to go to Koridallos prison to pay Ioannidis a courtesy visit. (Explain that the only visits allowed are those of family and of lawyers.) *Four.* The fact is that Averoff wanted that coup. It was the first step toward his objective. He could use it to dismiss from the army about forty officers who had understood his plan and were not prepared to support him. (Explain that with this coup stratagem he managed to expel thirty-seven.) *Five.* We must ask ourselves if Karamanlis has completely understood that Averoff is aiming at a dictatorial regime dressed in parliamentary clothing, that is, camouflaged by a Parliament that serves only to talk and not to direct the country's policy. (Explain that, dealing with the authors of the coup and handling them as he pleased, Averoff promised to give their gheddafism a civil European form.) *Six.* Even if he has understood, Karamanlis can't do much. He is not strong, as he would like to make people believe when he says there is no office of his government which he cannot enter whenever he feels like it. There is such an office: it is called the Ministry of Defense. (Explain that Karamanlis can't dismiss Averoff because Averoff commands the army and in Greece whoever commands the army commands the prime minister also. Explain that between the two there exists a tacit, secret, grim struggle.) *Seven.* What was Karamanlis referring to when, answering parliamentary questions on the coup, he said that besides the danger of fascism there existed other dangers and that his life was more in danger than anyone's? (Explain that the coup ended with a compromise: between Karamanlis and Averoff.) *Eight.* With a single move then, Averoff managed to outsmart them all: from Karamanlis to Ioannidis. Now the gheddafists have realized clearly that a coup d'etat can't take place without a political man behind it. A man with the political and intellectual skills of Averoff, not a crude soldier like Ioannidis. But for the gheddafists to realize this, Averoff had to lure them away from Ioannidis. (Explain that for this reason Averoff wasn't keen on arresting Ioannidis and begged him to flee the country, insisting that he himself would arrange for the secret flight and living expenses far from Greece. Explain that Ioannidis didn't accept Averoff's proposals partly out of pride and partly because he knows his own strength with the army.) *Nine.* Averoff is not a horse who runs easy races, to get to the line before the others. The facade of power doesn't interest him, and he knows how to be patient. The future dictator of Greece is named Averoff. (Demand the headline: Averoff equals future dictator of Greece.)"

I handed you back the notes, puzzled. "Are you sure you want to make an article from these?" "Very sure. And you will help me." "You realize they'll ask you for proof of what you say?" "I have it." "All of it?" "I'm missing only one thing: the evidence that under the junta he worked for the KYP. But sooner or later I'll find it. I know where it is." "Where?" "In the ESA files." "Good. Let's get to work." We got to work and the following week the article appeared, with the headline you wanted. But some people didn't like it. And the mysterious visitor who had made a cross with the dates November 17, 1968—November 17, 1974, left this time an even more grisly message on the door of your new office in Kolokotroni Street.

You had taken this new office at Christmas in order to have comfortable quarters, suited to your job, and a place to live in the city. You liked it especially because of the street, very close to Parliament, and because of the shabby, humble building, still full of charm, the melancholy charm of turn-of-the-century buildings with peeling walls, iron balconies, pots of geraniums on the windowsills. The entrance wasn't handsome because it had a glass wall which it shared with a shop selling textile machines and because the hostile and slimy concierge was always dozing on a little straw seat, but the charm resumed once one reached the elevator. An old elevator that creaked and groaned frighteningly as it rose, often got stuck between landings, and if it went straight to the fourth floor, you had to cry triumph. On the fourth floor there was only that one apartment and it consisted of five rooms, kitchen, and bath, along both sides of a corridor. The first three rooms you had fixed up as offices and waiting rooms for the people who came to see you, in the fourth you had set up your sanctum, your study; the last, facing the bath and the kitchen, you had chosen to make into a bedroom-livingroom like the one in the house in the wood. And we furnished it like the house in the wood, buying the furniture in Italy, and I had come at that time to help you arrange the objects in the exact same way, the rugs, the pictures, the curtains, the lamps. In the bedroom-livingroom the big sofa bed, the nineteenth-century bookcase, the eighteenth-century trumeau, the little round table, the art nouveau chair, and the French tapestry; in the study the long, heavy Florentine-style table, the high cardinal's chair, the comfortable seats for welcome visitors and uncomfortable ones for unwelcome ones, the cabinet with the secret drawers for hiding the documents that you said you would find one day "to screw Averoff." On the walls a sampling of your political independence: a reproduction of the painting by Pelizza da Volpedo, the peasants of the fourth estate, a copy of the first page of the United States Constitution, a bronze tablet reproducing the words of Piero Calamandrei on the massacre of Marzabotto, "Now and always resistance," a parchment with the first verses of the Divine Comedy, and a portrait of Sun Yat-sen. We worked until dark arranging things like this, then we went to dinner at Tsaropoulos's, and now we were coming home, arm in arm, laughing because the elevator hadn't got stuck between floors. "It made it! It made it!" Still laughing we stepped out onto the landing, turned on the timed light, went toward the door. And it was then that we saw it: a skull this time. A big black skull, drawn on tan paper and attached with adhesive tape under your name.

I remember well your movements. First your arm around my shoulders stiffened and for a few seconds you remained stony, staring at it. Then, with exasperated slowness, you moved away from me, tore off the adhesive, detached the paper, put it in the pocket of your jacket. Then you stuck the keys into the lock, and on tiptoe, your ears alert to every rustle, you went inside to inspect the rooms, to make sure nobody was hidden in there. Finally you went back and barred the door and, deaf to my protests—That's enough now, get some rest now—you abandoned yourself to an endless monologue made up of calculations, fears, reasoning. "This is strange business. We went out at ten and at ten the door of the building is closed. So it was somebody who got inside ahead of time and waited for us to go out. Or else someone who has the keys to the building. In either case somebody who means business. I must change the lock. I must also make sure I won't be caught alone, especially after dark. Tomorrow evening we'll have to find three or four people who will come to supper with us. There must always be witnesses with me. And not just one: at least three or four." Witnesses to what? "An accident, a provocation. Let's suppose some drunk or some fake drunk attacks me while I'm walking in a deserted street or somebody tries to hit me with a car and knock me off a bridge or down an embankment. If I don't have any witnesses, who can prove I was provoked or attacked. They can say it was an accident. And if I have only one witness, you for example, and that witness dies with me? I must also come home late at night. Never come home between midnight and two, those are the most dangerous hours. After two in the morning they get tired, they think I'm not coming home and they go away. On going out, always leave the lights burning, so they'll think there's somebody in the house. And keep an eye on the stairs. The stairs are the worst spot. No watchman, and that damned timer on the lights . . ." I was listening to you, incredulous: even in the days of the house in the wood you had never reacted like this, planning in such detail the precautions to be taken, considering every possible avenue of attack. Was it that suddenly danger no longer seduced you, no longer was your refreshing rain, the vital sap without which you would wither? Was this a passing crisis? Yes, it must be a passing crisis, I concluded. But the next day you really did take the precautions you had listed, never to abandon them until a few days before you were killed.

The most amazing thing was the caution with which you reentered the house after supper. In fact if no witness accompanied us, you wouldn't enter the house immediately: you would stop on the sidewalk opposite, study the scene for a couple of minutes, and only after you had made sure that you weren't risking any ambush, you would cross the street and quickly open the door of the building, then close it quickly behind you. In the hall you proceeded on tiptoe, withering me with evil glances if my heels made the slightest shuffle, as if the darkness concealed hordes of assailants, and this lasted until the corner, to the button of the timed light which you turned on with an imperceptible sigh of relief. But then if you didn't find the old elevator waiting there at the corner: trouble! Forgetting that relief, you would frown, curse, start grumbling—There, they've gone up, they're waiting for me upstairs—and, to make sure, you summoned the elevator, checking with your watch the time of its descent. You knew exactly how long it took from the fourth floor to the first, fifty-eight seconds, and if by chance your timing came to exactly fifty-eight seconds, you went pale, you put your forefinger to your lips, imposed absolute silence on me. "Ssh! Ssh!" Holding our breath we slipped then into the cabin, went up, cautiously stepped out of it, more careful than ever not to make noise, and circumspectly you inserted the key in the lock, opened the door, hissed again that imperceptible "Ssh! Ssh!" Then abruptly the scene changed. With the impetus of an infuriated cat you would fling yourself into the first room, into the second, into the third, into the fourth, hurling the doors open, looking behind the desks, inspecting the bath, the kitchen, the closets: and so on as far as the bedroom, always double-locked. Still that impetus didn't calm down even in the bedroom, because you bent to look for intruders under the bed, you started rummaging in the drawers, among the books, among the papers left in a precise position so you could tell if they had been moved. And every time I followed you, skeptical and resigned, saying in vain—

You see, there's nobody, nobody's been here—or asking myself if this wasn't a psychosis of yours, a persecution complex. You had also started using the hair trick again; you leave a hair here, a hair there, and if you don't find it afterward, that means someone has come in, has searched. One night the hair attached to the handle of the bedroom door was missing, and for hours you kept searching. "A hair is proof. If it isn't there, it means someone got in, searched." "But who, Alekos, who?" "I know who." The question about the possible intruders always remained without answer. And soon the matter lost importance for me: other questions were taking the place of that one.

After the skull you had changed in every sense: reality wounded you also in its most familiar, its most obvious aspects. So you reacted in an almost hysterical fashion, becoming more angry than necessary, suffering more than necessary, and giving way to sudden fits of obstinacy that left me bewildered. The sudden obstinacy with which you curtailed that trip to Moscow, for example.

"Hello it's I, it's me, I'm going to Moscow." "Moscow?" "Yes, they've invited me for an international youth congress and I'm going to take a look around." "Alekos, that isn't a place for you." "I know, but I want to satisfy my curiosity." "When are you leaving?" "Now, right away." "And when are you coming back?" "In two weeks, they invited me for two weeks." But then, three days later: "Hello . . . it's I . . . it's me . . ." A mortified, bored voice. "Are you calling me from Moscow, eh?" "No, I'm calling you from Athens." "Ah, then you didn't go!" "Oh, yes, I did go." "You went? What? We spoke less than three days ago. It's not possible." "It's possible, all right. Tomorrow I'll be in Rome and you'll see." The next day you are in Rome, passport in hand, and from the stamps it emerges that you really had been in Moscow. Three days. "Alekos! Three days!" "No, two and a half." "Did they kick you out?" "Certainly not, I ran away."

"Ran away? Without seeing anything?" "I saw everything." "Out with it. What did you see?" "I saw Red Square, with the spires that have red stars in place of crosses: it's the same thing anyway. I saw the Holy Sepulcher, I mean the tomb of Lenin. I saw the faithful standing in line to pray over the Holy Shroud, I mean the mummy of Lenin. Lined up like trained geese, the idiots. I saw the Congress Hall. And then I saw . . . I saw . . ." "What did you see?" "I saw three policemen beating a man just like Theophiloiannakos and Babalis beat me. And it wasn't at the Lubyanka during an interrogation, either, you know: in the bar of a hotel. The hotel for the rich and for foreigners with foreign valuta, the Rossia. They were beating him because he wanted to come in and he wasn't rich or a foreigner, he was an ordinary citizen who wanted to drink like a rich man or like a foreigner with foreign valuta. Heavy boots in his face, on the head, the genitals. They were slaughtering him. And he was shouting: 'Svobodu! Svobodu!' The Greek who was acting as interpreter for me explained that it meant: 'Give us freedom, give us freedom!' I choked on the wine I was drinking. I spat it all out of my eyes. I started crying. And I left the bar, went to my own hotel, packed my suitcases, and the next morning I went back to Athens." "Because of that?" "Because of that, cataramene Criste! In my country the dictatorship lasted eight years but in theirs they've been putting up with it for fifty, cataramene Criste!" "Well, didn't you know that?" "Of course, I knew that. But I cried all the same." "And if instead of crying you had stayed a few more days?" "I couldn't stand it, I really couldn't stand it. Svobodu, svobodu! And then they would hit him. All I could think of was that cry: Svobodu, svobodu! And then a little song that some sing but in a whisper because they're all coming apart in silence and fear. This is it, I had it translated for me." It was the ironic little song about the subway passengers in Moscow, who, to reach the door and get out, have to keep to the left: "In my subway I'm never uncomfortable / because since childhood / it's like a song / where instead of a refrain / there's a chant / Stand still on the right, move forward on the left / Eternal command, sacred command / he who stands still on the right stands still / But he who goes forward to get out must always stay to the left." And there was no way of making you tell me anything else, that day. To make up for this reticence, you would only repeat, shaking your head: "The trip was a mistake, pointless, I don't want to think anymore about it."

So I was to spend a lot of time reconstructing what happened to you on that mistaken, useless trip thanks to which an obvious, familiar truth had wounded you to the point of making you cry and run away. What had happened was this. A general aged seventy-four, dressed in medals from paunch to neck, welcomed you at the airport, saying he was the head of Soviet Youth. Then he escorted you in a black limousine to the Congress Hall where on the authorities' dais there wasn't one young person: there were only old generals like the airport general, dressed in medals from paunch to neck like the airport general. While no young people dared oppose them, the old men grimly followed one another at the microphones and spoke exclusively about Lenin, Marx, the battle of Stalingrad: never about other things. The business inflamed you with helpless rage, a sense of guilt for having accepted the invitation, and when the session ended you refused even the ticket for the Bolshoi. You didn't give a damn about the fucking Bolshoi, the ballet, *Swan Lake,* you wanted to be alone, and ridding yourself of the Greek acting as interpreter for you, saying, "I want to have a nap," you went roaming about the city. You wanted to see Mayakovsky Square, where in the 1960s Vladimir Bukovsky and the group of the Lighthouse used to read the poems of Jurka: "I am the one who / invites the truth and to revolt / I no longer wish to serve / and I break your black chains / woven with lies." You were thinking chiefly of Bukovsky because among the dissidents he was the one to whom you felt closest, but you were also thinking of Pliutch, of Grigoryenko, of

Amalrik, of the workers, the students, the unknown citizens, the anonymous beings, the thousands of yourselves who, for having demanded a bit of freedom of thought, of action, for having rebelled against the dogma, were languishing in their ESA cells, their Boiatis, crucified by their Malioses, their Babalises, their Theophiloiannakoses, their Hazizikises, their Zakarakises, ignored or betrayed by the fear and by the indifference of the people, that people who are silent or submit or collaborate. Suddenly, when you had been walking for about fifteen minutes, you realized you had taken the wrong street; you found yourself in a round square with a statue in the middle and a building opposite. Here you stopped, looking now at one and now at the other, in the grip of an inexplicable uneasiness, and a kind of chill that numbed your bones. The statue, high on its pedestal, inaccessible because of the traffic moving around it, was the statue of a man with an overcoat down to his ankles, was standing there, actually standing at attention. Tall, thin, severe as a monk. The building was a monumental building, gray, in nineteenth-century style or early twentieth century, and it had no windows on the first floor or on the top floor: at a glance it might have seemed a museum or an academy or a ministry, but your instinct told you it was none of these, that it was something tremendous, familiar, and closely linked with the statue of the monk with the overcoat down to his ankles. You turned back. You returned to your hotel, where you immediately asked what square that was, what building, what statue, and so you learned that the statue was that of Felix Dzerzhinsky, creator of the CEKA later the OGPU later the KGB, the square was Dzerzhinsky Square, and the building was the Lubyanka: cathedral of every ESA, of every torment, of every punishment for those who disobey and seek a bit of freedom. That's when your desire to run away began.

You wanted to run away the next morning. But the next morning the black limousine captured you again and took you again to Congress Hall among the old generals who talked exclusively about Lenin, Marx, the battle of Stalingrad, and here you stayed until afternoon when, on the pretext of getting a breath of air, you jumped into a taxi, had it take you to number 48B Chklova Street, where Andrei Sakharov lived. Let's hope there's no concierge, you said to yourself, getting out of the taxi, concierges are almost always police spies. There was no concierge, but the building at 48B Chklova Street was a hive of twelve stories: and which floor did Sakharov live on? You hadn't thought about it, and this error started a chain of errors. Looking for the board with the names of the tenants, you went in, then came out, then went in again, and you reached a floor at random, rang a bell at random: "Sakharov?" "Nyet!" At a second bell, the same: "Sakharov?" "Nyet!" At a third: "Sakharov?" "Nyet!" Disconcerted also by a language of which you understood only that no, that nyet as brutal as a slap, you came out yet again onto the sidewalk and you began to reflect whether it was a good idea to insist or not. Better not, you concluded, it had already been foolish to come on an impulse, attracting the attention of the three tenants who had answered "nyet." Thank heaven nobody had followed you. But as you were saying that to yourself, a man seemed to appear out of thin air. A man with a cigarette in his hand. Aiming the cigarette as if asking for a light, he came toward you, staring hard at you. "Spika. Light, please." You lighted it for him, staring at him in the same way, studying him carefully, deciding he wasn't a policeman. Everything about him, the callused hands, the dirty fingernails, the worn clothes, denoted the wretchedness of a poor mercenary bought by the KGB for a few kopeks or because of some blackmail. Then in the place of the rage that had gripped you at the Congress Hall, a great sadness rose up. With that sadness you walked to the subway station, the Kursk station, and with a few words of French you managed to catch the right train and get off at the right stop, reach your hotel, sink exhausted onto the bed, fall into a sleep charged with nightmares.

Ioannidis and Hazizikis and Theophiloiannakos at the Congress Hall, their tunics covered with medals, talking about Lenin and Marx and the battle of Stalingrad; Averoff in a room of the Kremlin meeting Jackson, the assassin of Trotsky and murmuring to him—My dear, you must do me another favor—Malios and Babalis coming out of the Lubyanka to hunt you in the streets of Cyprus, in the streets of Athens, and catching you right at number 48B Chklova Street, after having arrested Sakharov who didn't have the face of Sakharov, he had the face of Kanellopoulos on the dawn the junta had arrested him in his pajamas; and instead of taking you to ESA headquarters they took you to the Sierbsky Institute and they put you in a straitjacket and gave you an injection of amenzoin. "He's crazy, he dares protest against the regime, he's crazy!" Then they took you in a truck to Boiati to put you into a cell next to the cells of Bukovsky and Pliutch, and you yelled: "Vladimir! Leonid! Ime edo! I'm here! Imesta masi! We're together!" But they didn't understand you, because they didn't understand Greek, and Zakarakis laughed: "I told you it was no good studying Italian, didn't I? Why didn't you study Russian, which is a language of the great powers? Russian or English, no?" You woke up soaked in sweat, it was night, and immediately you called the Greek who acted as your interpreter: "I want to get drunk, bring me something to drink." You felt you had never had such a desire to drink, to get drunk, to forget that wherever you go it's the same shit, a shit that kills any hope, and the Greek came. But it was almost eleven, the hotel bar was closing, and there was no other place to drink in Moscow except the bar of a hotel. The search then began for a hotel where the bar didn't close at eleven, the absurd pilgrimage that ended at the Rossia, where you couldn't get drunk because, as soon as you had ordered the bottle of wine, the three policemen came in to beat the citizen who demanded to drink like the rich, like the foreigners with foreign valuta. "Svobodu! Svobodu! Svobodu! Svobodu!"

It was reactions like this one, so intense, so exaggerated, so desperate, that convinced me you had changed in every sense. And that isn't all, because after the skull incident something else exploded in you. An excessive, angry exuberance, a kind of gaiety lacking in any joy. The exuberance and the gaiety of Dionysus, who runs through the woods snickering, piping, gamboling with fauns and maenads, his head girt with ivy, his penis erect and eager, his eyes filled with tears.

Dionysus is not a happy god; on the contrary he is the most tragic of the gods because he is the one who expresses the frenzy of life and the inevitability of death. Dionysus is a god who dies, but then is reborn in order to be killed. In order for his body to form man, the Titans have to tear it to pieces and cook it, in order for the plant that will give man wine to sprout from him, Demeter has to bury the torn flesh. Dionysus is life that does not exist without death, he is the curse of being born, the unconscious refusal to die. It is no accident that his cult is a greedy and desperate orgy, his gaiety is steeped in suffering and his vitality in sorrow. Among your thousand faces there had always been the face of Dionysus, who runs through the woods snickering, piping, gamboling with fauns and maenads: "Shall we play?" There had always been that impetus of vitality. Suddenly, however, it had taken on an exacerbated, frantic quality, as if it were a comedy to deceive yourself, to tolerate the idea of death. You were never still anymore, never calm, reflecting; you could no longer stay away from the crowd and the hubbub. Even on the days when you didn't go to Parliament, you mixed from morning till evening with the people who crowded your office like the office of a smart dentist. Flatterers, perhaps, looking for a recommendation, good-for-nothings seeking a handout, typical of the political clienteles you despised. People whom you shouldn't even have allowed inside but with whom you adored passing your time drinking beer, orange juice, coffee, another beer please, another orange juice, another coffee. Twenty, thirty people a day. And if I bitterly asked you what's the point, you would answer fatuously: "Nothing! To live! I'm amused." Then, when the last visitor went off, leaving you exhausted, because by now it would be ten at night, the first part of the ritual began. With the excuse of witnesses you collected anyone who was available or who happened along, often parasites only interested in exploiting your generosity, and you assembled a party, took them all to eat in a tavern, and the more numerous the group the more pleased you seemed, the more avidly you ate, the more greedily you drank. Liters and liters of wine, plates and plates of food, while you preached, catechized, blustered, brilliant, rowdy, mercurial, unconquerable by weariness: if one of the party, overcome with sleep, dared ask—Aren't you going to bed?—you would be rude to him. Or else you would answer him sharply—When I'm dead I'll have an eternity for sleeping. And this would go on until two, three in the morning, until the moment when the waiters would turn up the chairs on the tables to remind you that everyone else had gone. Only then would you get up, and, paying for everyone, leaving a millionaire's tip, you would make up your mind to leave: "All right then, we'll clear out!" But the moment you were outside, your reasonableness vanished and, inflamed by a new vigor you would invent a thousand tricks to prolong the night, to drag your dazed, sleepy suite somewhere else: "Music! Bouzouki!"

Your favorite place was a night club on the outskirts of the city, vast and hateful. I hated it first of all because they played bouzouki so loud that merely entering, you were stunned by it, your eardrums shattered, and then because this noisiness had something macabre about it, something funereal: even visually. That play of spotlights for example that sliced the stage in red flashes, yellow, green, violet, until your eyes stung; that glitter of backdrops that changed constantly, obsessively, so that looking at them you felt you were on a carousel that spun and spun until your stomach heaved. But you insisted on a table near the orchestra! Where the infernal orgy of blasts, crashes, thuds deafened the most, and the evil storm of glare and flashes was the most blinding. That chaos was just what you were looking for, what you needed to feel alive, and immediately more wine, you abandoned yourself to the voluptuousness of morbid sensations. Those who didn't know you couldn't even guess the effect that horrible place had on you because the effect did not show in your behavior. Silent, composed, you allowed yourself the one excess of calling the flower seller and buying all the gardenias in her basket, to fling them then at the singers with broad, regal gestures. But the effect was savage, lugubrious. It was as if a sexual fever, a spasm, struck your body and your imagination, releasing unconfessed, repressed desires, the same you had dreamed on Aegina in the dawn when they were to shoot you and it seemed to you that you were a seed and the seed doubled, trebled, decupled, thus becoming so swollen that its husk could not resist, with an explosion it burst and flooded the earth with a thousand seeds each of which was transformed into a flower then a fruit then again into a seed which in its turn doubled, trebled, decupled in an inexhaustible process, so that you wanted to possess each woman who bloomed from those flowers, and knowing you didn't have time you clutched at random the closest, entered her quickly, ravenously, threw her aside to clutch the second, the third, the fourth, the fifth. I knew it and, knowing it, I suffered from it, and suffering, I avoided looking at you, but there was always a moment when my curiosity drove me to seek your face. And what I saw there had something bestial about it, despite the self-control you imposed on yourself, your face actually changed. Your eyes became smaller, your lips redder, and your nostrils dilated, throbbing, your breathing grew heavy. One evening on the dance floor a kind of female elephant was prancing around with an ephebe. She was fat, gelatinous, suety in a red dress. He, thin, agile, skipping, in too-tight blue jeans. And they began dancing to a rhythm both lascivious and hysterical; the elephant flaccidly swinging the mass of her soft and immense hips, the quivering exaggerated breasts; the ephebe wickedly shaking his fragile, effeminate body and his impatience to be possessed. A brazen spectacle, in my opinion, and I was about to say this to you when I heard a little crack. I turned: in your teeth you clenched the stub of the broken pipe stem, the bowl had remained in your hand. "Alekos!" A grim, panting voice answered me: "Don't disturb me. I'm screwing that pair."

On the nights when the demon possessed you like that, tearing you away from the damned club was an almost impossible undertaking. To succeed I had to wait until five, six in the morning, when many empty bottles were on the table. Thanks to some unknown physiological or psychological phenomenon, you could tolerate wine with a nightmarish resistance, never going past the invisible intoxication of the first stage, never falling into the excesses of the second or the catalepsy of the third, on the contrary, remaining charged with energy. And this was the worst thing because, on reaching home, having overcome the torment of the corridor to be covered on tiptoe, the agony of the elevator which was perhaps at another floor so we had to watch out for the fifty-eight seconds, then the torture of the checks to be run in the various rooms, the search for the hair possibly vanished, then the final part of the ritual had to be celebrated: Dionysus exorcizes death with the phallus and celebrates life grimly releasing his orgasm. Only after those furious and sinister embraces, loveless, cadenced to the invocation—i zoi, i zoi, i zoi, life life life—you would deliver yourself to sleep. Yet I remained with wide eyes and alert ears, thinking, listening to the street cleaners at dawn collecting the garbage of Kolokotroni Street, cursing, slamming, and as I was trapped by the usual formulas we use to explain existence, the arbitrary concepts of good and evil, I saw in all this a symbolism: to waste oneself like that, why? What sense was there in that roaming through taverns and night clubs, that self-degradation in humiliating emotions, unhealthy fantasies, that inflammation for a fat she-elephant and a skinny ephebe? What had become of the hero, what had become of the legend? Had you perhaps dropped anchor, brought your ship into the convenient port of renunciation? Or had I been wrong, had I mistaken Don Quixote for the most feckless of Peer Gynts? With such questions I tossed and turned, disappointed, and I became more and more convinced that I had attributed to you virtues that were nonexistent or had existed and were now extinct. It was in this period that I loved you less, and renouncing my Sancho Panza role, now useless and without meaning, I started working again, traveling, I returned to the existence that on a fatal August afternoon you had overwhelmed. We always forget that a hero is a man, only a man, and that resisting a tyranny, undergoing tortures, languishing for years in a cell without air or light is at times easier than fighting amid the ambiguity and the snares of normalcy. It would take me a long time to understand that your Dionysian madness was simply desperation, feelings of inadequacy born from the discovery of having committed yourself to an enterprise beyond your strength and in any case impossible. And only when you were dead did I realize that, after seeing the skull, you knew you were living your last summer.

"What's the name of the whale in that book, the white whale that never dies?" "Moby Dick." "And the captain of the ship, the one who dies hunting it?" "Ahab." "And the sailor, the one who survives the shipwreck and tells the story of Moby Dick and Ahab?" "Ishmael." "I'm going to call you Ishmael. And I'll sign myself Ahab. Give me the address." "Alekos, why do you always have to play conspirators?" "Give me the address, I said." I gave you the address. I was going to Saudi Arabia, I was to return on Thursday, two weeks later, and you wanted some place where you could let me know whether we would meet in Rome or Athens. But the telex that reached me in Jedda said neither Rome nor Athens; it said Lanarka.

In other words, Cyprus. "Ishmael noon Lanarka stop no confirmations repeat none stop be there stop Ahab." Strange. Not so much because of the rendezvous on Cyprus, where you hadn't set foot for seven years and where it seemed to be normal that you might want to see again places or people who had deeply affected your life; but because of the staging, the fact that you really did use the names Ishmael and Ahab, that you had employed these subterfuges avoiding mentioning the date or writing the word Cyprus. The only precise indication was the hour. And you wanted no confirmations. "Be there." Was it one of your jokes, one of your excesses, or was there a serious reason? I looked at the timetables. You had studied them very well before sending me the telex: from Jedda the only way to reach Cyprus was via Beirut, and the flight from Beirut landed precisely at noon. Then I shrugged, prepared to follow orders, and at Lanarka there you were on the field: triumphant, escorted by three strangers: "Good for you! You made it!" "Yes, but wouldn't it have been better to send me a less sibylline telex?" "No, they would have understood I was on Cyprus." "Who would have understood? Who wasn't supposed to understand?" "Somebody I wanted to put on the wrong track. I left Athens saying I was going to Italy, to Florence." "When?" "A week ago." "And for a whole week you've been in hiding here on Cyprus?" "No, I was hiding only three days of it. Long enough to send somebody on a wild goose chase to Italy. Now they all know I'm here. Tomorrow Makarios is making a speech in public and I'll be there with other members of Parliament." "Explain." "There's not much to explain. I got wind of something and I took my precautions. Come on." We stepped into the automobile that would take us to Nicosia and under the front seat my heels immediately struck a submachine gun. "What's this? Is this part of your precautions, too?" You shrugged. "No, no. The fact is that here weapons are a dime a dozen. They're all crazy about weapons on Cyprus. They have the mistaken notion that to defend a man all you need is a machine gun. Forget it. Look, what a lovely day it is!"

Your good humor was sincere. Anyone would have said that knowing yourself in danger, again, pleased you, revived you. Perhaps this is why I attached no importance to the whole business, I didn't even try to find out more about it, to ask you who the mysterious somebody was. In fact a little at a time I gave way to the suspicion that you had invented the whole scenario to fight off boredom. Moby Dick, Ahab, Ishmael: if you really heard a rumor that they were about to harm you and if you had believed in it sufficiently to send them off to Italy, why had you then chosen Cyprus, where it is easier to kill people than in other places? And besides had nobody seen you when you caught the plane for Cyprus, saying you were coming to Italy? The employees of the airline, the border police, all the people involved in a departure: hadn't they noticed? You had traveled under your own name, hadn't you, and with your passport? Nonsense! Probably you hadn't even come a week earlier but had arrived along with the other deputies invited to attend Makarios's meeting. "Let me see your passport." "You don't believe me, eh? Like you didn't believe me about the three days in Moscow!" "No." "Here it is." The stamp really had been put there seven days before, but my skepticism remained. It didn't diminish even at the discovery that the other deputies were staying in a comfortable hotel and you instead were in a kind of inn near the demarcation zone. "Alekos, why don't we go and stay in a decent hotel too?" "Because this one belongs to a friend I can trust. I feel safe here." There was only one entrance, and the three men whose machine gun had been under my seat guarded that entrance even at night, in shifts. As for the fact that a bodyguard followed you wherever you went, perhaps keeping a certain distance so as not to be noticed, hadn't you said that weapons on Cyprus are a dime a dozen? Only one evening was I alarmed. We went to visit Makarios, and the conversation had fallen on the ESA documents: the ones that during your scene with Averoff you had announced that you were going to find to give the lie to him and his government. "Your Eminence, there is a great deal to be discovered about the coup on Cyprus. I am told that Ioannidis fell into a trap set for him by the CIA and by some Greek politicians. The proof is in those documents." Makarios answered that to seek those documents then meant risking your neck, and he repeated it also to me: "Very risky! Very!" And returning to the inn, we argued about it: "Alekos, did you hear what Makarios thinks?" And then you said: "Don't forget it in the book." "What book?" "The book you will write after my death." "What death? You're not going to die and I'm not going to write any book." "I will die and you will write a book." "And what if I die before you or with you?" "You won't die with me or before me. Ishmael doesn't die before Ahab or with Ahab. Because he has to tell his story."

But you were laughing as you said it, and soon I laughed at it too. Only a year later, tracing the paths of your murderers, I was to discover a blood-curdling coincidence. The very week you left for Cyprus, and in Athens everyone thought you were in Florence, two Greeks arrived in Italy. And they stayed in Florence, put up by two fellow-Greeks, Cristos Grispos and Notis Panaiotis, students of architecture. The two newcomers said they were both on a holiday and had struck up a friendship, by chance, on the ship from Patras to Ancona. A curious friendship, since one called himself a Papandreist and ex-Communist sympathizer and the other defined himself as a Nazi. And a curious holiday, since they had chosen Florence but made no effort to see the sights. During the day they remained almost always shut up in the house waiting for a telephone call that never arrived, in the evening they went out looking as if they were hunting for something or somebody they couldn't find. And on returning home they seemed extremely dissatisfied. On the seventh day they left again, evidently disappointed. Disappointed by what? The Nazi was a blond with cold blue eyes, a blank face swollen with hatred. He spoke very little, greeted people by clicking his heels military-fashion and muttering, "Heil, Hitler"; he gave out the name of Takis and said he owned photocopying shops in Athens. From the portrait that Grispos and Panaiotis gave me of him, I thought I knew him. I had interviewed a character like him some months before, during an investigation of the ties between Greek and Italian fascists. In any case he was the same youth who in the spring had taken part in the beating up of the Communist deputy Florakis. As for the Papandreist, he was a fat, vulgar boy, with a round face like the boy I had seen from the hovercraft the day we went to Ischia with the Salamander tailing us. He wore blue jeans with a studded belt, he chattered a lot, especially about his automobile, a silver white Peugeot whose speed and response he boasted of. He called himself a great driver, unbeatable in pursuit and in controlled skidding, he went on a lot about his travels: at the time of the junta he had even been in Canada, where he had worked in a garage in Toronto and taken part in auto races. Grispos and Panaiotis didn't remember what these races had been or said they didn't remember though they knew a lot about him: all three were from Corinth. Yet, it wasn't hard for me to discover that these were races where the racers fling themselves against one another with frontal crashes or seesaw ramming. It was also easy for me to connect that detail with something the newspapers had already talked about, namely the fact that he had also been in Italy in the autumn of 1973 and in the spring of 1974. Milan, Rome, Florence. As for his chameleonlike political position, his being a friend of Takis, the admitted Nazi, and his calling himself a follower of Papandreou after having been a Communist sympathizer, he had a very interesting history: in the first years of the dictatorship he had been a designer in the atelier of Despina Papadopoulos. A link therefore between the extreme right and the extreme left: another son of the horrible marriage that begets excellent mercenaries.

I am talking about Michael Steffas. The same Michael Steffas who on the night of May 1, 1976, was to drive one of the automobiles that was to kill you: the silver gray Peugeot. It was he who, while you were on Cyprus, was roaming the streets of Florence, where you had led everyone to believe you were going to be at that time.

3

YOU KNEW THAT INCREDIBLE SUMMER WAS GOING TO BE your last. Every sort of thing happened during that incredible summer. To remind you of the appointment in Samarkand, Death also reappeared in the form of an automobile. The trial of Papadopoulos and Ioannidis and the members of the junta had barely begun, running parallel with the trial of Theophiloiannakos and Hazizikis and the band of torturers, and we had just come back from Cyprus to plunge into an Athens torn by riots instigated by the unions, as strange as they were inopportune. Inopportune because they took place in the very days when the city should have been demonstrating its joy at seeing the former tyrants before the bar; strange because they were characterized by an unaccustomed violence, paper bombs, Molotov cocktails, uprooted cobbles, a rain of stones which the police answered with tear gas, clubbings, brutal arrests, and also strange because the clubbings and the arrests never were inflicted on the most violent demonstrators. In fact the police seemed to be taking special care to overlook these demonstrators as well as a certain black Cadillac which for forty-eight hours had been driving by again and again, throwing the paper bombs and the

Molotovs. After first believing it was a strategic error of the left wing, blind to the bad timing of riots while the trials were being held, we soon began to suspect that it was all part of a plan, the right wing seeking the spark necessary to justify the usual coup restoring "law and order." At the same time catastrophic rumors were circulating and in your office many people seemed worried: they said that there was a war atmosphere in the barracks, the tank corps had been put on alert, some troop movements had been observed. You were the only one who seemed calm: "Let's not exaggerate. If the little group exists, it simply has to be isolated. If the black Cadillac exists, it only has to be identified. And discover who's in it, who's behind them, to whom they report. No use sitting here talking." Then late that afternoon you left the office only to come back, acting pleased with yourself: "Get dressed, we're going out on the town." "Out on the town? You think this is the right evening?" "Yes, and I want you to be elegant." "Why?" "Because if they arrest us we can protest that we have nothing to do with it: 'Look how we're dressed, we were going dancing.'" You even made me put on a long dress, high heels, jewels. You had picked out for yourself a blue suit, silk shirt, Hermès tie. "And got up like this, all decked out, we're supposed to mix with the demonstrators?!" "We're not mixing with anybody. And besides we have a car." "What car?" "The one I've hired." "Why did you hire a car?" "To go and take a look at the barracks and to hunt for a black Cadillac."

Our automobile wasn't really suited to its mission: to spend less you had hired a rickety old Renault that started with a coughing fit and threatened to break down every time you shifted gears. On the other hand, it seemed adequate for your reconnaissance which, not the least adventurous, consisted of stopping at a certain distance from the barracks, turning off the headlights, embracing me or pretending to be amorous if anyone approached, keeping eyes wide open and ears pricked up. By midnight, however, we had already spied on three barracks and nothing was happening that suggested the preparation of a coup. Nothing was happening downtown either, where the second day of rioting had ended in front of the Polytechnic with an explosion on the sidewalk. As for the black Cadillac, responsible for the explosion, there was no trace of it. "Alekos, do you realize it's like looking for a ring in the ocean?" "Yes, but I still feel I'll find it." "But where? How?" "I don't know. Let's go to the Polytechnic." "We were there less than thirty minutes ago!" "We'll go back." Jolting and creaking, the Renault took us back to the Polytechnic, to the students who were keeping vigil, locked inside the gates. Had anybody seen it again in the meanwhile? No, nobody had seen it. Were they sure? Yes, absolutely sure. They couldn't be mistaken? No, impossible. "Good, I'll wait." "But why, Alekos, why?" "Because I feel it will come along. I feel it, I tell you." You took out your pipe, you lighted it, and after a few puffs, there it was, coming from a cross street of Stadiou. It came toward us calmly, as if it were hesitant about what to do or as if it wanted to study the situation, and when it was alongside us it suddenly accelerated and went off. We barely had time to see the CD license, Corps Diplomatique, and to observe the four men inside: three about thirty, black hair, and an appearance both humble and aggressive; one about fifty, gray hair and an air of authority despite a curious short-sleeved shirt with a flower design. "Hurry up! Go!" You shoved me into the Renault, leaped to the wheel, and said let's have another look at this death, which in the place of hollow eye sockets has two headlights, in the place of the skull, a hood and a windshield, in the place of fleshless limbs, wheels, and the roar of the engine, its voice; and so you are all vibrant, happy at having found it again, at being able to flirt with it as on Crete, as in Rome, as always, to be able to gamble with your audacity, your love of the challenge, your madness which is the madness of Don Quixote, or the madness of Dionysus, or the madness of Ahab, but whatever face it assumes it is the same madness and whoever is beside you doesn't count, their life doesn't count, yours doesn't count, the only thing that counts is catching the black Cadillac, to know who is in it, who are the four men, who has sent them, and perhaps bring them to their knees, humiliate them, at the cost of dying.

That mad, senseless, lunatic chase, Stadiou Street, Patissiou, Alexandras, Kifissias, after an automobile going at twice our speed, only pretending to run away in order to draw us far out, lure us into the trap that soon would transform pursuers into pursued, pursued into pursuers, and the trick worked, now increasing its speed, now reducing it, a hundred and twenty kilometers, a hundred and thirty, a hundred and forty, and then down to a hundred, ninety, eighty, the familiar strategy of the fisherman who amuses himself by playing out the line and then pulling it in, to tire the fish. And you knew it. But you wouldn't give up. Your face pale, taut, your hands clenching the wheel, you pressed on the accelerator, more, still more, swerving, veering, skidding, as I begged you to let them go for heaven's sake, we'll kill ourselves, can't you see they're teasing you, they could get away whenever they want, they aren't escaping simply because they want to keep an eye on us and take us who knows where, you can't catch up with them and if you did it would be worse, there are four of them and two of us, they are certainly armed and we're not, and if we don't kill ourselves by running off the road then they'll kill us, and dying like this is silly, why do you want me to die too, didn't you say that sacrificing others along with yourself isn't right, isn't civilized? And terrified, outraged, I insulted you, I cursed you, I pleaded with you. But you, your face pale, taut, your hands clenching the wheel, continued pressing on the accelerator, swerving, veering, skidding, and you didn't deign to answer, not a monosyllable, not a gesture. You didn't even hear what I was saying, my feelings were no concern of yours, as if I were a bundle, not a person. You were interested in that car, nothing else, in those men, nothing else. They must have been experts in maneuvers of this sort, and the one at the wheel a real champion. At times allowing themselves to be passed and at times passing us, at times maintaining a considerable distance and at times only a few meters, from the sea road of Agios it led us to Rafina, then turned sharply to the left and took us up on Mount Hymettos, then turned again to the right and brought us down again toward the sea in the Voula area, and you never opened your mouth, never gave me a glance. At a certain point I even stopped protesting, I stopped pleading, resigned. Only at three in the morning, when the black Cadillac reentered the city and unexpectedly braked to let out the man with gray hair, a tall and heavy shadow that immediately dissolved in the darkness, I felt a whisper of hope. I thought you would want to get out and run after him. After an infinitesimal hesitation, however, you resumed the chase, and the trap they had set for us snapped shut. A blind alley that descended into an underground garage, where the car glided in, secure, straight. I heard my voice: "Turn back!" Then, finally, yours: "Too late." "We're trapped, Alekos." "I know." You continued driving, to the garage. You parked next to the black Cadillac that had stopped at the mouth of the garage. You held your pipe by the bowl. You got out. "Come." I obeyed. In the garage there was no one, except for the three. And no one in the alley. The only sign of life, the shadow of a cat that sprang away, silent, in the greenish light of the neon sign.

"Look at them." The three were waiting for us, one beside the other. Chest out, hands on hips, legs apart: the pose of professional sluggers. The third, awkward because of a cylindrical package he held in the crook of his left arm. They resembled one another, curiously: same sneer, same build, same olive complexion, same little moustaches, like commas. And the same poor-people's clothes: shapeless trousers, worn jacket, tie askew. It didn't take us long to realize they weren't the owners of the Cadillac and the brains of the whole thing was the gray-haired man. But because of the fact that they were mere tools, three wretches bought for a few drachmas, the danger was great, and instinctively I stuck my hand in my bag: pretending to grasp a weapon, which naturally didn't exist. A not completely useless gesture perhaps, but something your monstrous courage didn't need. Your eyes steady, your jaws clenched, you advanced slowly toward them, and every muscle of your face emanated a fury so icy and uncontrollable that you no longer seemed a human being but rather a wild animal dressed as a human. As you advanced, you were panting, you stared at them and panted, and when you were in front of them you stopped: to look them up and down, one by one, with exasperated slowness. After examining them you struck the stem of the pipe on the cylindrical package, and because none of the three rebelled or made a movement or said a word, you declared in my language and in yours: "You see, this is a bomb. It is not a bomb to throw at a tyrant: a bomb to throw at people. And this is a Greek fascist, a servant without balls. A servant of the CIA and of the KYP and of Averoff." Having said this, you moved around them twice, at your usual pace, your usual exasperated slowness, then you stopped in front of the middle one, you grabbed his tie, you jerked it repeatedly with sharp, contemptuous tugs: "This is also a Greek fascist. And this one too has no balls, you see. And this is also a servant of the CIA and the KYP and of Averoff." And still none of the three rebelled or made a movement or said a word: I couldn't believe my eyes, and kept on holding my hand inside my bag, and I thought it isn't possible that they are standing there numb, allowing themselves to be insulted, mocked, it's not normal, in a minute they will jump on him and massacre him. You then dedicated yourself to the third. You raised the pipe, held the stem against his heart, pressed it twice against his heart as if it were a knife, and said: "Him too. You wouldn't think so, would you? Look at those hands." You tapped the hands. "Look at the jacket." You tapped the jacket.

"Look at the face." You tapped the face. "You would say a son of the people. All three, you would say, are sons of the people. In a procession they would pass for sons of the people. And instead they are servants without balls, fascists. And you know what I do to servants without balls, to fascists. Do you know?"

There was nothing you could do to them. Absolutely nothing. You were alone with a pipe and a woman who, awkward in her long dress, was pretending to clutch a nonexistent pistol. If one of the three woke up, we would be slaughtered in a flash. And you knew it. But with the corner of your eye you had finally noticed my bluff and now you were making use of it to gamble on luck: rouge ou noir, le jeu est fait, rien ne va plus. Now or never. You live or you die. In either case what matters? What matters is to gamble, challenge, bet. Five seconds, ten. Twenty, thirty, forty. As the little ball spins in the bowl, around and around, then the pivot slows down, stops, and what I would never have hoped, never imagined, now happens. Suddenly the one with the package sank to his knees, the one whose tie you pulled made the sign of the cross, the one you taunted with taps of your pipe covered his face. "No, Alekos, no! I have a family, forgive me, let me go." "No, Alekos, no, there's a misunderstanding, we admire you, we respect you, I swear by my children, by the flag, don't kill us." And you hesitate, I can see your rage is deflated, I can see you have to make a terrible effort not to explode in the laughter tickling your throat, to maintain your composure and order him with your earlier voice: "Stand up, cowards. And into the car, hurry. Follow me closely." "What did you say, Alekos? What are you going to do?" "I'm taking them to the Polytechnic." "And you believe they'll come?" "Yes." They did come. Docile, hypnotized. As in a Western, where the sheriff manages to capture the whole band single-handed, bring them to the village, turn them over to the judge who will hold a proper trial, they obeyed you without a word; they followed you as you demanded. And you, in the rickety Renault that started with coughing fits and threatened to break down every time you shifted gears, dragged them all the way to the incredulous students. They were to confiscate the package, surely a bomb, and interrogate the men, discovering who they were, who was the character with gray hair, who owned the Cadillac with the CD license, no doubt a fake license, good luck and good night. "Alekos?! Are we going away like this?" "What do you mean are we going away like this?" "I mean: don't you want to know who sent them, who they are?" "I already know. Besides I don't like to see people interrogated, people on trial, people sentenced. Even when they're scoundrels. An enemy at the bar is always an ex-enemy."

What you meant would soon be clear. It was during that very summer, that incredible summer, that the extraordinary coherence emerged with which you cemented your apparent incoherences. And you showed that Papadopoulos, Ioannidis, the defeated whom the mountain, Power, was putting on trial, as enemies no longer interested you.

"I saw him! I saw them all!" "And did they see you?" "Yes, the first to sight me was Ladas. You know the one who thought I was George the morning of the attempt and said—Listen to me, Lieutenant, I know your brother Alexander, an intelligent sort, and if he were here, he'd give you a piece of advice, don't play the fool with Ladas, etcetera. And when he glimpsed me, he jumped as if a wasp had stung him. He went pale. Then he put his hand on Ioannidis's shoulder and whispered something to him. Ioannidis turned around, his eyes sought mine. With a hint of embarrassment, it seemed to me, and he promptly passed the news on to Pattakos, whose lips moved, as he was asked, 'Where is he?' and he waited a while before turning to look at me but when he noticed that I was also looking at him he straightened his head up at once like a kid caught listening at a keyhole. And he informed Makarezos, who bent over Papadopoulos and told him. Papadopoulos wasn't upset. He sat stiffly in his chair, erect, staring at the floor, a spot beyond his shoes, and for a few minutes he stayed like that: as if he had swallowed a stick. Then he moved his pupils, imperceptibly, without shifting his head an inch, without moving a muscle of his face. And he saw me. And it hurt me." "Hurt you?" "Yes. Those glazed, spent eyes, ash-colored. They were like a dead man's eyes. And that stony, earthen face. No, not earthen: green. You know the green color of water in a stagnant pond. And that . . . yes, that dignity. Maybe he did it deliberately, to show that he felt himself the chief and wasn't mingling with anybody, not even his colleagues, and finding himself the accused in a courtroom was a mere mishap: anyhow he behaved with dignity. And I thought—He's less ridiculous than I thought, he's a man. This surprised me, because I had never thought of him as a man, for me he had always been an automobile that was to blow up, an automobile with a tyrant inside, and I had to make an effort to recover the nausea I had felt on entering, thinking what a difference between my trial and his. Me, with handcuffs, held between two policemen, bundled into a uniform too big for me; he, all elegant, with his well-pressed clothes, his clean-shaven cheeks, his trimmed moustache, his chair with a cushion. But when I did recover it, the nausea, it was no use because that humiliated, defeated man, twice humiliated, twice defeated, since I was there looking at him, I, who had tried to kill him, was no longer an enemy. Or rather treating him as an enemy didn't interest me anymore." "What about Ioannidis?" "Uhm! Ioannidis is always Ioannidis. Cold, nonchalant, sure of himself. With that proud, closed face, like an Inquisition monk. He'll never give in, not Ioannidis. He'll never resign himself, he'll never behave like a humiliated, defeated man. Uhm! At heart I understand Ioannidis. Because certain dictatorships never occur by chance or whim, they are always the fruit of the political class that precedes them, of its blindness, its ineptitude, its irresponsibility, its lies, its hypocrisy. And among the bullies that think they can correct those disasters by murdering freedom there are not only types like Papadopoulos, there are also the types in good faith like Ioannidis. Violent and brainless, yes, even unable to realize they are tools of the power they want to overthrow, yes, but in good faith. In fact, they are the ones who pay afterward. The Averoffs, on the contrary, never pay. They are corks that always bob up again, even if you fling them into the sea with a lead weight; they always die of old age, in their bed: with the crucifix in their hands and their patent of respectability in their pocket. No, thank you, not even Ioannidis is my enemy anymore. I'm not interested in treating even Ioannidis as an enemy anymore."

You also wrote an article about this. You actually fought to keep Ioannidis and Papadopoulos and the other members of the junta from being sentenced to death: a verdict that was taken for granted at the outset. "In the spring of 1968 we of the Resistance also tried the junta, honorable judges. And we sentenced it to death with a sentence that I assumed responsibility for carrying out, in the case of Papadopoulos. However, we were trying men at the height of their power, but you are judging men who for some time have lost power or have spontaneously given it up; we did not belong to the political class whose errors had provoked the coup, you still belong to that political class, to that caste. So along with the twenty-seven defendants today in the courtroom of Koridallos, you, their judges, should also be sitting. You who applied their laws and sentenced their opponents. And with you there should also be the ministers, the undersecretaries, the lackeys who fell in behind the colonels, the industrialists who financed the regime with their money, the publishers and the journalists who supported it with their cowardice. To say nothing of the false resisters, the false revolutionaries who come in this courtroom today to testify as offended parties, to accuse, to play the victim, they who never did anything to fight the dictatorship and failed to cry 'Long live Papadopoulos!' only out of farsighted shrewdness. Really there are too many things about this trial that are unpleasant, from a formal standpoint, and from a moral standpoint; to begin with it is not pleasant that at the moment of preparing it you ignored a reality as bitter as it is historical: the tyranny did not fall as a result of the Resistance. It fell on its own, smothered by its outrages, it abdicated the night that Ioannidis allowed Gizikis to recall the politicians defenestrated by the coup. This is in Ioannidis's favor. We must remember that he controlled a great part of the army and the officers in the key posts of the state, he could have refused to give up his command or else could have demanded of the new government an amnesty for himself and for the members of the junta. We must also remember that the minister of defense, Averoff, retained Ioannidis as head of the ESA and then retired him with honor, leaving him for months to tend the roses in his garden. If the same Ioannidis had not made himself guilty of treason by joining Papadopoulos, it could be said that he has every reason to feel betrayed. I in his place would call Averoff and ask him: 'What game were we playing, Averoff? First you keep me on as head of the military police, then you retire me with honor and let me tend my roses, then you arrest me and try me on charges punishable by the firing squad.' I would also ask him why Gizikis is not standing trial. When the junta abdicated, wasn't he president of the Republic? This trial is really a joke, a stratagem to create a new virginity for the old bosses. As for the capital sentences you are writing, that you have already written, let us remember this: in the Piazzale Loretos the Mussolinis are hanged at once, or nevermore. If in a time of dictatorship tyrannicide is a duty, in a time of democracy pardon is a necessity. In a time of democracy justice is not done by digging graves."

You actually wanted to talk with them, with Ioannidis and Papadopoulos. You said that if you could penetrate the hauteur of the former and break the silence of the latter, you could learn where the ESA files were hidden and you could quickly procure the evidence against Averoff. Actually, approaching them wasn't hard; like the other defendants, they weren't in a cage but in the center of the courtroom and barely protected by a cordon of good-natured guards. But this plan did not weigh your shyness and your odd fear of offending them: as soon as you entered and felt yourself the target of the photographers' flashbulbs, the reporters' comments, the murmuring of the audience—There he is, he's here—you would huddle down behind a column and wouldn't step forward even when the hearing was over. "Did you do it?" "No, tomorrow." "Did you make up your mind?" "No, tomorrow." Then one morning, you clenched your teeth and took the plunge: aiming at Papadopoulos. You were so determined to speak to him, as you were to tell me, that after the first step you felt almost calm and you could record everything: the silence that had suddenly fallen, the beating of your heart, the amazed looks that followed you as you advanced toward him. He was also staring at you, for that matter, the green water of the pond was finally stirred by a breath of wind, by a kind of smile that you couldn't decipher, it could have expressed irony or liking; anyway it was an encouragement, an invitation. But just as you were reaching him and your eyes met his eyes, distant and yet precise memories, a black Lincoln moving along the Sounion Road, inside the black Lincoln someone you have never seen and yet must kill, remote and yet searing memories, who knows what he's like, let's look him in the face, if you look a man in the face and you realize he's a man like yourself you forget what he stands for and killing him becomes difficult and so better deceive yourself and think you are killing an automobile, this hateful automobile that is traveling at a hundred kilometers an hour, a hundred kilometers are a hundred thousand meters, an hour is three thousand six hundred seconds, every second equals twenty-seven meters, a tenth of a second equals about three meters, and how long is a tenth of a second, O Christ, not even the blink of an eye, a tenth of a second is fate, kilia ena, kilia dio, kilia tria, one thousand and one, one thousand and two, one thousand and three, just as you were reliving this and moving your lips to say what you would never have believed yourself able to say—Good morning, Mr. Papadopoulos, I would like to talk with you—from the enclosure of the invited public a woman's scream rose: "Papadopoulos killer! Ioannidis murderer! Filthy worms! To death with them!" And immediately your resolve vanished. You turned your back on him and went off, blushing.

"Why, Alekos, why?" "Because I felt so embarrassed, so ashamed. Lord only knows I insulted them, I threatened them, I cursed them, but at that time they were the masters and I was in chains. You don't insult a man in chains. Never. Not even if he was a tyrant before. I've had enough. I'm not going back to that courtroom, I'll never set foot in it again." And you kept your promise. You refused even to witness the reading of the sentence. "I've already heard it once, a judge pronouncing the death sentence. I know what it means to be sentenced to death." I went in your place. And it helped me to conclude, as usual tying the threads of the real with the cobwebs of the imaginary, that you had seen things that didn't exist or that existed only in your imagination. First of all, nobody risked the firing squad: even children knew that the death sentence would only be a formal verdict, and an hour later Karamanlis would grant pardons. And far from appearing the stage of a tragedy, the Koridallos courtroom seemed rather the foyer of a theater in the intermission before the last act of an operetta. The defendants chuckled idly, they exchanged condescending grimaces, they even amused themselves by glancing at me with morbid curiosity—He didn't come, she's come. As for Papadopoulos and Ioannidis, each concerned with avoiding the other like a pair of jealous prima donnas, seething with reciprocal hatred, they aroused no indulgence in me: in the former I couldn't see the dignified figure you had described to me, in the latter I simply couldn't imagine the honest soldier you had substantially and unpredictably defended. That flat face, without soul, that purposeless harshness. If anything there was something wretched about him, something pathetically clumsy. You know the clumsiness of army men who seem born in uniform, they wear it like a second skin, and when they take it off to wear civilian clothes they become plain or vulgar. He was vulgar: with his if-I-want-you-I-take-you expression, his too-tight checked jacket, his trousers held at his ankles with two incredible laundry pins. Papadopoulos was not vulgar, if anything he looked like a petty clerk caught with his hand in the till: Ioannidis, the terrible Ioannidis, was vulgar. I couldn't take my eyes off those clothespins. And at a certain point he noticed. He got up, folded his arms behind him and with a heavy robot's tread, he came toward me, seated where I was, in isolation below the public prosecutor's bench. Here he stopped, chest out and chin erect, in a uselessly hostile pose, warlike, and he began staring at me with icy, pale-blue eyes. I stared back at him, playing the stupid game of if-you-don't-look-away-I-won't-look-away, and this lasted an interminable time. It lasted until he murmured in his language something I couldn't understand and lowered his eyes and did an about-face: chest out, chin erect, his arms folded behind him.

"I wonder what he said." You had a strange smile. "I know." "You can't, nobody was listening." "I know all the same." "Oh, really? Come on then, what did he say?" "He said—Say hello to him for me." And, convinced of this, you took me out to supper with the usual swarm of fauns and maenads. To catechize them on the injustice of that verdict.

Words cast on the wind. Nobody understood you, naturally. Nobody approved the position you took toward the men who had wanted to kill you and whom you now treated with such mercy. He enjoys being contrary, they said, he himself doesn't know what he wants. And often I thought the same thing, that summer: never before that summer had I sensed so clearly the drama of accompanying into the desert a man whose essence eludes us because he is too many men at once, yet all of them unconnected, all enveloped in contradictions that can't be reduced to the duplicity of the hero with one good eye and one bad, a boy's face and an old man's face, one mind clinging to the past and one turned toward the future. It was only after your death, in reconstructing the mosaic of your figure, that I understood how every action I or others had considered incongruous had a reason. It fitted into a very precise line of conduct. Your attitude toward the trial against Theophiloiannakos, Hazizikis, the group of torturers, for example. This trial you did not disapprove of, you made a sharp distinction between it and the trial of Papadopoulos and Ioannidis and the members of the junta, and not only because the new trial was based on undeniable crimes but also because it served as a warning to those countries that used torture. And yet you had been summoned three times to testify and three times you had used pretexts not to appear—"I have a fever, I'm busy, I'm in Italy." "But you're the most important witness, Alekos, you're the one who's aroused the greatest expectation." "I know." "When are you going then?" "I don't know." Then, suddenly, a phone call: "Are you coming with me? Tomorrow I'm going there." Your decision had been made because of the rumor that they wanted to reduce to the minimum the publicity of your appearance and your testimony and that on the day you should appear the judge was going to forbid access to the courtroom to photographers and TV cameramen. "Incredible! Who can have asked him to do such a thing, Alekos?" "He." "He? Who?" "Why, Averoff, no? It's a military court, and military courts answer to the minister of defense." "And what will you do to prevent it?" "Nothing. It suits me this way."

I wondered how it could suit you, now that I was examining the scene where you would make your entrance. A rather sorry scene actually. Unlike the

Koridallos courtroom, vast and theatrical, this one lacked any atmosphere: it was a long and narrow little room, divided down the middle by an aisle that led to the witnesses' microphone and the judges' bench. To the left of the aisle as you came in, the public and the reporters. To the right, the lawyers and the accused. In the first row of the accused: Theophiloiannakos, recognizable because of his heavy build and his pock-marked apelike face. In the second row: Hazizikis, with his blue suit and blue tie, his spotless shirt, his face half-hidden by dark glasses. In the third: the doctor who was present at the tortures so the victim wouldn't die; shifty character, thin, with a nasty little mouth and eyes that flickered like a butterfly's wings. Beside each of them: the others, about thirty of them. Anonymous, innocuous faces: ordinary expressions. Rarely do the evil look evil. Not even Hazizikis did, in my opinion. Nor did Theophiloiannakos. If anything a touch of perfidy could be perceived in his wife, the lawyer: a beautiful blonde with spiteful features and a sarcastic smile. And all this played down the drama of this trial in which the chief judge, a bald, whining little man, swamped in a great black robe, wearily conducted the hearing. But then your name was called, along the aisle your steps resounded as you advanced, and Theophiloiannakos was again Theophiloiannakos, Hazizikis was again Hazizikis, the courtroom expanded, the tedium turned into electricity. You didn't advance, you progressed. And with a sangfroid so deliberate, disturbing, a pride so majestic, provocatory, that the confidence and the hauteur of the night you confronted the three fascists from the black Cadillac seemed by comparison briskness and good humor. One, two. One, two. One, two. But what was most impressive was not the rhythm of your tread. It was the way you accompanied that rhythm with the rest of the body and especially with your right arm which rose and fell in perfect synchronization with the left leg: as if you were marching to the cadenced tempo of a grandfather clock. Tick, tock. Tick, tock. Tick, tock. The other arm was bent in a right angle toward your heart, where your hand clutched the pipe. As for your eyes, they aimed, steady, at the chief judge as if at a prey: pointedly ignoring Hazizikis and Theophiloiannakos, as if you had never known them. You reached the microphone. You thrust your right hand into the pocket of your jacket. You put the spent pipe in your mouth, and said: "I must ask this court—" I saw the motionless masks of the uniformed judges flare up in amazement, and the president's little face went white: "You will not ask anything! It is the court that asks! Simply state when and where you were imprisoned! Facts, not opinions. Understand?" A sudden intuition. This is why the prohibition of photographers and TV cameramen suited you; this is why the moment you heard the news of that prohibition you agreed to come and testify, this is why you entered like that, without deigning to glance at Theophiloiannakos, Hazizikis: to start trouble and to say in a loud voice what you would have liked to say in the Koridallos courtroom, namely that the really guilty were not the scoundrels on trial but those who had brought them to trial for their own purposes. Well, all I could do was take a deep breath and wait for the explosion.

You took the pipe from your mouth. You held it up, like a lance: "I was imprisoned from August 13, 1968, until August 21, 1973, Your Honor, and I will state specific facts. Only facts, Your Honor, and facts which for that matter are already known to this court, because I did not have to wait for the regime to change in order to accuse the defendants in this room. To save time you have only to read my denunciations of seven years ago, obviously ignored by the magistrature in the service of Papadopoulos. These denunciations are in the file there under your nose. But I make one condition for repeating those facts: that you address me with civility, using my first and last name, calling me sir or rather calling me Honorable Deputy, and explaining why you have forbidden photographers and TV cameramen to witness my testimony. Did your minister of defense, Evangelos Averoff, order you to do this?"

"Witness!!" Heedless of the yell, you jabbed the air twice with your pipe: "I repeat the question, Your Honor. Did your minister of defense, Evangelos Averoff, order you to do this?" "Witness! I am the one who asks questions here!" "And I will answer them, provided you explain yourself." "Witness! You forget where you are!" "I'm not forgetting that. I am before a military court to testify to the crimes of men I fought for so many years, while magistrates like you were serving them. I am in a courtroom where they are trying torturers whose victims you sentenced, applying the laws of the dictatorship. A courtroom where I am treated with less respect than I received from the magistrates of Papadopoulos." "Be quiet!" "Again you are addressing me disrespectfully, Your Honor." "Be quiet!" "You continue addressing me disrespectfully, and if you continue, little averofaki, then I'll talk to you the way I spoke to the magistrates of Papadopoulos." The judges in uniform listened more and more astonished, cringing at every sentence. The defendants seemed made of stone, and so did their lawyers. The reporters were writing, writing, overwhelmed with excitement, and I was wondering when a truce would come. But the truce didn't come. In a confusion of overlapping voices, yours booming, the judge's shrilling, in a clash of shouts, barking, the quarrel went on. The battle you had planned and awaited. "Witness! I want to hear what happened after your arrest! That, and nothing else." "Not until you explain, averofaki, why you forbade the presence here of photographers and TV. Not until you address me with respect!" "My name is not Averofaki! What does Averofaki mean?" "You know very well, averofaki! It means servant of Averoff!" "The court is being insulted here. Silence!" "Are you saying 'silence' to me, averofaki? They couldn't make me keep silent with their tortures, their firing squad, and you want to put a muzzle on me? You?" "I am not putting a muzzle on you! I am questioning you according to proper procedure!" "Proper procedure does not allow you to address me as a boy, averofaki." "The facts! I want the facts!" "Reread them in your file there, averofaki!"

He gave way. Perhaps because he couldn't arrest you without the consent of Parliament or because the scandal would have harmed him, perhaps because he was beginning to tire and to realize that he could never hold out, he gave way. And he huddled in his seat, and now addressing you formally, he pleaded with you: "Do calm down, Mr. Panagoulis, I beg you. Don't take it like this, be so kind as to answer the question I asked you. If you please." And you accepted his surrender, you gave up trying to make him confess why he had forbidden photographers and TV in the room, you had said what you wanted to say anyhow, and lowering the pipe, taking your hand from your pocket, you began listing the sufferings undergone between August 13, 1968, and August 21, 1973. But in a spent, bored tone, as if you were playing a part whose necessity you couldn't see, and it all took less than thirty minutes. Others had spoken for five hours, six hours, illustrating details, lingering on minutiae, trivia; but in less than thirty minutes you condensed the calvary of one thousand eight hundred and thirty-seven days and one thousand eight hundred and thirty-seven nights when the hope of speaking as you were speaking now, of accusing in a courtroom those who today were sitting behind you, was the only thing able to keep you alive. In less than thirty minutes you squandered the opportunity you had longed for, and you told almost nothing of what you used to tell me whenever memory kindled the fever, and the fever brought on the delirium, with your head in flames and your legs of ice you wept in my arms until my face became the face of Theophiloiannakos or of Hazizikis or of the doctor who was present at the tortures, and if I begged you—Be calm it's me, look it's me—you thrust me away shouting—No, stop, no, enough, murderer, murderers, help! Even the most horrifying tortures you now reported with indifference, minimizing them, as if they belonged to a past so remote that every trace of it was lost in you, and as if

Theophiloiannakos and Hazizikis and the others behind you, seated a few meters from you, were millions and millions of miles away: canceled in space and time. Names, dates, bare information: nothing else. Lashes of the whip, blows of the club, stabbings, cigarettes burned against the genitals and all over the body, falange, smothering with the blanket and without the blanket, sexual tortures. With the two words "sexual tortures" you fell silent. "Continue please," the judge urged you with a new, almost affectionate voice. "No, that's enough." "That's enough?" "Yes, I have nothing more to add."

An incredulous silence fell. From the judges to the defendants, from the lawyers to the reporters, all seemed crystallized in amazement. "Perhaps you've forgotten something," the judge prompted. "I never forget. But now, as I said, that's enough." And the silence fell again. "Does anyone wish to ask questions of the honorable witness?" the judge stammered. After an interminable wait, the invitation was accepted only by a defendant wearing a captain's uniform: "I would like Mr. Panagoulis to say how I was during the interrogations." Perhaps he was hoping that you would absolve him of some responsibility, perhaps he really had behaved better than the others and deserved a bit of indulgence. But you didn't give him any satisfaction, barely turning your head, your eyes skipping over Theophiloiannakos and Hazizikis, you answered in a sibylline manner: "As you are now." For the third time the silence fell. "Nobody else wants to ask questions of the honorable witness?" the judge repeated. And it was then that Theophiloiannakos moved. Heavily, as if it cost him an unspeakable effort, he rose, his hands pressing on the back of the bench where his wife was sitting, in her attorney's robes. He seemed very tall, standing, very strong: a boxer's broad shoulders and short neck, bull-like, a weight lifter's. And yet there was something fragile about him, something sorrowful, or resigned, and whether you liked it or not, he inspired a great pity. The same that you feel before a dead elephant, a slaughtered rhinoceros. "Alekos—" Still gripping the back of the bench and grazing his wife's robes, as she angrily muttered something or other to him, he fixed his shining eyes on your back, cleared his throat, and in a hoarse voice, filled with sadness, he repeated your name: "Alekos—" More than a name, a prayer. A heartrending invitation to you to turn around, give him at least a very brief glance. "Alekos—" You remained motionless, deaf. "I have to make a declaration, Alekos." "Declarations are made to the court and not to the witnesses," the judge admonished. Theophiloiannakos bowed his head without taking his gaze from you, who, I knew, could feel it weigh on your back with the heaviness of a leaden cover. But you didn't turn and were not to turn. "Go ahead, what is your declaration?" the judge went on. Theophiloiannakos heaved a deep sigh. "This, gentlemen. Alekos . . . Honorable Deputy Panagoulis has not told everything he could have told. And what he has told is true. I beg him to believe that I am sorry, we are sorry for having treated him the way we treated him. I beg him to believe that I respect him very much, that I have always respected him, we respected him very much. Because . . ." Here his voice broke, but resumed immediately, stronger, more secure. "Because, gentlemen, he is the only one who stood up to us! The only one who never bowed his head!"

You didn't move a muscle of your face, of your body. You didn't bat an eye, you gave not the slightest sign you had heard. In this attitude you waited for the court to dismiss you and when the moment came for you to leave, to walk down the aisle again, you turned away from Theophiloiannakos, so that you could still have your back to him or show him only your profile. Then with the same sangfroid as before, the same cadence, your left arm bent over your heart, your hand clutching the pipe, your right arm swaying like a pendulum to accompany your walk, and your head erect, your eyes staring, you left the room. One, two. One, two. One, two.

And Zakarakis? Now that the mountain had ascertained the usefulness of the farce, the trials followed one another in a chain reaction. The moment one ended another began, the extension or the repetition of the first, of the second, of the third, and so even those who had been ignored at the beginning because they weren't sufficiently important now appeared on the benches of the accused. And so the turn of Zakarakis came, and toward him I thought you would behave differently. Could you possibly have forgotten his snicker on the night he caught you with half your body outside and half of it inside the hole in the wall? Could you possibly have forgotten his smile when he showed you the tomb and the cypress, forgotten the confiscation of your shoes, pen, paper, the beatings, the straitjacket? Yes, it was possible. You had only to see again his ignorant face, his little porcine eyes, to remember instead the promise you made him when he discovered that X didn't stand for Khania, Y didn't stand for Yemen, and Z didn't stand for Zurich, and he brought you the red and blue ballpoints to solve Fermat's last theorem. "Listen, Zakarakis. You're an incredible shit, but it's not your fault. And when you're on the defendants' stand, when I come to testify against you, I will say exactly this. That you were an incredible shit but it wasn't your fault." In fact your words were not so much testimony as a defense speech. "Yes, what I suffered in Boiati I owe to Zakarakis. He was the one who kept me in handcuffs for weeks, who beat me and ordered others to beat me, who took away my books and newspapers and pens and writing paper, who insulted me and persecuted me with spiteful cruelties. But I wasn't gentle with him either. I answered his insults with worse insults, his cruelties with provocations. Once he ordered my head shaved and I said to him: 'Everything or nothing, Zakarakis. You can't just shave my head without depilating me under the arms and on the balls. If you don't shave under my arms and my balls, I'll repeat my hunger strike. My hunger strikes were an obsession with him, and he gave in to my blackmail. He sent a soldier to shave under my arms and around my balls. I refused him: 'No, Zakarakis has to lather me, because he's a faggot and gets a thrill.' I always called him a faggot or an idiot. 'You're such an idiot, Zakarakis, that when you're dead your skull will be used as a spittoon for the pupils of the military academies.' So there is no use in being overharsh, Your Honor, especially since Zakarakises can be found in all regimes, they are bastards who count for nothing. They are the sort that if you tell them to shout long live Papadopoulos they shout long live Papadopoulos, or long live Ioannidis and they shout long live Ioannidis, or long live the king and they shout long live the king. If Theophiloiannakos had carried out a coup d'etat, Zakarakis would also have shouted long live Theophiloiannakos. People like him are the wool of the flock that bleats and goes where the master wants. People who simply obey, at ease only under the heel of an authority. The streets are full of them, the squares where they hold rallies. Poor Zakarakis. If I were in your place, I would inflict on him only one week's confinement in my cell so he would know what it feels like in there." "Don't listen to him!" Zakarakis yelled. "I am not an idiot, I am not a fool who counts for nothing! I am the commandant, I was the commandant, the head! the head! I assume my responsibilities!" But thanks to your speech he was absolved. And naturally you went on behaving like this toward everybody. Suddenly you seemed no longer to believe in the things you had always believed in, the principles that had always been the foundation of your political morality: worship of the individual, refusal to absolve those who manufacture the M16 bullet because that's what the industrialist wants and who then fire it because that's what the general wants, contempt for anyone who takes refuge behind the refrain "I'm obeying orders." In all your testimony you repeated that refrain. "It's true that

Corporal So-and-So took part in torturing me, but he was carrying out orders. And at Aegina, when I was waiting to be shot, he fell on his knees and asked my forgiveness." "It's true that Sergeant So-and-So beat me almost to death, but he was carrying out orders. And in Boiati he smuggled messages to my mother, he saved my poems." In the end you even repeated this for Theophiloiannakos. With all the consequences that it caused.

His appeal was being debated, and this time the chief judge was a good man, not at all intimidated by the dragon. He issued no prohibition of photographers and TV cameramen, he treated you with a respect downright obsequious: without admonishing you "facts not opinions," without reproaching you because you supplied more opinions than facts, and moreover addressing you as honorable deputy. "Continue, Honorable Deputy." "I was saying, dear judge, that the guilt of the soldiers must be separated from the guilt of the officers. I say that the soldiers must be absolved because they can't refuse to carry out orders. For that matter not even the officers can refuse to carry out orders. Did you perhaps refuse to sentence men of the Resistance when you were serving the junta and were part of a court-martial?" An unjust question, a gratuitous insult. And he reproached you for it with great dignity: "You are mistaken, Honorable Deputy. I never served the junta. I was never part of any court-martial, I have never sentenced any member of the Resistance." "No? Then why did they give you the rank of general, averofaki?" A moment of confusion, then a shout: "Bravo Alekos! Congratulations, Alekos!" It was Theophiloiannakos who shouted. In fact on this day he didn't look like a shot rhinoceros. Swollen with arrogance, full of initiative, he was drinking in your words like the nectar of the gods, and when you were dismissed, he rushed toward you. "May I present my wife to you, Alekos?" With a smile more sarcastic than ever on her painted lips, the blonde blocked your way and held out her right hand. A moment of emotion, then you held it. "My pleasure." And before you could realize what was happening, in the place of her soft fingers, there were the hard fingers of Theophiloiannakos: "Dear Alekos, allow me too to shake your hand."

"And you shook it!" "Yes, shook it. I answered him: 'Well, it isn't the first time I've touched shit.' And then I shook it." "Oh, no!" "Oh, yes. We even embraced. Or rather, he embraced me. 'You've repeated this word so many times to me,' he smiled, 'that I'm hardened to it by now.' And then he embraced me." "Oh, no!" "Oh, yes." "But what need was there . . . I don't understand you, Alekos. I don't understand you anymore." "Because you don't understand men in struggle. Reread Sartre." "What's Sartre got to do with it?!" "*Dirty Hands*. Fifth act, scene three. I learned it by heart: 'How important you consider your purity, my boy! How afraid you are of soiling your hands! Very well, remain pure! What good will it do? And why do you come to us? Purity is an idea for fakirs, for monks. You intellectuals, bourgeois anarchists, use it as an excuse for doing nothing. Do nothing, remain motionless, press elbows to your sides, wear gloves. My hands are dirty up to the elbows. I have plunged them into shit and into blood.'" "But your hands have always been clean, Alekos. Always!" "In fact I have always lost." "Alekos, what are you up to?" "Nothing that I hadn't decided a long time ago. Even if now I'm just looking, just listening. Eh! Interesting things are said in these trials, interesting things happen." And your bad eye flared. But I had no need to ask myself why. It was so obvious. Like a hurricane that is announced by a livid sky, the stifled moan of the wind, and after a long incubation it descends on the motionless world, flooding, breaking boughs, uprooting trees, ripping away roofs, so you were preparing to break forth: to condense your thousand faces into a single face. The face of Satan, who, disappointed in God, rebels against his dictatorship and in the illusion of winning, chooses to become a devil. The infernal corrida with the black Cadillac, your defending Papadopoulos, your explaining away Ioannidis, your absolving Zakarakis, your shaking the hand of Theophiloiannakos had only been a prelude, a livid turning of the sky, a stifled moaning of the wind.

PART FIVE

1

All banners, even the most noble, the most pure, are filthy with blood and shit. When you look at the glorious banners displayed in museums, in churches, venerated as relics to kneel before in the name of ideals, dreams, have no illusions: those brownish stains are not traces of rust, they are dried blood, dried shit, and more often shit than blood. The shit of the defeated, the shit of the victors, the shit of the good, the shit of the bad, the shit of heroes, the shit of man, who is made of blood and shit. Where there is one, unfortunately there is the other, one needs the other. Naturally much depends on the amount of blood shed, of shit spattered: if the former surpasses the latter, they sing anthems and raise monuments; if the latter surpasses the former, they cry scandal and celebrate propitiatory rites. But to establish the proportion is impossible, since blood and shit in time take on the same color. And in appearance the majority of flags are clean: to know the truth we would have to question the dead slain in the name of ideals, dreams, peace, the injured and outraged creatures who were defrauded on the pretext of making the world more beautiful, from such testimony then compose a statistic of infamy, or barbarity, of filth sold as virtue, clemency, purity. There exists no enterprise, in the history of man, that did not cost a price in blood and shit. In war whether you fight on the so-called just side (just for whom?) or whether you fight on the so-called unjust side (unjust for whom?) you're not firing roses. You are firing bullets, bombs, and you are killing innocent people. In peace it is the same, every great exploit reaps victims pitilessly, and mind the heroes combating dragons, mind the poets tilting at windmills: they are the worst executioners because, vowed to sacrifice, destined to torture, they do not hesitate to impose sacrifice and torture on the others; as if an uprooted tree were less uprooted, a bared roof were less bared, a broken heart less broken because the goal is good and the result positive. This is what I forgot when, materializing fears that had been dulled by waiting or hope, the hurricane burst. And unable to grasp the true reason that was overwhelming me, the reason I would understand after your death, I withdrew from you, horrified.

Autumn was upon us, and I had come back to Athens without enthusiasm: drawn by a letter, not by a desire. The traumas of the last trip weighed on me like undigested food, the tangle of excesses and ambiguities I had witnessed tormented me with a thousand doubts, and something in me had snapped. Too often in those fourteen months of life together I had grown tired of walking in your desert, alleviating your loneliness without lessening my own; too often the figure I loved had disintegrated into other figures, perhaps to be recomposed in an inexplicable, unrecognizable individual. You no longer wrote poems, you leafed through books instead of reading them, you got by on facile slogans instead of facing debates, you no longer bothered about Parliament, which you mentioned in an absent or ironic tone: nothing interested you now except your promise and your dragon. You spoke only of him, of the evidence to be collected against him, ignoring any other problem, any other reality, and if I changed the subject, if I said after all Averoff isn't the center of the universe, the ESA documents can't be your only interest, your only commitment, you became angry: "You don't understand, you don't want to understand!" And to make matters worse those torpid nights continued: thermometer of your every discontent, your every desperation. No longer confined within the noisy boundaries of the bouzoukis, the circle of the maenads around Dionysus had extended and now included squalid creatures with whom you seemed to experience a perverse pleasure in debasing yourself. Generally they were the sort you called "one dive and out," watch in hand to measure its speed, but at times the dive became complicated and drew you into hateful situations, spiderwebs from which you were unable to disentangle yourself, and all this diminished you in my eyes, killed my wish to be with you. "When are you coming?" "I don't know." "Then I'll come there." "No, wait. I have to go to London, to Paris, to New York." It was as if keeping far away from you helped me to get over the crisis, to protect a love that was tottering. At a distance, in fact, I could see you through the filter of memory, discard defects and squalor, rediscover the figure I admired and who, I repeated to myself in disappointment, was going to pieces. At the beginning you didn't realize it and, displaying archaic forms of male pride, you took to accusing me of inconceivable treacheries; after the handshake with Theophiloiannakos, however, and the argument about dirty hands, you understood that it wasn't a rival that led me to avoid you but a weariness, and with the instinct of an endangered animal, you sent me an irresistible letter: signed Unamuno and composed entirely of sentences from Unamuno. "If I evade him so much, believe me, it is because I love him. I flee from him and yet I seek him. When he is near me and I see his eyes and I listen to his voice I would like to blind him, make him dumb, but as soon as I go from him I see two trembling flames appear which shine like stars lost in the depths of the night. They are his eyes, his words purified by absence. His soul is nearer to me as his body is farther away. Postscript: when are you coming?" I gave in. I rushed, but accompanied by a presentiment of evil that meeting you at the Athens airport did nothing to dispel. If anything, the presentiment grew, like a fever whose cause can't be discovered. And now we were lying in each other's arms on the bed, for some minutes you had been looking at me as if you wanted to say something, I could feel that the cause was about to be revealed in words that I would have preferred not to hear.

It began like this: "That scorpion. He wasn't a man, that one, he was a scorpion. I won't shake his hand, no, not even if it would bring heaven to earth. There's a limit to everything, even to dirty hands, and besides how can you shake hands with a scorpion? A scorpion doesn't have hands, he has pincers!" "Who are you talking about?" "I'm talking about Hazizikis. About Major Nicholas Hazizikis. Theophiloiannakos was a little angel compared to him. Because with Theophiloiannakos I could defend myself, or groan, yell, faint. Theophiloiannakos only beat me, only tortured my body. But that scorpion! He would thrust out his sting, stick it into my soul, and wham! He had injected his poison into me." "Alekos . . . Why are you thinking again of these things, Alekos?" "And the way he mocked me after they had sentenced me to death. Good morning, Socrates. Or should I call you Demosthenes? No, the comparison to Socrates seems more right to me! I wanted to cry. And the more I told myself not to cry, not in front of him, no, the more the tears swelled in my eyes." "Alekos . . . What does that have to do with anything now, Alekos?" "And at a certain point I couldn't restrain them any longer. And it was a terrible thing: to cry like a baby in front of a scorpion. It was terrible also because he redoubled his irony—Who would have said you know how to cry?—and things like that. I lost my head. I shouted at him: I won't die, Hazizikis, and one day I'll make you cry because you'll end up in prison, and while you're in prison I'll screw your wife, Hazizikis, I'll screw her and screw her until she pisses blood, until her guts fall out, and you won't be able to do anything about it, Hazizikis, nothing except cry the way I'm crying now." "Alekos, please!" "And he started laughing. He answered that he wasn't married." "Alekos, do you want to tell me why all of a sudden you're thinking again about these things?" In all those months you had never talked about Hazizikis. Never. "Because . . . remember when I told you that interesting things happened in the trials?" "Yes." "Well, I had realized the key was there. His lawyers behaved too insolently. Always threatening revelations, waving papers they then didn't submit as evidence, didn't include in the proceedings. So I conducted a little investigation and I found out that in jail he was treated with special consideration. Radio, TV, visits from relatives and friends, including a certain Kountas, who works for a billionaire who finances the fascists. And each of the visitors came with packets of photocopies that the major studied and studied. They were photocopies of the ESA files. They are the documents I want." "Ah!" "And I'll get them." "Do you know where he keeps them?" "No, but I know who keeps them." "Who?" "His wife." "You said he wasn't married." "He wasn't then. He is now. Married and in love. A beautiful girl, it seems. Much younger than he. The daughter of a Resistance fighter, imagine. They met when her father was in prison, they were married three or four years ago." "Do you know her?" "No, never saw her." "Well then?" "Well then, it's simple: I'll get to know her." "And if she doesn't want to get to know you?" "She will, she will." "If she doesn't want to tell you where she keeps the documents?" "She'll tell me, she'll tell me. A speech is missing in the third scene of the fifth act of Sartre's play: a prick sinks into shit and blood easier than hands do." "Alekos!" "Which, translated into clean language, means: nothing is unworthy when the end is worthy." "Alekos!"

"Exactly what Sartre's character means." "Alekos!" "I've got a fine job ahead of me, yes. I'll say this to you: there's only one thing that worries me about this job: not having transportation, to be able to move when I have to, instead of always having to rely on taxis or borrowed cars. Even your Don Quixote never went on foot. So I need a horse, I mean a car. Will you give me a car?"

The airport was almost empty. Most of the flights had been canceled because of a strike which had started the day before, and in the departures lounge there were only three Arabs waiting, cloaked in white tunics, five or six irritated Westerners, and two nuns with their rosaries in their hands. At the check-in desk the clerks had tried to discourage me, saying there was little likelihood of my getting off, better to postpone it till tomorrow, but I insisted I had to reach Rome that evening and then they suggested a flight that would be stopping in Athens, coming from Asia, no telling at what time because it was very late already. All right, I answered, and went through police control and down into the embarkation lounge. I had taken refuge at the bar, where an American had tried in vain to strike up a conversation. Was I also waiting for the jumbo from Bangkok? "Yes." A real bore, eh? "Yes." Did talking bother me? "Yes." I needed to be alone, to meditate undisturbed on what had happened from the moment when you asked: "Will you give me a car?" Nothing had happened that could allow you to guess what an earthquake you had provoked inside me. Without answering you, I had lain there staring at a spot on the ceiling, a damp stain that soon became a smear of slimy sperm, and for a few minutes I was only able to think—It looks like a smear of slimy sperm. Because that too, I forgot to say, is on the banners soiled with blood and shit, on the glorious flags displayed in museums, in churches: the sperm of the heroes who fight for freedom, for truth, for mankind, for justice. In the name of those beautiful dreams, of those beautiful words, one lowers his pants and out comes the sperm. Guess how many creatures have been outraged, wounded, killed like that! There are those who have written history like that. Then I got up abruptly, avoiding your gaze which was questioning me, puzzled, I started talking about things that had nothing to do with automobiles or the ESA files. I went out on some pretext. For a couple of hours I wandered at random through the city, trying to calm myself, to persuade myself that such a reaction was excessive, unsuited to a modern woman: we had had the conversation about dirty hands after all, I had seen your torment as you told me again the scene of Meletus with Socrates and explained again your hatred for the scorpion. But reasoning, wandering served only to indicate to me the only possible choice: leave. I had to leave and in the meanwhile I had to avoid being alone with you. So as not to argue. On returning, I was to find two journalists in your office. This was a help and I made them stay on to lunch: we didn't remain alone even for a minute and the time came when you had to go to Parliament, to take part in the debate on I forget what law. "Will you come with me?" "I'm sorry, I can't." And the journalists said: "We'll go with you." You went out with them saying we would meet again after six: the debate would end around six. "All right." "And tonight we'll eat without witnesses, the way you like." "All right." "And without staying out late." "All right." "What is it? Something wrong?" "No, why?" The elevator went down, creaking, through the glass panes you smiled at me, and only then did I have second thoughts, an impulse to run after you, hug you, feel your moustache against my cheek, confess I'm going, I can't take any more. But I remained motionless, uttering only a very cold good-bye.

I looked at my watch: five o'clock. I imagined you in the chamber, intent on following the debate without following it, nervous, dazed by my ambiguous behavior; and a longing to cry rose in my throat. I cleared it with a cough which echoed in the silence of the half-deserted hall. A nun turned, the American gave me an odd look. He was a very handsome man, tall and thin, with gray hair and blue eyes, the vigorous refinement that certain purebred horses have, and I looked back at him thinking how much more difficult it would have been if you had had gray hair and blue eyes, a tall and slim figure, the refinement of a purebred horse. Paradoxically I wasn't in love with you. I never had been, not even during the seven days of happiness or in the period of the house in the wood, at least not in the sense this word usually has. I am talking about that physical desire that glazes the eyes and stops the breath at the very sight of the beloved, the shudder that numbs and melts at merely grazing a hand, a cheek, as everything in that person becomes unique and irreplaceable, even the smell of his breath, the sweat of his skin, his very defects which instead of defects seem charming qualities. You need that person as you need air, water, food, and in this slavery you die a thousand deaths but always to be resuscitated, to be enslaved again. I knew these symptoms, but honestly I couldn't say that I had ever felt them at any moment with you. Your body didn't really attract me, I didn't understand the women who considered it handsome and fell madly for it, betraying husbands, humiliating themselves just to be flung for five minutes against a wall or on a bed, to be able to tell the others or themselves that they had touched you; from the first moment I considered you somewhat ugly and I went on seeing you like that. Those little eyes, one different from the other in shape and position, one higher and one lower, one more closed and one more open, that flat boneless nose, that short and spiteful chin, those cheeks that puffed out the minute you put on the slightest extra weight; that thick oily hair you never combed, that squat body, with shoulders too round, arms too short, hands too stubby, the nails torn away instead of cut. You learned to tear them away in prison, where you had no scissors, and you kept on tearing them in spite of my horrified protests. How many things about you irritated me!

Your way of eating, for one: so coarse, so greedy. You stuck certain morsels into your mouth that not even a horse would have managed to swallow. Your way of taking a bath, for another. Taking a bath for you meant nestling in the water like a duck, dozing for hours without using the soap, abruptly emerging to jump into bed all wet, soaking me, yelling joyously—I'm cold, I'm cold! And your exaggerated vitality, your avid, growling sexuality, which attacked me with feline outbursts, arousing in me an impulse to flee; I had to control myself, lie, so you wouldn't know my participation was a cerebral act, sustained by a mysterious tenderness, heartrending, lacerating, a transport born I don't know from what but not surely from the senses. I hadn't come to you pulled by a call of the senses. I remembered well the anguish I had felt hearing you pacing up and down outside the opaque glass door, wondering whether to enter or not, I remembered well the cold that had numbed me glimpsing your fingers on the knob and the relief that had eased me when the fingers withdrew. Could this possibly have been due only to the presentiment of a tragedy to come? I remembered just as well the uneasiness that penetrated me the evening I had come back to find you in the hospital, my secret dismay at the idea that it was up to me to fill a five-year gap, to submit to a voracity so unappeased. No, the senses had not had any influence even on the enchantment of the first night, it would have been dishonest to say your passion had aroused mine, and afterward it had been the same: in our wild or sweet embraces it was not your body I sought but your soul, your thoughts, your feelings, your dreams, your poems. And perhaps it's true that a love almost never has a body as its object, often we choose or accept a person for the inexplicable spell he casts on us, or for what he represents to our eyes, our convictions, our morality; however, the vehicle of a love relationship remains the body, and if that doesn't seduce you, then something else must seduce you. The character, for example, the way of living or of behaving. And with time I had discovered that I didn't much like your character either: with its excesses, its ferocities, its rages, wicked and meaningless, its intoxications of the first stage, second stage, third stage, its rock-hardness, its oysterlike closing. The more I tried to open the oyster to extract the pearl, the more it resisted me, expelling a black liquid, the more I dug into the rock in search of rubies and emeralds, the more I found stone and coal. Your forest was full of undergrowth, thorns; whenever I plucked a flower I scratched myself, I bled. And the arrogance which assumed that everything was permissible to you, the superficiality with which you dismissed situations and problems, the contradictions into which you fell. All defects I deplored. But then why had I had that impulse to rush after you, embrace you, feel your moustache against my cheek, why now did I have to clear my throat and repress the tears?

I looked at my watch again: five thirty. If the debate really ended at six, soon the apartment in Kolokotroni Street would vibrate as you rang the bell, and you would press your nose to the wrought iron of the peephole, waiting to see me open the door, then to announce to me joyously: "It's I! It's me!" The little peephole would remain closed, silence would answer you, and at first you would pay no attention. Convinced it was a joke, you would let yourself in with your key, on tiptoe to take me by surprise, on tiptoe you would search from room to room. "Where are you hiding?" And you wouldn't find me. Then, disappointed, you would look for a note saying—Gone out, be right back—such as I often left for you, but you wouldn't find that either. I had left nothing written, I had preferred to explain by annulling every trace of myself. After the elevator had gone down, taking you away with the two journalists, I emptied the drawers of all my belongings, the wardrobe of all my clothes, I filled two big suitcases and a box and hid them in the closet along with the more insignificant objects, almost-empty bottles of perfume, toothbrushes, hairpins, tweezers, so scrupulously that not a hair remained, finally I stuffed the essential things in a traveling case and put the keys on the bed to show you I didn't need them anymore because . . . a spasm of vomit clenched my stomach. And yet, I wasn't physically jealous of you. I never had been, not even at the beginning, when I realized that arousing desire tickled your vanity, not even later when your Dionysian rituals destroyed our nights and I saw you bite off your pipestem staring at the she-elephant and the skinny ephebe. I am talking about the jealousy that empties the veins at the idea of the beloved's entering another body, the jealousy that makes the knees weak, dispels sleep, destroys the liver, inflames the mind, the jealousy that poisons the intelligence with questions, suspicions, fears, mortifies dignity with investigations, complaints, traps, making us feel robbed, ridiculous, transforming us into policemen, inquisitors, jailers of the beloved. Perhaps out of cerebralism, adherence to the principle that love relationships must be reinvented and above all scraped clean of the barnacles, the burdens that in the long run make them stifling, I had always forbidden myself to feel such sufferings for you. To know that you were desired actually flattered me, to see you open to temptations amused me, at times the two things actually aroused the pleasure of fighting for you against a greed that I myself fed by being your companion. Only in recent times had your excesses grieved me, and not because I knew I had been replaced for an hour or a night but because of the wrong you were doing to yourself, exposing yourself to gossip, accepting the ways of a society you wanted to change, adjusting yourself to the filth of a subculture whose phallus worship humiliates the intelligence. Still I hadn't given way even then to that indignation which silences and drives us to close the door after us, having left the keys on the bed. So why had it happened today?

For the third time I looked at my watch: six o'clock. An intuition told me that the debate really had ended at six and you were heading for the house, or rather going upstairs in the elevator, or rather ringing at the door, or rather entering on tiptoe to take me by surprise, and I saw you searching from room to room, looking for a note that wasn't there, frowning, opening the drawers, finding them empty, realizing everything was gone, finally opening the closet, noticing the two suitcases and the box, pale, turning to stone with certainty. Mouth shut, jaws clenched, nostrils flaring. And your gaze? The gaze of a wolf preparing to claw something to death or of a dog kicked because he peed on the rug? My head swam, a spiral of mist encircled the American with the gray hair, the nuns with the rosaries, the Arabs shrouded in their white robes. I clung to the table, I lighted a cigarette with trembling hands. Perhaps I wasn't in love with you, or I didn't want to be, perhaps I wasn't jealous of you, or I didn't want to be, perhaps I had told myself a pack of truths or lies but one thing was certain: I loved you as I had never loved any creature on earth, as I was never to love anyone. Once I had written that love doesn't exist, and if it exists it's a fraud: what does it mean to love? It meant what I was feeling now as I imagined you turning to stone! I loved you, by heavens. I loved you so much that I couldn't bear the idea of hurting you even though I was hurt, of betraying you even though I felt betrayed, and loving you I loved your faults, your sins, your errors, your lies, your ugliness, your pettiness, your vulgarity, your contradictions, your body with the too-round shoulders, your arms that were too short, your hands that were too stubby, your torn nails. And certainly love's object is not a body, but even when an ocean was separating us I took that body to bed with me, in my memory I embraced it as I had when we lived in the house in the wood, in winter, and at night it was cold and we warmed ourselves like that, my head against your head, my belly against your belly, legs entwined, or else when we were lying in the bedroom of Kolokotroni Street in summer, and the afternoons were sultry and we moved apart laughing—Go way hot stuff—but there was always a moment when your strange little eyes, one higher and one lower, one more closed and one more open, intoxicated me with sweetness, so I bent to kiss your swollen eyelids, those almonds of flesh, to stroke with the tip of my forefinger your comical nose, your prickly moustache, and your curled lips with so many little wrinkles, an old man's lips you used to say, and running my finger along your chin, then your jaw, then over your cheekbone, I moved up very slowly to the ears, these were perfect, well set, and you submitted happily to my admiring your ears at least: "What ears! What ears!" And perhaps I didn't like your character, or your way of behaving, but I loved you with a love stronger than desire, blinder than jealousy: so implacable, so incurable, that now I could no longer conceive of life without you. You were as much a part of it as my breathing, my hands, my brain, and giving you up was giving up myself, my dreams which were your dreams, your illusions which were my illusions, your hopes which were my hopes, life! And if love did exist, it wasn't a fraud, it was rather a disease, and I could list all the symptoms of this disease, all the phenomena. If I talked about you with people who didn't know you or who weren't interested in you, I knocked myself out explaining how extraordinary you were, what a genius, how great; if I passed a shop selling neckties and shirts I instinctively stopped to look for the tie you would like, the shirt that would go with a certain jacket; if I ate in a restaurant I ordered without realizing it the dishes you liked best and not the ones I liked best; if I read the newspaper I always spotted the story that would interest you most, I clipped it and sent it to you; if you woke me up in the heart of the night with desire or with a telephone call, I always pretended to be as wide awake as a chaffinch singing at dawn. I threw my cigarette away angrily. But a love like this wasn't just a disease, it was a cancer!

A cancer. Like a cancer that little by little invades the organs as the cells multiply, its slimy plasma of sickness, and the more it grows the more you realize that no medicine can stop it, no operation can remove it, perhaps it would have been possible when it was a little grain of sand or rice, a voice that shouts, Ego s'agapo, an embrace while the wind is rustling through the olive limbs, now instead it's impossible because it is stealing your every organ, every tissue, it is consuming you to the point where you are no longer yourself but a substance fused with him, a single magma that can be undone only by death, his death which would also be your death: this was how you had invaded me and were consuming me, killing me. There is a lugubrious characteristic in cancer patients: as soon as they understand that the disease has won or is about to win, they stop fighting it with drugs, scalpels, willpower, and they submit to being killed, without cursing it, not even reproaching it for the pain it demands. "My disease," they call it with affectionate indulgence, as if it were a friend, a master, or a possession they can't do without, and that "my" at times has a sweet sound: the sound that bubbled in my voice when I said your name. There, to this stage I had come because I hadn't removed you when you were a grain of sand, of rice, even though my instinct had warned me that anyone who entered your sphere would lose all peace forever. And still I had had chances to escape you, I could have seized them by the dozen in the period before the excursion to the temple of Sounion and the commitment made by accepting the two charges of TNT. But I had always rejected those chances and so the cancer had continued its course, to show me that to love means to suffer, that the only way not to suffer is not to love, and that when you can't help loving, then you are destined to succumb. My problem was insoluble, my survival impossible, and escape achieved nothing. Nothing? I raised my head. It did achieve something: it saved my dignity. You can't say to a person who loves you and whom you love—I'll screw the wife of so-and-so, I'll screw her and screw her until she pisses blood and her guts fall out, for this joy I need a horse, will you give me a car? And all your heroism, your desperation, your genius, your poems would not suffice to erase the disgust I had felt on hearing you repeat the dusty old slogan, "Nothing is unworthy if the end is worthy," the tired old talk of necessity. The necessity invoked by generals who send their soldiers to be slaughtered in order to take a railroad junction, a hill, anyway a nice telegram is sent afterward—Dear sir, dear madam, we are sorry to inform you that your son was killed in battle. The necessity claimed by the revolutionaries who empty pistols into anyone who comes along, and destroy and slaughter like bomber pilots, anyway afterward they write a tuneful little march about the sacrifices that it costs to win equality and overthrow czars. The necessity always allowed men who struggle and who in the name of the goddamn struggle can perform any perfidy, trade Briseis, enslave Cassandra, sacrifice Iphigenia, abandon Ariadne on a desert island after she has helped you defeat the Minotaur. Anyhow breaking one woman's heart, cutting open the belly of another, are trifles in the face of history and the revolution, aren't they? Enough. It's all very well to say that serenity puts you to sleep, that happiness makes you an idiot, while suffering wakes you and gives you ideas. Suffering paralyzes, extinguishes the intelligence, kills. And with you I had really suffered too much. Except for little oases of joy, brief hailstorms of gaiety, our union had been a river of anguish, danger, madness, neurosis: being with you was like being in the front line. It was a constant rain of rockets, grenades, napalm, an endless digging of trenches, patrols over mined paths, attacks, wounding and being wounded, yelling, sobbing, calling the stretcher bearer, pass me the ammo, Captain, I can't make it. No one can stay at the front forever, live forever in drama. Finally one loses a sense of proportion.

Six thirty. The loudspeaker crackled, a soft voice announced that the plane from Bangkok had landed. Good, soon we would be boarding, and even if you thought of looking for me here, you wouldn't have time to find me. Or would you? Suddenly fear condensed in images that followed one another with mad rapidity. You saw the keys on the bed, you understood. You grabbed them, went out to look for a taxi, got into the taxi, told the driver to take you to the airport, you arrived, came in, went to police control, showed your deputy's pass, reached the stair to the embarkation lounge, headed for the bar, and for the column where I was hidden, and the more I refused to believe it the more I felt it was happening, I thought I could catch the sound of your tread, heavy, cadenced, pitiless—one two, one two, one two. I kept my head down and asked myself if it wouldn't be better to go stand in line with the Arabs and the nuns and the American who were already by the gate to the runway, but I couldn't move and now that tread really was resounding, more and more distinct—one two, one two, one two—now it stopped and beneath my eyes there was a pair of dusty shoes that I knew well because you never shined them, above the shoes there was a pair of trousers that I knew equally well, rumpled, without a crease, above the trousers there was the checked jacket, the one with the bottom button missing. Aghast, and determined to ignore you, I didn't look beyond the tangle of thread in the button's place, and I pretended I hadn't seen you. But, like war trumpets, the keys I had left on the bed jangled at my ear and your voice rose, hoarse: "What did I do?" Immediately I raised my head to seek your gaze. No, it wasn't that of a kicked dog, it was the gaze of a wolf ready to claw. And the wolf's lips were trembling, strangely red, and at every twitch they revealed teeth clenched in a wrath so icy that for a moment I was afraid. "Tramp. I don't need your automobile. I don't want your automobile. I don't need anything or anybody. And stand up when I talk to you!" I remained seated, staring at you. Over the loudspeaker the soft voice announced the departure of the flight, asking the passengers to board, and I had to move. But I wouldn't have obeyed you, by standing up, for anything in the world. You went pale. You aimed the ring of keys at me. "If you move, if you take that plane, I'll kill you." Then I stood up. I collected my bag, I broke my silence: "Damn me and damn you if I ever set foot in this dirty city again." Then I turned my back on you, I headed for the gate, and I was a few paces from my flight group when a violent fist struck me in one lung: "Stop right here!" I went on, and immediately the second fist arrived, in the same lung, so sharp this time, murderous, that my breath failed and I arched backward and one of the two nuns murmured, bewildered: "Jesus help us!" But the American blushed and started to rush forward to intervene. I stopped him with a sign, I looked hard at your face. Drops of sweat were rising on your brow, your nose, the moustache, your eyes were two pools of alarm. Very bright. It looked as if you were about to cry. And so a few seconds passed before I could say those two words. In the end I said them: "Drop dead." And with this wish I left you, not turning back.

Eight months later when I entered the morgue to look for your body and my torment was a wounded animal's incessant repressed cry, the memory of having wished death for you, even in a trivial remark, rent my consciousness and stunned it and from that moment on it began tormenting me like the drip from a leaking faucet—drop dead, drop dead, drop dead. Naturally there were other accusations, other condemnations, with which I lashed myself; and soon you will understand which. But that "drop dead" summed them all up and in it I steeped myself, damned myself, I asked myself the question: Why had I so exaggerated that day, leaving you and denying you any explanation? Could the candid announcement of your plan and then the ingenuous request for an automobile possibly have driven me to such an excessive and definitive reaction? Unable to absolve myself, but at the same time pressed by the need to do so, I gave myself answers, and denied them immediately afterward. Yes, I had felt offended, I had given way to the human need to revolt, to free myself from a yoke that had become too heavy; but hadn't I always shown you that I accepted your carefree attitude? And with whom could you have talked if not with me, your companion? No, the real reason for that reaction must have been another, submerged and buried in the darkness of my unconscious. A fear, yes, a superstition I was unwilling to admit or was unaware of. Something must have gone off in me as I listened to that talk about necessities: something had snapped, a spark was ignited. And this spark had kindled other sparks causing a chain explosion like mines connected to one another and attached to the same detonator so that if one explodes they all explode. The mine of wounded pride, of unconfessed jealousy, of gagged boredom: they had remained inert for months, years, with no engineer to defuse them. Then suddenly one night it was clear: the automobile, the word automobile. I hated automobiles, I had always hated them, so much that I had never owned one, but the hatred had swollen monstrously since I had known you because from the beginning there had been a nightmare in our life: the automobile. The automobile that had attacked us on Crete, driving alongside us and forcing us toward the edge of the road to fling us down the embankment. The automobile on our return from Ischia that had waited for us outside the restaurant to strike our taxi. The automobile that threw the paper bombs at the Polytechnic, the black Cadillac that for me had become the sum of all horror experienced with the automobile because of an automobile. And there was the automobile that you had tried to blow up, Papadopoulos's Lincoln, the same you had tried to throw yourself under at the end of the week of happiness. Death in the form of the automobile, the headlights in the place of the hollow eyesockets, the muzzle in the place of the skull, the wheels in the place of the fleshless limbs. And you had asked me to give you death. That was the first spark. But why had you asked me, specifically me? You didn't need me to buy you an automobile. And why did you need an automobile to finally capture the documents? What did the automobile have to do with the ESA files and the wife of Hazizikis and the evidence against Averoff? It had plenty to do with them, as I was later to see. Besides the hero in the legend never faces the final duel without his horse: the horse has an almost religious function in his last challenge. Even in the myths of ancient Greece, the obvious texture of your culture, there is always the horse. Because without his horse the hero cannot enter the realm of the Underworld: it is the enchanted object, the gift indispensable to dying. And the giver of that gift, of that enchanted object, that vehicle of death, is always he or she who loves the hero.

We always understand afterward, as if understanding in time would serve to ward off the already-written fate. And certainly I wasn't thinking of this as I boarded the plane that was to take me far from you, or as I sat beside the American who had wanted to help me and now tried in vain to strike up a conversation. He knew New York well, did I know New York? Yes, I knew New York. He lived in New York, had I ever lived in New York? Yes, I had a house in New York. Really? How nice. What a coincidence. Then I was going to New York also? No, I wasn't going to New York. Actually I was, not telling anybody, convinced it was the only place where you wouldn't be able to catch me. The very idea of seeing you again, in fact, appeared to me that afternoon as an unspeakable disaster, a terrifying threat.

It's extraordinary the invention you thought up to catch me again, to use me as instrument for your death. Afterward I was to ask myself, incredulous, through what fit of idiocy had I let you hoodwink me so thoroughly. Especially since, better than anyone else, I knew your cleverness, your gifts as an actor capable of every kind of histrionics. And putting an ocean between us had not brought regrets: every day New York reinforced my determination to tear you definitively from my existence. There I worked, there I met people from a world that belonged to me and that excluded you, there I spoke a language familiar to me and unknown to you, there I found an environment in which I had always felt at ease. In the evening, when I came home and looked from the tenth floor windows at the glittering city, the handsome skyscrapers, the handsome bridges over the East River, gazing at them as I added up the positive results of a day spent without the torment of those names, Hazizikis, Theophiloiannakos, Averoff, I didn't miss you. And not even at night, when I lay in my comfortable bed thinking what a relief to sleep alone, warmed only by the electric blanket. It did happen that your image assailed me every now and then, summoned by a name or a sound or a food, or even a neon sign, Alexander's, Acropolis, Olympic, Greek Restaurant, but to thrust it away I had only to remember those two blows in the lung. It even happened that a glimpse of the ring exchanged at Christmas, now taken from the ring finger on my left hand and put away in a drawer, would bring a lump to my throat; but it could be cleared promptly with a bit of reasoning: in a desert where every tree is a mirage, every wisp of breeze an illusion, the desert of utopias, we had met, forgetting to ask each other who we were and where we wanted to go; dogs without tags, we had clasped hands, and stumbling over the sand dunes, falling, rising, falling again, we had kept each other company, bound by the ambiguous leash of love. But now the leash was broken, and there was nothing worse than mending it with lumps in the throat; nothing worse than disturbing my equilibrium, my detachment. There was only one chance of that happening, and it lay in the risk of hearing your voice. That voice that ensnared me, captured me like witchcraft. It was not so much a chance as a fear. Though the plane you had tried to keep me from boarding had been bound for Rome, not New York, it wouldn't take you much effort to discover I had come here. A phone call would have been enough. Still the fear lasted only one week, and the second week I had already stopped believing in it. Grave mistake. The dawn of my seventeenth day of escape was breaking when the telephone rang: "Hello! It's I! It's me!"

There is something intimidating about surprise. Good or bad, it's always an intrusion, an imposition, a bullying. Because it shatters an equilibrium and forces the recipient to submit to it: whether he likes it or not, whether he's prepared or not. And you loved surprises. The unexpected attack, the sudden whim that dumbfounds, the unprogrammed action: these were your specialties: I had forgotten that. For better or worse you fell upon others like a thunderbolt, like a child who bursts into a room disturbing a dialogue or work or rest: I had forgotten. But you hadn't forgotten in the least that, faced with a surprise, I became helpless; you had carefully calculated that if you called the first week you would find me on guard, but calling later you would catch me unprepared. "Hello! It's I! It's me!" That voice. The walls of the room started spinning with the vehemence of a centrifuge, the bed sank into a lake of bewilderment, and the handsome skyscrapers, the handsome bridges over the East River, the glittering city, the world that belonged to me and excluded you, everything dissolved abruptly. Useless, almost grotesque, the faint barrier of distrust I flung up against you: "What do you want? Where are you?" "I'm here, in Madrid! Listen! I'm in trouble! I need help!" "In Madrid? In trouble? I don't believe it." "You've got to believe it, cataramene Criste! It's true, true, true! Bad trouble, real trouble! Why would I call otherwise? You think I like telephoning you? Listen to me!" "Who told you I was in New York?" "Nobody. I guessed, I tried! Don't waste time talking, cataramene Criste! I've only got a few minutes: listen to me!" "All right, I'm listening." "The trouble is I came here with a fake passport, you understand? And I forgot my wallet with my real passport at the police control, you understand?" "What the devil are you saying?" "This is what I'm saying, don't interrupt me, cataramene Criste, this is what I'm saying! And I didn't notice I had left it there, you understand? I realize when they called me over the loudspeaker and a policeman came in here in the room where you wait for the planes!" "Oh, no!"

"Oh, yes. And he had my wallet in his hand! And what was I to do, was I supposed to let him have it? I took it back, obviously, but now if they're not stupid they know I'm me and I'm here, you understand? And my flight was canceled because of engine trouble, I have to wait for another one, they offered to take us back into the city, but it's best for me to stay here." "Oh, no!" "Oh, yes. Now I'll tell you what you have to do." "Me? Alekos, what can I do, from New York? Do you realize that there's the Atlantic between Madrid and New York?" "Of course, I realize, cataramene Criste, I know, I don't care. Let me talk. Listen to me!" "All right, I'm listening." "You must absolutely, I said absolutely, take the next plane leaving for Europe that stops off in Madrid. From New York there are lots of flights that stop in Madrid. I won't move from this waiting room unless they arrest me. I'm counting on the confusion. There's a lot of confusion. It will last till tomorrow morning because they're canceling other flights, I don't know why. The waiting room is also the transit lounge. You get off and come into the transit lounge. Without attracting attention you come over to me and slip me your transit card. When the plane leaves again, I'll board it in your place. Meanwhile you go to the ladies' room and you stay there until the plane has left. Then you pretend you've lost your card and you act all upset for a bit. You understand?" "It seems absurd to me." "Absurd?" "Yes, to make me come from New York. Why don't you look for somebody in Madrid?" "Who, in Madrid? Who?" "Well, in Europe then." "Who in Europe? Who?" "Why don't you take the first plane that leaves?" "Why? Why? Do you think this is the moment to ask questions, cataramene Criste? How many times do I have to tell you the same thing? You want me to go to prison?" "No, Alekos, I'll come." "Right away!" "Right away." "If you don't find me, don't give yourself away. It means they've arrested me. Continue the trip, go on to Rome, rush straight to my embassy, and from there let them know in Athens. Understand?" "Yes, but what sense is there in going to the embassy in Rome if they arrest you in Madrid? Wouldn't it be better if—" "Don't argue, cataramene Criste, don't argue. If I tell you to do something, that means it has to be done that way! I can't talk! I've talked too much already! If you don't find me, don't give yourself away, go on to Rome! Please!" "All right. Good-bye. I'm coming."

I hung up, torn by conflicting thoughts. On the one hand it seemed improbable and on the other more than possible. Let's suppose that after the shock of my leaving, you decided to give up the capture of the documents. All of a sudden, the way you gave up the Acropolis plan. That would have created a terrible void in you and also the need to embark at once on another enterprise. Not in Greece, however, and not in the politics of politicians: in a reality where white was white and black was black and red was red, namely in a country oppressed by a dictatorship. Spain. You had a score to settle in Spain, a promise that went back to the days when the Basques had imitated your Papadopoulos attempt, perfecting it and blowing up the automobile of Carrero Branco. You hadn't liked the idea of the Basques succeeding where you had failed. Deaf to my efforts to console you—There were lots of them but you were alone, they had an organization and you didn't—you shut yourself up in your jealousy: "It was my plan, my plan." Then you said that you would show them whether or not you were any less capable than they were. Had you then gone to Madrid to get your own back? No, no: Francisco Franco was dying, they were predicting a return to democracy, and your rejection of violence was too firm by now. Your conviction that any fool is able to press a trigger and the real bombs are ideas. On thinking it over I actually dismissed the possibility that you had given up the documents enterprise: you must have gone to Spain for something connected with the ESA files. Some paper in safekeeping in Madrid, some person who had fled to Madrid with the help of Averoff and the KYP. This explained the detail of the fake passport, your worries about being discovered by the Spanish police: obviously now that you were a deputy, an interpreter of legality, you couldn't let yourself be caught red-handed at your old tricks. Yes, you had to be rescued from that airport. With an ocean between us or not, you had to be saved from this trouble. And as my imagination raced, trampling on doubts, hesitations, incredulity, I looked for a flight going to Rome via Madrid. I found it. I quickly packed a case. I put the diamond wedding ring back on my finger. And a few hours later I was on the plane: I'm coming, Don Quixote, I'm coming, Sancho Panza is still your Sancho Panza, will always be, you can always count on me, here I am, agapi, here I am! It was only when I was over the Atlantic that my sleeping brain had a weak flash of lucidity: certainly it was quite a strange idea to make me come from the other side of the earth for a boarding pass, a job that anyone in Madrid could do in a couple of hours! Was it an excuse to make me come back? You were capable of everything, even of playing a paradoxical joke on me. And this suspicion, now substantial, made me flush. But since it was too late to do anything about it, I thrust it away and surrendered to a liberating sleep that lasted until the plane reached Madrid.

In the transit lounge you weren't to be seen, nor was there any sign of the confusion you had mentioned. There was, however, an unusual movement of police, and this made me nervous: I asked a hostess if some incident had occurred during the night. The hostess looked at me with a strange flash in her eyes. Incident? What sort of incident? She was supposed to give flight information, nothing else. Yes, I understood, please forgive my curiosity: muchas gracias, adios. And I continued the journey, to reach Rome two hours later. If you had really been arrested, as it was legitimate to suppose from the strange flash that had brightened the hostess's eyes, I was to follow your instructions to the letter. A quick dash to the hotel and then on to your embassy. I rushed to our hotel and I was so tired, so distraught, that I paid no attention to the words of the clerk and then of the concierge. Something about double keys or a package that had arrived. What package? I wasn't expecting any package. Mechanically I went up to the room, the one they always gave us since the splendors of the suite were past. I went in. The curtains were lowered but in the semidarkness I could discern a big basket of red roses, those buds I liked so, and a handsome bowl of fruit: apples, pears, oranges, grapes, candied fruit. Who could have sent me such presents, since no one knew of my arrival? I frowned. And immediately a shape moved in the bed, and that voice rang out: "Did you like the surprise?"

Now that the basket of roses had slammed against the wall and fallen in a rain of mortified petals, and the apples and pears and oranges lay scattered over the bed along with a shoe that had missed its target, and a bunch of grapes crowned your brow like a Bacchus garland, and the mocking grin that had curled your lips when I hurled the flowers and the fruit had died in a seraphic smile, and my dry throat was no longer emitting any sound because in the place of anger there was a stagnant, resigned impotence, I could listen to your explanations. "Let's hear them!" You took the bunch of grapes from your head, you began to pluck at it calmly. "Number one, I really was in Madrid: with a fake passport. There it is. I wanted to meet some members of the Spanish Resistance, to learn about a certain fascist group that's operating in Greece, in Spain, in Germany, and in Italy. A group founded by Otto Skorzeny, the one who freed Mussolini. I hoped to find the key to a mess I have my doubts about. Number two, I really did forget my wallet with my real passport and my money. I was tired, angry because I hadn't learned anything, and so I left it on the police desk. They really did call me over the loudspeaker and a policeman really did give it back to me. Number three, my flight really was canceled and I really did call you from the airport, while I was waiting for another flight. I was there, I was asking myself what I could invent if they started inquiring into the business, and I got the idea. It appealed to me, and I used it to make you come back. Number four, if I hadn't used it you wouldn't be here. And I need you." "To buy an automobile?" "No. For more. Much, much more." You became serious. "Soon I'm going to have them all on me, right, left, center: those documents won't help anybody. Evidently he isn't the only one who collaborated; there is even a pig from my own party among the traitors. I'll be more alone than ever then, and—" "Did you meet her?" "I met her lover. Eh! She has a lover!" "And when will you meet her?" "Soon. As soon as I go back to Athens. But I have to be careful, strange things have been happening for about ten days now. I have the impression, yes, that I'm being specially watched, I often have somebody after me who knows what I'm doing. A bad business." "And you plan to go through with it anyway?" "Of course. That isn't the problem. The problem, as I said, is that I can't count on anybody, not even on the party, and I'll be more alone than ever."

And at that point all my bitterness vanished. I collected the roses that had survived my fury and arranged them in a vase, I replaced the fruit in the bowl, then I said: "Let's think about the automobile." And with those words I surrendered again to the role the gods had chosen for me before we met: to be the instrument of your fate, and thus the accomplice of your death.

2

Like a boat cut adrift, unable to combat the river's current, not knowing whether the water will toss it on the shore or drive it to the sea, I went along in your existence during that autumn. My battle against love, against the cancer, was lost by now. My flight had been in vain. Oppressed by the sensation of having made an irreparable mistake, I tried to ask myself where I had gone wrong. Understanding it, for that matter, wouldn't have done me much good: the automobile had become an irreversible reality for you. You had actually convinced yourself that the capture of the documents depended on whether or not you had an automobile of your own: "I simply can't use a taxi to wait in front of Hazizikis's house or to shadow his lawyer Alfantakis! Taxi drivers are often police informers!" Or else: "I can't go on borrowing cars from other people, or hiring them. And I have to be always on the move, traveling from one end of the city to another!" Probably, if I hadn't said, "Let's think about the automobile," you wouldn't have given it another thought. But now that I had reminded you, the idea obsessed you: every conversation of ours ended with words like cylinders, rods, breaking in, international permit, registration tax, purchase price, license, customs sheet, color. Especially the color. You wanted a Fiat 132, and the range of colors was fairly wide but you never found the one that suited you: almost every day there were arguments about the virtues and defects of blue, of metallized gray, of milk white, of liver red, of green drab and apple green. The only point on which we agreed was the rejection of apple green. I, out of superstition, because green aroused memories connected with unpleasant or distressing sensations, and you because of your unswerving dislike of Andreas Papandreou, who during the campaign had chosen green as his party's color. And besides we couldn't ignore the fact that this was the new color for automobiles, in Athens apple green Fiats still didn't exist, and with apple green you would be followed all the more easily by those you felt were after you. Better a gray or a tan or a blue which at night, moreover, would blend with the darkness. The subject of the automobile absorbed us in such an exaggerated way that we talked of nothing else, least of all the drama which you were hurtling into and which for that matter I knew nothing of because, true to my invective against "ever setting foot in that dirty city again," I didn't go back to Athens. You came to Italy, and if I asked you how things were back there, you would evade the issue: "At the right moment I'll tell you, right now I don't want to think about it." The only time you referred to it was the afternoon the question of necessity came up again. We were walking along Via Veneto and it was the hour the birds come to sleep on the trees that line the street. They came by the thousands, in the violet sky they made a kind of blackish cloud, and we stopped to watch. One by one, detaching themselves from the cloud like drops from a faucet, they outlined a broad curve and then dived headlong onto a linden: always the same one. As they plunged, they shouted in triumph, shrilly, and along with the constant flapping of wings, this caused a deafening sound: the sound of evil. The most impressive thing, however, was not the noise: it was the helplessness of the linden: tall and strong, it was still anchored in its immobility, and it seemed to undergo a massacre, a torture. That torture was endless, that cloud never grew smaller. Inexhaustible, it continued spilling birds that flung themselves on the tree with the greed of piranhas that tear the flesh from a cow, and its branches were so teeming that under the excess burden some boughs cracked and even broke. The sidewalk all around was a carpet of ripped leaves. "Alekos!" You nodded with a mysterious smile: "There's an example of necessary perfidy. They know they are hurting it, perhaps destroying it, but they can't help it." "Yes, they could. There are other lindens on Via Veneto." "But they don't need the others, they need this one. I know." "What do you mean?" "I mean that Ioannidis would also have what I want: you think the former head of ESA hasn't preserved somewhere a copy of the ESA files? And Theophiloiannakos too or rather the wife of Theophiloiannakos has them. Even Alfantakis has them. But they would never give them to me. So I have to fling myself on who will give them to me, tear the flesh from the person who will give them to me." "I see: the job has begun." "You might say it's off to a good start." "Alekos, doesn't it make you uneasy to deal with people who you would have spat in the face of before?" "Eh, I suppose Bakunin asked the same thing the day Nechayev answered him: 'In politics everything is legitimate if it is necessary. Alliances with bandits, with the depraved, with thieves, seduction, betrayal. In politics anyone, and especially an enemy who can be useful, is a capital to be spent.'" Then you changed the subject, and I didn't bring it up again. Perhaps because, after hearing so often the words cylinders, rods, international permit, registration, I had convinced myself that in that period you were hovering in a limbo where your dreams took on the form of an automobile.

And the automobile came. It descended upon our life with the winter frosts. Someone had suggested that you buy it at a reduced price, already broken in, already registered, and from the factory they called us to say that at the reduced price they had two. Almost new, a splendid bargain. The only problem: the color. One was a cornmeal yellow and the other apple green. Definitely rejecting the apple green, you started illustrating the merits of the cornmeal yellow, which in

Athens was the same yellow as the taxis—"Nothing is better camouflage than a yellow that's the color of taxis, don't you think, let's go!" We went. And just as I was telling you that it really was the right color, it wasn't so much a cornmeal yellow as a mild and discreet hazel, I heard a joyous yell and I saw you dart toward a great green spot that glowed in the semidarkness. "My spring! My beautiful spring! My meadow! In May the daisies will bloom on this meadow, violets, verbena! I want it!" A few minutes later it was yours. "And no more talk, no more superstitions. What if it can be seen from a distance? Too bad. We'll take it right now, we leave in an hour, look at the blue sky, I ordered it for my spring, I sent a telegram to the clouds, I told them to vanish when I drive my spring." The rest is a sequence of images, sounds, colors that sting the memory like a fresh wound: you signing the contract of purchase, you sitting at the wheel, throwing the suitcases in the trunk, turning on to the superhighway, and it is a morning ripe with sunshine, at the sides of the superhighway the grass fields run toward us swiftly and then are lost swiftly behind us in stripes of green identical with the green of your spring, and so you burst out singing: "Green on the green! Long live life!" We went to Tuscany, to spend Christmas in the house at the top of the hill where we had spent all our Christmases, but the memory of your last Christmas and of the days that followed isn't among those walls, those woods: it is inside that green automobile. You couldn't keep away from it. "Let's go for a drive! Let's go and warm up the engine!" You drove without destination, never tired, and any time was right, any route, provided that it supported four wheels and your frenzy. You stopped only if you saw a service station or a shop where they sold dolls. You bought them by the handful: little, big, cloth, plastic. And I couldn't understand why. "What's come over you, Alekos? Who are you going to give them to?" "To children, to grownups, to people." "To people? To play with?" "Dolls aren't to play with. They're to remember who gives them to us." Then, on the seventh day, you asked me to go with you to Athens: "You can't mean to erase Athens off your map!" I let myself be convinced and with the absurd cargo of dolls after more hours and hours inside the green automobile we went to Brindisi to board ship with it for Patras, to land with it the next evening at Patras, drive in it along the road from Patras to Corinth and from Corinth to Athens. The same road, this last, that Michael Steffas was to take four months later in his Peugeot. To come and kill you, with the help of two accomplices in a red BMW.

You had been lighthearted during the trip, talkative. On the boat you joked, conversed in a lively tone with the officers and the captain, you even went down into the hold "to say hello to spring so she won't feel lonesome," but once we were on that road, an unexpected melancholy came over you and you fell silent. You drove with a strange absorption, your head bent toward your left shoulder, and every now and then you reached out to stroke me, sighing. "What is it, Alekos? Are you tired?" "No, no." "Do you feel ill?" "No, no." "Then what is it?" "I don't know. I'm sad." "Why?" "I don't know. Maybe the darkness, the road." "What about the road?" "Nothing. It's as if . . . nothing." You were in a bad humor also when we got to Kolokotroni Street and, after having parked askew on the sidewalk, you started unloading the dolls: as if having come back irked you or owning the green automobile worried you. Along with the bad humor, a kind of resigned indifference. Despite what you had said in Rome, "I have the impression I'm being specially watched," you attached no importance to the fact that the elevator wasn't at the ground floor, and entering the house you didn't assume your usual cautious attitude. "You've changed methods!" "Uhm! What was the use anyway? What has to be has to be, what will have to be, will be." Finally in the study-bedroom you were yourself again, and having lowered the curtains, from a secret drawer in the bookcase you took out a flat little metal box more or less the size of a wallet. Then you stuck into it a wire attached to a kind of button, then slipped the wire inside the left sleeve of your jacket, and attached the button to the cuff of your shirt. Finally, you thrust the strange instrument into the inner pocket of the jacket: "Now you tell me if you could guess I have a tape recorder on me!" "No. But who are you going—" "I'll have to learn to use it, it's very delicate, anyway it's already produced results." "Who with?" Without answering you went back to the drawer, took out a letter written in a clear, refined hand, dated February 24, 1975. "Who wrote it?" "Hazizikis. To his wife. Tomorrow I'll make a photocopy for you to keep in Italy." "Is it so important?" "Yes." And you translated it for me. It said: "My love, I am writing you from prison to inform you about the actions for which I am accused and to explain to you that I am the victim of political interests. Interests of brief duration for that matter, since my arrest will cause grave harm to the man who ordered it. The care with which they treat me, the consideration with which I am surrounded, show that he who decided to put me on trial knows the overwhelming consequences it will have. This was clear from the face of the public prosecutor as he was informing me, and I said to him: 'You're doing something wrong, and that is obvious from your white face. Look at yourself in the mirror, there's a mirror over there.' A little while ago the television announced that some units in Attica are on standby alert, and that some officers are preparing to rise up against the government. In his usual style Averoff has declared that the number of diehards, as he calls them, is less than five percent. Averoff knows perfectly well that his words are false. Averoff is a deceiver, it's no accident that he abandoned the good path for the bad. He always acts in the same way. After having deceived us, he deceives the people. I can be sure, even leaving a large margin for error, that the lieutenant colonels and colonels in favor of insurrection come to more than sixty percent, that among the captains the figure rises to eighty percent, among the lieutenants and noncommissioned officers, ninety percent. Under these circumstances, it's obvious that, if I were free, some people would not sleep easily. That's why they arrested me with such haste and such irregularity, apart from the pleasure in vengeance that moves him and the dirty politicians like him. But I hope soon to emerge from the isolation where they are trying to keep me . . ."

The attempted coup of which you had accused your dragon in your article eleven months before. The connections he was supposed to have had thanks to his so-called bridge policy. His fears of arresting Hazizikis and the other members of the junta. And this was only the beginning, the faint prologue to heaven knows what hornet's nest. How had you managed to make someone give you that letter? Had she handed it over to you, or her lover? In either case, who except you would pay the price for it? I couldn't breathe, just thinking about it. And paying no attention to the curtains, which you wanted down, I flung the window wide open, looked out on the balcony. But it served only to increase my uneasiness: on the sidewalk of Kolokotroni Street your spring parked askew, phosphorescent, seemed another cry of alarm. No, I shouldn't have bought it for you. I shouldn't have defied the gods, coming back to Athens. "Alekos . . ." You came over to me, you put your arms around my shoulders with affectionate irony: "Eh! But if it makes you suffer like this, I won't tell you anything from now on!" "Let's agree on that, Alekos: unless it's indispensable don't tell me anything. I don't want to know anything."

Whether this was really what decided my angry disinterest in the capture of the documents is hard to tell because, to the traumas of that day, I have to add the consequences of the crisis over my flight to New York. Great loves are also indigestions, which at intervals must be worked off with fasting: you can't keep eternally swallowing dishes of hare, pike, pheasant, lobster, partridge, capon, venison, stuffed veal, as in a Renaissance banquet where dogs bark, guests belch, drums roll, harps and violins accompany the songs of the minstrels. To avoid falling victim to such abundance, such gargantuan nourishment, you have to skip some courses: catch your breath again, leaving the great hall. And the seventeen days spent in New York had surely not been enough for me to catch my breath again, work off the indigestion, especially since the banquet had resumed at the same pace, with the same menu. And so that autumn, when I hovered in your existence like a boat adrift, resigned and aware of having lost my battle with the cancer, those consequences had been revealed in all their inevitability, causing relapses of weariness, germs of new revolts, as well as the discovery that loving you took time and space from every other commitment. Was it possible, I kept saying to myself, that everything turned on your enterprises, on your way of translating the dream? Was it possible that since we had met, even my work had been pushed into the background? And the discovery had made me dismiss the alarm bells: the purchase of the dolls "to give to children, grownups, people to be remembered," the mysterious sadness that had come over you on the road from Corinth to Athens, even the sense of anguish I had felt on looking down at spring parked in Kolokotroni Street, not to mention the justified fear that had taken my breath away when you translated the letter of Hazizikis, his accusations of the dragon. Result: Sancho Panza was never so far from her Don Quixote as in the two months in which you worked out the final challenge. I never asked you how far you had got, I deftly ignored your attempts to tell me, I never read the papers you entrusted to me from time to time. The original transcript of the dialogue recorded during the meeting with Fany, the wife of Hazizikis, for example. Before putting it in the pink folder I barely glanced at it.

Here it is, on four little sheets of airmail paper, with some gaps because a defect of the machine made some sentences incomprehensible, but still there is enough to understand the plan you were following. It bears the date of January 16, 1976, and the Tsatsos of whom you speak is Deputy Demetrios Tsatsos, member of your party, nephew of the president of the Republic. "Tell me, Fany, you married Hazizikis in 1972?" "No, in 1971." "When he was at the Infantry School?" "No, he was there from September to December of seventy-two." "And when did he go to the War School?" "In seventy-three." "Was Spanov there too?" "He was vice-commander of the EAT." "So, when you were at Kalkida, Hazizikis was already commander of the EAT." "Yes, in the morning he went to the War School and in the evening, after ten, he went to the EAT." "I've heard someone say that in those days Theophiloiannakos wanted a civilian government, of political men." "No, he wasn't the one who wanted that: it was Hazizikis." "Tell me, Fany, the person you talked to me about a little while ago and who downtown—" "Dimitri Kamonas." "—has a car park?" "Yes, right near here. Why do you ask me?" "Oh, just asking. And Fotakos, do you know if he just helps him out in a friendly way?" "Yes, in a friendly way. Like Potamianos and the others." "Uhm! I'll check on him. Tell me about Hazizikis, Fany: how was he the last time you saw him in prison? Did he talk just about your personal matters?" "Yes, he didn't say anything about the other matters." "It's obvious that he has no more faith in you and won't ever talk to you again about certain matters. And besides he wants to be optimistic." "What do you mean?" "I have the impression he's preparing something that the others who are in prison also know about." "That I (incomprehensible)." "Ah! And what about the wife of Theophiloiannakos, do you see her?" "Her? Even if I did see her, I wouldn't speak to her." "They say that Alfantakis is courting her." "I didn't know that. He throws himself on all women." "And what do you know about Demetrios Tsatsos? Do you know if his letters to Hazizikis are among Hazizikis's documents? Or did they end up somewhere else?"

"Tsatsos (incomprehensible). And mention the name of Pantelis, of Kostantopoulos." "Fany, earlier you told me of having been present the day Tsatsos denounced the students." "Yes, but (incomprehensible). And he really does have plenty of information on Tsatsos!" "But when you and Hazizikis used to go out to dinner with Tsatsos, was he the one who invited you?" "Yes, with his wife." "Is it true that his wife asked if she could bring her knitting needles?" "Yes, one evening we actually changed the light bulb so she could see better. That was the evening when Tsatsos (incomprehensible)." "Did he say that before or after the junta?" "After, after." "Then don't tell me you think it's impossible that you have anything of interest in the house, Fany! That cousin of his, Kountas, is here in Athens, isn't he?" "Yes, but—" "Listen, Fany, in this business I'll be categorical. I'll make photocopies, the documents will stay where they are, and nobody will know I got them from you; if there's anything against your husband, I promise you I won't use it. After all, he's been sentenced to thirty-one years, so what more do they want from him? They just want him to stay in prison five or six years and come out when there's no further danger of a coup. The state has no desire and no interest in keeping him inside for thirty-one years, it doesn't aim at vengeance. Vengeance is the aim of those who, as you said, tell how they were in the Resistance, when instead they made fools of themselves. They are the only ones who desperately want certain people to stay in prison: they are full of hate because they are ashamed of themselves. You have to look at this business from every side, Fany, you have to understand why I have to have the documents that show their responsibility. Not necessarily documents that incriminate them: documents that show who are the men who occupy or will occupy high positions of the state. These documents exist and we have to prove that certain people acted badly in the difficult moments, that when they were put to the test they didn't save even their own dignity. They are the ones, I tell you, who will go on harboring hatred against a group of officers like your husband. Officers who, in my opinion, committed crimes against the country, but still we should understand them. Yes, we should have the courage to understand them and to show them clemency, to avoid having this situation continue." "But I—" "Listen, girl: I really believe I can look at those papers without causing you problems and without anyone ever knowing a thing. And one of these days, say Sunday morning . . . Sunday morning, in fact, I have a meeting at eleven. What time does your mother-in-law go to church?" "At nine, nine thirty." "And what time does she get back?" "At eleven thirty." "Uhm! Any others? Give me the exact address. Is number twenty toward Patissia or toward Kifissia?" "Toward Patissia." "All right, I'll find it. And as I said: I won't use anything that might make the position of Hazizikis more difficult. Now I'll take you home and I'll leave you there because I have an appointment at seven."

I didn't read even the two little pages with the transcription of a dialogue between you and Fany's lover. Undated, this one, though it took place obviously after the first meeting with her and after the capture of some papers that hadn't satisfied you. Here it is: "But what did she say to you? That there were no more documents in there?" "She said that (incomprehensible)." "Anyway, if she's sincere about wanting to help me, she can come here." "She'll come tomorrow if you set a time." "Tomorrow I have to leave, I have an engagement." "In any case she can come after eleven in the morning." "All right, now tell me how she reacted to the matter and what you said to her." "I told her what you told me to tell her: that about ten people arrived, that the whole quarter was occupied, that they had cut the telephone wires, that they all went inside together, that after a few minutes Panagoulis also arrived and told me not to be afraid because he would protect me if I helped him in some way." "Good, but there is one point to clear up. At eight thirty for how long a time was she not with you?" "We went down together and we went to the corner where I realized I had forgotten something and (incomprehensible)." "Listen, boy: even if they cut off my legs, I'm going to get to the bottom of this business. So the problem is: how sincere are you being? At eight thirty a girl and a young man left the house, I tell you, and the girl was very much like Fany and the young man really seemed you. They were carrying a suitcase. They went to Taxiarcas Street, they went into a house. If you were the young man, we had better put our cards on the table." "But I (incomprehensible)." "And tomorrow it's best to tell Fany to watch out if by any chance she has other documents at home. Naturally I've taken my precautions: both in the eventuality that the house is watched, and if the business should become known through negligence or gossip. You understand?" "Yes, but I have some doubt, Alekos: is it possible that he really left so many documents in the house?" "It's possible if you tell me that Fany made the photocopies there and gave them to Kountas." "Fany didn't give photocopies to Kountas." "She did give them to him. As for your doubts, you've been in her house so much: didn't you have enough curiosity to look or at least to ask?" "Yes, but she said it shouldn't interest me, so I never asked anything. A lot of people are always coming to that house, but I don't go around asking who's this one or who's that one. I only know that at the War School he had packs of those documents and he arranged them in folders." "What time did she go to visit Hazizikis in prison yesterday?" "Yesterday was Thursday and she went at seventeen minutes before noon. I know because I was waiting for her in a bar. Why do you ask me that?" "And at what time did you go to her house?" "Yesterday I didn't go there at all, I tell you. She called around noon and said to me: 'Iannis, my parents are arriving between twelve thirty and one. What do you say: should I go?' 'Of course, go,' I answered. 'Then come with me,' she said. So I went by and picked her up and (incomprehensible)."

"Listen, boy: don't tell me the automobile was mine. And don't tell me you don't like certain things. You know full well that until this business is cleared up I'm going to know every move you make!" "Alekos, why do you talk to me like this?" "And I'll say something else: those papers about Averoff (incomprehensible)." "You really think he was in the KYP?! The authorities (incomprehensible)." "Boy, the authorities don't know anything. If I had known that the files were there I would have sent the attorney general, I told you that. But I also said a move like that is no longer wise, the way things are today. And from there you haven't brought me one paper." "But Fany's the one who—" "If Fany is the way you say, if she really won't let her husband screw her, if she really acts so nobody will catch on to anything, and if she manages to look on me as a brother . . ."

As for Hazizikis's letters to Fany, more and more numerous after the one you had handed me in Athens, it upset me even to have them in my possession, and I couldn't manage to touch them without the uneasiness of an involuntary pity. The summary translation you made of them one day, laughing, convinced me that only the first one contained news of a political nature; the others were only the heartrending pleas of a husband in love, willing to do anything to hold on to a wife who wants to leave him. I didn't even understand why you collected them so scrupulously: vengeance on the scorpion who had tortured your soul, mocked you after your death sentence? Fidelity to the vow you made to yourself that terrible night? And I wouldn't have believed my own ears if you had told me that, now, neither vengeance nor vows interested you anymore, that in those lines full of desperation, helplessness—My darling don't leave me, my child don't go—you saw only material for your strategy. You used them with absolute detachment, with the ghastly coldness that derives from the principle that nothing is unworthy if the end is worthy, you read them to extract information, rational arguments. First: if he went on begging her, then she hadn't decided on the divorce. Second: if she hadn't decided on the divorce, he maintained control of the documents he had entrusted to her. Third: for him to lose possession and control of them, the divorce would have to materialize. So there you are, the great director of their tragedy, the great puppeteer who pulls the strings of his marionettes to make them dance as he pleases; there you are on Corfu looking up her parents, who, as the letters show, are in favor of the divorce; there you are suggesting lawyers, legal loopholes, insisting how cruel it is to keep the poor girl bound to a husband who is going to spend thirty years in jail; there you are manipulating the lover with promises and proposals, kindling his ardor, suggesting he flee abroad with her and the child born of her marriage. And when you realize that he is a weakling, a poor bastard unable to fight the influence Hazizikis still has over his young wife, there you are falling on the tastiest prey: advising her, coaxing her, courting her, seducing her until every residue of a conjugal bond is dissolved, and the lover himself liquidated, no longer of any use. All this during the two months when I am busy working off the indigestion of hare, pike, pheasant, lobster, partridge, capon, venison, stuffed veal; and toward the damned documents I display that angry disinterest, evading your attempts to confide in me, rejecting your requests for help. "I have to go to Corfu, you know. Come with me, please! That way it'll look like a holiday." "Corfu? No, I don't want to, I can't." "You have to lend me a hand, I have a problem: finding a place for three Greeks in Italy. A couple and a child." "Who are this couple? Who is this child?" "Guess." "Ah, no! Not on your life!" "I'm nervous, you know, I can't get into that house. I found out she was looking for a babysitter and I was sure I could make her hire a nurse I know, but she didn't hire her. What if I got a wax impression of the keyhold?" "I don't want to know about it!"

The only time I paid some attention to you was when you described the capture of the first packages of documents, thanks to the young man's complicity. Needless to say, things weren't as he had told Fany, following your orders, and as you had told the press in April. No occupied quarter, no telephone wires cut, no commando of ten people who rush in ahead of you. You went in alone, at nine in the evening, fifth floor, door to the right of the elevator, alone, you found the room, the first on the left, a dining room, and picked out the right piece of furniture, a kind of credenza with shelves, and discovered the packages hidden on the top shelf. Alone, you stole them, in several trips, and each trip an agony because at the beginning you thought there was nobody at home but then you realized that Hazizikis's old mother was sleeping in the bedroom at the end of the corridor. You heard her snore. Terrified at the idea she would wake, you then started working faster, holding your breath, and it seemed to you that the trip from the room to the stairs, from the stairs to the automobile, from the automobile to the stairs, from the stairs to the room again, would never end. Your heart was pounding hollow cannonades, your body was spitting off icy sweat, you were shaking, and on the fourth trip, a package fell to the ground with a heavy thud. The old woman woke up: "Iannis, is that you, Iannis?" Answer or not? And if I answer, what if she realizes that my voice isn't Iannis's voice? A long sigh and then: "Yes, it's me." "Ah! Don't make any noise, Iannis. I want to sleep." Afterward you felt bad about this, at night you had a nightmare. You dreamed of an octopus. Among all the fish the octopus was the one that for you more than any other symbolized bad luck and death. You can't elude an octopus, you used to say, wherever you run, it'll overtake you and catch you. And this octopus was immense, monstrous, its head was as broad as a square, its tentacles as long as the avenues of the city, in fact it wasn't in the sea, it was in the city. Its suckers stuck to the walls of the buildings, it filled every void, swallowing anything that got in the way of its expansion: automobiles, bodies, wagons, buses, and in the meanwhile it was roaring. A grim, angry roar, a kind of invocation that rose to the heavens and then fell down like a rain, forming a word you didn't understand. A word that gave both joy and sadness. "I think it was like the word for life, zoi. Or alive, zi. And yet it seemed to me that I was dead." But I attached no importance to that dream at the time.

The fact is that we never realize in time what is important and what isn't. As long as the beloved oppresses with demands, with bonds, we feel stolen from ourselves and it seems that to give up a job for him or a journey or romance is unjust; openly or in secret we harbor a thousand resentments, dreams of freedom, we long for an existence without affections in which to move like seagulls that fly through the golden dust. What an unheard of torment are the chains with which the beloved ties us, preventing us from spreading our wings, what boundless wealth is the space whose doors he seals with the same chains. But when he is no more and that space is flung open, infinite, so we can fly in the golden dust as much as we like, seagulls without affections and without ties, we sense a frightful void. And the job or the journey or the romance we sacrificed so reluctantly now appears in all its futility, we no longer know what to do with our regained freedom, like dogs without masters, sheep without a flock, we wander in that void weeping over lost slavery and we would give our soul to go back, to live again in the demands of our jailer. Because remorse chokes, remorse is an incurable wound. In vain we try to allay it with attenuating circumstances, justifications—If I had known, if I had guessed—in vain we try to ignore it, declaring we failed him as much as he failed us, so the score is even. At first the wound seems to heal, dissolve, but there is always a moment when a sound or a smell or a color, the sight of a sheet of paper, of an automobile going by, opens it again with new feelings of guilt, self-accusations, the incontrovertible fact that he is dead and we are alive, and therefore the score is not even.

I am not referring only to the remorse for not having

understood that in those documents your death was written. I refer also to the remorse for not having understood that everything around you was collapsing, flinging you back inside the ghastly solitude of the years when you were buried in Boiati.

The word "everything" also includes the illusion that in the politics of politicians there was room for you. Hazizikis's files were now in your hands, and the cruel enterprise had been concluded in a cruel way, when you realized that in the politics of politicians there was no room for you and your worst mistake had been joining the party. For the simple fact that a party is a party, an organization, a clique, a mafia, at best a sect which does not allow its adepts to express their own personality, their own creativity: on the contrary it destroys them or at least it twists them. A party does not need individuals with personality, creativity, imagination, dignity: it needs bureaucrats, functionaries, servants. A party works like a business, an industry, where the general manager (the leader) and the board of directors (the central committee) hold unattainable and indivisible power. To hang onto it they hire only obedient managers, servile employees, yes-men, in other words men who are not men, robots who always agree. In a business, an industry, the general manager and the board of directors have no use for intelligent persons, endowed with initiative, for men and women who say no, and the reason for this goes even beyond their arrogance: thinking and acting, the men and women who say no represent a disturbing element, sabotage, they put sand in the gears of the machine, they become monkey wrenches thrown into the works. The system of a party and of a business is that of an army in which the private obeys the corporal who in turn obeys the sergeant who in turn obeys the lieutenant who in turn obeys the captain who in turn obeys the colonel who in turn obeys the general who in turn obeys the supreme command who in turn obeys the minister of defense. Priests, monsignors, bishops, archbishops, cardinals, curia, pope. And too bad for the deluded person who believes he can make a personal contribution through discussion and exchange of ideas: he ends up expelled or demoted or liquidated, as is right for one who is unable to understand that in a party, a business, he is allowed to discuss only orders already given, choices already made. Provided, it is understood tacitly, the discussion respects the two sacred principles: obedience and loyalty.

All this assumes different nuances according to the party. Obviously a party with a precise ideology, a crystallized theory, is the fiercest in demanding obedience and loyalty, in repressing the creative contribution of the individual: the more a church is severe, the more it rejects protestants and condemns heretics to the stake. Paradoxically, however, the abuses and the infamies that such a church commits on its adepts have a sense, a justification: the power of its faith, the apparent nobility of its programs or plans—I crush you because I want to create the kingdom of heaven on earth, I crush you because I want to create it thanks to the doctrine of historical materialism. But a party that has no theory and no ideological model, a party that doesn't know what it wants or how it wants it, cannot claim ideal motives to exculpate itself. Its abuses and infamies and demands of obedience and loyalty are imposed by personal opportunism, by private ambitions. Cliques within the clique, mafias within the mafia, churches within the church, and with the aggravation of a disease that in parties without doctrine is contagious as the plague: the corruptibility and the corruption of the yes-men. While the doctrinaire party crushes with its principles those who protest or disobey, the party that doesn't know what it wants expels, like foreign bodies, those who do not adjust to its absence of principles, that is, to its lies, its hypocrisies, its clienteles.

Well, this was exactly the sort of party that you had considered capable of receiving your imagination, your dignity, your creativity. But your error also included the monotonous illusion to which we abandon ourselves, out of helplessness or lack of choice, all of us who believe in the mirage of a world that changes: the illusion that we can still struggle while leaning for support on the barricade called the left. In fact, except for the brief period of the campaign, of the rallies at which you gave the lie to the Papandreous, the general managers, the boards of directors of the official left, and except for that trip to Moscow, which only your friends knew something about, you had not done much to recall that the shit is the same on the right, the left, and in the center. You had never committed yourself to waging the battle on several fronts at the same time. On the contrary you had chosen the strategy of fighting one enemy at a time, you had concentrated your energies against the right, and only the right, against the dragon, and only the dragon. "Now I have to worry about him. Later, if I'm alive, I'll deal with the others." You had deliberately renounced acting according to your convictions and would not remember that the left is the best ally of the right, that in the countries where the left is in power it represents the boulder at the top of the mountain, that in the countries where it isn't in power it supports that boulder, the Averoffs, imitating their game or becoming a part of their system. The same professionals, the same opportunists in peacetime; the same traitors and often the same cowards in time of war. So you had behaved as if the dragon were not a dragon with two heads, as if you didn't know that it is useless to cut off the first head if you don't also cut off the second, that only a double and simultaneous decapitation can achieve the disappearance of the monster, after which you can plant a new tree. Assuming, mind you, that a new tree bears good fruit, that the mirage of a world that changes contains a bit of green, a bit of water. Isn't it perhaps true that human beings don't change, that only the scenery in which the mirage dazzles us changes? For millennia we have pursued the mirage, weeping, dying, yet we find ourselves always at the same point, perhaps with one more union or party, one more ideology or technological discovery, to weigh down the luggage of our perfidy and our stupidity, to remain where we were a hundred thousand years ago, with a two-headed dragon. When you did remember that the dragon has two heads it was too late to turn back and resume the only possible battle: the one that takes place on several fronts at the same time. The only thing to do was turn your back on the politics of politicians, on the business in which you had got stuck, forgetting that it hires only obedient managers, servile employees, yes-men, never men and women who say no and put sand in the gears of the machine. And you did just this. You renounced all support, you recovered your independence. But you thus restored yourself also to the solitude that would make you vulnerable, bring you to the logical conclusion of your legend: to be physically and morally killed by all, at the hands of mercenaries from this side and that.

This developed, or rather precipitated, with the proofs of the collaborationism of that Demetrios Tsatsos, deputy, nephew of the president of the Republic, member of your party, and with the inevitable cowardice that your party showed. Fany had not lied that evening when you questioned her with the recorder hidden in your jacket and the microphone in your shirt cuff. Not satisfied with visiting their house and inviting husband and wife to dinner, Demetrios Tsatsos had also denounced students of the opposition. The sort of person he was emerged from the little letters to Nicholas Hazizikis and to the chief of the torturers of Baboulinas Street. "Dear Nicholas, Papadopoulos's speech at the press dinner was marvelous! It is a real outrage that certain mudslingers don't recognize that." "Dear friend Dascalopoulos! I have heard of your promotion and I want to be the first to congratulate you! Promoting a man of your culture and your civility is something exceptional in this country of mediocrities, and your position at the head of the police represents a hope for the future! Yours, Demetrios Tsatsos." You asked then that the steering committee of the party be called to meet and, your lance in rest, you plunged headlong into the tourney: what stuff was this, and who were these people!? What? You were looking for the evidence against Averoff and with it you found more against a member of your own party? He should be expelled at once, without hesitation. "Either he goes or I go." And there were the cliques within the clique, the mafias within the mafia, the churches within the church, the clienteles, the lies, the hypocrisies, the opportunism: take it easy, my boy, easy! Don't dramatize, let's give this some thought. Go slow, my boy, slow, let's see what it's all about, let's examine the matter. To expel like that, without forewarning, a member of the party who wasn't Mister Nobody after all, he was an important figure, a deputy, a university professor, nephew of the president: what the devil! Assuming that your information is correct, what had the man done after all? He had shown himself to be weak: it isn't obligatory to be born a hero. And what was this business of the secret files of the ESA? Who had authorized you to stick your nose into such a delicate business? When a man belongs to a party he can't just act on his own initiative without informing the party! Discipline, by Christ, discipline! Grave documents about Averoff. Eh! Let's examine them, consider the pros and cons. They could help the party and they could harm it. The most disgusting were the members of the board of directors, the leaders of the little churches, the factions, the various wings of the party. Some of them, besides, accepted financing from the German Social Democrats. And Demetrios Tsatsos was one of the protégés of the German Social Democrats: touching him meant a risk of losing their contributions. And tell me if, having to choose between an honest man and a nice pile of deutsche marks, a party like that would choose the honest man.

"You know how they answered me?! You know what they want to do with my documents?! They want to hide them!" "Alekos, why are you so amazed? Parties always act like that: they want the documents in order to hide them and, if needed, to use them for blackmail —If you don't give me this I'll screw you by spilling all about how you betrayed, how you stole, how you're a faggot. Any party would have answered you in the same way. Even a more respectable party than yours. We have to see if it helps the party, they would have said to you. And your party—" "It's not my party anymore. I smashed a chair on the table, I've handed in my resignation." "Ah! And did they accept it?" "No, they rejected it. But that doesn't change anything. As far as I'm concerned it's over." "I understand. And now what?" "Now I'll stay on in Parliament as a left-wing independent." "Without a party backing you. Or rather with enemies in the party that continues to consider itself your party." "I don't care." But as you were saying this there was a hint of anguish in your eyes: you knew very well that without a party behind you and with enemies within the party that should have supported you everything would be doubly difficult. What, for example, should you do with those papers for which you had suffered so much and made others suffer? Hand them over to the magistrature so that they could ignore them? Deliver them to a parliamentary committee so that it could shelve them? Publish them? Publish them of course. But where? What newspaper would have the courage? "Uhm! I know. I ought to have a newspaper all my own. What if I founded a newspaper? A little sheet. A weekly or a biweekly that would last three or four months: the time to publish what I have. I have so much stuff, you know? And what I don't have yet, I'll have soon. Besides the ESA files there are also the KYP files. And I've discovered a friend at the KYP. A democratic officer, an honest man. The husband of a girl who helped me at the time of the attempt on Papadopoulos. He said to me: I'll give you a trunkful of documents! Just think: the papers of the Cyprus coup, on the CIA! On the ties between the KYP and the CIA! Between Averoff and the KYP and the CIA! Tsatsos's little notes to Dascalopoulos and Hazizikis aren't in it! If I could prove that Averoff knew about the Cyprus coup, that in agreement with the KYP and the CIA he deceived even Ioannidis . . . The problem is to lay my hands on that trunk. I don't want to get my officer friend into trouble. He isn't a torturer or a whore, not him!" "Alekos—" "Yes, a newspaper. On the front page the documents about Averoff: some that I have now and some that I'll find in the trunk—" "Alekos, forget about the trunk. You know what it means to start a newspaper? You know how much it costs? Only people who have power, financial or political power, can start a newspaper. It takes a lot of money to start a paper, lots." "I'll borrow it." "Who from, Alekos? If you don't have money, you can't borrow money. Debts are a luxury of the rich. No paper plant will sell you the paper. No journalist will write for you. No printer will print it for you, knowing you don't have the money." "I'll find it." "Where? From the very people you're fighting against? A party should help you, you should turn to another party—" "I'll never have a party again! Never! I don't even want to hear the word party! The word party makes me vomit!" And now the anguish in your eyes wasn't just a hint: it shed long tears, wet your cheeks, your moustache, soaked your necktie.

A few days later I learned that your helpless isolation had already borne its fruit. On two occasions mysterious night visitors had entered the apartment in Kolokotroni Street where, recklessly, you kept the photocopies of the files. Once they had got in while you were having supper in a restaurant outside the city and once when you were sleeping in the house with the garden of orange and lemon trees at Glyphada. They hadn't found anything because everything was in the locked bedroom and they hadn't been able to force the lock. But they had turned the office inside out and left a note covered with insults. "How do you plan to defend yourself, Alekos?" "No way, alitaki. What has to be is. What has to come will come. I'll simply try to see this business through." And it was then that my love for you revived completely and the banquet was resumed with hare, pike, pheasant, lobster, partridge, venison, veal seasoned with desperation. Hand in hand we would celebrate it for twenty-eight days. The last twenty-eight days the gods granted us.

3

A STRANGE THING HAD HAPPENED. YOU HAD TURNED UP in Rome without warning. "I've found somebody who'll publish the documents for me!" "Who?" "An afternoon paper, *Ta Nea.*" "When?" "Soon. In a few weeks' time. The *Ta Nea* journalist is already working on them." "Thank heaven! So what are you doing here in Italy?" "I came to write the book." "The book? What book?" It was true that you had once said you would like to write a book on the assassination attempt on Papadopoulos and the trial and Boiati, but rather than a plan, to me it had seemed simply a wish. Could you possibly have revived the idea all of a sudden, and while you were up to your neck in the business of the documents? "The book I talked to you about, of course. Publishing the documents isn't enough, things have to be taken further, I must explain why a man who began with bombs ends up fighting with paper. Listen, there are all these people who turn out books even though they have nothing to tell, shouldn't I tell the story I have? It's a terrific story, for Christ sake! So I packed my bag and here I am. Let's go to Florence." "Florence?" "Of course, to be peaceful. I certainly couldn't start writing in Kolokotroni Street or at Glyphada! Too many problems, too many distractions." "Yes, but—" "You think I can't do it? You're wrong. I've got it all clear in my head, this book of mine, divided into chapters and everything; I've always considered myself a writer, really. I even know how I'll begin it: with the scene of the attempt. There I am trying to untangle the wire, he's leaving his villa at Lagonissi, the sea breaking on the rocks . . . And if I have any problems, you'll help me." "Yes, but—" "How long will it take? Eight months. I need only eight months. In May I'll ask for a leave from Parliament, and in November I'll deliver the manuscript. The important thing is for me to start at once and for nobody to disturb me, I mean for nobody to know where I am. If I begin tomorrow morning and keep at it for three weeks or four, I can break off for a while when the documents appear, and—" "Tomorrow morning?" "Yes, we leave tomorrow morning." "Alekos, I can't leave tomorrow morning. I didn't know you were coming and I have some appointments." "You surely wouldn't let me go alone? What if I need advice, suggestions?" "No, of course not. But what sense does all this haste have?" "I can't wait; it's burning me up. Besides I don't want to show myself in Rome. Otherwise they'll be after me, they'll distract me. Nobody must know I'm here: I told you that!" There was really no way of dissuading you. Ignoring my protests, insisting that inspiration can't be commanded, that my presence was indispensable, that I couldn't refuse it to you, you forced me to leave for Florence with you. "And ask the concierge to reserve seats on the Paris plane, so they'll believe we're going to Paris."

How strange I thought. But I didn't let myself go in conjectures or suspicions now that, shut up in the house in the wood, you devoted yourself to the book seriously and steadily. Seeing you bent over those papers, anyone would have believed they were the real purpose of your trip to Italy, that only the book had driven you to exile yourself in that room. In the morning you woke early, arranged the paper on the desk along with ballpoints, pipes, tobacco, lighter, then you asked me to leave you alone, and you stayed there writing, earnest as a student preparing for his exams. You wrote slowly, without second thoughts, more like someone finding release than like a writer obeying an inspiration; you never sought the advice for which you had dragged me to Florence, and in the evening there were always two or three new pages tightly filled with your precise handwriting, almost without cancellations. Each time I was amazed. Was it the house in the wood? You had always liked going back there, finding again the atmosphere and the objects that recalled a past of intimacy and tenderness, the rocking chair, the Tiffany lamp, the big wardrobe with the mirror in which the trees were reflected and the birds would dart to rest on a branch that didn't exist. Not even the memory of the nights we were tormented by the spotlight, or the night you wanted to confront our persecutors and we lost the baby when I tried to prevent you, had ever managed to lessen the spell that refuge cast on you. Even in Athens you were homesick for the park with the pines and cypresses and the horse chestnuts that grazed the balcony, with chestnuts to pick or caress, and the laurel hedges, the rose arbors, the clumps of lilac. But why did you never go out for a stroll, why did you never look out of the window for a moment, why did you always keep the shutters closed? Every day before going out I would fling them wide; every evening, on returning, I would find them closed. At the beginning I didn't attach too much importance to it, believing that an open window is always an invitation hard to resist: the heroism of writing while the sun beckons to us requires the discipline of a professional, not of a schoolboy. But soon I became alarmed, and I noticed other eccentric details. In the evening the windows were also firmly closed and the curtains drawn so carefully that not a thread of light could filter through: the only lamp burning was the one on your desk. Finally there was the telephone. You never answered the telephone, you who worshiped that instrument with such passion. If I was out and wanted to tell you something, the only thing I could do was go home.

"Alekos, I called you all afternoon, dammit! You didn't pick up the receiver once!" "How was I to know it was you calling? Didn't we decide that nobody must know I'm here?" Then the business of the key. The house in the wood had one flaw: the door didn't close with a rim lock, but with an old knob lock so elementary that, if it was locked from the outside, anyone inside remained trapped. Unless he had a second key. You had forgotten our second key in Athens, and one day when I told you I wanted to have a copy made, you objected: "No! One key's enough. I don't need one anyway. Keep it, and when you go out, lock the door carefully." "And what if you want to go out?" "I won't go out." "And what if somebody comes?" "I'm not expecting anybody to come." "Suppose somebody comes anyway?" "If somebody comes, I won't have any temptation to open the door, and I avoid bad encounters." Finally your behavior at suppertime. Eating in a restaurant had always been a pleasure you couldn't forego, you liked restaurants because you could choose the foods, and you liked the noises, the crowd, but now all this irritated you: you wanted to eat at home. "I like it better here, it's so beautiful staying here." "Don't you feel any need to move about, see a few people, amuse yourself?" "No." "All right, so much the better."

So much the better. Nothing is more egoistic than love, of course. At times, in order to be alone with the beloved, we would stoop to any self-deception, any blindness; there is an almost abject joy in having him exclusively for ourselves, and I had shared you too long with others. Besides without others we were never bored: the meeting of two solitudes is also the meeting of two imaginations, and our fantasy was able to fill every silence, every void. How the room expanded when you stopped writing and allowed yourself to rest! If you put on a record, the place became a night club with orchestra; if you turned on the television, it became a theater; if you moved the desk, it became a dance floor; if you pushed the table in front of the mirrored wardrobe, it became a vast hall where two duplicates of us were eating and dancing and laughing so that you could pretend to complain: "Silly parrots!" There were evenings when I felt a kind of gratitude for that absurd exile and its unknown causes, a secret hope that it would last as long as possible, and those were the moments when my blindness plunged into the depths of stupidity. If I had only turned the conversation to the files or to your disagreement with your party or to the mysterious night visitors in Kolokotroni Street I would have realized that you were lacerated by an agony as secret as it was desperate: the waiting for something horrible that perhaps you couldn't identify and perhaps you already identified in a mortal defeat. Actually you also always avoided those subjects: whatever you said was concerned with the book, you did not want what you had suffered to be completely lost. You did nothing but discuss it, to untie the knots that tangled in your mind, to dissect the episodes of the characters that should be underlined without playing anyone else's game. The trial, for example, which you wanted to present as a symbol of all the trials that tryannies stage left and right, exploiting fake confessions, invented evidence, intimidated witnesses, pusillanimous journalists, so the defendant has nothing left but the pride of demanding to be sentenced. Or jailers like Zakarakis who without realizing they themselves are imprisoned, as much victims as their victims, sum up all the blindness of the flock that silently obeys Power. Or the problem of opposing violence with violence: at the time it seems legitimate but then you discover it is wrong because it replaces one abuse with another abuse, it prepares a new master in the place of the old master. And the parallelism of the ideological barricades which conceal a grotesque football-team fanaticism, both aiming at the same exploitation of the individual, of man. You believed so deeply in that book that you seemed to have forgotten, as I had, the protagonists of your last great effort. But you hadn't forgotten them at all.

On the tenth day the pace of your work slackened.

The three daily pages became two, though much denser, written in a much smaller hand. Then they became one, still more dense, in a still smaller hand. Then half a page and at this point you threw away almost everything to start over again, but usually without following the logical development of the narration. "Today I sketched a little scene that I'll stick in, six or seven chapters from now." "Why?" "Just because." "Do you want me to help you, Alekos? You want us to write together for a little while?" "No, because even if we wrote very small, we'd get there too quickly." "We'd get where too quickly?" "To page twenty-three." "And why in the world don't you want to get to page twenty-three?!" "Because . . . I had a dream." "What dream?" "I dreamed I was writing the book. And in the dream the book broke off at page twenty-three." "I don't understand." "It broke off because at page twenty-three I died." "But that's ridiculous!" "Eh!" "Is that why you threw away almost everything and now you're dawdling, not going ahead?" "Actually I am going ahead. But it's useless, I feel I'll never get past page twenty-three." "Don't number the pages, that way you won't realize when you're at page twenty-three." "All right, I'll try." You tried. But two days later, when I came home, instead of finding you seated at the desk, I caught you in bed. And with all the lights burning, all the windows wide open. On the floor, crumpled and torn in half in an access of fury, there were the pages you had written. I gathered them up, I counted them. Twenty-three. "Alekos! Wake up, Alekos!" "I'm awake." "What have you done?" "I finished it." "You haven't finished it: you numbered the pages!" "I didn't number them. But I got stuck, so I counted them, and I discovered I had reached page twenty-three." "Alekos, be serious. What does that mean?" "It means that there is nothing more to say." "Nonsense." I handed you the last page. "Read this, translate it." "No." "Please." "No, I said." "Why not? Did it come out badly, is it ugly?" "No, it came out splendidly, it's beautiful. It's the most beautiful of all." "Then what reason do you have not to read it?" "The reason is that it makes me feel . . . makes me feel . . ." "You see? You don't even know it yourself. Come on, do it for me." You took it, sighing, adjusted the pillow behind you, stalling for time, to delay as long as possible the nausea that you obviously felt in having to look at it. "Go on, start. What part of the story is it?" "The beginning. It's still the beginning of the interrogation when they think I'm George, and they're beating the life out of me to make me tell who gave me the explosive." "All right, I'm listening." You hesitated a little and finally you translated.

"There were many officers. They had come in with the quartermaster who was bringing coffee to Malios and Babalis. They didn't belong to the ESA. Some wore the insignia of combat units, others of an infantry regiment, others of the navy. They seemed overcome by a furious rage. Theophiloiannakos sneered: 'You see, Lieutenant? The whole army's in an uproar. If I handed you over to some of the barracks, they'd tear you to pieces.' Suddenly an officer spat on me, and that gave the signal for the lynching. They fell on me all together: to spit on me, beat me, insult me. Walls of uniforms formed around the cot where I was bound. The door was wide open and they kept coming, more and more of them all the time, like wasps drawn to a pot of honey. I don't know how many they were. I don't remember how long it went on. But I do remember that I answered almost every blow with a contemptuous remark. I did it mechanically, my thoughts were elsewhere. Instead of the wall of uniforms I was seeing again the angry sea, the wire of the fuse that is tangled and won't come undone, the spray that is soaking me, the automobile of Papadopoulos approaching, the explosion, the flight. And swimming underwater, my breath leaving me, forcing me to surface. That race over the rocks, toward the boat going off along with the months, the disappointments, the toil expended for nothing. Nothing because of a wire that got tangled and became too short. An error of calculation, an extra fraction of a second, and the tyrant drives past. Alive. So I am caught and end up in the midst of the wasps, while a vulture holds the revolver, aims it at me, shouts at me: 'Why haven't they killed you, dirt?' Then Theophiloiannakos, visibly afraid the man will shoot, knocks the hand aside. At the same moment another makes his way forward, starts looking at me, asks: 'Do you regret it, at least?' 'No. I only regret I didn't succeed.' It is my voice that answers. What a strange, remote voice. Where does he come from? From another world? The polite officer also seems strange, remote. Where does he come from? Also from another world? Now he goes off in silence, and the moment he has left, the uniforms become furious again. More, always more. They beat me on the soles of my feet, on my eyes. I say again: 'I only regret I didn't succeed.' Yes, I only regret I didn't succeed. Then a terrible blow. From whom, with what? I feel a paradoxical force against my stomach, and my neck, chest, heart press into me, as if they were breaking all together, exploding. And I can no longer discern anything. I close my eyes and . . ."

It was the scene of your death, as it was to happen a month later, on the Vouliagmeni Road, when your lungs and liver and heart exploded all together, in the impact, and you would close your eyes forever. I stammered: "It's a death scene." You nodded. "I know." "Is this really what happens during a beating?" "I don't think so, it doesn't seem so to me." "Then why did you write it?" "I don't understand. At a certain point the words came on their own. It's as if my fingers were moving independently of my will. I got to the end of the page and there I realized I couldn't go on because every thought stopped with the last four lines." "Cross them out and go on." "Impossible." "I'll help you." "It wouldn't do any good. The dream ended there too." "But you're not writing a dream, you're writing your own story!" "Maybe my story will end like this." Then you got up, lighted the pipe, went out on the balcony illuminated by the burning streetlamps whose glow reached the lawn. Your shadow, unmistakable, was printed on the lawn. Even your profile could be made out, with the pipe in your mouth: anyone could have recognized it. But it was clear that you didn't care about being seen now because you knew that the end wasn't awaiting you here but elsewhere, and there was no way you could oppose events, fate. Fate is a river no dam can arrest as it flows to the sea. It doesn't depend on us. The only thing that depends on us is the way we navigate it, fight its currents, not letting ourselves be carried along like an uprooted tree. "Ah, well." "Ah, well what?" "You'll write it for me. We already talked about it." "Stop, Alekos!" "You'll write it for me, promise!" "Stop Alekos!" "Promise me!" "All right, I promise." "Good. Where shall we go and eat tonight? I want a nice restaurant full of noise and crowds. And I want to drink wine, lots of wine."

You emptied the second bottle and ordered a third. "Too bad, I would have liked to become an old man, to satisfy that curiosity. And besides I've always thought old age is the most beautiful season of all. Childhood is an unhappy season. They do nothing but scold you, in childhood, tyrannize you. The beatings I took, as a child! My mother always had a broom in her hand. But she held it by the broom end: the handle was for me. Once, to escape her I let myself down from the window. I cut a sheet into strips, tied them into a rope, and let myself down. But when I reached the sidewalk, I found her there waiting for me: with the broom in her hands, holding the broom end. Uhm! I've never been lucky in my escapes. But my father didn't beat me. Never. Not even when we lived in the house with the movie theater. In the summer they showed the movie outdoors and from the bedroom balcony I could see it all. So I invited the neighborhood kids and charged them admission. With a discount, you see? In the end the theater manager caught on and asked my father to reimburse him. And my father paid without beating me. He was good, my father was. Because he was old. The old are always indulgent, and good. Because they are old, and they have figured things out. Growing old is the only way to figure things out." "Alekos, stop drinking." "Adolescence is an unhappy season too. Maybe when you're a boy they hit you less than when you're a child because as a boy you rebel. But to make up for it they bully you in other ways, worse than beatings. You must become this, they say, you must become that. Even if you don't want to become anything and you just want to live. To make you become this, make you become that, they send you to school, which is a terrible unhappiness. Because at school you study and you fall in love. At fourteen I fell in love. She was a girl in my class, blond, and she said I looked like James Dean. I really did look like him. Same mouth, same eyes, same hair, same build. I never answered her when she said I looked like James Dean. Because I didn't want to ask her for a date until I had long pants. And they would never give me a pair of long pants. In the end I borrowed George's. I took her out in a boat and kissed her. The next day they kicked me out of school, I don't remember why. But I remember how sad I was, because I landed in another school and never saw her again. Then I heard she was dead. In an automobile, like James Dean. How you suffer when you're an adolescent! When you're old you suffer less, even if you die. Because for the old, death is something normal. Am I wrong? I'll never know if I'm wrong. To know if I'm wrong I would have to grow old and I'll never be old." "Alekos, stop drinking." You emptied the third bottle and ordered a fourth. "But the most unhappy season of all is youth, young manhood. Because in youth you begin to understand and you realize that human beings aren't worth anything. They aren't interested in truth or freedom or justice. These things are uncomfortable, and human beings feel more comfortable with falsehood and slavery and injustice. They wallow in them like pigs. I realized that as soon as I went into politics. You have to go into politics to realize that human beings aren't worth anything, that they are like charlatans and imposters and dragons. A man goes into politics full of hopes, marvelous intentions, telling himself politics is a duty, it's a way to make men better, and then he realizes it's the exact opposite, that nothing in the world corrupts more than politics, nothing in the world makes people worse. One day, when I was twenty, I went to the political man I most admired. He was a great socialist, and they said he was the only one with clean hands. I went to him to tell him about the dirty dealings of some of his companions, I thought he was unaware of them. On the contrary he knew all about them. He started laughing at me and he said: young man, you surely don't think of conducting politics with ideals? Then he said I had come to the wrong address. That day I wept, I got drunk and I wept. Before then I had never gotten drunk, I didn't like wine. I liked orangeade. Even now I like orangeade better. But I learned to drink wine at twenty, I learned to get drunk, because when you're drunk you weep better." "Alekos, stop. Please, stop!" "You know? It's easier to bear the fact that human beings aren't worth anything, that the more you understand them the more difficult it is to love them. I can manage to love human beings only when they are children or when they're old. I like children, I like old people, I would have enjoyed staying in politics only for children and for old people. Because nobody in politics ever thinks of them. Politicians don't care about children and old people: children and old people don't even vote. Since I have already been a child, then I would have liked also to be old. A handsome old man with a fine moustache and a cough. When they were going to shoot me, I felt that regret: not to become old. Because it's not true that growing old is a bore. Growing old is a pleasure. And it's right. Everybody should grow old, satisfy that curiosity. Waiter, another bottle." "Alekos, stop drinking." You drank with cold determination, the kind that led to the third stage, and your eyes were very bright, your lips very red, your voice very thick. But the brain remained clear. "Alekos, please stop, let's go home." "No, I want to drink." "We have to leave: look, the restaurant's empty." "But I have to tell you why maturity is unhappy, why all of life is unhappy." "Tomorrow. You'll tell me tomorrow." "No, now! Let's go someplace else." "It's late, Alekos, very late." "It's never too late to live a bit more. Even unhappily."

To live a bit more, even unhappily, there was a place you loved. It was a little bar on Piazzale Michelangelo, where we used to go after dinner when you were in exile in Florence. We would go there to linger in the square, which is an immense terrace suspended over the city, between trees and sky. At night, a moving view. The river winds in a ribbon of light, which is the light of the streetlamps reflected in the water, each lamp a glitter of gold and silver sparks, and over the river the rainbows of the bridges, on either side of the river the rooftops that spread out in carpets of red tiles, and from those carpets rise the spires, the towers, and the domes swell illuminated by spotlights against the black sky. On arriving you would linger, delighted, to admire the scene and you used to say that the sky had emptied its stars on earth, beauty exists only if the sky empties them on earth where we can look at them without getting a stiff neck. This time you didn't look at any of it. You dragged me at once into the little bar. "Two glasses of ouzo, big, double. No, four glasses of ouzo, big, double." "Yes, sir." With ironic obsequiousness the waiter lined up the four glasses of ouzo, excessively big and excessively double. You drained two at once while somebody at the next table snickered, and immediately a tear flowed down your nose, drowning in your moustache. "Don't cry, Alekos, why are you crying?" "Because I've done everything wrong. I trusted people. I got it all wrong. I thought people cared about truth, freedom, justice. I got it all wrong. I believed they understood. I got it all wrong. What's the use of suffering, fighting, if people don't understand, if people don't care? I've done everything wrong." "Hush, Alekos. Hush!" "I shouldn't have left my cell. The minute they put me out of my cell I should have gone back to it. And back again and again. Then they would have understood. When I was in my cell they understood. When you're in prison they understand. Afterward they don't understand anymore, unless you die. To make them understand me now I should die." "Hush, Alekos. Hush!" "A funeral, a good funeral is what's needed. They would come from the villages, from the islands, they would jam the streets, perch on the roofs like crows. And they would understand. You see? You don't love me and you don't understand me. To be understood at times you have to die. And to be loved at times you have to die." "Hush, Alekos, what are you saying? Hush! They're looking at you, they're listening to you." They really were looking at you, they really were listening to you, and from the nearby tables some murmurs came: "Drunk. He's drunk." "So what? What do I care about a handful of idiots who tomorrow will tell people they saw me crying in a bar? What do they know about my crying, about my drinking? They have too many automobiles. And you know what they use their automobiles for? To drive to football games. You know what they'll do, those idiots, on the day of my funeral? They'll go to the football game. And between goals they'll say: Guess who died! And after the football game maybe they'll go to a political rally, the rally of some jackal who's made a goal without fighting, without suffering. And they'll applaud him, all enthusiastic. For them even dying is no use. They understand only football games and automobiles. I hate them and their automobiles. Now I'll piss on their automobiles." You got up, staggering. You threw some money on the table to pay for the ouzo. You went outside, heading toward the cars parked in the square. You freed yourself from me, as I was trying to restrain you, and you reached them. Then you unzipped your pants, without haste. You took out your penis, without haste. You held it like the pole of a flag and calmly, determinedly, you began inundating with urine the sides, hoods, windows of the automobiles. I tugged at you, begged you please to stop, but the more I tugged, the more I begged, the more you resisted, and that jet continued, insistent, impudent, the jet of a fountain, as if your bladder contained an inexhaustible supply of liquid, and every drop freed you from a desperation that had surpassed every limit, an obsession that had forgotten every control, and while you did this you recited your poem, the one about those who never disobey, never compromise themselves, never risk. "You, walking graves / living insults to life / murderers of your thought / dummies in human forms / You who envy the animals / who offend the idea of Creation / who ask refuge of ignorance / who accept fear as your guide / You who have forgotten the past / who see the present with clouded eyes / who are uninterested in the future / who breathe only to die / You who have hands only to applaud / and who tomorrow will applaud / harder than all, as always / and as yesterday and as today / Know then, all of you / living excuses for every tyranny / that I hate tyrants as much as / I feel disgust for you / And your lousy automobiles."

Shyly at first, then nervously, the men from the nearby tables had come to the door of the bar and were observing the scene dumbfounded. Out of the corner of your eye you were well aware of them and you realized that if one of them moved, the others would follow him, to attack you in their indignation. But this served only to strengthen your contempt, your arrogance, and as the group hesitated, you had time to recite your poem to the end, drain your bladder to the last drop, replace your penis, zip up your pants, turn on your heels. A taxi was going by. I stopped it, pushed you inside: "Hurry, drive on!" At the same moment we heard a cry: "Stop him! Catch him!" But the driver realized he had to save you and he accelerated, reaching the house in the wood a few minutes after. He even volunteered to get you up the stairs, since you were now as limp as a ragdoll. "You want me to help you? Just say the word, eh? It's always a pleasure to help somebody who pisses on some shits' automobiles." But I answered him no thanks, and by myself I dragged you to the fourth floor, every step a mountain, by myself I dropped you on the bed, where you sank with a blissful grunt: "I gave them a good wash, uhm? I baptized them. In the name of the Father and of the Son and of the Holy Ghost." But the limbo of oblivion, the third stage, was still far off. You belched, snickered, grumbled confused protests about the accomplices of murderers who kill without soiling their hands, then about me because I didn't know how to love you, had never known how, because I loved not you but my idea of you, and for me to understand that you were you and not my idea of you then you would have to die, as a dead man I would love you perfectly: "Get out. I don't want you here, get out. Out, I said. Out!" In the end I lost patience. It was so disheartening to see you in that condition, even the idea of sleeping in the same bed became unbearable. And when you began to snore, I really did go away. The next morning, coming back, I found the room half-wrecked.

It was as if a cyclone had burst through the windows, falling on objects, uprooting them like trees, ripping, shattering. The precious Tiffany lamp was broken, the desk overturned, the rocker upset, and also the chairs. One painting had fallen from the wall, another was hanging crooked, and the pink folders with the documents were scattered everywhere. As for you, you were lying on the floor, motionless, next to the telephone with the receiver off the cradle. Had there been a struggle, had they killed you? Thinking they had killed you, I stood staring at you, petrified, until you opened the good eye and your lips parted. "I'm sorry about the lamp. That fell on its own." I didn't answer. And even if I had wanted to answer, to ask you what had happened and why, I couldn't have: a stifled sob paralyzed my vocal cords. With that stifled sob I replaced the telephone, the chairs, the rocker, I began collecting the broken glass, the wretched remains of the Tiffany, of what had once been a masterpiece of grace and harmony. I threw them in the garbage can. Still motionless on the floor, you followed my movements with your good eye and a flash of interest seemed to kindle it when I picked up the pink files. You stood up. Your pale and swollen face, your rumpled hair, your wrinkled suit stained with vomit, narrated a drama that had approached the borderline of madness. "Where have you been?" "In a hotel. You told me to get out. You were drunk." "So much the better. I could have hurt you too, after that phone call." "What phone call?" "I called Athens. *Ta Nea* has postponed publication. Postponed is what they said." "Until when?" "Until never, unless I go back. I have to leave." "I thought you wanted to stay well away from Greece." "I did. But I have no choice." "I'll leave with you." "No, I need you here." "Here?" "Yes, because if something happens to me, you'll have to put those documents to use." "I don't even know what they're about." You righted the desk, which was still overturned. "You'll know soon."

You sat down in front of the pink folders, to tell me finally what was in them, and now you seemed unassailable by emotions, all reason. Your face shaved, your hair combed, your skin relaxed after a good bath, in clean clothes, you looked like a professor preparing to give his pupil a lesson. Or a notary preparing to draw up his own will? There was a hint of pained contempt in your eyes, but your voice was steady as it said, Here they are, the damned papers for which you had disrupted so many months of your life and mine, the existence of other human beings, treacherous or silly, but human. What did they tell? Nothing but the usual story of the boulder that falls from the mountain only to return to the mountain: the same as before and more solid than before. The usual story of Power, the eternal power that never dies, and that even when it seems to fall doesn't fall, even when it seems to change, doesn't change: only its representatives fall, only its interpreters change, and the quantity or the quality of the oppression. It has always been so, it will always be so, the history of mankind is an endless jest about regimes that are swept away and remain the same as before: in every period and in every country the papers to prove it have been or will be more or less like these, only the dates are different and the names and the language. Yes, even in the healthy and strong democracies, assuming that a healthy and strong democracy exists: every democracy is weak and ill simply because it is a democracy, because it is a system based on the lesser evil. Yes, even in the countries which have undergone a revolution: every revolution contains within itself the germs of what it has overturned and with time it proves to be the sequel of what it overturned. From every revolution an empire is born, or reborn. Look at the French, the example that poisoned the world with its lies—Liberté, egalité, fraternité. Rivers of blood and dreams, seas of atrocities and chimeras, and then? Napoleon Bonaparte and the Empire, privileges identical with the privileges of the past, if anything perfected, abuses identical with the abuses of the past, if anything sealed by a code written according to principles of logic. Look at the Russian Revolution, new example of new poisons, new rivers of blood and dreams, new seas of atrocities and chimeras. And then? An empire of little czars like the eliminated czar, privileges identical with the privileges of the past, if anything perfected, abuses identical with the abuses of the past, if anything sealed by a document formulated according to criteria of the sciences. Philosophical science, mathematical, medical: a psychiatrist who declares you insane because you have disobeyed. There they not only destroy your body with prison and the firing squad, they also destroy your brain with amenzoin. Look at America, this America that was born of the desperate people in search of freedom and happiness, that rebelled against England because it didn't want to be its colony. And then? It exploited slavery, human flesh sold by weight like the meat of cattle, it crushed other desperate people in search of freedom and happiness, and finally made half the planet its own colony. Look at the countries that in Europe led the Resistance and that today live under the same regimes that paved the way for fascism and Nazism: the same leaders, the same police forces. If the evidence you can see with the naked eye is not enough to deduce this, you have only to read the secret papers of their ministries. Why suffer, then, why struggle, why risk being struck by the volley that comes from the mountain and flings you down in the well among the fish? Why, because it is the only way to exist when you're a man, a woman, a person, not a sheep in the flock, cataramene, Criste! If a man is a man, not a sheep in the flock, he has a survival instinct in him that leads him to fight even if he realizes he's fighting in vain, even if he knows he will lose: Don Quixote who tilts at windmills, not caring that he is alone, indeed proud of being alone. And it doesn't matter whether he's acting for himself or for mankind, believes in the people or doesn't believe in them, it doesn't matter whether his sacrifice produces results or doesn't: as long as he struggles and at the moment when he succumbs physically he is the people, he is mankind. And perhaps a result does exist: it lies in the fact that he leaves the flock behind, he refuses to belong to the river of fleece, he upsets the flock for an hour or a day. At times a man, a woman, has only to move away from the flock and then the flock scatters a bit, the river of fleece interrupts its flow along the course marked by the mountain. I was to remember this, you said, I was to use well these poor pages that repeated a rule as ancient as the world, as vast as the world. I was not to present them to this barricade or that, to the general managers, the fake makers of fake revolutions, to the opportunists, that is, to the pseudo-revolutionaries. I was to give them to the poor bastards who fight alone, free of formulas and doctrines, from theological disquisitions and useless violence. They were to collect your little truth, sought and found this time in a small country that counted for nothing, that interested nobody, that could now offer only a handful of islands scattered in the great blue sea, and its outdated legends, its forgotten wisdom, its dead. "Alekos, why are you saying these things to me?" "Because . . . Let's start."

You picked out a letter dated January 5, 1968. "This is the proof that I asked of Averoff for months and Averoff always refused me. It confirms that George was sold to the Israelis in exchange for some advice on killing other people. It doesn't concern His Excellency, the minister of defense, or at least it concerns him only because it shows how much he wanted to protect the officers of the junta, keeping them in key positions, doing their misdeeds, protecting along with them a foreign government that in 1968 didn't have diplomatic relations with Greece but still sold George to the junta for thirty pieces of silver. The policy of international equilibrium. In that respect this letter is a gem." Then you translated: "To the supreme command of the army. Urgent. Secret. Following the orders of the prime minister and the minister of defense, George Papadopoulos, the unit of fifty-six officers chosen for the role of advisers to the special Israeli units fighting the Palestinian commandos will leave on special flight for Tel Aviv January 13 next. The officers are particularly expert in sabotage activity thanks to experience gained in our army during the 1946-49 war. They will also utilize the experience gained in this sort of fighting by the Israeli army and they will present a detailed report on their mission. The commander of the unit, Lieutenant Antenor Mpitsakin has been given the necessary instructions so that the mission can maintain due secrecy, also with regard to the tasks assigned to it during the Greek officers' tour with the Israeli army. To avoid protests from the Arab countries, stern measures have been taken to guarantee total secrecy. The prime minister and the minister of defense, George Papadopoulos, has also ordered Lieutenant Antenor Mpitsakin to express to the proper Israeli secret services the warmest thanks of the Greek government for the close collaboration shown in the case of Lieutenant George Panagoulis. The prime minister has also asked

Lieutenant Mpitsakin to renew the promise that such collaboration will be constantly strengthened in the reciprocal interests of the two countries. Signed: F. Roufogalis, vice-director, KYP."

You gave it to me, your hands trembling slightly, then you looked for other papers. "These ones, on the other hand, concern him. They show that even before screwing with the colonels and setting up his bridge policy to take over control of the country, Evangelos Tossitsas Averoff was a big son of a bitch. It's not true, in fact, that in the forties he fought the Nazis. Here, stamped and signed, is the report presented on August 29, 1944, by a certain Ziki Niksas. It shows that in 1941 the present minister of defense became part of the notorious Rumanian Legion and began to collaborate with the Italian occupation troops. Here is also the accusation presented on September 23, 1944, by one Elias Skiliakos, a lawyer from Larissa, which shows that in the same period Averoff helped the invader by trying to set up a Greek-Italian alliance with Consul Giulio Vianelli and the then prime minister Tsalakoglou. In his estate at Ioannina he actually arranged for all guns to be confiscated, then handed over to the Italian occupation troops, to combat the Resistance. And here finally is a series of letters and denunciations that illustrate other wild oats of his youth, what he calls 'my antifascist past.' At a certain point he was taken prisoner and sent to the Fieramonte camp in Italy. Here he immediately became an honored guest: chicken or turkey instead of the usual rations, a comfortable private cell which he could leave at will, using the commandant's automobile, freedom to see anyone he liked. And you know why? Because he was an informer. They asked him to provide a list of Communist prisoners and he supplied it. They asked him for the names of other dangerous prisoners and he gave them. Then from Fieramonte they transferred him to Arezzo and there he didn't even enter the camp: he went to live in a first-class hotel. A really special prisoner. Nobody could receive more than a hundred lire per month from Greece; he received a thousand at a time, several times monthly. Nobody could buy lire at less than three or four hundred drachmas, he bought them at eight drachmas. In return for his services the Italians assigned him also to maintaining relations with the Swiss embassy and the International Red Cross, so he was the one who distributed packages or money. And he did this, rewarding only those who collaborated. Finally he went to Rome. He rented an apartment near Piazza Venezia and settled there with a lawyer from Samos, Nikolarezos, who was the trusted agent of the Italian authorities in Greece in the espionage sector. With Nikolarezos he managed to prevent the return home of three hundred Greek prisoners because the group included a hundred and ten patriots of the Freedom or Death Group. Naturally the magistrature shelved these denunciations. 'The law is equal for all.' But finding them at the ESA, the foresighted Hazizikis put them aside. Everything can be useful, even little escapades, for blackmail. These are still escapades, as I said, the venial sins. The big stuff comes later, it starts with the documents concerning his arrest in 1973, when the navy revolt failed, and knowing that our Averoff was in it up to his neck, Hazizikis picked him up and brought him to ESA. And here Hazizikis didn't even need to scare him, because the future defense minister spontaneously revealed names, addresses, dates, meetings, responsibilities that the ESA had no evidence on, even the way the Resistance was organized in Crete, Larissa, Epirus. The revelations are contained in personal statements written in his own hand. Here they are."

You translated for me the introductory part of the second statement: "On the day of my arrest I wasn't well. This was verified also by the commander of EAT-ESA. In the afternoon I fainted in his office, where I was given medical assistance, and it was thanks only to their treatment that I felt better. However, my health remained precarious and my mind was not clear when I heard the commandant's questions, his accusations, his requests for clarifications. I didn't understand, in other words, that the interrogation covered also the political aspect of what had happened and dealt with the responsibility of many officers of the navy, not only those with whom I had been in contact. And so, on my word of honor, I confined myself to denying that I knew the facts to which the commandant referred. But today I feel better, also thanks to the medicines which the commandant kindly procured for me, the walks he has courteously allowed me to take in the open air, and I believe I am no longer bound by my word of honor. Others have talked, supplied details, so I can confess that it was not because of bad faith but the brevity of our conversations that I did not explain all the details with the proper attention. I do so now, convinced that it is my right, my duty to the country and toward those involved in this matter. And I withdraw my statement of the seventh of the month in order to tell the whole truth about the events within my knowledge." You picked up a page at random to translate another passage: "I asked him then what he meant to do in the event of failure. He answered that they would go to a foreign country and they would leave the ships there so that those which had not taken a direct part in the conspiracy could be returned to Greece. The others, however, would remain under the protection of the foreign country. I pointed out to him that in such an eventuality they would have been wisest to choose Cyprus and I informed them that Leonidas Papagos had just got back from Italy, where he had met the king, who had expressed reservations about the enterprise. Some time went by before we had another meeting and toward the middle of May I decided to see him again. I sent Mr. Foufas to the house of Papadogonas and the latter set an appointment for the morning of May 21 at Lake Marathon. One reason why I wanted this meeting with Papadogonas was that Constantine Karamanlis had sent two messages to tell me he had been told about the business and if it was not a serious undertaking then it had to be canceled. The other reason was that Papadogonas had revealed to me the possible days of the revolt. One of these dates was near and I feared they were about to make a grave error of political tactics. I feared also that the secret would leak out. In fact, from a certain remark of the industrialist Cristos Stratos I had inferred he knew everything. Papadogonas confirmed this to me: he himself had met Stratos, who had promised modest financial aid to the families of the noncommissioned officers taking part in the revolt. Stratos was even aware of the date chosen: the night between May 22 and May 23. But the go-ahead sign had been given, the preliminary operations were under way, and it would have been impossible to call them off."

"Here." You handed me the pack of the two statements, you added a letter: "Put this with them." It was a handwritten letter, dated July 26, 1973, and addressed to Major Nicholas Hazizikis, commander of EAT-ESA. It was signed, "Most respectfully yours, Evangelos Averoff," and it thanked Hazizikis for his kindness in sending him seven copies of the fascist newspaper *Estias*. I took it and, simply touching it, I experienced again the uneasiness of the day when the dragon's eyes met mine, to search them for a long, cruel moment, then his hands imprisoned mine like the valves of a shell, and a shudder went through my body because the hands were smoother than a girl's but their contact caused a kind of horror. The same horror you feel in grazing nettle leaves, soft at first, and then just as you are thinking how soft they are, you feel a nasty sting. Yet it wasn't the contact of his hands that upset me, nor the sound of his voice that at times cracked in metallic shrillness, nor the liquid and slimy gaze of his round eyes black as olives swimming in oil: it was his reference to the bridge policy. Now you sensed what I was thinking: "Yes, we're coming to the bridge policy, we're getting there. We're also getting to the proof that I was right to attack him in Parliament on the question of the reserve officers, to say that he was keeping the democratic officers in the reserves because they made him as nervous as they made Papadopoulos and Ioannidis. Here it is." And you showed me two pieces of letterhead: his name printed in the upper-left corner, Evangelos Tossitsas Averoff, the text typewritten, a note added in his handwriting. Then you translated: "Athens, January 21, 1974. To General Phaedo Gizikis, president of the Republic. Dear Mr. President, I have the honor of submitting to your attention the enclosed note. If I do not sign it and if I write it in the third person, it is because I presume you will want to show it to others without saying who sent it to you. I am, however, not denying in any sense my authorship, and you can clearly see that this paper bears my name. The note I enclose is a compendium limited in the first part to general, but essential lines. It does not touch on, does not analyze everything. Since this can create the impression that I have a prejudiced attitude toward the present government, I underline the facts that: (1) It is quite correct and in many ways just and useful to eliminate numerous reserve officers from the highest positions in the administration. (2) The government has faced, not in an orthodox fashion but in the best possible way, the drama of our venerable church. I believe that the attempt will bear fruit. (3) I hail the restoration of the council for the appointment of prefects. (4) It is useful to repress abuses insofar as this can be done without exceptions and on objective bases. And with this, Mr. President, I beg you to accept my most sincere esteem always, yours, Evangelos Tossitsas Averoff." There was then a postscript dated February 1, 1974: "Having sought in vain a person of our common acquaintance who would kindly deliver this letter and the enclosed notes, I am bringing them myself to your house. It is possible also that I will send you a copy by mail. In view of the conditions under which I send it to you, I would be grateful if you would ask your aide-de-camp to acknowledge receipt." Under the postscript, another three notes apparently written by someone else, perhaps an aide to Gizikis, on the copy sent by mail: "The sergeant of the guard at the palace, stationed at 51–53 Plankedias Street refused to receive this. It was delivered the next day, February 2, 1974, by Mr. Zizis Foufas, to Mr. Spiropoulos, secretary to the presidency of the Republic, in 17 Stisicorou Street at 9:30 A.M." "Monday, February 4, 1974. At 8:30 A.M. a telephone call from Mr. Bravacos informed the office of Mr. Atanasakos that the envelope had been received by the president." And then the final note: "Mr. Bravacos of the presidency of the Republic called the office to confirm that the president had received the letter."

"Here." You gave me also the letter to Gizikis, and an amused smile made your moustache twitch. "Eh! After all Averoff is a genius. A provincial genius but a genius. If instead of being born in a small country that doesn't count he had been born in Russia or America or China, by now he would be deciding whether World War III should break out. And if he had been born at least in a more central and richer country, somehow he would end up in the history books. Poor Averoff, he was unlucky: to be born in Greece in the twentieth century. Anyhow the proof that Averoff is a genius, a provincial genius but a genius, is here." And you waved the eight closely written pages of the Enclosed Note. "This is a little masterpiece. It begins with vague references to liberalism, cautious protests about the risks the government is running, then it moves on to flattery, saying that a feeling of joy, of lively optimism for the future, of affectionate sentiments toward the armed forces dominated Greece on November 25 and 26, 1973—the days following the massacre at the Polytechnic when Ioannidis deposed Papadopoulos—then from flattery it goes on to an examination of the situation, and listen carefully, because the skill with which he offers himself as savior of the country or rather its man of destiny is simply diabolical." You found page two and then translated: "The fact that at the head of the armed forces there are honest men, something of which the writer is convinced, does not count. The people still see only a determination to maintain for an indefinite time an oligarchy based on the armed forces. So the mere sight of uniforms irritates them, and many who formerly wore their uniform with pride are now cautious about displaying it in public. This is sad and dangerous, Mr. President; at this rate the young will follow anyone opposed to the regime. And unfortunately we know that those opposed to the regime rarely have healthy thoughts: in recent months the Greek Communist party has become active, and anarchist thinking, incoherent and destructive, has begun to seduce the young who are easily influenced and seek to act in a violent fashion. There is a slide toward the left, toward highly dangerous forms of anarchy, pernicious for the young who will be called tomorrow to lead the country. And abroad Greek communism is very energetic, more energetic than ever. According to reliable foreign sources, in Germany alone, where the Italian Communist party has founded two workers' federations, one with headquarters in Cologne and one in Stuttgart, there are two strong Greek Communist groups: the ESAK and the EESKEI, which collaborate. In the preliminary conference at Stockholm, where emigrants of all nationalities met last year and where it was decided to hold a conference in March 1974 in Copenhagen, the most outspoken representatives were the Greeks . . ." Here you stopped translating: "Next comes a pompous analysis of the economic situation and then comes the best. Because what Averoff proposes to Gizikis to solve the troubles of the colonels is precisely what happened in July 1974 when everybody believed that the junta had fallen. These pages supply the proof that the junta abdicated according to Averoff's advice and with the method Averoff desired: apparently transferring power to the politicians, actually hanging onto it through him who, on taking over the Ministry of Defense, would become the heir and interpreter of the past regime or at least of its interests. You understand? I mean that in January 1974 Power had no use for the colonels, it needed a changing of the guard, for example, a formal democracy, where the key posts were in the hands of the most reactionary right wing, and that could happen only through the return of a Karamanlis chosen and imposed by an Averoff, now master of that army from which the democratic officers had been purged. So I was wrong to believe that Averoff had won his battle at the last minute tricking Kanellopoulos and Mavros, saying—See you later, I'm going to have a pee. He really did have a pee, he really did trick them, but what happened on July 23 had been decided months before. The only point where Averoff failed was with the related-parties fraud. The fraud consisted of a trick the monarchy had exploited from 1963 to 1967 to keep the right wing in power, and it worked like this: every party had to declare itself related to another party, that is, to the party ideologically closest, and only related parties could make coalitions among themselves to take part in a government. But nobody wanted to consider himself related to the Communist party, and this hampered the left, forcing it always to ally itself with the right. Only George Papandreou had rebelled, setting up a popular front in which the whole left was joined with the center. And the right had replied with the Papadopoulos coup. Although he failed with the related-parties fraud, Averoff knew he was winning. In fact he knew he could count on Karamanlis, on the meticulous way Karamanlis would follow the plan outlined in the letter to Gizikis. And this was the plan." And you resumed translating.

"First: the president of the Republic will choose a person who is able and who inspires trust. Namely an old officer or an old statesman or a technocrat. Second: the president of the Republic will entrust to this person the position of prime minister, and the prime minister will appear on television announcing the platform but not the composition of the government. Third: the platform will reflect the chief lines not subject to change. Nuances and minor variations will be examined with ample exchange of ideas. Here are the chief lines: (a) the new prime minister announces that the armed forces have entrusted to him, through the president of the Republic, the restoration of democratic legality; (b) the new prime minister expresses his admiration for the armed forces underlining the fact that they come from the people, respect the people, defend always the internal and external security of the country; (c) the new prime minister declares that he has deliberately not yet formed his government. But now you must see the Top Secret Enclosure." The Top Secret Enclosure: "(1) It is not advisable that this be known, but we must come to an agreement about the ministries of Defense and Public Safety and make sure they are given to respectable, influential people, who possess the confidence of the president of the Republic as well as of the prime minister. (2) There must be a loss of credibility in those who insist that elections be held under the control of the local authorities appointed by the junta, thus in a position to apply psychological pressure in favor of the same junta. (3) Local elections must be avoided until after the general elections; to do otherwise would be dangerous for many reasons but especially because in some places there would be a risk of having town councils capable of influencing the national elections in favor of the left. (4) Public opinion and foreign opinion must be convinced that the new regime is conducting the elections honestly (see principal text); only in this way will it be possible to exclude the nomination of subversive candidates. (5) The articles of the electoral law must make it clear that: every party will be obliged to deposit with the supreme court a declaration containing its basic principles and its related parties; every party will be considered related to another only if the latter accepts a similarity of principles; parties not related to other parties cannot participate in the formation of the government nor support it; a deputy cannot shift from one party to another if the party he is leaving is not related to the one he is joining. (6) The Greek Communist party can be legalized only on condition that those who travel beyond the iron curtain cannot return to Greece and must be considered guilty of having spilled the blood of their brothers in order to conquer power. (7) Since this is a delicate subject, the problem of the monarchy can be debated by an assembly that will provide for the revision of the constitution. But how to resolve it, seeing that those who worked actively on the referendum that established the Republic define that referendum as false? For reasons that do not concern this note the writer considers a constituent assembly the best way out of the dilemma. But that requires a verbal explanation."

"Here." The enclosure was added to the other pages, and your voice shook briefly with anger: "There was a verbal explanation. The farce was enacted as Averoff had arranged in the script written for Gizikis: the facade of power to Karamanlis, the real power for himself, the status quo almost intact. The only thing he failed to achieve was ridding himself of Ioannidis and the various Hazizikises and the various Theophiloiannakoses without sending them to jail: needless to say, the trials were not part of the agreement in the so-called verbal explanations. And this became his Achilles heel; this is why he hesitated to arrest them. But he found the solution to the problem. Directly or indirectly he summoned them one by one and offered them escape abroad: either you go away or I'm forced to arrest you, put you on trial. The majority refused: some out of pride, some because they deceived themselves thinking they could regain power with a coup of the gheddafists. But others accepted. And this paper proves it." You waved a handwritten letter, addressed to Karamanlis and signed by a border guard at Ezvonoi. It bore the reference number 2499 and had been sent on December 6, 1974, received on December 17. It said: "Mr. President, the undersigned believes it necessary to bring to your attention the following facts. Between November 15 and 20 of this year, one morning at about five thirty, the vice-commander of passport control entered the above-mentioned office. This was contrary to his habitual appearance at nine. The vice-commander said nothing about the arrival of a bus, and when the bus arrived at about six, we saw that it was escorted by the director of the foreigners bureau of the Salonika police. The director was in civilian clothes. We were not allowed to board the bus, not even to control valuta. The driver of the vehicle carried the passports to the officer assigned to examine them and who was also supposed to look at the passengers. Then the bus left at once and entered Yugoslav territory. According to reliable information, on board there was the former KYP lieutenant Michael Kourkoulakos, who was traveling on a false passport. Please, Mr. President, consider this letter genuine and accept my respects." A bitter smile: "He wasn't a little fish, this Kourkoulakos. He was also the CIA agent in Salonika and he had been accused of killing two members of the Resistance, Tsaroukas and Kalkidis. Now he's apparently in Munich or some other German city and is managing a fascist organization founded in 1960 by Otto Skorzeny, the man who rescued Mussolini from confinement at Gran Sasso. An organization called Die Spinne, the Spider—in Greek, the Arachne. It seems also that he often meets Panaiotis Cristos, minister of public instruction at the time of Ioannidis, and Evangelos Sdrakas, another junta big shot, and a friend of Averoff's as well. He taught at the University of Ioannina, Averoff's city. Sdrakas also got away on that bus. A neat trick, that bus, a neat trick. As for the Spider, Arachne, Die Spinne, it seems to have offices all over Europe: Germany, Spain, Britain, France, Italy. If I can just get my hands on that trunk the KYP officer promised me, you'll hear some great things: I tell you the next dictator of Greece could be called Averoff if somebody doesn't unmask him in time. Sombody or something. A dictator in civilian clothes, the kind that last, like Salazar. Yes, I really have to get my hands on that trunk. If they give me time—" And, grinning, you waved the last paper. "Here's the koh-i-noor." "The . . . what?" "The koh-i-noor, the diamond above all diamonds, the gem of gems. Something that's kept me awake for weeks, something that makes me hate even the light of the sun. The proof that he was spying for the junta. It comes from Hazizikis obviously, from the list with information and opinions on the people whose names were on file at ESA." I cast a glance at it, and this time there was no need for you to translate. Everything was frighteningly clear. In the second column the professional status. In the third the ideological status. In the fourth comment. There were seven names, the numbers went from seventeen to twenty-three. On the twenty-third line you read: "Evangelos Averoff—former deputy—supporter of the bridge policy between the national government and the former politicians—already collaborates and reports to high-level officials of the KYP, so far with very positive results."

There is a mysterious expression on the faces of those who know they are going to die, a shadow that gathers in the eyes and is transmitted to their movements. We can see it in the ill who leave the hospital to die in their bed or in soldiers who leave for a battle from which there is no returning. At first it is difficult to focus because we do not so much see it as sense it: only after death, in memory, it comes back to us, as clear as a sharp photograph, and we suddenly understand what it was. It was the nostalgia for the future that will not come, the sudden awareness that without a future even the present is illusion, and only the past is existence. That was the very expression in your eyes the day you left the house in the wood forever. The suitcases were already loaded into the taxi, the taxi was waiting, the train would leave soon, and you lingered, left hand stuck into the pocket of your topcoat, right hand raised to hold the pipe clenched between your teeth, head bent toward one shoulder, you walked up and down the room, silent, absorbed, observing every object with the look of someone who wants to impress it deep in his memory, retain it with the regret for a piece of life, the moments of a time that seemed destined to last forever. A rocker, an ashtray, a picture you will never see again. I was jittery, impatient: "What are you looking for, Alekos, what do you want? Come on, it's getting late, let's go." But you didn't answer, as if you didn't care about missing the train, about wasting time which was abundant for you because before very long you would have eternity at your disposal. And at a certain point you sat down on the bed, your lips curved in a mysterious smile, saddened by a shadow that descended over your whole face, blackening the thick eyebrows, then you took the pipe from your mouth, stroked the pillow, murmured: "We were well here. We were alive." "We'll be here again, Alekos. Come on. Let's go." "Yes, let's go." But you said those three words, as I would understand a month later, with the tone of the ill person who knows he has reached the end and answers yes to those who say—You'll get well, dear, you'll get well—with the tone of a soldier who knows he's going into a battle from which there is no return and replies yes to those who say—You'll make it, you'll make it. Other strange things happened that day, things that were repeated and intensified in the days that followed. Hesitations, uncertainties, postponements. "I want to be in Athens within twenty-four hours, so we'll stay only one night in Rome. I won't even unpack my bags," you said in the train. Reaching Rome, however, you emptied them promptly and didn't even reserve a seat on the plane. "Alekos, we have to reserve the seat on the plane." "Tomorrow." And the next day: "Day after tomorrow." And the day after tomorrow: "There's time." A constant putting off, as if the problem of *Ta Nea* no longer existed, and any excuse was good to keep from repacking the bags, from reserving the seat. The first was the arrival from Athens of a tailor friend who wanted to establish a trade in fabrics between Italy and Greece. The second was an invitation to Capri for the birthday of an eighty-year-old woman, mother of an admirer of yours. The third was a party at the Greek embassy, where you had never set foot. The fourth an appointment with the publisher to whom you had promised the book. And naturally you cared very little about the tailor friend, still less about the eighty-year-old's birthday, and absolutely nothing about the embassy party, and the appointment with the publisher made no sense since you refused to continue writing the book. Still you saw the tailor, you visited the old woman, attended the party, met the publisher, never mentioned having to return to Athens, to hasten the agreed publication of the documents, but instead you seemed distracted by an unexpected and inexplicable heedlessness. Once the desperate anguish that had blocked you on page twenty-three was past, once the grim melancholy that had caused the apocalyptic binge and the jet of urine on the automobiles had vanished, once the solemn drama of the morning when you read and handed over to me the documents of the dragon was ended, it seemed that those episodes had never taken place, that the future was a long promise to be enjoyed without haste and without fears, that your commitment to reveal the truth was no longer pressing. After the meeting with the publisher you were actually excited, and insisting that you had changed your mind, you said you would start writing again from page twenty-three, by the end of August you would deliver half the manuscript to him, within the year the whole book. "You know what I'm going to do? I'll take that leave of absence from Parliament the minute I arrive in Greece. I'll stay there two weeks, then you join me, and we'll come back here with my spring."

I was happy at this and at the same time irritated. It cheered me to see you cleansed of the lugubrious grief that had half-destroyed the house in the wood and I blessed those days of calm, of earned rest, but on the other hand I concluded then that your problems weren't as serious as you had said, so what whim or hysteria had driven you this time to torment me with your difficulties, your histrionic scenes, the obsessive reading of those boring files? And in these mixed feelings I vacillated, sometimes refusing to go with you to your absurd engagements, sometimes making myself the accomplice of your idle diversions, never suspecting that you were postponing the trip to Athens because suddenly the instinct of survival was overcoming the passion of defiance. I only began to sense that things were not at all what they seemed when you said: "It's time I stopped putting it off." In fact the very moment you said this your mood changed and something very odd happened. We were about to cross Via Veneto and the red light came on. I stopped, knowing how much it annoyed you to see me cross on the red light, and immediately a brutal shove flung me into the midst of the traffic: "Go on! What are you afraid of? Anybody not ready to cross on a red light isn't ready to die, anyone not ready to die isn't ready to live!" Then you abandoned me on the opposite sidewalk, and it was late that night when you came back to the hotel with your jacket ripped, your hands skinned and bleeding: as if you had had a fistfight with all the trees along the street. But it wasn't trees you had hit: it was a poor pimp who was offering you a prostitute. You had struck him with such violence that the police had rushed up and wanted to arrest you. "Alekos, you've been drinking again!" "No, not a drop." "Then why did you do it? Why?" "I don't know. I swear to you: I don't know. I was seized by a desire almost to kill him, a need to release all the anger I have inside me." Then you shut yourself into the bath for at least an hour and when, alarmed by your silence, I came to see if you were ill, I found you immersed in the tub with your eyes closed and your arms folded over your chest: the position of a corpse in a coffin. "Alekos, what are you doing, for heaven's sake?!" "Rehearsing. I'm rehearsing. You know, death isn't necessarily so bad. After all, death is the friend of someone who's tired. It's also a great ally of love. No love in the world lasts unless death intervenes. If I were to live a long time, you'd loathe me in the end. But since I'll die soon, you'll love me forever."

And the last day we spent together arrived, the day that for months and for years my memory would probe most deeply, in the stubborn search for every detail, every instant, as if that served to give me back a drop of what I had lost; but never succeeding, on the contrary losing myself in the helpless stupor that grips us when we wake from a dream we can't remember. It was an important dream and yet we don't remember it, a curtain has fallen on too many details, a veil of shadows has extinguished the images, the sounds, and that veil cannot be torn, or dispelled. In vain you pursue the echo of a sound, a gesture, in vain you tell yourself you have caught it; at the very moment you think you are clasping it in your hand, it dissolves and you have to resign yourself: the dream has really vanished. The last day we spent together is like that. In some well of my unconscious there must be the film of all the things we did, all the things we said, but oblivion seals off the well with a darkness heavier than a marble slab. A darkness that goes from dawn to dusk. The memory of the last night, in fact, is very clear, it flares up like a firework along with the music of your beautiful voice telling the fairy tale of the stars swallowed up by the black holes of the cosmos. We are in your favorite restaurant on a little square in old Rome, and the tiny room is narrow with a vaulted ceiling, warmed by a wood fire burning in violet flames, the tables are lighted by candles stuck into green bottles on which the wax melts making bizarre reliefs, white stalactites. We are sitting in a corner marked off by a railing and hidden by a column, the candle blanches your white face and lengthens your forehead which seems higher than ever, your moustache seems thicker than ever, and on the left side there are three gray hairs. I had never noticed them, they weren't there before: when did they turn gray? The gray lock at your temple has also become more gray. Strange, when did it become more gray? I pretend to pull it out, you shield yourself, tilting your head in a movement charged with sweetness. You are gentle this evening and your gaze is mild. "Tomorrow you're really leaving," I whisper. "Yes." "I would like to come with you." "No, I need you here, I told you. And besides we'll see each other again soon, we'll see each other at

Easter. I'll bring my spring back and we'll change her color. We have to change the color. If somebody wanted to harm me . . ." A stab in the heart: because of the last words or because of the macabre and terrifying image the automobile evokes in me? Strange, since New Year's Eve, three months now, I haven't seen the car and haven't asked you about it: if it's working well or badly, if you still like it. Every time you've mentioned its name I've changed the subject: as if it hurt me to be reminded that it exists, that I have never been back to Athens after that voyage on the ship that landed us in Patras. Have I never been back because of the betrayed oath or because of the automobile? "We could make it blue or gray or tan," you are saying. And the stab comes again: yes, because of it, I can't bear for you to talk about it. I can listen to your talk about death, I'm used to that by now, you talk about nothing but death, but not your talk about the automobile. In fact I shift and, unaware, you change the subject. You tell me in your own way, inventing, the story of the stars that are swallowed up by the black holes in the cosmos. Astronomers' theories don't interest you, you say, nuclear condensation, nonsense, gravitational attraction, nonsense, you know what the black holes in the cosmos really are. They are actual holes, rents in infinity, and they are very tiny holes, the diameter of a glass, it seems inconceivable that a star can enter because a star is immense, but in order to enter, it contracts, through millions and billions of years it thickens and condenses until it becomes a fist, a lemon, a pebble, and the spell is fulfilled. Fate. A great wind springs up, and more than a wind, it is a monstrous tornado that calls the star, summons it, pleads with it, to lure it into the black hole. The star is reluctant. For millions, billions of years it has lived only to enter that hole, that is why it has thickened and contracted to become a fist, a lemon, a pebble, and now that the moment is approaching, it is reluctant. Because it would like to become old, fade away in peace, adrift. Frightened, it rejects the invitation, opposes it with all its will, all the strength of its weight which is monstrous, condensed and monstrous. It runs away, goes off in very slow turns, to the edges of the universe, hides behind the stars that the wind isn't calling, defends itself, denies itself, as if unaware of the fate that has loomed over it since birth, or as if its courage had failed. But the wind cannot be resisted, is capable of defeating the most boundless weight, the most stubborn will, so the flight of the star becomes weaker and weaker, its spirals more and more narrow, tightening always in the direction of the hole, and at a certain point the limitless space is reduced to a deep, narrow vortex, a whirlpool within which infinity slips down with silence, silence that turns and enfolds itself to coagulate around a mystery, and all of a sudden that hole becomes a tunnel without light, without exit. Or perhaps the exit exists, but so remote that it can't even be glimpsed. And the star, exhausted, resigned, defeated, allows itself to be swallowed: it plunges headlong into the darkness, into the mystery that will lead it Lord only knows where. On the other side, tell me, what is there?

Your eyes shine anxiously in the glow of the candle, your voice vibrates: "On the other side what is there?" The stab strikes me again and I shiver. And yet this time you didn't talk of the automobile, you only interpreted poetically a scientific theory in order to extract a fairy tale from it, and you are not the escaping star. "It's a stupendous fairy tale," I stammer. "No, it's a terrible reality," you answer. "It depends on how you understand it, Alekos." "There is only one way to understand it: the black holes are death." "If the black holes were death, all stars would fall into them. Instead they swallow up some stars and not others. Why?" "Because not all stars have to be punished. The black holes swallow those that must be punished." "Punished for what?" "For having sought different worlds where everybody is somebody and where justice exists, and freedom and happiness." "It's not a crime to seek different worlds where everybody is somebody and where justice exists, and freedom and happiness." "No, but it's a luxury that the dictatorship of God cannot allow, nor can the mountain. God wants to make us believe that his is the only universe possible. And anyone who rebels ends up in a black hole." "You talk as if you believed in God." "I do believe. I don't know what he is but I believe. And I forgive him because he has no choice, therefore he has no guilt. It's human beings who have choice, and therefore have guilt." I smile: "I once knew somebody who said exactly the opposite. Human beings are innocent, he said to me, because they are human." "Who was that?" "A Vietcong prisoner." "He had never been before a firing squad then. When they were about to shoot me, I forgave even God. And when I die, I'll forgive him again." I can't manage to smile anymore. You notice and you stroke my hand: "Don't take it too hard." Then with your usual gesture you call the flower woman who has come in with a basket of roses and you buy all the roses and fling them in my lap. We go out, forgetting about stars that die, you tease me because the great bunch of roses makes me awkward. We walk off along the narrow little streets with sooty walls and here memory is composed of muffled sounds, scattered images, sensations that last for the batting of an eye. Our footsteps echoing on the cobbles, a dog that comes by wagging his tail, your thumb tickling the palm of my hand as you whisper: "All the same, life is beautiful. It's beautiful even when it's ugly. And she doesn't know it!" She is a prostitute who is strolling, bored. "Give me a rose." I give you one, you hand it to her, and get yourself insulted as a result. "Nut! Are you some kind of nut?" Walking, we have reached Via Veneto, under the tree where the afternoon of the automobile the birds were plunging by the hundreds. They have plunged there today too, thick as berries, sleeping on the branches. "And Nekayev?" "He is trying to escape the wind." "And Satan?" "Satan is in paradise." We go into the hotel and in the elevator you amuse yourself by pressing all the buttons: "I'm driving the plane that's taking us to paradise!" In the corridor you steal the whole bunch of roses from me and you stick one in the handle of each door. In the room you calm down. You undress with pensive slowness, you stretch out on the bed, you fold your arms behind your nape, you lie motionless and stare at the ceiling. "But on the other side, what is there?" "Stop it, Alekos, stop!" "Answer me: on the other side, what is there?" I answer: "If the swallowed stars are seeking better worlds, on the other side there must be a better world." "No, there is nothingness. The extreme punishment for anyone seeking better worlds is nothingness. But perhaps it isn't a punishment: it's a reward. You try so hard to seek what doesn't exist that in the end you feel the need to rest in nothingness." Then a flash: "Shall we play?" And carried away by an uncontrollable gaiety, you fling your legs over me saying you're not a star, you're a comet and these legs are the tail of the comet, and since the light of a comet is dazzling there's no need to leave the lamp on. You turn it off and we love each other as we had loved each other on a distant August night in the room with the peeling red armchairs, the plates of pistachios on the table, as the wind sang among the olive branches. The same movements, the same sensations. From a past that the years have not corroded, the harmonious embraces return, the silken caresses, the joy of drowning together in a dazzling river of sweetness, once more and again, and again and again, as if it were to last forever, to be repeated until old age. My old age, your old age. And instead it will last only this final night. "Don't forget me. Don't ever forget me. You mustn't forget me!" purls a voice I don't recognize, hoarse and heartrending, while your body enfolds my body. A long time afterward, when our tragedy was to end also in the torment that seemed incurable, and in its place there was to be a scar that hurts even if one doesn't touch it, a different and worse solitude, in it I would ask myself useless and absurd questions, why old age doesn't arrive for all, and what is death, especially the death that strikes before old age, and why you were so in love with death, frightened of it, yes, but in love, so seduced that I was jealous of it as if it were a person, a woman, the memory of the last evening and of the last night would hit me with the force of a revelation. There is no doubt: you knew. You possessed the mathematical certitude that the vortex had begun, and that the black hole was about to swallow you.

We left the hotel at three in the afternoon, and your plane was to take off at four. The taxi was in bad shape, it proceeded at an exasperatingly slow pace, and you urged the driver on: "Go a little faster, please, you'll make me miss my plane." But he answered rudely: "This is the fastest I can go: you should of started sooner!" Suddenly when we were at the outskirts of the city the engine started coughing, then died. "I'm out of gas." "Out of gas? You accept a passenger for the airport with no gas in your tank?!" I intervened, to stave off a quarrel: "Look there's a service station near here, try to get to it." Amid grumbles and curses, crashing of gears and angry stamping on the accelerator, we reached the place and filled up. But to no avail "It won't go anyway. It's broken down." "Broken down?!" I looked at you, fearing an explosion of wrath: having used up your store of prayers, incitement, you had observed the scene in a silence which, as a rule, heralded an outburst of fury. But no, all of a sudden you sat there calmly, as if the matter didn't concern you: had you failed to understand? "Alekos, he says it's broken down." "So much the better." "Better? Don't you want to leave?" "Uhm!" "Tell me, because if you really want to leave, we have to do something." "Uhm!" Nastier than ever, the driver interrupted the discussion: "Whether you want to leave or not, I can't keep you here. Now I'll call for another taxi." "Whatever you like!" He liked that. He went, telephoned, came back: "Can't find one, there aren't any. Shall I stop one on the road for you?" "If you like." He liked. Huffing, he planted himself in the middle of the road, but no taxi came by, and it was almost three thirty. "Alekos, let's go back to the hotel, you can leave tomorrow." "Maybe you're right." But just as you were saying this and I was feeling a disproportionate relief, an exaggerated pleasure, not so much because you would be staying another evening as because there was something wrong about this departure, an empty taxi went by. And our driver stopped it; mollified, he shifted the luggage, mollified, he opened the door, saying hurry up, he's got a good engine, he can go fast. We headed again for the airport, it was now three forty. "Alekos . . . do I have to explain to him that we have only a few minutes?" "No, no, why do you want to force things, force fate? What has to be, is; what will have to be, will be. If it's written that I catch that plane I'll catch it even if I arrive after four o'clock. If it's written that I don't make it, I won't make it even if I arrive on time." Then you put your arm around my shoulders, gravely. "You'd like us to be together another day, I know. I'd like it too, but a day more or a day less, a month more or a month less: what would that change? We've had a lot, the two of us, and another day or another month wouldn't give us what we haven't had." "Why do you say this?" "Because you've been a good companion. The only possible companion."

We reached the airport at four on the dot. The flight was closed, the plane was about to take off. However, an airline official recognized you and gave instructions for them to hold the flight. Then, considerate, excited, he took your luggage, gave you the boarding pass, thrust you toward passport control: Hurry, run, hurry. You followed him without haste, lingering at every step, as if you wanted to force fate or as if now it revolted you to go back to Athens, and at the glass door beyond which only passengers are admitted, you actually stopped, to play with the koboloi. "Ciao then," I said and held out my hand. In public we never embraced. You locked it in yours, for a long time, avoiding my gaze. "Ciao, alitaki." The official was beside himself: Hurry, run, hurry. You nodded and reached passport control, then passed the police control. You went on for a few meters, without turning, you were almost at the gate. And here, abruptly, with the determination of someone obeying an impulse he can't reject, you came back. "What are you doing? Where are you going?" the official yelled. Two policemen reacted, tried to block you. "You can't!" You eluded them without looking at them, without listening to them, haughty, you were again at the glass door, you came over to me. You clasped me in a long, intense, silent embrace. You kissed me on the mouth, on the forehead, on the temples. You took my face in your hands: "Yes, a good companion. The only possible companion." Then, more haughty than ever, calmer than ever, you went back past the dumbfounded policemen and the amazed official. The last image I have of you is a moustache standing out black against a marble pallor and a pair of gleaming, steady, overpowering eyes that stare at me from afar, penetrating mine. I would never see you alive again.

[illegible] lucky [illegible] sorry. You [illegible] and [illegible] [illegible] country. [illegible] went on for a few pages without moving; you were [illegible] at the [illegible] with the exception of [illegible] some [illegible] because [illegible]. You came back. "What are you doing? Where are you going?" the official yelled. Two policemen reacted, tried to block you. You [illegible] You chased them without looking at them, without listening to them. [illegible] you were again at the glass door; you came over to me. You clasped me in a long, merciless, silent embrace. You kissed me on the mouth, on the forehead, on the temples. You took my face in your hands. It's a good conclusion, the only possible conclusion. Then, more haughty than ever, calmer than ever, you went back past the dumbfounded policemen and the amazed official. The last image I have of you is [illegible] standing out clearly against a marble pillar and a [illegible] clear, overpowering [illegible] that stare [illegible] from afar, [illegible]. I would never see you alive again.

PART SIX

1

DEATH IS A THIEF THAT NEVER TURNS UP BY SURPRISE, that's what I've been trying to tell you. Death always announces itself by a kind of scent, impalpable perceptions, silent sounds. Death is perceived when it approaches. Even while you were embracing me at the airport you knew I would never see you again alive. You had courted death too often with your challenges, sung of it with your poems, invoked it with your anguish too often not to recognize it, sniff it, be convinced it was coming. But, and this is the point, the other times you had rejected it or sidestepped it a moment before it caught you; after that embrace, on the contrary, you went toward it like an impatient lover, anxious to allow himself to be stolen. Was it deliberate, was it weariness of living, weariness of losing? All three. The deliberation was born from weariness of living, the weariness of living was born from weariness of losing; the night when you destroyed the house in the wood you realized that every stage of your legend had ended in a defeat. You had only to look back and you were convinced that the curse of failure loomed over your existence with the inexorability of a tumor, you had only to retrace the path of eight years to see that your victory had been never surrendering to anything or anyone, never giving way even in moments of dejection or of doubt. The attempt on Papadopoulos had gone wrong; the calvary of the arrest, the trial, the sentence had not stirred Greece. The escapes from prison had failed, to see the sun again you had to accept the tyrant's clemency. The Acropolis plan had remained a fantasy, your clandestine trips to Athens had served only to make you suffer, the hope of organizing an armed resistance had collapsed. And the return to the village, a mortification; the decision to enter the politics of politicians, an error; the electoral campaign, a disaster; your activity as a deputy, a failure. And also the effort of adapting yourself to a party, your insistence on expelling unworthy men from it; and also your attempt to write a book. As for your great notion that ideologies don't stand up because every ideology becomes doctrine and every doctrine clashes with the reality of life, life's refusal to be cataloged, or as for your discovery that the formulas "left" and "right" have no meaning, if anything they are equal because both are supported by a false alibi and both aim at an identical goal, the Power that crushes, you had not been able to formulate these ideas in philosophical terms or to maintain them rigorously with actions. Now condensing them into poetic slogans, now neutralizing them by giving in to the filthy blackmail of the opposing barricades, namely by joining the side of the liars who wear underpants with the word "people" on them but by people they mean the crowd that applauds them, you had relegated these principles to the refrigerator of uncompleted ideas or impossible enterprises. Only through your personal story, too unique, had you declared that every human being is an entity that cannot be generalized and cannot be forced into the concept of the mass, and so salvation must be sought in the individual who revolutionizes himself.

Whatever you undertook, you found yourself empty-handed and everything had gone wrong for you, everything: as dynamiter and as conspirator, as tribune and as thinker, as politician and as leader. Even as leader, since no one ever listened to you except for a few followers won by your fascination and not by your message, and only a few people had followed you the afternoon of the procession, inspired by a misunderstood gesture. Never a disciple, never a true accomplice on whom you could lean. The only interlocutor you had in the desert of those years was I, who based our bond on the ambiguous foundations of love and, as you had rightly reproached me, I loved you not for what you were but for what I wanted you to be and you were not, Nguyen Van Sam and Huyn Thi An and Chato and Julio and Marighela and Padre Tito de Alencar Lima, the patterns of my past which had been lived on patterns, so at the breaking of every pattern I ran away disappointed, making demands, rebelling, absent just when I should have stayed with you. And solitude continued to be your real companion. True, this is the fate of Don Quixote, the fate of heroes, poets. But the day always comes when a man, no matter how great a hero, how great a poet, can no longer bear the torment of wandering alone in the desert. The moment always comes when he tires of living because he tires of losing, overwhelmed by nausea, he says to himself—I have to win at least once—and in saying this he thinks of death (now close with its scent) as if it were a winning card. An ace up the sleeve, a prize. Why grow old? Why continue the effort that is called existence? To undergo the same defeats, to repeat the same mistakes? Or to adjust and wither in the grayness of renunciation, of normality? "He's no longer a crazy anarchist, a restless rebel, he's got sense into his head, he's grown up." "I think I recognize him; isn't he the one that planted the bomb and stole the ESA files?" Dying, on the contrary, you would give a meaning to your sacrifices, your sufferings, your failures. And people would finally listen to you, understand you. Even expressing themselves badly, with flowers and banners and shouts, "his sacrifice," "his example," they would be with you, would show that the flock need not be flock, that doctrines crumble under the initiative of the individual, the disobedience of the individual, the courage of the individual, that everyone is somebody provided he wants to be, that salvation lies in the individual who revolutionizes himself. And perhaps the mountain would tremble a little, perhaps the boulder on its peak would teeter. No living hero is worth a dead hero, the ancients also said as much. The heroes of myth never waste away in the afflictions of old age, they never die of illness in a hospital bed: they go off in the bloom of youth, violently, and almost always the last act of their adventure is a virtual suicide committed through the one who kills them. To die in order not to die, to let oneself be killed in order to win at least once, this is the horrible and brilliant calculation you made, mixing abnegation and pride, altruism and egoism, your good eye and your bad eye, accepting without last-minute evasions your appointment in Samarkand, giving yourself to Death in a suicidal embrace.

The horrible and brilliant calculation ripened in the space of a month. The month of April. Were you aware or not? The line that separates the conscious from the unconscious is so fine. Coming back to Athens, I was to learn, you seemed drained of all vivacity, dejected in a mysterious listlessness. You spent a great deal of your time in the office, where your secretary often caught you with glazed eyes, mouth clenched, arms folded, sitting with the look of someone pursuing an obsessive thought. You didn't shift your eyes even if the phone rang or if she spoke to you, she had to come over and tug your sleeve to make you bestir yourself and answer: "Who is it? What?" When the boy from the bar downstairs came in with hot coffee, you didn't notice him or the cup he set on the table, and afterward, seeing it, you examined it, bewildered: how had it got there, who had brought it to you? At times you stood up, very slowly, sighing, and you would start pacing through the rooms. Hands in your pockets, shoulders bent, head bowed, three paces forward and three back, as in Boiati. If the paces brought you to the secretary's desk you would stop and stare at her without seeing her, and your eyes were so glassy that she was frightened: "Mr. Panagoulis! Do you feel ill, Mr. Panagoulis?" You felt ill. You told everybody so. Your stomach hurt, your legs hurt, you couldn't sleep. "I took two sleeping pills and they didn't do any good." Or else: "I dozed off at five and at seven I was awake." Or else: "I can't stand on my feet, and my esophagus burns. I can't swallow anything." You ate very little, nothing before evening, you had suddenly stopped drinking, insisting that the smell of wine made you sick. You quenched your thirst with orangeade and your suppers were no longer jolly symposia destined to drunkenness, but excuses to take a bit of nourishment, spend some time in the company of others. A passing friend or an insistent courtier or a lusting maenad. But even with them you were taciturn, absent, as if your mind were thousands of miles away or shrouded in a fog that protected a secret. And, horrifying detail, you now evinced a kind of inexplicable hatred for your spring. You slammed the doors, drove angrily, took pleasure in crashing the gears, scraping the tires against curbs, parking badly and thus exposing the car to traffic and the bumps of other automobiles, you delighted in getting it dirty. Outside it was always dusty, mud-spattered; inside a receptacle of papers, rags, butts, magazines, trash of every sort. And you even lent it to anyone who asked you for it, displaying total indifference if they brought it back with more scratches or dents: as if it had become the symbol of your soul that was disintegrating.

I didn't know it, I didn't even suspect that your soul was disintegrating. I believed you were serene because you had convinced *Ta Nea* to cut the delay and to publish the documents within the month. In the first ten days of April the only time I worried was when you called to tell me they had broken into your apartment again, and again they had tried to steal the documents. "Hello? It's I! It's me! Guess what happened. Last night when I came home, I found one of them there." "One of them there?" "Yes, I caught him while he was trying to force the bedroom door." "And what did you do?" "I jumped him and gave him a good beating. Then I held him fast, took him prisoner, and I locked him in a cellar. I'm interrogating him." "And who is he? Who sent him?" "That's what I'm trying to find out, for the moment all I can tell you is that his name is Erodotou." "Maybe he's just a thief, Alekos." "No, he isn't just a thief. He knew the photocopies are in the bedroom." "What? You're still keeping them there? You still haven't put them in a safe place?" "Where can I put them? In Averoff's villa?" "Listen to me, Alekos—" "No sermons. Good-bye." I wasn't only worried: I was puzzled. Was it conceivable that you continued keeping your treasure in that room, at anyone's mercy? Wasn't it strange that you talked about the alarming episode almost gaily—Guess what happened, last night I found one of them in the apartment, I took him prisoner and I've locked him in the cellar. From the tone of your voice it sounded as if the thing amused you. Or was I wrong? To make sure, I waited a few hours, then called you back. But this time your voice betrayed a disheartening resignation: "Yes, it's me, what's new?" "Nothing, Alekos. You're the one who must tell me." "What?" "About that Erodotou you locked in the cellar, dammit! Has he talked?" "Ah, yes. He's talked." "And who sent him?" "Uff, this isn't something to discuss over the phone. Anyway, who gives a damn? It isn't important." "Isn't important? A stranger breaks into your place at night, you catch him as he's forcing the bedroom door, you telephone to let me know, and then it's not important?" "It's not, because it doesn't change anything. As for him, he's only a poor devil. I'm sorry I gave him a beating." "Aren't you going to turn him over to the police?" "No." "Aren't you going to tell the newspapers?"

"No." "Alekos, I don't understand you." "Eh! Maybe I'm becoming wise. Life is already so difficult, why complicate it with useless things? I caught him, I found out what I wanted to find out, I've decided it isn't important. That's all." And with these words you closed a subject to which formerly you would have devoted rivers of words, oceans of rage. And I would never be able to tell you how seriously worried I was: every time I tried, you reacted rudely. "Nothing new about your prisoner?" "What prisoner?" "Erodotou, of course." "Forget Erodotou, Erodotou doesn't matter." "He does matter, Alekos, he does matter." "If he does, it's my business." "What kind of answer is that?" "The kind of answer a man gives when he has a pain in the ass. You've given me a pain in the ass, you and Erodotou. Good-bye. I can't listen to you. And don't telephone about every little trifle! If you only knew the problems I have!"

You did have problems. The party, to begin with. After they rejected your resignation, you arrived at a kind of armistice with them. But in the following days more evidence of Tsatsos's collaborationism came to light, and the war was resumed, aggravated by the fact that he shamelessly suggested removing you from the presidency of the party's youth group, and to bring it off, he used the support of the faction that the German Social Democrats were financing in return for an ultramoderate policy. So the effort of fighting was made worse by the outrage of being attacked by that bunch of unscrupulous professional politicians, opportunists, yes-men. Then there were the troubles with *Ta Nea*, obstacles you hadn't foreseen. One concerned advertising announcements, which the radio and television refused to accept for fear of being compromised; the other, the sequence in which the files were to be published. You insisted, rightly, that the documents on Averoff should open the series because they were the most grave and because, otherwise, he would have time to seek cover through some legal stratagem. The journalist to whom you had entrusted the editorial part, Iannis Fazis, insisted that those documents should appear last because the expectation would enhance them, make them more dramatic. Fazis, whom you liked, was backed by an editor whom you disliked so much that you called him Mr. Malaka, Mr. Shit, and this exacerbated your black moods, your lack of appetite, your insomnia. Still these problems did not explain your disinterest in Erodotou and your detachment toward me: there was the mysterious listlessness whereby you took refuge like a snail that curls into its shell to sleep inside itself. This is what happens to the dying in the phase before the state of coma. There is a phase, before the coma arrives, during which they shut themselves off in an almost mystic isolation: rejecting the persons they loved, ignoring the things that excited them, stripping themselves of affections, curiosity, desires, of everything that represents a bridge to life. Yet it is not the decisive phase because, at the very moment that they believe themselves freed of every bond, every residue of temptation, an angry sob explodes in them, like a nostalgia for life, which is beautiful even if it's ugly; in life there is the sun, there is the wind, there is green, there is blue, there is the pleasure of food, drink, a kiss, there is joy which compensates for tears, there is good which compensates for evil, there is everything, the opposite of nothingness; otherwise there is stillness, there is darkness, nothingness. So they regain the wish to love, to desire, to fight. Especially to fight. It is a dark desire, painful, fragile as a crystal. And very brief. But for a hero it suffices to make the final effort.

The final effort began the week fate used me once again, a cog in the gears, a link in the chain. It was mid-April, Easter was approaching, with different dates in my country and in yours, Catholic Easter would be April 18, Orthodox April 25, and then the telephone rang offering the old, festive voice: "Hello, it's I, it's me! Kalimera, good morning, alitaki!" "Thank goodness, you sound pleased with yourself today. Things going well?" Yes, you answered, they were going splendidly because you had resigned from the party a second time and forever: you had nothing more to do with the politics of politicians. "Really?" Really, and your throat hurt because of the yells with which you had deafened them, you felt like Demosthenes, after the things you had said to them. What an address, no, what a riot! First you had shut Tsatsos's mouth, flinging in his face his love letters to Dascalopoulos and his informer reports to Hazizikis; then you had shut up his pals by reading an interview with Willy Brandt in which Brandt admitted financing their clique; finally you asked what kind of socialism was this Union of the Center talking about when it jabbered about socialism. The elusive, indefinable socialism of the German Social Democrats? The garrulous and lying socialism of the demagogue Papandreou? The totalitarian and sectarian socialism of the fanatics who wanted to transfer Cambodia to Europe? All socialists, for Christ sake; except for Christianity, there was no currency more inflated than socialism. So inflated, so defaced, so degraded that all the gold of Fort Knox wouldn't suffice to give it back a bit of value, a bit of authority. And the most horrible thing was that, though they carried it in their wallets, though they spent it blindly for every trifle, none of them knew what the hell it meant except what had been written in a book read only by a handful of scholars. And assuming that it meant what you hoped, a dream to go forward and make the world a bit more free, a bit better, was this the way they wanted to bring it about? Selling themselves for a handful of deutsche marks, retaining a sack of shit because he was the nephew of the president of the Republic, giving you a pain in the ass because you wanted to denounce the filthy right wing, the right wing of the Averoffs? "After which I broke the chair on the table and I went out slamming the door and I tore it off its hinges." "Ah!" "And now they hate me unanimously: right, left, center, extreme right, extreme left, extreme center." "Ah!" "I'm happy." "Happy?!"

"Yes, because I like life. In life there's the sun, there's the wind, there's green, there's blue, there's the pleasure of food, drink, a kiss, there's joy that makes up for tears, there's good that makes up for evil, there's everything, and I love you." "So do I." "And besides there's the radio that at this moment is broadcasting the advertising of *Ta Nea*: 'Alexander Panagoulis reveals the secret files that the government couldn't find.'" "Alekos, this really is good news! So you made it! When does the fun begin?" "In three days. Sunday. Uhm! Too bad I won't be in Athens on Sunday. I'm coming to Italy, Sunday. I'm coming with my spring and I'm staying until Thursday or Friday." "Alekos—" "So I'll be well away from the uproar and I'll change spring's color, I'll have it painted blue. Blue can't be seen in the dark, and if we have to change the name, too bad. We'll call it autumn." "Alekos—" "Reserve a sleeper for Brindisi, I'll take the ship at Patras, I land in Brindisi, we meet in the port, and drive together to Rome and then to Florence." "Alekos!" "What is it? Don't you want to come to Brindisi." "No, Alekos. It isn't Brindisi. The fact is that Sunday night or Monday morning I'm leaving. I'm going to America." "But Sunday is Easter, Catholic Easter, and Monday is Easter Monday!" "Yes, Alekos." "We've always spent Christmas and Easter together. Always!" "Yes, Alekos, but this time it was understood we wouldn't spend Easter together because I have to go to America! We talked about this, Alekos!"

We had talked about it often. On April 18 or 19, I had told you, I was going to New York and from there to Massachusetts, to give a lecture at a college. The subject of the lecture was the art of journalism and the formation of political consciousness in Europe through the press, and after a few skeptical remarks, you had decided that it was a good subject: you had actually suggested some research I could do on the scribes who in the sixteenth century went from fief to fief with their scrolls of political information. "Don't you remember, Alekos?" "I remember so well that I said: I'll arrive

Sunday the eighteenth and stay almost a week. Your lecture is the twenty-sixth. You still have plenty of time if you leave the twenty-fourth or the twenty-fifth or even the twenty-third." "No, Alekos, no, because on the days before the lecture I've made all sorts of appointments in New York: we talked about that too!" "That's simple: cancel your New York appointments." "That's impossible, Alekos." "Nothing is impossible, except not dying." "Listen to me, Alekos: why don't you come right away, by plane? That way we can be together until Sunday evening or Monday morning and—" "No. If I come, I come to stay almost a week. If I come, I come with my spring to change the color. And to get it out of here, to avoid the temptation of using it during the uproar." "All right, bring it. We'll see each other for twenty-four hours and—" "Twenty-four hours, no." "Be reasonable, Alekos. Try for once to adjust to my problems, don't make a fuss." "You're the one who's making a fuss." You're the one, no you, it's your fault, my fault– when we got into such quarrels, our antagonism ran riot and neither of us wanted to give in. In the end you yelled for me to go ahead and go to America, to the moon, to hell, you wouldn't come anyway, you wouldn't change any color, you'd keep your spring in Athens, and you hung up, leaving me with the image of a great green muzzle that speeds, two immense burning yellow eyes, followed by other yellow eyes. The usual humanized, sinister image of death in the guise of an automobile. Then I began telling myself that perhaps I really could postpone my New York appointments, leave six days later, and do what you asked, and that night I called you back to say—You win, dear, all right I've changed plans. But the phone rang unanswered: you had gone to a bouzouki to work off your anger. You had gone there with a Greek from Zurich, and he says that you seemed wild, you did nothing but buy roses, gardenias, and throw them at the orchestra to make them play the song that had haunted you two years earlier—Life is short, very very very short—and at a certain point you wanted to pick up two prostitutes, take them to Kolokotroni Street. You didn't take them there because the Greek from Zurich prevented you: "You're worn out, get some rest, do you want to die?" And you said: "Uhm! Can you imagine the funeral they'd give me if I died now? A million people, at the very least. And even Papandreou would bend down to kiss the coffin, even Tsatsos would say he was sorry. The only one who wouldn't say anything, maybe, would be Averoff." But you weren't drunk, you talked about Camus, about Epicurus, about the happiness people seek in pleasure, in wine, in prostitutes, forgetting that happiness exists only in atarassia, in the absence of pain, and since death is the absence of everything, it is also absence of pain and therefore happiness. "The happiness of stones, Camus says." You seemed obsessed with this remark, the happiness of stones. Everything you said contained a reference to the happiness of stones.

But I didn't know that by now you desired the happiness of stones, nothing could have led me to such a suspicion, and not finding you at home irritated me. At dawn I stopped calling. I swore I would stick to my American plans, and we didn't talk again until Sunday, April 18. From that moment our telephone calls become important, tesserae indispensable to recomposing the mosaic of your final effort. An effort so cruel, so superhuman, that it confuses the memory and the mind. "Hello, it's I, it's me." "You really didn't come, eh? You made your fuss and you stuck to it." "So much the better, alitaki, so much the better. You can't imagine the work I have here, the worries. Besides, if I had come, I would have brought my spring, and I need it here because I'm not sleeping in Kolokotroni Street anymore, I'm sleeping at Glyphada. How could I travel twice a day between Athens and Glyphada without an automobile?" "That's why I couldn't reach you the other night, Alekos! You could have told me, eh?" "I did tell you!" "When?" "Yesterday." "But we didn't talk yesterday!" "Ah, that's right." "Anyway, why are you sleeping at Glyphada? Another Erodotou?" "No, a precaution. *Ta Nea*'s appeared, you know. There's a long article today. The whole front page is my documents. But tomorrow is the big day. The real publication begins tomorrow." "With the documents about Averoff?" "No, unfortunately. No, Mr. Malaka wouldn't give in; he's shitting his pants with fear. It begins with the diary of Hazizikis." And then, immediately, the fog. "You know why I'm calling you?" "To wish me Happy Easter and apologize for being so stubborn." "No, to tell you that we'll spend Orthodox Easter together, next Sunday! In Paris!" "In Paris?!" "Yes, Friday the twenty-third I have to go to Paris, to a congress of Chilean exiles and—Didn't I tell you that? Funny, I thought I had told you. Anyway, I've promised to go, and you'll join me in Paris. We'll stay until Monday or Tuesday and then we go to Cyprus." "To Cyprus?!" "Yes, I have to pick up something that—I can't explain on the phone, but you can imagine. First-class stuff." "Alekos—" "You like the idea of Paris and Cyprus? Do you? You like that?" "Alekos, tomorrow I'm going to America. Have you forgotten that?" "To America?!" "Yes, dear, America. Isn't that what we quarreled about, three days ago?" "Uhm. Yes. Now I remember." "Now you remember?" "Yes, I'd forgotten. What are you going to America for?" "Alekos! What's happening to you? The lecture at the college in Massachusetts. Have you forgotten that too?" "Uhm. Yes. Now I remember. So you aren't coming to Paris with me." "No, dear, no!" "Or to Cyprus, either." "No, dear, no." "Too bad!" "Alekos, are you feeling all right? Alekos?" "Yes, yes. When are you coming back from America?" "On May 5 or 6." "Uhm. Yes. Now I remember. Then we'll see each other May 5. I'll come to you on May 5. No, you come to me on May 5. We have a date for May 5. That's settled: May 5." You repeated the date May 5 like a broken record playing the same notes over and over, as if to retain that date cost you a tremendous effort, as if even to think were an agony. Yet even in the moments of greatest tension your brain had always remained more lucid than a polished mirror and you had a fantastic memory for dates. Even during our quarrel, you had remembered very well that my lecture in Massachusetts was on April 26. Strange. Really strange, I said to myself. And I hung up, in the grip of an uneasiness that surpassed even my amazement.

I would have been much less amazed if I had known that, agreeing to begin the publication with the diary of Hazizikis, you had betrayed your pledge to Fany: "If there is anything against your husband, I assure you I won't use it. Believe me, girl, I am sure I can take the files without creating problems for you, and without anyone's ever knowing anything . . ." But more important was the fact that in those very days you had come into possession of the document that I would receive after your death: a paper identified by the reference number 98975. In the upper-left corner, typed: "From KYP headquarters to Minister of Defense Evangelos Averoff. Top secret. Personal. Urgent." In the upper-right corner, written by hand: "Received, April 6, 1976 at 9:30 A.M." In the center, also by hand: "Graf. H. E. the Minister. 463." And it said: "We have the honor to inform you that on the basis of your verbal order of recent days the colonel Constantine Kostantopoulos and another officer of headquarters will join our group in Cyprus to recover the secret documents of the EAT and the ESA of Athens which are in the hands of a collaborator of the deputy Panagoulis. This office is at your orders and awaits further missions from you."

It was after that document and the choice made by *Ta Nea* that things precipitated. Especially the threatening phone calls: "If you don't get wise, Panagoulis, you'll be sorry. If you don't pull your horns in, Panagoulis, you'll pay." Then the harassment of the magistrature which through a judge by the name of Giouvelos opposed the publication. Giouvelos, an ambitious character, full of initiative, had already sounded the alarm when the advertising announcements had been broadcast. He had promptly telephoned *Ta Nea* to find out what it was all about, and naturally you hadn't taken him seriously. "I'm convinced he doesn't really mean to block us," you said to Fazis. "He'll calm down, you'll see." Sunday April 18, however, the day that heralded the diary of Hazizikis, there he was, calling again: to serve notice on you. And again on Monday the nineteenth, again on Tuesday the twentieth. This time, to summon you to his office, with Fazis. And yet there was nothing sensational in that diary, nothing that cast dishonor on any member of the government; despite the dramatic tone of the announcement, the diary simply explained the methods by which the KYP every day delivered to the ESA the files on citizens under special surveillance. The readers had been downright disappointed: "Is that all?" As for the reports that Fazis and his editor had chosen as examples, they concerned people whose consciences were completely clear, Resistance men like Mavros and like Kanellopoulos. So the summons on April 20 irked you more than the others. Why was he getting so upset, this Giouvelos? What was he afraid of? Perhaps seeing the document that listed number twenty-three: "Evangelos Averoff—former deputy—supporter of the bridge policy between the national government and former Politicians—already collaborates and reports to high-level officials of the KYP, so far with very positive results." The irritation, however, became outrage when you noticed that Giouvelos had summoned you for the next day, April 21, anniversary of the Papadopoulos coup. "Giouvelos! Do you want to celebrate April 21, Giouvelos?" was the yell with which you answered him. And he wasn't to expect you, you wouldn't answer his summons, if he wanted to speak to you then he would have to come to you, but with tanks, because you wouldn't even open the door to him. You asked Fazis to do the same. Then, on Thursday April 22, Giouvelos came to the paper. He spoke with Fazis and with the editor, he put his demands on the table: *Ta Nea* was to suspend the publication at once, and the files were to be handed over to him. This was the demand also of the minister of defense, who, being responsible for the ESA and the KYP, was the only one in a position to authorize the circulation of such documents. If *Ta Nea* did not obey, he would issue an order of confiscation. They were to inform you. They did inform you and your reply was adamant: "Tell Giouvelos I'll take his order and wipe my ass with it."

Yes, your fighting spirit was aroused again. But at what cost. Those close to you say that it was enough to look at you to understand the effort it cost, the tension that was devouring you. You were never still, one minute you would take off your jacket saying, "I'm hot," then you would put it on grumbling, "I'm cold," first you would loosen your tie, then you would unbutton your shirt, then you complained about pains: "I have a fever. I feel bad. I'm old. Ah, how old I am!" Sometimes you would point to the houses in Kolokotroni Street, saying: "Uhm! From one of those windows they could really shoot me easily." The idea that someone wanted to kill you never left you for a second. Was this what caused the states of confusion that clouded your mind? The night between Wednesday and Thursday, when I called you from New York, in Athens already Thursday morning, you seemed to be groping in a fog: "You've arrived already? Good! Fine! I'm arriving tomorrow, at two in the afternoon, with Olympic. Will you come and meet me at the airport?" "The airport, Alekos? What airport?" "What do you mean, what airport? Paris, of course. Then from there we'll go to Cyprus and—" "Alekos, where do you think I am, Alekos?" Silence. Then a bitter sigh: "Where are you? Where are you calling from?" "From New York, Alekos. I'm in New York!" "Oh, no! I thought you were in Paris." "Alekos, what are you saying? Didn't I call you yesterday from New York?!" "Uhm. Yes. Uhm. But what are you doing in New York? Why are you in New York? Weren't we supposed to meet in Paris, spend Orthodox Easter together, and go on to Cyprus Monday?" I could have cried. "No, Alekos, no.

You've forgotten again!" "Yes, I've forgotten again." "What's happening to you, Alekos?" "Everything. I'm tired. So tired. I'm fed up. So fed up. I can't go on. They're cutting the ground from under my feet, you know, that's what they're doing. You know what I say? Once I've finished with this business, I'm going to quit Parliament too. And I'll go back to studying mathematics. Instead of going back to writing the book, I'll go back to studying mathematics. Writing books is no use anyway. And staying in Parliament is no use either. Oh, what a headache, what a headache. Did you receive the photocopy of the paper?" "What photocopy? What paper?" "The one I sent to you in Florence two days ago?" "But, Alekos, if I'm in New York, how could I have received a photocopy you sent two days ago to Florence?" "Of course. You're right. You see how tired I am? As soon as you receive it, put it in the bank." "We'll take it there together when I come back, Alekos." "Yes, when you come back. But when are you coming back?" "May 5, Alekos, you know that! We've talked about it a hundred times!" "Uhm! Yes, right. May 5. We'll see each other on May 5. And have you received the three numbers of *Ta Nea*?" "Received them where?!" "Ah, I was forgetting again, you can't have received them, I sent them to Florence. So much the better. There's nothing in them anyway. They keep on publishing trivia, I've fallen into the hands of idiots. Good-bye, we'll talk tomorrow. Tomorrow I'm in Paris, at the Hotel Saint-Sulpice. No, not at the Saint-Sulpice, at the Louisiana. At the Saint-Sulpice or the Louisiana? I can't even remember that, cataramene Criste! That bastard Giouvelos is breaking my memory, along with my balls."

Giouvelos issued his order on Friday April 23. "Inasmuch as the court-martial has opened an inquiry concerning the ESA documents, inasmuch as a newspaper is publishing those documents, inasmuch as those who have taken possession of them will not hand them over to the magistrature though they had been invited to do so in accordance with the law, inasmuch as it has not been possible for us to requisition them, inasmuch as aforesaid publication can hinder the operation of justice, we have decided to prohibit such publication as of today." The text reached *Ta Nea* while you were flying to Paris, unaware that the threat had materialized, in fact convinced that it would not materialize. During the flight, as I would be told by the passenger sitting next to you, a businessman friend of Karamanlis, you seemed relaxed. You conversed in measured, affable tones, criticizing the excesses of the young, praising the good sense of the old, quoting proverbs. A couple of times you quoted a saying of Mao Tse-tung: "When you point a finger at the moon to indicate the moon, instead of looking at the moon, the stupid ones look at your finger." The fact that your mood was good that day and your mind wasn't confused is confirmed also by the two Greeks who were waiting for you at Orly, two members of your Dionysian entourage. "A bit pale, yes, and he had hollows under his eyes. Somewhat weak because, he said, the passenger sitting beside him had made him talk too much. But almost jolly. At table he ate with an appetite and laughed, telling about the Giouvelos–Averoff couple." You were also lucid and lighthearted when you telephoned me to explain that your hotel was the Louisiana, not the Saint-Sulpice: you even joked about your recent memory lapses. "I'll bet you're in New York!" But Saturday you were again groping in the fog and in your apathy. It was seven in the evening, in Paris, when I called you from New York to wish you Happy Easter, and I didn't even think I would find you. At this hour, I thought, he'll be at the congress of Chilean exiles. You weren't at the congress, you answered me in a voice thick with sleep: "Yes, I was sleeping . . . I'm sleeping." "At seven in the evening?" "Yes . . ." "And what about the Chileans?" "The Chileans are in Chile." "Very cordial you are! Happy Easter." "It's not Easter for me, there's nothing more for me. He issued the order, he's suspended publication. Yesterday." "And now what are you going to do?" "I don't know. I'll decide

Monday. I'm flying back Monday." "Without going to Cyprus?" "There's no use now." You didn't feel like talking, I couldn't get a conversation going, you refused to write down the address of the college where I would be the following evening. "I won't call you there anyhow, too complicated. You call me. And if you can't call me, don't worry. We'll see each other on May 5. Our date for May 5 holds." It was the only thing that never sank into the darkness of oblivion, the date of May 5. "But what does May 5 have to do with the address of the college? May 5 is a long way off, Alekos." "No, it's near. Very near." "All right, it's near. Good-bye, Alekos. Until tomorrow." But the next day, when I called again, the concierge of the Louisiana said you had left. Left? Oui, madame, le monsieur est parti. And there was no message for me? Non, madame, pas de message pour personne. No messages for anyone. Le monsieur était pressé, très pressé. The gentleman was in a hurry, a great hurry.

2

SUNDAY IS SO QUIET AND DISQUIETING IN NEW YORK. THE world seems to stop, life falls into catalepsy. On Sunday in New York people are silent, the streets are deserted, the only sound that stirs the silence is the muffled glide of wheels on the asphalt, an automobile, a truck, or the chatter of a helicopter flying over the city. Who said that one can relax and rest on Sunday in New York? On the contrary it is more a day for thinking, for drawing up a balance sheet of our errors and our regrets, for self-torment. Numbed in that void, in that silence barely stirred by rustling, chattering, I tore my brain with reproaches, doubts, questions, and the sensation of having made a tragic mistake by putting an ocean between us grew from minute to minute. True, the lecture I was to give the following day couldn't have been canceled without committing an unforgivable discourtesy; true, you had often said I was useful to you far away from Greece; true, my presence in Athens would probably have been an encumbrance. But every time we spoke you seemed so alone, so sad, so confused, and how had I been able to leave you at such a moment? We hadn't seen each other for twenty-four days. Suddenly twenty-four months, twenty-four years. We had never gone twenty-four days without seeing each other, never. The longest interval had been my flight: seventeen days. And you were well, then: well as Satan rebelling against the dictatorship of God, as Dionysus garlanded with pleasures and grape leaves. But this time: "There is no Easter for me, there is nothing for me anymore." "Le monsieur est parti. Le monsieur était pressé, très pressé." And the paper that you had sent to Florence? What paper was it? What did it talk about? Whom? And that farewell, that public embrace, that solemn sentence: "You've been a good companion, the only possible companion." Why had you used the perfect tense? And why was I now thinking of that good-bye as a farewell? Nonsense. The melancholy of a New York Sunday. We would talk about it on May 5. "We'll see each other May 5." "Our date for May 5 holds." Everything you said ended with the words May 5, the date May 5. It was becoming an obsession. May 5 was beginning to make me nervous. As if something special or rather something bad were to happen on May 5. And why had you left Paris a day early? I called Athens, nobody answered. Then I rebelled. To hell with these guilt complexes, fears, anguish: even when I was on the other side of the earth, in a landscape that didn't belong to you, in a reality that excluded you, you succeeded in conditioning my existence, determining it, seizing it. Free of you, I had to be free of you! I would go straight to Amherst where I was to give the lecture. I packed my bag, and four hours later I was in Amherst, the little college town.

Trimmed lawns, cool. Leafy, green trees. Red houses with white-columned front porches and blue slate roofs. And outside the window of my room, a splendid peach tree in blossom, a pink cloud that stuns with its perfume. Welcome to our midst, welcome, see how tender the world is here, how easy. No ESA files, no Hazizikis diary, no heroic enterprises, no passions. We have overcome everything here, even pain. We are never hungry, we are never cold, theological controversies don't interest us, we don't believe in fate, in superstitions, presentiments. We are logical here, rational. Also charming, hospitable, civilized, in spite of the occasional war, the occasional denied visa. Come, rest with us, we'll give you a bit of anesthetic. A handsome auditorium with plush seats, a round well of motionless faces, listening. A loudspeaker that broadcasts a metallic voice, my voice, a language that finally erases you from my thoughts. "Good evening, ladies and gentlemen, it's a pleasure to be here with you. The subject of this lecture will be the art of journalism and the formation of political consciousness in Europe through the press." Where is Athens? Who is Sancho Panza? And Ishmael? Afterward in the hotel there is a telephone beside my bed. I would only have to pick up the receiver, dial an international code, then the number, and say to you: "Since I've been going on about political consciousness, and skipping love for the moment, why did you leave Paris a day early?" I do pick up the receiver, and I say: "Hello, may I have a coke?" What a relief, this fat peace, this well-being, padded with oblivion. Would you like to stay another day or two? Yes, thank you! Thank you very much. To postpone the torments, to suspend them. To rest some more, to prolong another twenty-four hours this delightful narcosis of the soul. Is this how we prepare ourselves for the pain that screams when we wake from anesthesia? Because meanwhile, beyond the ocean, death was coming closer. The irresistible wind that swallows the star and sucks it into the vortex sweeping away every residue of hope, of illusion. By now you had only five days left to live.

Monday April 26, fifth-to-last day. You seemed a bird swooping in a room without doors and windows, Fazis was to tell me. You paced up and down, up and down, desperate, infuriated, seeking a way out, and there was no way out. On coming back from Paris the night before, you had called Giouvelos and a roar had shaken Kolokotroni Street: "Giouvelos! You too are a servant of Averoff, Giouvelos! You too take orders from that faggot, Giouvelos!" But Giouvelos had answered, icily, that he took orders only from justice and justice would follow its course. Then you had called the KYP officer. The trunk full of documents on Cyprus, the trunk! It had to be taken away at once, there was no time to waste! He was to send it to you as soon as possible. No, he should come at once to your office: you had to explain to him what was happening. Panic-stricken, the officer stammered no, it was no longer possible, too risky now to be seen with you: Averoff suspected him, was preparing to transfer him to a post on the Turkish border. Transfer? To a post on the Turkish border? So they didn't just want to cut the ground from under you, they also wanted to chop off your hands, tear out your tongue! Shaking with rage, you whispered an address to the officer, the house of a trusted friend: he was to meet you there. The officer did meet you there and for hours you argued, but at the moment of separating, you and he had concluded nothing. Worse, as you were driving in the darkness, along the road leading to Glyphada, you thought you were being followed by two cars: one very pale, almost white, and one red. You only thought this, because, when one appeared, the other vanished; still any doubt was faint: you were almost sure. With this thought, you went into your mother's house and there too the telephone rang three times: "If you don't get some sense into your head, Panagoulis, you'll be sorry." "If you don't draw in your horns, Panagoulis, you'll pay." "We know every move you make, Panagoulis, every action. You won't escape us." They didn't let you close your eyes. And now, exhausted by lack of sleep and by helplessness, a bird swooping in a room without doors and windows, you slammed your wings in vain against the wall and the ceiling of your office in Kolokotroni Street. If only you weren't so alone! If you had a party behind you! If parties were something serious, something worthy! If the word "left" had a meaning! If instead of the politics of politicians, the politics of opportunists, hacks, climbers, demagogues, demiurges, pseudo-revolutionaries, there were real men, ready to fight, to lend you a hand! If the people had been people, if you had been able to address them, call on them: companions, friends, brothers, help! Help! And yet there had to be a way out: you had escaped from Boiati, you would escape also from this maze. You would, yes. You would talk with Karamanlis to tell him what you had and what you knew about Averoff and what Averoff was plotting against you: secret services, magistrature, disciplinary provisions against your friends. You would offer Karamanlis two solutions: either intervene with his minister of defense to make him leave you alone and with Giouvelos to make him revoke his order or face a confrontation with you in Parliament: to undergo the extreme embarrassment of seeing himself handed the proofs of what you were declaring. The swooping of the crazed bird calmed down. You sat at the desk, you telephoned Moliviatis, personal secretary and adviser to Karamanlis. You asked him for an appointment with the prime minister: very grave matters, you said, made the meeting urgent. Moliviatis answered that the prime minister was very busy these days: problems with Turkey, with NATO. The chance of seeing him was scant. In any case he would try and would let you know.

Was it Moliviatis who told Averoff? Monday April 26, Averoff seemed well informed of your attempt to see Karamanlis. In the afternoon he was at Goudi, in the army camp at Dionisos, for the Easter Monday ceremony, and he was conversing with an officer. At a certain point the officer mentioned your name, and it was like putting a match to a fuse. All unctuousness, all softness vanished, and Averoff flushed in a paroxysm no one would have believed him capable of, he even forgot that hundreds of people were watching, listening, and with his little eyes bloodshot, he yelled: "That insolent dog! That cursed beast! I'll crush him! I'll crush him, I'll crush him! Exonthoso, exonthoso, exonthoso!" Tongues of fire and roars, hysterical lashes of the tail, severed heads and gnawed bones: the remains of those who dared approach the bridge that protects the realm and fire a little arrow, throw a pebble at the mountain. On your knees, varlets, on your knees, all of you who dare defy those who command, who count! Exonthoso, exonthoso, exonthoso! They all heard him as he yelled that verb. And the officer who had involuntarily sparked the scene was so embarrassed that, blushing, he said: "Your Excellency, allow me to turn my back on you, to show them I'm smiling. Otherwise they'll believe it's me you want to crush."

Tuesday April 27, fourth-to-last day. You came into the office, complaining that you had spent another hellish night: no sleep and plenty of migraine. You hadn't been able to sleep also because, as you were driving toward Glyphada, the red automobile and the pale, almost-white one had reappeared in the darkness. On the Vouliagmeni Road, near the filling station, the red one had almost touched you. A red BMW with two men in it. Policemen assigned to checking your movements, or mercenaries paid to harass you, perhaps to teach you a lesson? Sooner or later you would face them, to satisfy your curiosity; you would transform yourself from pursued to pursuer and you would force them to stop. But not now, now you had important things to attend to. First of all the appointment with Karamanlis. The phone rang, you grabbed it anxiously: Moliviatis? No, the usual mocking voice: "We always know where you go and where you are, Panagoulis. Just keep on like this and you'll see the party we give you." The secretary heard you shout: "Faggot! Malaka! Come here, come here and tell me to my face, if you have the courage!" She spoke up: "Be calm, Mr. Panagoulis! Who was it, Mr. Panagoulis?" "The same fool who thinks he can frighten me." And what about Mr. Moliviatis? The phone rang again, and again you grabbed it anxiously. No, it wasn't Moliviatis. It was Fazis, who told you about Averoff's scene on the parade ground of Dionisos. "Did he really say, 'Exonthoso, I'll crush him?'" "Yes, three times." "Eh! Who would ever have thought it? I like that: he has more guts than I believed. Now I really will drive him crazy. And you'll have plenty of things to write, Fazis! A novel, my friend, a novel!" As if the story amused you. But hanging up the receiver, you looked at your watch, impatiently. And what about Moliviatis? Why didn't Moliviatis call? A few more minutes and you would call him yourself. You did call him. Oh, he said, pompous and obsequious, you caught him with his hand on the receiver. He was just about to call you, to tell you that he had been right: the prime minister's book was crammed with appointments. There wasn't a single gap into which he could slip an appointment with you. That Turkey, that NATO! So sorry. You would have to wait. "I can't wait, Mr. Moliviatis! I mustn't wait! I don't want to wait!" "But do try to understand, Mr. Panagoulis, questions of state—" "My business is a question of state too, Moliviatis! Tell him, cataramene Criste!" "I'll tell him, I'll try." Did he really try? Had he tried at all? A few months after your death I talked with the businessman friend of Karamanlis who had traveled to Paris with you, and I told him the incident, I asked him to ask Karamanlis why he hadn't received you that week. The businessman did as I asked, and when I saw him again, he swore to me that Karamanlis seemed sincere when he said he had never known about your asking to see him and said it with such insistence. Whether he told the truth, I don't know, but I do know that the refusal was a mortal blow for you. You sank down on the desk and kept repeating: "There's nobody, I have nobody. I'm alone, alone, alone! I can't take anymore! I can't go on."

It's clear also in the photograph that they snapped of you that evening in a restaurant. The photograph of a man now clinging to life by his teeth. The cheeks are so haggard that the cheekbones stand out more sharply than the jaws; the circles under the eyes are so livid that you look as if you had been beaten up; the nose is so sharp that it no longer has the same form, the double chin has vanished, and the neck is so scrawny that it's lost in the collar. You are speaking to two people who listen to you soberly, and from the way you move your hands it is obvious that you are mastering a ghastly nervous tension. The two have eaten, their plates are almost empty, but your plate is still piled high with food. And your glass of wine is untouched. No, you really couldn't go on. Because, wherever you looked, all roads were closed to you and the future caved in on you with the weight of a falling house.

Wednesday April 28, third-to-last day. Not only had Moliviatis not kept his promise to tell Karamanlis that you were asking to see him, but now he wouldn't even answer calls. All right then, you would shift your battle into Parliament. You took pen and paper, you drafted the first version of a superquestion to ask Karamanlis. "Why does the prime minister retain in his government —and in a position of such capital importance as the Ministry of Defense—Mr. Evangelos Tossitsas Averoff, namely a person who collaborated with the junta, who under Papadopoulos was a spy for the KYP, who under Ioannidis betrayed the navy by revealing every detail of the revolt to his inquisitors, who after the junta assisted criminals of the regime in leaving the country?" Then you wrote down what you would say, approaching the benches where the members of the government sit, and holding out the pack of papers: "I hand over to the prime minister the proof of what I have declared: the

EAT and ESA files which Evangelos Tossitsas Averoff wanted to recover through the secret services and whose publication he suspended, utilizing the magistrature. Here they are, and the Parliament is my witness." You told me this when, waking from the narcosis of the soul, from the anesthesia of Amherst, I came back to New York and telephoned you. "I'm writing something important, very important." "What is it?" "A superquestion for Karamanlis. I'll read it to you. Listen." "You mean to say you're handing the documents over to him?" "Yes. Next week the bomb explodes. In Parliament this time. And it will make more noise than the one I presented to Papadopoulos eight years ago." "Don't tell anybody, Alekos." "On the contrary a thing like this has to be publicized." Then you told me about the threatening phone calls and the two automobiles which, you had no doubts now, were following you at night. The torment of always having to look in the rearview mirror; you look for a car that sometimes is there and sometimes isn't, sometimes is red and sometimes pale, almost white, and you occasionally wonder if you are seeing things, you tell yourself you're not, no, not at all, and then you feel like an enraged boar, or the next minute like a fly that has fallen into the spider's web. "Every night, by Christ, every night when I go to Glyphada. My spring, you know, is visible in the dark. That goddamn phosphorescent green." "Alekos, do you really have to go to Glyphada every night?" "It's better than Kolokotroni. I found somebody forcing the lock of the bedroom, you remember?" "And who goes with you at night when you go to Glyphada?" "Nobody. Who do you think would go with me? I have no escort. I'm not His Excellency Papandreou after all. I don't have his bodyguards!" "Alekos, who do you think it is, this time?" "Who could it be? Somebody who loves me." "Alekos, I'm coming to you. I've done what I had to do here and I don't feel like waiting for May 5." "No, we'll see each other on May 5." "But why are you fixed on May 5?" "Because it's settled, isn't it? It's definite. On May 5 we'll be together, you'll see." "But I feel you're so depressed—" "I am. Oh, what wouldn't I give to go back, to my cell at Boiati."

That faint thread of a voice. The resignation that soaked that thread of a voice. Because this happened on Wednesday April 28: the dissolving of your resistance, the collapse of your indestructibility, the onset of resignation. The final effort never lasts too long. At a certain point the weariness of living returns, soul and body relax in the resignation that looks back: the impulses now are involuntary flashes, the shouts, the superquestions you will never ask. It is also in the poem you wrote that night, going back to Kolokotroni Street. Thoughts of a man who from exile regrets the past, the past being the only support he can grasp, returning to the times when solitude was a cell without space and without light, a mad desire to speak with someone, but the future was a hope. Here it is, on four little pages of your notebook. What convulsive, distorted handwriting. Verse after verse, it becomes more convulsive, more distorted, as if holding the pen in your hand were a terrible task. "How they went roaming in the past / poets / and how they recited their truths / truths dressed in beautiful words / by tales baptized / so I also went roaming / in unknown places / but beautiful as our own / and I wanted to believe that / I was not turning my back on the world / I do not travel / I speak to myself / through woods mountains valleys / I do not travel / it is the lands that speed / and my memory bound to the friends / who in some place / were waiting / to see me turn up suddenly / to the distant days when / with the strength only of dreams / we constructed hopes / and sorrow / accompanied us everywhere always / Trees mountains valleys travel / and I / bound to those who suffered because I suffered / who wept because I wept / who demanded bars because I was behind bars / alone / Years have gone by and I / without forgetting the sorrow / but without becoming unjust in recalling it / along the same roads am walking / roads that only he who has suffered knows / and for my cell I long with homesickness / when I think that in those days I gave something / that all understood / And when I think of what I know / that happens now / now more than then / without the others being able to understand it / or even to guess at it / I say: / My end will come in the way desired by those who have power."

I was to find it forty-eight hours later under your pillow, along with a fifth page on which you had copied the words of Socrates before he gave himself death: "The hour of departure has arrived, and we go our ways—I to die, and you to live. Which is better only the god knows."

Thursday April 29, next-to-last day. You came into the office without looking anyone in the face, and you told the secretary you didn't want to be disturbed: you had to make a phone call. It was the call to Averoff, the final attempt to prevent the transfer of the KYP officer. You had even asked a lawyer's advice on this, and the two of you had come to the same conclusion; it was pointless to react to the threats that Averoff had yelled on Monday afternoon at Goudi: it would serve only to hasten the transfer. Best to pretend to ignore the episode and reach a compromise, best to imitate his customary tactic. The Averoff who always won was not the Easter Monday Averoff, he was a polite, rational man, a master in the art of hypocrisy: and he didn't fight with cold steel but with the poisons of intelligence. So you had to do exactly the same. You dialed the number of the minister of defense. You asked for His Excellency the Minister. His Excellency did not pretend to be out: "Dear friend! Distinguished colleague! What a pleasure to hear your voice, what an honor!" The sarcasm vibrated audibly in the mellifluous voice. But you were not discouraged. Thank you, Mr. Minister, His Excellency was too kind, you hoped you were not disturbing him. "My illustrious friend, what are you saying? What could make you suspect such a thing? Disturb me?" Yes, disturb, you repeated. Also because you were calling to ask a favor and favors are always a bore. "Please, dear friend. Please! What is it in reference to?" It was in reference to an officer whose fate was important to you, you said, a KYP officer. In fact his wife was a friend who had helped you in 1968 when you fled to Cyprus. At that time she was working at the embassy in Cyprus. "I understand, dear friend, I understand." This lady adored her native city, like a true Athenian she couldn't give it up, and the point was that His Excellency had given orders to transfer her husband the KYP officer to a village on the Turkish border. "Do go on, dear friend, go on." What was the lady's dilemma? To leave Athens and follow her husband to the village on the Turkish border or stay in Athens and live far apart from her husband? A cruel thing especially because the two loved each other very much. "Very clear, my friend, very clear. And how can I help you, dear friend? Tell me." You went pale. "I'm telling you, Mr. Minister. I am asking you not to transfer the officer." "And I will answer that I am here to satisfy you, dear friend, distinguished colleague. I will station the officer wherever you like. Where shall I station him, dear friend, dear colleague?" The cat-and-mouse game. He the cat, and you the mouse. A game you didn't know how to play. Also with Hazizikis it had almost always failed because you reacted, you would tolerate it and then suddenly you would explode. For that matter it was clear you were about to explode from the pallor of your face and the purplish swelling of the scar on your left cheekbone. You tried to control yourself: "I wish him to stay where he has always been and where he is, Mr. Minister: in his office at the KYP, in Athens." A squeak: "Illustrious friend! Who would dare deny you a favor? Your wishes are my commands. Athens is impossible, I fear, but tell me where you prefer him to be transferred and I will obey you." You put the receiver down on the desk, closed your eyes, forced yourself to take a breath. One more effort, Christ in heaven, one try. Make it work. You picked up the receiver again: "Perhaps I haven't made myself clear, Excellency. I was asking you to . . . In short, I don't want the officer transferred. Anywhere." "You don't want, illustrious friend? You don't want it?" "No." "And why not, pray, why not, if I'm not being too indiscreet?" "Because, as I was saying, the wife of this officer—" And here the dam broke, the fragile dikes that were restraining the ocean of your fury. They broke with a yell that rattled the windowpanes, in the next room everyone crouched down, the secretary made the sign of the cross. "Averofakiii! Little Averoff! Akusa, Averofaki, skulikaki! Listen, little Averoff, little worm! Den isse t'afendiko tis Elladas! You're not the master of Greece! And you won't become it! Ke den tha ghinis! Because I, I will prevent you! From my grave I'll prevent you, from my grave!" And then Averoff also, forgetting all prudence, succumbed to the anger that had overwhelmed him at Goudi. And repeating the same words, adding others, shouting: "Ego tha s'exonthoso, Panagoulis! I'll crush you, Panagoulis! Ego tha se katastrepso, Panagoulis! Katastrepso. I'll destroy you, Panagoulis! I'll destroy you!"

I knew it immediately afterward, when we talked again, and I didn't recognize your voice. Because it wasn't your voice, your beautiful sensual, guttural, deep voice: it was a kind of rarefied chirp that seemed to come from a cavern millions and millions of light-years away. Like an echo of memory. Every now and then it actually disappeared, leaving voids of silence. "Hello, Alekos? Hello? I can't hear you, can you hear me?" "He then . . ." "Hello, Alekos. Hello." "I'll destroy, he said . . . crush . . ." "Hello, Alekos. Hello. The line's no good, dammit!" "No, the line is working. I'm the one who isn't working anymore." "Why, Alekos, why? What's wrong, Alekos? Tell me. Do you feel ill, do you have a fever?" "No. Yes." "Yes or no? Explain yourself, don't frighten me, you're frightening me! And I'm over here, I can't do anything for you. Hello!" "Yes, I feel ill. Very, very ill . . ." "Where? Why?" "Because I am very, very, very sad. Very, very, very worried." "Alekos, enough of this business, stop it! You're killing yourself, they're killing you! I'm coming to Athens, I'm coming immediately, now. I want to see you, I want to take you away, I want—" "Come, if you want, but you can't do anything agapi. Nothing. We'll see each other May 1, you'll see me on May 1. Good-bye." And you hung up, leaving me amazed. May 1: had I understood correctly? Had you said May 1? Yes, May 1, not May 5. Now you didn't even remember the date of our meeting! Or had you perhaps changed your mind, did you really want me to arrive on May 1, the day after tomorrow? I should call you back. No, no calling you back. These calls serve only to make me suffer, and I didn't want to hear again that voice, that voice that wasn't your voice. I would really be in Athens on May 1, that was it. I would leave tomorrow, that was it. And I did. I boarded the plane at the very moment when you were dying. Six fifty-eight on the evening of Friday April 30. In Athens one fifty-eight in the morning on Saturday May 1. At seven sharp I was on board, I looked at my watch surprised by the punctuality of a flight that was usually delayed. During the flight I was uneasy, oppressed by a nervousness I couldn't manage to define. The nervousness mounted when they showed a film that smelled of ill omen: the story of a mad and brave poet, misunderstood by everyone and always involved in impossible adventures, always pursued by death, covered by a white shroud, luring him, holding the scythe. Every now and then the scythe filled the screen and the poet had to run off. To flee he took refuge in new enterprises, new follies from which he emerged miraculously unharmed. But in the end he grew tired of running away, of denying himself to death, who wanted him so insistently, and he went to meet death and had himself killed. Then the two went off, singing and dancing together on a broad meadow as green as the green of your spring.

The contemporaneity of actions is only apparently a coagulated mystery of accidental and independent episodes. In reality it is a texture composed of episodes which are necessary one to the other and strictly linked among themselves. It is a well-oiled machine. I would become convinced of that as I reconstructed the events that made up the last day of your life, when everything coincided and contributed to oiling the machine, entwining the parallel ways of your actions and the actions of Steffas, so that the now irreversible process of your death would go forward without errors or delays or obstacles and would conclude at a precise point, already fixed in space and in time. The black hole under the garage with the Texaco sign, one fifty-eight in the morning on Saturday May first nineteen hundred seventy-six.

The last day of your life broke in a gray, leaden sky. During the week there had been a summer sun and not one cloud had dulled the blue. But the previous evening, abruptly, the horizon had grown livid with an icy light and a great wind had sprung up, the sea had swollen, slamming against the shore, and a storm had come down, from Athens to Corinth. All through the night, as in a brawl of gods turned bestial, lightning bolts had rent the air, rain had flooded the streets, and only at dawn had calm descended with that gray, leaden sky, messenger of misfortune. You work early. Strangely, you had slept well, and when your mother brought your coffee you were already up, looking absently at the garden, at the damage done to the plants. The storm had decapitated the roses and mutilated the trees, oranges and lemons lay on a carpet of torn leaves and branches, the clump of garlic heads tied to the palm tree to ward off bad luck had also fallen. Falling, it had scattered bulbs of garlic over the path and on the muddy clods, some heads had opened: the cloves looked like the remains of an unstrung necklace. "Your garlic!" you exclaimed. She looked out, saw them, and grunted in horror: the clump had never fallen before; even when they had taken you off to be killed, it had remained hanging. Then she set down the tray, ran outside to collect one head of garlic after the other, one clove after the other, and came back into the house, prepared another, larger, clump, tied it tight with string, went again to tie it to the trunk of the palm tree. She tied it very well, but the moment she turned her back the knot came undone and the clump fell a second time, scattering more bulbs, more cloves: as if the devil were amusing himself by insisting on signs of ill omen. Looking out of the window, you watched her intently, and an inexplicable smile curled your lips. "You'll never manage, not even if you nail it there," you said, as she went back to collect the bulbs and tie them in a clump, obstinately. Your voice was limpid that morning, the beautiful voice I loved, and the high brow was without wrinkles. You seemed rested, fresh. A mysterious serenity, suddenly, had taken the place of the desperation which had undone you until a few hours earlier.

You washed and dressed well, as if you were going to a party. You chose fresh linen, your best shirt, and the suit you liked most: jacket and trousers of a hazel gabardine. With meticulous attention you shaved, trimmed your moustache, filled your pockets with the objects you always carried with you: pipe, little cigars, tobacco, pens, engagement book, notebook, scissors, newspaper clippings. In your inside pocket you hid a document about Averoff you were hesitating to have photocopied. You had told one of your squires: "It's too important. Copying it is risky. I better carry it with me." You moved without haste, lost in thought, with the calm of one who has stopped measuring his existence by the hands of a watch. After you were ready you began wandering up and down the house as if you didn't feel like going out or as if you were looking for something. A regret, a memory? Dragging herself in her slippers and sticking hairpins into her straggling hair, your mother followed you, surprised: "Ti theles? What do you want?" "Tipote, nothing. I was thinking. One month and two days from now it will be my birthday. Thirty-seven on July 2. I'm an old man." Finally you went out, casting a glance at the clump of garlic heads that now hung firmly from the trunk of the palm tree. But on reaching the gate, you stopped, retraced your steps, and with a sharp movement you tore it away, hurled it on the ground: "It's wrong to be superstitious!" She grumbled again, horrified, indignant, as you climbed in behind the wheel of your spring and set out, taking the Vouliagmeni Road: the road you had taken thousands of times, which you knew every meter of, every curve, every hole. Did you turn in front of the garage with the Texaco sign? When we passed by together, you always turned there, muttering that the absence of a wall made the ramp dangerous, a trap you could get your head banged in. You used to point to the sign over the ramp, Kalon Taxidi, Good Journey and say: "Good journey, with your head broken!" At nine you were in Kolokotroni Street and you parked your spring just outside the textile machinery shop, the one next to the front door of your building, with the common glass wall along the corridor leading to the elevator. The shop was open, inside there was already a customer: a young man with a round face, marred by moles. He was the same one that in July 1975 had come to Florence with the Greek Nazi and had stayed there a week: the very week you had left Athens saying you were going to Florence and had gone to Cyprus instead. The same one who in Florence had boasted so much about his kamikaze exploits, the complicated maneuvers he was capable of with his Peugeot: a tap with the front wheel, a tap with the rear wheel, and the other automobile skids off like a bullet. The same one who had worked during the junta in the atelier of Despina Papadopoulos and traveled a lot in the countries where there were opponents of the regime to be shadowed, especially in Canada where he had taken part in the terrible races in which the aim is to destroy the other automobiles with seesaw ramming and the one who wins is the one who has the coolest brain, the quickest eye. It was Michael Steffas. At present a Papandreist Socialist, employed in a dress firm, Heim Fashions, and owner of a silver gray Peugeot 504. What a coincidence! He had come to the textile machinery shop other times, those past few days.

You entered your office and the lawyer was waiting for you. You told him about the quarrel with the dragon and said: "As you see, I followed your advice, but it's impossible to deal with him. I have no choice now but to see this business through to the end, whatever it costs. Monday I'll put my superquestion to Karamanlis." "You'll gain very little." "I know. Karamanlis can't allow himself the luxury of firing him, and there's nobody with me. Nobody." "Well then?" "Well then, nothing. There are cases when to win you also have to lose your breath." "And after the superquestion?" "I'll go to Italy for a few days, then to Cyprus." The lawyer was observing you, perplexed: you were extremely tranquil that morning, confident. Even in reporting the insults traded with Averoff, your voice betrayed no passion. But what did you mean with that sentence—there are cases when to win you also have to lose your breath? Seized by a suspicion, the lawyer shifted the conversation to the threatening calls, the automobile harassment, the inadvisability of driving alone through deserted streets every night going to Glyphada. "How tiresome you all are," you answered him. "Would you also like me to travel about with a bodyguard, making myself ridiculous?" Then you picked up the receiver of the ringing telephone and talked with someone, your lips twisted in a bored grimace. What a nuisance. A woman named Sougioulzoglou was inviting you to supper on behalf of her brother-in-law, Victor Nolis, a Greek from Melbourne. You had met him in Rome in 1968, this Nolis, and a few months ago he had got in touch again through this Sougioulzoglou woman, his wife's sister. Now he was in Athens and he wanted to take you out to supper with the two women. "Today of all days! The last thing I want to do is spend the evening with three dimwits." "Come and have supper with me. I'll pick you up with my car and afterward I'll take you to Glyphada, so for once you won't be driving around alone at night," the lawyer suggested, bringing the conversation back to where it had been before the Sougioulzoglou woman's call had interrupted it. "No, thank you. If I don't go out with them, I have to eat with the general manager of Olimpia Express: it comes to the same thing. I'll see you tomorrow." "All right, we'll meet tomorrow, but I repeat: don't drive around alone at night, and go to Glyphada as little as possible. I'm not keen on this business of the two cars that follow you as soon as it's dark." "What has to be is, what will have to be will be." You separated with these words and later on you called Nolis: he was to come to your office about five in the afternoon, and then if you could get out of the appointment with the general manager of Olimpia Express, you would have supper with him, his wife, and his sister-in-law. Meanwhile Michael Steffas had left the textile machinery shop and had taken a taxi to Heim Fashions. He used a taxi because for a month he wasn't keeping his Peugeot in Athens, he would say. He kept it in Corinth, outside his parents' house, because the license plate was still French and the car had to be nationalized. A month before, in Athens, because of the license he had almost had to pay a very heavy fine.

You left the office around two thirty, came back at three thirty to cancel the appointment with the general manager of Olimpia Express, and at this point your actions and the actions of Steffas become contemporary. At five Nolis came and you told him yes, you would see him at supper, but you were inviting him with his wife and sister-in-law to a restaurant in Glyphada. At the same hour, five sharp, Steffas pulled down the shutter of Heim Fashions and was ready to play his role. At six you said good-bye to Nolis, arranging to pick him up before supper at 8 Alkionis Street, where he was staying, and at the same hour, six sharp, Steffas went to see Basil Georgopoulos: his friend and his alibi. At nine Mrs. Sougioulzoglou telephoned you to say her car had broken down: before going to Alkionis Street could you come by her house at 15A Androtzou? At the same hour, nine sharp,

Steffas got into the bus for Corinth to go get the Peugeot and bring it to Athens. And what about the French license plate to be changed? And the risk of being fined? Georgopoulos, he would explain, had suggested the two of them spend May 1 with a couple of girls on Aegina and this had made him forget every precaution. But isn't Aegina an island? Doesn't one go to Aegina by boat? What sense does it make to rush from Athens to Corinth by bus, there take an unlicensed Peugeot, bring it to Athens, put it on a boat, land with it, put it back on a boat, land again, and take it again to Corinth the next day? No sense, obviously. But who says that the Peugeot was really needed for an excursion to Aegina with the girls? It could be needed for something quite different, a job for example, a favor that demands a cool mind, quick eye, skill in ramming, bumping, demands even a past as kamikaze trained on Canadian tracks, and a sturdy automobile, more resistant to bumps than a certain pale, almost white automobile which in recent days has proved unequal to the task. At nine thirty you left Kolokotroni Street to go by Mrs. Sougioulzoglou's house and then on to meet Nolis and his wife. At ten you were at Alkionis Street with the couple, who detained you there long enough to have a drink, a sip of whiskey which, however, you didn't like and it remained untouched in the glass. At quarter past ten you went out with them. And it was then when Steffas's bus arrived in Corinth, Steffas got out and ran to the square where he kept the Peugeot. It was ten fifteen then he reached the square, climbed quickly into the Peugeot. It was ten twenty-five when he turned onto the Corinth–Athens superhighway. It was the same hour when you parked your spring outside Tsaropoulos's, then with Nolis and his wife and Mrs. Sougioulzoglou you went into Tsaropoulos's, the restaurant you had chosen for the two of us three years before, the evening when I had come back to you and you had escaped joyously from the hospital, restored to life, and you had given me the poem, and the week of happiness had begun.

You ordered supper, excited. All of a sudden the calm which had encased you since morning, the tranquil equilibrium, the absence of passions gave way to an unexpected euphoria. You seemed excited. You talked constantly, joked, laughing as you told about the files and Averoff and Tsatsos, about the superquestion you were going to put to Karamanlis on Monday, about the earthquake you would cause by handing over the documents prohibited by Giouvelos. You even confided that you were writing a book: you had already begun it, you said, then some problems had made you interrupt it, but in the month of May you would take it up again and finish it within the year. "I'll work steadily in the summer and fall, I'll go to Italy to work, I'll ask for a leave from Parliament. It's a book that begins with the attempt on Papadopoulos and ends with the documents. It's the story of an effort, the story of a man." You promised also to make a trip to Australia: "Yes, I want to move, to know the world. Once the book is finished, I really will come to Australia." It seemed you had an endless future before you, laden with promises and successes and joy; it seemed that your horrible plan, your unconscious calculation, to die in order to live, was forgotten. And your eyes shone, your hands trembled, you liked everything. The company of the three old people, the food, the crowd. The two ladies looked at you in silence, seduced, Nolis listened to you, fascinated. What vitality in this man, what warmth, what fire! You didn't even have to drink in order to feed that fire: one bottle sufficed for the four. At a certain point, raising the glass to your lips, you said that your relationship with wine had deteriorated: you had rediscovered the virtues of orangeade. "And, I'm not sorry, because the darkness is full of traps, of shadows always in ambush. One has to have a clear mind and quick reflexes." Meanwhile Michael Steffas was driving, cursing the rain that had started pouring down again between Corinth and Megara, the rain that prevented him from speeding as he would have liked. But he still went fairly fast, because at ten minutes to midnight he was again at the house of Georgopoulos, his alibi until one thirty. (Curious this return to him at midnight, this procuring witnesses for himself right to the minute.) And the red BMW? It was there too, it was there and it wouldn't wait for Steffas's Peugeot before coming after you. After following you to the restaurant, it went off to await the proper time without attracting attention and it made a significant mistake. It was about midnight when a terrified citizen went to the police to report that along the Vouliagmeni Road a red BMW had followed him at a distance for several kilometers and then suddenly had come straight at him, had sideswiped him, obviously meaning to run him off the road. He had avoided disaster by clinging hard to the wheel, stopping as soon as he could. No: it wasn't accidental. He could prove it because, while he was catching his breath, wondering what the reason for the attack could be, the BMW had reappeared. And had stopped. And the two men in it had taken a good look at him, then they had made a gesture of dismay: as if they had mistaken his identity and were calling themselves idiots. Remembering that if they had left you at Tsaropoulos's you couldn't already be on the Vouliagmeni Road. The terrified citizen had a moustache and a green automobile. Not apple green, but in the dark almost the same color as yours.

You left Tsaropoulos's a little after one in the morning, and at the door of the restaurant there was a slight argument: you wanted to drive your guests home and they insisted on taking a taxi. You were staying at Glyphada and the restaurant was at Glyphada, the three of them repeated, it was absurd for you to go all the way to Alkionis Street and Androtzou Street, both in distant neighborhoods, and then come back to Glyphada. Nevertheless you forced them to get into your spring, first stop Alkionis Street, and it was in a cross street of Alkionis, after saying good night to the Nolises, that a strange thing happened: a taxi passed you, blocked your way and braked in the center of the street. You also braked and got out, saying: "Even the taxis now! I want to see who it is." Then you went toward the driver and Mrs. Sougioulzoglou saw you argue with him for a few minutes. But when you came back, you seemed relieved: "No, he wasn't following me. He's from Glyphada, I know him." You started the car again and turned into Poseidonos Street. "The fact is that I'm so suspicious now with automobiles." "Why?" Mrs. Sougioulzoglou asked. You didn't answer. Perhaps you didn't even hear her. Your lips clenched, your brow furrowed, you were looking into the rearview mirror. Suddenly: "Heleni, do you feel like dropping into a bouzouki place? Just long enough to drink an orangeade and enjoy a bit of music. There's one near here, in the opposite direction." Mrs. Sougioulzoglou didn't understand and tried to make excuses. No, thanks, it was late, at her age one didn't go to bouzoukis with handsome young men. "Come, come, Heleni." "No, thank you, really." "All right then." And with your eyes still on the rearview mirror you accelerated, turning into Leoforos Sigrou Street at great speed. When you were in front of the brewery you suddenly put on the brakes, hastily apologized: you weren't in the habit of abandoning ladies on the sidewalk at night but Androtzou Street wasn't far and number 15A was just around the corner, would she mind getting out here and walking the rest of the way? Again Mrs. Sougioulzoglou didn't understand. It was only after your death that she realized you didn't want to enter Androtzou Street, narrow and dark, and you were very impatient to be alone. She said no, she didn't mind at all, then she got out, as you made no move to do the same or to open the door for her. One hand on the wheel and the other on the gearshift, you were ready to zoom off. "Thanks, Heleni. Sorry, Heleni." "Thank you, Alekos. But why don't you go and sleep in Kolokotroni Street? It's so near, and is it worth having to drive another twenty minutes to Glyphada?" "Better to sleep four hours at Glyphada than eight at Kolokotroni." "Good night then—" "Good night." You didn't even wait till she had crossed the street and reached the opposite sidewalk. You drove off at once. And it was one thirty-five, one forty at most, Mrs. Sougioulzoglou was to say. She was to say this, explaining that at one forty-five she was home: to walk the two hundred meters to 15A Androtzou Street, open the door of the building, ring for the elevator, go up to the fourth floor, enter the house, couldn't have taken her less than eight or ten minutes. True, but at night and with the streets half-deserted, to go from that place on Leoforos Sigrou Street to the place where they killed you on the Vouliagmeni Road takes only five or six minutes. And the clock in your spring was to stop, with the crash, at one fifty-eight: a time confirmed by the witnesses. Between the moment when you said good night to Mrs. Sougioulzoglou and the moment of the crash then there is a gap of eighteen or twenty-three minutes, let's say twenty minutes, that nobody has been able or willing to explain. They are the twenty minutes of the corrida you fought with your murderers.

They appeared together, punctual, as if they had a specific appointment. They appeared immediately, as you were turning into Diakou Street. A red BMW and a silver gray Peugeot. And you certainly weren't surprised: you had realized it was going to happen, in Poseidonos Street, when you wanted to stop and turn around with the pretext of the bouzouki, then you had become further convinced in Leoforos Sigrou Street when you let Mrs. Sougioulzoglou out. In fact the witnesses that the police would later ignore or silence (except for one who never gave in, a driver by the name of Mandis Garoufalakis) said the next morning that behind the apple green Fiat there wasn't just the Peugeot: there was also a red car, rust color or maroon, maybe a Jaguar or maybe a BMW. You found yourself between the two like a mouse in a trap, and it's possible that at first you wanted to run away. But immediately you felt the irresistible impulse to confront them, to see them face to face, to discover who they were, to fight, in the same way you had fought in Crete and in Rome and in Athens and every time they had tried to scare you or provoke you or kill you with an automobile; the weariness of living surfaced again, born of the weariness of losing, and so the need to win at least after death, the unconscious calculation that no live hero is worth a dead hero, and the corrida began. The kind which at a particular moment reverses roles and transforms the pursued into the pursuer, the pursuer into the pursued, and then reestablishes the roles so that the pursuer is once again pursuer and the pursued is once again the pursued. Where the arena of this corrida was before the Vouliagmeni Road I don't know, but retracing the streets of your agony I was to conclude that the route could only have been Diakou Street, Anarafseos, Logouinou, Mousourou, Imitti, Ilioupoleos, that is, first in the direction of the cemetery and then skirting the cemetery, because if from Leoforos Sigrou Street you don't take the Vouliagmeni Road at once but turn down the one-way street ignoring the sign, then you inevitably have to take those other streets, and those streets lead to the cemetery and reaching the cemetery you can only skirt it with the circular motion of the star caught in the vortex that will pull it into the black hole. I see you, tensed at the wheel, pale, chasing them as they chase you, attacking them as they attack you, in a mad succession of swerves, acceleration, deceleration, bumps. The bumps, the collisions described in the expert's report that the magistrates of Power were not to accept, the traces of a rust brown that could have been rust red or maroon, and at what moment did you feel the futile impulse toward survival, the flare of the star that to escape the vortex surrenders to the whirlpool? At what moment did you think of heading toward the Vouliagmeni Road, to reach the house with the garden of orange and lemon trees, the only escape? Suddenly there you are eluding the horrible roundabout, slipping into the same street by which you had come, Anarafseos, bursting into Vouliagmeni, where the witnesses I mentioned were to tell of having seen a green automobile dart past and a red automobile and a silver gray one after it. Four witnesses: a taxi driver who was two hundred meters behind, the passenger he was carrying, a second taxi driver who was ahead of you, a third who had stopped at an intersection. They were to tell it, presenting themselves voluntarily to the police, and at first the police didn't even ask their names, then they did ask, and three witnesses would change their account, forgetting the red automobile. Only Mandis Garoufalakis would insist, but no one would listen, and he was dissuaded, that is, threatened; in fact to the reporters who wanted to know more he talked with increasing reluctance, with the shyness that is the daughter of fear. "Yes, a red one and white one . . . White no, tan . . . No gray." First one then the other, on the right and then on the left, they passed you and blocked your way, they sat in front of you, and you had to avoid them both, then pass them both, and the moment you succeeded, they would repeat the maneuver. With method, with precision, with perfect synchronization. "But I don't know anything, gentlemen, I didn't see anything, for heaven's sake. I don't want trouble, I have a wife and children, I have a family, don't get me involved. If you don't get me involved, if you swear you won't use my name, I'll tell you that the green automobile was always trapped between the red automobile and the pale automobile, in the red automobile there were two people, and at a certain point the red automobile did the worst: it crashed into the green automobile from behind, right on the license plate. Then the green automobile skidded, straightened out miraculously, and went on speeding in the direction of Glyphada. But I don't know anything gentlemen, I didn't see anything, I haven't said anything, for Christ sake." All three were going very fast. A hundred and ten kilometers, a hundred and twenty, a hundred and thirty, and at this speed you reached the Church of Saint Demetrios: after it the houses end and the street rises in a slight hump. After the hump the Vouliagmeni Road widens into a double avenue with an island down the middle. Fifty meters farther, on the right, there is the garage with the Texaco sign.

It was at Saint Demetrious that thc rcd automobile struck you on the license plate. And it was after the hump that it passed you a final time, then went off, vanished in the darkness. But as they were passing you to go off and vanish in the darkness, did the two men inside the red automobile use the gas pistol or not? A pistol identical to the one that the investigating magistrate shelved so casually in August. Registration number 159789, made in West Germany, short barrel, heavy grip. The magazine contains five cylinder bullets, five metallic cartridges with a little hole for emitting a gas, which evaporates almost without leaving a trace. (And if there were traces, at the morgue they didn't go to the trouble of looking for them. They made no analysis that would serve to find traces of hallucinatory agents, of volatile narcotic substances.) Did they use this gas revolver or didn't they? Circumstances allowed it, since you were driving with the left window rolled almost completely down. If they didn't use it, if that magistrate was right in dismissing so casually the revolver with the registration number 159789, what was it that dazed you, enfolding you in a shroud of stupor and sleepiness? What clouded your sight and numbed your will? You were veering and skidding when the Peugeot overtook you, you were already losing control of the car, so it was easy for Steffas to complete the job. First he slammed the right front fender against your left rear fender, then he pressed against your left flank and dragged you for a few meters, then pulling hard on the wheel he detached himself and inflicted the mortal ramming: a blow of his car's rear against your front left fender. And you skidded off like a bullet while, with a great kamikaze's maneuver, the maneuver of a killer trained on the racing tracks of Canada, he veered almost at a right angle to enter the opening in the traffic island that divides Vouliagmeni. You skidded off obliquely, mounted the broad sidewalk, on the pavement next to the garage with the Texaco sign, missed a lamppost by a few meters, and through the shroud of stupor, of sleep, you tried in vain to slow down, braking. Your spring by now had taken off. High and determined, it was flying inexorably toward the ramp down to the garage, the trap with the sign Good Journey, Kalon Taxidi, and nothing could have stopped it. If the flight had been two meters longer, perhaps it could have leaped over the void of the ramp and landed again in the world of the living: you could have been saved. But this was not part of the god's plans, of your fate already written, and the automobile quickly lost altitude, its muzzle dropped, aiming at the wall that a moment before hadn't been visible and suddenly was visible, it was falling on you with insane speed, it stopped being a wall and became a crash, the roar of an exploding bomb, the end. And as you held up your arms in a sign of surrender, of victory and of surrender, as the palms of your hands touched the entrance to nothingness, everything happened as it was to happen, as you had foreseen it would happen in your unconscious calculations, in your clairvoyance, in the last lines of the book interrupted at page twenty-three: "'I only regret I didn't succeed.' It is my voice that answers. What a strange, remote voice. Where does it come from? From another world? The police officer also seems strange, remote. Where does he come from? Also from another world? Now he goes off in silence, and the moment he has left, the uniforms become furious again. More, always more. They beat me on the soles of my feet, on my eyes. I say again: 'I only regret I didn't succeed.' Yes, I only regret I didn't succeed. Then a terrible blow. From whom, with what? I feel a paradoxical force against my stomach, and my neck, chest, heart press into me, as if they were breaking all together, exploding. And I can no longer discern anything. I close my eyes and . . ."

The first person to rush up was the driver of the taxi with the passenger inside, and at first he saw nothing but a dense cloud. At the moment of the crash a great dust cloud had risen, and it covered everything with darkness. The driver went forward groping in the cloud, in the darkness, and when he was on the edge of the hole he covered his face, incredulous and horrified: it seemed impossible that an automobile could have thrust into such a small space. But just like a star that is dying and to be swallowed by its black hole it contracts and tightens until it becomes a fist, a lemon, a pebble, so your spring had contracted and compressed and reduced itself until it was a little pile of twisted iron, ripped metal, shattered glass. In the midst of that you lay, still alive and apparently intact. You raised your eyelids, you moved your lips: "Ime . . . I am . . . Mou . . . echun . . . Me . . . they have . . ." "Hush, hush," the driver begged, not recognizing you. "Isan . . . They were . . . " "Hush, hush, we'll pull you out." And with the help of the passenger he extracted you from the tangle, dragged you up the ramp, laid you on the sidewalk. Here he recognized you and realized that you weren't intact: the blood was pouring from your wounds, irrepressible, soaking the asphalt. "To the hospital, quickly, to the hospital!" he stammered. "To the hospital or to the morgue?" the passenger answered. And without conviction they lifted you by the arms, that were broken, by the legs, that were shattered, they settled you on the rear seat of the taxi. Two pupils now blind. Two lips that tried in vain to move, to say something. The hospital was very far, anyway it was no use now. Halfway there, you moved your lips the last time and called clearly: "Oh Theos! Theos mou! Oh, God! My God!" Then you drew a breath, very long, very deep, and your heart burst.

3

I ARRIVED SEVENTEEN HOURS LATER. OUTSIDE THE morgue a large, silent crowd was standing. I was pushed into a big room, dimly lighted by a bulb hanging on a wire, the storeroom with the refrigerator cells, and immediately the flash of a camera blinded me, a sharp order struck the silence: "Get the photographers out! Everybody out! Bar the windows!" Then somebody opened a door, cast a glance inside, and shut it again with a grunt: "Ne, aftos. Yes, this one." It was the last door to the left, bottom row, there were two other doors beside it, and three above. Shining, smooth, of metal. They looked like the doors of a safe. "Etimi, ready?" a voice asked. I nodded and the door opened wide, letting out a gust of ice. Inside a white bundle could be seen, set on a slab also of metal. "Siguri, are you sure?" the same voice asked. I nodded again and the slab glided toward me, it became a sheet stained with blood, wrapping a body. Your body. The form of the head could be distinguished clearly, the hands folded on the chest, the feet. They raised the sheet and I saw you. You were running. You were crossing the beach and you ran with the broad strides of a happy colt, your trousers clung to your strong thighs, the T-shirt stretched over your strong shoulders, and your hair flowed, light, in black waves of silk. The night before we had loved each other for the first time in a bed, marrying our two solitudes, and in the afternoon we had gone to the sea where the summer blazed in a glory of sun, of blue. Flooded with sun, with blue, you yelled happily: "I zoi, i zoi! Life, life!" I knelt to look at you, incredulous. From the groin to the neck they had opened you to steal your heart, your lungs, your viscera, then sewed you up again with black knots that marred you like roaches clinging to your skin, in a line, to devour you. A horrifying gash ran irregularly along your right arm from elbow to wrist, a monstrous swelling deformed the thigh shattered by the broken femur. But the face was unharmed, only a bluish shadow blanched it at the temple. I called you, shyly, I touched you hesitantly. Stiffened in the haughty and scornful immobility of the dead, you proudly rejected every word and every gesture of love: I had to overcome a fear of offending you in order to stroke the icy brow, the icy cheeks, the stiff moustache covered with frost. I conquered it, to warm you a little. But it was like trying to warm a marble statue, all that remained of you was a marble statue with the form, the lineaments, and the memory of what you had been until seventeen hours earlier, and an impotent fury pierced me, a certitude that had the flavor of hate: they hadn't killed you by chance, they hadn't killed you by accident, they had killed you so you would disturb them no more. I stood up. Somebody covered you again with the sheet and gave a kick to the slab, which, rustling, slid again into the darkness. The door closed on you again, with another gust of ice, then a thud.

Outside it was night. Smearing the slime of their curiosity on me, people were saying: "She isn't crying!" In Kolokotroni Street there was your poem: "My end will come in the way desired by those who have power." There were the words of Socrates: "The hour of departure has arrived, and we go our ways—I to die, and you to live. Which is better only the god knows." There was the grief that finally explodes in a scream like a wounded animal's. There was my task of living and my promise to keep. "You'll write it for me, promise me!" "I promise." There was the waiting for May 5, the day set for your funeral. "We'll see each other on May 5, we'll be together on May 5." There was the agony of the morning I would return to the morgue to dress you, to exchange rings a second time, to face the octopus that roars zi, zi, zi. And meanwhile the mountain remained in its place, unshakable, meanwhile the vultures were preparing to feast on your corpse waving underpants with the word "people," the word "freedom," we salute our noble comrade, we venerate the noble opponent. And in Corinth Michael Steffas was going to his favorite café to meet his friends for a cup of good Turkish coffee and a dish of pastries.

It hadn't been easy, after the fatal ramming, to swerve and turn into the passage through the traffic island, to enter the other lane of the Vouliagmeni Road, and to escape in the opposite direction, toward the center of the city. It hadn't been easy because the passage, very narrow, was designed for cars that, coming from Glyphada, wanted to change direction and go back along the lane of the garage with the Texaco sign. For automobiles coming from this direction then, the passage was a reversed curve which one could enter only the wrong way, climbing over the elbow edge of the traffic island. Climbing over it, or moving around it very slowly because taking it at great speed, you would risk turning over. And although it was going at a hundred and thirty kilometers an hour, the Peugeot had not turned over. Making a serpentine maneuver, Michael Steffas had managed to slip into the passage with the skill of a skier dodging the stakes in a slalom, the precision of an acrobat who, coming out of his somersault, seizes the pole of the trapeze to repeat his leap. Holding the same speed, Steffas had managed to slip through the two columns that narrow the passage at the end, then to swerve a second time and take Olga Street. A double slalom, a double somersault, circus stuff. Or the stuff of a mercenary accustomed to such feats, sustained by an extraordinary sangfroid? The same sangfroid that he was to reveal in the following days and months, with the police, with the press, with everybody. Passing three intersections on Olga Street, he got out to check the damage done to the Peugeot, then walked back to the Vouliagmeni Road, and at the top of the rise he stopped to take a look, to realize what was happening. What was happening was what was supposed to happen, in the great dust cloud two men could be discerned dragging an inanimate body and a third who was shouting: "He's dying, he's dead, he's dying!" Also a taxi could be discerned, and windows were coming alight, people were stepping out on their balconies to ask who was dying, who was dead. This didn't upset him in the least and after two or three minutes he retraced his steps, took the wheel of the Peugeot again. It had behaved really well: the damage done to it was not serious, a few dents on the right front fender and some scratches along the side. Nothing to prevent him from going back to Corinth. (And what about the trip to Aegina? And what about Georgopoulos who was expecting him in the morning, along with the girls? Was it all forgotten, all discarded?) At three thirty in the morning, Steffas arrived again in Corinth. He parked in his usual place and then went to bed, falling asleep at once. He woke at one in the afternoon, had dinner, took another little nap, and now he was going to his favorite café to meet his friends for a cup of good Turkish coffee and a dish of pastries. He had to show himself, furnish the proof of his presence in the city.

He reached the café around seven and sat at a little table where some friends were already sitting: the son of the mayor, another man named Dimitri Nikolaou and, sure enough, Cristos Grispos and Notis Panaiotis, the two students who had put him up in Florence along with the Nazi named Takis. Hi, look who's here, are you in Corinth for Easter vacation? Yes, and what about you, Michael, why have you been hiding? Hiding, hell, I came home yesterday from Athens on the bus, I've been here since yesterday. They chatted also about the weather, which had turned fine again, they could go to the sea tomorrow, and then the brother of Grispos arrived: "Hey, you guys, have you heard the radio?" "No, why?" They've killed Panagoulis." "Panagoulis? Killed?" "Boy, they've killed Panagoulis!" But Steffas was silent. "Who killed him? Who?" "They don't know. They ran into him and flung his car off the road. Two of them, it seems: a white Mercedes and a red Jaguar." "What do you mean, it seems?" "Because there's one guy who says the Jaguar wasn't a Jaguar and the Mercedes wasn't a Mercedes. Anyway he crashed in a garage on Vouliagmeni. Dead. On the spot. Or almost. His liver burst in nineteen pieces, his right lung was a rag, and his heart exploded like a bomb. Bang!" Steffas continued to remain silent, calm, as if the news didn't interest him. Two months later, Grispos and Panaiotis were to tell me they saw no reaction on his face or in his actions. He seemed completely indifferent, normal, if anything a bit bored. He yawned. "Anybody arrested?" "No, a blank." "But was it an accident or not?" "The papers don't come out today. Isn't this May 1?" "Right." "Who could it have been?" "Hm." And with that sound they closed the subject, they started talking again about the excursion to the beach: "Well, are we going to the beach tomorrow?" "Of course, we'll go to Loutraki." "Who'll take us there?" "Steffas'll take us there, with his Peugeot. By the way, Michael, where's the Peugeot?" Steffas emerged from his silence, and his voice was the same as always: "It's here, where else? In the parking lot." "Then why did you walk? Is it broken down? Did you have an accident?" "Accident, my foot. It's because of the license plate. I haven't driven it for months because of the plate. You have no idea of the fine they'd hit me with, not being registered?" "Oh, who notices license plates, on a holiday. From here to Loutraki—" "No, I can't." "Come on—" "I can't, I said." "All right, I'll take you. I have a car too," the mayor's son volunteered. "Who's coming?" "I am," Grispos said. "Me, too," Nikolaou said. "I'm busy," Panaiotis said. "And you, Michael, are you going?" "Of course," Steffas said. "Okay, you guys, we'll meet tomorrow morning at ten." "Right, ten." And so it went. A jolly excursion, very pleasant, Grispos was to tell me. Both going out and coming back, Steffas was in fine humor, the life of the party. He laughed, joked, went on about automobiles, clothes, girls, especially girls. He never mentioned your death. And neither did the others.

He came back to Athens about four in the afternoon of Sunday May 2, and according to his statements, he went to the movies, then home. But whom he saw and what he did afterward nobody knows, who urged him or advised him or forced him to present himself to the police twenty-four hours afterward. Only one fact is sure: nobody, absolutely nobody, suspected him. They were looking for a Mercedes, moreover, not a Peugeot. But the rumor that you hadn't been killed by chance, that you hadn't been killed by accident, that you had been killed deliberately and on someone's orders, was growing like a swelling river, threateningly: it had to be stopped. And on Monday afternoon Steffas presented himself at police headquarters with his lawyer, a certain Kaselakis, who in 1973 had defended a certain Nikos Moundis: accused of having killed an English journalist, Anne Chapman, who was investigating the ties between the junta and the CIA. Also in that case the murderer had offered himself on a silver platter, also in that case Kaselakis had convinced the jury that it wasn't a political crime: in fact he had managed to show that Nikos Moundis had killed Anne Chapman after having raped her, in a fit of temporary insanity. And who cared if, after the sentence, Moundis had withdrawn the confession, repeating it was all balls, he had confessed to the crime because they had paid him and he needed money, or something of the sort? Steffas, Kaselakis said, was presenting himself simply as a witness and out of pure love of truth, so they would stop hinting at a political crime. It had been a common accident, the typical accident where the victim himself is entirely at fault, why, Steffas himself almost got killed. He was calmly driving along Vouliagmeni, poor Steffas, when a green Fiat had started swerving out of control and had bumped into him, passing him on the right. In fact poor Steffas had barely had time to veer and save himself by turning into the passage through the traffic island, the wrong way. Afterward he had heard a crash, and coming back, he had glimpsed a great dust cloud, two men dragging an inanimate body, but he really had never imagined he was leaving a corpse behind him. He learned that the man was dead and the corpse was Panagoulis only Monday morning, reading the papers. No, neither before nor after the accident had there been a red automobile, these were the fantasies of those who had some motive for insisting on a political crime: the only thing red here was himself. Michael Steffas, former Communist sympathizer, now Papandreist Socialist, and was it possible that a Socialist, a comrade of the left, would want to kill Panagoulis? The police indicated they were convinced, and instead of arresting him, they put him under their protection. They even allowed him to hold a press conference in the course of which he amazed everyone with his self-control, his confidence. No question managed to embarrass him, or even discomfit him. He didn't lose his composure even when someone reminded him that the laws of dynamics are universal and unchangeable: if Panagoulis had struck him instead of being struck, he, Steffas, would have been flung off the road. To this reasoning he answered, with a pair of unperturbable, cold eyes, and said that they could believe what they liked: dynamics or no dynamics, he had nothing to reproach himself for. They should think, by Christ, use their heads: if he had had anything to reproach himself for, would he have presented himself to the police, or wouldn't he? He didn't bat an eye either when somebody else answered that he did have something to reproach himself for, seeing that he hadn't bothered to lend assistance to the dying man he had left behind him. Why hadn't he lent assistance? "Because the wounded man had already been put in a taxi, and there was no need of me." And Corinth, why had he gone back to Corinth instead of following that taxi or staying in the city? "Because I was seized by a kind of panic and by a comprehensible desire to return to Corinth. That's simple." But the next day wasn't he supposed to go to Aegina? "Obviously I no longer felt like going to Aegina, I didn't care then about going to Aegina." And the red automobile: why did he make such a point of denying the presence of the red automobile, ignoring the fact that some witnesses had seen it? "Because I didn't see it and because, as I said before, I'm irritated by this story of a political crime, an organized crime." Just a moment: if his innocence was so complete, and if he was a Socialist, a Papandreist Socialist, a comrade of the left, why was he so irritated at talk of a political crime, an organized crime? Why, in order to contradict it, had he turned himself in? A logical question, correct, and dangerous. But once again he handled it calmly, actually answering with an expression full of annoyance: "I am not here to be tried by you, and you are forgetting that I didn't turn myself in. I offered myself as a witness. In fact I have not been arrested." Even when those suspect details emerged, his employment in the atelier of Despina Papdopoulos, his skill as a driver, his racing exploits in Canada, he continued repeating: "I'll manage, you'll see. I always know what I'm saying and what I'm doing."

He knew. He certainly did know. In fact the magistrates of Power paid no attention to the report made by Italian experts which showed, unequivocally, that you had been rammed by the Peugeot in a seesaw maneuver, and had been rammed also by another automobile with two impacts that had left traces of rust brown or maroon paint. They paid no attention to Steffas's past and to the detail that he had been in the textile machinery shop, in Kolokotroni Street, also on the morning of Friday April 30. It paid no attention to the fact that in July 1975 he had gone with the Nazi named Takis to Florence and had stayed there apparently looking for something or somebody that couldn't be found. They paid no attention to the testimony that for eleven hours at one stretch I gave the judge in charge of the investigation, reporting what I had heard from Cristos Grispos and Notis Panaiotis, listing the threats and the harassment you had undergone for three years, the attempts to kidnap you or to kill you with an automobile on Crete and in Rome and in Athens, the things you had told me in our last telephone calls, the documents you had captured in the last days and whose contents, I said in conclusion, I would reveal in the courtroom. They paid no attention, but instead dismissed with remarkable haste the story of a certain George Leonardos, a former criminal from Salonika, according to whom on the night between April 16 and 17, in Omonia Square in Athens, there had been a meeting of four members of the fascist group Arachne, Spider, the same one you had told me about after the reading of the documents and before waving the gem of gems, the koh-i-noor diamond. They had met and had decided to teach Panagoulis a lesson so he would draw in his horns and shut his trap, Leonardos said, in fact it was supposed to be only a lesson: things had gone beyond that by accident. Saying this, he supplied dates and names, precise details, and among the names there was that of Basil Kaselas, physician, right-wing extremist, CIA agent at Salonika, then that of Anthony Mikalopoulos, another former criminal from Salonika, previously involved in the murder of the Communist deputy Lambrakis, and also owner of a red BMW. In his testimony to the investigating judge, Leonardos said plenty of things. He even underlined the fact that a few days after your death Kaselas had moved to London, at that time the refuge of many fascists. He even handed over one of the gas revolvers that the Arachne bullies used to daze their victims. The revolver made in West Germany, registration number 159789. But Kaselas and Mikalopoulos cried slander, they answered that Leonardos was an exhibitionist, a lunatic, a well-known liar, already sentenced for calumny, and he became frightened. He retracted everything. Or did they make him retract everything? And yet some journalists had indeed discovered that he wasn't all that crazy, wasn't all that much a liar: Arachne really did exist, Kaselas really had gone to London, and by way of Munich, where he had met Sdrakas, the former minister who had fled across the Ezvonoi border with Kourkoulakos. Other journalists had also ascertained that Mikalopoulos really did have a red BMW. And they had gone to him, in Salonika, asked him where this red BMW was. And he answered that he had sold it. Then they asked him to whom he had sold it, and he answered well, he hadn't exactly sold it: he had given it away. They asked him to whom he had given it and he answered well, to an institution run by some nuns. They asked him what institution run by nuns and he answered that he didn't remember and get out, damn you all, get out! No, the magistrates paid no attention, the magistrates of Power. Nor did the so-called left pay any attention, this ineffable left that never listens to anyone who contests it or denounces it or criticizes it, and to renew itself it can only produce pistoleros John Wayne-style, pseudo-revolutionaries. And so, with the automobile accident thesis, only Steffas was brought to trial and sentenced. At the first trial, to three years, suspended, for manslaughter. In the appeal, to a five thousand drachma fine for failing to lend assistance. Five thousand drachmas which he had no trouble paying since in the meanwhile he had become co-owner of Heim Fashions, he had made his fortune. Five thousand miserable drachmas.

And meanwhile other things were happening: with Judge Giouvelos now the apostle of courage and democracy and freedom, divulging the files that he had forbidden you to publish, naturally the files that did not concern the dragon or the dragon's pals, no reference to the memorandum sent to Gizikis, no mention of the list with the number twenty-three; while the dragon remained minister of defense, undisturbed and undisturbable, invulnerable; while your party regained its virginity by expelling Tsatsos, accepting post mortem your request; while Papandreou used your corpse as a defenseless orphan is used and waved it like a rag at rallies; while your relatives and friends and companions ended up with him to a man in return for a cozy seat in Parliament; while the fascists beat up Fazis with savage fury, shattering his skull and his memory; while I was also threatened with letters and phone calls—Just try writing certain things and you'll see, publish your book and you'll see—while the people accepted this, again, submitted to this, again, blind and deaf and silent, again, bent in obedience or self-interest or helplessness, again; while nobody dared say you're all murderers, left right and center, you murdered him all together, filthy assassins who live on the alibis of law and order, of moderation and of balance, of justice and of freedom; while the whale of evil, Moby Dick, moved off unharmed and the waters became calm, soft, oblivious, over the vortex of your sunken voice, Power won another time. The eternal Power that never dies, that falls only to rise again, the same as before, different only in hue. But you had clearly understood it would end like this, and if ever you had a doubt, it vanished the moment you took the deep breath that sucked you to the other side of the tunnel: into the well where those who would like to change the world are regularly thrown, those who would like to bring down the mountain, give voice and dignity to the flock that bleats inside its river of fleece. The disobedient. The misunderstood and solitary. The poets. The heroes of senseless fables but without which life would have no meaning and to fight knowing that to lose would be pure madness. And yet for one day, that day that counts, that salvages, that often comes when you've given up hoping, and when it comes it leaves in the air a microscopic seed from which a flower will bloom: even the flock understood this, bleating within its river of fleece. No longer a flock, that day, but an octopus that strangles and roars zi, zi, zi! Alekos lives, lives, lives! This is why you were smiling so mysteriously now that you were descending into the grave where the high priest covered with gold and necklaces, sapphires, rubies, emeralds, symbol of every power present past and future, was tumbling grotesquely, breaking the crystal, trampling on the marble statue, thinking this was all that remained of a dream, of a man.